FRANCINE RIVERS

The Scarlet Thread & Leota's Garden

A CONTEMPORARY COLLECTION

TYNDALE HOUSE PUBLISHERS, INC.

CAROL STREAM, ILLINOIS

Visit Tyndale's exciting Web site at www.tyndale.com

TYNDALE and Tyndale's quill logo are registered trademarks of Tyndale House Publishers, Inc.

Francine Rivers: A Contemporary Collection

This special edition includes the following titles:

The Scarlet Thread

Scripture quotations taken from the *New American Standard Bible,* © 1960, 1962, 1963, 1968, 1971, 1972, 1973, 1975, 1977 by The Lockman Foundation. Used by permission.

Leota's Garden

Scripture quotations are taken from the *Holy Bible,* New Living Translation, copyright © 1996. Used by permission of Tyndale House Publishers, Inc., Carol Stream, Illinois 60188. All rights reserved.

ISBN-13: 978-1-4143-1456-3
ISBN-10: 1-4143-1456-6

Printed in the United States of America

12   11   10   09   08
 7   6   5   4   3   2

FRANCINE RIVERS

The Scarlet Thread

Tyndale House Publishers, Inc.
Carol Stream, Illinois

To Sue Hahn, Fran Kane, and Donzella Schlager . . . my traveling companions

ACKNOWLEDGMENTS

Three very special people helped bring this story into being: Sue Hahn, Fran Kane, and Donzella Schlager, adventurers all, who shared a dream with me of traveling the Oregon Trail. With the blessings of our husbands, we took off in a Suburban and drove from Sebastopol, California, to Independence, Missouri. From there we followed the Oregon Trail to The Dalles, Oregon. Over five thousand miles together. We saw the beauty and vastness of our country, stopped at every historical landmark (and rest stop) along the road, visited every museum we could find (small town and large), and collected enough information to keep us reading for years to come.

Thanks, gals. It was one of the best times of my life.

When do we do the Lewis and Clark trail?

Many thanks as well to Ryan MacDonald, for sharing his expertise in computer games and trade shows.

ON THE OREGON TRAIL

Mary Kathryn McMurray's Journey

1

The Call

1

SIERRA CLANTON MADRID COULDN'T STOP
shaking. Her stomach was quivering. Her head had begun
throbbing with a tension headache the moment Alex had told
her the news.

She hadn't had a headache like this since prom night during
her senior year of high school. Alex had come to pick her up in
his father's beat-up Chevy three minutes before her father turned
into the driveway. It was the first time in her life her father had
come home *early* from work. She might have known it would be
on that night. She could still remember the look on her father's
face when he saw Alex—a drop-dead handsome, long-haired
Hispanic boy dressed in a rented tuxedo—standing on the wide

porch of her family's Mathesen Street Victorian. As if that wasn't bad enough, Alex was reaching forward to pin an orchid to the front of her fancy prom dress. When Sierra heard the slam of her father's car door, she almost fainted in fear.

The headache had started then and was only compounded by the inquiring look on Alex's face. "What's the matter?" he asked. What could she say? She had told her father about Alex; she just hadn't told him everything.

Words were exchanged, but, fortunately, her mother was there to intercede and calm her father down.

In the end, Alex escorted her to his borrowed car and helped her in while her father stood on the front steps glaring at him. Alex didn't so much as look at her as he put the Chevy in gear and pulled away from the curb. They were halfway to Santa Rosa before he said anything.

"You didn't tell him who was taking you to the prom, did you?"

"Yes, I did."

"Yeah, right. You just left out a few important details, didn't you, *chiquita?*" He had never called her that before, and it boded ill tidings for the night ahead. He didn't say anything more on the drive to the expensive restaurant in Santa Rosa. She ordered something cheap, which made him even madder.

"You think I can't afford to buy you anything more than a dinner salad?"

Her face aflame, she ordered the same prime rib dinner he did, but he didn't look any happier.

Things got worse as the evening wore on. By ten, Alex wasn't speaking at all, not to her, not to anyone. She ended up losing the nice dinner he bought her in the bathroom of the Villa de Chanticlair.

She'd been crazy in love with Alejandro Luís Madrid. *Crazy* being the operative word. Her father had warned her. She should have listened.

Sierra's eyes smarted with tears now as she drove along the Old Redwood Highway, which linked Windsor with Healdsburg. For all of its turmoil, she preferred clinging to the now-romantic past rather than facing the uncertain, terrifying present and future.

Prom night had been such a disaster. When most of her friends were going to all-night parties in Santa Rosa, Alex took her home well before midnight. The front lights were turned on, and not discreetly. Her father had probably changed the 60-watt bulb to a 250 while she was gone. Even the inside lights were on that night.

There was plenty of light for her to see how angry Alex was. But his expression revealed something deeper than just anger. She could feel the hurt that lay hidden behind the cold, remote expression on his face. She thought he'd just walk away then. Unfortunately, he didn't intend to do so before he had his say.

"I knew it was a mistake to ever ask you out."

The words struck like a shotgun blast to her heart. He wasn't finished. "I'm not some character in a Shakespearean tragedy, Sierra. I'm not Romeo to your Juliet. And I didn't ask you out because I wanted to play around!" He turned away with that and almost reached the steps before she could speak past the tears choking her.

"I love you, Alex."

He turned around then and looked at her. "What'd you say?" His eyes were dark and hot, still mad at her—with good cause. She hadn't considered what her silence would cost him. All she had thought about was avoiding a confrontation with her father.

Alex stood waiting.

"I—I said I love you."

"Say it in Spanish," he told her in the same tone he had used when tutoring her.

She swallowed, wondering if he only meant to humiliate her

more before he walked out of her life. *"Te amo, Alejandro Luís Madrid. Corazón y alma."* She started to cry then, hard wracking sobs. He caught hold of her and poured out his feelings in Spanish. Though she didn't fully understand the words, she saw in his eyes and felt in his touch that he loved her.

Infrequently over the years, he had fallen back into his first language during times of powerful emotions. He had spoken Spanish when he made love to her on their wedding night and again when she told him she was pregnant. He had wept and spoken Spanish in the wee hours of the morning when Clanton had pushed his way into the world, and again when Carolyn was born. And he had spoken Spanish in tears on the night her father died.

But that night on the porch, they both forgot about the lights. In fact, they both forgot everything until the front door was jerked open and her father ordered him gone.

She was forbidden to see Alex. At the time, it didn't matter to her father that Alex was ranked number four in a class of two hundred students. What mattered was that Luís Madrid, Alex's father, was "one of those beaners" who worked as a laborer in the Sonoma County vineyards. Her father didn't care that Alex was working a forty-hour week at a local gas station to save money to put himself through college.

"I wish him luck," he said, and it was clear that luck was the last thing he wished Alex.

She reasoned, cajoled, whined, and begged. She appealed to her mother, who promptly refused to take her side. In desperation, she threatened to run away or commit suicide. She had gotten their attention with that.

"You so much as talk to that beaner on the phone and I'll call the police!" her father had yelled. "You're fifteen. He's eighteen. I could have him arrested!"

"You do and I'll tell the police you're abusing me!"

Her father called her aunt in Merced and made arrangements for her to spend a few weeks there "cooling off."

Alex was waiting when she returned, but he proved less malleable than her male parent. He had a few succinct Spanish words to say about her idea of meeting him in secret. Alex was a fighter who preferred facing wrath head-on. She had never expected that he would deal with the situation on his own. He just showed up at the house one day five minutes after her father had come home from work. She learned later from a neighbor that Alex had been waiting down the street for more than an hour. Her mother, sympathetic to their plight, invited Alex into the foyer before her father got to the porch and could order him off the property.

Clutching the steering wheel of her Honda Accord, Sierra remembered how she had felt that day, seeing Alex standing in the front hallway between her mother and father. She had been so sure her father would kill him or at least beat him to within an inch of his life.

"What's *he* doing here?" She could still hear the anger in her father's voice as he dumped his briefcase on the floor. Sierra had been convinced he was only freeing his hands so he could get them around Alex's neck.

Alex stepped around her mother and faced him. "I came to ask permission to see your daughter."

"Permission! Like you asked permission to take her to the prom?"

"I thought Sierra cleared it with you. My mistake."

"You're right about that! A big mistake. Now get out of here!"

"Brian, give the young man the chance to—"

"Stay out of this, Marianna!"

Alex stood his ground. "All I ask is a fair hearing." He didn't even notice her standing above them on the stairs.

"I don't want to hear anything you have to say."

13

They were like two dogs with their hackles up. "Daddy, please
. . . ," she said, coming down the stairs. "We love each other."

"*Love.* I doubt that's what he feels for you."

"You don't understand!" she wailed.

"I understand plenty! Get back to your room!"

"I'm not going anywhere but with Alex," she said, reaching
the hallway and taking a position beside her boyfriend, and she
knew in that instant that if her father came at him, she'd do whatever she had to do to stop him. She had never been so furious!

Alex clamped his hand on her wrist and firmly pulled her
behind him. "This is between your father and me. Stay out of it."
The whole time he spoke, he never took his eyes off her father.

"Get out of my house."

"All I want is a few minutes to speak to you, Mr. Clanton. If
you tell me afterward to back off, I'll back off."

"All the way to Mexico?"

"Brian!"

As soon as her father uttered the words, his face turned beet
red. Alex, with his own prejudices, had no intention of letting
him off easily.

"I was *born* in Healdsburg, Mr. Clanton. Just like you. My
father took his citizenship test ten years ago. Not that it makes
much difference. He passed with flying colors. Red, white, and
blue. He's never taken a dollar of welfare in his life, and he works
hard for what he makes, probably harder than you do in that
plush real estate office you have downtown. We don't live in
a Victorian," he said with a swift, telling look around, "but we
don't live in a shack either."

His little speech hadn't made anything better.

"You finished?" her father said, embarrassment burned away
by anger.

"You might enjoy knowing that my father and mother disapprove of Sierra as much as you disapprove of me."

Her mouth fell open.

"Disapprove of Sierra?" her father said, insulted. "Why?"

"Why do you think, Mr. Clanton? She's white and she's Protestant."

"Maybe you ought to listen."

"I do listen. I've got a lot of respect for my parents, but I've got a mind of my own. The way I see it, a bigot is a bigot, no matter what color he is."

A long, hot silence filled the foyer.

"So," Alex said bleakly. "Do we talk or do I walk?"

Her father looked at her for a moment and then back at Alex with resentful resignation. "We talk." He jerked his head toward a room off the hallway. "But I doubt you're going to like what I have to say."

They spent the next two hours in the small office at the front of the house while she sat in the kitchen with her mother, alternately crying and raging about what she'd do if her father wouldn't let her go out with Alex. Her mother hadn't said much of anything that day.

When her father came into the kitchen, he told her Alex was gone. Before she had time to scream recriminations, he informed her she could see him again, *after* she'd agreed to follow the *rules* the two of them had established. One phone conversation a night, no longer than thirty minutes and only *after* her schoolwork was finished. No dates Monday through Thursday. Friday night she was to be home by eleven. Saturday night by ten. Yes, *ten*. She had to be well rested for church on Sunday. If her grades dropped a smidgen, she was grounded from Alex completely. If she missed church, same consequences.

"And Alex agreed?"

"He agreed."

She hadn't liked any of it, but she had been so much in love she would have agreed to anything, and her father knew it.

"That boy's going to break your heart, Sierra."

Now, fourteen years later, he was doing just that.

Wiping tears from her eyes, Sierra drove across the Russian River bridge and turned right.

She knew her father had hoped things would cool off if he gave the relationship time to develop cracks. He hadn't known Alex then, nor did he see the determination and drive that burned in him. Alex graduated with honors from high school and entered the local junior college. Sierra had wanted to quit school and marry him, thinking it would be romantic to work and help put him through college. He squashed that idea. He told her in no uncertain terms that he intended to finish college *on his own,* and he sure didn't want a dropout for a wife. He completed two years of work at Santa Rosa Junior College in a year and a half and transferred to the University of California, Berkeley, where he majored in business, with an emphasis in computer technology. She finished high school and entered a local business college, counting the days to his graduation.

As soon as Alex returned to Healdsburg, he found a job with Hewlett-Packard in Santa Rosa, bought a used car, and rented a small bungalow in Windsor.

When they couldn't get their parents to agree on the kind of wedding they should have, they eloped to Reno. Nobody was very happy about it.

They had been married ten years. Ten wonderful years. All that time she'd thought Alex was as happy as she was. She never suspected what was going on beneath the surface. Why hadn't she realized? Why hadn't he told her straight out that he was dissatisfied?

Sierra pulled her Honda into the driveway of the Mathesen Street Victorian and prayed her mother was home. Mom had always been able to reason with Daddy. Maybe she could help

Sierra figure out how to reason Alex out of his plans for their future.

Unlocking the front door, Sierra entered the polished wood foyer. "Mom?" She closed the door behind her and walked back along the corridor toward the kitchen. She almost called for her father before she caught herself.

With a sharp pang, she remembered the call she and Alex had received at three in the morning two years ago. She had never heard her mother's voice sound that way before. Or since.

"Your father's had a heart attack, honey. The ambulance is here."

They had met her at the Healdsburg General Hospital, but it was already too late.

"He complained of indigestion this morning," her mother had said, distracted, in shock. "And his shoulder was aching."

Now, Sierra paused at his office door and looked in, half expecting to see him sitting at his desk reading the real estate section of the newspaper. She still missed him. Oddly, so did Alex. He and her father had become close after Clanton and Carolyn were born—amazing the way grandchildren seemed to break down walls between people. Prior to her pregnancy, she and Alex had seen little of her parents. Her father always found some excuse to turn down dinner invitations; Alex's parents were no better.

All that changed when she went into labor. Everyone was at Kaiser Hospital the night she gave birth. Alex had kissed her and said maybe they should name their son Makepeace. They had settled on Clanton Luís Madrid, forging both families together. By the time Carolyn María arrived a year later, the Clantons and the Madrids had had plenty of opportunity to get to know one another and find out they had a lot more in common than they ever thought possible.

"Mom?" Sierra called again, not finding her in the kitchen. She looked out the window into the backyard garden, where her mother often worked. She wasn't there either. The Buick Regal was in the driveway, so she knew her mother wasn't off on one of her many charity projects or at the church.

Sierra went back along the corridor and up the stairs. "Mom?" Maybe she was taking a nap. She peered into the master bedroom. A bright granny-square afghan was folded neatly on the end of the bed. *"Mom?"*

"I'm in the attic, honey. Come on up."

Surprised, Sierra went down the hallway and climbed the narrow stairway. "What are you doing up here?" she said, entering the cluttered attic. The small dormer windows were open, allowing a faint sun-warmed breeze into the dusty, dimly lit room. Dust particles danced on the beam of sunlight. The place smelled musty with age and disuse.

The attic had always fascinated Sierra, and she momentarily put aside her worries as she looked around. Lawn chairs were stacked at the back. Just inside the door was a big milk can filled with old umbrellas, two canes, and a crooked walking stick. Wicker baskets in a dozen shapes and sizes sat on a high shelf. Boxes were stacked in odd piles, in no particular order, their contents a mystery.

How many times had she and her brother gone through their rooms, sorting and boxing and shoving discards into the attic? When Grandma and Grandpa Clanton had died, boxes from their estate had taken up residence in the quiet dimness. Old books, trunks, and boxes of dishes and silverware were scattered about. A hat tree stood in a back corner on an old braided rag rug that had been made by Sierra's great-grandmother. The box of old dress-up clothes she had donned as a child was still there. As was the large oval mirror where she had admired herself with each change.

Nearby, stacked in her brother's red Radio Flyer wagon, were a dozen or more framed pictures leaning one upon another against the wall. Some were original oils done by her grandfather during his retirement years. Others were family pictures that dated back several generations. Paint cans left over from restoration on the house were stacked on a shelf in case touch-ups were needed to the colorful trim. One bookshelf was filled with shoe boxes, each labeled in her father's neat printing and holding tax returns and business records going back twenty years.

A tattered, paint-chipped rocking horse stood in lonely exile in the far back corner.

Her mother had moved some of the old furniture around so that Grandpa Edgeworth's old couch with the lion-claw legs was sitting in the center of the attic. Opposite it was Daddy's old worn recliner. Two ratty needlepoint footstools served as stands for the things her mother had removed from an old trunk that stood open before her.

Marianna Clanton had a tea towel wrapped around her hair. "I thought I should go through some of these things and make some decisions."

"Decisions about what?" Sierra said, distracted.

"What to throw away, what to keep."

"Why now?"

"I should've started years ago," her mother said with a rueful smile. "I just kept putting it off." She looked around at the cluttered room. "It's a little overwhelming. Bits and pieces from so many lives."

Sierra ran her hand over an old stool that had been in the kitchenette before it was remodeled. She remembered coming home from kindergarten and climbing up on it at the breakfast bar so she could watch her mother make Tollhouse cookies. "Alex called me a little while ago and told me he's accepted a job in Los Angeles."

Her mother glanced up at her, a pained expression flickering across her face. "It was to be expected, I suppose."

"Expected? How?"

"Alex has always been ambitious."

"He has a good job. He got that big promotion last year, and he's making good money. They gave him a comprehensive health package and retirement plan. We have a wonderful new house. We like our neighbors. Clanton and Carolyn are happy in school. We're close to family. I didn't even know Alex had put out word he was looking for another position until he called me today—" Her voice broke. "He was so excited, Mom. You should've heard him. He said this new company made him a fantastic offer, and he accepted it without even talking to me about it."

"What sort of company?"

"Computers. *Games*. The sort of stuff Alex likes to play around with at home. He met these guys at a sales conference last spring in Las Vegas. He never even told me about them. He says he did, but I don't remember. Alex has been working on an idea he has for a role-playing game for an Internet-type program. Players could link up with others and create armies and battle scenarios. He said it's right up their alley. And it doesn't even bother him that they haven't been in business four years yet or that they started business in a garage."

"So did Apple Computers."

"That's different. These guys haven't been around long enough to prove they can *stay* in business. I don't see how Alex can throw away ten years' seniority at Hewlett-Packard when people are being laid off of other jobs left and right! I don't want to go to Los Angeles, Mom. Everything I love is here."

"You love Alex, honey."

"I'd like to *shoot* Alex! Where does he get off making a decision like this without even discussing it with me?"

"Would you have listened if he had?"

She couldn't believe her mother would ask such a thing. "Of course I'd listen! Doesn't he think it has anything to do with me?" She wiped angry tears from her cheeks. "You know what he said to me, Mom? He told me he'd already called a Realtor, and the woman's coming by tonight to list the house. Can you believe it? I just planted daffodils all along the back fence. If he has his way, I won't even be here to see them bloom!"

Her mother said nothing for a long moment. She folded her hands in her lap while Sierra rummaged through her shoulder bag for a Kleenex.

Sierra sniffled into the tissue. "It's not fair. He never even took my feelings into consideration, Mom. He just made the decision and told me it's a done deal. Just like that. Whether I like it or not, we're moving to Los Angeles. He doesn't even care how I feel about it because it's what *he* wants."

"I'm sure Alex didn't make the decision arbitrarily. He's always looked at everything from all sides."

"Not from *my* side." Restless and upset, she walked across the room and picked up an old stuffed bear her brother had cuddled when he was a boy. She hugged it against her. "Alex grew up here just like I did, Mom. I don't understand how he can turn his back on everything and be so *happy* about it."

"Maybe Alex wasn't treated as kindly as you were, Sierra."

Sierra glanced back at her mother in surprise. "His parents never abused him."

"I wasn't referring to Luís or María; they're wonderful people. I mean the assumptions too many people make about Hispanics."

"Well, he can add all that to the other things Los Angeles will have to offer. Smog. Traffic. Riots. Earthquakes."

Her mother smiled. "Disneyland. Movie stars. Beaches," she recited, clearly seeing a much more positive side to things. Daddy used to call it her Pollyanna attitude, especially when he was irritated and in no mood to see the good side of a situation. The way Sierra was feeling now.

"Everyone we love is here, Mom. Family, friends."

"You're not moving to Maine, honey. It's only a day's drive between Healdsburg and Los Angeles. And this *is* the age of telephones."

"You talk as though it doesn't matter to you that we're leaving." Sierra bit her lip and looked away. "I thought you'd understand."

"If I could make the choice, of course, I'd rather you were here. And I do understand. Your grandparents were far from overjoyed when I moved from Fresno to San Francisco." She smiled. "It was a ten-hour drive in those days, but you'd have thought I'd moved to the far side of the moon."

Sierra smiled wanly. "It's hard for me to see you as some sort of beatnik living in San Francisco, Mom."

She laughed. "No less hard than it is for me to see you as a young woman with a wonderful husband and two children in school."

Sierra blew her nose. "Wonderful husband," she muttered. "He's a male chauvinist pig. Alex probably hasn't even bothered to mention this to his parents."

"Luís will understand. Just as your father would have. I think Alex has stayed here for ten years because of you. It's time you allow him to do what he needs to do to make full use of the talents he has."

It was the last thing Sierra wanted to hear. She didn't reply as she ran her hand along the books in an old shelf. She knew what her mother said had merit, but that didn't mean she wanted to listen. Alex had received other offers and turned each down after discussing them with her. She had thought the decisions mutual, but now she wondered. He had sounded so excited and happy when he talked to her about this job. . . .

She plucked *Winnie the Pooh* out and blew dust off the top. Stroking the front of the book, she remembered sitting in her mother's lap as the story was read to her. How many times had she heard it? The cover was worn from handling.

Just thinking about leaving and not being able to see her mother or talk with her every few days left Sierra feeling bereft. Tears blurred her vision.

"Alex gave notice this morning." She pushed the book back into its space. "It was the first thing he did after he got the call from Los Angeles. *Then* he called me with the *great* news." Covering her face, she wept.

Sierra felt some comfort when her mother's arms came around her.

"It'll be all right, honey. You'll see." Her mother stroked her back as though she were a child. "Things have a way of working out for the best. The Lord has plans for you and for Alex, plans for your good, not your destruction. Trust him."

The Lord! Why did her mother always have to bring up *the Lord?* What sort of plan was it to tear people's lives apart?

She withdrew from her mother's arms. "All our friends are here. *You're* here. I don't want to move. It makes no sense. What does Alex think he'll find in Los Angeles that he doesn't already have here?"

"Maybe he wants the chance to prove himself."

"He *has* proven himself. He's succeeded at everything he's ever done."

"Maybe he doesn't feel he's done enough."

"He doesn't have to prove anything to me," Sierra said, her voice choked.

"Sometimes men have to prove things to themselves, Sierra." She took her daughter's hand. "Sit, honey." She drew her down onto the old faded couch. Patting her hand, she smiled wistfully. "I remember Alex talking with your father about all the frustrations he felt in his job."

"Daddy was the one who told Alex to settle in and stay put so he'd have all the benefits."

"Your father was worried Alex would do the same thing he did."

She blew her nose and glanced at her mother. "What do you mean?"

"Your father changed jobs half a dozen times before he settled into real estate."

"He did? I don't remember that."

"You were too young to notice." Her mother smiled wistfully. "Your father intended to be a high school biology teacher."

"Daddy? A teacher?" She couldn't imagine it. He wouldn't have put up with anything. The first student to shoot a spit wad would have found himself upside down in a garbage can outside the classroom door.

Her mother laughed. "Yes, Daddy. He spent five years in college preparing to do just that and after one year in a classroom decided he hated it. He said the girls were all airheads and the boys were running on testosterone."

Sierra smiled, amazed and amused. "I can't even imagine."

"Your dad went to work in a lab then. He hated that, too. He said staring into microscopes all day bored him senseless. So he went to work for a men's clothing store."

"Daddy?" Sierra said again, astounded.

"Yes, *Daddy*. You and Mike were both in school when he quit. After that, he trained to become a police officer. I was as strongly against that as you are against moving to Los Angeles." She patted Sierra's hand again. "But good came out of it. I used to lie awake at night, worrying myself sick over him. I was so sure something would happen to him. Those years were the worst of my life, and our marriage suffered because of it. And yet the greatest blessing came from it, too. I became a Christian while your father was working the eleven-to-seven shift as a highway patrolman."

"I didn't know all this, Mom."

"Why would you? A mother hardly shares these kinds of struggles with her young children. You were four and Mike was seven. Neither of you were happy. You sensed the tension between us and didn't understand. You didn't see that much of your father when he was home because he had to sleep during the day. I spent most of my time telling you two to be quiet and trying to keep you busy with games and puzzles and long walks. The hours and stress were bad enough for Daddy, but I think it was missing you and Mike that finally made him quit. Before he did, he studied for his real estate license. He gave it a try and loved it. As God would have it, he started at the time when real estate was booming. It was a seller's market. Within two years of getting his license, your dad was one of the top Realtors in Sonoma County. He became so busy, he dropped residential and specialized in commercial properties."

She squeezed Sierra's hand. "The point I'm trying to make is this, honey: It took your father sixteen years to settle into a career he enjoyed." She smiled. "Alex knew what he wanted to do when he went to college. The trouble is he's never had the opportunity to accomplish it. The greatest gift you can give him is the freedom to spread his wings."

Again, this wasn't what Sierra wanted to hear. "You talk as though I've put a ball and chain around his neck." She stood and began pacing again. "I'd like to have been consulted, Mom. Is that so hard to understand? Alex didn't even discuss the offer with me. He accepted it and then informed me of his decision. It's not fair."

"Who ever said life was fair?" her mother responded, hands folded.

Sierra felt defensive and angry. "Daddy didn't make you move."

"No, he didn't. I would have been delighted if he had."

Sierra turned and stared at her. "I thought you loved Healdsburg."

"Now I do. When I was younger, all I could think about was getting away from here. I thought how wonderful it would be to live in a big city like San Francisco where lots of things were going on. You know I grew up on Grandma's farm in the central valley, and believe me, it was anything but exciting, honey. I wanted to go to the theater and attend concerts. I wanted to immerse myself in museums and culture. I wanted to walk through Golden Gate Park. And, despite warnings and pleadings from my parents, I did just that."

"And met Daddy."

"Yes. He rescued me from a mugging on the Pan Handle."

Sierra thought of the wedding photo on the mantel downstairs. Her father's hair had been long then, and his "tuxedo" consisted of worn Levi's and heavy boots; her mother, dressed in a black turtleneck and Capri pants, had woven flowers in her waist-length auburn hair. The photo had always jarred with the image she had of her parents. They had been *young* once—and rebellious, too.

Her mother smiled, remembering. "If I'd had my way, we would have settled in San Francisco."

"You never told me that before."

"By the time you and your brother came along, my ideas about what I wanted had changed drastically. Just as your ideas will change. Life isn't static, Sierra. Thank God. It's constantly in motion. Sometimes we find ourselves caught up in currents and carried along where we don't want to go. Then we find out later that God's hand was in it all along."

"God didn't make the decision to move to Los Angeles. Alex made it. But then, I suppose he thinks he's God." Sierra could hear the resentment in her voice, but she hardened herself against any regret or guilt. Emotions raged and warred within her: resentment that Alex had made such a decision without talking to her beforehand; fear that if she fought him, she'd lose anyway; terror of leaving a life she loved and found so comfortable.

"What am I going to do, Mom?"

"That's up to you, honey," her mother said gently, tears of compassion in her eyes.

"I need your advice."

"The second greatest commandment is that we love one another as we love ourselves, Sierra. Forget yourself and think about what Alex needs. Love him accordingly."

"If I do that, he'll walk all over me. Next time, he'll jump at a job in New York City!" She knew she was being unfair even as she said it. Alex had given her two beautiful children, a nice three-bedroom home in Windsor, and a secure, happy life. Life had been so smooth, in fact, she had never once suspected the turmoil within him. Realizing that frightened her. It made her feel she didn't know Alex's heart or mind as well as she thought she did.

She couldn't see a way out. Part of her wanted to pick up the children from school and come back here to the Mathesen Street home and let Alex face the real estate woman alone; he couldn't sell the house if she didn't sign. But she knew if she did that, he'd be furious. The few times she had unintentionally hurt him, he had retreated into anger, putting up a cold front and withdrawing into silence. He didn't come from a family of yellers. She didn't even want to think about how he would respond if she hurt and angered him deliberately.

"It might help to take your mind off the matter for a few hours and then try to think about it later," her mother said.

Heart aching, Sierra sat down on the sofa again. She looked at the open trunk and piles of boxes. "Why are you doing all this now, Mom?"

Something flickered in her mother's eyes. "It's a good winter activity, don't you think?" She glanced around. "It's such a mess. Your father and I meant to go through all this stuff years ago, but then . . ." She looked sad. "Time has a way of getting away from us." She looked around the room at the odd assortment of treasures, some ratty and from long-forgotten sources. "I don't want to leave all this chaos for you and Mike to have to figure out."

She rose and walked around the attic, brushing her hand lightly over an old rocking chair, a bookshelf, a baby's pram.

"I'm going to sort and put all of Mike's and your things over there in the north corner. You two can decide what you want to keep and what you want to throw away. Special things from your father's family and mine, I'll repack. Most of your father's papers from the business can be burned. There's no point in keeping them. And Grandpa's paintings . . . some of them are disintegrating."

"Some of them are really bad," Sierra said, grinning.

"That, too," her mother agreed with a laugh. "It kept him occupied." She stopped near the window, glancing out at the front lawn, her expression pensive. "There are a lot of family papers. I'll have all winter to go through and organize them for you and Mike." She glanced back at Sierra and smiled. "It's a big job, but I think it'll be fun and interesting."

She came back and sat down on the old flowered sofa. "This trunk belonged to Mary Kathryn McMurray. She was one of your ancestors. She came across the plains in a wagon in 1847. I was just glancing through her journal when you came," she said, taking up a leather-bound volume from the trunk and brushing her hand over it. "I hadn't gotten very far. Apparently, this was an assignment book and then it became her diary."

She set the volume between them on the couch. Sierra picked it up and opened it, reading the childish scrawl on the first page.

Mama says livin in the wildurnes aint no resun to bee ignurant. Her papa wuz a larnud man and wud not want fuls in his famlee.

"The trunk was part of Grandpa Clanton's estate," her mother said. "I haven't gone through these things in years." She lifted out a small carved wooden box. "Oh, I remember this," she said, smiling. Inside was an embroidered silk handkerchief. She unfolded it carefully and showed Sierra the antique gold chain and amethyst cross.

"Oh, it's beautiful," Sierra said, taking it and admiring it.

"You may have it, if you'd like."

"I'd love it," Sierra said, opening the small clasp and putting it on.

Her mother took out an old tintype in an oval frame. The couple were dressed in wedding clothes, their expressions solemn rather than joyful. The groom was handsome in his dark suit and starched shirt, his dark hair brushed back cleanly from chiseled features and intense pale eyes. Blue, Sierra decided. They would have had to be blue to be so pale in the picture. The bride was very young and lovely. She was wearing a gorgeous white lace Victorian wedding dress. She sat while her husband stood, his hand firmly planted upon her shoulder.

Sierra took out another box. Inside, wrapped in tissue paper, was a small woven Indian basket with designs. Around the top edge were quail plumes and beads. "I think this is a gift basket, Mom. It's worth a lot of money. They have them in the Indian Museum at Sutter's Fort."

"Is there anything inside the box to tell about it?"

Sierra removed everything and shook her head. "Nothing."

"Look at this old Bible," her mother said, distracted. As she opened it, a section slipped free and fell onto the floor. Her mother picked it up and placed it on the sofa beside her.

Sierra picked up the paper yellowed with age and read the pretty script.

Dearest Mary Kathryn,

I hope you have changed your mind about God. He loves you very much and He is watching over you. I do not know what hardships and losses you will face on the

way to Oregon or what will happen once you reach the end
of the trail. What I do know is God will never leave you
nor forsake you.

You have my love and are in my morning and evening
prayers. The ladies from the quilting club send their love
as well, as do Betsy and Clovis. May the Lord bless your
new home.

Aunt Martha

Sierra's mother thumbed through the black, cracked leather Bible and then picked up the portion that had fallen. "Look at how worn the pages are." She smiled. "Mary Kathryn favored the Gospels." She took the note from Sierra and read it. Folding it, she tucked it in the loosened pages and set the Bible carefully beside Mary Kathryn McMurray's journal.

Sierra took out a decaying flowered hat box. She found a note on top saying simply, in beautiful black calligraphy, "Save for Joshua McMurray." The box was full of animals, carved of wood, each wrapped carefully in a scrap of flowered calico or checked gingham. She unwrapped a fierce-looking wolf, a majestic buffalo, a coiled rattlesnake, a prairie dog standing on its hind legs, a comical jackrabbit, a beautiful antelope, two mountain goats locked together in fierce battle, and a grizzly bear standing on its hind legs, ready to attack.

At the bottom of the trunk was a large package wrapped in butcher paper and tied with string.

"I don't remember this," her mother said and slipped the string off so she could remove the wrapping. *"Oh,"* she said in wonder and excitement. "I think it's a crazy quilt." She unfolded it enough so that Sierra could take one end of it and then stood, spreading the folds to reveal the full pattern.

It wasn't a crazy quilt, but a picture quilt with squares made of hundreds of different scraps of cloth, each with a different scene, each framed with an edging of brown, and all stitched together with vibrant scarlet thread. Each picture block was surrounded by a different stitch: blanket, crosses, herringbone, doves, fern, olive branches, feather, open cretan, fly, zigzag chain, wheatear and sheaf filling stitches, Portuguese border, and star eyelets.

"It's beautiful," Sierra said, wishing she could have it.

"If I'd known it was here, I would have had it cleaned and hung on the living room wall years ago," her mother said.

Sierra looked at the squares one by one. Along the top row was a homestead with a man, a woman, and three children. Two boys and a girl stood in the open space between the cabin and barn. The second square was bright with consuming flames. The third showed a baby in a manger, a young girl watching over him while darkness surrounded them both.

The telephone rang downstairs. A second later, the portable phone rang from nearby. Sierra's mother handed her the other end of the quilt and went to pick up the phone from the top of a box and answer it.

"Yes, she's here, Alex."

Sierra's heart lurched. Hands trembling again, she folded the quilt while listening to her mother's side of the conversation.

"Yes, she told me. Yes, but that's to be expected, Alex." Her mother's tone held no condemnation or disappointment. She was silent for a long moment, listening again. "I know that, Alex," she said very gently, her voice husky with emotion, "and I've always been thankful. You don't have to explain." Another silence. "So soon," her mother said, resigned. "How are your parents taking it? Oh. Well, I imagine it's going to be a shock to them as well." She smiled faintly. "Of course, Alex. You know I will. Let me know after you've spoken to them, and I'll call."

Marianna cupped her hand over the receiver. "Alex wants to talk to you."

Sierra wanted to say she didn't want to talk to him but knew that would put her mother between them. She laid the folded quilt back over the trunk and crossed the attic to take the phone from her mother's hand.

"I'll make us some coffee," her mother said with a gentle smile.

Sierra watched her go down the stairs, knowing her mother was allowing her privacy to speak with Alex. She felt a tangle of emotions, from relief to despair. Her mother hadn't said one word to discourage Alex from his decision. Why not?

"Yes?" she said into the receiver, her voice coming out thin and choked. She wanted to scream at him and could barely draw breath past the pain in her chest. Her throat was tight and dry.

"I was worried about you."

"Were you?" Why should he worry about her just because he was ripping her life apart? Resentment filled her and hot tears welled again in her eyes.

"You're not saying much."

"What do you want me to say? That I'm *happy?*"

He sighed. "I suppose that would be expecting too much, especially considering this is the biggest opportunity of my career."

She heard the tinge of disappointment and anger in his voice. What right had he to be angry with her after making a life-changing decision without so much as hinting it to her?

"I'm sure the children will be thrilled to hear they're being uprooted and torn away from their friends and family."

"We're their family."

"What about Mom? What about your parents?"

"We're not moving to New York, Sierra."

"I guess you're saving that for next year's big surprise."

Silence followed. Her heart picked up speed; she could feel his growing anger.

Stop this now, an inner voice cautioned her. *Stop before you go too far. . . .*

She wasn't interested in stopping. "You might have hinted what was going on, Alex," she said, clutching the phone.

"I've done more than hint. I told you about this company weeks ago. I've been telling you for the last four years what I want to do. The problem is you don't listen."

"I listen."

"And never *hear.*"

"I do too hear!"

"Then hear *this.* You've had it your way for ten years. Maybe, just for a change, you could cut *me* a little slack."

Click.

"Alex?" Dead silence filled her ear. Sierra blinked, shocked. She stared at the phone in her hand as though it had turned to a venomous snake. Alex had never hung up on her before.

More distressed than when she had arrived, Sierra went downstairs. The tantalizing aroma of freshly ground caramel au lait decaf filled the kitchen. Her favorite. So, too, were the Tollhouse cookies her mother had put on a dessert plate in the sunny alcove overlooking the back garden. Clearly Mom wanted to cheer her up. Fat chance.

She plunked the portable phone down on the pretty flower-embroidered cloth covering the small table and sank down onto the chair. "He hung up on me." Her mother poured coffee for her. "He's never hung up on me before," Sierra continued, her voice breaking as she looked up at her mother. He'd made a decision he knew would tear her life to pieces, and then *he* hung up on *her?* "He said I don't listen."

Her mother set the carafe on a sunflower trivet and took the seat facing her. "Sometimes we only hear what we want to hear." She picked up her coffee cup and sipped, distracted.

"You look tired, Mom."

"I didn't sleep very well last night. I kept thinking about your father." Her mouth curved faintly, her expression softening.

33

"Sometimes I imagine him sitting in his chair watching the news on television. The house creaks and I awaken, thinking he's coming along to bed." She smiled sadly and looked down into her coffee as she set the cup back in its porcelain saucer. "I miss him."

"I miss him, too." He might have been able to talk Alex out of going to Los Angeles.

Her mother lifted her head and looked across at her with gentle humor. "Your father wasn't an easy man either, Sierra, but he was worth it."

"If Alex insists, I'll go, but I don't have to smile and pretend to be happy about it."

"Maybe not, but it'd be better if you came to terms with his decision. Resentment and anger eat away at love as quickly as rust is corroding that metal lawn chair out there in the backyard. One of life's great tragedies is watching a relationship unravel over something that could've been resolved in one intelligent, adult conversation."

Her mother's words hurt. "One conversation isn't going to change Alex's mind."

"Then it depends on what you really want."

Sierra raised tear-soaked eyes to her mother's clear hazel ones. "What do you mean?"

Marianna reached out and took her daughter's hand. "It's simple, Sierra. Do you want your own way, or do you want Alex?"

2

SIERRA LEFT HER MOTHER IN TIME TO DRIVE TO Windsor and pick up the children from school. They slammed into the car and immediately began vying for her undivided attention. She was often amused by their antics. Today their youthful exuberance and competitiveness irritated. As she drove along Brooks Road toward the foothills, she heard only bits and pieces of their day, distracted by her own turbulent thoughts. She longed for a quiet place to lick her wounds.

Her heart began beating a battle rhythm when she saw Alex's Honda in the driveway. He never came home before five-thirty.

"Daddy's home!" Carolyn said, dashing out the car door toward the front steps, her backpack forgotten in the front seat.

Sierra pressed the garage door opener and watched the door lift slowly. She drove in, shifted into park, put on the brake, and turned off the engine — each movement carefully measured and controlled. "Take Carolyn's things in, would you please, Clanton?"

"Let her come out and get 'em herself."

"It wouldn't hurt you to help —"

"I'm not her personal servant. Besides, she was just bragging about girls being better than boys. So let Little Miss Wonderful carry her own backpack!"

"Don't argue with me. I'm not in the mood for it."

Clanton grumbled, but one look at her face silenced further protests. Sierra gathered her own things and followed him into the kitchen. She could hear Carolyn chattering happily and Alex's deep laugh. A sharp pang shot through her, though whether it was pain or anger she couldn't tell. Maybe both. How could he laugh at a time like this? Didn't he care at all how she felt?

"Why are you home early, Dad?" Clanton's excited voice carried easily, as did the *thud* of the two backpacks hitting the living room floor. Alex answered too quietly for her to hear what he was saying, and she clenched her teeth. As she opened a cabinet and took a can of coffee down from the shelf, she listened to the quiet murmur of voices, subdued now. Was he telling the children he had decided to uproot them and take them away from friends and family? How were they taking it? She knew she should be there, helping them understand . . . but how could she do that when she didn't understand herself? Her hand trembled as she measured grounds.

Her throat closed tightly when she heard Alex enter the kitchen. She didn't look at him. She couldn't and still maintain any semblance of control. She poured water into the coffeemaker and then turned her attention to the package of chicken she had left to thaw on the counter.

"I'm sorry I hung up on you." His deep voice was low and quiet.

Her eyes burned. She removed the plastic wrap from the chicken and turned on the water. "Did you tell them?"

"Yes."

She took a thigh from the open package and began washing it meticulously. "And?"

"Carolyn's going down to Karen's house. Clanton's riding his bike over to David's."

"I never let them go anywhere until they finish their homework."

"Well, I think this is a day for exceptions to the rule, don't you?" He sounded so in control. It grated on her nerves. "I told them to be home by five." He leaned against the doorframe and crossed his arms. "I thought it might be a good idea to have them both out of the house while we talk things over."

"Talk?" she said stiffly. "It's a little late, isn't it? I was under the impression you'd already decided everything."

"Fine," he said tightly. "We'll do this your way. We *won't* talk."

Glancing back, she saw him go back into the family room. Her heart pounded heavily, her stomach tightened. It was the second time today he had flung an unfair accusation at her! She pitched the last piece of rinsed chicken onto the cutting board, washed her hands with soap, and slapped off the tap. Snatching the towel from the oven door handle, she dried her hands quickly, then flung the towel in the direction of the counter before following him, trembling with anger.

"*My* way," she said. "You're the one who called and said we're moving. Oh, and by the way, Sierra, a Realtor's coming by tonight to list your home!"

"*Our* home," he corrected, his dark eyes narrowing.

"That's what I thought until you dropped your bomb!"

"I made a judgment call."

"You just got a promotion *and* a raise. When most people are shaking in their boots about the possibility of being laid off, you have job security, pension, health coverage. We have a nice home. The children are happy—"

"Most people never get an opportunity like this, Sierra."

"An opportunity for what? To work for a new company that may go broke in a year?"

"I don't think that's likely."

"But you don't know for sure."

"No, I don't know for sure," he said, angry now. "I haven't got a crystal ball. But I have a strong feeling about where they're going, and I want to go along for the ride."

"A *feeling?* And you talk about me basing everything on emotions."

"This is different," he said through his teeth.

"What's different about it? You've worked so hard for security—"

"Security isn't everything."

She closed her ears to his remark. "And now you're throwing everything away on a whim."

"I'm not throwing anything away! You still don't get it, do you? Everything I've done up to now has been to prepare myself for an opportunity like *this*. I'm not going to spend the rest of my life building someone else's ideas. I have my own!"

"Why can't you do what you want on your own time *here?*"

"Because I don't have the equipment it takes."

"And what if it doesn't work out, Alex?"

"I'll cross that bridge *if* I come to it."

Shaking violently, she sank down onto the sofa, her hands clenched into fists as she fought her tears. "I don't want to move, Alex."

"Don't you think I know that?" he said, sounding torn between frustration and understanding. "You'd be happy if we stayed in this place for the rest of our lives."

She met his troubled gaze. "What's wrong with this place?"

"I want more out of life than a thirty-year mortgage on a tract house."

A tract house? Was that how he saw their home? He made it sound like a cardboard box. She thought of the time she had spent painting, hanging wallpaper, planting and tending the front and back yards so that it looked like an English garden. Hurt beyond words, she covered her face and wept.

Alex said a short, foul word under his breath and sat down on the sofa beside her. "My little homebody," he said tenderly, touching her hair. She jerked away and started to get up. He caught her wrist and jerked her down again. "You're not going anywhere."

She cried harder, and he pulled her firmly into his arms, swearing softly under his breath again. "I know you're scared, Sierra. You've spent your whole life in Healdsburg. What do you know about anything else? You think this place is the end-all of creation."

"Most of the people in Los Angeles would probably think they'd died and gone to heaven if they could live where we do."

"People who aren't going anywhere, anyway. I should've taken you to Berkeley with me. Then maybe you'd understand how a place can hum with ideas and excitement. That's what I feel when I'm around these guys. *Energy.*"

She didn't know what he was talking about, but she felt the excitement running through him.

"I graduated with honors, Sierra, and what am I doing with what I learned?" He gave a dismal laugh under his breath. "Nothing."

She struggled free. "How can you say that? You've been

working only ten years, and you've already accomplished what most people spend their whole lives trying to do."

"Yeah," he said cynically. "A three-bedroom, two-bath tract house that looks like every other house on the block. Two children. Two cars. All we lack is the dog and cat to fit into the mold of middle-class America. Big deal!" His eyes burned with intensity.

She went cold inside at the way he described their life.

He searched her face. "Don't look at me like that, Sierra," he said, softening. He cupped her face. "I'm not criticizing you or what you've done to make this place a home. I didn't make this decision to hurt you. I *love* you." He kissed her. "You know I love you. I've done everything so far to make you happy."

"I am happy, Alex."

"I know," he said grimly, his hands sliding away. "The trouble is, I'm not."

His softly spoken words struck a stunning blow. Fear and confusion gripped her. He was telling her she wasn't enough; he wasn't satisfied.

"I want more, Sierra. I'm still hungry. I want to explore new frontiers in computer technology. I want a chance to do something meaningful." He smiled wryly. "And maybe even get rich while doing it."

When she remained silent he spent the next hour telling her all the details of his new job. She couldn't remember ever seeing him so excited about anything. Depressed, she said she needed to start dinner.

"I'll fly down to Los Angeles on Saturday," Alex said, leaning against the doorframe and watching her work. "Steve Silverman made an appointment for me with a Realtor who handles rentals in North Hollywood. He knows everyone in that area."

Good for him, Sierra thought rebelliously. Her hands shook as she peeled potatoes. "How soon do we have to move?"

"I start on the first of the month."

"Three weeks?" She could feel the blood draining from her face. "But the house will never sell in three weeks," she said shakily, looking for any excuse to delay his plans.

"Probably not, but that's OK, too. One of the guys at work is going to rent it."

Sierra blinked. "Rent it?"

"His wife's expecting a baby, and they've been looking for a bigger place." The telephone rang in the family room. "Our house payments are less than what they're paying to rent a two-bedroom apartment," he said over his shoulder as he went to answer it.

She could hear Alex speaking in the other room. "We were just talking about it. No, but I didn't expect her to be. Don't worry about it." Silence for a long moment.

Sierra looked out the kitchen window at the rose bushes she had just planted along the back fence. She'd never see them bloom.

"I land in Burbank at ten fifteen. No, but thanks for the offer, Steve. I'm going to rent a car. I want to drive around and get a feel for the area." He laughed. "I have a good sense of direction."

Tears ran down Sierra's cheeks as she finished preparing their dinner. Normally she enjoyed cooking; right now, even the sight of food made her stomach churn.

Alex was still talking on the telephone. Discussing terms. He sounded very cool, very much in control.

He was going through with this. Nothing she'd said had gotten through.

Oh, God, she prayed frantically. *If you're really there, don't let Alex do this to me. Put stumbling blocks in his way. Open his eyes to what he has here. Make him satisfied. Don't let the house sell. Change his mind. I don't want to move! Jesus, I want to stay right here where I am. Oh, God, please don't let this happen!*

Slamming the head of lettuce on the counter, she pulled out the core. She put the plug in the sink and ran cold water and then pulled the head of lettuce into pieces.

With each action, she whispered brokenly. "Oh, God. Oh, God, oh, God, oh, God." Her shoulders shook with her quiet weeping as she listened to Alex shattering her life with his plans.

2

The Wilderness

3

EXHAUSTED, SIERRA PULLED HER HONDA IN behind the big U-Haul truck Alex had rented to move all their possessions and to tow his car. Clanton got out the passenger side of the truck and looked up at the big stark white apartment complex. Sierra followed his gaze.

The place had all the charm of a fortress.

She rolled down her window, not eager to get out into the cold, driving January rain. She could hear the roar of traffic from two intersecting freeways half a block away. "Is this it?"

"It looks a lot better inside. Come on. I'll show you around."

She leaned across the seat and kissed Carolyn, awakening her. "We're here, sweetheart."

Carolyn looked out at the apartment house. "It's ugly," she said glumly. Sierra didn't disagree.

Clanton was already going through the iron gates into the complex. "Hey! There's a pool! Can I go swimming, Dad?"

"Sure, if we can find your suit," Alex said, laughing.

As Sierra climbed out of the car and came around for Carolyn, she was certain she could smell and taste the smog despite the rain pouring down on her head. She took her still-sleepy daughter by the hand and followed Alex through the gate. The inside courtyard was sterile: a gray cement patio, white stucco walls, and a black iron fence. Three stories of apartments were stacked together like crates in a warehouse. Geometric. Ultramodern. Cold and impersonal.

Sierra didn't see any signs of life until a woman peered out at her from a first-floor living room window. Sierra forced a smile. The woman drew back sharply and let the sheer drapes fall into place once more.

Welcome *home*, Sierra thought bitterly, following Alex.

"We're on the second floor, apartment D," he said. Clanton was first to the stairs, eager to see his new home.

The apartment was as white inside as the building was outside, except for the rug, which was a pale beige. The living room was roomy enough, but the kitchen was cramped and utterly utilitarian. The small dining area was barely large enough to accommodate a table and four chairs. Sierra wandered into the hallway. To the left was the bedroom Clanton and Carolyn would share. It was only big enough for twin beds and one dresser. The other dresser would have to go into the closet. Sierra's mouth thinned. Clanton and Carolyn were going to love this; they were fighting already.

A glance into the bathroom revealed walls, tiles, and a commode in antiseptic white. She continued down the short hallway into the master bedroom. Most of their furniture would fit, though Alex's armoire would probably have to go inside the closet. Sierra caught her reflection in the mirror on the closet doors; she did not look pleased. Turning away, she went to open the drapes covering a large window and discovered a view of the courtyard and pool below. Just like a hotel.

Depressed, she went back into the living room.

Alex hung up the telephone that Steve Silverman, his new boss, had been kind enough to have installed before their arrival. Steve had told Alex to call as soon as they arrived, and he and Matt would come with helpers to get them settled. "They'll be here in ten minutes," Alex said, grinning. Either oblivious to or ignoring her mood, he caught hold of her shoulders and kissed her before heading for the door.

In less than two hours, all their furniture was in position and boxes stacked high against the living room wall. Steve had a couple of pizzas delivered. Matt had brought a six-pack of beer and another of soda. Clanton and Carolyn tucked away the food eagerly while Sierra pleaded no appetite and escaped into the bedrooms to hide her angst. She made the beds, hung pictures, laid out the bathroom rug and towels. Then she set to work on the master bedroom, the sound of the men's laughter irritating her more with each passing minute.

Clanton found his bathing suit. Her first *no* brought out his debating skills. Her mother always said Clanton would make a good lawyer. "I said no, Clanton. It's raining and . . ."

He followed her out into the living room and appealed to Alex. "Dad, can I go swimming? The rain isn't going to hurt me."

"Sure. Go ahead," Alex said, pausing in his conversation with Steve and Matt long enough to gainsay her. He saw her expression after the fact. "What's the big deal?" he said as Clanton charged out the door before she could say anything. "He's going to get wet anyway, and the pool's heated."

"Fine. You stand out in the rain and keep an eye on him," she said, her fury far exceeding the incident. Swinging around, she went back into the master bedroom and plunked down on the bed.

Alex came in a moment later, tight-lipped. "We're going out for a while."

"Out?"

"For an hour or two. To talk business."

She clenched her hands, wanting to scream. "Is Clanton back from his swim?" she said with icy sweetness.

He stalked across the room. "You can sit nice and cozy where you are and keep an eye on him while you're sulking."

Raw and exhausted, she looked at him. "What about groceries, or will there be enough pizza left for breakfast?"

"If you look out the front gate, you'll see the back of one of the biggest supermarkets in North Hollywood. You've got a car, and you've got the checkbook. Get what you need." He went to the door and stopped. He uttered a soft curse and slammed the heel of his fist against the frame. "I'm sorry," he said bleakly.

Blinking back tears, she looked away.

"This is only temporary, Sierra."

Still she said nothing.

"I'll hook up the TV before we leave."

"Great. That'll be a real comfort," she muttered under her breath as he left the room. A few moments later she watched him walk by the bedroom window with Steve and Matt. They were so intent on their conversation that he didn't even spare a glance at her. She was already forgotten.

Clanton and Carolyn were asleep in bed before he returned.

"An hour or two?" she said when he walked in the door.

He shrugged off his jacket and tossed it on the sofa. "We had a lot to talk about."

She snapped off the television. She hadn't even been paying attention to what she was watching, so intent was she on the time. "It's after midnight, Alex. I've been worried sick. You could've called."

"I would've if I could've remembered the number. We're unlisted."

An excuse, not an apology. "I'm going to bed," she said in a choked voice and left him standing in the living room.

She brushed her teeth and washed her face, then went into the bedroom to undress. Alex came in as she was pulling on her nightgown. "It's been a long day," he said.

"The longest of my life."

She got into bed and pulled the covers up to her chin, staring up at the dark ceiling. She heard the whisper of clothing as Alex undressed. The bed dipped slightly when he sat down on it. He didn't say anything more. What could he say? Swallowing hot tears, she turned her back to him while he set the alarm clock. When he lay back, he let his breath out slowly.

She felt his hand curve over her hip and squeeze slightly. "I'm sorry."

His apology brought a rush of feelings and a flood of tears. She dug her fingers into her pillow, trying to stifle her sobs. Alex turned to her. Curving his body around hers, he pulled her into him, holding her firmly when she resisted his comfort. He stroked her long hair back and kissed the curve of her neck. "I love you."

She cried harder.

He turned her to him gently. "Trust me," he said raggedly and kissed her, comforting her in the only way he knew how.

And for a while, Sierra was able to forget everything but the fact that she loved Alejandro Madrid above all else.

ARMED WITH A MAP AND AN ADDRESS, SIERRA SET
off to enroll the children in school. She missed a turn and got
lost. By the time she found what she was looking for, she and
the children had seen North Hollywood, a portion of Studio
City, eaten at a McDonald's, and toured most of Sherman Oaks
and San Fernando Valley. They arrived and entered the school
building just as the bell rang to end the day.

Children poured out of classrooms and filled the hallway. The
cacophony of squeaking tennis shoes, friends calling to friends,
and the general rush for the buses assaulted them. Carolyn
clutched frantically at Sierra's hand as they went against the flow,
while Clanton plowed ahead and led the way to the main office.

A secretary greeted them. She was polite, but cool, clearly tired and ready to go home. "Fill these out," she said briskly and went in to speak with the principal. Returning, she informed Sierra that Clanton would be in Mr. Cannon's fourth-grade class and Carolyn in Mrs. Lindstrom's third grade.

"Both teachers have after-school meetings today, so you'll have to wait to meet them until tomorrow morning. School starts at eight-thirty." The secretary turned the forms around and looked them over. "Kling Street," she said. "That's only a few blocks from here." Sierra's face went hot with humiliation at the disclosure.

"We have a list of parents who take turns walking their children to school each day."

"I'll be driving mine," Sierra said, unwilling to entrust her children to anyone. Clanton groaned expressively, and she gave him a quelling look.

Back in the car, she sat studying the map before starting the engine. She didn't want to get lost again and end up in Watts this time.

Alex laughed when she told him about it. "I wondered where you were," he said. "I called twice today and got no answer. I was afraid you'd packed up and gone back to Windsor."

She didn't think his remark amusing.

"Don't worry about it," he said, leaning his hip against the counter. "My first trip down here, I had an appointment in Burbank. I got on the wrong freeway and ended up in Agoura. It's not hard to do."

His words were hardly comforting.

They went to Steven's house for dinner. Alex's new boss had even made arrangements for a professional babysitter to look after Clanton and Carolyn. She came complete with references and a list of classes in first aid that she had completed at Northridge.

Alex found his way to their Sherman Oaks home without difficulty. Steven answered the door and ushered them into a spacious, elegantly decorated living room. His wife, Audra, was perfectly charming and courteous, but Sierra felt an undercurrent of disdain that nullified the show of warmth and hospitality. Audra wore a fine, lacquered veneer of friendliness, leaving Sierra to wonder at what lay beneath the flawless surface.

Alex seemed perfectly at ease with both of them, making Sierra wonder if she was imagining the crosscurrents and undertow. But within the course of the first ten minutes of conversation, she knew it was not her imagination. Somehow Sierra had been made fully aware that Audra was a graduate of USC who had studied—and mastered—liberal arts and who had been a member of one of the more prestigious sororities.

Then Audra turned her perfect, elegant gaze on Sierra and asked where she'd gone to college. It was the first time in Sierra's life that she was embarrassed to admit she had only graduated from high school and finished a year at a secretarial college.

"Oh," Audra said, looking utterly taken aback. There was a brief, mortifying lapse in conversation, until Steve jumped in.

"Do you like the theater, Sierra?"

"I haven't been to many plays."

"What have you seen?" Audra inquired, her eyes lighting with interest.

Joseph and the Amazing Technicolor Dream Coat," she said, not telling Audra it had been a high school production. "And a few concerts," she added, which was true—in just the last six months she'd gone to a country western concert and to hear a few Christian singers who had visited local Santa Rosa churches. Of course, she didn't think Audra needed to know the details.

And yet, even without the details, the other woman laughed. "Well, we'll have to correct that. Los Angeles has a great deal of culture to offer."

Sierra felt like a country bumpkin.

While the men talked business, Audra gave Sierra a rundown of the current cultural events. It seemed she had attended every major play and concert in the area and had a critique for each one. She quickly reviewed every theater company and artist currently performing, until Sierra wondered if she was dining with a normal woman or with some odd, sophisticated, upper-class incarnation of Siskel and Ebert.

Dinner proved spectacular. Any critic of fine cuisine would have given Audra a ten-star rating. She accepted all compliments with an air of casual amusement, skillfully turning the discussion to restaurants. Audra knew all the finest. She also knew where to shop for the highest quality meats, vegetables, and fruit. Prices never came up.

Sierra glanced at Alex and saw he was impressed with everything—especially with Audra. Was that the kind of wife he wanted now? Depressed, she ate the fluffy spinach soufflé. It melted in her mouth and made her heart sink into her stomach. What on earth was she going to serve these people for a reciprocal dinner? Her specialty was meat loaf and mashed potatoes. Oh, *that* would go over big! Or perhaps Clanton and Carolyn's favorite: tuna casserole. There was a meal custom-designed to impress high society!

"You were pretty quiet tonight," Alex said on the drive home.

In her mind, she had been busily packing and moving back to Windsor. She didn't appreciate his interruption of her daydream.

He didn't seem to notice. "Audra was trying to make you feel welcome."

"Is that what she was trying to do?" she snapped, surprised herself at the coldness in her tone.

Mouth tightening, Alex stared straight ahead, the headlights

from the oncoming traffic casting a glow over his handsome features. "She was offering to take you under her wing."

"I'm not a chicken."

"Give it a break, Sierra. She grew up down here. She could
show you around."

"I'll remember to thank her properly next time, but I'll find
my own way around, thank you very much. You gave me a map,
remember?"

"A lot of good that did. At least try not to get lost again. I won't
have the time to come find you in the middle of the day."

They didn't say another word to each other for the rest of the
drive home. In fact, they said very little to one another over the
next week. Alex left early, came home late, and always brought
work with him. They shared a perfunctory "How'd your day go?"
"Fine. And you?" "Fine"—and then he would settle in front of
the television, studying the papers he spread out over the coffee
table while she cleaned up the dinner dishes, saw to the children's
baths, read them stories, and tucked them into bed.

It was a perfect life—for someone who adored misery.

Ten days and four telephone calls to her mother later, Sierra
received a package in the mail.

"What's this?" Alex said, picking up a worn leather book from
the coffee table before he spread his work across it.

"It's a journal. Mom sent it as a housewarming present."

He handed it to her.

"It looks old."

"It is," she said warmly. "It belonged to an ancestor of mine.
Mary Kath—"

"Mm-hm," he replied absently, cutting her off as he turned
to concentrate on the papers spread out in front of him. "That's
nice."

Hurt swept over her at his casual dismissal. It shouldn't have surprised her that he wasn't listening. He seldom listened anymore. All that mattered to him was his precious work.

She left the room in bitter silence. She entered the bedroom, not even bothering to turn on the light. Enough light filtered through the window for her to see. Besides, the darkness fit her mood better. She prepared for bed, then slipped between the cool sheets. As she turned on her side, the journal, which she'd laid on the bed stand, caught her eye. She reached for it, fingering the soft leather wistfully.

At least Mary Kathryn wouldn't mind spending some time with her.

Mama says livin in the wildurnes aint no resun to bee ignurant.

Her papa wuz a larnud man and wud not want fuls in his famlee. The preechur brung buks and jurnals to rite in frum Ant Martha and now with snow up to the windows, we got time. Papa sits by the fire smokin and Mama reeds to us frum her Bible.

Matt dont like to rite much. He draws wulfs with big bludy dripin fangs that giv me nitmars. He drew me a hair once. I stil got it hung up over my bed. It iz nis. I wish he wud draw birds and flouerz stead of wulfs. He only seen one wulf his hol lif and it was ded. Magots wuz eting it.

Lucas does not draw nor rede nor rite. He says Papa dont no how an he dont need to neether. Papa tuk him to the wud shed fur sasing Mama,

but he wernt no better wen he cum bak. So Papa
giv him the gun and told him to go huntin. He
wuz gon three daz. Mama wuz sure he got kilt by
injuns or a bar, but he cum bak dragin a dear on a
palot fixt up. Papa laft and gav him a cup of rum.
Mama was mad as a wet hornet, but she dont tel
Lucas to rede or rite no more.

Dearest Mary Kathryn,
  *Please practice spelling the following words and then
write an essay using them. I love you and have grand
hopes for you.*

Mama

  *living journal life whole read choice
dead learned wolf/wolves come journal
back flower*

If you want to be learned, you got no choice. You
got to read and write your whole life until you
are dead. You can not be a wolf or a flower who
jest enjoys living. You got to come back to the
table and werk in your journal until yer fingers is
crampt and aking.

just	cramped	your	are	work	aching
just	cramped	your	are	work	aching
just	cramped	your	are	work	aching
just	cramped	your	are	work	aching

Stubbornness is unbecoming to a lady.
Stubbornness is unbecoming to a lady.
Stubbornness is unbecoming to a lady.
Stubbornness is unbecoming to a lady.
Stubbornness is unbecoming to a lady.

"Spring"

Spring is the time when snow melts and flowers
come up. Papa and Matthew plow them under
and I have got to go to the wuds to pik some. I
like to pik flowers in the wuds but Mama worrees
I mit get took by injuns. One come to the house
once askin fur food. Mama give him sum and I
aint seen him since. I gues he didnot think much
of her cookin.

Spring is also wen Matt turns the dirt in
Mama's vechtable gardin. Every wurm he turns
up I put in a kan fur fishin. I like catchin fish but
I hate eatin em. Lucas told me he new a boy who
chokt to deth on a fish bone. Mama said he wuz
foolin me but I aint et fish since.

Papa says spring is a time for courtin. I askt
him wat courtin wuz and he said it is when a yung
mans blud comes up like sap in a tree. Wen I askt
him what he ment, Mama giv him her look and he
laft and wud not tell me. I askt Matt later but he
turned red and wud not say. Lucas said courtin
was wen Papa took the cow over to Graysons

bull. Matt told him to shut his dirty mouth and
Lucas hit him in his and Papa come runnin to
stop them before they kilt each other. I am more
and more interested in what courtin is.

Spring is wen the preecher comes and stands
on a stump and screeems holy murder at us. He
yells about GAWD and SALVATION and the
BLOOD OF CHRIST. Peepull come from all
rownd to see him. He gits so wurkt up his face
turns red as fire. Frum up or down I aint sure
witch. Mama says he is zelus for the Lord. Papa
says he is plum crazy. But every tim he comes we
go and watch with every one else. He is the best
entertanmunt a rownd.

We always end up at the river with the preecher washin peepul clean of sin and buryin them
and razing them up with Jesus. Mama says
amen and creyes every time someone gets dunkt
and Papa comes bak from the wuds smellin of
whiskey and tobako.

Mama and I plant corn and squash and turnups
and carots. Mama gave me a handful of seeds and
askt me what I saw and I said seeds. She askt
if they looked alive and I said they looked like
stones. She said that is rit but when we bury them
they will grow and bar frut. I said they will bar
squash. She said when you plant a seed, God will
soften it and water it and make it grow. She said
people are like that.

Old Schmidt died last summer and they planted him but nothing come up that I can see cepting weeds. Lucas said worms ate him. So I reckon that is why.

"The Well"

The well is very deep and very dark. It is cool when you first go down but if you stay it is cold. The walls are wet and slimy and you can hear dripping. When you look up you can see a circle of blue sky unless Lucas puts the cover over. Then you dont see nothing. You just hear yourself screaming all around you. Lucas took the cover off and called down that I was a bludy coward. I hollared back up I wasnt. He said prove it and put the cover back. I sat in the bucket all day so he'd know.

Matt found me when he tried to get a bucket of water for Papa. He looked down and said what in hades are you doing down there. Mama is going crazy looking for you. Thinks injuns stole you. He hollared he had found me and Mama come running thinking I wuz drowned. My backside had no feeling and was stuck fast in the buckt. It hurt bad when Papa popped me out. Lucas was leaning against the house laffing. I yelled I aint no coward. No, you are a fool he said.

Papa took him to the wood shed and Mama cried and took me in the house. She made me sit

in the tub of hot water and drink whiskey. I dont
see what Papa likes about it. It burns all the way
down and then comes right back up.

Dearest Mary Kathryn,

*Please practice these words on your slate until you are
ready for me to test you. Use ten in an essay. And do not
ask anyone else about courting.*

I love you,

Mama

Go   witch/which   people   worry/worries
zealous   Indians   woods   garden
choked   liked   laughed   asked
death   pick   when   might
from   some/sum   wood/would   catching
running   washing   raising   cooking

God loves *zealous people* in the *woods*. He *might* love
some Indians. Mama loves *washing, cooking,* and
raising chikins.

Mary Kathryn McMurray,

*You will have no supper until you write chickens
twenty-five times on your slate, and "A penitent heart is
a humble heart" fifty times.*

Mama

5

"WHAT TIME DO YOU THINK YOU'LL BE HOME?" Sierra said, trying to keep her voice neutral as she clutched the telephone receiver.

"Five-thirty or six," Alex said, sounding distracted. She could hear him punching the keys of his computer.

Couldn't he stop working long enough to talk to her for two minutes? "What would you like for dinner?"

"Something light. I had a big lunch with Steve."

"Where'd you go?" she said, wanting to draw out their conversation.

"La Serre. It's a French place. Classy."

"Expensive?"

"Very." Alex chuckled. "It's nice when the boss picks up the tab."

Must be nice to have a fancy lunch and then ask for something *light* for dinner. She looked at the breakfast dishes in the sink. She hadn't even had lunch yet. She opened the refrigerator while talking to him. Maybe she could open a can of peaches and finish off the carton of cottage cheese sitting on the top shelf.

"We were celebrating."

"What?" she asked, feeling left out.

"Vigilantes went into production today," he said, clearly proud of the game he had created. "Steve said they'll be sending out trial copies to game reviewers around the country by the middle of next week."

"What if they don't like it?"

"They will. Look, honey, I've got to go. I've got a call coming in, and I'm right in the middle of something important. We'll talk tonight."

He hung up before she could utter a word. She held the silent receiver and felt more bereft than when she'd called. Why had she bothered? He was always busy and it was always important. More important than she was, anyway.

Celebrating. He hadn't even bothered to share the news with her. *La Serre. Classy. Expensive.*

Angry, she took a package of frozen hamburger from the refrigerator freezer and tossed it on the counter. She'd fix spaghetti *again.* It was easy, and the children loved it.

Turning on the television, she set the basket of clean laundry in front of her. She had made a habit of doing the wash right after she dropped the children off for school, and then saving the folding for now. At least then she could overcome her feelings of guilt for watching a soap opera. She plunked down on the sofa and began folding T-shirts, towels, and underwear while watching the episode unfolding before her. She used to scorn soap operas. Now she found solace in them. For an hour, she could forget how miserable she was and lose herself in the convoluted lives of television characters. Their problems were more tragic and complex than hers, their passions a lot more exciting. How many times had Erica Kane been married anyway?

The laundry was folded and set aside well before the third commercial promoting some new feminine hygiene product. She put the towels and clothing away. Sitting down again, she kicked her bare feet up on the coffee table and leaned back into the sofa. She *should* be doing *something*. But what?

They'd been living in this apartment house for three months, and she didn't even know the family next door. She knew they had children. The little boy ran along the corridor right outside the living room window a dozen times every day, even when it was raining. And there was that woman down on the first floor who peered out her curtains all the time and then ducked back in when someone chanced to notice her. What was her problem anyway?

Sierra didn't want to find out. There were twenty apartments in this complex, and she didn't know a single soul living in one of them. Everyone protected their privacy. They probably had guns in their side tables. She remembered having a phone conversation with her mother, in which her mother said, "Reach out, Sierra. You can never tell who God has just waiting for you to say hello." So she'd said hello to one woman who came into the laundry room, and the woman had barely acknowledged her attempt at friendliness. She just dumped diapers into one of the washing machines, poured in soap, twirled the controls, and left.

Rebuffed, Sierra didn't make the attempt again. If God had someone waiting for her, he'd have to tell them to make the first move.

She didn't leave the sofa until the credits were rolling, and then clicked off the television. Collecting her things, she went out the door. She had it all perfectly timed. If she left immediately after the soap opera, she'd pull into Carolyn and Clanton's school just as the other children were boarding school buses.

The kids pleaded for McDonald's on the way home, and Sierra gave in. She didn't feel like making spaghetti anyway, and Alex had already said he wouldn't be hungry. Something light. Fine. She'd stop by the grocery store and pick up packaged salad fixings and dressing.

She straightened up the kitchen while the children settled at the table to do their homework and talk about their day at school. At least they were making new friends.

Clanton dug through his backpack and produced a fistful of school announcements, sign-up sheets, and graded homework. "Can I sign up for Little League, Mom?"

"You'll have to talk to your father about it," Sierra said, putting the last rinsed dish into the washer.

"You think Dad'll coach again this year?"

"I don't know, Clanton. You'll have to ask him."

Clanton did the minute Alex walked through the door. "Not this year, champ," Alex said, ruffling his hair. "I'm not going to have the time." He leaned down to kiss Carolyn hello.

Flipping the kitchen towel over her shoulder, she approached as he stood loosening his tie. "Did you have a good day?"

"Great." He gave her a firm kiss and pulled his tie free. Unbuttoning the collar of his shirt, he headed toward the bedroom. "I'm going to change and take a quick run."

Jogging was another new thing in Alex's life. Steve and Matt jogged; they claimed it was great as a stress reliever. So, of course, Alex had followed suit.

By the time Alex returned, Clanton and Carolyn had taken their baths and were dressed for bed. She read to them while Alex showered and put on his worn Levi's and UCB sweatshirt. When she came out to straighten the living room, he went in to say good night to the children. She supposed she should be thankful he spent the next half hour talking with them.

"Jack called me just before I left the office," he said when he came out.

Jack and his pregnant wife had rented their Windsor home. "Problems?"

"On the contrary. He's got enough for a down payment on the house."

"They're buying it?" she said weakly. As long as they still owned the Windsor home, she held out the hope that they'd return. Alex's words tore the crumbling foundations right out from beneath her.

"That was their hope when they moved in. I told him what the house was worth before we left. He said today his parents decided to give him a portion of his inheritance early. He's contacting your father's old partner to take care of the paperwork. They shouldn't have any problem qualifying for a mortgage. We'll have the money in our hands by the end of May."

He cupped her face. "I know how much that little place meant to you."

That little place. He said it so casually, as though it had been a shack or a hole in the wall. He couldn't have any idea what it meant to her, or he wouldn't be so quick to sell it.

"Matt gave me the name of a good Realtor. I want you to start looking at houses. Four bedrooms, three baths, with a pool. Get together with Audra. She knows all the best areas. I want us in a *good* neighborhood."

"We were in a good neighborhood."

He let his hands slide away. "We'll be in a better one. Steve gave me a raise today. A *big* raise. He's that sure Vigilantes is going to be big."

She saw how bright his eyes were, aglow with ambition and

plans. "Was all this the reason you spent a whole twenty minutes with your children?"

Alex didn't move, but Sierra could feel the cold front move in worse than an Illinois winter.

The tongue is a restless evil, full of deadly poison ... her mother's voice echoed in her mind, and Sierra felt a stab of shame. But before she could apologize, Alex spoke in a glacial tone.

"They like the idea of having their own pool."

"Do they also like the idea of changing schools again?" she shot back, trying to keep the edge of sarcasm out of her voice and failing.

"Audra suggested a private school. I have the name she gave me written down."

Naturally. "Has she offered to pay for it, too?"

Alex's temper came surging to the surface. "What have you got against her? You haven't liked her from day one, and she's done nothing but be nice to you."

"Is *that* what you call it? Remind me to kiss her feet the next time I see her!" Sierra moved away from him, filled with resentment and feelings of betrayal. She had tried to explain to Alex how Audra made her feel: uneducated, uncultured, and from the lower classes in a supposedly classless society. Alex insisted it was her imagination; she knew it was deliberate.

Every time she was with Audra, the woman made a point of mentioning this course or that course that she had taken at USC, any of which made her an expert on any given subject. Sierra might have an opinion, but it was an uneducated one.

"Oh?" Audra had said only two days ago in response to a comment Sierra had made. She arched her elegant brow. "And how did you come to *that* conclusion?"

They had been discussing the abortion issue, and Sierra had said she believed it was wrong to end the life of an unborn child.

Clearly what her mother had taught her just didn't cut the mustard in Audra's eyes.

"Sounds like fundamentalist brainwashing to me," she said with a pitying glance that dismissed Sierra's lifetime of learning from her mother's knee. Then Audra launched into a dissertation complete with "facts" proving the nonentity of the human fetus.

"Why didn't you go to college, Sierra?" Audra finally said. "You learn how to think for yourself at college. If your parents couldn't afford it, you could've gone to a junior college and then finished at a four-year university." She said it so sweetly it sounded as though she genuinely felt sorry that Sierra had lost out on the opportunities she herself had been given.

"Money was no problem. I just wasn't interested."

"Not interested?" Again the eyebrow arched. "Steve said Alex graduated with honors from UC Berkeley."

"Yes, he did."

"You might think about taking some night courses," she said seriously.

Sierra waited for more, but it wasn't forthcoming. Apparently, Audra felt she had said enough, and indeed she had. Even now, several days later, Audra's implication rankled: Alex would lose interest in her because of her lack of education. Sierra looked out the window at the line of cars ahead, two lanes to the right and two to the left. Just because she hadn't gone to college didn't mean she didn't keep up on what was happening in the world. She read the newspaper. She read magazines. She watched CNN!

Yet, even with all that, she was left feeling as though she were standing on sinking sand.

Shopping was even more excruciating. She had accepted three invitations from Audra because Alex insisted. Each time when Audra arrived, she tapped her long, coral-colored acrylic fingernails on the door and jangled the keys of her silver Mercedes when Sierra answered.

"Ready to go?" she said as though speaking to a recalcitrant child.

Chatting gaily, Audra drove to stores far beyond any ordinary citizen's budget.

"Aren't you going to buy anything, Sierra?" Audra said the last time while signing the slip for an eight-hundred-dollar dress. "That blue dress you were looking at would make you look wonderful."

"At six hundred and fifty dollars, even a chimp would look wonderful in it."

Audra had laughed at her remark, but Sierra felt the full force of an affronted glare from the elegantly attired saleslady. One just didn't say such things on Rodeo Drive.

Actually, Sierra had wanted to say more. She wanted to add for both women's benefit that if she had an extra six or seven hundred dollars lying around, she certainly wouldn't put it all on her back!

Audra offered to treat her to lunch at Lowry's. Sierra declined. She had been taught to reciprocate, and she doubted Audra would feel suitably recompensed at Denny's.

"I'm sorry, but I need to get home, Audra. The children will be getting out of school soon." She'd glanced at her watch to make her point. "I always pick them up."

"You should get involved in a car pool," Audra had commented, shooting the Mercedes in and out of traffic with the skill of an experienced Indianapolis 500 driver.

Sierra was tired of Audra "should"ing all over her. "Chauffeuring children to school is one of the delights of motherhood."

"Delights?" Audra laughed. Weaving smoothly across three lanes of dense traffic, she glided down an off-ramp. "That doesn't say much for the quality of your life." Her eyes twinkled merrily. "We'll have to do something to give you a little excitement."

And now it seemed she had.

Was it really Alex's idea that they look for a house so soon? Or had Audra through Steve advised they do so? Once they were under the weight of a mortgage, it would be pretty hard to change their minds about working in Los Angeles.

She pushed thoughts of Audra away and tried to reason with Alex. "I think it's too soon to think about buying a house," she said.

"You like living in a cramped apartment?"

She bristled anew at his sarcasm but remained calm. "You haven't even been at your new job for four months, Alex. What if you decide you hate it?"

"I *love* it."

"I'm saying *if* you changed your mind. You're having a honeymoon at Beyond Tomorrow right now. The whole thing may come down around your head like a house of cards."

"Thanks for your vote of confidence."

"I'm confident in *you*, Alex, but I don't trust *them*. Everything's moving too fast. It's all too easy. We should wait at least a year, Alex. So much can change—"

"Get it through your head, Sierra. I'm not changing my mind about anything." Face rigid and pale with anger, he glared at her. "I'm getting pretty tired of you walking around with a black cloud over your head all the time." He picked up his briefcase and went to his computer. Opening the briefcase, he took out a diskette. He turned on the computer and slipped the diskette into the slot. "Either you can look around for a house and help make the decision, or I'll just take care of it myself," he said, his back to her. "The choice is yours."

So much for priorities, she thought, tears brimming as she went into the kitchen.

She called the Realtor the next morning and made an appointment. Roberta Folse said she would be by at ten, which would give Sierra enough time to drop off the children at school and do her grocery shopping.

Roberta had penny-red hair, dark brown eyes, and was slightly overweight. She was elegantly dressed in a green suit with a gold silk blouse and a string of pearls.

"Your husband said you moved recently and you were having a difficult time settling in," she said when they were on their way in her sleek black Jaguar. "He didn't mention where you lived before."

"We both grew up in Healdsburg," Sierra said, wondering how much else Alex had confided in this attractive stranger. "It's about seventy miles north of San Francisco, in the wine country."

"I'm familiar with the area," Roberta said and smiled with complete understanding. "God's country. No wonder you're having trouble. Culture shock. This area must seem like another planet to you."

Sierra warmed to her at once and felt herself relaxing. From that point on, they talked easily. Roberta had four children, all grown-up and in college or married. She had gotten her real estate license when the market was booming. "I've always loved looking at houses," she said, driving along pretty tree-shaded streets with charming ranch-style houses and some with a hint of Victorian. "You know, most people I know dream of retiring in the wine country or farther north in the redwoods. I like Garberville myself. It has an old-fashioned feel to it."

"My brother owns a place there. He has twenty acres out near White Thorn on the way to Shelter Cove. He likes to go up on weekends and relax."

"Heaven." Roberta sighed. "Well, we'll see if we can't find you a house down here that'll have the country feel. Why don't we take a look at this one?"

Roberta showed her four homes, all with four bedrooms, three bathrooms, and a pool. The prices made Sierra's head spin and her stomach drop. They were four times what she and Alex had paid for their Windsor home! What was Alex thinking? Sierra confided her concerns to Roberta.

"It is a shock, I know. Your husband told me what you're going to make from the sale of your home and what he's currently making. It'll be tight, but I don't think you'll have problems qualifying. Especially with Steve Silverman cosigning."

Sierra could feel the blood running out of her face. "Cosigning?"

"It'll speed up the process of you and your husband having a new home. Steve simply guarantees the loan."

"So they would own part of our home?"

"Oh no, but should you fall into financial difficulties, which is very unlikely, Steve would have to assume responsibility for the mortgage. Alex told me his primary concern is location, which is wise. Should you decide to resell after a few years, any one of these homes would be snapped up quickly."

Warning bells were going off in Sierra's mind, but she couldn't pinpoint the cause. She tried to talk to Alex about it that night, but he thought she was suspicious of Steve's motives in offering to guarantee their loan and took offense.

"That's not what I said!" Sierra protested, upset.

"Pretty close."

"You don't *listen*."

"Then try making sense. Try thinking things through before you open your mouth."

"Forget it," she said, hurt. Did he think she was stupid just because she wanted all the facts? "Just forget it. We'll buy a house. After all, it's *your* money. Right? This marriage isn't a partnership. I'm just the stupid, uneducated little homebody who happens to be your wife!"

"I didn't say that!"

"You didn't have to."
Alex said barely a dozen words to her over the next week.

James Farr has come to live with us.

He talks to me sometimes when Matthew has
other things to do. He is laid up with a broken leg
and he is very sad because his mother and father
was both dead from a terible Tragedy.

I herd him tell Matthew what happened.

James and his mother and his father was
riding home from the camp meeting when his
father says he sold out and they were moving
West. James said his mother got crazy. She said
she was tired of moving and had roots. She said
if she was moving anywhere, it was back east to
her family. His father said thar was better land
West, and she said it werent land he was after.
Her crying and his shouting made the horses
start running. They wud not stop. A wheel brok
off and the wagon turned over. God tuk mercy
on James and threw him on soft ground. But his
fathers head got cracked open like a melon and
his mother got crushed when the wagon rolled
over her.

I am sorry his mother and father are dead, but
I am not sorry James is with us. I hope he stays
forever.

When I grow up I am going to marry him.

James let me sit with him today. He did not say much to me and I did not know what to say to him. I read him two chapters from Exodus about Moses in the bullrushes and pharaoh's daugher finding him. James said thank you very much. He took my hand and kissed it.

I will never wash my hand again as long as I live.

God says we are to love one another, but it is very hard to love Lucas.

Lucas told Mama he wuz in the barn when I got locked in the henhouse. He's a liar. He always lies and Mama is so good she dont know the difference. I saw Lucas close the door. I heard him drop the bar. And I heard him laffing while I was screaming at him to let me out. He knows I am affeered of chickens.

Mama asked me why he wud do such a thing to his sweet little sister. I said he done it because he is mean. She said that was a very bad thing to say about my own brother.

Sometimes Mama dont want to hear the truth because then she will have to do something about it.

Matthew wud have done something. But Matthew was out in the fields with Papa.

Sometimes I wish I was a boy so I could grow big enuf to punch Lucas hard enuf to nock him down like Matthew does. Lucas needs nockin down.

Mama says that jest cause the devil nocks at your door dont mean you have to answer.

I think Lucas opened his door and invited the devil in a long time ago.

We went to camp meeting again. I did not like it much this time. Sally Mae Grayson and her yellow hair came. She has not been to a meeting in two years because she has bin living in Fever River with her grandmama and going to school. I wish she had stayed in Fever River with her grandmama.

Even Matthew who thinks girls are stupid and empty headed looked at Sally Mae like he was a sick calf. All the boys were following her around and wanting to talk to her. The only one she pad attention to was James. They sat together during meeting and ate together at supper. Sally Mae kept looking at me and saying little pitchers have big ears. James told me to go and get him another mug of cider and when I did and came back with it he was gone. So was Sally Mae.

I looked and looked until I found them.

Now I know what courting is.

I never want to talk about courting or hear about it again. No one is ever courting me like that.

Mama found me down by the crek washing my hand. She askt me why I wuz crying. I told her. I thot she wud go and make them stop what they

wuz doing or at least tell Mister Grayson. All
she did was hold me and rock me for a long, long
time. She said idols always have feet of clay.

Sally Mae is not going bak to school in Fever
River. James told Matthew that her grandmama
wrote a letter to her father saying she was ailing
and could not take her. She said Sally Mae wud
be better off staying at the homestead with her
papa. James said her schooling was lost on her
anyway. He said Sally Mae knows more than she
shud all ready.

I am going to die. My heart hurts so much
I know I will be in the grave soon. James is
goin. I'm never going to see him again. The only
consolashun I have is Sally Mae wont get him
either.

He thanked Mama and Papa over supper and
said he cud never repay them for their kindnes
to him. He said he is sixteen and old enuf to fend
for himself. Papa said Fever River is a big place.
James said he wants to be in a big place. He said
maybe he will even go east. He said he wud like
to see Boston and New York. He said he wud like
to see England and maybe even China.

He and Matthew talked the hole nite before
he left. I heard him tell Matthew he did not love
Sally Mae and it wud be smart if Matthew did

not love her either. You are not like me, James
said. She will cut yor heart out and feast on it.

I walked with him to the crek bridge. I did not
cry. I askt him strat out what he thot he wud find
better in Fever River or China for that matter. He
said he was not looking for better. He was looking
for different.

Mama said he is lost.

I know I am.

———————

6

"BECAUSE IT'S THE WAY THINGS ARE DONE DOWN here," Alex said, irritated. "When are you going to stop worrying about money? I just got a bonus. We can afford to have a professional decorator."

"It isn't just a matter of if we can afford it," Sierra said, though that did concern her. Alex was spending money at an alarming rate, eating out at fancy restaurants every day for lunch, buying expensive suits. Why wouldn't he listen to anything she said anymore? "What's the matter with the way we've decorated? People are comfortable —"

"Nothing goes together. Look around you, Sierra. Does Steve's house look like this? Does Matt's? Most of what we have are hand-me-downs given to us by our parents when we first got married. That old armoire in the bedroom, the hatch-cover table in the family room, those ridiculous brass lamps!"

"The armoire was the first piece of furniture your parents bought when they came to California."

"So what?"

"It has a family history to it! It meant something to them."

"It means poverty to me. I don't need reminding."

"That hatch-cover comes from an old merchant ship that sailed around the Horn and into San Francisco Bay in 1910. My uncle refinished it for us as a wedding present. Those brass lamps are almost a hundred years old."

"And look every day of it."

"I can get some new shades."

"New shades won't help. Don't you get it? Everything we've got is *junk*. If you buy something from a discount store today and save it for a hundred years, it's just hundred-year-old junk. That's what we've got. Old junk!"

Sierra stood there, stunned. Had he always felt this way? She remembered how nice everything had looked in their small Windsor house. Maybe he figured what they had just wasn't good enough in a 5,000-square-foot, upscale, ranch-style house owned by an up-and-coming young executive.

"Look, Sierra," Alex said, his tone gentling, "there's a right way and a wrong way to decorate a house, and hiring a professional is the *right* way."

"Who told you that rubbish?" she said. But she knew without even asking.

His dark eyes flashed with anger. "*I'm* saying it. All right? Does that make it go down easier? I'm sick of living with other people's discards around me. I'm making good money. I bought this beautiful house for you."

Rolling her eyes, she turned away.

"I don't want it looking like it was decorated by someone running a flea market," he said through his teeth.

She wondered if he knew how much his words hurt. She had always done their decorating. People had always said she had a knack for it. Friends had asked her advice, and one even offered to pay her to decorate her house. She liked reupholstering old couches and chairs, tole painting, and making wreaths. She liked *country!*

Alex opened his daily planner and jotted some notes on her grocery list. "I'm giving you a couple of names of interior decorators. The one in Beverly Hills is the best. Call him first. If he's not available, call the second one." He tore the slip off the pad and handed it to her. Stepping past her, he picked up his briefcase. "Get it done today," he said, like he was giving a subordinate a command. It was all she could do to not salute him as he headed for the door.

It wasn't the first morning of late that he had neglected to kiss her good-bye. Sierra followed him, slip of paper in hand, and stood in the doorway to the three-car garage. Maybe he'd remember.

"I want it done as soon as possible," he said, opening the door of his new Mercedes. It was silver with black leather interior, complete with tape deck, CD player, and car phone. Tossing the briefcase onto the passenger seat, he slid in and slammed the door. Tapping the garage door opener, he turned away, slinging his arm over the passenger seat as he started backing out.

She looked at the white BMW sitting in the garage. Alex had bought it for her birthday last month. He'd been so proud when he drove it home.

"Where's my Honda?" she'd said weakly.

"I traded it in," he said, grinning and handing her the keys.

He'd fully expected her to weep with joy over having a new car. She'd wanted to weep, all right. The Honda was the car her mother and father had given them as a wedding present. Clanton and Carolyn had ridden around in it from the time they were babies. It was like an old family friend. The BMW was an unwelcome houseguest.

Alex had never spent much time keeping up the Honda. She'd vacuumed and washed it every few weeks. Now Alex spent every Saturday vacuuming, washing, and hand-drying both cars; first the Mercedes, then the BMW. He even rubbed the already shiny dashboards with Armor All. He used a toothbrush to scrub the spoked hubcaps, for heaven's sake!

Three days ago, Alex had told her he didn't have time to make Clanton's Little League game—but he had two hours to spare for the cars. And she couldn't even remember the last time she'd received an eighth of that much time and attention from him.

A stab of pain ripped through her as she remembered the days, less than a year ago, when Alex couldn't wait to come home to her, to talk with her, to share and laugh and love. She remembered how it felt to sit together, sharing dreams and ideas. And the wonder of melting into each other's arms after a day apart. How could life change so dramatically in the space of six months? How could a man change so much?

She had always known Alex was ambitious and determined. What she hadn't realized was that his work could become the driving force and focus of his life. He was consumed with his career, impassioned by it, obsessed with it. It was as though the success of his first game, Vigilantes, merely whetted his appetite to do better on the next. Apparently success gave him an adrenaline rush she and the children couldn't.

Sierra readily acknowledged that Alex was making more than four times what he had made in his job in Santa Rosa. Two magazines had done articles on him in the past two months giving glowing forecasts of the future of Vigilantes. She had seen ads on television.

"Sick of what's happening in the world?" the announcer's smooth voice would ask. "Become the law!"

Industry columnists were predicting Vigilantes would be the most popular arcade game of the decade. In the interview for the second article, Alex said Beyond Tomorrow would be releasing a new 64-bit CD-based system called The Monolith by the new year. The system would come complete with a code breaker that would allow owners to play any CD game on the market. The Monolith was aimed at the older teens and adults and would come packaged with Vigilantes. Stores were already calling Beyond Tomorrow and placing orders before the system had even hit the market. And Alex was working day and night on a second game, The Chameleon, a role-playing computer game utilizing the modem peripheral and the Internet so that players from around the world could link up.

No doubt about it. Beyond Tomorrow was booming. "Changing the future of gaming!" their company motto, was becoming a catchphrase; Alex was determined to make it come true.

But Sierra felt little pleasure at what was happening. It was too much. Too fast.

Granted, Steve had proven himself a man of his word. He'd kept every promise he made to Alex. Bonuses, salary increases, benefits . . . He even hired a personal secretary for Alex and added several new employees to the marketing and distribution departments. Alex's place and position were guaranteed; he was a key in Beyond Tomorrow's incredible success. He was on top of the professional world.

And Sierra had never felt less secure in her life.

She and Alex barely talked anymore. He was constantly over-worked and preoccupied. She tried to talk to him about it one night, but he wanted to know what she *needed* to talk about. The minute she said there wasn't anything specific, he returned his attention to his computer screen and immersed himself in work for the rest of the evening.

The next morning, she tried to bring it up again.

"So, go ahead," he said, sounding impatient. "What's on your mind?" He hadn't even bothered to lower his *Wall Street Journal.*

"Nothing in particular," she said. How did you start a good talk when you needed to talk about not talking?

"Pour me another cup of coffee, would you?" he said from behind the paper.

She wanted to pour the entire pot over him. "We used to talk about all kinds of things from the minute you walked in the door until we went to bed."

"We still talk."

"About business. About the games you're working on. About the kids."

At last he lowered the paper and looked at her. She could see him putting on his armor, getting his weapons ready. He had always been better equipped for fighting than she was. "What are you getting at, Sierra?"

God, what do I say? What do I do? she screamed inside her head. When Alex presented his cold front, she felt incapable of reaching him — and that seemed to be the case almost all the time now. Tears of frustration pricked at her eyes. He used to sense when she needed him. Now, he didn't seem to care what she was feeling or thinking. She wanted to say she missed him. She wanted to say she was lonely. She wanted to tell him she was afraid they were drifting apart, and that Audra was right: She was boring, uneducated . . . and losing him.

The very thought filled her with a bleak terror. But she was even more terrified to say those things aloud and find that he was indifferent.

Her eyes pled with him. *Just tell me you still love me, Alex. Don't make me ask you if you do.*

He just sat looking at her, eyes narrowed, posture defensive.

And so she leaned back in her chair, overwhelmed with a sense of defeat. "I'm not getting at anything," she finally responded, aching inside for the connection she had always felt with him.

How could you be with someone you loved so desperately and feel so alone?

He stared at her, as though he were studying a particularly curious insect on the window screen. He shrugged. "I guess we haven't been out for a while," he conceded, folding his newspaper and tossing it onto the coffee table. His gaze drifted from hers. Restless, he glanced at his wristwatch and got up. "I wanted to get into the office early this morning. I've got a lot to do." He downed his coffee and headed for the kitchen. "Why don't you figure out where you'd like to go and make the reservations?"

He sounded so offhand, so uninterested. . . . She closed her eyes against the pain swelling inside her. Alex had always been the one to suggest places they could go and things they could do. Several times, he'd surprised her with tickets to a show at the Luther Burbank Center. He used to take her and the children to pizza and a movie. Once, he'd even made arrangements for her mother to take care of the children so he could whisk her off for a romantic weekend at a bed-and-breakfast in Mendocino.

Now, he sounded as though the whole idea of taking her out was just one more responsibility he needed to handle.

She suggested a rib place.

"Too much fat and cholesterol."

Since when had he worried about fat and cholesterol?

They agreed on a movie, but that night Alex called and said he had some work to do. She asked him to reserve Friday night for dinner out with the children, but he called from the office at the last minute Friday and said he had an important meeting he couldn't miss.

She gave up making plans.

Now, it seemed, he didn't think she had the ability to decorate their home properly.

The whine of the garage door closing and the roar of Alex's Mercedes as he floored it toward work brought Sierra back from her dismal reverie. She needed to awaken the children soon so they'd have plenty of time to get ready for school.

Carolyn was invited to a birthday party this weekend. Her little friend, Pamela, lived somewhere in Studio City. Sierra went back into the kitchen and jotted down a note to buy a birthday present.

She glanced at the slip of paper Alex had given her: *Bruce Davies Interiors*. She tacked it to her noteboard beside the phone. She didn't make the call until later that afternoon, after Alex called and asked if she had done it yet.

The designer's receptionist had a rich, velvety voice with a heavy New England accent.

"I'm under orders from my husband to hire a decorator," Sierra said.

The woman was polite and efficient, making no promises and hinting that Bruce was in high demand and terribly busy. Too busy, Sierra hoped. "Please hold." Yanni played softly in Sierra's ear.

The receptionist came back on the line. "Is your husband employed by Beyond Tomorrow?"

"Yes, he is." Had Alex called ahead?

"One moment, please," the receptionist said, and Sierra heard Yanni playing again. Plucking a pencil from the kitchen drawer, she doodled flower and leaf patterns along the top edge of her grocery list. But she'd barely gotten started when the receptionist was back.

"I apologize for the wait, Mrs. Madrid. Mr. Davies will be pleased to speak to you."

Before she could protest, Bruce Davies was greeting her with the familiarity of a long-lost friend.

"Sierra, I'm *so* glad you finally called. I knew anyone with such a charming name wouldn't let me down. Of course, I expected your call several days ago, but this works out just as well. I've just finished a stunning home only a few blocks away from you, and I'm ready for something new and exciting! And believe me, the ideas I have for your home are definitely that!"

After a two-minute conversation with Bruce, Sierra felt she had been run over by a steamroller. He made the appointment for late Thursday afternoon and informed her he would bring an assistant with him. He knew who Alex was because Audra Silverman had faxed him an article from a well-known computer game magazine.

"Decorating for a game designer will be a challenge," he said, clearly eager.

"I'm not sure Alex will want to have much involvement, Mr. Davies."

"Oh, but he must. I *insist.*"

Surprisingly, Alex didn't quibble and assured her he would be home early Thursday.

Bruce Davies turned out to be an attractive man in his late forties, trim and elegantly dressed, who absolutely exuded energy. His assistant attended him in silence, writing notes as they walked through the house, Alex at Bruce's side.

It became apparent very quickly that Sierra was going to have little say in what was done to the house. Country, Bruce informed her, was a definite "no-no," and anything even remotely Victorian "just wouldn't do, darling." Bruce was interested in the architecture, made suggestions for some changes, and poured forth with decorating ideas. Alex had his own, and Bruce listened as though every word was genius.

"A man who is going to change the future of gaming must have a house that reflects his creativity," Bruce said, his eyes sparkling as he surveyed the entryway.

By the time Bruce and his assistant left, Sierra was convinced the house would bear the stamp of Bruce Davies Interiors, a slight mark of Alejandro Madrid, and absolutely nothing of her.

"It's going to be expensive," Alex said, not noticeably worried about it, "but it'll be worth it. Bruce said he'll have sketches within a week, and decisions can be made."

She knew who would be making the decisions.

The next morning, after dropping the children off at private school, Sierra drove to the closest mall to look for a suitable present for Carolyn's new friend. Nothing looked right to her: The selection was too wide and the prices too high.

Depressed, she purchased a cappuccino and sat watching the hustle of people in the mall. Most were women. Some strolled at a leisurely pace, looking lonely and bored as they paused at window displays. Others moved with quick efficiency, looking for all the world as though they knew exactly where they were going and what they were doing.

Sierra longed for home. She wished her mother were sitting across from her so she could pour out her heart and ask her advice. But she'd done enough of that lately over the telephone. Her mother's parting words after their last conversation still echoed in her ears: "Remember, honey, God is in control."

If that was true, why did she feel so desperate?

Shaking her head, she turned her thoughts back to the matter at hand. What was she going to do about that blasted birthday present? When she was Carolyn's age, she had liked nothing better than taking her friends up into the attic so they could spend hours dressing up in her mother's and grandmother's old clothes, high-heeled shoes, hats, and jewelry—all perfect props for pretending to be Cinderella or Snow White or some other fairy-tale character.

Did children do that sort of thing anymore? All the dress-up Carolyn had ever done was back in preschool. The Windsor School had provided plenty of clothes to choose from: surgical gowns, nurses' uniforms, suit jackets and briefcases, a fireman's hat, a policeman's uniform. Nothing frivolous or fanciful. Everything geared to answer that all-important question: What are you going to be when you grow up? Sierra could still remember her frustration when she'd discovered the teacher was asking Carolyn and her classmates this. Was it really necessary to know at the age of four or five what one was going to do for the rest of one's life? It seemed so long ago. Now she wondered.

Wasn't being a wife and mother enough anymore?

Feeling defiant, Sierra finished her coffee and drove to Cost Plus, the area warehouse store. Wandering through, she found an intricately carved box imported from India. It was pretty and inexpensive. She bought it and drove to Kmart, where she purchased three beaded necklaces, a gold-tone charm bracelet with African animals on it, and two bright rhinestone pins, as well as a long, thin multi-colored scarf. Pleased with her choices, she headed home.

While watching her soap opera, she used the scarf to wrap the gift. Twisting the tied ends, she curled them around until they looked like a plump flower on top of the box. During a commercial, she rummaged through her wrapping-paper box in the hall closet and found some gold ribbon. Cutting a long strip, she tucked it around the fabric flower and wrote on the ends: "Happy Birthday, Pamela. From Carolyn." She sat back and smiled, perfectly satisfied with the gift.

Then she drove Carolyn to the birthday party on Saturday.

Pamela's house was near the top of the hills with an iron gate in front. The gate was open, but a uniformed guard was on duty. He asked their names and checked his list before nodding them through. Other cars were already parked: two Cadillacs, three Mercedes, and a little red sports car the likes of which Sierra had never seen before. Everything reeked of money.

Sierra walked Carolyn to the front door, where a maid answered their ring. She was Spanish and dressed in a crisp black uniform with white collar and apron.

Carolyn's hand tightened. "Don't leave, Mommy. Please." Sierra forced a reassuring smile, but her daughter didn't loosen her grip until they entered a huge room with cathedral windows at the back and she spotted Pamela with several other little girls. Sierra spotted the mothers.

They were all standing near windows that provided a panoramic view of San Fernando Valley. Every one of the ladies looked as though she had just stepped out of a fashion magazine. Sierra cringed inwardly, wondering what they thought of her in her faded teal sweat tunic, black leggings, and scuffed Reeboks. *Oh, God*, she thought, *please don't let Carolyn be embarrassed by me.* One of the women glanced toward Sierra and Carolyn. Smiling, she said a word to the others and left them.

"You must be Sierra and Carolyn Madrid," she said, her tone warm and welcoming. "I'm so glad you could come." She touched Carolyn's hair lightly. "Pamela has talked of little else since you came to school, Carolyn. She insists you're kindred spirits just like the girls in *Anne of Green Gables*."

Marcia Burton had class and grace and dissolved every bit of Carolyn's shyness. Smiling, the little girl held the present out to Marcia. "Why, it's perfectly lovely," she said.

"My mother wrapped it," Carolyn told her proudly, and Sierra's face went hot. She could see the other gifts on the polished mahogany coffee table nearby, all obviously from expensive stores and professionally wrapped. She thought of the wooden box and cheap, gawdy jewelry inside it. She wished she could snatch it back and run.

As Carolyn joined the other children, Sierra thanked Marcia for inviting her and made her excuses to leave.

"Oh, please stay," Marcia said, sounding as though she actually meant it. "Pamela said your son plays on the school's baseball team, and I know they're practicing today."

She was right. Sierra had dropped Clanton off before bringing Carolyn to the party. The coach had invited all the boys back to his house for a barbecue and movie.

Marcia smiled, her blue eyes amused as she confided her belief that Pamela had developed a crush on Clanton. "She says he's the most handsome boy in school."

Sierra wasn't surprised her son made female hearts flutter. Clanton had Alex's features and coloring, and her light green eyes. It made for a startling combination that had always attracted attention from the time he was a baby.

"I really had better go," Sierra said.

"At least stay long enough to meet the other mothers."

As Marcia Burton put her hand lightly beneath her elbow, Sierra resigned herself to further humiliation.

All the ladies were polite. Only one looked her over as though she were convinced Sierra had just crawled out of a homeless shelter. Marcia, appearing not to notice, remained warm and friendly to all, while staying close to Sierra's side.

But the woman's efforts did little to ease Sierra's discomfiture. After what seemed a polite interval of stilted small talk, she made her excuses and left.

She breathed far easier after driving out the gate and heading down the winding road out of the rarefied air of the Studio City hills to the bank of smog in the flatlands of North Hollywood. One thing was certain: She wouldn't step foot over the threshold when she returned to pick up Carolyn.

Sighing, Sierra focused her thoughts on Alex. He actually had an afternoon free, and they were going to spend it together. When he had asked her if she'd like to do so, quick tears of gratitude had sprung to her eyes. It had been so long since they'd really been together, just the two of them. Maybe this would be a chance for them to bridge the chasm that had developed between them. Sierra wasn't sure if they could, but she wanted to. Oh, how she wanted to.

When she unlocked the door and went inside, she felt almost lighthearted. "Alex? I'm home," she called.

Silence met her.

"Alex?" she said again, going into the kitchen. The room was empty, but there was a note on the refrigerator. Cold fingers of disappointment closed around her heart as she moved forward and took it down.

> *Sierra,*
> *Steve called. A big client is in town unexpectedly, so we're taking him out to dinner. I'll probably be home late.*

That was it. I'm gone, I'll be home late. No apology. No regret at not being able to spend time with her.

Angry, Sierra crumpled up the note and tossed it into the garbage. She vacuumed, dusted, and made preparations for dinner for three. She considered changing her clothes before going back to pick up Carolyn, and then rebelled against the idea. She was who she was. Besides, even dressed up she wouldn't fit in with that crowd.

Steeling herself, she headed back to Studio City. As she pulled up before the palatial house, she saw that all the cars were exactly where they were when she had left three hours before. Apparently, they had all stayed through the entire party, sharing the catered hors d'oeuvres and luncheon and the beautifully decorated cake, and enjoying the magician who had come to make sure the children were properly entertained. She got out of her car as several of the women and their little girls came out, each child holding a bag of party favors.

"Our girls are playing in the family room," Marcia said, greeting her at the front door.

"I'm sorry if I'm late."

"You're not late at all. Come in, please. Would you like some coffee?"

"Thank you, but I'd better not. I'm in something of a rush. I need to pick up Clanton soon."

Marcia's expression flickered with understanding and disappointment; it was an excuse, and both women knew it. "I'll show you the way," she said quietly. "Pamela loved the treasure box and scarf."

Polite to the end, Sierra thought sarcastically, then felt a twinge of shame for her critical attitude. *Shrew,* she chastised herself. *Marcia's shown you nothing but kindness. But then, maybe you don't know how to react to kindness anymore. . . .*

The girls were leaning close together and talking like little conspirators. To Sierra's surprise and pleasure, Pamela was bedecked in the scarf and jewelry. Carolyn laughed happily at what her friend was saying and then noticed her. "Oh, Mommy," she said, obviously disappointed. "Couldn't I stay a while longer? Please?"

"We have to go, Carolyn."

"Clanton's staying at—"

"*Now,* Carolyn."

Carolyn rose obediently. Remembering her manners, she thanked Pamela and her mother for the lovely time and for the bag of party favors and treats.

"Why don't we get together sometime?" Marcia said as they walked back upstairs.

"That'd be nice," Sierra said, giving the proper innocuous response. She knew sometime meant never. The girls were talking again and going ahead of them out the front door, obviously trying to find another way to delay the inevitable.

"Are you free Monday?" Marcia said.

Startled, Sierra looked at her. "Monday?"

"For coffee," Marcia said and smiled. "Or tea. Or water. I don't care." She laughed at Sierra's look, then reached out and squeezed her wrist gently. "What I really want to do is get to know you better."

She spoke so sincerely, Sierra didn't doubt her. Quick tears burned her eyes, and she wondered that a casual invitation for coffee could affect her so deeply.

"Monday sounds perfect."

Mister Grayson cum over today, mad as a grizly.

He said Matthew is going to marry Sally Mae
or he is going to shoot him dead. Papa said no
son of his is going to marry a harlot. Matthew
said Sally Mae is no harlot and they are already
married in the eyes of God.

Lucas laughed and called Matthew a fool.
Matthew hit him in the mouth and nocked him
down. He got on top of him and kept pounding
until Papa pulled him off.

Mama has not stopped crying for two days.

Papa said Mister Grayson is sending a rider
around to tell every one who comes to camp
meeting that his daughter is getting married to

94

Matthew Benjamin McMurray. Papa said he is actin proud about it.

Mama said some people have no sense of shame.

Matthew married Sally Mae today. She wore her dead mother's white wedding dress. I have never seen Matthew look as happy as he did when he put Mama's ring on her finger.

Sally Mae almost did not have a ring at all. Papa wud not let Matthew have Grandmama McMurray's ring. I heard Papa and Matthew yellin at each other in the barn. Matthew said he loves Sally Mae. Papa said no one like Sally Mae was ever going to wear his mother's ring. He said he wuz sorry he listened to Mama. He said he shud have taken Matthew to Fever River a long time ago to let him larn some facts of life about women and then maybe he wud not have fallen prey to one.

So Mama give Matthew her own wedding ring. Papa has not said a word to her since.

I wonder if James is still in Fever River and what he's doing there.

I got no time for writing in this journal, but it is the only place I can put down my feelings. And such feelings! Sometimes I think I will burst.

Mama is sick, bad sick. Sally Mae dont do nothing to help. She and Matt fight all the time.

Or rather Sally Mae does all the fighting. He does
all the taking. She says she is bored with her life
and bored with him. All he does is work in the
fields beside Papa and does nothing fun with her.
Sometimes I hate her so much I wish her dead.
Then she cries and tells me she loves Matthew and
wants to be a good wife and I feel guilty. She just
dont know how to be good cause she never had a
mama like mine who wud not let her be anythin else.

Mama coughed up blood today. I dont know
what to do. Papa dont spend much time with
her because he cries every time he does. He said
he can't bear to see her suffering. He told her
he dont know what to do without her. He dont
believe in God. He dont believe in nothing but
what he can do for himself and he can't do nuthin
for Mama.

Mama said today she is not afraid to die and
I shud not be afraid to let her. She smiles when
I sit with her. She says she is getting closer to
God every minute. I tell her we need her more
than God does, but she says maybe she is in the
way. In the way of what I asked, but she coughed
so long and hard she had no strength to tell me.

Mama died today. She said she could smell the
lilacs through the window. She wanted to hold
some. So I went outside and cut some for her.
When I came back, she was dead.

I was with her three days knowing her time
was near. Why did she send me away right then?

Papa and Matthew buried Mama yesterday
morning. We could not wait another day for
Lucas to cum home from hunting. Sometimes he
is gone for a week.

The sun is going down again and Papa is still
sitting by the grave with his jug.

I dont think much of Sally Mae being the woman
of the house. She dont cook. She dont clean. She
just tells me what to do. Matt says she is older
and has the right because Sally Mae is his wife.
I told him that dont make her my mother. He has
never slapped me before. I told him he had better
not do it again.

Papa spends all his time in the fields and dont
know whats going on in this house. Only time
he comes in is when the sun is going down. Then
he just sits before the fire with his jug of whiskey
drinkin until he dont know nothin anyway.

Matt went huntin with Lucas. I herd Lucas
talking to Sally Mae before they went off. He
said maybe he wud take his brother to Fever
River and show him the sights. They have been
gone five days. Sally Mae dont say much. Papa

dont say nothing. Sometimes I feel like the old
hoot owl and this journal is my only company.

Matt and Lucas came home today. They had no
meat with them. Sally Mae did not say anything.
So I asked Matt if they went to Fever River. He
said yes. I asked him if he saw James. He said no.
I asked him what it was like in Fever River and
he said there were too many people. He did not
say anything after that. Lucas wuz smirking at
Sally Mae. He said they learned a lot while they
was in Fever River, but he did not say what they
learned. Sally Mae did not look well. She said she
was going outside for air. Matt went out to help
Papa in the fields.

When I went outside to do the wash I saw
Lucas talking to Sally Mae. When he laffed at
her, she slapped his face. He slapped her back
and she ran off crying.

Papa sent Lucas to Fever River with the corn.
Matt did not go with him this time because Sally
Mae wanted him home. Papa said thar will be
enuf money to pay the taxes, buy supplies, and
put some by for hard times.

I gotta bad feelin, but Papa dont listen.

Lucas came bak from Fever River today wile
I was workin in the garden. He and Papa had

words. Lucas said the corn did not sell well this
year, that he paid the taxes but thar was not
much left for supplies. Papa said he is lying. He
said Lucas must have spent the money gaming or
on women. Lucas said it is a poor thing when a
father dont trust his own blood.

Lucas is gone. He tuk Papas best horse and gun
and left before sun up. I never herd such cussing
as Papa did when he found out what he dun. Matt
said he did not think Lucas wud come back this
time. Papa said he wud kill him if he did. Papa
said nothing after that. He did not eat breakfast
or supper. All he does is wurk in the fields and
drink.

I wud not grieve if I never saw Lucas again. As
far back as I can remember, ther has been a mean
streak in him Papa never cud beet out. Mama
tried to talk it out of him. But I dont think Lucas
ever herd a word she said. Mama believed we
shud treat others the way we want to be treated.
Lucas saz that is fools thinkin. He says take what
you want or you dont get nothing.

So I guess Lucas tuk what he wanted. He
tuk Papas money. He tuk Papas horse. He tuk
Papas gun. The only things he did not take were
Papas land and Papas house. And he wud have
tuk them too if he cud have put them in a saddle
bag.

Sally Mae is going to have a babee come winter. Matt is happy about it. It is nice to hear him laugh again.

Papa dont say much about it. Papa dont say much about anything these days.

Today is my birthday. I am fourteen. Not even Matt made mention of it. I guess he forgot jest like Papa.

———————

7

SIERRA SENT THE TENNIS BALL ZINGING
across he net. It bounced far right of where Marcia was waiting
for it, gaining her the winning point. "Yes!" she cried and jumped
into the air, raising her racket in triumph.

"Devious," Marcia said in good humor. "Since you won, you
have to jump the net."

"Not on your life," Sierra said, laughing. She walked over to the
bench and picked up her towel. Dabbing the sweat from her face,
she grinned at Marcia as she walked over to drink from a bottle of
Calistoga water. "Maybe now I'll be some competition for you."

"You're getting better every time you play," Marcia said, her
tone enigmatic.

"You're a good teacher." Sierra bent down to roll the cotton overshirt she had left on the bench. She tucked it into her canvas bag and set the racket on top.

"Well, I'm not teaching you anymore," Marcia laughed.

Two men entered the court, one older than the other, both dressed in white tennis shorts and shirts, both reeking of affluence.

"First time I've ever seen you lose, Marcia," said the younger and more attractive of the two.

"She tossed the game," Sierra said with a laugh.

"Not likely," he said, a grin making him even more handsome. "Marcia puts her all into everything she does." He winked at Marcia and then looked pointedly at Sierra. "Aren't you going to introduce us?"

Marcia put her towel around her neck. "Sierra, this is Ronal Peirozo, a longtime family friend. Ron, this is Sierra Madrid. She's married to Alex Madrid, game designer for Beyond Tomorrow."

"My pleasure," he said, extending his hand.

"It's nice to meet you." Sierra felt cool strength in his fingers as they closed firmly around her hand. His eyes were Paul Newman blue, and the way they rested on her was decidedly unsettling. He introduced her to the older gentleman with him, but, flustered, she failed to catch his name.

Marcia grinned at her as they walked along the pathway to the dining room. "Don't be embarrassed. Ron has that effect on most women."

"What effect?"

Marcia laughed. "Fine. We'll play it your way."

When Alex had been given the club membership as a Christmas bonus, Sierra had resisted coming to Lakeside Country Club. Not until Marcia invited her for lunch one afternoon had she even admitted being a member. "You're kidding. And you don't go?"

"No. I don't go."

"For heaven's sake, Sierra. What are you going to do? Sit home watching soap operas for the rest of your life? I've never known anyone to be so resistant to success and the benefits it brings."

Resigned, Sierra had accompanied her to the club. She had had so much fun meeting Marcia's friends it had become a part of her daily routine. She met Marcia for tennis or golf or racquetball, depending on the weather, worked up a sweat, showered, and then relaxed for a few hours. Sometimes they sat in the salon and had a manicure or pedicure. More often than not, they joined others in the women's lounge for drinks and lunch.

As they reached the patio outside the dining room, Sierra saw that Nancy Berne and Edie Redmond were already sitting at the table they usually occupied. It was considered a primo spot, located as it was near the windows overlooking the golf course, but then, having the best was par for the course for these women. Both were married to high-powered executives. Beside them, Ashley Worrell—who was recently divorced from her well-known, extremely wealthy plastic surgeon husband—was sipping mineral water. Lorraine Sheedy, a close friend of Ashley's, sat next to her, looking grim. Lorraine's husband was an attorney who had made a fortune handling divorce cases for movie stars. The last of what Marcia jokingly called "The Rat Pack" was Meredith Schneider, an heiress who was four-times divorced, five-times married.

As Sierra took her usual seat near the tall ferns, she greeted the others with easy camaraderie. Wylie, the waiter who always took care of their orders, came to the table. He picked up Meredith's empty martini glass, replaced the napkin, and set a fresh martini before her.

"Thank you, Wylie," Meredith said, and Sierra could tell she had been drinking for some time. Meredith smiled benevolently around the table. "You girls going to have something? My treat."

Marcia glanced at her watch. "It's not even noon, Merry. Aren't you starting a little early today?"

"You're an hour too late with your warning, dear." She glanced at her Rolex. "Eleven forty-five. If you wish to be legalistic, wait fifteen minutes. Then you may order a drink."

Marcia ordered a gin and tonic with a twist of lime.

Nancy and Edie both ordered espresso. Ashley grimaced delicately. "How many times do I have to tell you girls what caffeine does to the skin?" she said and ordered a rum punch.

"And rum's good for it?" Nancy said, amused.

"Rum is made from sugarcane and molasses, both natural substances. Add a little fruit juice and you have a nutritious noontime libation."

"And a buzz," Edie said dryly.

Lorraine quietly ordered a double Scotch on the rocks. Everyone at the table looked at her in surprise. She never drank anything but white zinfandel. Meredith popped the green olive into her mouth, eyes amused.

Sierra ordered an iced tea. She had learned early on that she didn't like the taste of alcohol or its dizzying effects.

They talked of mundane things until the drinks were served. Lorraine finished the double Scotch with two swallows. Shuddering, she set the empty glass down before Wylie had taken three steps from the table.

"Feeling better?" Marcia said softly, astonished.

"Wylie," Lorraine said firmly, "bring me another, please."

"Yes, ma'am," he said, brows lifting in surprise.

"Doing some serious drinking today, are we?" Meredith cooed.

Lorraine gave a humorless laugh, her eyes glittering. "Frank's having an affair."

Ashley set her rum punch down hard and uttered a short, exceedingly foul word. "I swear. All men are pigs."

"Darling," Meredith said, too inebriated to be distressed by anything. "You're looking at it all wrong. Haven't you read *Men Are Just Desserts*?" She looked at Lorraine. "Did he fess up, sweetie, or did you have to pry the information out of him with a crowbar?"

"I asked him point-blank. He tried to worm his way around the issue with his usual legal jargon. He might be able to fool everybody in a courtroom, but I always know when he's lying."

"Are you filing for divorce?" Ashley said, her own having only recently been declared final.

"Actually, I was thinking about castration."

"Here," Meredith said, delighted. "Take the butter knife."

Ignoring Meredith, Marcia put her hand over Lorraine's. "Don't make any decision too quickly, Lorry. Try to work it out."

"Work it out!" Lorraine's dark eyes welled with tears. "I put the jerk through law school. Four years I worked two jobs just to get him through. You know who the woman is? That airheaded blonde bimbo I told you about, the one in the last divorce case he handled."

"Be thankful," Meredith said. "At least it wasn't the husband."

Nancy laughed before she could stifle it. Looking sheepish, she apologized quickly. "Stop making jokes, Meredith," she whispered. "It's not funny."

"Of *course* it's funny. It's hilarious!" Meredith said. She lifted her martini in salute. "To marriage, the biggest joke man ever played on womankind. I should know. I've been on the merry-go-round often enough." She downed the martini with a flick of her wrist.

"At least Eric's faithful," Lorraine said bitterly.

"Oh, of course, he is, darling. As long as I give him everything he wants, he performs like a trained dog, though I daresay a dog has more loyalty." Her mouth curved in a cynical smile. "That little sports car Eric is driving cost me one hundred and fifty-seven thousand dollars." She gave a bleak laugh. "Fidelity comes at a high price these days."

Sierra saw the sheen of tears in Meredith's eyes.

"I'd kill myself if John cheated on me," Edie said.

"Ah, now there are wise, comforting words," Meredith said, her tone hard-edged with derision. She flagged Wylie for another martini. "Far from an original idea. Attempt suicide, and your unfaithful husband will be wretched with guilt. I tried that with my second husband. Charles called an ambulance and had my stomach pumped. A completely disgusting experience, I can tell you. And did he beg forgiveness and tell me how much he loved me and what a mistake he'd made? Ha! He moved out while I was in the hospital." Pain flickered across her face as she revealed this old, obviously still unhealed, wound.

"I told Frank a long time ago that what's good for the gander is good for the goose," Lorraine said as the waiter moved away.

"Meaning what?" Edie said. "You're going to cheat on *him* now?"

"Why not?" Lorraine said fiercely, eyes brimming with tears. "Let him have a taste of what it feels like to be betrayed."

"That's the spirit!" Meredith said with an overbright laugh. "And I know just the lad to instill jealousy in any husband. James! Come over here this minute, dear."

Lorraine, fully aware of just how outrageous Meredith could be when she'd been drinking, blushed as a handsome young waiter turned slightly to look over at them. "Don't you dare, Meredith!" she hissed.

"Isn't he a dish?" Meredith said, waggling her bejeweled fingers at him playfully. "Gorgeous, ambitious, and *half* Frank's age. In far better shape, too."

"If he takes one step in this direction, I'm leaving."

Meredith shrugged dramatically toward the young man. "Another time, dear. Lorraine's changed her mind."

"I swear, Meredith. You're completely incorrigible," Lorraine said.

"Comes with the territory," Meredith said, a bleakness seeping into her blue eyes. She quickly tried to hide it behind a bright, brittle smile.

Ashley glanced at her watch. "I'm going to have to get to the gym."

"She has to work off the rum," Meredith said dryly.

Ashley worked out an hour each morning at home and then spent another hour each afternoon at the club with a personal trainer who specialized in body shaping. She had a perfect body already but was convinced if she missed a day of exercise, she'd blow up like a balloon. Sometimes she ate nothing but salad without dressing, while at other times she gleefully devoured every dessert on the menu. Sierra had never known anyone so obsessed with her body and caloric intake.

"Can't you forgo it just this once?" Lorraine said, annoyed.

"Why don't you come with me? A good workout will do you a world of good."

Meredith smiled drolly. "Treadmills are wonderful things, aren't they? They reduce a normal human being right down to the mentality of a hamster in a wheel."

Ashley gave her a sharp glance. "A good workout would be better for her than obsessing about Frank and getting drunk like *you.*"

Meredith arched an elegant brow. "The kitten has claws today."

Ignoring her, Ashley got up. "Are you coming with me, Lorry?"

"No. My heart already aches. I don't need my body aching, too."

"Fine." Swinging around, Ashley walked quickly across the room and out the exit into the lobby.

"That girl's so uptight she could turn coal to diamonds," Meredith said, shaking her head. "I say we spike her mineral water. Maybe she'll enjoy life a little more."

Sierra lifted her iced tea and sipped, wondering if any of these women enjoyed life at all. They had everything the world counted important, yet she couldn't see any evidence of *joy* in their lives. They were all hungry for something more.

Just like you . . . a voice echoed in her head. She shifted uncomfortably, knowing it was true. The same hunger ate away at her and left her feeling restless and insecure.

Something was missing, but she didn't know what.

Marcia put her hand over Meredith's. "What's the matter with you today?"

Meredith gave a bleak laugh. "Nothing that isn't wrong with me every day of my life." She gave the waiter a radiant smile as he set another martini in front of her. "Thank you, Wylie." She lifted the drink to Marcia. "Cheers, sweetie."

"Did you ever see Dr. Worth?" Marcia said.

Meredith gave a derisive laugh. "I don't need a psychiatrist."

Sierra had been amazed to find out that the totally together Marcia had ever been to a psychiatrist, let alone that she'd been in ongoing therapy for ten years. Marcia claimed that was why she felt so at peace within herself. Dr. Worth had taken her on a journey into her past, where she had come face-to-face with the causes of problems in the present. Apparently, her parents had said and done things, seemingly unimportant at the time, that had had profound effects on her ability to function as an adult.

"Once I'd discovered what—and who—was responsible, I found I was free to move on," she'd told Sierra, that calm smile on her face.

Whenever difficulties arose in her marriage or life, Marcia simply returned to the refreshing, comforting counsel and couch of Dr. Worth. Once there, she received a booster shot of self-esteem, absolution, and direction.

"Don't you see, Meredith?" Marcia continued. "You'll never be truly happy until—"

"I don't think getting in touch with my 'inner child' would help much," Meredith said flatly, cutting her off.

"It would help. I guarantee it. It's helped me tremendously."

"Has it?" Meredith gave a mirthless laugh. "If it's so helpful, why are you back in therapy every other month?"

"Dr. Worth gives me a fresh view."

"Darling, I could give you a fresh view, and I wouldn't charge you two hundred and fifty an hour."

Marcia drew back with graceful calm. She gave a slow sigh, a sign she was striving for patience. "Why don't we order lunch?"

"Ah, ah, ah. I'm sure any self-respecting psychiatrist like Dr. Worth would tell you substituting food for a good fight is stuffing your feelings and counterproductive to your mental and emotional health."

"I'm hungry," Marcia said with a beatific smile.

"No, you're not. You're *mad.*"

"No, I am not."

Though Marcia sat in her usual, elegantly relaxed pose, Sierra could feel the tension radiating from her. She had seen the same thing happen before when Marcia was faced with a hard question.

Meredith gave her a bald grin. "You're getting angry."

"I'm sure you'd like me to be angry," Marcia said coolly, "but it's not constructive."

"Constructive?" Meredith smiled, her lovely, perfectly made-up face showing nothing of the inner turmoil that was clearly raging. "I'm always curious to see how deep your serenity goes, Marcia. I suspect not very."

Marcia arched her brow. "What do you mean?"

"You're not serene at all, despite appearances. I admire your control. Really I do. You're always so cool and so calm. Your husband never strays. Your children are a perfect little lady and gentleman. Not a single rapid in the river of your life, is there, sweetheart? Not so anyone can see, that is." Meredith twirled her beautiful, aristocratic, bejeweled hand gracefully in the air, adding sardonically, "And all because you've embraced the light, become one with the universe, and live on a higher plane of consciousness than the rest of us poor mortals." Her hand took rest beside the martini, her eyes shrewd. "Tell me, dear. Does the Valium help?"

Two spots of color appeared in Marcia's cheeks. "I face my problems head-on, Meredith."

"Oh yes, and wrestle them to the ground and choke them to death with the sheer strength of your will. I *know*," Meredith said. "I've seen the hunted look on Tom's face. I imagine if the poor man ever felt free enough to wear an open-necked shirt, we'd see the bite marks on his throat."

Marcia's face flushed beet red. She went rigid for a moment, then let out her breath very slowly and audibly, a yoga technique Sierra recognized. "I prefer your company when you're sober," she said with icy calm.

"And less honest, too, perhaps?" Meredith's blue eyes flashed with disdain. "Solve your own problems, dearie, before you try to fix mine."

Marcia rose regally and cast a stiff smile at the others seated around the table. "Why don't we all go in for lunch, ladies?"

Edie, who loathed conflict, rose quickly. "I think that's an excellent idea."

"We'd be delighted if you joined us, Merry," Marcia said as she gathered her white tennis sweater and canvas bag.

"Liar," Meredith said and raised her martini in mocking salute.

Sierra followed Marcia into the dining room. Nancy and Edie

joined them; Lorraine, preferring the heiress's acerbic wit, ordered another bourbon and remained behind.

"I swear. Merry is turning herself into a drunk," Nancy said, taking her place at the table.

"What do you think Lorraine will do?" Edie said, accepting a menu from a waiter.

"Get sick and cry a lot," Nancy said with a pitying glance back toward the lounge. "Ending a marriage is bad enough, if it comes to that. If you happen to be married to one of the leading divorce attorneys in the country, you can expect to lose everything, including your children."

"If he wants them," Marcia said blandly. "You've heard Lorry say often enough that Frank hasn't shown any interest in the children since the day they were born."

Sierra thought of how little time Alex had for the children these days. When was the last time he'd played baseball with Clanton or talked with Carolyn? She had been shouldering the full responsibility of parenting since their move to Los Angeles. Then, when things didn't go right, such as Clanton's report card showing two Cs and a D, Alex always had her to blame.

"What about Ashley's situation?" Edie said. "Gerry demanded joint custody just to make her life miserable."

"I don't think that's true," Marcia said, closing the menu and setting it aside. "Gerry was concerned for the children, and rightfully so. Ashley is so obsessive about weight, and poor little Veronica is going through her plump stage. Can you imagine what it's like for a child of ten to be dragged to aerobics classes every afternoon after school? That's what was happening until Gerry stepped in."

"An hour of exercise each day won't hurt her, will it?" Edie said, looking at Marcia for answers. Her own children were enrolled in various sports programs and resisting attendance.

"It's not the exercise that's harmful, Edie," Marcia said, sounding as though she were explaining a basic equation to a slow-witted pupil. "It's the experience of being *forced* to do what she doesn't want to do. That will leave terrible scars on her psyche."

Sierra could imagine Veronica grown-up and spending a hour twice a week in Dr. Worth's office exploring her "inner child." Still, would any child do anything if not pressed? Didn't Marcia press her own children to excel? Where was the difference?

"Have you *seen* Veronica?" Nancy said, shaking her head sadly. "All that child does is sit around and eat snacks in front of the television. She doesn't talk; she whines."

Uncomfortable with the course of the conversation, Sierra stared at the menu. She couldn't help but wonder if the women talked about her and her children when she wasn't present.

She ordered lobster thermidor and let the current of conversation swirl around her without diving in.

"You've been very quiet," Marcia said at last.

Over the past half hour, Sierra had listened to her three companions dissect Meredith's, Lorraine's, and Ashley's lives. They had laid bare every dysfunction, past sin, and private anguish, seeming to relish the action far more than they were enjoying their food.

She met Marcia's calm gaze. "My life is so full of problems, I don't feel I've any right to talk about theirs."

Silence fell around the table, and she felt the three women staring at her with a mingling of expressions.

Marcia blinked, her eyes widening in surprise. "You think we're *gossiping,*" she said in quiet accusation.

Sierra glanced from Marcia to Nancy, whose eyes were hot with indignation. Edie, on the other hand, looked embarrassed.

Sierra felt surrounded. Sometimes her friends acted like a pack of hounds. They had the veneer of sophistication, but they'd proven many times just how savage they were beneath. They didn't use their teeth to rip a person apart—they didn't need to.

Their soft-spoken words were sharp and barbed and effectively shredded one another with regularity. Didn't they realize what they were doing?

"I think you're concerned," Sierra said, wondering if that was only the guise beneath which they hid less altruistic motives.

"Of course we're concerned," Marcia said. "We *love* Meredith."

"And Ashley," Nancy said.

"And Lorraine," Edie added. "You know we do."

"Yes, I know," Sierra conceded, but she couldn't help hoping they wouldn't love her in the same way. "It's just that talking about their problems like this doesn't change anything."

"Then what will?" Nancy said.

"I wish I knew." She looked around at them, not knowing what else to say. Seeing their bleak eyes and defensive postures, she suddenly wished she were more like her mother. She would have had something to offer, some wisdom or encouragement.

From the beginning, she had found the company of these women stimulating and challenging. They made her laugh. They made her think. They opened her eyes to the way the world was. She wasn't the innocent, small-town girl Alex had brought to Los Angeles over a year ago. And she was thankful for that. But sometimes, she felt that despite the sophistication, knowledge, and wisdom about life that these women seemed to have, they really didn't know anything at all. Nothing that mattered. Nothing that changed anything. If they did, wouldn't their lives reflect it?

The fear of the Lord is the beginning of wisdom, Sierra.

She frowned at the remembered words; her mother had quoted them to her often. She looked at the women around the table again. It was bad enough that her words had brought an end to the conversation. There was no way she was going to try to bring God into this! That might work for her mother, but Sierra wasn't as confident as her mother that God had all the answers. If he did, he certainly didn't seem eager to share them.

Not with her, anyway.

She shifted again in her seat, wondering why she suddenly felt so depressed. Maybe it was because the discussion had revolved around the disintegrating lives of three women she liked and admired. Maybe it was because so many people all around her seemed to be hurting.

Maybe it was because her own life felt so empty and out of control.

"What's bothering you?" Marcia said, sensitive to her mood. Nancy and Edie were looking at her, too.

How honest could she be with these women? Was she the only one struggling with a sense of hopelessness? "I don't know. A lot of things, I guess. I'm not even sure I can explain."

They sat waiting.

Sierra plunged in, taking the risk. "I'm so *busy* all the time. Yet, at the end of the day, I feel . . . empty, as though time has passed, but I didn't accomplish anything that mattered."

"What do you expect of yourself?" Nancy said. "To find the cure for cancer?"

"No. Just *something.*"

"The best thing we can do is be happy," Edie said.

"Within ourselves," Marcia said in gentle admonition. "If we can't manage our own lives, how can we expect to manage those of our families?"

Manage. The word jarred. It was discordant. Sierra pictured a company president issuing memorandums to her employees. Meredith's words flashed back in her head; they had been harsh, but true. Sierra had seen the dynamics of Marcia's family. Watching her interaction with Tom and the children was like watching a master puppeteer working marionettes. Marcia always knew exactly what to say and do to get her family members to do what she expected of them. Both of her children were A students, active in sports, popular. Her husband worked hard, made good money, and came home from work every night at precisely five-thirty. Marcia's life seemed to run so smoothly.

Was that the secret to having a happy family? A woman who could *manage* everything?

If that was the case, she was doomed to perpetual failure.

Manage Alex? What a laugh! She could hardly even get her husband to sit down long enough to talk anymore. When he did, they ended up fighting. He had a will of steel. Over the past year, that will had run over hers like a steamroller flattening macadam.

Edie changed the subject. She mentioned a play she'd seen, and Nancy chimed in to agree it was wonderful. Marcia talked about her plans to accompany Tom to a business convention in Detroit. When asked by Nancy, she admitted most of the other men from his company weren't taking their wives. Smiling, she said Tom had agreed it would be a nice time for them to get away by themselves.

"By yourselves?" Nancy said. "With Tom in meetings most of the day? What are *you* going to do?"

"I'll relax and read and have lunch and dinner with Tom. I imagine there'll be time to take in a museum or two between meetings."

"Are there museums in Detroit?" Nancy said.

"There's Henry Ford's Fairlane Museum," Marcia said with a bright laugh, but Sierra couldn't help wondering if her friend's real reason for going with Tom was to keep him under her ever-watchful eye.

Well, what if it is? she wondered, almost defiantly. *Is that such a bad idea in this day of disintegrating and broken marriages?*

Poking at her lobster thermidor, Sierra remembered Alex asking her to go with him to the Consumer Electronics Show in Las Vegas last year.

"What about my mother?" she had said.

"What's CES got to do with your mother?"

"She's coming down for a visit. You knew that! I told you weeks ago."

"You knew about CES, too!" He'd sworn in Spanish. "I gave you the dates."

"You did *not!*"

"Call your mom and ask her to hold off for a week."

"She's supposed to juggle her schedule just to please you?"

"She's *retired.* What sort of a schedule has she got to juggle?"

As it turned out, she didn't go to CES, though she did call her mother and change their plans. Instead of her mother coming south, Sierra drove north with the children and spent eight days in Healdsburg. Her mother had lost weight and looked tired, but otherwise she'd been in good spirits. They'd had long talks while sitting on Memorial Beach watching the children swim in the Russian River. Sierra had returned to North Hollywood remorseful, almost afraid of the greeting she would receive from Alex. Their telephone conversations had been stilted and uneasy while she was in Healdsburg. She apologized and things had been easier between them for a while.

Easier, but not the same.

Audra had mentioned CES just the other evening when she and Alex were all having dinner at Matt and Laura's house. Steve said several new members of the staff were going along this year. Alex didn't even look at her as he sipped his wine and said he was looking forward to a trip to Vegas.

Stabbing a piece of lobster, Sierra decided it might be to the best interests of her marriage if she went along this time.

"You wouldn't be interested," Alex said that evening when she brought up the subject.

"What makes you so sure?"

"It's all glitz and meetings, and a lot of people you don't know. Those you do, you can't stand."

"I suppose you mean Audra will be there."

"Yes, Audra will be there. She supports Steve wholeheartedly."

She heard what he didn't say: She didn't support him. Anger poured through her; it was always just beneath the surface these days. But whose fault was that? Alex was always cutting her down. She wasn't supportive. She wasn't a good mother or her children would be getting better grades. She wasn't doing anything other than spending his money at the club. Whose idea was it to go to the club in the first place?

"I'd like to go with you this year," she insisted.

He looked at her enigmatically. "You said you hate Vegas."

What she really hated was the way he remembered every word she ever said just so he could throw it back in her face. Breathing slowly, she clung to her self-restraint. "I've never been to Las Vegas, Alex. I'd like to see what it's like."

He didn't say anything. He just looked at her. She wondered why the decision was so hard for him to make. Hadn't he wanted her to accompany him last year? Didn't he want her along this time?

"Fine," he said, gaze flickering away, "but I don't want the kids coming. These shows are work, not play. You'd better keep that in mind, too. I won't be able to entertain you."

Gracious to the last. "I'll ask Marcia if she would mind having the children spend the weekend at her house."

"Don't expect to play tourist," he said. "We're going to be attending a lot of business dinners and company parties."

"Will I need some new clothes?"

"Ask Audra."

———————

God, dont you listen when peepul pray?

Dont you care? Mama told me you did, but

I dont see how with the Terrible Truble we got.

I got doubts you are even there.

117

Sometimes I dont think things cud get worse. Then they do. First James leaving. Then Sally Mae coming here as Matts wife. Then Mama dying, then Papa turning to whiskey. If all that aint bad enuf, Lucas had to leave and take the best horse with him. God, what more you gonna take?

Mama used to say you had control of everything. So what I wud like to ask is why you are giving us all this Sorrow and Grief?

Sally Mae is sick most of the time. She is scared all the time. Nothing makes her happy. She is either crying when Matt is out working or screaming at him when he is not. She says she wants to go home to her grandmama in Fever River. Matt will not tak her and her pa washt his hands of her the day she wed.

Papa works all day and drinks all night til he sleeps. And even with all his work it dont look like it will be a good year.

Weve had no meat in a month and since Lucas stole Papas gun no way of getting any.

Things cant get wurs.

I wuz wrong.

I aint settin hope on god no more. There is no god. There is only hell on earth. Mama is the lucky one. And Sally Mae too now that she is dead. They have no worries. The rest of us have got the wate of what they dun. Mama and her

hopes of heaven. And Sally Mae knowing she
wuz on her way to hell.

I dont know what I am going to do now with
this babee.

Matt burned Papas fields yesterday. He had
good reason. Sally Mae told him the babee werent
his. She knew she was dying and it made her
crazy scared. So she told the awful truth. *Do you
think you are the father, Matthew? You had to go off to
Fever River with Lucas, didnt you? I knew what you wud
think of me when you come bak. I wanted to hurt you
before you hurt me and I did. O, I did. I wasnt goin to tell
you but I can't die with this sin on my head. I dont want
to go to hell. You hear me?* Matt said what are you
talkin about? And Sally Mae said *The babee aint
yours. Your father put it in me.* Matt called her
a liar and she said to go and ask him. So he did.

Papa said he was drunk when she come in
to him and lay with him like a wife. He did not
know what he was doing. Matt went crazy. He
beat Papa until I thot he wud kill him. He nocked
me down three times before I cud stop him. And
Papa just lay in the dirt bleeding. Matt set the
fields afire. I aint seen him since.

Sally Mae was screaming somethin awful. It
raised the hair on the bak of my neck. The babee
come with the flames. Thar was so much smoke it
burned my eyes. The fire did not tuch the house.
The wind changed and sent the flames across the

fields to the woods and creek. If it had not, Papa, Sally Mae, the babee and me wud all be ded.

The babee come out of her at nightfall, and blood come too. I never seen so much. It soaked through the straw mattress and pooled on the floor underneath. She stopped screaming then. Papa cum inside the house when I called, but he jest stud in the doorway. I kept cryin for him to help me. He said leave that devil child to die with her. He said they cud both go to meet the devil together.

I cud not do it. I can't let this babee die. His mother was a wanton and his father a drunken fool. Does that mean he has to die for it?

Papa said he will not have Sally Maes devil spawn in his house. I said it was no devil, but his own son. He laid a curse on me. He said I am not his daughter no more. He said if I did not leave the house he wud kill me and the babee with me.

I can hear Papa digging her grave. Thar aint going to be a ceremony or a marker and he is burning all her things and the bed she and Matthew shared.

He ought to be burning with it.

I hav deecided to call the babee Joshua. It is not a famly name like Matthew or Lucas. But why would anybody want to be in this famly? I like the sound of Joshua. I read it in the Bible. Mama wud sing about Joshua blowing his horn and the walls of Jericho came tumbling down.

Maybe Joshua's crying will make Papa's walls come tumbling down. And he will let us come back and live in the house before winter hits.

Maybe Joshua is not a good name for this babee. He has not come into this world to bring his famly to the Promused Land. He has stirred up nothing but trouble since the day he was born.

The preecher came today.

He said a lady acros the river wants a babee bad. I told him she shud talk to her husband about that and not send a preecher to me. Preecher said if I give the babee up, Papa might forgive me my sins and let me come back to the house. I asked the preecher what he knew about what happened and he said he knew all he needed to know and I told him he did not know much. He got all puffed up like a toad and turned red. He said an unwed girl with a babee shud not talk to her betters the way I was talking to him and it was no wonder Papa threw me out. He said Papa did rite. He said in the old days I wud hav ben stoned to deth for what I dun. So I did not say nothing else until he left.

Nobody is taking Joshua away from me.

I tried to talk to Papa today but he walked right by me like I was not thar. I followed him out into

the blackened fields and begged, but he did not
let on he herrd nothing until Joshua started cryin.
Then he turned around and looked at me. I never
seen such a look on his face. I never seen such
a look on nobodys face like that. He said to git
away from him or he wud kill us both.

I said winter is coming, Papa. You want us to
die?

He said yes.

First snow came today. The goat is going dry.
Seems like I did not save this babee from deth at
all. Just made him suffer.

The right reverend came again today. He said if I
do not send the babee to that lady across the river,
Papa is going to send me and the babee to Mamas
sister in Fever River with the Reinholtzes, the
German family moving out. Preecher says they
lost two children to fever a month ago and can not
bear to stay another winter. It wud be Christian
kindness to give them my babee. I said if they cud
have two babees of their own, they could have
more, but I was not giving my own blood away to
strangers for any reason. He said I was unrepentant
and arrogant. When I did not say nuthin he askt
if I knew what arrogant meant. I said it is when
someone already thinks he knows everything there
is to know and dont know nothing at all.

He said I am hell bent. Maybe I am. All I know
for certain is the right reverend wud find truth
harder to swallow than the lies hes chewing on.
The truth would choke him to death.

I aint going to tell him what happened. Better
he thinks Joshua is mine than know where he
cum from. It is bad enuf God knows without
havin the hole county hear of it.

God dont care.

I did not think Aunt Martha wud let me in the
door of her fine house. The Reinholtz told me
to wait an hour before coming into Fever River.
The town is called Galena now after the ore they
mine hereabouts. Reinholtz did not want anyone
knowin they had anythin to do with a girl who
had a babee and no husband and did not even
know where she was going. So I did what he askt
and waited til nightfall before comin into town.
I askt the first person I saw whar Martha Werner
lived. The boy tuk me strat here. I almost died
when I saw the house. It is so grand and up on
a hill street. Two stories of wood and block with
steps up one side.

A black woman answered when I nocked.
I askt for Martha Werner. She called for Clovis.
A black man come runnin and started untying the
rope around my wast. I got scared and said I wud
not let him take my goat. My baby needs milk or

he will die. He said he wud not take him far and
he wud see the goat was fed and watered.

Aunt Martha is the prettiest woman I ever seen.
She was wearing a yellow dress with white lace.
She knew me rite off. She said I look like Mama.
She tuk Joshua from me. A good thing she did
because I cud not stand no more. It is a long walk
from the home place to Fever River or Galena or
whatever it is called. Worse when you are eatin
wagon dust. I did not want to sit on her furniture
in my dirty clothes but the black woman picked
me up from where I sunk down and put me on
the sofa anyway.

The black womans name is Betsy. She carried
me into the kitchen and set me near the stove.
Aunt Martha had Joshua. Clovis fetcht water
from the town well and Betsy heeted it in big
pots. I askt about the goat. He said the goat
is fine and eatin supper and went out again
for another bucket of water. Betsy tuk off my
clothes and put me in the tub. I aint never felt
anythin as good as that warm water comin over
me. She washed me like a babee wile Aunt
Martha washed and played with Joshua. Betsy
said stop worrying about that goat. My man
Clovis will take good care of her.

When Joshua started in fussin, Betsy went
out bak and milked the goat. Aunt Martha sat in
a rockin chair near the stov feeding Joshua and

singing Mamas song. I cried. I cud not stop. I just
sat in the warm water and the tears kept running.

Aunt Martha give me a real bed to sleep in and
a room of my own. Joshua slept with me. He aint
never ben in a bed before. For that matter, I aint
never seen one the likes of it. It is shiny brass like
gold with a lacy tent over head. Aunt Martha
said it belonged to Mama before she run off with
Papa. She said her own Papa ordered it and had
it shipped all the way from New York.

I wunder if James ever made it to New York
like he wanted. He mit even be in China by now.

Aunt Martha dont ask me a lot of questions.
And she dont look at me like most foks do. The
Reinholtz were in church today and they wud not
look at me at all. On the way home I told Aunt
Martha Joshua is Sally Maes son. It is half-true.
She cried and kist me. She said she loves me and
I can liv with her forever if I want. She said *You
are not to worry what people say. The truth always comes
out in the end.*

I hope this truth dont.

Aunt Martha thinks as much of edukashun as
Mama did. She says I got a good mind that needs
fillin with good things. To that end, she is tutorin
me in reding, riting, and numbers and teachin me
the Bible. She says that the only way to do well in

this life is to know the word of God. Mama knew the Bible front and back and it did not do her much good at all. I did not tell Aunt Martha this. I wud rather eat stones than hurt her feelings. Life does that easy enuf as it is.

8

SIERRA WANDERED DOWN THE CROWDED aisles of the Consumer Electronics Show by herself. The convention center was a beehive of activity. It reminded her of the state fair with its carnival atmosphere, but here few people were over the age of thirty and everyone dressed in suits.

Big booths lined both sides of the carpeted aisle. Videos of new games were going. Neon and vibrant-colored cartoonlike artwork was everywhere. It was dizzying to the eye and ear. She saw a short man wearing funky clothes and glitter-framed glasses talking with several taller men in suits. She could tell by the deference paid him that he was somebody important in the industry.

Sometimes she could tell who was important, sometimes not.

Alex had introduced her to a man at a party the night before. He'd looked ordinary enough until he'd left them, then Alex informed her the man's company had built a two-million-dollar studio in his home just so he could work on sound for games.

Someone bumped her, glanced at her badge, mumbled an apology, and moved on. Everyone looked at badges. Alex could sniff out sales reps and reporters like a hound in the hunt. Not that he had to work very hard at it. Reporters from *Game* Informer, Blaster magazine, and *Next Generation* were fighting to make appointments with him.

Lost in the maze of booths and people, Sierra tried to get her bearings and figure out how to get back to the Beyond Tomorrow booth. It was almost five o'clock and Alex had told her to meet him there. They needed to go up to their room and change for a business dinner. The Beyond Tomorrow booth was near the center with big television screens displaying Alex's new game: Camouflage.

Everywhere she turned she heard computer jargon.

"They've got the best FMV in the business," one man crowed, referring to full-motion video. Alex had explained to her that with FMV, actors did the fighting and then the sequences were plugged into the computer to make lifelike graphics. Companies then used cut-and-paste methods to stick the FMV on top. She heard people talking about "texture mapping" and "polygon graphics" and hadn't the foggiest idea what they were talking about.

Over dinner, she had listened to Alex talk about his work and his new game. He exuded confidence as he answered questions and explained his theories and plans. He held his guests' rapt attention, fanning their interest. This was a side of her husband she'd never witnessed before. She was proud of him, of his obvious achievements and his ability to sway others. Yet she had felt set apart as well—like some kind of nice-looking but totally unnecessary adornment. After the introductions and pleasantries, she sat listening. The conversation went on around her, but hardly a word was directed her way. Half the time she didn't even know what they were talking about.

"Do you play your husband's game, Sierra?" one of the young men asked her as their dinners were being served.

"No. I'm not much for video games. They're too quick and complex for me."

Alex laughed. "Sierra prefers physical pursuits, like tennis at the country club, manicures, and shopping."

The other men laughed with him. She laughed, too, pretending to share the joke while doing all she could to conceal the surprise and hurt she felt at his remark. He said it lightly, as though affectionately amused. Yet she felt belittled.

Was that how he saw her? As a shallow young woman with nothing important to do?

The thought had plagued her all night and most of the day.

God, I don't even know who I am anymore.

Ahead of her now was a big screen with vividly colored warriors using medieval weapons to hack at one another. One split the other in half with an axe, sending splashes of neon-red blood in a shower. Repulsed, Sierra looked away and kept walking. At least she knew where she was now. Beyond Tomorrow was down two aisles to the right.

Alex was talking with two men in business suits, while Elizabeth Longford, Beyond Tomorrow's hotshot merchandising director, stood alongside him with a clipboard. The young woman was dressed in a designer suit of deep green. It fitted her slender body like a glove. No sign of a single wrinkle or crease, even after a full day of standing on the floor and talking to sales reps. Elizabeth's long blonde hair was permed into kinked tendrils that tumbled down her back.

Sierra had only met Elizabeth a few times and found her cool and remote. She was very attractive, professional, and ambitious.

Sierra felt uneasy around her, even more so when she saw Alex talking with her so easily.

"Yes, she's young," Audra said that evening at a party. Sierra stood beside her near the hors d'oeuvres, sipping champagne. "She just turned twenty-six a few weeks ago."

Alex and Steve stood not far away talking business to several sales reps, who seemed more interested in admiring Elizabeth in her sleek low-cut black gown. The simple, elegant design bespoke money. Lots of it.

"She graduated from Wellesley," Audra said, setting her champagne down so she could put caviar on a small circle of melba toast. "She took her masters in marketing at Columbia." Sierra watched the younger woman move out onto the dance floor with one of the reps. Elizabeth's graceful undulations were in stark contrast to the enthusiastic gyrations of her partner.

"She's very lovely," Sierra said, noticing how Alex and Steve were both watching her.

"Indeed," Audra said enigmatically. "She knows how to present herself. She went to finishing school in Switzerland and was a debutante." She took up her glass of champagne again. "I asked her about it, but she disdains the whole thing. Family pressure. Understandable." She ate the cracker delicately. "Her father is a descendant of one of the crew of the *Mayflower.*" She looked at Sierra. "She works very closely with Alex."

Somehow, Audra's words held warning. They planted doubt and fear.

"Do you like Elizabeth?" Sierra asked Alex later in their hotel room.

"She's good at her job," he said, loosening his tie.

Hanging up his suit jacket, Sierra waited for him to say more. When he didn't, she looked back at him standing near the windows overlooking the lights of Las Vegas. He was so handsome, her heart ached. What woman wouldn't be attracted to him? He pulled his shirt free of his suit trousers and unbuttoned his collar.

Sierra's stomach fluttered. How long since they'd come together in passionate need for one another? How long since he'd held her and kissed her and said he loved her? She loved him so much. She needed him. Yet he seemed so distant, so distracted. Whatever thoughts were running through his mind clearly troubled him. Hadn't things gone as well as expected tonight? Or was it something else?

Her throat ached. She wanted to say something but couldn't trust her voice. They had been fighting so much lately, usually about the most trivial things. She wasn't sure what Alex would do if she reached out to him. She wanted to be close to him again, the way they used to be when they could talk about anything, when just being together and touching one another had been heaven. Now it took all her courage to cross the room.

Brushing his hands away, she unbuttoned his shirt for him. "I love you, Alex." He didn't say anything. He didn't touch her. But he didn't turn away either. When she finished, she looked up at him. "I'll never stop loving you."

Frowning, he searched her eyes.

She couldn't read his expression. Fear suddenly overwhelmed her, and she couldn't even say why.

His eyes softened. Sighing, he cupped her face. "You've always driven me crazy, Sierra," he said, his voice deep and rough as his fingers stroked her skin. He didn't look happy about it.

"*Te amo muchísimo,*" she whispered.

He loosened her French braid. Combing his fingers into her hair, he kissed her.

Sighing in relief, she let the passion sweep through her. *Nothing has changed, not really,* she told herself, wanting desperately to believe it.

It has been a long time since I wrote in this journal.

I have had little time to do anything over the past months except complete the work Aunt Martha prepares for me. I am not complaining. She says she has Great Expectations for me. When I do well, she is more pleased than I. While everyone else in this town seems to look upon me as Mary Magdalene still possessed of demons, Aunt Martha sees me as Pure Delight. It is beyond me why. I question everything she teaches me. She listens and makes no condemnations while others would not even give me the time of day.

Aunt Martha tells me I was God's gift to her. She has never been married and therefore has never had children of her own. Now, she has two, me and Joshua.

Joshua is growing so quickly. Sometimes I am afraid. I can see Sally Mae in him. He has her blue eyes and gold hair. I see Papa, too. But it is the other things in him I see that disturb me. He has Papa's hot temper and Sally Mae's lust for life. I love Joshua so much. But I wonder what he will become.

Everyone in Galena thinks Joshua is my child.

It is well they do. They think less of me, but treat
him kindly. I think they do so for Aunt Martha's
sake. She is a Strong Force in this community.
Everyone loves and respects her. She is the
Gentlest of Ladies and given to Good Works.
They tolerate me for her sake. They love Joshua
for his own. He is beautiful like Sally Mae and
as charming as Papa used to be. Aunt Martha
said it was Papa's charm and good looks that won
Mama's heart.

I am restless tonight. I dont know why. I have
the oddest feeling something is going to happen.
Whether good or bad, I do not know.

Thomas Atwood Houghton is what was about
to happen. He is an old and dear friend of Aunt
Martha's who has come to visit. Everyone was a
twitter when he came to church. He is very Well
Known because he has Money and Land and
Connections. Why he is here I am not certain. He
told Aunt Martha he was in Galena on Business,
but what kind of Business is Unclear.

I was a shock to him. He looked at me in the
strangest way when first we met. Calf's eyes, Aunt
Martha said. She believes he is taken with me. She
is very pleased, but I am filled with Misgivings.

Thomas is as kind as Aunt Martha. Joshua
adores him. Everyone in Galena is taken with

Thomas. I like Thomas also, but he has made it
clear he is thinking in terms of Matrimony. He
spoke to Aunt Martha about it and she spoke to
me. Why he wants to marry me I do not know.
There is not a young unmarried woman in this
town who would not be delighted with the
prospect of being Thomas Atwood Houghton's
wife. He is a contrary man to court a girl who aint
interested.

I gathered my courage and asked him straight
out what he was thinking. He said he did not
want a simpering maid, but a girl who spoke her
mind. I said Aunt Martha speaks her mind. He
said Martha is his dearest and best friend. I said
he would be wise to marry her. She is more suited
to him and closer to his own age. He said it is a
matter of love and not practicality.

It seems to me the harder I resist the more determined he is to make me his wife. So I am going to
simper and sigh. Perhaps this will shake him loose.

The announcement of my betrothal to Thomas
has changed my life completely. People speak
to me now. They are even Polite. Some pretend
to be friends. Elmira Standish *insisted* I come to
her afternoon tea and visit with the ladies of the
Women's Society. Aunt Martha is a member. She
has not gone to any meetings since I came to live

with her, but she attended with me yesterday.
I am thankful she did.

Several young ladies spoke with me now that
I am considered *acceptable* company. Their mamas
watched, but did not call them back. The girls
were full of questions, not about Thomas, but
about Joshua's father. I could feel my face go
all hot. One girl said they heard my child's papa
was a mountain man who spent the winter at our
homestead. Another heard he was a drummer.
One girl said her mama was very Upset because
I had charmed Thomas the same way Sally Mae
Grayson had charmed poor Noah Carnegie. I
asked about that.

Sally Mae is remembered. Her poor grandmama
died before I got here. One girl said old Missus
Grayson passed on to heaven just so she would
never go through hell with Sally Mae again. I
asked her meaning, and another said Sally Mae
was the sort of girl who bewitched men that were
her betters. She was looking straight at me when
she said it and I got her meaning clear enough.
Another said Sally Mae's last beau was Noah,
son of one of the elders in the church. He came
confessing to Sally Mae's grandmama about what
they was doing on their Sunday rides together.
The other girl glaring at me said you know what
a girl like that will do to get a man. The other
said Noah was a foolish boy and wanted to marry

Sally Mae and make things right. I thought of poor Matthew making things right. But Noah had poor Missus Grayson come to his rescue. She sent Sally Mae packing. After she did, Missus Grayson did not come out of her house again. The doctor went to see her, and people asked after her. But it was clear to everyone that the poor woman pined away out of pure shame over having Sally Mae for a granddaughter. As for poor Noah, he finally came to his senses and realized what sort of girl Sally Mae was. When he did, he was so overcome with shame and grief, he stood up in church and confessed his sins to the entire congregation. That is how everyone in town came to know about everything.

One of them said she wondered if Sally Mae would ever come back to Galena after the Great Scandal she had caused. I held my tongue. My feelings were over large right then. I almost said Sally Mae had destroyed my family. But had I said it, they would have descended on me like a flock of crows pecking and wanting to know the gory details of how and why. If I answered, they would have spread the Terrible Truth all over town like manure on a field.

It is better for Joshua if everyone goes on thinking he is mine than to know he came out of Sally Mae Grayson.

Poor Matthew. I cry every time I think of him.

I miss him something fierce. Just like I miss
Mama. I wonder where he went after he burned
Papa's fields. I wonder if I will ever see him again.
And if I did, what would he say to me about
Joshua? Would he hate me the same way Papa
does? I think he would. But that does not change
my mind about what I did or why.

Aunt Martha says daily God is in control. If
that is so, God has made a fine mess of things.
Aunt Martha says there is a good reason for
everything that happens. She says God has a Plan
for everyone. I wanted to scream when she said
it. Was it God's plan that Mama die alone choking
on her own blood? Was it God's plan Papa turn
into a drunk? Was it God's plan Matthew marry
Sally Mae who brought grief to everyone? Was it
God's plan Papa father a child on his son's wife?
And what of kind, loving, faithful Matthew?
What did he do to deserve what he got? What
good reason is there for any of the Terrible things
that happened?

Aunt Martha does not know everything. I
would be the last to tell her so. She is happy in
her Ignorance. I hope Aunt Martha stays blind. I
would not like for her to know about the dirtiness
and meanness of life. I would rather die than have
her know about the shame Papa brought upon
us all. Aunt Martha's Jesus heals the sick, raises

the dead, and feeds the five thousand. Just like Mama's Jesus. Let her hold to that fine fairy tale.

The Jesus I know stands by and does nothing. He dont save nobody or put out fires. He starts them. Maybe he is like the gods on Olympus that I have been reading about. They enjoy playing with people too. When they get tired of someone, they throw him away. Maybe that is what God did. He got tired of Mama and Sally Mae and Matthew and Papa. Maybe our Father who art in heaven is like those other gods. I couldn't help thinking it would be better if Jesus just sat and watched the play unfold beneath him, but took no part in it, either good or bad.

And then sometimes I wonder if Jesus is just a man in a big black book.

I do not know anymore. I cannot bear to think about it much.

When I was a little girl and Mama and I picked flowers in the meadow, I thought God was there with us. I loved him and talked to him the way Mama taught me. I thought God was everywhere, even inside us. Mama always said it was so. And I believed her. I always believed everything Mama said.

I do not believe in anything now. It hurts less.

9

"YOU'RE GOING TO HAVE TO GET A JOB." ALEX'S dark eyes were grim.

"A job?" she said, astonished. She hadn't had a job since they got married. "Why?"

"Because the bills have been stacking up for the past six months, and I don't see any other way around it."

"You said we had more than enough money."

"That was before you started having lunch at the club every day of the week. The bill last month alone was fourteen hundred dollars!" He tossed it onto the desk, where he'd been working on their accounts.

"Fourteen hundred dollars?" she said weakly, feeling the blood drain from her face.

Alex swore in Spanish. "Don't you even bother to look at the slips you sign or keep track of what you're spending?" he said in disgust.

Hand shaking, she picked up the bill and looked at it. Running her finger down the column, she saw she wasn't entirely at fault. "Green fees and dinners account for more than half of this bill."

"Those are business expenses!" he said hotly.

They still came out of their pocket until the end of the year and taxes. Last year, they'd ended up paying more. That had been a shock after ten years of getting refunds. "Alex, you were the one who encouraged me to go and meet —"

"Not *every* day of the week! I thought going to the club would give you something *constructive* to do with your time. You were sitting around every day watching soap operas, reading romances, and feeling sorry for yourself."

She dropped the bill from the country club back onto the desk. He was making her the cause of all their financial problems. How convenient. "I'm not the one who gave Bruce Davies carte blanche and ended up with eighty-six thousand dollars in decorating expenses. *That's* when the problems started."

A muscle jerked in his jaw and his eyes darkened. "The trouble started when you decided you needed a closet full of clothes so you could keep up with Marcia Burton and the rest of her bourgeois friends."

"If anyone's bourgeois, it's *us.*"

Alex's face hardened.

"You're the one who told me to buy some clothes," she went on, lowering her voice.

"I want your credit cards."

"You're not being fair about any of this! You always blame everything on me! You go out to lunch in expensive restaurants every day of the week and pick up the tab for whoever comes along. You bought three tailored suits and half a dozen shirts just last week. And then you say *I'm* spending too much on clothes!"

"I *work* for a living."

She froze at the look of contempt on his face.

She worked, too, not that he ever noticed. She drove the children to and from school, sports activities, and doctor and dentist appointments. She attended parent-teacher meetings and open houses. She planned menus, shopped, and cooked dinner, though he was seldom ever home to enjoy it. Who did he think kept the house neat and clean during the week? A maid? Who did he think washed and ironed their clothes and saw that his expensive suits were cleaned and hanging neatly in the closet? She ran the hundred and one errands he gave her every day of her miserable life, and he never even bothered to say thank you!

Hot tears filled her eyes. "Fine." Anger and resentment filled her until she was shaking with it. She got her purse, took out her wallet, and extracted four credit cards. She tossed them on the desk.

"What're you going to do?" Alex said. *"Cry?* That'll solve a lot, won't it!"

"No. I'm going to get a job."

Alex raked a hand through his hair in frustration. "Keep the cards. Just don't use them for a while. And forget about getting a job. I don't want Steve getting wind of this mess." He gave a derisive laugh. "What would you find anyway? You've got a few months of business school. Big deal! Any job you'd get would pay a pittance." He swore. "Just back off on the club for a while until I can figure out how to juggle things around and pay some of these bills down."

Sierra stood in stony silence. When he left, she cut up the credit cards and tucked them into the bill box, where he was sure to find them. Then she called Marcia. "Do you know anyone who might have a job opening?"

"A job?" Marcia said in surprise.

"I'm sick of being made to feel like a parasite," she said, her voice wobbling.

"Did you and Alex have another fight?"

"Do bears live in the forest?"

"I'm sorry, Sierra."

"I'm tired of this, Marcia. Sick to death of it." She stopped, clutching the telephone receiver so tightly her hand ached.

"Ron Peirozo was over yesterday telling Tom he's in dire need of a secretary right now. Judy's baby is due at the end of the month. Do you have any secretarial training?"

"I went to business college before marrying Alex, but I didn't graduate."

"Well, charity organizations should be charitable."

"A charity? Didn't you introduce me to Ron Peirozo a few months ago at the club?" Sierra said. He didn't have the appearance of someone working for a charity.

"As a matter of fact, yes. I'd forgotten." Marcia laughed. "I can hear what you're thinking. No, he wasn't spending charity donations. He has his own money. His grandfather died and left him a lot of money, as well as a heart for philanthropy. The first thing Ron did was give several hundred thousand dollars to his alma mater for scholarships for minority students. Then he set up Outreach. As long as I've known Ron, he's been involved in community work of some sort. He's generous and brilliant. Besides that, his family connections bring him in contact with some of the most influential and wealthy people in the country. He could charm money out of the meanest miser and make them feel good about writing the check."

"I don't think he'd be interested in someone like me," Sierra said, positive she lacked the qualifications to work for a man like Ron Peirozo.

"Nonsense. He's looking for someone to handle office details.

I'll call him. If the position's still open I'll let you know, and you can see about making an appointment with him for an interview."

"I don't know, Marcia."

"Nothing ventured, nothing gained. You have to take control of your life."

Sierra did her grocery shopping and picked up two of Alex's suits at the cleaners. On the way home, she stopped by the post office for more stamps. She'd put the last one on a letter to her mother this morning.

The telephone was ringing as she came into the kitchen from the garage. She laid the suits over the counter, deposited a bag of groceries beside it, and made a lunge for the telephone as it rang again. "Hello," she said breathlessly, dumping her purse and keys on the counter.

"Sierra? Sierra Madrid?"

"Yes," she said, frowning slightly. The man's voice was vaguely familiar, but she couldn't place it. "Speaking."

"This is Ron Peirozo. Marcia said you might be interested in a job."

She felt her face go hot. "Yes," she said simply, heart thumping nervously. "I thought I should do something more important than play tennis and drink iced tea at the club."

He laughed. "Still beating Marcia?"

She relaxed slightly. "Once in a while, when her guard's down."

"Would it be convenient for you to come in tomorrow morning for an interview?"

"That would be fine. What time?"

"Nine, unless that's too early at such short notice."

"Nine is perfect."

"I'll outline the position for you. Once I've done that, you may have second thoughts about working for me."

143

"I doubt that, Mr. Peirozo, but *you* may have second thoughts. How much did Marcia tell you?"

"Just that you were looking for a job."

"I went to business college but didn't finish. Basically, I've been a wife and mother. That's it."

He chuckled. "Seems to me that's a pretty big responsibility."

"I thought so," she said dryly. "Some people wouldn't agree."

"All right," he said slowly, mulling over her remark. "Are you willing to work hard?"

"Yes."

"Are you willing to learn?"

"Yes."

"Will you take directions?"

"Yes."

"Can you type?"

"Yes."

"Shorthand?"

"Some."

"You've got the qualifications. I'll see you at nine."

Alex called at six that evening. "I'm going to be late." Big surprise. Dinner was already on the table and the children were eating. "Steve and I are going over the new promo stuff," he went on when she didn't say anything.

"Do you want me to keep your dinner in the oven?" she said, proud of how calm she sounded.

"No, thanks. We'll order something in."

At ten-thirty she gave up waiting for him and went to bed. She awakened at one in the morning when she heard the garage door open. She had left the bathroom light on so he could find his way around the room.

"Did you and Steve get everything done?" she said groggily, watching him go into the walk-in closet to take off his clothes.

"Sorry," he muttered. "I didn't mean to wake you."

Shrugging out of his suit jacket, he tossed it over a chair and headed into the master bathroom. She heard him turn on the shower. The glass door snapped closed. He let the water run so long, she fell asleep again and didn't awaken until the alarm went off at five-thirty.

"Didn't you reset the alarm?" she said sleepily.

"I'm getting up."

She brushed some hair back from her face. "You worked until one o'clock in the morning, Alex. Is Steve turning into a slave driver?"

He sat up and raked his hands back through his hair. "Steve'll be in the office by six-thirty," he said, his back to her.

She sensed something was wrong. Was it the fight they'd had yesterday? She'd had time to think things over and cool down. She reached out to touch him, but before she could, he got up and left the bedroom. Pushing the comforter back, she got out of bed, pulled on her robe, and followed. She found him in the kitchen, watching the stream of coffee filling the carafe. She knew he was aware of her standing there, but he didn't look at her. He pulled the carafe out and poured himself a cup of coffee.

"What's wrong, Alex?"

"Nothing," he said, a muscle clenching in his jaw.

"If it's the bills, I—"

"Look. I'm tired. I didn't get a lot of sleep last night."

"You're still angry with me. You still think it's my fault."

He winced. "I don't want to talk about it, Sierra."

She could feel him building the wall between them. "You don't want to talk about anything, do you?"

He looked at her, his eyes brooding. "Not now."

"Fine. Maybe this will please you. I have a job interview this morning. You could wish me luck." She turned around and headed for the bedroom before he could see the tears in her eyes.

Alex swore and slammed his cup of coffee down. "I told you *not* to get a job!"

She slammed the bedroom door. Dragging in her breath, she clenched her fists. She wanted to scream and cry at the same time. What was happening to them? They couldn't say two sentences to one another without getting into another fight.

Alex came into the bedroom, looking upset. "You don't have to go to work. We'll just cut back on spending until we catch up. I want you to stay home."

"Why? So you have a convenient scapegoat? You told me the bills are my fault, Alex. You said I spend too much on clothes. You told me when I'm not spending all your money at the club with my bourgeois friends, I'm sitting around watching soap operas, reading romances, and feeling sorry for myself!" She could hardly see through the sheen of hot tears.

"I was mad, Sierra. I said a lot of things. So did you!"

"I'm sick of being made to feel I'm on the dole! You think I don't do anything around here. Well, you're not around to see what I do! The only thing that matters to you anymore is how much money a person makes. And I don't make any, do I, Alex? So that makes me less than nothing in your eyes."

He grimaced. "I didn't say that."

"You say it every day in a hundred ways." Her voice cracked. When he took a step toward her, she took two back. "You were so worried about what Steve might think if your wife had to get a job. Well, if I am lucky enough to get this job, you can tell him I work for a charity organization. Maybe he'll think I'm volunteering." She went into the bathroom and locked the door.

Paradoxically, she hoped he'd knock and tell her to come out so they could talk. She hoped he'd say he was sorry for blaming her for their financial problems and admit that some of them were of his own making.

He did neither.

"We'll talk it over later," he said flatly. She heard the doors to the walk-in closet open and knew he was getting dressed to go to work.

Sierra sat down on the commode lid and wept silently.

"I'll call you later," Alex said.

It sounded like another empty promise.

When she had no more tears, she took a long shower and decided what to wear for her job interview with Ronal Peirozo. Suddenly, getting that job mattered more than anything.

Clanton and Carolyn said little over breakfast. Sierra knew they were aware something was wrong, and they didn't want to know what it was. She tried to be reassuring, but tears were too close to the surface, anger just beneath it.

She pulled into the gates of the private school, kissed each of them good-bye, and said she'd see them later.

Half an hour later, she walked through the front door of L.A. Outreach. It was precisely nine o'clock by her watch. A middle-aged lady in a flowered dress sat at the reception desk. Still speaking on the telephone, she glanced up and smiled warmly. As she put the phone back in its cradle, she said brightly, "Good morning! My, what a lovely suit."

"Thank you," Sierra said, put somewhat at ease by the lady's warmth. She had chosen an expensive golden brown suit and cream silk blouse. On the lapel, she'd pinned a gold brooch of three children holding hands. "My name is Sierra Madrid. I have an appointment with Mr. Peirozo."

"Yes. We've been expecting you." She rose and extended her hand. "My name is Arlene Whiting. I'll show you the way, Mrs. Madrid." She led Sierra down a corridor and tapped on a door. As she opened it, Sierra saw a much younger woman, obviously pregnant, rise from the chair in front of Ron Peirozo's desk. She smiled warmly.

Sierra immediately felt overdressed. Judy was in a simple cotton maternity dress.

Ron was wearing Levi's, a lightweight pale pullover sweater, and a navy blue sport coat.

"Ron, this is Sierra Madrid," Arlene said, ushering her in. "Sierra, this is Ron Peirozo and his secretary, Judy Franklin." Brief pleasantries were exchanged, and the two women went out, leaving her alone with Ron.

"Right on time," he said, grinning. "I like that. Please sit down."

"Thank you," she said and took the seat Judy had just vacated. She crossed her legs carefully and folded her hands in her lap, hoping she didn't look as nervous as she felt.

"Let me tell you a little about Outreach to start off," Ron said. He spent the next half hour explaining the mission of the organization he had founded less than five years before. The primary goal of Outreach was to place homeless children in safe housing and encourage them to become responsible, productive citizens in the community. Ron raised money and dispensed it to shelters and foster families. Equally important, he maintained a list of professional counselors who volunteered a portion of their time as arbitrators between parents and runaways.

"We want to restore these children to their families whenever possible. Sometimes that takes time. Sometimes they need protection."

He also maintained an extensive list of agencies and services available to families in trouble. Many of the children who came in contact with L.A. Outreach were referred to drug rehabilitation programs, medical treatment, and counseling for incest, physical and emotional abuse, and any number of other serious problems.

Several major denominational churches were involved in the program, supplying volunteer tutors.

"We've had good luck. Twenty children passed high school equivalency exams last year. Four times that many have returned to grade schools and high schools throughout the county. Six started college in September. Twelve are in trade schools. Twenty-seven got jobs this year. The numbers aren't big, I know, but every case is important."

Each child who entered the Outreach program was required to spend two hours a day, Monday through Friday, in community service. "They groan about it in the beginning, but they cooperate. After a while, they learn that helping others makes them feel better about themselves. That's when the incentive changes and things get exciting."

His eyes glowed as he spoke. There was no doubt about his love for his work or for the children he hoped to help.

"The churches are instrumental in helping us with this part of the program. These kids aren't picking up trash along a road somewhere. They're mowing lawns for the elderly, helping at day-care centers, serving meals to shut-ins, assisting at convalescent hospitals, any number of things that bring them into contact with people in the community." He grinned. "You'll hear people talking about 'going AWOL.' Don't let it throw you. It means they're going on 'a work of love.'_"

"Do the children come here in order to get into the program?"

"Not very often. Unfortunately. Frankly, finding these kids was one of our main problems in the beginning. I used to go downtown with a friend of mine and talk to the kids we found living on the streets. Some of them didn't have any reason to trust an adult, let alone listen to one. It's getting easier the longer we're around. We've employed six kids who've come through the program to go back on the streets and spread the word we're here and ready to offer help to those who want it. Kids listen better to kids."

Ron leaned forward, his blue eyes filled with warm intensity and passion for what he was doing.

"The whole idea of the program is to get as broad a base of community people involved with these children as possible," he said. "At the same time, we try to keep a low profile. I want people sincere in their concern, not people out to get plaudits. It's one-on-one. Personal. We don't send out mass mailers asking for donations. We don't do radio or television spots. We don't have celebrities heading up committees or movie stars acting as spokesmen. We don't give out plaques or public congratulations. And we don't go door-to-door asking for donations."

"How do you raise money to fund all this?"

"Fund-raisers. Word of mouth mostly. Some of my friends helped me in the beginning. I speak to different congregations and community groups. People spread the word. We don't always meet our budget, but God always sees we have enough money to meet our needs."

Ron Peirozo mentioned God as easily as her mother did, as though the Almighty was personally involved in his life and work. She felt herself relaxing even more.

He leaned back slowly and smiled at her. "You finally unclenched your hands."

Sierra blushed. "I was hoping you wouldn't notice."

"I notice a lot of things," he said cryptically, studying her.

"You haven't said what the job I'm applying for would entail."

"Simple," he said, all business again. "You'd assist me in everything I do."

"I'm sure there's a lot more to it than that, Mr. Peirozo."

"Call me Ron. I intend to call you Sierra. We're not formal around here."

She could feel herself growing excited as he talked. He had important work to do, and he wanted her to help. She couldn't remember the last time she had felt so good. She knew she would like working for Ron Peirozo. If he hired her.

"I haven't much in the way of qualifications," she said frankly, wanting to get to the bottom line. Maybe it would hurt less if she got the whole thing over.

He smiled, his eyes warming. "I thought we already settled that. You can type."

"Ninety words a minute."

"And take shorthand."

"Yes, but it's been ten years since I used it."

"Don't worry about it. I tape most of my letters while I'm trapped in five o'clock traffic. You'll find a tape on your desk each morning."

He talked as though he'd already given her the job.

Ron picked up a pencil and tapped it lightly. He had strong, nicely shaped hands. Sierra noticed he wasn't wearing a wedding ring.

"The pay isn't great. You'll start at fourteen hundred a month."

Enough to pay last month's country club bill, she thought, though she doubted Alex would appreciate the gesture. "Then I have the job?"

"If you want it."

She laughed. "When can I start?"

He grinned. "How about tomorrow?"

"Tomorrow will be fine," she said, relieved and elated. "Nine?"

"Nine it is." Ron stood as she did.

"Thank you," she said, extending her hand as Ron came around his desk. He enclosed her hand firmly but didn't linger as he had the first time they'd met at the club. "I appreciate the opportunity you're giving me, Ron. I hope I won't disappoint you."

"You won't," he said with such certainty, she felt bolstered.

She spent a few minutes talking with Judy and Arlene. Both seemed genuinely delighted that she was coming to work for Outreach. "Ron is a terrific boss," Judy said.

As Sierra walked out to her BMW, she realized what it was she liked so much about Ron Peirozo. He made her feel like an attractive woman. Not only that, he made her feel worthwhile, intelligent, and capable.

She hadn't felt that way in a long, long time.

––––––––––

James Farr is in Galena.

I saw him in the mercantile today and almost fainted. Aunt Martha had sent me for some white ribbon. Thomas accompanied me and Joshua. He likes to stroll through town with me on his arm. Or so he says. We went into Coopers and he took Joshua to the counter to buy a stick of candy. I was looking at some new bolts of cloth.

And then there was James, standing in the doorway. My heart beat so fast. He must have felt me staring at him, for he looked around and saw me. He smiled. He has never smiled at me like that before. He came to say hello. I could not draw breath when he did. Thomas saw him and came over to stand beside me. When he picked up Joshua and handed him to me, James tipped his hat to both of us and left the store.

I dont think he even knows who I was.

James came by the house today. Aunt Martha was not home. She had gone to market with Betsy. Clovis drove them. So it was I who opened the door to him. Joshua went right out to him as if James were an old friend of the family. James laughed and picked him up. I didn't know you the

other day in the mercantile, he said. Little Mary
Kathryn McMurray all grown up and pretty as
a princess. I said I could not invite him in as no
one was home and it would not look proper with
me betrothed and all. He is too old for you, Mary
Kathryn, he said. It is all decided, I said. Who
decided, he wanted to know. I took Joshua back
from him and said it would be better if he called
when Aunt Martha was home. He said he would
do that.

Thomas left for his homestead today. He must
take care of his business. He kissed me before he
left. It was a first kiss and chaste. I feel guilty for
my lack of feeling. I care for Thomas, but wonder
how we will fare together as man and wife. He
told Aunt Martha to watch out for me. I told him
not to worry. I can watch out for myself. It is a
wonder why he wants me as a wife when he treats
me like a child.

James came today. I introduced him to Aunt
Martha. He stayed for a full hour talking about
home and Matthew and Mama and Papa. He
asked so many questions. I could not answer many.
I gave him the facts. Mama died of consumption.
Papa still grieves. Sally Mae and Matthew
married. Sally Mae died in childbirth and Matthew
went away. I have not seen my brother since.

James did not ask a single question about how I came to have Joshua. I wonder what he thinks about that.

Aunt Martha was very quiet when James left. I asked her if something was wrong. She said I must be careful where James is concerned. I did not ask why. I know.

A mere look from James touches something deep inside me. When he is close, my heart pounds and I can scarce draw breath. Thomas Atwood Houghton loves me and I feel nothing at all.

I am in a terrible quandary. I dont know what to do.

This morning, I was feeling so restless. Perhaps it was a portent of what was going to happen. Joshua was fussing and Aunt Martha needed rest. So I took him out for a walk. Everything is in bloom. I think the scent of spring went straight to my head. I walked far from the road and let Joshua play in a small meadow.

James followed me. I thought I imagined him at first standing at the edge of the wood, watching me. He has been so much in my thoughts of late. I cannot get him out of my head no matter how much I try. I try to think about Thomas and our approaching wedding, but my heart betrays me and it is James who comes to mind. But James was not conjured by

my imagination. He was real. All too real, as it
turned out.

James came to me, and while Joshua played,
sat with me in the soft grass amidst the flowers.
He spoke of casual things at first. I did not stop
to think why he came upon me as he did. I was
so pleased to see him. Pleased and afraid. My
stomach was trembling and my heart pounded so
hard. I asked him about his travels to New York
and the Carolinas and England. I delighted in
his voice and the look in his eyes as he talked. It
made me sad in part, too. I kept wondering how
long it would be before he left again, breaking my
heart as he did before.

James took my hand.

I said it was not proper for him to do so. He
said he did not care what was proper. He said
I could not marry Thomas Atwood Houghton.
He will never make you happy, he said. I told
him Thomas was a good and kind man. James
said that may be, Mary Kathryn, but you are not
in love with him. I said love will come in time.
James said it took us no time at all. I knew I
should leave right then, but instead, I said I did
not know what he meant. He told me not to lie.
He said we both knew the moment we saw each
other in the mercantile. He said Thomas knew
it too. I said I did not know what he was talking
about and he said he would show me.

155

James kissed me. It was not a kiss like Thomas
gave me. It was not chaste or gentle. James shook
me so badly inside I could only think to get away
before I was consumed by the fire he set inside
me. I pushed him away and got up. I told him he
could not court me like Sally Mae Grayson.

I ran to fetch Joshua, but James caught up
with me. He said he never wanted to marry Sally
Mae and it was an awful pity Matthew did. I told
him to let go of me. He said he would hold onto
me as long as he lived. You belong to me, Mary
Kathryn McMurray. You have since you were a
child and well you know it. I told him he was a
bad bargain. And he said not as bad a bargain as
it would be if you marry a man you do not love.
I shud of run then. But I didn't and he kissed
me again. When I could get my breath back, I
told him to leave Galena. He said he would leave
when I was ready to go with him and not before.
I said he was crazy. He laughed and said he was.
Crazy in love.

And now, here I sit in the quiet of my room,
trying to think of a way out of this mess I am in.

Aunt Martha has been weeping all afternoon.
Thomas came to call this morning and I told him
I could not marry him. I told him why. He said he
would give me time to come to my senses. I said
I should have stuck with my senses in the first

place and never agreed to marry him. I told him
I never intended to hurt or anger him. I admire
and respect him as a dear friend. I said I did not
love him. He said it was not love I was feeling for
James Farr. He said I should marry him and put
away childish fantasies and passions. He said he
would leave me alone to think about what I will
be giving up.

I feel guilty for breaking my word to him. It
would be worse if I married him and broke my
heart and his and James in the bargain. But
Thomas does not see things the way I do.

I went down on my knees before Aunt Martha
and tried to explain. She said she knew very
well what had happened. She said you are your
mother's daughter, Mary Kathryn. She said some
men are like strong wine that go straight to a
girl's head and then they spend the rest of their
lives paying for the pleasure. If you do this thing,
Mary Kathryn, your life will be a trial. James will
take you into the wilderness. She said she had
hoped and prayed for better to happen to me than
happened to my mother.

James and I have been married for seventy-three
days, nine hours, and fifteen minutes and I have
not suffered one bit! He has made me so happy
I have had no time to write. I have delighted in
every minute with James.

We almost did not get married at all. It was
Aunt Martha who insisted pastor perform the
ceremony. He did not want to do it, but Aunt
Martha said I must be joined to James before
the Lord and if pastor refused, it would be on his
head when we went off and lived in sin together.
So he did the ceremony short as he knew how.

Aunt Martha, Betsy, and Clovis stood up with
us. No one else came. I am a pariah once again,
but I do not care. We are living in a small cabin
on the edge of town near the mill and I see little
of people anyway. James said we will go live in
Chicago as soon as he has enough money to get us
there.

. This rented cabin is just fine. James makes me
happy. When he holds me, I forget everything but
how much I love him. I dont care what they all say.

James has taken work at the sawmill. He leaves
early in the morning and does not come home
until sunset.

There is little to do in this small cabin and only
Joshua to keep me company. I spend most of the
day thinking about James and waiting for him to
come home. I have started a little garden.

James brought Aunt Martha. He is worried
about me because I have been sick so much of
late. Aunt Martha made me chamomile tea and

we talked for a long time about many things. She asked me Questions. Some of them surprised me they were so personal. She kissed me like Mama used to and said I was not to worry. Everything is fine, she said. She called for James. When he came in, Aunt Martha told us what was wrong with me.

I am going to have a baby this winter.

Or die trying.

I am afraid. I never been so afraid before. Not when Mama died. Not even when Papa kicked me out of the house with winter coming. I was not this afraid when I tended Sally Mae during her last hours on this earth. But then what happened to her wasn't happening to me. Now I wonder if it will.

Sally Mae was a fine one for letting her passions rule her and so it appears am I. James knows how to make me happy. He said that is the way it is supposed to be between a man and wife. He said it says so in the Bible. I asked him where. He could not show me but swears its true. I do not dare ask pastor. He thinks I am a Jezebel and treats me so. I will go to hell if he has anything to say about it and he talks to God all the time.

I cannot tell James about my fears. James knows something is wrong but he will only worry. I learned early worry changes nothing.

I spoke with Aunt Martha yesterday. I could
not tell her either I was so ashamed. She agreed
to take Joshua when my time comes. She said
she would keep him until I was settled with my
new baby. I know now even Aunt Martha thinks
Joshua is mine. She mustve thot I wuz lying
when I told her Sally Mae had him. I cried. I
could not help it. She asked me why but I would
not say. It hurts when people think the worst of
you. I told her if I die I want Joshua to stay with
her forever. She said I am strong and healthy and
should have no problems. It was on my tongue
to tell her Sally Mae was strong and healthy, too.
Aunt Martha says I must trust the Lord. She said
God loves you, Mary Kathryn Farr.

I have no reason to trust God and little proof
he loves me. I could not tell Aunt Martha that.
She is so *convinced* and she would ask Questions.
Even if I told her the whole truth, she probably
would not believe it. She would probably think I
was lying about the trouble like she thinks I lied
about Joshua. Sometimes I have difficulty when
I think on the matter. When I think of Papa, I
remember the way he used to be when Mama
was alive.

I wrote a letter to Thomas Atwood Houghton
and asked him to forgive me. Maybe my mind will
be at rest if he does. Right now, I feel all manner
of demons coming to rest upon my head.

It has been a month and Thomas has not responded to my letter. I went into Galena yesterday with James. I asked him to take me to church with Aunt Martha. So he did.

Only pastor spoke to us. Briefly. About the weather.

I reckon God feels the same.

The leaves are turning red and yellow. Joshua is my comfort all day while James is gone.

Aunt Martha came yesterday day to visit. I did not feel up to talking much.

Aunt Martha came back this morning. She brought books with her. She said just because I am married does not mean I must let my mind go to waste. I am glad of her company. While I study and write lessons, she plays with Joshua.

Henry James Farr was born at sunup on December 11. He entered the world with a strong pair of lungs.

James fainted dead away before his son was born. He lay on the cabin floor, no use to me at all. I washed Henry and wrapped him in the cotton blanket. More came from me. It seemed it would not stop. I have never been so weak. By the time I washed myself, changed my nightgown, I had barely the strength to crawl back into bed.

I fell asleep with my son. When I woke up next day, James was in bed with us, his arm around us both.

Joshua came home today. I have missed him terribly. He is my child. It dont matter how I came to have him. He may look like his father and mother, but that dont mean he will be like them. Henry is a week old and a fine, strong baby. Joshua tries to crawl into my lap when I nurse him.

I am joyful tonight. James is asleep on our bed. Our son is sleeping soundly in the cradle near the fire. Joshua is sleeping beside it bundled in his blankets. He scorns his bed because he wants to be close to his baby brother. Sometimes I think Joshua guards him the way Matthew guarded me. Everything is so peaceful. Especially me.

Aunt Martha brought me a package today labelled Master Henry James Farr care of Martha Werner. In it was a beautiful silver spoon and small cup. And this note.

My dearest Mary Kathryn, May God always bless you and your family. Always your friend, Tom.

I wept when I read it.

My heart is full to overflowing.

Henry James turned four months old today. He will have a sister or brother come late fall. James

is pleased. Aunt Martha is mortified. She turned
dark pink when I told her. She said it is too soon.
What of your health? And think what people will
say. I said I was stronger than most and she could
tell everyone it must be God's will James and I be
fruitful and multiply.

The truth is I have few pleasures in this world
and no wish to shun James embrace. I told him
what Aunt Martha said. He laughed. I said it was
not funny. He said she is innocent and modest. As
to the rest, they are jealous. He said everyone will
get used to us having a baby every year and think
nothing of it.

Martha Elizabeth was born midday November
20. She is healthy and beautiful. Aunt Martha
was here at her coming into the world. She was
first to hold her.

James says Beth has my blue eyes and red hair.
Little Hank had blue eyes too when he was born.
Now they are dark brown. His blond hair all fell
out when he was barely a month old. I was afraid
he would be bald. Then it all grew back in black
as Papas.

Betsy came to the cabin today. She said I look
tuckered out. I felt better for her visit. A good
talk can bolster spirits and renew strength. It gets
lonely when the only people you have to talk to

all day are a five year old boy and two babies. I love them dearly but they have not the makings yet for Stimulating Conversation. And Aunt Martha is often too occupied with Good Works to spend much time with me. When she does come, it is little Hank and Beth who have her attention. Betsy was like a breath of spring air even though she bossed me the whole hour she stayed.

I know I should not complain. Aunt Martha is ever kind to me and mine. I remind myself that I am more Fortunate than some.

I love James.

He loves me.

I have three beautiful children.

I am healthy.

I have a roof over my head with only a few leaks.

I have food on the table.

Yet there are times when I feel something is lacking. I despair. I *yearn.* I cannot put my finger on what I yearn for or why. It is just an ache inside that wont go away.

Maybe I am just tired. I weary of washing diapers. I think about the African women I read about in a book Aunt Martha brought me. They let their children grow up naked. Maybe their way is better. Seems to me it would save time better spent on other things.

———

ARLENE WHITING BUZZED SIERRA AT HER
desk. "You have a call on line one. Michael Clanton?"

"My brother," she said in surprise and punched the button.
Mike never called. He wasn't at ease on the telephone and left it
to Melissa, his wife, to keep in touch. "How's everything down
there in la-la land?" Melissa would always say and make her
laugh.

Nothing short of an emergency would get him to lift a receiver
to his ear. "What's wrong, Mike?"

"Mom's sick."

"Sick?" she said, alarmed.

"She's got cancer."

Sierra couldn't believe it. "She can't have cancer. I just saw her a few months ago." She had noticed at Christmas her mother had looked thin. She'd even asked about it. "She's lost some weight, but she said she was fine."

"She didn't want you to know."

Sierra clutched the telephone receiver more tightly. "You're sure?"

"She's known for quite a while," her brother said quietly. "She's just kept it to herself until recently."

"What do you mean she's known? When did she find out?"

Her brother was silent for a moment. "She was diagnosed with breast cancer just before you and Alex moved south."

"What?" Sierra felt her blood chilling with shock. "That was two years ago, Mike." In a blinding flash she remembered hints that something was wrong. She had wondered why her mother was so intent upon going through all the things in the attic. What was it she had said? She didn't want to leave the chaos to her and Mike. *Oh, God.* Sierra's eyes filled with hot tears. "Why didn't she say something?"

"You know how Mom is, Sierra. She doesn't want anyone worrying about her."

"What's being done for her?"

"She had a lumpectomy when the doctor first diagnosed her. They found out in the tests afterward that the cancer had already metastasized into her bones."

"Oh no," Sierra murmured. "And she didn't tell you?"

"She didn't tell anyone until a few days ago."

Alarm filled her. "What happened a few days ago?"

"Her right leg hurt so much she couldn't drive. She called Brady and asked if he could take her into the doctor's office." He was quiet for a few seconds. "They did another MRI. It looks bad."

Sierra closed her eyes, panic bubbling inside her. Her mother was her rock of strength. She couldn't lose her! She was only sixty-five. They'd always laughed and talked about how they'd celebrate her hundredth birthday when it came. "Is she going to have chemotherapy?"

"No."

"What do you mean *no?*"

"She said she didn't want it."

"But—"

"It wouldn't do any good at this point, Sierra."

"They have to do *something*. What about radiation? Couldn't they do that?"

"It'd already metastasized into her bones when she was diagnosed. It's spread to her liver."

Sierra lowered her head and covered her mouth for a moment until she could get control of her emotions.

Mike didn't say anything for a minute. "She's undergoing palliative treatments," he said hoarsely.

"What's that?"

"They're giving her radiation to ease the pain in her right leg."

Tears ran down Sierra's cheeks. She swallowed, trying to keep her voice steady. "Is she in a lot of pain, Mike?"

"Not that she talks about," he said with difficulty. "You know Mom." He was quiet for a minute. "I think she's been on pain medication for months. Melissa was putting dishes away in the cabinet the other day and found the prescription bottle tucked in the corner." He cursed softly, and she knew he was crying. "I'll call you back in a few minutes." He hung up abruptly.

Sierra put the receiver in its cradle and covered her face. She tried to fight down the rush of emotions: grief, fear, the desire to get in her car and start driving north right this instant. She was shaking and felt cold.

"Bad news?" Ron said, standing in the doorway that joined his large office to her smaller one.

"Yes," she said without looking up. She was afraid if she said anything more, she'd break down.

Her intercom buzzed. She snatched up the telephone and punched the line-one button. "Mike?"

"Sorry," he said hoarsely.

"It's OK," she said, clutching the phone tightly, keeping her other hand up to shield her face from Ron's perusal. Her throat was so hot and tight, she could hardly breathe. "How long do we have?"

"A month. Probably less."

She swallowed convulsively. Her vision blurred with tears as she stared at the calender. If that was true, her mother wouldn't even make it to her sixty-sixth birthday. Her chest ached with the weight of fear. "Is she at home?"

"No. She's in the hospital. Just until she finishes the treatments. Five days, maybe six. Then she comes home."

"Which hospital?"

"Community." He gave her the number.

"I'll call you tonight, Mike." Her hand shook as she hung up the telephone. Ron was still standing in the doorway. He didn't say anything, but she sensed his deep concern. Over the past four months of working with him, she had learned he was a perceptive and caring man. "My mother has cancer."

He let out his breath slowly. "How bad?"

"It's in her liver," she said huskily, afraid if she said more, she'd start crying. She felt Ron's hand slide over her shoulder and squeeze gently in comfort.

"I'm sorry to hear that, Sierra."

She recalled how her mother had looked six months ago, thin, her hair graying. She had asked straight out if she was all right, and her mother had said everything was fine. Fine? How could she have kept such a secret? "She never said a word, Ron."

"What do you want to do?"

Her hands felt like ice. "I want to go home."

"Then go," he said simply.

She thought of the chaos she'd leave behind if she did. Her desk was piled with work. And what about the children? Who'd take care of Clanton and Carolyn? Who'd drop them off at school? Who'd take Clanton to his baseball practices or Carolyn to her piano lessons? Alex was gone by six-thirty and never home before seven.

Maybe she should pull the children out of school and take them with her. But how could she do that when she didn't even know what she would be facing when she got home? What would they do while she was taking care of her mother?

"I don't know what to do," she said shakily. "I don't even know where to start." Her brother's words rang in her ears. A month. Maybe less.

Oh, God! God, where are you?

She wanted to be with her mother. She wanted that so desperately, she shook with fear that it wouldn't be possible.

Ron sat on the edge of her desk. "Call Alex."

She dialed Beyond Tomorrow. Alex's secretary told her he wasn't in the office. "He had an appointment at one."

"Can you page him?"

"He told me not to—"

"This is important! When you get in touch with him, tell him to call me here at work. Please." She hung up. Every time she called Alex lately, he was out.

Shaking, she began shuffling the papers around on her desk, wondering how she could get everything sorted out and finished by the end of the day. And what about tomorrow? She had the schedules to type up. She had calls to make. She had letters to write.

She couldn't concentrate.

Ron's hand stopped her agitated movements. "I'll call Judy.

She said she and Max are saving for a down payment on a house. I'm sure she'll agree to stand in for you while you're gone."

"She can't, Ron. She's nursing Jason."

"She can bring her baby with her. I won't mind. And Arlene loves getting her hands on the little guy. If things get too hectic, I think we could track down a couple of responsible teenagers who'd pitch in."

"Miranda," Sierra said immediately, thinking of a fifteen-year-old runaway who'd entered the program about the same time she'd started working with Ron. "The day-care center says she's wonderful with babies."

Ron smiled and brushed his knuckles lightly against her cheek. It was an oddly intimate and tender gesture that made her blush. "We'll take care of things around here. You go see your mother." He straightened from her desk.

When Alex didn't call back by one-thirty, Sierra left him out of her arrangements. Marcia gave her the name of a professional nanny. Sierra called Dolores Huerta and explained the situation. Dolores agreed to meet her at the house that afternoon at four so they could go over the children's schedules and her household duties and fees.

Sierra was packing her bags when Alex came home. He stopped just inside the bedroom door and stared at the two open suitcases on the double bed. "What's going on?" he said, his face paling. "What're you doing? Where're you going?"

"If you'd bothered to return my call this morning, you'd know." She yanked open a drawer. "I'm going home."

He uttered a soft curse and came into the room. "Look. Let's talk about—"

"There's nothing to talk about," she cut him off. "My mother's in the hospital. She has cancer." She swallowed convulsively as she put the sweater on top of a pair of dark gray slacks.

He let out his breath. "I thought . . ." He shook his head. "I'm sorry," he said heavily.

She spun to face him, pain etched in her features. "Sorry about what, Alex? That you're never around when I need you anymore? That my mother has cancer? That all this is going to complicate your precious work schedule?"

He didn't say anything.

She looked at him, hurt and embittered. "Where were you? Your secretary said she'd page you. Did she?"

"Yes."

"Why didn't you call me?"

"I was busy." He moved farther into their bedroom. "Look. I figured if it was really important, you'd call back."

She turned back to her suitcase in frustration. "It's nice to know where I stand on your priority list."

"You want a fight before you go? Is that what you really want?"

She went into the closet. When she came out with two more pairs of slacks, Alex was standing in the middle of the room, rubbing the back of his neck. Shaking, she dropped the clothing on the bed. "I needed you, Alex. Where were you?"

Turning, he looked at her. She saw something in his expression that made her sick. Guilt. Shame. And not just because he hadn't returned her call. It was something more, something deeper. His eyes flickered, stark and raw, and then the expression was gone, hidden.

"What can I do to help?" he said flatly.

She wanted to say he could hold her. He could tell her he loved her. He could promise to call her and talk with her each day. He could reassure her that everything would be fine with the children while she was gone.

"I don't know," she said bleakly. "Pray for a miracle, maybe?"

For whom, Sierra? an inner voice asked. *For your mother or you . . . and Alex?*

What had brought them to this impasse? They couldn't even talk to one another anymore. It was as though a wall stood between them, four feet thick and a hundred feet high. She was tired of trying to hack her way through it.

He shrugged out of his suit jacket and tossed it over a chair. "What are you going to do about the kids?"

Anger surged through her, twisting her stomach into a hard knot. Hadn't he just asked her what he could do to *help?* What a laugh. All he cared about was that he not suffer any inconvenience.

"Don't worry. I've already hired a nanny. You won't have to look for one. Her name is Dolores Huerta. She'll be here by seven each morning. I figured you wouldn't mind staying home an extra *thirty* minutes until she gets here. Dolores has agreed to cook and do the washing and take care of the house. She drives, so she'll drop the children off at school and pick them up. She'll also see that Clanton gets to baseball practices and Carolyn gets to her piano lessons. I knew you wouldn't have the time or inclination to be there for the kids. I gave her a hundred dollars for gas money. She gets three hundred dollars a week salary. You'll need to pay her on Friday." She looked at him, waiting for a response.

His face was rigid. "How long do you think you'll be gone?"

She bit her lip, fighting back the tears. "As long as it takes," she managed bleakly, turning away. She couldn't remember what she'd already packed and what more she needed.

"You can't take all of it on yourself, Sierra."

She wished she could believe he was concerned for her, but she couldn't. What was he really worried about?

"Mike said the doctor told Mom she has a month, maybe less. I want every minute with her I can have."

"You don't think I understand that? I love your mother, too."

Do you? she wanted to say. If he did, he never would have moved the family to Southern California. She wondered sometimes if he even loved his own father and mother. When was the last time he'd called them? He seemed to resent the time he took off to make two short visits home to family in the course of a whole year.

What he loved—apparently the only thing he really loved—was his work. Nothing else seemed to matter to him anymore, least of all her or the children. Her mother didn't even enter the equation.

"You don't believe me, do you?" he said, defensive.

"Should I? I hope you'll call and tell her while you have the chance." She glared up at him, hurt and anger spilling over into each other, flooding her with the desire to retaliate. "People *need* love when they're hurting."

His eyes cooled. "I'll leave you alone so you can pack." He walked out of the room.

⸻

The right reverend came by to talk to me today.

Seems he's in Galena preaching at the market place. First thing he did was look at my babies and my rounding belly and ask how long I had been married. Long enough I said. He told me Mister Grayson died last spring. He fell and cut himself on the plow blade and died two weeks later, jaws locked and body twisted like a pretzel. I asked him if that was what he had come to talk about. He said Papa is ailing and the homestead is going to seed and he thought I should know

about it so I could do something to help. I said
most likely Papa is not ailing but drunk. He said
in Bible times Papa could have had me taken out
to the gates and stoned. I said as near as I could
tell the only people Jesus ever got mad at were
church folk who were so busy looking for slivers
in other peoples eyes they missed the logs in their
own. He left none too happy.

Now I am left to wonder what to do. Even
drunk, Papa never neglected the land.

I am staying with Aunt Martha while James is
gone to the homestead to see how Papa is.

I had forgotten how nice it was to sleep in a
big bed with a lace canopy and beneath a roof
that does not leak. No wind blows through the
windows and the walls are painted white with a
framed picture of a Grecian girl pouring water
from a jug. Beth sleeps with me in the feather bed
while Joshua and little Hank sleep in the small
room next door. I miss James.

People come and go quite often in Aunt
Martha's house. She has her door open to all. She
invited a drummer in yesterday to supper. He
looked tired and worn down to bones. He looked
better when he left. She gave him money to pay
for a room at the hotel. Aunt Martha and three
lady friends quilted all afternoon. She invited
me to join them and I did. Betsy took charge of

Joshua and my babies. They fared well beneath
her wings. She made pound cake for Joshua and
applesauce for Hank. The ladies were pleased to
watch the children play. Their own are grown and
gone off to who knows where.

I did not think it possible to enjoy womens
company so much though I have always enjoyed
Aunt Martha. But she is not like most I have met.
These women were like her. They laugh about all
manner of things, but not one unkind word did
they utter about anyone.

Life is hard and cruel.

James said Papa is ailing and we have to go
home and tend things for him. I did not dare ask
if Papa's heart has changed toward me. I will
know soon enough.

Truth is I am glad to be going home though I
will miss Aunt Martha and Betsy and Clovis.

———————

11

A METAL TANK HUMMED IN THE UPSTAIRS MASTER bedroom, the soft tick signaling an influx of oxygen that passed through a clear tube to Sierra's mother. Sierra checked the tube frequently, making sure it was in place beneath her mother's nose so that the pure oxygen would be infused into her mother's straining lungs. Edema was causing the difficulty with breathing. Over the past few days the edema had gone down. Her mother's breathing had eased and slowed. So, too, had the trickle of urine into the catch bag attached to the side of the bed. The hospice nurse had told her it would change color as death approached.

Sierra rose from the wing chair beside the bed and checked the tube again. She touched her mother's hair, once soft and dark auburn, now streaked white and oddly coarse. Her mother's skin felt dry, like fallen leaves. She was awake.

"Can I bring you some soup, Mom?" She was desperate to do something, anything, to make her mother comfortable, to keep her alive.

"You can move me near the windows."

The rented hospital bed had wheels, but Sierra knew moving it would jar her mother and cause her more pain. She hesitated.

"Please," her mother whispered.

Sierra did as her mother asked, gritting her teeth each time the bed jiggled. Her mother didn't make a sound. "Is this all right, Mom?"

"Hmmm," her mother said, her thin fingers loosening their grip on the pillow. Her body slowly relaxed again. "Can you open the window?"

"It's cool today."

"Please."

As Sierra did so, she couldn't stop worrying. What if her mother caught cold? Even as she thought it, she knew it was irrational. The hospice nurse said yesterday that it wouldn't be long.

"Brady's mowing his back lawn," her mother said, and Sierra noticed her speech was faintly slurred. The morphine patches were doing their work. She noticed other things, too. Her mother's hazel eyes had lost their twinkle. Her skin was no longer tan from the long hours she'd spent tending her beautiful garden. "I always wanted skin as white as alabaster," her mother had teased a few days before. Sierra hadn't been able to laugh with her.

White. The color of purity.

The color of death.

"I've always loved the smell of cut grass," her mother said quietly. She reached out and took Sierra's hand. Sierra felt the tremor of weakness in her mother's grip. "This is my favorite time of year. The cherry trees bud, and the daffodils come up. Everything's so green and pretty." She sighed, and it was a sound of contentment, not sadness. "How can anyone fail to see God's hand in all of it?"

Sierra's throat closed. She stared out the window as the clouds moved slowly across the blue sky. Her mother wouldn't want her to cry. She had to be strong. She had to be *brave*. But inside, she could feel pieces of herself crumbling.

"Every year, Jesus shows us the Resurrection," her mother said and squeezed her hand lightly.

"It's a pretty day," Sierra said mechanically, thinking that was what her mother wanted to hear. She couldn't say what she was really feeling. How could her mother talk about Jesus now? She wanted to curse God, not praise him! Her mother had served the Lord for as long as she could remember, and this was her reward? To die slowly, in pain? Her mother saw God's hand in everything. But where was God's hand in *this?*

"Can you raise the bed?"

"I think so," Sierra said and went to the controls. She pressed a button, and the bed came up. When it stopped, her mother had a good view down on the garden below.

"Oh, that's nice," she said, content.

Sierra checked her oxygen tube and readjusted the elastic straps looped behind her mother's ears. One had left a crease in her mother's cheek.

"Would you pick me some hyacinths?"

"Hyacinths?" Sierra said bleakly.

"I can see a few down by the walk, near the birdbath." Her hand trembled weakly as she tried to point. "The clippers are in the bucket under the steps."

Sierra hurried downstairs and out the back door to the porch. She found the clippers exactly where her mother said they'd be.

She had always been one for believing a place for everything and everything in its place.

Walking quickly along the brick path, Sierra was dismayed at the state of the garden. Even during the winter, her mother had weeded and raked and kept everything neat. Now it was clearly neglected.

Sierra found a patch of the pretty blue flowers near the back of the garden. Hunkering down, she selected two stalks of perfect blooms and cut them for her mother. When she returned to the upstairs master bedroom, she saw her mother had the controls in her hand. She had raised the head of the bed a foot higher, giving her a better view.

What must her mother feel looking out at the sorry, deserted garden below?

"Thank you, sweetheart." She touched the flowers with her fingertips. She moved restlessly, pain flickering across her face. "It always amazes me to think how God made the garden and then placed man in it," she said, her words coming slowly, sluggishly. "Everything he made, from the bottom of the seas to the heavens, was for us to enjoy. Like hyacinths and blooming cherry trees and sunshine. Sweetness, hope, light."

Hope, Sierra thought. Where was hope when her mother's cancer advanced like an avenging army, ravaging her body, sapping her strength? Where was hope when death was imminent?

She readjusted the oxygen tube. "Is that better?" she said, touching her mother's face tenderly.

"It's fine, honey."

At night, when Sierra lay on the cot she'd set up near her mother's bed, she'd listen to her mother's breathing. And count seconds. One. Two. Three. Four. Five. Her own heart would stop after six and then beat faster at seven. Eight. Nine. Sometimes ten. And then her mother would take another precious breath, and Sierra would find herself relaxing for an instant before she started the count all over.

"Spring's coming," her mother said, gazing out the window. "The garden's always so beautiful."

All Sierra could see were the weeds that had come up and the suckers sprouting at the base of several unpruned rose bushes. The fall leaves from the birch trees had never been raked and lay like a heavy black blanket over the uncut lawn.

Over all the years the family had lived in this beautiful house, it had been her mother who had kept up the flower gardens and pruned the roses and trimmed the bushes and trees. It had been her mother who had been the gardener to loosen the soil, mulch in the compost, plant the seeds, and tend the young seedlings. Her mother had been the one to lay out the design so that flowers bloomed all throughout the year, filling the yard with a profusion of brilliant color.

Sierra remembered the hours she had spent with her mother outside in the sunshine, playing with her small tin bucket and little spade while her mom plucked weeds, thinned seedlings, and snipped dying blooms. She could remember the day her mother had planted the trumpet vine, gently tying green shoots to the lattice. The vine now covered the back wall.

Without her mother, everything would go wild.

Clouds moved across the sun, casting shadows over the yard below. "I hope it doesn't rain again," she said softly.

"It can't be sunshine all the time, or flowers wouldn't grow for lack of rain."

Even now, hurting, dying, her mother saw the brighter side of things. Sierra's eyes burned. Her throat ached with tears. She put her hand against her chest, wishing she could lift the weight of grief that grew heavier every day. She was choking on it. Suffocating. If it hurt this much seeing her mother slip hour by hour, what would life be like when she was gone?

"Sierra," her mother murmured softly.

Seeing her hand fumble weakly, Sierra took it. "What, Mom? Are you uncomfortable? Can I get you something?"

"Sit down, honey," she said.

Sierra did as she was asked and forced a smile as she enclosed her mother's hand in both of hers.

"I want you to do something for me," her mother said softly.

"What, Mom? What can I do?"

"Let me go."

Sierra's throat closed up. She had to press her lips together so she didn't cry out. She used every bit of willpower she had and still the hot tears bubbled into her eyes. "I love you," she said brokenly. Leaning down, she put her head against her mother's breast and wept.

Her mother stroked her hair once and then rested her hand weakly on her head. "I love you, too. You've always been God's blessing to me."

"I wish I could go back to when I was a child, sitting out on the patio in the sunshine while you worked in the garden."

Her hand trembled in weakness. "Each stage in our lives is precious, Sierra. Even now. The door isn't closing on me, honey. It's opening wider with each breath I take."

"But you're in so much pain."

Her mother stroked her hair again and spoke gently. "Shhhh. Don't cry anymore. I want you to remember that God causes all things to work together for good to those who love him, to those who are called according to his purpose."

Sierra had learned those words as a child when she was in Sunday school. Her mother had helped her memorize them as they worked in the garden. But the words held no meaning. What good was there in suffering? She breathed in the scent of her mother and was afraid. Wasn't God supposed to heal those who had faith? Her mother had faith. She'd never doubted. So where was God now? She wanted to cling to her and beg her to fight harder, to hang on to life; but she knew she could not speak those words aloud and add to her mother's burden of pain. It was selfish to even think of asking her to endure more.

Anguish filled her. What would she do without her mother? Losing her father had been hard enough, but her mother had always been her counselor, her fountainhead. How many times had she run to her mother for help? How many times had her mother walked through troubles with her, gently guiding the way, showing her the higher road?

Sierra listened to the beat of her mother's heart. No one in the world knew her as well or loved her as much as her mother did. Not even Alex, her own husband, who should. Sierra's lips thinned. Especially not Alex, who hadn't even bothered to call in the past three days, the hardest of her life.

"Oh, Mom, I'll miss you so much," she murmured, wishing she could lie down beside her and die with her. Life was too painful, the future so bleak.

Her mother's hand moved slowly against her hair. "God has a plan for you, Sierra, a plan for your welfare and not for calamity, a plan to give you a future and a hope." Her voice was so weak, so tired. "Do you remember those words?"

"Yes," Sierra said obediently. Her mother had taught them to her as well, and like the others, they'd made no sense to her either. It had been her father and mother who took care of her. Then it was Alex. God had never come into the equation.

"Hold to them, honey. When you turn, you'll know I'm no farther away than your heart."

Sierra thought her mother had fallen asleep. She could still hear the slow, steady beat of her heart. She remained where she was, her head resting on her mother's breast, taking comfort in the closeness, the warmth. Exhausted, she stretched out beside her, arm around her, and slept.

She awakened when Mike came by after work. He stood beside the bed. "Her breathing sounds different." His expression was grim and controlled. "Her hand's cold."

Sierra noticed other things. The fluid level in the catch bag hadn't changed in hours. Her mother's skin color had changed.

She called the hospice, and a nurse was sent. Sierra recognized her, but couldn't remember her name. Her mother would have remembered. Her mother always remembered everyone by name. She remembered things about them, too, asking after family members and job situations. Little things. Personal things.

"It won't be long," the nurse said, and Sierra knew the woman was saying her mother wouldn't be waking up again. The nurse adjusted the blankets and lightly stroked the hair back tenderly from her mother's temple. She straightened and looked at Sierra. "Would you like me to stay with you?"

Sierra couldn't make a sound. She shook her head. She just kept watching her mother's chest rise and fall slowly and counted seconds. One. Two. Three.

"I'm going to call Melissa," Mike said and left the room.

Soon after Melissa arrived, Luís and María Madrid came in. Alex's mother embraced Sierra and wept openly, while his father stood with tearless, grave dignity at the foot of the hospital bed.

"When is Alex coming?" he asked.

"I don't know that he is," Sierra said dully, standing by the window. "I haven't talked to him in a while." She listened to the click of the oxygen machine and counted.

She didn't want to think about Alex or anyone else just then. She didn't want to think about anything.

Seven. Eight.

Alex's father left the bedroom.

Melissa came in a few minutes later and stood beside Sierra. She didn't say anything. She just took her hand and held it in silence.

Eighteen. Nineteen. Twenty.

Melissa let go of her hand and moved to the bedside. She touched Marianna Clanton tenderly and checked her wrist pulse. Leaning down, she kissed her forehead. "Good-bye, Mama."

Straightening, she turned slowly to Sierra. "She's with the Lord," she whispered, tears running down her cheeks.

Sierra stopped counting. Her heart felt like a cold stone inside her chest. She didn't say anything. She couldn't. She just turned and looked down into the moonlit garden and felt the stillness closing in around her.

"She's not suffering anymore, Sierra."

Why did people always feel they had to say something? She knew Melissa meant to comfort her, but no words could. She heard another click as the oxygen machine was shut off.

Everything fell silent. Everything was still . . . so still she wondered if her own heart had stopped beating. She wished it would.

She couldn't think. She felt numb, so numb, she wondered if she was becoming exactly like the little statuette of the Virgin Mary her mother-in-law had brought and set on the windowsill. Bloodless. Hollow.

Mike came into the room again. He didn't utter a word. At least her brother understood. He just stood at the foot of the hospital bed, looking down at their mother. She looked peaceful, her body completely relaxed. When he turned away, he touched Sierra's arm. It was the merest brush of his hand, but enough to let her know she was there, alive.

Crossing the room, Mike sat down in the chair and leaned forward, hands loosely clasped between his knees. Was he praying? His head was down. If he wept, he did so silently. And he didn't leave the room or her, not until the men from the mortuary arrived.

Sierra followed the men downstairs as they took her mother away. She stood in the front doorway watching until the doors of the hearse closed. She'd still be standing upstairs if Melissa hadn't made the call.

Her mother had made all the arrangements two years ago, without anyone knowing. No fuss. No bother. Everything like clockwork. She would be cremated by tomorrow morning. Nothing but ashes left.

Sierra closed the front door and leaned her forehead against the cold wood. She was so tired, her mind whirring like an engine in neutral, going nowhere.

The telephone rang. She heard Luís answer. After the first word, he spoke in hot, hushed Spanish. The words might as well have been spoken in Greek for all the sense they made to her, but she knew he was speaking to his son.

He came into the parlor where she was sitting. "It's Alex," he said and held out the portable telephone. "He's been trying to reach you."

A lie, kindly offered, but unconvincing.

She took the phone and held it to her ear.

"Sierra? I'm sorry about your mother." He was silent, waiting. She shut her eyes tightly. What did he want her to say? Did he think one call and a little sympathy absolved him of days of neglect? She'd needed him. "I tried to call you yesterday, but the phone was busy." She couldn't speak, not with the weight of grief bearing down on her. "Sierra?" One word and she'd shatter. Worse, she'd say things she'd regret.

"I'll make reservations," he said at last. There was no inflection in his voice to give away his own feelings. "The children and I will fly up to San Francisco tomorrow. I'll rent a car. We should be in Healdsburg by evening." He sounded as though he was making business arrangements. Silence again. It stretched. "Are you all right?" His voice was almost gentle. It filled her with infinite sadness and memories. "Sierra?"

Pressing the off button, she put the portable telephone down on the side table.

James works hard as Papa ever did.

He goes out at dawn and comes in for the midday meal. Then out again he goes until dusk. I am left alone to care for Papa.

Papa has changed much in the four years I have been gone. His hair has gone white and he is so thin and weak he can not get out of bed. I thought he was blind when first we came, but when Joshua came to stand in the doorway I knew he was not. His face got all red and awful. He started shouting loud enough for Aunt Martha to hear him all the way back in Galena.

He said—Keep that devil child away from me or I swear before God I will kill him.

Joshua ran out of the house. If I had not heard him crying, I would never have found him inside the hollow burned out tree. It was at the edge of the fields Matthew burned.

When I came back to the house, James asked why Papa would say such a terrible thing. I said he is crazy.

I know what's killing Papa. Hatred. It is eating him alive.

Sometimes I wish Papa would die and there would be an end to all his pain. And mine.

He is so weak and sick, he can do nothing for

187

himself. And nothing I do for him helps. It makes things worse. He will not look at me or speak to me. He would not even take food from my hand until necessity and hunger made him. James does not ask for explanations. He thinks Joshua is my babee just like everyone else thinks it. I never told him otherwise.

James moved Papa into the little bedroom off the kitchen. We need the big bed for ourselves. Papa did not say anything, but I saw tears in his eyes.

I felt strange sleeping in the bed Papa shared with Mama. James wanted to love me the first night and I could not. All I did was cry. He said he understood, but I do not think he did. He thought I was tired and sad. What I feel is so much worse than that.

Papa and Mama made Lucas and Matthew and me in the bed James and I are sharing. Papa and Sally Mae made Joshua. That was on my mind too. I could see her sneaking in during the night while Papa lay drunk and unawares. She was just like Lots daughters. And look what come of that. My only comfort is remembering that Ruth was a Moabite.

I am all mixed up inside. Papa hurts me with his silence and meanness. But I am angry, too. And grieving. I wonder what Mama would think of all this. And me. I wonder where Matthew is and what he is doing. I hope he is well and happy wherever he is. But I doubt it. Matthew took everything to heart.

Seems to me Papa is the one who should answer for the pain he caused. Sally Mae did not do what she did without him helping. Being drunk is no excuse. I have not said so to Papa. It would do no good and he is Determined I done wrong by keeping Joshua alive. Papa does not think he is to blame for anything. It was all Sally Maes fault. And when she died, it was all Joshuas fault. When I took him up, it is all my fault.

So be it. I am stronger than Joshua and can take the heat of silent hell Papa pours down on me. Like God. I can feel it every time I walk through his door. Hatred is a powerful thing.

Joshua will not even come into the kitchen because he knows Papa is in that little back room. I am glad of it. I think Papa would kill him if he had the chance. And I do not intend to give him one. But at night I lay wondering what will come of all this.

When Joshua grows up he is going to want to know who his father is. What do I tell him if he asks?

I heard tell once that the sins of the father are

189

visited on the sons. Does that mean Joshua must pay for what Papa did?

Life is not fair.

I put a marker on Sally Maes grave.

Papa is worse. His mind is going. Today when I went in to wash him and change the bedding again, he thought I was Mama. He said—Where have you been Katie love. I have missed you so much.

I took his hand and said I have been with Jesus these long years.

And Papa said real soft with tears in his eyes— Put in a good word for me.

I cannot stop crying. He was a good man once for all his drinking and wild ways. And he loved Mama more than life. Hearing him talk today made me remember what he was like when Mama was alive. And remembering made me miss her so much my body hurts with it. Everything inside me is clenched tight, aching and lonely.

It seems to me when God took Mama from us, Satan waltzed in the door and he has been living in this house ever since.

Papa is fading away. He does not eat. He sleeps most of the day. When he is awake, he does not speak. He looks at the corner of his room

as though someone is there visiting with him.
Sometimes he smiles and mumbles something.

I am afraid. His curse still lays so heavy upon me.

Papa died this morning.

He was restless last night. He kept moving and
moaning. I did not know what to do to comfort
him. He could not breathe easy. He was better
when I raised him up and sat behind him and held
him in my arms. I stroked his hair and talked to
him just like I do my babies when they are fretful.

And then near dawn a thought came into my
head so powerful and clear it was like a real voice
talking to me. I knew what was wrong with Papa
and what he needed. I struggled against it but it
was like a hand squeezing hard around my heart.
I laid him back and went down on my knees
beside the bed.

I said—Papa I forgive you. Do you hear me
Papa? I forgive you.

His fingers moved. Just a little. So I took his
hand and kissed it. I said—I love you Papa. And
I meant it. Just for that minute after all the time
before and between up to now. I meant it. I forgot
how much he hurt me and saw how much he was
hurting. Be at peace, Papa, I said. I couldn't say
no more than that.

And he seemed so. He did not say anything.

Not one word. He just gave one long sigh and was gone.

We buried Papa in the suit James wore when we were wed. I sewed Papa inside the wedding quilt Mamas friends made for them. With Mister Grayson dead, there was no one to come see Papa laid to rest beside Mama and the babies they lost. It was just me holding Beth and James holding Hank and Joshua who stood beside the grave. I read words from the Bible. Mama would have liked that.

It has been raining ever since. Fitting weather for my feelings.

I cannot help wishing Papa had said something to me before he passed on to whatever was waiting for him. Even my name would have been enough. Or if he had looked at me before he died. Maybe then I would not feel this awful ache inside me.

Papa didn't say a word to me. Not from the day he cast me out to the day he died. But at the end, when he had no strength left, I think he wanted to. I hope so anyway.

Oh, what foolish creatures we are. Cursed with our pride! Cursed with our stubbornness!

No wonder God has forsaken us.

12

SIERRA SAT IN THE FRONT PEW OF THE CHURCH with Alex on one side and Carolyn and Clanton on the other. Mike sat on the aisle, Melissa at his side, his three children next to her. The sanctuary was packed with people. As the pastor offered the eulogy, Alex took her hand. He had hardly touched her since arriving three days ago. She'd saved her tears for privacy, unwilling to share them with him or anyone else.

She couldn't stop thinking about the small polished wooden box placed on her father's stone at the cemetery. Was that all there was to a human being? One small box of ashes that weighed less than a newborn baby? The pastor had met them there and led the solemn but brief ceremony. Only family members had been present: she and Alex, their children, Mike and Melissa and their children, and Luís and María Madrid. So few. Too many.

Her mother's ashes would be mixed with her father's, and in a few days a stone carver would come and add the date of her death to the slab that would cover them both.

Now, half listening to the pastor's homily, she wondered if the forget-me-not seeds the children planted around the marble would come up.

"Marianna Clanton walked in the Spirit," the pastor said, using the opportunity to proclaim the gospel. Tearful, he rejoiced for his friend and parishioner. "Marianna will be sorely missed, but we can take comfort in knowing she's in the arms of her beloved Savior. And those of us who share her belief have the comfort of knowing she isn't lost to us. We will see her again."

One of the church ladies sang "Take my life and let it be / consecrated, Lord, to thee. . . ."

Numb with grief, Sierra stared at her mother's picture on the linen-covered table at the front of the sanctuary. She would have chosen a different photo. On each side were vases filled with bright yellow daffodils. In fact, the sanctuary was full of flowers—not funeral wreaths, but spring arrangements bursting with color and a mood of celebration.

"It was your mother's wish," the pastor had explained upon their arrival and her question. "She brought me this picture several months ago."

Far from the usual formal portrait used in solemn services, her mother had chosen one when she was years younger, laughing, with a bucket of yard trimmings in one gloved hand and her clippers in the other. She'd left a note as well. "Rejoice with me."

Finishing his homily, the pastor opened the service for sharing. One by one, friends stood and talked about Marianna Clanton and what she had meant in their lives. Some of the stories were funny, making people laugh. Others brought a hush and quiet tears. When all who wished to had spoken, Melissa went forward and spoke briefly on behalf of the family. More hymns were sung by all. Her mother's favorites. "Amazing Grace." "Ave Maria." "Standing on the Promises of God." And last, drawing tearful laughter, "Father Abraham." Everybody was on their feet, waving their arms and turning around. Even Sierra pretended to join in the spirit of rejoicing.

"Rejoice in the Lord always," the pastor said in benediction. "Again I will say, *rejoice*. Let your forbearing spirit be known to all men. The Lord is near." Sierra felt him looking down at her as his voice softened. "Be anxious for nothing, beloved, but in everything by prayer and supplication with thanksgiving let your requests be made known to God. And the peace of God, which surpasses all comprehension, shall guard your hearts and your minds in Christ Jesus."

A reception followed in the social hall.

Steeling herself against her inner turmoil, Sierra smiled and thanked everyone who came through the receiving line. The kind words slipped like water off a duck's back. She couldn't afford to let them sink in. Not now. Not here in front of everyone. Later, when she was alone, she'd bathe in the pool of tears.

Alex stood beside her, close but not touching. He was like a handsome stranger in his dark suit — polite, distant, but not indifferent. Everyone was impressed with his obvious success. They didn't know the cost.

Clanton and Carolyn sat with their three cousins across the room. They talked among themselves, sharing refreshments.

Sierra was ready to leave before the others. She asked Melissa if she'd mind watching Clanton and Carolyn. She knew the children wanted to visit as long as possible. "Why don't you let them spend the night?" Melissa said.

"I didn't mean —"

She cut her off with a gentle touch on her arm. "We'd love it. We see so little of them since you and Alex moved south." As soon as she said it, Sierra could tell she wished she hadn't. "Just don't worry about them. You need to rest."

Alex had driven his rented Cadillac to the cemetery and church. She debated asking him to take her home and decided against it. He appeared to be deep in conversation with his father.

She spoke briefly with the pastor and slipped unnoticed out the side door of the social hall. It was beautiful outside, everything in bloom. Her mother would have loved a day like this.

Three blocks away Alex pulled up beside her. "Why didn't you tell me you were leaving?"

It wasn't concern that tinged his tone, but impatience, anger. He didn't ask if she was all right. "You were busy." He was always too busy.

Alex got out of the car. When he touched her, he did so with gentleness. Then he put his hand beneath her elbow, his expression shadowed with sadness. "Get in the car, Sierra. Please."

She did as he said. Putting her head back against the black leather seat, she closed her eyes, feeling utterly bereft.

"What do you think people are saying about us when you just walk out the door without so much as a word to me?"

She looked at him. Was that it? Was that why he'd come after her? "Since when did you ever worry about what *other* people say?"

"You ought to care. Those people are family and friends."

"Don't worry, Alex. I didn't tell anyone you only called me three times in the past month." Ron had called more often than her own husband.

"The phone works two ways."

"It does, doesn't it? But then, every time I called you, you weren't home."

A muscle jerked in his cheek and he didn't say anything more.

196

When he pulled into the drive alongside the Mathesen Street house, he turned to her. "I'm sorry. Sierra, I—"

"Forget the excuses, Alex." She got out of the car and walked along the cobblestone pathway to the front steps. Fumbling for her key, she shoved it into the lock and opened the door.

Shaking, she walked along the corridor toward the kitchen. Maybe a cup of coffee would brace her against whatever came.

The kitchen smelled of lasagna. The Pyrex dish still sat on the butcher block where she'd placed and forgotten it this morning. Sally Endecott had dropped the lasagna off along with a cellophane-covered bowl of tossed salad and a chocolate cake. Every day someone from the church came with food—spaghetti one day, the next a turkey dinner complete with dressing and cranberry sauce. Another brought roast beef and mashed potatoes, creamed carrots, and peas. Other friends brought home-baked apple pies and Tollhouse cookies.

No one wanted her to worry about having to cook. No one wanted her to worry about anything.

Not the least hungry, she measured coffee into the filter-lined holder and slid it in place. As she poured water into the top of the coffeemaker, she heard Alex come into the kitchen. He stood for a moment, saying nothing. When she kept her back to him, he went to the windows. She knew he was looking out at the back porch and garden.

"The house doesn't feel the same without her, does it?" he said quietly.

Sierra swallowed hard. She couldn't shake the feeling that her mother was still upstairs or down the hall. If she called aloud, her mother would answer.

But it wasn't true. She had to remind herself her mother was dead. The ceremony in the cemetery this morning should have driven that fact home. Ashes to ashes, dust to dust. A few pounds of it equaled a human life.

One moment she felt numb inside. The next she felt a debilitating anguish and fear.

Pressing the heels of her hands against her eyes, she tried not to think about it. "How long can you stay?" she said, hoping Alex would say as long as she needed him.

"I made reservations for tomorrow."

She lowered her hands slowly, despair filling her. Alex had given her three days of his precious time. She supposed she should be thankful.

"The kids said they want to stay with you."

"That's fine," she said in a brittle voice. She took down a cup and saucer from the cupboard. "Do you want some coffee?"

"Sí."

She glanced back at him and saw he was still staring into the backyard. Maybe her mother had meant something to him after all. She filled another cup and brought both to the table near the windows.

"Mom and I sat here together only a few weeks ago, before she was too weak to leave her bed." The cups rattled slightly as Sierra set them down and took a seat. "Roy Lubbeck is coming over at five to go over Mom's will."

Alex sat down across from her. "I'll stay another day or two if you want me to, Sierra."

Sure, she thought bitterly, he'd stay and resent every minute of it. She shook her head.

"What are you going to do about the house?"

"Do?" she said blankly, glancing up at him.

"You're going to have to rent it out or sell it. You can't leave it vacant. The place will fall apart. The garden's already going to seed."

She could feel the blood flowing out of her face. "I grew up in this house."

"I know how much the place means to you, Sierra, but you

have no idea what it costs to keep up a place like this. Your mother was working on it all the time."

"I buried my mother this morning, and now you want me to give up this house?"

"Don't make it sound like it's my fault your mother died of cancer," he said, his eyes glittering.

"I didn't, but it would've been nice of you to wait a few days before telling me I should get on with disposing of my mother's property!"

"*Bien, chiquita.* Take all the time you need. Stay for another month! Keep the place if you want. I don't care what you do!" He scraped his chair back and grated out the rest. "Just don't expect me to foot the bill for maintenance costs and taxes!" He left her sitting at the table.

A moment later, Sierra heard the roar of the Cadillac's engine. He revved it loudly and then sent gravel flying as he backed out of the driveway.

Pushing the cup and saucer back, Sierra put her head in her arms and wept.

Mike pulled his van into the driveway an hour later. Carolyn and Clanton piled out with their three cousins. After a quick kiss hello, they went into the family room to watch a movie with their cousins. Melissa put her hand lightly on Sierra's shoulder and then took the lasagna out of the refrigerator and put it into the oven to warm up.

"Alex drove his mom and dad home," Mike said, pouring himself a mug of coffee. "He said he was going to stay and visit for a while, but to tell you he'd be back here before five. You told him Roy's coming by?"

"Yes." Sierra kept her gaze on her cold coffee. "I'm sorry I left the way I did."

"Don't worry about it. Everybody understood."

Except Alex.

Melissa came back and took the seat Alex had left vacant. "You look tired, Sierra. Why don't you rest for a while? I'll wake you when dinner's ready."

Sierra nodded and rose. She felt her brother looking at her and wondered if he'd guessed how bad things were between her and Alex. If he did, he was sensitive enough not to say anything.

As she climbed the stairs and walked along the upper hallway, she glanced at the narrow passageway to the attic. She remembered finding her mother there on the day Alex had turned life upside down. It hadn't turned right side up since.

She went up the steps and opened the door. Standing there, she looked in, amazed at the change.

The attic was swept and dusted, new Nottingham lace curtains hung over the four small windows. The old sofa had a new forest green slipcover and four bright throw pillows, two of a deep golden yellow, two white with embroidered sunflowers and green ruffles. The coffee table had been refinished. On it were several old picture albums. The old brass lamp, now polished, stood between the sofa and her father's old worn leather recliner.

The walls had been painted pale yellow, the open-beamed ceiling white. On the south wall hung a dozen paintings and pictures. Sierra took one down. Not recognizing the face, she turned it over and saw that her mother had written the pertinent historical information on a card and glued it to the newly papered back. She smiled. Her mother had always been a stickler for detail.

The bookcase where her father's old files had been stored was now full of old books. The top three rows were designated for Mike, among them *Robinson Crusoe, Treasure Island, The Collected Works of H. G. Wells, The Earth Abides*. The bottom three were for her. She pulled out a worn copy of *Little Women* and leafed through it. Tucking it back in the shelf, she ran her fingers over

Anne of Avonlea, Daddy Long Legs, Captain from Castile, The Black Rose and looked away.

In the far east corner of the attic, standing in a beam of sunlight, was the ornate wood-framed oval mirror. The old braided rug had been cleaned, the trunk of dress-up clothing repainted white with tole-painted flowers and leaves. She opened it and saw everything had been washed, ironed, and neatly folded away. Nearby was a small bookcase with children's games and books.

When she turned around, she saw two distinct stacks against the west wall, one for Mike, one for her. Her brother's red Radio Flyer wagon was neatly packed with other mementos, favorite books, an old worn teddy bear, a baseball bat and glove. Next to it were boxes neatly labeled: "College Texts," "Trophies," "Comic books," "High School Mementos/Block sweater."

Her own things were sorted, consolidated, and labeled as well, "Clothing/Prom dress," "Dolls," "Scrapbooks/Albums," "Stuffed Animals." In one container was clothing she'd tired of but had been unwilling to give away. Mary Kathryn McMurray's trunk sat next to the new white boxes, a white envelope taped to the top. "Sierra" was written in her mother's familiar handwriting.

Sierra removed it and opened it carefully, extracting the note.

> *My dearest Sierra,*
>
> *This trunk and all its contents were meant for you. I read the journal before I sent it and couldn't help but feel you and Mary Kathryn McMurray share a great deal in common. The quilt has a message for you. You may not see or understand it now, but one day it will come to you like a star bursting in the heavens. And what a day that will be!*
>
> *I love you.*
> *Mom.*

Kneeling down, Sierra ran her hands over the clean wood and metal braces of the trunk. She could smell the linseed oil her mother had used. Unlatching the top, she opened the trunk. The scent of mulberry sachets rose and surrounded her. The beautiful antique quilt lay on top, cleaned and carefully refolded. Sierra lifted it out and saw the gift wrap–covered boxes beneath. In one was the Indian gift basket. In another were the carved wooden animals with the note saying they were for Joshua. A blue velvet box held half a dozen wedding rings, each tagged with a name of the relative who had worn it. Her throat closed when she found two tied together with a small tag reading, "Brian Philip Clanton, Marianna Lovell Edgeworth, married December 21, 1958, in San Francisco."

Sierra put everything back the way she had found it. She folded the note and put it on top of the quilt. Closing the lid, she ran her fingertips over the wood-and-metal braced surface. She walked to the small attic window and pushed it open. A bracing spring breeze fluttered the lace curtains.

"I'm no farther away than your heart."

Grief tore at her, and Sierra went back to the sofa and sat down. She opened the top album. On the first page were two pictures of her father as a young man. One showed him with shoulder-length hair and dressed in worn Levi's and boots. Right next to it was another picture of him clean-shaven, hair shorn, and wearing a policeman's uniform. She smiled at the contrast. On the next page were pictures of her mother. In one, she appeared to be dancing in a meadow. Her arms were outstretched, her head back, her waist-length hair swirling. In another, she sat on a beach gazing pensively out at the surf. There were pictures of Mike, a bundled baby asleep on his father's shoulder, a baby playing in his crib, a toddler playing in the sandbox in the backyard. On the next page were pictures of her, wrapped in a blanket in her mother's arms, another of her sitting in a high chair with her face covered with spaghetti, yet another of her toddling along the cobblestone pathway in the backyard garden.

Each year was chronicled in pictures. Stretching out on the sofa, Sierra paged through the albums, seeing her mother and father in the early years of marriage. She smiled over pictures of Mike from infancy to his wedding. She went through her album, reliving memories as she saw herself in the garden with her mother, playing dress-up with friends in the attic, swimming at Memorial Beach, playing baseball, wearing her cheerleader's uniform. She came across a picture of Alex in cap and gown. She was standing with him, and they looked at one another with open adoration. Young love in full bloom. She had forgotten her mother came to the high school graduation ceremony. Her father had ignored the invitation. On the next page, she saw herself in the full bloom of her first pregnancy. The next picture showed her in a hospital bed, looking tired and happy, Clanton in her arms. María and Luís were on one side of the bed, her mother and father on the other. Beneath the picture was written, "Reconciliation."

Outside the attic window, a nest of baby birds chirped excitedly. Sierra laid the album against her breast and listened. She knew when the mother bird was close and when it flew away by the sounds of the chicks. Closing her eyes, she drifted.

"You can't let it go." Her mother smiled at her as they both worked on their knees in the garden. "You need to take notice each day. See how they've come up already. If you give these weeds a day or two, they'll begin choking the flowers." She sat back on her heels and brushed strands of dark hair back from her temples. She looked young again, healthy and happy. "It's like that with life, too, honey."

Sierra awakened abruptly when the album was lifted from her chest. Alex stood over her. "Roy Lubbeck is downstairs."

"Oh," she said sleepily.

Alex closed the album and put it back on the coffee table. He moved away slightly as she pushed herself up and raked her hands back through her hair. She felt unkempt. Her church dress was rumpled and creased. "I need to freshen up before I come down." She was so tired. She wished she could lie down again and sleep here in the attic, where she was surrounded by happy memories. Maybe she'd dream of her mother again. Meeting with Roy Lubbeck would merely drive home the fact that she was gone.

Staring out the window, Alex shoved his hands into his pockets. "I'm sorry about what I said earlier."

Sierra didn't want to talk about it. "I can't make any decisions yet, Alex."

"I can understand that."

"I grew up here."

"I know."

His response was clipped, neutral. The wall was still firmly in place between them. The first brick had been laid when he took the job in Los Angeles. More had been added since, day by day, month by month, over the past two years. She didn't even know anymore who was inside the wall and who was outside.

"I miss you," she said softly, brokenly. "I miss the way things used to be."

He looked at her then, his eyes bleak. She knew he was deeply troubled, that he wanted to say something of import. Maybe he was as worried about their marriage as she was.

"I'm going to leave tomorrow. I think it'd be better that way. It'll give you the chance to think things over."

What things? She wondered. The house? Or was there something he wasn't saying?

He left the window. "I'll go down and tell the others you'll be with us shortly."

"Alex?"

When he turned, she stood. Gathering her nerve, she took the risk and let her feelings show. "Would you hold me? Just for a minute." He came to her and did as she asked, but she felt no comfort. His arms were around her, but it was as though he withheld himself, his heart.

How could he be standing there, holding her, and yet seem so very far away?

When she joined the others in the parlor, she sat in the wing chair near the cold fireplace. Alex took his proper place beside her. He didn't so much as put a comforting hand on her shoulder. Mike and Melissa sat on the couch, holding hands.

She tried to listen as Roy Lubbeck talked. He was explaining that after her father's death, her mother had put all the family assets into a living trust so that, in the event of her death, their inheritance wouldn't be tied up in probate.

Her mother had put the house in Mike's and her name two years before. The taxes, which amounted to a considerable sum, were paid through the year. She had also set up an account intended to take care of any minor problems that might arise, such as plumbing, appliance repair, and the like.

Sierra remembered that shortly after her father had passed away, her mother had hired a contractor to reshingle the entire roof. She'd spent a great deal to have the southern eaves and back porch torn out and rebuilt after termites were discovered. Roy went on to explain that the rest of her mother's assets were in certificates of deposit and treasury bills, including fifteen thousand earmarked for each grandchild, the money to be held in trust until their eighteenth birthdays.

Closing his briefcase, Roy cleared his throat. He looked at Mike and then her. "Your mother was a remarkable woman. It was my good fortune to call her and your father friends." He started to say more and couldn't. As he rose, he took an envelope from his suit jacket and held it out to Alex. "Marianna asked that I give this to you."

Disturbed, Alex took the letter, folded it in half, and pushed it into the front pocket of his slacks. "I'll walk you out," he said.

Sierra heard the murmur of their voices. After a few moments the front door closed, but Alex didn't return. Glancing at Mike and Melissa, she rose and went into the foyer. She could see through the leaded window on each side of the door. Alex stood outside on the front steps, his hands shoved into his pockets. As Roy Lubbeck's Thunderbird pulled away from the curb, Alex went down the steps. Her heart began to beat heavily in dread, but he didn't head for his car, which was parked in the drive alongside the house. He went out to the sidewalk and headed for the Plaza where they used to sit and listen to the summer concerts in the bandstand. Relieved, she rested her forehead against the door for a moment and then went back into the parlor.

"We've already eaten," Melissa told her. "Do you want something?" Sierra closed her eyes, shaking her head. The thought of food was enough to make her stomach lurch.

✳✳✳

"Try to get some sleep," Melissa said when the mantel clock chimed eleven.

Sierra went upstairs to bed. Lying in her canopy bed, she tried to think of happier times. Her mind was consumed with "what if" scenarios. When she awakened in the morning, Alex wasn't beside her.

Donning her robe, she came downstairs to the kitchen and found Melissa making waffles for the children. "Have you seen Alex?" she said.

"Daddy left for the airport," Carolyn said, pouring syrup on her waffle.

206

"When?" Sierra said, heart sinking. Had he really left without even saying good-bye to her?

"About an hour ago, I guess. He came in and talked to Clanton and me while we were watching television."

Turning away, she blinked back tears.

Melissa poured batter into the waffle iron. "He said he didn't want to awaken you," she said quietly. "He felt you needed sleep."

When Melissa looked at her, Sierra knew Alex hadn't fooled anyone with his excuses. Sierra gave her sister-in-law a cynical smile, poured herself a cup of coffee, and sat down with the children.

If this baby is not born soon, I will burst like an overripe melon.

James is worried sick. He makes me nervous. There is no midwife and I am too far gone to go back to Galena by wagon or any other way. So we will have to manage by ourselves. I cannot even bend over to pick up the babies I have and there is no lap left for them to sit on. Some days this baby kicks so much I wonder if there are not two inside me. Maybe they are contending with one another just like Esau and Jacob.

Matthew Lucas Farr was born mid-morning May 5 or thereabouts. He is as strong and loud as his older brother ever was. Deborah Anne followed her brother into the world straight away. They do not look at all alike, but sound pretty near the same.

James is back at work in the fields. He is much relieved to have me up and around again. He has not the patience for tending toddling and crawling babies, though he had charge of his offspring for three whole days. I could not help but laugh at his Frustration. Joshua had to show him how to change a diaper, but washing soiled ones is a chore James would sooner die than do. Does he think I like it?

I am beginning to feel like our poor milk cow.

It has been two years since I wrote a word in this journal. Where has all the time gone? Back on the homestead, by the time the day is done, I am too tired to put two thoughts together in my head let alone put anything sensible on paper. Now, I am visiting Aunt Martha and my Burdens are lifted. She is enthralled with the twins and Delighted to have Joshua, Hank, and Beth back under her roof. Betsy and Clovis are pleased, too. Joshua is Clovis's shadow. Hank and Beth spend most of their time in the kitchen with Betsy. They have discovered her fine cooking. The only time Aunt Martha gives up the twins is when they need nursing.

Galena is so much bigger than it was three years ago. Aunt Martha said there are more

than ten thousand souls living here now. I think
it more likely that four thousand of them have
no souls at all from what I've seen. The river is
busy with ships from the Mississippi. Irishmen
and Germans swarm the docks and negras as
well. Betsy said there is a new African Methodist
Episcopal Church. She and Clovis go there to
worship Jesus. There's so much noise now you
can't hear yourself think.

Aunt Martha has a new cistern. She said too
many people use the town well and it is too long
a wait for water.

James and I saw a man haul a box out onto the
sidewalk near the marketplace today. He stood on
it and talked about Oregon. He talked about the
Preemption Act of 1841 saying every person head
of a family can have 160 acres of prime free land
in Oregon. James insisted we stay and hear what
the man had to say. The man claimed Oregon is a
land flowing with milk and honey on the shores of
the Pacific. He said there are great crops of wheat
there that grow as high as a man's head. He said
pigs run about under great acorn trees, round
and fat, and already cooked with knives and
forks sticking in them so you can saw off a slice
anytime you have a mind to do so. Some believed
his hogwash and were ready to sign up and go

right off with him in their farm wagons. I am glad
James had more sense.

James sold our corn crop today. Prices are down.
He has worked hard the past few years paying
off Papas debts and making improvements on the
homestead. If Papa could see the land now, he
would be proud of James.

We will go home soon. I will miss Aunt Martha
and Betsy and Clovis. I will miss the good
cooking, the feather bed, the piano, and the ladies
from the quilting club.

For all that, I can hardly wait to be home again.

James has westering fever. He talks of nothing
but Oregon.

What is it about men that they always think the
grass is greener on the other side of a mountain?
The grass is green enough right here. I told
James we have land all paid for, a sturdy house,
a barn, two horses, a milk cow, some goats, and
a flock of chickens. We have our health and our
babies and we are happy.

He said—You are happy, Mary Kathryn. The
way I see it we will be living hand to mouth all
our lives as long as we stay in Illinois. In Oregon
there is a chance. A chance for what I wanted to
know. To build something that will last he said.
And the winters are milder.

I told him when something sounds too good to be true, it most likely is.

But all he said to that was—Free land, Mary Kathryn. Think of it.

I said—Free land two thousand miles away. Free land we have not seen and know nothing about. We have land right here already.

He said—Poor land full of rocks and roots and heartache.

Sometimes James sounds just like he did when he was talking about going off to New York and England and China.

I am sick of hearing about Oregon.

———————

3

The Surrender

13

THE HOUSE FELT VACANT WHEN SIERRA UNLOCKED the side door from the garage. Carolyn and Clanton followed her in, lugging their suitcases through the kitchen and down the hallway to their bedrooms. Sierra set her own down in the living room and wandered through the house.

Something didn't feel right. Sierra couldn't put her finger on it, but a strange foreboding filled her. At first, she wondered if the house had been burglarized, but nothing was missing. She opened the drapes in the living room and let the spring sunshine in, but that didn't help dispel the dark atmosphere.

Picking up her suitcases, Sierra went down the hallway to the master bedroom. Her brows lifted slightly when she found the bed made. In thirteen years of marriage, Alex had never made a bed. The rugs had been vacuumed. Clean towels hung in the bathroom. She put her hand on the doorknob to the walk-in closet and then hesitated, irrational fear gripping her. Taking a deep breath, she opened it and breathed in relief when she saw Alex's suits hanging to the right. The shelves at the back were neatly stacked with shirts.

She went back into the bedroom, where she had put her suitcases. Hefting one onto the bed, she unlatched it and began unpacking. As she tucked her clothing back into the dresser and put her toiletries into the bathroom, she couldn't shake the doubts and fears that had been building since Alex had left Healdsburg.

The children had raised them.

Over the past two weeks while she'd remained in Healdsburg to make some decisions with her brother, little things had come out in conversations with the children. During the time Sierra was in Healdsburg by herself, Dolores had spent the night babysitting four times, and Clanton and Carolyn had spent one weekend at Marcia Burton's.

"Daddy!" Carolyn cried out in the other room, and Sierra heard Clanton chattering away as their father returned early from work. Sierra's pulse skyrocketed. She looked around the bedroom again and bit her lip. Had he hired a maid service? If so, why now when he never had before? Closing the empty suitcases, she lifted them off the bed and set them near the door. She would put them away in the garage later.

Her stomach knotted with tension. Trying to calm down, she sat in the chair by the window. Resting her hands on the arms, she waited.

It seemed an hour before Alex stood in the doorway. "I'm glad you made it back safely." His tone and expression were enigmatic.

"Thanks." Her heart drummed harder, not in the way it used to when she looked at him, but with something deeper, something primeval. "Where are Carolyn and Clanton?" she said, keeping her tone neutral.

"Carolyn's on the telephone with Pamela, and Clanton's down the street playing soccer with some friends. He'll be in before dark." His eyes narrowed slightly. "What's the matter?"

"You tell me, Alex," she said without inflection. When he said nothing, she drew in her breath slowly to keep herself from shaking. "I heard Dolores had to spend four nights with the children while I was gone." His expression flickered slightly. "And they spent a weekend with Marcia." A pink hue seeped up from his collar and filled his face.

Sierra closed her eyes.

Alex came into the bedroom and closed the door quietly behind him. He leaned against it for a moment, saying nothing. When he spoke, his voice was low and heavy. "I didn't want to talk about this. Not the first day you got home." He sat down on the bed and leaned forward, clasping his hands between his knees. "Things aren't working between us anymore."

She opened her eyes and looked at him. His eyes grazed hers and shifted away.

"You don't understand what's important to me," he said.

"What is important, Alex?"

He looked at her then, coolly. "My work. You've resented what I do from the beginning."

"Can you tell me truthfully it's *work* that kept you away for six nights while I was gone?"

The small lines around his mouth deepened. "We've got nothing in common anymore. Our marriage started disintegrating a long time ago."

"We have two children in common," she said quietly. "We're married to one another. We have that in common."

"Then let me put it to you straight. I'm not in love with you anymore."

Sierra hadn't realized how much it would hurt to have Alex say those words straight out. She remembered listening to Meredith talk about her ex-husbands. *"They always say you never understood them, that you don't have anything in common anymore. But it usually boils down to one thing. Another woman."*

Her heart sank into the pit of her stomach.

"I'm sorry, Sierra. I—"

"Who is she, Alex?"

He looked away from her and sighed. Standing, he moved restlessly, finally stopping near her dresser. "What difference does it make?"

"I'd like to hear the news from you before I hear it from someone else."

Alex pushed his hands in his pockets, reminding her of the night Roy Lubbeck had given him a letter from her mother. Had he ever bothered to read it?

"Elizabeth."

"Elizabeth?" Her heart plummeted. "Elizabeth Longford?" she said weakly, cold clarity washing over her like a tidal wave. "The woman from Connecticut?"

"Yes."

"The one who graduated from Wellesley?"

"Yes."

Alex said she didn't understand him. Oh, but he was wrong, so wrong. She knew him better than he knew himself. She saw him so clearly in that instant. It was as though all the veiling had been ripped away, leaving his soul bare for her to see.

"You finally made the grade, didn't you?" she said softly, hurt beyond anything she could ever have thought possible.

Alex turned slowly and looked at her. Sierra watched her husband's face change. Shock. Pain. Rage. She knew her words had struck true, right to the very heart of the matter. He knew exactly what she meant. The poor farm laborer's son who had never felt good enough had finally bagged himself a worthy trophy. Beautiful, well-educated, accomplished Elizabeth Longford, daughter of the American Revolution. Maybe he didn't fully realize she had always understood his insecurities and loved him despite them. Certainly she had never expected to throw them in his face. But then, she had never expected him to betray her with another woman.

"*Bruja,*" he said through his teeth.

"And what are you, Alex? A cheat and a liar."

Had Alex been another kind of man, he would have struck her. She saw how much he wanted to. She almost wished he would. Maybe then she wouldn't feel this sick anguish. She'd be glad to see him leave. She wouldn't care. It wouldn't feel like he was ripping her heart out. Looking into his eyes, she saw no hint of tenderness or regret. She saw a man determined to be free, eager to be gone.

"This farce of a marriage is *over!*" he said, enraged.

Pain gripped Sierra until she could hardly breathe. She knew Alejandro Luís Madrid so well. If she apologized, it would make no difference. She had done the unthinkable by putting light on his secret pain. If she begged, it wouldn't change anything. He would never forgive her. His very blood would cry out against it.

"It's not over for me, Alex. It never will be."

Crossing the room, he opened the door. "That's your problem," he said and walked out.

Lucas came back today.

   If I could wish a man dead, it would be him. He
was a bad seed as far back as I can remember and
he has grown up tangled and full of treachery.

He rode right up to the house on a good
animal and dressed in fine clothes, claiming the
homestead belongs to him. I told him he was
a thief and a liar. He laughed and said it dont
matter. What is important is he is Papas firstborn
and I am disinherited. He has a letter from Hiram
Reinholtz to prove it.

And then he said bold as brass — But since
James has done such a fine job working the
place, I will be generous and allow you to stay
on as sharecroppers. And if you don't like that
arrangement, Mary Kathryn, you can pack up
and go straight to hades.

James said he will not fight Lucas over the land.
No matter what I say, he will not listen. This land
is my home. I was born in this house. James has
done more work in the fields than Lucas ever did.
And now my no-good brother shows up after all
these years and says the homestead all belongs to
him. Not without a fight, I say.

James says no. He says we are going to Oregon.

Lucas came to the house today and he brought
a man and woman with him. They all were in a
wagon. I stood on the front porch with a rifle,
but James took it from me before I could shoot
my brother dead. Lucas brought Elder right into
my house. The man had his hat in his hand and

would not look at me. It did not help knowing he
is ashamed for taking my home from me. Lucas
said he has a contract with Elder. Elder will work
the land and share profits.

I am writing this in the barn by candlelight as
I am pushed out of my own home and my own
husband helped. I am sleeping in the hay with
my babies. Where James is sleeping I don't know
and I don't care.

Aunt Martha welcomed us with open arms. So
did Betsy and Clovis. I had not cried a tear until
I saw them and now I cannot stop.

It was a long ride here by farm wagon from
the homestead. Not in miles. The children fretted
and kept asking how long it would take to get to
Galena. James was short-tempered. If it's like
this for two days travel, what does he think it will
be like on a two-thousand mile journey through
Indian infested wilderness?

He said — You will see I am right when we get
to Oregon, Mary Kathryn.

I did not answer or even look at him.

I hoped in vain that by the time we got here,
he would change his mind. I hoped he would see
I am right and he would turn this wagon around
and go back and fight for what belongs to us.

He didn't change his mind about nothing. He's
dug in his heels deep as Papa ever did. He went

right down to the market place and sold our wagon and used part of the money to buy passage on a steamboat. He says we're going down the Mississippi the end of this week and getting off at Independence Landing.

I said—Good bye, James Farr. It was nice knowing you.

He said—You are going with me if I have to hog-tie and carry you! I told him he would have to do just that. So he went out and got so drunk Clovis had to fetch him home. Poor old Clovis had to carry James home slung over his shoulder like a sack of grain. I told Clovis he could dump James in the potato cellar and leave him there until he grows eyes and rots. He is not welcome in my bed.

I reckon that is what Clovis did with him.

I can barely see this page for the tears. How is it possible to hate a man I love so much?

Aunt Martha says God's hand is in this. If that is so, then I have a bone to pick with God. Not that he will listen. Not that he ever did.

Aunt Martha and I sat all day today talking and crying. I asked her if I and my children could stay and live with her when James goes to Oregon. She said no. She said she cannot come between a man and his wife. She said God joined us together

and she will not help me split the sheets. So I am
stuck with James Addison Farr and his dreams of
Oregon.

I should have married Thomas Atwood
Houghton.

Aunt Martha bought me a trunk. James is
outfitting us in Independence. So for now, all I
have is a medicine box with Quinine, bluemass,
opium, laudanum, whiskey, hartshorn for
snakebites and citric acid to treat scurvy, books,
slates, chalk, and ink aplenty. I do not want my
children growing up ignorant like their father.
The ladies from the quilting circle packed pieces
of fabric in every color and pattern imaginable so
I can make my own quilt someday. I have packed
stout linen thread, large needles, beeswax, buttons,
paper of pins and 2 thimbles and packed in a pretty
candy box Thomas gave me a long time ago.

If I had married Thomas I would not be going
to Oregon.

Pack three sets
1 linsey-woolsey dress
1 wool dress
unmentionables
4 pairs of woolen socks
2 pairs of walking shoes
1 good shawl

1 bonnet
comb, brush and 2 toothbrushes

Pack two sets
2 flannel overshirts
2 woolen undershirts
2 pairs thick cotton drawers
4 pairs of woolen socks
4 color handkerchiefs
2 pairs of walking shoes
1 pair of boots
1 gutta percha poncho
1 coat
comb, brush, 2 toothbrushes each

frying pan
kettle
coffee pot
pie tin
butter churn

2 saws
2 shovels
2 axes
3 belt knives
1 whetstone
1 rifle
1 pistol
ammunition

James says he has the money to buy the rest of what we need when we get to Independence. I think it would be cheaper to buy supplies here, but he said it would cost too dear to freight it down the river. So we will go with what little we have, which is not much.

Aunt Martha offered money to James, but he would have none of it. I was not so proud.

I said Good Bye to Aunt Martha this morning. It near broke my heart. It is breaking still as I sit on this miserable shallow draft steamboat taking me down the Mississippi away from her and Betsy and Clovis and my home. Aunt Martha kissed me and took off her cross necklace and put it on me. It is the pretty one with amethyst stones I admired when I first come to Galena after my father cast me out. She has worn it every day of her life since her papa give it to her on her fourteenth birthday. She said—I want you to have it in memory of me. Let it remind you I am praying for you every day. She said— God is with you, Mary Kathryn Farr, and don't you ever forget it.

I was not comforted.

I will never see them again. She says I will, but she means heaven and I am not going there. I am not going anywhere God is.

I got God and James Addison Farr to blame
for all this heartache.

Joshua asked me today why I will not speak to
Papa. I said it was nothing for him to worry his
mind over, but he is worried all the same. I said
I was busy making sure Beth and Hank and the
twins do not fall overboard into the river. But he
said that is not so because Papa has Matthew and
Hank with him and the twins are asleep and Beth
is too scared of water to get close to the edge of
the boat.

He said—You will see Papa is right when we
get to Oregon. I told him if I heard those words
again, his papa will find himself in the muddy
Mississippi. And he can't swim!

We got off the boat at Independence Landing
two days ago. It has been cloudy and cold. James
found a holding place for our possessions until we
have a wagon to store them. It is a good thing it
is not raining because we are camped without so
much as a tent over our heads.

Independence is the wildest place I have ever
seen. It is full of people from every walk of life,
most I would not want to venture down. I have
never seen so many people. Everyone is buying
and selling something. Everyone is in a hurry

to get ready to go to Oregon or California or
Santa Fe.

It is dusk and I can still hear hammers
pounding as wagons are being built and oxen
bellowing and horses neighing. It is impossible to
get a wink of sleep in this jumping off place.

James left me with the children so he can go
walking around the town square and—get a feel
for what is happening—as he put it. I am getting
feeling enough from sitting by and watching.
Most people hereabouts are as crazy as he is.
The men at least. I have not seen a happy woman
since we landed.

James talked all day to men camped near us with
their wives and children about whether it is wise
to buy oxen or mules. He came back and laid out
all he had learned and then said—What do you
think, Mary Kathryn?

He would not want to know what I think.

He said—You gotta talk to me sometime.

Not in this lifetime I don't.

James bought 4 teams of oxen today at $25 an
ox! They are good sturdy animals and gentle, but
not worth that much. He should have bargained
harder. James said he will send me next time. He
said if things get bad on the trail, we can eat them.

I would like to know how he thinks he could do that with Beth taking these beasts of burden to her heart already.

I met Nellie Doane today. She and her husband Wells are camped near us. She was washing clothes in the creek same time I was. I am not the only one weeping about going to Oregon. We cried together and laughed some too. We both had some fine ideas about what to do with our husbands. She said she supposed we would have to make the best of what comes. She has three children all eager to go westering. Joshua and her son Harlan are already fast friends.

Other people are gathering near us. Virgil Boon for one. He is a cooper from Pennsylvania and up in years. He is at least forty if he is a day. There is also Judge Skinner and his wife. He is older still. Forty-three, he said. He figures they will need Law and Order in Oregon. His wife is not friendly so I do not know her name. Ruckel Buckeye is from Kentucky and only fifteen. I asked him what his mother thinks about him going off to Oregon by himself and he said she told him to go and make a better life for himself out west. I cannot imagine a mother telling her son to leave her knowing she will never see him again. She must be a hard woman.

It has been raining near every day. Our clothes
are as damp as my spirits. I must trek through
mud to get to the mercantile. James said he
needs me to do an accounting or we will not have
money enough to make the journey.

He said—You're going to have to help me unless
you want to live in this wild place for the rest of
your days, Mary Kathryn. He cant write or read
and there are men in this town that skin you for the
pure pleasure of it. He said we have $854.22 to our
names and it took him all the years we worked the
homestead to save that. Aunt Martha gave me $120
that I have hidden in the trunk for safe keeping and
Dire Straits. I did not tell him about it.

James brought Mister Kavanaugh to our
campfire today. I saw this man two days ago in
the mercantile. Or rather he saw me. He was
standing at the counter and buying powder, lead,
and shot when I come in with the children. He
is a big man and hard to miss. He looks wild as
an Indian in his buckskins. His hair is long and
dark and held back by a piece of rawhide. He was
carrying a Sharp's buffalo rifle and had bluer eyes
than I have ever seen before and staring right at
me from the minute I walked in the door.

Joshua wanted to talk to him but I told him to
stay put by me and watch that Hank and Beth did
not stray. I turned my back for one minute and

next thing I knew Joshua took Hank and Beth
right up to him. I should have been paying better
attention, but I had the twins and was bargaining
with MacDonald who is a thief and must be
watched. When I turned around again, there was
Joshua asking this rough stranger all manner of
questions and him looking at me with those blue
eyes of his. I shooed the children away from him,
apologized, and left quick as I could.

I knew I would see him again. I did not know
how or when. I just knew. How James met him
I don't know and will not ask. I offered Mister
Kavanaugh supper and he accepted. James
did most of the talking while they ate. I did
not say anything. I listened and learned Mister
Kavanaugh has had commerce with the Kansa,
Pawnee, Cheyenne, and Sioux. He lived with the
Cheyenne two years. He has great respect for
the Indians and not much for those he has seen
getting ready to head west. He said most are ill-
prepared for what awaits them.

I said—Do you mean us, Mister Kavanaugh?
And he said—Depends.
On what I asked to know. He just looked at me
and did not say.

James and Wells and half a dozen other men are
meeting with John MacLeod tonight. A contract
will be drawn up and signed and fees set for

his hire. James said he Highly Recommends Kavanaugh as a scout but doubts the man will agree. Kavanaugh has an affinity for Indians and little use for his own kind.

James said Kavanaugh has agreed to go with us to Oregon. He said John MacLeod was surprised and pleased. He said—Kavanaugh knows this country like the back of his own hand.

All the ladies are Impressed with him. They think he is Very Handsome and Mysterious. The men ply him with constant questions. I wonder sometimes if James and the others are not having second thoughts about this madness of going west.

It is raining again today and making mess of our camp. Last night, the wind blew rain right into the wagon. It is too wet for a cookfire. I wish I was at home at Aunt Martha's with my children cuddled into that big brass bed.

I asked James what we would do if the children get sick. He says we got Doc Murphy. What if the wagon breaks down? He says we have spare parts and the wheels are made of osage orangewood. What about Indians? He says Kavanaugh knows what to do about Indians. James says I worry too much, and I say he doesn't worry enough.

We ate cold beans and hard biscuits tonight.

I kept thinking about Betsy's fine cooking and that warm kitchen. I wonder if I will ever know those Comforts again.   By the time we get to Oregon, it will most likely be too late to plant Crops. We will all starve by springtime.

I wonder if any of us will be alive in a year.

EXPENDITURES

Concord spring wagon of white oak . .	$85.00
Cotton duck covers	100.00
4 teams of oxen	200.00
harnesses	25.00
6 barrels of flour	25.00
600 pounds bacon	30.00
50 pounds chipped beef	8.00
50 pounds lard	2.50
100 pounds dried fruit	6.00
50 pounds salt and pepper	3.00
100 pounds coffee	9.00
200 pounds beans	8.00
75 pounds rice	3.75
10 pounds of saleratus	1.00
5 pounds mustard	1.00
150 pounds sugar	7.00
powder, lead, shot	20.00
30 pounds tenting	5.00
matches	1.00
50 pounds candles	3.30
3 pounds castile soap	2.00
100 feet heavy rope	4.00
45 pounds bedding	22.50
Total	$572.05

Savings. 854.22
                                        -572.05
                                         282.17
Share for captain/scout
MacLeod and Kavanaugh. . . . . -44.00
Savings. 282.17
                                         -44.00
                                         238.17

Members

John MacLeod Wagon Company to Oregon
   Territory

Scout—Mister Kavanaugh

James and Mary Kathryn Farr—Illinois/ farmer
   children: Joshua, Henry, Beth, Matt, and
   Deborah

Virgil Boon—Pennsylvania/ cooper

Judge Skinner and wife Mary—Carolina/ lawyer

Reese Murphy—New York/ doctor
   sister: Susan

Cal Chaffey—Maine/ farmer

Mary and Marcus Sweeney—Ohio/ blacksmith

Mittie Catlow—Illinois/ farmer
   son: Calhoun

Franklin and Paralee Sinnott—Missouri/ merchant
   children: Frank and Patricia

Werner Hoffman—New York/ farmer
   son: Herbert

Kaiser Vandervert—Massachusetts/ tailor

Ernest and Winifred Holtz—New York/wheelwright
   children: Ernst, Louisa, Alicia, Gottlieb

Melzena and Arbozena Pratt — Alabama/
seamstresses
nigra servant: Homer

Wells and Nellie Doane — Missouri/ baker
children: Robert, Harlan, LeRoy

Lot Whimcomby — Massachusetts/ clerk

Paul Colvigne — Delaware/ teacher

Binger Siddons — Indiana/ farmer

Oren and Aphie McKenzie — Virginia/ farmer

Dunham and Celia Banks — Connecticut/shoemaker
children: baby Hortense

A. J. Wright — Tennessee/ harnessmaker

Wyatt Collins — Vermont/ farmer

Cage Baker — Kentucky/ farmer

Ruckel Buckeye — Ohio/ hunter

Artemesia and Athena Hendershott — Georgia/
drayage
brother: Apollo

Stern Janssen — Sweden/ sailor

Matthew Odell — Illinois/ gunsmith

Less Moore — South Carolina/ gambler

Payment rendered in advance to John
MacLeod — $800.00

Payment rendered in advance to   Bogan
Kavanaugh — 300.00

The sun has finally come out. We were busy all
day repacking to John MacLeod's instructions.
Our flour is now stored in canvas sacks instead
of barrels, 100 pounds per sack. Our bacon
supply is repacked in boxes, 100 pounds each.

We surrounded the bacon with bran. JM says
this will prevent the fat from melting and keep the
bacon from spoiling.

I am too tired to write more.

It is raining again. We have moved to higher
ground. Everyone is Wet and Cold and Agitated.
JM says we will not move out until the grass is
four inches high. Right now, our stock is feeding
on what grass there is which is not much.

No one is happy, not even James who had this
fool idea of going to Oregon.

I long for home. I cannot think about Aunt
Martha, Betsy and Clovis without crying.

James bought a milk cow for $20. Beth will have
charge of it. Joshua will help herd the stock the
company has bought from the common fund.

We have been on the trail three days. We left
Courthouse Square at sunup May 12. There are
twenty-eight wagons in our company and fifty-
eight souls counted among them. We crossed
the Missouri border and left the United States
of America. The only law and order we got now
is what we have agreed to among ourselves. We
have traveled over muddy roads past a great big
blue mound and then crossed Bull Creek. Heading
due west, we saw a sign saying The Road to

Oregon. We had a hard crossing at the Vermillion.
A. J. Wright lost a wheel coming down the steep
bank.

Crossing creeks is always trouble. Near the
mission the Shawnee Indians helped me while
James helped A. J. The children and I had a
smooth crossing though my heart was in my
throat the whole way.

Franklin Sinnott has two wagons, one for
family and supplies and another loaded with
goods he intends to sell in Oregon. He is driving
it himself and leaving his wife Paralee to drive
the other. She is scared of driving and with good
reason. She is not much good at it and Very
Fragile. When we were at the Wakarusa, she
pulled out of line and waited. Franklin yelled at
her something fierce, but she would not get back
behind and follow him across. She would not
budge. He had to come back and drive the wagon
across himself. He was so mad, he made her get
off and walk. Little Patricia screamed for her
mama all the way across the river. Paralee came
across in a bull boat with a Shawnee.

We crossed the Kansas and have followed the
Little Blue for three days. James is letting Joshua
drive the wagon. I am thankful. It is easier on a
body to walk.

Someone pushing a wheelbarrow followed us

all day yesterday and today. MacLeod said it was probably a Mormon and went out to see. I can see the glow of a campfire in the distance.

Artemesia and Athena Hendershott have asked Kavanaugh to share their supper. They are very nice ladies. Perhaps he will take a liking to one. Apollo would be delighted to see one of his sisters wed.

John MacLeod just returned and told James it is a woman out there. He told her she is a fool and should go back, but she said it is a free country and she can go where she pleases.

It is beyond my thinking why any woman would choose to go to Oregon let alone work so hard to get there.

I wonder who she is and why she is so Determined to leave Civilization behind.

James said the woman following us is French and from New Orleans and I am to have no discourse with her. I asked him why and he would not tell me. I said I would talk to whom I please and he said I would not. I asked how he come to know so much about her and he said Kavanaugh told him. I told him it was his rotation on guard duty and he should go. Ruckel Buckeye and Apollo Hendershott are also on duty tonight. Kavanaugh told us from the start the Indians have a fondness for stock and the men must keep their Eyes

Open. James was mad enough when he left the
fire that he will have no trouble staying awake.

We have reached Alcove Springs. There were
so many wagons, we felt we were right back
in Independence. We will move on tomorrow
for better forage for the animals. I spent the
afternoon washing clothes.

I can hear fiddles playing on the night air.
James wants to dance. He has not said so,
but I can tell because his foot is tapping. He
keeps looking at me and waiting for me to say
something.

I would like to say something, but he would not
like to hear it.

———————————

14

THE INTERCOM ON SIERRA'S DESK BUZZED. SHE pressed the button. "Yes, Arlene?"

"You have a call on line two."

"Thank you." Sierra pressed the button, thinking it was the counselor she'd been trying to reach. "Sierra Madrid speaking."

"It's Alex."

Her heart leaped, and then crashed when he got straight to the point. "The house is yours. My attorney says I'm making a mistake, but I want you to have it. I've already had the deed changed over into your name. Same for your BMW. You'll get the papers certified mail in a day or two."

His voice was so cold, her fingers felt icy around the telephone receiver. "Do you feel absolved now? Do you think giving me a house and car makes everything *right?*"

"I think I'm being more than fair."

"Fair?" Her throat closed. "I never realized you thought adultery and desertion were fair."

"As soon as you get an attorney, we can get all the details of the divorce settled. The quicker it's done, the easier it'll be on all of us."

She had no intention of making it easy for him. Trembling, she put her hand over her eyes. "I won't give you a divorce, Alex. I already told you that."

He swore in Spanish. "I'm not coming back, Sierra. You'd better understand that here and now. I want *out!*"

"You're already out. You just don't have the legal documents to prove it. And you never will." She slammed the phone down.

She was shaking violently, her heart hammering. Clenching her fists, she pressed the heels against her eyes and tried to push the emotions down deep inside her.

"Are you all right?" Ron said from the doorway.

She didn't answer. Breathing slowly, she stuffed the feelings deeper and deeper, until she felt cold and still inside. She couldn't even feel her heart beating. "Yes," she said and turned away, finding her place on the schedule she'd been typing for the next week.

Ron came over to her desk and pressed the intercom button. "Hold all calls until I tell you otherwise, Arlene. Sierra and I need to have a conference." Releasing the button, he put his hands on the back of Sierra's chair and rolled it two feet back from her desk. "Let's talk about what's going on."

She didn't move; it was better if she kept her back to him. "I'd rather not."

"If you keep any more stuffed inside you, you're going to explode."

"I talk about it."

"With Marcia," he said simply. "I don't think she's helping much."

"And a few others."

"Meredith?"

"I've talked the situation over with her attorney," Sierra admitted. "Alex can't get a divorce, not without my help, and I'm not going to give it to him."

"You've lost weight in the last month, Sierra. You look like you aren't sleeping."

"Thanks, Ron. I needed to hear that," she said and looked away. Carolyn had come into her bedroom again last night. It seemed she came in every night, crying over another nightmare.

She felt his hand on her shoulder. "I care about you, Sierra. I hate to see you hurting like this."

The gentleness in his voice was almost her undoing. "I don't think there's any way around it."

"I want to help."

Maybe she did need to talk to someone other than Marcia. She was always so full of ideas on how to force Alex into coming home and taking up his proper responsibilities as husband and father—ideas that Sierra knew would be a waste of time. Manipulation wouldn't work with Alex.

It wasn't the first time Ron had offered his shoulder to cry on. She had hesitated to take up the offer, not wanting to bring her problems into work. But wasn't she doing that already? Ron cared about her. God knew, she needed someone to care. Alex certainly didn't.

"Come on," Ron said.

Letting out her breath, she rose and followed him into his office. He closed the door behind her.

"Didn't someone from the school call you this morning?" Ron poured a mug of coffee and held it out to her.

"Clanton was in another fight," she said, taking it. She sat in the wing chair in front of his desk.

Ron poured himself a mug of coffee and leaned on the desk in front of her. "That's two fights this week, isn't it?"

"The school counselor knows what's been going on. She says he's 'acting out his anger.'_"

"Has Alex spoken to him?"

She gave a bleak laugh. "Even if Alex tried, Clanton wouldn't talk to him."

"Why not?"

She shook her head. "I told the children why Alex left. The first time he called, Clanton answered and said he hated him and never wanted to see him again. Alex asked to speak with Carolyn, but she was crying too hard to even talk to him." She held the coffee cup between both hands, wishing the warmth would seep through enough to stop her shaking. "Alex blamed me, of course." She took a slow breath, trying to control her voice. "He said I'd turned his children against him."

"What'd you say?"

"He didn't give me a chance to say anything. After he said his piece, he hung up." Alex had cursed her in Spanish before doing so. "All I did was tell them the truth. What else could I say when they asked why their father hadn't come home for three days? I told them their father had decided to live with another woman. Those are the facts. I told them it wasn't because he didn't love *them* anymore. It's because he doesn't love *me*. I'd like to know how else I could've broken the news."

"Take it easy," Ron said with a sympathetic smile. "I'm not criticizing you."

"I'm sorry, but I'm just sick and tired of having Alex blame me for everything. He says all the problems the children are having now are my fault. *He's* the one having the affair. *He's* the one who deserted his family. And yet everything is my fault."

"It's human nature to want to blame someone else."

Just as she was blaming Alex for everything? Was that what he was saying? She pressed her lips together. Well, wasn't it Alex's fault? If he hadn't left her and the children and moved in with his mistress, everything would be fine.

Speak the truth, Sierra.

Her face burned at the remembered admonition. Whenever she or Mike had tried to justify something they'd done as children, Mom would always look them right in the eye and say those quiet words.

Speak the truth. . . .

The truth. Things hadn't been right between her and Alex in a long, long time. She knew it, but she also knew she wasn't ready to face it. She quickly averted her thoughts from that path and focused on the children instead. "I'm not sure what to do about Clanton. He's been in the principal's office four times over the last two weeks, and his report card is a disaster. He quit baseball without even telling me. When I asked him why, he said he didn't care about it anymore. He used to love it, Ron. Now, all he does is sit in his room and play video games."

"What about Carolyn?"

"She's the exact opposite. Clanton tells me every afternoon that he has no homework, whereas she works on assignments for hours. She was devastated the other day when she missed one word on a spelling test."

"Is she still having the nightmares?"

Sierra nodded. "She had another last night. She came into my room at one in the morning, crying and saying she'd dreamed I'd died in a car accident."

"Poor kid."

"Marcia says it's fear of losing both parents. With Alex gone, she's afraid something will happen to me, too."

"Marcia's spent enough time in counseling to be an expert,"

Ron said with a faint smile. "Listen, I think you all need a break. Why don't you and the kids go with me to Catalina on Saturday?"

Startled by the invitation, she looked up at him. "Catalina?"

"We're having great sailing weather."

"Sailing?"

"Yes, sailing. Don't look so doubtful. I'm good at it. I sailed to Fiji by myself when I was twenty-three."

"I had no idea," she said for the sake of conversation. Her mind was whirring. She felt vaguely uncomfortable, but she couldn't pinpoint why. Her cheeks grew warm as he continued to study her.

"I wasn't suggesting anything inappropriate," he said, his tone sincere.

Her face went hot. "Oh, I know that!" she said quickly, "but . . ."

"But what?"

"You're my boss."

His mouth tipped. "I'm also your friend." He straightened and went around his desk, sitting in his swivel chair. She wondered if he sensed she needed distance between them to feel at ease with him again. "I'll ask Marcia and Tom and their children to come along," he said. "They've been to Catalina with me several times. Pamela and Reed are good little sailors. They can teach Clanton and Carolyn how to man the ropes."

Sierra smiled bleakly. "It'd be a relief not to sit around the house all weekend obsessing about Alex and Elizabeth Longford." As soon as she said it, she wished she hadn't. Somehow, pairing their names aloud brought up all the pain and humiliation. Feeling the warning prick of oncoming tears, she looked away briefly. "I think the children would enjoy it, too," she said when she'd regained her self-control.

"Good. I'll pick you up at five on Saturday."

"Isn't that sort of late?" she said, rising and taking his empty coffee cup. She'd rinse them out in the kitchenette down the hall. "It'll only give us a couple of hours before dark."

He laughed. "Five in the *morning*, Sierra."

"You've got to be kidding!"

"I'm being kind to you. I usually like to get an earlier start. I'll tell Marcia to give you a call. She can tell you what to wear."

It rained all day.

Aphie McKenzie had a baby boy as we were traveling. The road was mud and hard pulling. The jouncing made it even harder on poor Aphie. She is not a strong girl, and it was a Difficult Birth and she is in a Very Bad Way. Rain was blowing in on us as we helped her. Doc Murphy did what he could to make her comfortable. Oren gave the baby to Winifred Holtz to nurse.

Nellie is praying hard for Aphie but I don't think it will do much good.

We have had a week of good weather. I never imagined the prairie to be so boundless and beautiful. It stretches as far as I can see and not a tree in sight. Green grass waves and flows and wild flowers are growing everywhere and making splashes of every color of the rainbow clear to the horizon. The great distance scares me. There seems no end to it.

The Platte River is before us. I have heard much
of this great river that runs like a line from east to
west. It looks to be running bottom side up it is so
brown. The islands in the middle have willows and
cottonwoods. We are in need of firewood. James
and some of the other men have gone across to
get some. Others are making do with what they
have. Werner Hoffman burned his wife's Gothic
bookcase yesterday. She is still grieving over it. It
did not comfort her that Cal Chaffey broke up a
mahogany secretary that has been in his family for
over a hundred years. His grandfather brought it
over by ship from England.

Binger Siddons found a piano that had been
dumped along the trail. Athena Hendershott
asked to play it before the men put axes to it. She
made it sound pure heaven. Cal Chaffey joined in
on his mouth organ. I sang The Orphan Girl and
Sweet Charlotte. James asked if she could play
Are You Still Mad at Me, Darling, and she did.
I did not think it funny. Athena played until the
sunset and then left the men to break it up. Kaiser
Vandervert cried when he put his ax to it.

We are camped at new Fort Childs. It is named
in honor of Colonel Thomas Childs. Some think
the fort should be named Fort Kearny to honor
General Stephen Watts Kearny and after the other
fort that was on Table Creek. I do not much care

who it is named after or where it was before. I am
glad the old Fort Kearny was moved here from
Table Creek and we have some sight of Civilization
before we head out over the Great American
Desert to face God knows what.

There are Grand Islands in the center of the
Platte and more than 170 military men Working
Diligently on the fort. A few sod shelters are
finished. Prices at the trading post are High. The
soldiers are making adobe bricks and there is
much cutting and sawing going on.

Indians are here in large number. Kavanaugh
said they have come to trade. They have conical
houses of poles and hides. Kavanaugh said they
can take down the "tipis" and be on the move
quicker than James can harness the teams of
oxen. He said the Indians live this way because
they follow the buffalo. I said there are no buffalo
here and he said there will be plenty soon enough.

Joshua was very interested in the Indians.
Kavanaugh said we are crossing their land and
eating their game and leaving nothing in return. A
day will come when they will not be so hospitable.

James found a carved bed and chopped it up for
fuel. I could not help but wonder who slept in it.
It was such a grand headboard with leaves and
vines. What a shame to burn such a costly thing,
but we have to eat and need a fire to cook over.

Beth and my sweet little Deborah just brought
an armload of flowers to camp. They both have
Mama's love of flowers. Beth is busy weaving
garlands for our hair. The children seem to think
we are on a long picnic! I am so tired by the time
the sun goes down that I can hardly put two
words together. James said we made 18 miles
today. It feels more like 100 by the time we make
camp, but he is pleased. He says if we keep the
pace, we will reach Oregon in plenty of time
before winter sets in.

I long for a bath. A week ago I was soaked to
the skin with rain and my skirt was caked with
mud. Now my skin is raw and itching from the
dust that seeps under my dress. My shoes are
already wearing out. I long for Sunday when we
will have a day of rest. Virgil Boon preached last
time. I did not agree with a word he said, but he
was entertaining.

Poor little Aphie McKenzie died last night. Oren
is Heart Broken.

The men dug her grave right in the trail so
the wagons could go over it. Kavanaugh said no
wolves would catch the scent nor Indians see the
signs of a grave that way. It makes me sad that
not even a marker bearing her name will be left,
but it would make me feel worse to think wolves
dug her up and ate her or Indians stripped her

clean of the pretty wedding dress Oren insisted she wear to meet her Maker.

Oren is just nineteen. James says he will mend, but I am afraid for him. He has no interest in his son. I asked James to keep close watch over Oren. James said he would be pleased to do so as long as I keep talking to him. I said I would talk to the devil himself if he agreed to make sure that boy does not hang himself to whatever tree he can find.

The baby seems to be faring well in Winifred's care. She has milk aplenty and a good heart. Perhaps she will give him a name.

I have not seen the French woman's fire burning the last two nights. I asked MacLeod what become of her. He said he did not know. I hope Indians did not take her.

I never thought I would see the day that I would be cooking over a fire of animal dung. We have not seen a single buffalo yet, but are burning their leavings and thankful to have them. Kavanaugh said buffalo "chips" are good fuel and he is right. The cook fire is hot and there is no smell. Joshua shot two rabbits. I spitted and roasted them. The sparks that shot up made them taste lightly of pepper.

Harlan Doane was killed today. It happened just before our usual nooning. It was hot and he was dozing. He fell off the high wagon seat and broke his neck. No one knew anything happened until Nellie started screaming.

All I could do was hold Nellie and cry with her. I did not know what to say to comfort her. If I had a word of wisdom I could not have gotten it out. Joshua is just sitting against the wagon wheel not saying anything. Harlan was his best friend.

Death comes sudden and awful on the trail.

I am so afraid of losing one of my own.

We reached the South Platte this morning. Kavanaugh went across ahead of the wagons and drove long poles to mark the way. Ruckel thought he knew a better place to cross and almost lost his wagon in quicksand. MacLeod shouted loud enough to be heard back in Galena he was so mad. He said next time they would leave Ruckel in the river rather than risk life and limb for a fool who could not listen to those more experienced.

Kavanaugh came back to ride with us on the way across. He had James water the animals before starting out. He said not to let them stop or the wagon would sink into the sand. The Platte may be shallow, but it is treacherous.

We all made the crossing with no Disasters.
Nellie gave thanks to God on the other side.

Beth and I doctored one of our oxen during the
nooning. The poor animal was chaffed from
being in harness. The wound was crawling with
blow fly eggs and worms. I cleaned it out and put
bacon rind over the chaffing. MacLeod said it
will soothe the wound and keep the harness from
rubbing more. Beth walked beside the animal
until we made camp. The poor beast seems better
this evening.

We had a terrible lightning and thunder storm
last night. The children were all crying and
carrying on. It struck so close you could smell
Hades breath.

And then we heard a sound like rolling thunder
only it did not stop. The ground began to shake.
Kavanaugh rode in fast and shouted for the men
to get their guns quick. A stampede of buffalo
were coming straight for us.

I have never seen so many animals. They are as
numerous as the stars in the heavens. Kavanaugh
rode out with James and six others and fired
their guns to turn the stampede. That was hours
ago and the buffalo have been running by us all
that time. Dawn broke an hour ago. The sound
of those hooves is Deafening. I cannot keep

my hand steady for the pounding and my own
trembling heart.

Joshua wants to ride with the men and I will
not let him. He is angry with me. I said he had
to stay. He asked why and I said we needed
him to keep watch over us. He is not appeased.
MacLeod is here.

The truth is I am afraid he would get himself
killed. It is bad enough to be worrying about
James without wondering what is happening to
my son.

The men have been busy all day butchering the
buffalo that were shot during the stampede.
They did not shoot many as they shot in the air
most times to turn them. I told Joshua he could
go help the men do that but he has stomped off
to pout. Kavanaugh brought back a hump and
tongue and some marrow bones for us. The meat
was very tasteful and tender. He told me to roast
the bones which I did and found the marrow was
delicious. Kavanaugh has been good to us. He
seems to watch over my family more carefully
than the others. James likes him. Joshua thinks
he is next to God Almighty. He is always inviting
Kavanaugh to sup with us and then asks him
a hundred questions.

Kavanaugh said the Indians do not waste
anything. They use buffalo hides to build their

homes. They eat the meat. He cut squares of hide
and showed James how to wrap the hooves of the
oxen. Beth is delighted. Our animals now have
shoes to wear! I could use a new pair myself but
will wait until we reach Fort Laramie.

Before leaving our campsite, Kavanaugh spoke
to James away from the fire. They did not want
me to hear. I know enough from watching that
they have doubled the guard. James saddled one
of the horses and tethered it to the end of the
wagon a few minutes ago.

Kavanaugh expects trouble.

Sioux Indians came today. Two of them were
wearing magnificent warbonnets. I near died
of fright when I saw them riding toward us.
MacLeod called the alarm and we circled the
wagons. The men took up defensive positions
while Kavanaugh rode out to talk to them. I was
sure they were going to kill him, but he showed
no fear of them and spoke to them at length.
Joshua said young braves are dangerous because
they have to engage and defeat an enemy in order
to take their place on the tribal counsel. I asked
him how he knew so much about it and he said
Kavanaugh told him. He quotes Kavanaugh
like Scripture about everything. Joshua said
Kavanaugh told him prairie Indians are seldom at

peace with their neighbors. That did not set my
mind at rest.

Kavanaugh brought the Indians to camp. I have
never seen such fierce faces. Kavanaugh said we
are crossing their land and eating their buffalo.

Joshua pays no heed to my fears and
warnings. He ignored me and went off with
Kavanaugh. If that was not bad enough, while
he was about it, he invited the Sioux to eat
vittals at our fire! I was afraid they would not
like my cooking. They did not care much about
food. It was my red hair that impressed them.
Joshua told me to take off my bonnet and let
my hair down so they could see it. What for I
wanted to know. To see if it would make a fine
scalp? James laughed and said I have a temper
to match my hair. Kavanaugh explained so the
Indians would not think James was laughing at
them. I was so mad, I let down my hair. They
seemed to admire the color. So I cut six curls off
and gave one to each of the braves. Kavanaugh
told them it is strong medicine. I hope they are
satisfied with what I gave them and will not
come back for the rest of it! MacLeod gave them
gifts of blankets, sugar, and tobacco from stores
the company bought for such purposes. The
Sioux seemed satisfied with the tariff and left.

Joshua just told me the Indians earn each

feather in their warbonnets by killing an enemy.
I am glad he did not tell me earlier!

MacLeod has posted extra guards around the
stock. I am keeping close watch on my children.
I want every one of them within sight and reach.
I have heard Indians will steal children quicker
than they will steal a horse or mule and Beth and
Deborah both have hair the same color as mine.

Kavanaugh said a most alarming thing to me
tonight. He said one of the Indians asked how
many horses James would take for me. I asked
him how many he said. Enough that he will be
making no offers, he told me. He also said not to
wander too far away from camp.

I am not certain he was serious, but I will take
no chances. James will be surprised when I sleep
beside him tonight. It will be the first time I have
done so since we left home.

Two wagons were lost today.

We made a slow climb up a California hill to
the top of the plateau. Kavanaugh and MacLeod
had warned us of the Hard Descent to come, but
no one was expecting a drop past perpendicular.
Flocks of birds were rising and dipping in the
wind. When I saw that hill, I wished we could
sprout wings and fly down. As it was, the men
rigged a windlass to lower the wagons one by one.

Paul Colvigne was snakebit before the first one made it down. That Event was a sign of other catastrophies to come. The ropes pulled free of Matthew Odell's wagon and the whole lot went crashing down the hill and made a sorry mess at the bottom. The noise startled the horses. As our luck would have it, Less Moore was in charge of the watch over them. He is better with cards than animals. Joshua and four others are still out rounding them up.

It is near dusk and the men are lowering Stern Janssen's wagon. It is the last one. The rest of us are camped in a hollow with many ash trees and good water. I have supper cooking and have hung wash on the wagon to dry. There is little wind here which is a relief from the last few days up on the prairie. I am tired of dust in my eyes and mouth and under my clothes.

This was one hill and we have yet to face the Rocky Mountains.

Joshua has returned. He said they found all but three horses. The Best Ones. Sinnott's Arabian was not recovered. He will be fierce about its loss. The other two were company bought prime stock. Kavanaugh said the Arapahoe are a little richer for our foolishness.

The hartshorn Doc gave Paul did no good. So Kavanaugh made an indigo poultice for him. He said the Indians use it to draw serpent bites. It may be too late. Paul is addled and doing poorly. I gave him whiskey to ease his pain.

We buried Paul Colvigne at sunup. The company voted to give his outfit to Matthew Odell.

———————

15

SIERRA SAT WITH HER BARE LEGS DANGLING over the side of Ron's sailboatas she watched Clanton and Carolyn swim in the cove with Pamela and Reed. It was a perfect early summer day, the sun high overhead, not a cloud in the blue sky. Looking back toward the mainland, she could see the haze of smog that lay over the metropolitan area of Los Angeles. Here, she could fill her lungs with clean, sea air.

"It's heaven, isn't it?" Marcia said with a contented sigh as she lay basking on a deck chair.

"Hmmmm," Sierra said dreamily. How long had it been since she had heard Clanton and Carolyn laugh or seen them having so much fun? Clanton was trying to catch Ron. Each time he came close, Ron disappeared beneath the surface and came up well out of reach. The four children tried working together and still failed to tag him.

"All I need is something to eat," Marcia said.

Sierra turned her head. Reaching up for the railing, she started to pull herself up. "If you'll watch the children, I'll—"

"No, no," Marcia said, adjusting her dark glasses as she got up. "I'll see about getting lunch. Stay where you are. There's not enough room in the galley for two people. Besides, Ron didn't leave much to do this time. He called a caterer. All I have to do is take off the plastic wrap. Stay and enjoy the sun." She shrugged into a lightweight hip-length terry-cloth robe that covered her bikini. "Tom can help keep an eye on the children." She flicked the hat off his face. Grunting from the shock of sunlight, he awakened abruptly. "I said you can help keep an eye on the children," Marcia repeated. "I'm going below."

"Yeah, yeah," he said.

"Go back to sleep, Tom," Sierra laughed. "I'll watch them."

"Thanks," he said and sagged back, picking up the hat and putting it over his face again.

Ron came up next to the ladder he had put over the side after dropping anchor. Shaking his blond hair back, he started to climb. Sierra couldn't help noticing he had a perfect body. Looking away, she kept her eyes on the children.

"You're getting burned," Ron said, toweling himself off a few feet from her.

"I put sunscreen on."

"It probably washed off when you took that two-minute swim," he said, grinning.

Two minutes in the cold Pacific had been all she needed to know she preferred toasting on the deck.

"You need another basting." Ron uncapped a bottle of lotion Marcia had left next to her deck chair. Squirting some into his palm, he rubbed his hands together and hunkered down behind her. The scent of coconut and tropics filled her senses as he rubbed the lotion into her skin. "Where's your hat?" he said, his strong fingers kneading her shoulders.

"I think I left it below."

"Deliberate disobedience." Unlooping the towel he'd put around his neck, he covered her head with it. "I don't want you getting sunstroke the first time you sail with me."

Laughing, she folded it up so she could see. "You're worse than a mother, Ron."

He flipped her French braid over her right shoulder and finished rubbing the lotion into her back and shoulders. "You're enjoying yourself, aren't you?"

"Very much."

His hands slowed. She felt his thumbs moving up her spine. He gripped her shoulders. "It's good to see you smile and mean it," he said. Releasing her, he straightened.

Marcia called for Tom and began handing up the food. There was a large platter of cut vegetables and dip, another of sandwiches, bowls of potato and fruit salad, and bags of chips. "How are we doing with the drinks?" she called from below.

Tom opened the ice chest that had been set on the deck when they got under way. "We could use some more wine coolers. We've plenty of everything else."

Ron gave a piercing whistle, drawing the attention of the four children, who were still splashing around in the cove. "Anybody out there hungry?"

Four voices gave a short *yes!* and started swimming for the boat.

"You'd better get what you want before they get here," Marcia said. "There's something about swimming and salt air that seems to triple the appetite."

Laughing, Sierra rose from her post. The only one who hadn't served himself was Ron. He nodded for her to go ahead while he kept an eye on the children, who approached like hungry barracuda.

Clanton clambered onto the deck first. Shivering, he threw a towel around himself. Taking a plate, he heaped it with two sandwiches and two scoops of potato salad. Tucking a soda under his arm, he grabbed a bag of chips and headed for the bow. Reed, Carolyn, and Pamela poured onto the deck and raced for the food.

Ron laughed. "It's like watching sharks in a feeding frenzy."

"Take some vegetables, Reed."

"Aw, Mom."

"You heard me."

Glowering, Reed took a couple of carrot and celery sticks and put them on his plate before heading for the bow.

Shaking her head, Marcia glanced at her daughter and noticed she was about to take a handful of potato chips. "Pamela," she said, sounding weary. "You know very well what grease does to your complexion. No, take some of the fruit salad instead."

Cheeks stained red with humiliation, Pamela put her plate down and fled below.

"Oh, for heaven's sake!" Marcia said, annoyed. "I don't know what's gotten into her lately."

"I wonder." Tight-lipped, Tom leaned down and took another wine cooler from the ice chest.

Marcia raised her brow. "You've had four, Tom."

"Then I guess this one makes five." He headed for his deck chair.

Marcia stared after him in consternation. Clearing her throat softly, she glanced back at Ron and Sierra. "Well, I guess I'd better go below and see what's upset Pamela *this* time." She gave Ron a beseeching smile and whispered, "Would you please keep an eye on Tom?"

"He's a grown man, Marcia."

"Yes, but I think he's had enough to drink, don't you?"

Sierra noticed that as soon as Marcia went below, Reed pitched the vegetable sticks into the water and dug into the bag of chips Clanton had commandeered.

She and Ron shared a quiet lunch together, talking about Outreach and some of the children they were helping. Tom fell asleep in his deck chair while the boys rummaged through a waterproof case on the deck where Ron had laid in a supply of games. Carolyn sat with her legs dangling, waiting for Pamela to come up from below. When she did, her face was splotchy from crying.

"Mother says she has a splitting headache," she said as though delivering a rehearsed message. She picked up her plate and dutifully added a small scoop of fruit salad before she went to sit on the bow with Carolyn.

Sierra went below and found Marcia rummaging through her tote bag. "I know I brought them," she said in frustration. Upending everything onto the couch built into the bulkhead, she spread things out, searching again. Letting out her breath in relief, she picked up a small prescription bottle and uncapped it. Shaking out two capsules, she recapped the bottle and dropped it on the couch. Tossing the pills into her mouth, she headed for the galley. Sierra heard the hiss of tonic being shot into a glass.

"I don't know what to do about that girl," Marcia said from the galley. Sierra heard the thunk of a glass on the counter. "All I'm trying to do is protect her. Children can be so merciless to someone who's fat and has pimples." She came back into the chamber and sat down on the couch built into the bulkhead. She began to collect and toss the things back into her tote bag. "She misunderstands everything I say to her. Sometimes I think she does it deliberately in an effort to make me feel bad. Either that, or she's stupid."

Dropping the tote bag onto the floor, she leaned forward, her elbows resting on her knees as she kneaded her temples. "And now this headache. . . ."

"Can I get you a cold compress?" Sierra said, feeling sorry for her.

"Please," she said and stretched out on the couch.

Sierra went into the galley and dampened a cloth for her. "Thank you," Marcia said and pressed it against her eyes and forehead. "Would you please tell Tom I'm not feeling well? I must have a touch of sunstroke."

"Tell her to take a nap," Tom said when Sierra delivered the message. Yawning, he pulled the hat down over his eyes again. Clearly, he had no intention of going below and speaking with his wife.

Ron went in his stead and talked with Marcia while the children went swimming again. Sierra leaned on the railing near the bow and watched them.

When Ron came up again, he gave her a rueful smile and shook his head. "Sorry to desert you."

Sierra had enjoyed the solitude. She felt guilty that Marcia's problems made her feel less a failure for her own. She had always thought Marcia's family was perfect. She knew there were times of tension, of course. What family didn't have them? But what she'd seen today was clear evidence that all was not well in Camelot.

"Is she feeling better?"

"She's going to stay below and rest on the way back." Ron gave a loud whistle to catch the children's attention. "Wrap it up, mates. We're hauling anchor in half an hour."

Four children groaned expressively and went back to their game of water tag.

Under his tutelage, the children, with Tom's assistance, manned the sails. When the wind caught the sheets, the boat sped across the water toward the Long Beach pier. Closer in, they battened down the sails, and Ron used the engine to bring them to dock.

"We had a wonderful time, Ron," Marcia said, kissing his cheek while the children gathered their things. While Tom shook hands with him, Marcia turned to Sierra and gave her a hug. "Sorry I made a scene below," she said, kissing her cheek. "I'll call you tomorrow." Sierra saw her take the car keys from Tom's hand as they headed for the parking lot.

Ron took Sierra and the children to an expensive seafood restaurant. He laughed when Clanton and Carolyn both ordered hamburgers. Over dinner, he talked about sailing to the South Seas and spending two years exploring islands that were barely a spot on a map. Clanton was enthralled; Carolyn, quiet.

It was late when Ron finally pulled up in front of Sierra's house. She was sorry the day was over. The children had fallen asleep in the backseat of his Mercedes. They'd only lasted fifteen minutes from the restaurant before dozing off and leaving her and Ron to talk alone. And talk they did, about everything from his travels to her growing up in a quiet country town to racial prejudice, social climbing, education, and the importance of family. He'd grown up the only son of a Greek businessman and a Swedish actress. His mother died in a car accident when he was only fourteen. "My father never got over her death," he said quietly. "Now he's gone, too. I'm the only family I've got left. And I find myself craving the connection of family all the time." He smiled at her in the darkness. "All in God's timing," he said.

Sierra couldn't help feeling a twinge of jealousy. The woman he married would be lucky indeed. She didn't know anyone as caring and sensitive to others as Ron Peirozo.

He turned off the ignition, then glanced into the backseat. He chuckled. "If you have a wheelbarrow in the garage, I'll unload your children for you."

Sierra laughed. "I may have to take you up on that offer."

She reached over the seat and tapped each of them. "Come on, sleepyheads. We're home."

As she unlocked the front door, she heard the children thanking Ron for taking them sailing. Clanton asked if they could go again. "Sure," Ron said, a hand on his shoulder. "I'm out as often as I can be when the weather's like this."

As the children shouldered their tote bags and headed down the hallway to their rooms, Ron turned to her again. His mouth tipped slightly as he reached out and lightly brushed her cheek with the back of his knuckles. "You got a little color today."

Ron always knew what to say to make her feel better about herself. "Maybe I'll actually look like a southern Californian one of these days," she smiled, drawn to him.

"You look just fine the way you are, Sierra."

He couldn't have said anything kinder. Bruised and battered by Alex's desertion, she believed herself a complete failure as a wife, as a mother, and as a woman. Looking into Ron's eyes, she saw he valued her. She wanted to thank him for everything—for taking them sailing, for sharing so much of himself with her, for listening, for caring. She felt closer to him than she had felt to anyone in a long, long time.

An inexplicable shiver of alarm raced along her nerve endings at the realization.

His eyes flickered, and the warmth that stirred within her had little to do with sunburn.

He took a slow step back. "I'll see you Monday morning," he said, his smile both casual and tender. He closed the door behind him as he went out.

Disturbed, Sierra frowned, perplexed by her feelings. What had just happened? Was she so desperate to feel like a woman again that she could imagine a man like Ronal Peirozo was attracted to her? Ridiculous! The poor man had only been acting out of kindness and friendship. There was no reason to read anything more into it.

Stepping to the door, she opened it. "Ron!"

He paused halfway down the pathway.

"Thank you," she said, smiling.

"Any time."

Feeling a little better, she stood in the doorway until he got into his Mercedes. He gave her a wave as he pulled away from the curb.

Closing the door, she set the dead bolt. Gathering her things, she headed down the hallway to say good night to the children before she took a shower and went to bed.

Deborah is feverish and complaining of stomach pain.

I asked if she had eaten anything along the way and she says no. She has suffered often of stomach aches when she eats too many berries. The pain seems worse on her right side. I have bedded her down in the wagon where it is less dusty and am sitting with her until the fever lets up. Reese Murphy is looking in on her again in a little while.

I am so afraid and I do not know what I fear most. In the beginning, I thought it was just anger plaguing me. I was wrong. It was fear underneath. I knew what I had back home. I knew the face of my enemy. Out here, I do not know from one day to the next where the danger lies. It could be a fall from a wagon seat or a snake. It could be Indians or sickness. Or being tired unto death.

As tired as I am I know the men have the
worst of it. They are the ones hauling the wagons
across the rivers. They were the ones lowering
the wagons down that dreadful hill. They are the
ones digging the graves. But it is the men too who
dream of Oregon. It is as though Heaven itself
beckons them and we must all cross hell to get to it.

Aphie McKenzie. Harlan Doane. Paul
Colvigne. Three gone already. I think of the hard
trail and how many wagons will pass over these
fine people and never know of their existence.
How many more will we bury before we reach
our destination?

I am afraid for my baby.

I dreamed of Aunt Martha last night. She seemed
so close. We talked as we used to do. I wept when
I awakened. Has she died? Is that why I dreamed
about her? Is that why she seemed so near to me?
Oh, that she were here with me now. The thought
of never seeing her again makes my heart ache
and my throat close up. When my father turned
me out, she took me in and loved me. When I
jilted Thomas, she loved me still. Even when I
said I did not believe in God anymore, she did
not forsake me. She cried but she did not turn
me out. She said she loved me no matter what. I
have never known anyone so good and kind and
constant.

She said she would pray for me every day. I know she is a woman of her word. I think of her every day and feel perhaps in thoughts at least we are still connected.

I wish I could ask her right now to send up prayers to heaven on behalf of my little Deborah. God would listen to her.

Our precious little Deborah is gone from this life. Doc Murphy did no good at all. Neither could Kavanaugh with his Indian medicines. I hope the next life is better. She passed away last night as the sun was setting on the bluffs above us. They look like the ancient ruins of a once wondrous city. I will think of her playing up there with the angels.

I cannot cry. I cannot let myself. If I do, I will never stop.

———————————

16

THE TELEPHONE RANG ON SIERRA'S DESK. Flipping over the page on her notebook, she picked it up. "Good afternoon, Los Angeles Outreach," she said pleasantly, hoping Arlene would return from her dentist appointment soon. The telephone hadn't stopped ringing since she left, and Ron was champing at the bit to get some dictation done.

"Sierra, it's Audra."

Startled, she stammered an innocuous hello, irritation quickly following. What did *she* want?

"How are you?"

How *was* she? "About as well as can be expected."

"Can we have lunch?"

"I don't think so," Sierra said stiffly, surprised that the woman would even ask. What were they going to talk about? Shopping? Audra's charities or the plays she'd seen? Beyond Tomorrow? Alex and Elizabeth Longford?

"Are you really going to throw in the towel?" Audra said.

Sierra's body went hot. "I beg your pardon?" Of all the nerve!

"Your marriage. Are you just going to quit?"

"I don't think it's any of your business."

"Steve asked me to call you."

"Should I care?"

"So much for having any kind of reasonable conversation with you!" There was enough anger in Audra's tone to keep Sierra from hanging up. "Do you think any of us are happy with this situation? It makes me sick! It makes Steve and Matt sick. It's the worst thing that can happen in an office."

So that was it! "What's the matter? Is the work suffering?"

"You could say that. Everyone's suffering."

"Maybe you should talk to Elizabeth about that."

"Elizabeth isn't the problem!"

"Good-bye." Sierra slammed the telephone down, shaking with fury. It rang again in less than ten seconds. Taking a deep breath, she forced herself to be calm and businesslike. "Good afternoon, Los Angeles Outreach."

"Well, that was childish," Audra said. "But then, that's where you excel, isn't it, Sierra?"

Sierra's heart pounded like a war drum. She wanted to hang up on her again, but that was what Audra was expecting. The last thing Sierra intended to do was what Audra expected or wanted. Picking up her pencil, she tapped it on the notepad, trying to calm down, determined to wait her out.

Audra let out her breath. "I should've known you wouldn't listen. I told Steve there was no use in trying to talk to you. You've been hostile from the first second I met you. Every overture I ever made to be your friend was met with a cold shoulder. You always acted as though I was beneath contempt. You've done nothing but criticize me and everyone else at Beyond Tomorrow from the day you arrived. And why? Because you were so determined to stay in your narrow little comfort zone!

"Three years I've watched you wallow in self-pity and keep up your temper tantrum. And it's been something to watch, Sierra. A real show! I can't even count the number of times I've wanted to shake you until your teeth rattled!

"You've made Alex feel guilty over everything, especially the crime of using his talents. God forbid that he should be happy in his work! Not once did you ever think to congratulate him for what he's accomplished. He buys you a house. He buys you a car. Were you ever grateful for anything he did? Did you ever *once* notice how desperate he was to make you happy? You resented anything he did that didn't put you in the center spotlight. You even resent who he *is*. And you're surprised the man turns to another woman!"

Sierra felt cold with shock over Audra's diatribe. She couldn't even think of one word to say in her own defense.

Audra let out a deep breath. "I swore I wasn't going to lose my temper, and now I have. Well, so be it. I called to give you some advice, Sierra. Here's a piece of it. *Grow up!*" Sierra heard the click as Audra hung up. Stunned, she put the receiver quietly back in the cradle. Ron was standing in the doorway. He looked as upset as she felt.

"Why do you keep holding on?" he said softly.

She started to tell him the call wasn't from Alex, but he came over to the desk. "You're not in love with him anymore, Sierra."

Wasn't she? Had she stopped loving Alex? She couldn't fathom the idea. She'd loved him for as long as she could remember.

Ron leaned down and put one hand firmly over hers. "Give him a divorce, Sierra. You don't need him." His eyes were intense, his feelings raw and clear, so clear she couldn't misunderstand what he was telling her.

"I'm back," Arlene said from the doorway to the corridor. Her bright smile died when she saw Ron's hand over Sierra's. Arlene's expression registered shock and embarrassment as she looked between the two of them. "Excuse me," she said, the disturbing question clear in her eyes. "I didn't mean to interrupt. . . ."

"You didn't," Sierra said, snatching her hand from beneath Ron's. She fumbled, banging the file drawer open. "I just had a disturbing call," she said, grabbing her purse.

"Sierra," Ron said, a wealth of feeling in his tone. "Wait a minute. Let's talk—"

"I've got to go," she said, stepping around him. She couldn't look into his eyes. Arlene stepped back so she could go into the hallway.

"Can I do anything to help?" Arlene said, following her. "I don't think you should drive when you're this upset."

"I'll be fine. Really." She pushed open the front glass door with the words Los Angeles Outreach printed in bold black letters. Fumbling with her keys, she ran across the parking lot to her car. Alex's birthday present to her. Audra's words still rang in her ears. She found the right key and opened the door. Sliding in, she slammed it, turned the ignition, threw the car into reverse and then back into drive. She gulped for air, not even bothering to stop to look before she pulled out of the parking lot. Someone blasted their horn just behind her.

Running the yellow light, she turned onto the main thoroughfare and headed for the freeway entrance. The BMW revved loudly as she sailed up the ramp. Another horn blasted, but she was crying too hard by then to notice. She darted between two cars into the second lane, then moved into the third and pressed down even harder on the gas, shooting into the fast lane.

"Oh, God," she said, gripping the wheel. "Oh, God, *God!* I

didn't mean to make such a mess of things!" Choking on a sob, she slammed on her brakes so she wouldn't plow into the Mercedes in front of her. She whipped around to the right, passed it, and shot back into the fast lane.

Where was she going?

What did it matter?

She felt like driving straight off a cliff. Where was the closest one? Mulholland Drive? Maybe the canyons on the road to Malibu would be better.

She wanted her mother, but remembered with a sharp pain that her mother was dead. She needed Alex. No, not Alex. He was gone, too.

"Jesus, oh, Jesus," she cried, dashing tears out of her eyes. She wanted to dump everything at his feet and give up the fight. But how could she do that? What right did she have to ask God's help *now?* "Oh, Jesus, what can I do?"

She could hear a siren but paid no attention, not until a black-and-white highway patrol car pulled up alongside her, lights flashing. Her heart stopped when the officer jerked his thumb for her to pull over.

"Great! Just what I need!"

He slowed, moving in behind her. Traffic gave way as she moved over, lane by lane, until she was driving slowly along the shoulder. She rolled to a stop, put the car in park, and shut off her engine. Then, gripping the steering wheel, she rested her forehead against it and sobbed.

The officer tapped at her window. She had to turn the key before she could lower it. The roar of freeway traffic was deafening. Only the lane closest to them had slowed at all. Just enough so everybody could get a good look at her as they drove by.

Could a person die of humiliation?

Leaning down slightly, the officer looked at her face.

"I'm sorry I was speeding," she said, tears running down her face. She hiccuped, making matters worse. He probably thought she was a drunk on a crying jag.

"Your driver's license and registration please."

Fumbling through her purse, she found her license. The registration was in her glove compartment. As soon as she handed them over, he stepped back, his hand resting almost casually over the handle of his gun. Did he think she was dangerous?

"Get out of the car, please, Mrs. Madrid."

"I haven't been drinking. I swear. I'm not smuggling drugs or firearms—"

"Get out of the car, Mrs. Madrid."

She obeyed, trying to get hold of herself as she did so. She couldn't stop crying. When the officer put his hand firmly beneath her elbow as he closed her car door, she wondered what he thought she was going to do. Try to run away? Where could she go? Into the ice plant? Or was it ivy growing alongside the freeway? She couldn't tell through her tears. It was *green* whatever it was.

Sierra could just see the headlines: "Woman Has Nervous Breakdown on Hollywood Freeway."

She could see herself being hauled away in cuffs.

She cried harder.

Opening the back door of the squad car, the patrolman told her to get in. She had thought things couldn't get worse, but now, on top of everything, she was getting arrested and hauled off to jail for reckless driving! She did think of running into traffic then and putting an end to everything. The officer's fingers tightened slightly as though he read her thoughts and had no intention of letting her get off that easily. "Get in the car, ma'am."

Her thoughts went ballistic as soon as she was in the backseat. Who'd bail her out? She couldn't call Ron. Who'd take care of the children while she was moldering in jail? Alex? Oh, not Elizabeth Longford!

Hunching over, she covered her face and hiccuped more sobs

as the officer got into the front seat and reached for his radio. He said her name and several numbers and then put the speaker back. While he waited for a response, he had her take an alcohol breath test.

"I clocked you at ninety-five," he said, making a note of the test results on his clipboard.

"I'm sorry," she whimpered. "I've had a *very* bad day."

The officer pushed his sunglasses down and looked at her over the rims.

"I know," she moaned. "You've probably heard that excuse a million times, but it's true." She let everything pour out. She told him about nursing her mother through her last weeks of cancer and how much she missed her. She told him about Alex leaving her for another woman the day she got back from northern California. She told him about Clanton getting into fights at school and Carolyn turning into a basket case over her grades. She told him about Audra calling to say it was all her fault.

"Ron was the last straw," she said, sniffling.

He didn't ask who Ron was. In fact, he didn't say anything at all. He just looked at her and listened with that frown on his face.

What was the use? The highway patrolman knew she wasn't drunk, but she'd convinced him she was crazy.

Would he call an ambulance and have her taken away in a straitjacket? Where would they take her? Bellevue? Where *was* Bellevue? His radio crackled. He picked up the speaker. She felt some relief hearing the information given. At least he knew now she had no prior tickets or outstanding warrants for her arrest. She wasn't armed or dangerous, unless flooding his patrol car could be held against her.

Rummaging through her purse, she tried to find a Kleenex, muttering under her breath when she couldn't find one. Her nose was running. Her eyes were running. Her face was a watery mess. Desperate, she took her notepad out, tore out a page, and blew her nose into it.

Grimacing, the patrolman pulled a clean handkerchief out of his pocket and handed it over the seat to her.

"Thanks," she muttered, dabbed her eyes, and blew her nose. She started to hand the handkerchief back.

His mouth tipped up on one side. "You can keep it."

She blushed. "I'll wash it and return it to you." Maybe she'd be working in the laundry section of the jail. Or would she be making license plates? She felt better for having purged herself of everything that'd happened over the past few months, but she doubted that was going to change the consequences of barreling down the highway like a bat out of Hades. She could've killed somebody, not to mention herself. "You can take me in now."

He tipped his sunglasses down again. "Take you in?"

"To the slammer."

His mouth twitched. "I'm not taking you in to the slammer, Mrs. Madrid. I just thought it'd be wise to calm you down before turning you loose on the freeway again."

"But you *are* giving me a ticket."

"Yes, ma'am. I am giving you a ticket." He handed the pad to her and gave her a pen. Sighing heavily, she signed her name at the bottom and handed it back. He tore off the yellow copy and gave it to her. "Sorry to add to your grief."

She sighed. "My first ticket," she said, looking at it dismally. And it was going to cost her plenty. Folding it, she tucked it into her purse.

"Feeling any better?"

She gave a shuddering sigh and smiled. "Yes, but that's not saying much. I'll keep it at fifty-five. I promise."

"Good." He studied her for a moment longer and then got out of the patrol car. Opening the backdoor for her, he offered his hand to help her out.

Shouldering her purse, she looked up at him. He was young, probably no more than thirty or thirty-five. He had kind eyes. "You know what I was doing when you pulled up beside me, Officer? *Praying*. So much for divine intervention." Shaking her head, she started back toward her car.

She had just put the key into her ignition when the patrolman walked up to her car window again. He handed her a small slip of white paper folded in half. "My wife and I'll meet you on the front steps at quarter to ten. Bring your kids. Oh, and pull into traffic easy, Mrs. Madrid. I'll put my lights on and clear the way for you."

"Thanks," she said, confused. She watched him in the side mirror as he walked back to his patrol car.

Opening the slip of paper, she read the name and address of a church.

The trail is clearly marked ahead by the great rock formations.

We passed one a day back that looked like a courthouse with a jail beside it. The one ahead is like a giant funnel set upside down on the prairie.

We ate dust all day. It was our turn to be at the back. Tomorrow we will be at the head.

Water and grass are plentiful. So are the mosquitoes.

I had words with Oren McKenzie today. He was talking about Aphie again and crying with every word he uttered. I lost patience with him and told him he was not the only one who had lost a

279

loved one. I said Aphie would be ashamed of him for his endless carrying on. She was a good and sensible girl and would not think kindly of him if she knew he had not even bothered to give her son a name! He said I do not understand how bad he feels and I said understanding was not what he needed. What he needs is a good hard kick in the backside.

When Oren left our fire, James looked at me and said—It is amazing, Mary Kathryn, how you can see the sins of others so well, and your own not at all. I asked him what he meant. He said Oren has been grieving over the loss of a wife and has only been crying a few weeks while I have been grieving over not having my own way for months. He said—You only know in part, not the whole of his pain. He said I close my ears to anything that does not suit me. I said he was wrong. He said—You closed your ears to me before the first word was out of my mouth about Oregon and why we had to go. He said—It never even occurred to you that this journey is for your own good!

I said what good was there in Deborah dying. I said we should have stayed in Illinois. He said he wished he had left me there. He said he would sooner listen to Oren's weeping than my endless carping.

David Alexander McKenzie was christened by
his father last evening and I am sore ashamed.
James is right. I told Oren I had no right to speak
to him as I did. He said he was glad of it. He
had never held his son before today and doing
so eased the pain of losing Aphie. He said David
looks like her.

It never occurred to me that I could lose James
as easy as I lost my daughter or Oren lost his
sweet wife. Life is so uncertain. I do not know
where James went to spend the night.

When he came back this morning, I told him I
was sorry. It has done no good. The wall I built
up still stands between us.

Kavanaugh sighted buffalo across the Platte
to the north. Joshua insisted on going hunting
with the men. He would give no ear at all to my
fears. He came back a short while ago. Without
so much as a word, he slid off his horse, took a
couple of steps and fell face down on his bedding.
He was covered with so much blood I thought he
had been shot and stripped him like a baby to see
if he was wounded. He will not thank me when
he finds out. Kavanaugh rode up as I was doing
it and laughed. I did not think it funny and told
him so. He said Joshua is unharmed. I asked him
what he had done to my son that he would have
so much blood on him. He said he made Joshua

dress what he killed. He said the boy needed to
learn hunting is not all glory. It is hard work.

I could soak his clothes for a month of Sundays
and not get all the stains out.

We are nooning longer today than usual because
of the terrible heat. The land we are passing
through is fertile for rocks and sagebrush and not
much else. Some of the animals are sick from the
heat.

MacLeod said we will move on in another hour
and keep going until dusk. We will be lucky to
make 15 miles today.

Joshua shot two rabbits. I will stew them for
supper.

Kaiser Vandervert gave whiskey to his oxen.
It seems to perk them up. Had we whiskey left I
would try some myself.

We crossed the Laramie River this morning
and made camp at the fort. There are Indians
camped near by. Kavanaugh said they are
Cheyenne. They are a fine looking people dressed
in buckskins like Kavanaugh and wearing bear
claw necklaces and eagle feathers. The chief is
a handsome fellow. Joshua is impressed with
them. Kavanaugh knows them well and speaks
their language. He took Joshua with him when
he spoke with them. When he came back he said

they are at the fort to trade buffalo hides and
furs for tobacco, sugar, and blankets. We have no
sugar or blankets to spare.

The soldiers have invited us to a dance in the fort
this evening. The men drew lots to see who would
stay behind with the wagons and keep watch.
Ruckel Buckeye, Wells Doane, Oren McKenzie,
Ernest Holtz, and Werner Hoffman lost. Artemesia
is feeling poorly and is remaining behind as well.
Nellie said nothing will keep her away.

James said he will not go. He knows how
much I love to dance. This is just his way of
punishing me.

James is speaking to me again. I did not expect
him to forgive me for another five hundred miles
considering how many it took me to come to my
senses. When he said he did not want to go to the
dance last night, I knew what he meant was he
did not want to go to the dance with me. I said
that was fine by me and went anyway. There is
little enough fun on the trail without giving up
what Opportunity comes along because a man is
pouting. James came later. Of course, he did not
dance with me because he was still mad. I had
partners aplenty with soldiers and MacLeod and
some of the other men traveling with us. I even
danced with Oren McKenzie. I have not had so
much fun since I was engaged to Thomas Atwood

Houghton and considered Acceptable Company in
Galena. James cut in when Lieutenant Heywood
danced with me a third time. He said it was not
proper for me to dance with that soldier again. I
said it was as proper as him dancing four times
with Nellie. He said Nellie is good and married.
I said I am good and married too though my husband appears not to notice. He hauled me outside.

I said—What do you think you are doing, James
Farr? I don't want to leave. I was having fun.

He said to shut up and kissed me the way he
used to do. We went down to the trees along the
river. I am glad the fire has not died in him or me.
I was feeling soft inside and said—I am glad you
have forgiven me, James Farr.

On the walk back, James said—You do not
long for home anymore, do you, Mary Kathryn? I
said I would be lying if I said I did not miss Aunt
Martha and all the rest. I would be lying too if I
said I was pleased with the way things turned out
at the homestead. I told him I accept his decision
and will not CARP anymore. We will wait and
see what there is in store for us in Oregon.

James said Oregon will speak for itself when
we get there. And then he said in a quiet voice—
Or maybe California. I said what do you mean
about California? He said he had been thinking
Oregon might be too crowded in a few years
with the numbers going and we ought to think

about California instead. I could not get air to say anything but he went on real fast telling me that others are talking about it. I said like who? He said Ernst Holtz, Wells Doane, Binger Siddons and Stern Janssen have been mulling it over. I wonder if Nellie knows what is on Wells mind.

James said Kavanaugh has never seen the Pacific Ocean and has a desire to do so. Oh Grand I said. That is good reason for going someplace. Just because you have never been. Just to keep on to the ends of the earth until you have seen it all! Next he will want to see China!

James said—Stop talking, Mary Kathryn—but I had a lot more to say. So he kissed me again. He kissed me hard and for so long I forgot what my upset was about until now that I am writing my thoughts into this journal. When we all went back to the wagons after the dance, we bedded the children down in the tent so James and I could sleep under the wagon together. We slept last night like two spoons in a drawer the way we used to.

I don't have a house or land. But I have my James back and my children. They are home enough.

We all went down to the chalk cliffs. James does not know how to write. So I carved his name next to my own, and then carved Henry, Beth, and

Matthew underneath. I carved Deborah last and a cross next to it. She will not be forgotten.

Joshua ignored my call and climbed up high to carve his name. I was sure he would fall but he would not listen and come down. Kavanaugh said the boy is sure footed as a mountain goat.

Joshua has become so difficult of late. I feel him pulling away from me and James and drawn to Kavanaugh. Kavanaugh encourages him. He told me just the other day that he was not much older than Joshua when he left home and headed west for the first time. I asked him why he left so young. All he said was he had reasons.

I am not ready to let my son go.

James did not leave my side all day today. We walked together while Joshua drove the wagon. I have missed talking with James. He is so full of dreams. I never thought any of them would come to anything but this one of going west has. We will see about the others.

As long as I have James I am safe and happy.

It is so terrible hot. The dust coats all of us. The ground is sandy and makes hard pulling for the oxen. Beth is sick. We made a bed for her in the wagon and she is sleeping. I asked Nellie to pray for her.

Dunham Banks was bad hurt today. A rattle-

snake frightened the horses. His own pitched him
off and he hit his head on a rock. Doc Reese said
his chances are not good. Celia rigged a cradle
and had two men help her rig a big sling inside
her wagon. Baby Hortense and Dunham both
rocked all day while she drove. Celia is a fine
strong girl with good sense. She will need both
for the long haul ahead.

We are Plagued with Tragedy. Little Patricia
Sinnott wandered off this evening and can not be
found. Paralee is crazy with fear that the Indians
have stolen her. Frank Sinnott, James, and four
other men have gone out looking for little Patty.
I have my children near the fire where I can see
them. Joshua is not pleased with staying here
to watch out for us. He said he could ride after
Kavanaugh. The scout would know what to do.
I told him Kavanaugh and Ruckel Buckeye are
hunting game and there is no telling in which
direction they went.

Kavanaugh and Ruckel came back and went out
with the men again. They looked for little Patty
all day and found no trace of her. MacLeod said
we can not stay another day. Paralee says she will
not go on without her little girl. Franklin said it
was her fault the child is lost. It was a harsh, cruel
thing to say and not much different from what I

said to James not long ago. I cringe thinking of
it. Sinnott's son is from his first wife who died.
Paralee is the second wife. She told me a few
nights back Franklin has poured all the money
she inherited into what he is carrying in those
two wagons. Two of his oxen have died already
from pulling the load. It appears to me Franklin
Sinnott is more worried about getting his goods
to Oregon than he is about little Patty lost in the
wilderness.

We made 20 miles today. Paralee did not come
out of her wagon even for the nooning. Everyone
thought she was grieving in quiet. They did not
know until we camped that Franklin had her
tied so she could not get free and gagged her so
she could not cry out. MacLeod is fit to be tied
himself now that he knows what the man did to
his wife. Franklin insists he did it for her own
good. He said she would have run off looking
for little Patty otherwise. Kavanaugh told
Franklin and Paralee yesterday the Cheyenne
do not have their little girl. I sat inside our
wagon and cried. It was what he did not say that
grieved me so. Little Patricia Sinnott is dead.
Everyone but Paralee knows. The nights are
bitter cold and the days hot and dry. The child
had no blanket or water. And there are coyotes
and mountain lions and grizzlys and wolves.

No three year old child could have survived one
night out there.

Nellie asked me to pray with her that little
Patty was taken home to heaven quickly and did
not suffer long. I said I can not remember a time
when God heard anything I said to him. The
last time I tried was for Deborah and look what
came of that. Nellie was shocked and said—God
loves you, Mary Kathryn Farr, and you have got
to believe that. I told her that God loves those
he wants to love and I am not one of his chosen
people. I told her that it was all right because
I have no love for him either.

I did not mean to make her cry.

We are camped near a great rock that looks like
a giant turtle. Almost everyone has carved their
names upon it. Even me. Joshua and some of the
others have climbed to the top.

Devils Gate is not far from here. Joshua is riding over for a closer look. I can see it fine from
where I sit writing in my journal. It looks like a
giant ax cut through the stone mountain to let the
Sweetwater River run through. And sweet water
it is after the muddy Platte. It tastes so good. We
will follow the river west.

James had to shoot one of our oxen yesterday
it was suffering so. Beth is grieving over it. She

asked why everything has to die. I had no good
answer for her. Nellie was sitting with us and said
death is just a door believers walk through to be
with Jesus. Her words did not cheer Beth nor
I. Why does she have to keep on talking about
Jesus? Her words just raise a jumble of questions
and heartache. Beth said Old Tom was just an ox
and how could he know what to believe. Nellie
knew she had raised trouble. Beth said it was not
fair that people go to heaven and animals do not
because animals are nicer than a lot of people.
She is right about that but I could not let her go
on with such thinking. A child needs a little hope
in this world.

I told Beth Aunt Martha read to me about
heaven once and I remember it said the lion
would lie down with the lamb. Nellie said that
was right. She looked it up in her Bible right
there on the spot. And I said I remember Aunt
Martha reading that Jesus would ride down to
earth on horseback. Nellie found that too. I told
Beth there had to be animals in heaven for any
of that to happen. Lions and lambs and horses
maybe Beth said. She wanted to know if Werner
Hoffman would see his dog again in heaven. I
said likely so if Werner could get himself there.

We buried Dunham Banks today. Celia would
not let him be buried in the road. The men dug

as deep as they could but we are going over hard
rocky ground. MacLeod said words over him.
Celia gave baby Hortense to Beth to hold and
started gathering rocks to stack on top of poor
Dunhams grave. I helped her until the job was
done. So did Nellie.

It is dark now and Celia is still sitting by the
mound.

17

SIERRA RECOGNIZED THE HIGHWAY PATROL man even though he was dressed in a Sunday suit instead of a black uniform. He was waiting at the front steps just as he said he would be, and beside him was a young woman holding a baby. He grinned when he saw her.

"Be polite," Sierra said to her own children who stood glumly beside her, annoyed at being dragged off to church. Their father hadn't taken them to Mass more than three times in three years. In fact, the last time they had been inside a church was for their grandmother's memorial service.

"Welcome, Mrs. Madrid," the officer said, extending his hand. "I neglected to tell you my name. I'm Dennis O'Malley, and this

is my wife, Noreen. The bundle she's holding is our son, Sean."
As people moved around them to enter the church, Sierra introduced herself and her children. Rather than be annoyed at them
for blocking a portion of the steps, people smiled warmly.

Over the last several days, since her experience on the freeway, she'd had a growing sense of . . . something. All the pain,
all the crying out, had left her feeling empty. Drained. She had
reached the end of her endurance, the end of her abilities to
deal with the mess her life had become. And yet, much to her
surprise, she wasn't depressed, or hopeless, or any of the things
she'd expected to be. Instead, she felt . . . *directed*—as though a
gentle hand rested on her shoulder and guided her. With love.
She knew whose touch she felt. She'd heard her mother talk
about the "presence of God" more times than she'd cared to listen. But now she understood better. She didn't know exactly
what it all meant, but she was ready. She'd spent enough time
trying to figure things out for herself, and look where that had
gotten her. Now she wanted answers. Real answers.

And for some reason, she felt a certainty that this was the place
where she'd find them.

The O'Malleys ushered them into the church and selected a
pew near the back. Clanton sat on one side of Sierra, muttering,
"What a bore," under his breath. Carolyn sat on her other side.
Dennis sat nearest the aisle, while Noreen sat at the far end of
the pew beside Carolyn and near the outside aisle.

"Just in case I have to leave," she said with a smile. "Sometimes Sean wakes up hungry. He's small but he makes a big
noise." Her blue eyes were full of warmth. Seeing Carolyn's look,
she smiled. "Would you like to hold him?"

"Could I?"

People turned around from the pew in front. Dennis made
more introductions. Everyone was so friendly. They looked
happy to see Sierra and her children, and she felt the oddest sense

of connection, as though she'd finally come home. The feeling was even more poignant when the service began. Everything was so familiar, yet different. It wasn't that the pastor said anything she had never heard before. She had heard the gospel from her mother since she was old enough to remember. Yet now, inexplicably, it all made sense. It filled in the gaps of her life. *Oh!* Her soul sighed. *Ohhhhh.*

The pastor spoke and the words pierced her. Her throat closed even as her heart opened wide. Parched from wandering in the wilderness, she drank in the living water of the Word.

"Why're you crying?" Clanton whispered, embarrassed and worried.

She shrugged, smiling at him. There was no time now to explain how she felt. *Connected.* A part of something tremendous and exhilarating. *Whole.* She tried to stop the tears, but they flowed like cleansing balm. Sorrow poured over and through her, filling her and bringing with it a deep hunger for the Lord. In its wake came hope and reassurance that everything would work out.

Forgive me, Father, for I have sinned mightily against thee. Mea culpa, mea culpa. Oh, God! Oh, God!

How was it possible to feel so *alive* today, when only two days ago she had longed for death?

The congregation rose to sing, and she rose with them, fumbling through the hymnal and mouthing the words when emotion kept her silent. She couldn't read the words or even utter a sound, but it didn't matter. Her heart *sang.* Carolyn stood beside her, oblivious and enthralled with baby Sean in his mother's arms while Clanton, on her other side, fretted, convinced she was going nuts. She uttered a soft laugh and put her arm around him.

"I love you," she whispered.

"Let's *leave,*" he hissed back.

"No, we're staying." Forever.

It was Dennis who served her Communion. She smiled up

at him, remembering what she'd said to him as the traffic had streamed past them on the Hollywood Freeway. *You know what I was doing when you pulled up beside me, Officer?* Praying. *So much for divine intervention.*

God had been intervening, all right. Mightily. He had brought her to a screeching halt on the dusty shoulder of a Los Angeles freeway rather than allow her to hurtle herself off the nearest cliff. And he did it because he loved her and would not let her go.

She almost laughed as realization came, bringing joy with it. She had been standing on sacred ground and hadn't even known it!

"Bless the Lord, O my soul, and all that is within me, bless his holy name . . . ," the congregation sang, and she sang with them, unable to remember a time when she had felt so happy.

"Boy, am I glad that's over," Clanton said on the way home.

"You'd better set your mind to get used to it. We're going back."

"Oh, good!" Carolyn said.

She earned a glare from her brother. "You want Mom blubbering again?"

Sierra smiled at him. "I'll try to contain myself."

Lying in bed that night, Sierra knew she needed to make some changes in her life. Immediate changes. For one thing, she couldn't work for Ron anymore, not knowing how he felt about her. She realized her own feelings for him were confusing. She had always found him profoundly attractive. Several times, she'd thought how much better her life would be had she been married to Ron rather than Alex. That stopped her.

She was too vulnerable right now to think rationally. With Alex gone, she was needy. She was afraid of so many things. Ron was strong and confident. It would be too easy to turn to him for solace. Seeking solace could lead her into an affair.

She was still married. She needed to remember that, despite the present circumstances. For better or worse, Alex was her husband. Until death. Right now, she imagined Alex was wishing for hers. Not that she was feeling particularly fond of him, either. But feelings didn't make any difference.

She didn't want to think about Alex now. She couldn't and continue to feel the sense of comfort and rightness she had experienced this morning. "Do not be anxious for tomorrow," the pastor had read this morning, and here she was obsessing again. She couldn't do anything about Alex or her marriage. But she *could* do something about herself and her circumstances.

Ron looked sick when he came in Monday morning. His eyes were shadowed.

"Can we talk?" she said before he went into his office. He paused and looked back at her bleakly. She didn't have to say a word. He knew.

"You've decided to quit."

She blushed. "I'm sorry. I'll stay until you can find a replacement."

"And feel uncomfortable every minute," he said, expression grim. How odd that this man, after only a few months, could know her better than Alex seemed to know her after thirteen years of marriage. Ron knew her better than anyone, except her mother.

"I knew when you left Friday this would happen. I talked with Judy. She can stand in for you until I find a permanent replacement. What are you going to do?"

"I'm not sure yet. I think I'm going to sell the house." It hadn't even occurred to her until that instant.

"Are you going home to Healdsburg?"

"No," she said, surprising herself again. "I'm not sure what I'll do. I hadn't even thought about it until now."

"You never even guessed how I felt about you, did you?"

"Briefly, but I thought I was being foolish."

"I should've waited a little longer."

She met his gaze, her eyes compassionate. "It wouldn't have made any difference, Ron."

"It would've made all the difference in the world."

Looking into the blue depths of his eyes, she knew he was right. *Thank you, God,* her heart breathed. *Thank you that Ron waited. Thank you for sparing me and Ron from what could have been a terrible mistake. And forgive me. All the while I was casting stones at Alex, I was tumbling into the abyss myself.* "I'm married, Ron."

"Until Alex can find a way out."

His words hurt, for she knew Alex was doing everything he could to gain that end. Every time he spoke with her, he felt the need to drive home two facts: He wasn't coming back, and he didn't love her anymore.

Regret washed over Ron's face. "I didn't say that to hurt you, Sierra."

"I know, but it does."

"I'll call you when it's over." He went into his office and closed the door.

Gathering her things, Sierra left. On her way out, she gave Arlene her ivy plant and a hug.

Instead of going home, she went to the mall. She bought a cappuccino, sat on a bench next to a big fern, and watched the hustle-bustle of people shopping. She supposed she had the qualifications to be a clerk, but was that what she wanted to do? Alex was sending a check once a month to cover expenses, and every time she opened the envelope, she wilted at the sight of his bold signature. Somehow, gut-level, she knew that check wrote her off.

Not once in her life had she supported herself. *Father, can I do this?* she prayed, feeling overwhelmed.

Ask and you shall receive, Daughter.

The assurance washed over her, and she settled back, sipping her cappuccino. She'd told Ron she was putting the house up for sale. She didn't know why she'd said that at the time, but it seemed a good idea now that she thought about it. If she remained where she was, it was certain she'd never be able to handle the finances herself. House payments were bad enough, but add to that the BMW payments and private school for the children and the sum was far beyond any expectations of earnings she might have.

Sierra could see herself living out her life at the mailbox, waiting for whatever money Alex doled out to her. She could imagine his resentment. He adored his children and wouldn't begrudge a dime to them, but every penny he sent for her support would be another matter.

She spent the day wandering in the mall, thinking. When she picked up the children, she took them to their favorite fast-food restaurant. "I've decided to sell the house," she told them, knowing her announcement was abrupt, but unable to think of any other way to break the news of her decision to them.

"Are we going home to Windsor?" Clanton said.

"No. We're going to look around San Fernando Valley and see what we can find near the church. We might even look at condominiums. There's a complex just down the street. I saw a swimming pool and tennis courts. We'll have to see what we can afford."

"Can we still go to the same school?" Carolyn said.

"No, honey. It's too expensive." She didn't want to ask Alex for any more money than she had to. "It makes more sense to go to a school in your own neighborhood."

"So I won't get to see Pamela?"

"You can see Pamela as often as we can arrange it, and you can call her whenever you want."

Sierra prayed that night, frightened by the speed with which

299

her life was changing, but in the morning, she stepped out in faith and called Roberta Folse. She explained Alex had signed the house over to her before leaving her. Roberta was sympathetic but warned her not to expect a profit.

"You haven't been in the house long enough to build much equity, Sierra."

"We decorated. Maybe that'll help."

"You'll be lucky to break even. And then you're going to have to pay capital gains out of whatever you do get if you don't reinvest in something of equivalent or higher value in eighteen months. Is there any chance Alex will come back?"

"No."

"If he's keeping up the payments, you might do better staying where you are. I'd love a commission, Sierra, but not at the expense of your well-being. Why don't you take a few more days to think things over and give me a call in another week or two?"

Sierra did take a few more days. She prayed over it. She talked to Dennis and Noreen and got their opinion. The answer seemed clear. She needed to stand on her own two feet, trust the Lord, and stop depending on Alex. She called Roberta again.

Roberta came over the following afternoon.

"Oh, my word!" she said upon entering the house. "You didn't tell me Bruce Davies decorated your living room."

Roberta's remark absolved any doubts Sierra had ever had about Bruce Davies leaving his own stamp on everything he did. "Not just the living room, Roberta. The entire house."

"The *entire* house?"

"Yes."

"That must have cost you a bundle." Roberta sat down on the dark brown leather couch and put her briefcase carefully on the thick glass-topped table.

Sierra grimaced, seeing how Roberta stared at the muraled wall with a perplexed expression. It was one of the reasons she usually avoided the living room. "It's one of Alex's video games," she said.

"I'd swear there's someone watching me."

"There is. Actually, if you look at it long enough, you'll see six men and one woman hiding in that jungle. It's called Camouflage. If I turn out the lights, their eyes glow red."

"How much did you put into decorating the house?"

Sierra told her.

"We'll add ten thousand to that and see what happens."

Roberta called Saturday morning. "Be sure you take a look at the *Los Angeles Times* tomorrow morning."

Sierra forgot all about it until Carolyn came in the next morning while she was blow-drying her hair. "Daddy's on the phone," she said and held out the portable.

Surprised, Sierra shut off the dryer and took the phone, wondering why he was calling her so early on a Sunday. "Yes?"

"Is that our house on the cover of the real estate section?"

She could feel the heat of his anger through the wires. It all but melted the telephone in her hand. Her defenses rose. She almost reminded him he'd signed the house over to her, so it wasn't *their* house anymore. It was *her* house. Instead, she managed a mild, "Yes, it is."

"What do you think you're doing?"

"I can't stay here, Alex. It's too—"

"You're not selling that house."

"I have to move, Alex. I've thought it all over and—"

"You have to move where?" he sneered. "To Healdsburg so I'll never see my children again! Over my dead body, Sierra! You hear me?" He swore at her in Spanish. He used a word so foul her face heated.

"I hear you, Alex, but I'm not—"

He didn't give her the chance to get further than that. Cursing again, he blistered her with the same accusations Audra had leveled at her a few weeks earlier, only adding personal and private faults on top. If Audra's words had shocked, Alex's battered and bruised. He meant to annihilate her, and he was doing a good job of it. He spoke in Spanish, which made it all the worse. He never spoke Spanish unless his emotions were out of control. Unfortunately, she understood every single word he said.

"I've called my attorney," he said, falling back into crisp English again. "I'm going to fight you, Sierra. No matter what it takes, I'm not letting you walk away with my children. I'm sick of this situation. I'm sick of *you!*" He told her she could hold her breath until Hades froze over before he'd send her another dime. "It's bad enough Clanton won't talk to me. Now you think you can put four hundred miles between me and my daughter!"

He took a breath, and into that brief space of time Sierra said with miraculous calm, "We aren't moving north, Alex."

"Where then? East? New York, maybe? That's three thousand miles instead of four hundred. Or Hawaii. Right! Hawaii. That's it. That'd put an ocean between us!"

The storm of his anger blew about her like a tornado around a bruised reed. "I'm hoping to buy a condo in Northridge."

Silence.

She looked in the mirror and wondered how much makeup it would take to put color back in that stranger's face. Looking away, she swallowed hard before she tried to say anything else. "I have to go," she said quietly, trying to keep her voice steady. "Church starts in less than an hour." She took a slow breath, squelching the desire to cry. She had cried enough over the past few years. Buckets of tears. Mostly for herself. "Alex, I promise you'll know everything as we do it. Clanton and Carolyn will never be out of your reach. I promise."

Pressing the button, she set the telephone on the bathroom

counter. Nauseated, she thought about going back to bed and pulling the covers up over her head. But what good would that do?

Three years I've watched you wallow in self-pity and keep up your temper tantrum. It's been something to watch, Sierra. A real show!

Shuddering, she turned her thoughts to Dennis and Noreen and a dozen others who welcomed her and the children every Sunday. She had a choice. She could stay home and do exactly what Audra and Alex would expect her to do, or she could finish getting ready and go to church. She could learn something and, with God's help, start putting her own life back in order.

The house sold the first week. Full price.

When escrow closed thirty days later, the check Sierra received looked like an obscene amount of money. It dwindled fast when she sent half of it to Alex, made a 20 percent down payment on a modest three-bedroom condominium in Northridge, and paid her capital gains taxes out of what remained. If it weren't for her inheritance, she wouldn't have qualified for a loan in the first place. As it was, most of her assets were tied up in the Mathesen Street house in Healdsburg.

The telephone rang while Sierra was in the kitchen packing boxes. She avoided answering the telephone whenever possible. Alex had called several times during the past month. Luckily, Carolyn always flew to the phone when it rang, hoping it was her father. Clanton never picked it up, for the same reason. Carolyn spent two Saturdays a month with Alex, but she never said much about their day together. And Sierra didn't ask any questions.

"It's Daddy," Carolyn said now, holding the portable phone out to her. "He wants to talk to you." The hope in her eyes made Sierra want to weep.

"Thanks, honey." She took the phone, knowing exactly why he had called. She hadn't spoken with him since he'd read her the riot act over putting the house up for sale in the first place, and this conversation was destined to be no more pleasant.

"Why'd you send this check to me?" Alex said hotly.

Her heart gave a flip at the sound of his voice. "It's your half of the proceeds from the house."

"I signed the house over to you. Remember?" He sounded bitter about it.

"I remember, but I didn't feel right about keeping all the money."

"That's a big surprise. It never bothered you to keep my money before. Why change now? And while we're on the subject, why'd you send my check back last week?"

"Because you said you'd never send me another dime, and I thought I'd hold you to your word."

He spat a short, foul expletive. "So what are you going to do, Sierra? Make the kids eat at the local mission?"

"I have a job."

"Yeah, right. Working for Ron Peirozo at Los Angeles Outreach. I don't imagine it pays much."

"I don't work there anymore."

"Got fired, huh? Well, six months is something, I guess. That's longer than any other job you've held in your life."

Pushed to the limit by his scathing sarcasm and condescension, she almost blurted out the truth. *I left because Ron is in love with me and wants me to forget about you, to leave you in the dust like you've left me! He wants to be with me! He wants to marry me, Alex. He's a millionaire and he wants me! I left because it was the right thing to do, not that you care!*

But she didn't. He wouldn't believe her anyway. As much as he hated her, he'd find it impossible to think any other man would find her attractive or intriguing. And she wasn't about to humiliate herself by trying to convince him.

What does the Lord require of you?

She could hear the verse as clearly now as she'd heard it on Sunday, when the pastor had read it—and it brought her thoughts to an abrupt halt. What did the Lord require? Justice, kindness, humility . . . yet here she was, wandering down the familiar path of bitterness and self-pity again.

She drew a steadying breath. *Lord, I hurt him. I know I did. Please forgive me. I can't tell him I'm sorry right now because he won't listen, but you know how I feel. You know what I did to start this war. I don't want to be part of it anymore.*

"So, what are you going to do?" Alex demanded when she made no response to his last insult.

"I'm going to be a secretary in an insurance agency."

"You'll last two weeks, tops."

"Is that an estimation of my abilities or of how boring the industry is?" she said, trying to instill some lightness into her tone.

"Take a wild guess."

His meaning couldn't be more clear.

"I'll send you another check, Sierra. You'd better hang on to this one. You'll need it."

Hot, bitter anger swept over her, surpassing hurt and obliterating wisdom. "I have a better idea, Alex. Don't send the check. *Eat it!*" The words were out before she even knew they were coming. They passed her lips, flying up from her heart and roosting like vultures in the charged air, pecking at her head. She slammed the phone down, more angry with her own lack of control than with Alex's contemptuous laugh.

When a check did arrive in the mail two days later, it came in an envelope with an embossed return address that read Madrid/Longford. She tore up the envelope and check and flushed both down the toilet. She'd stand out on a street corner holding a sign that said Homeless and Hungry before she'd take another nickel from Alejandro Luís Madrid.

Pride did have its place, didn't it? What had she just heard at the last Bible study? Those who won't work, won't eat. Well, she'd work *and* eat. And so would her children. Whatever money Alex sent for the children would go in their college funds.

Dennis and several other men from the church helped her move into the condominium. The complex was within walking distance of the church, and Dennis invited Clanton to play baseball when they finished unloading the pickup trucks. "We've got a team, but we're short some outfielders. Do you think you could help us out?"

"Sure. Easy!" Clanton looked more eager than Sierra had seen him in a long time.

"As soon as we get all this stuff lugged inside, we'll head on down to the field. Can he stay out until nine, Mom?" Dennis said, winking at her over one end of a couch he was carrying.

"I'll have to fix him some dinner first."

"We can get McDonald's."

"Great!" Clanton said, before she could respond. He dumped the box he was carrying onto the top of a coffee table and ran back for another.

"Mom!" Carolyn said, running up, her face flushed with excitement. "Susan lives here. Susan from church! She lives in the condo just down from us. See! Right over there. Can you believe it? Can I go play with her? *Please."*

Susan's mother, Frances, came over an hour later. Clanton and the men had gone, leaving Sierra surrounded by boxes. Frances surveyed the chaos. "Why don't you join us for dinner?"

Removing the newspaper wrapping, Sierra set another plate into the built-in dishwasher. She brushed damp tendrils back from her face and glanced around at the unpacked boxes, Mary Kathryn's trunk, the furniture dumped anywhere and nowhere in particular. It would take her all night to get half the unpacking done.

"Believe me," Frances laughed. "It'll still be here when you come back. Susan and I can help."

By the time Sierra had finished her spaghetti, Frances had talked her into joining the choir. "It only makes sense," Frances said. "We meet on the same night as the youth group. We can walk down with the children, stay for practice, and walk back with them at nine."

"What if I can't carry a tune?" Sierra laughed.

"Then you'll just have to make a joyful noise!"

The telephone was ringing when she unlocked the front door and switched on the lights later that evening. Carolyn ran to the kitchen and answered it. Sierra could tell by the look on her daughter's face that it was Alex. She watched Carolyn hop up on a stool as she began telling her father everything that had happened that day. She sounded so happy and excited.

"Oh, and Mom's joined the choir. She's going to be practicing the same night Susan and I go to youth group. Susan? She's a friend from the church. She lives in a condo right down the path from us." She listened for a moment, her excitement dimming slightly. "He's not here, Daddy. He's playing baseball with Mr. O'Malley. Dennis is so neat! He leads the youth group, and he's a highway patrolman. He met Mom when he pulled her over on the freeway for speeding. You should see his baby. Sean is so cute, and Noreen lets me hold him in church."

Sierra went into Carolyn's bedroom. So much for keeping a few secrets, she thought, taking the sheets from a box. She made up Carolyn's bed, and then went into Clanton's room and made up his bed. Carolyn was still talking when Sierra went into her own bedroom and began making up her own bed, the one she'd slept in all through her growing-up years in Healdsburg.

She smoothed the comforter and plumped the pillows. Leaning against the bedpost, she looked around the room.

She'd had to get rid of the king-size bed she'd shared with Alex. After measuring the master bedroom, she'd realized it would fit but leave little room for anything else. Giving it up had been difficult. She'd mentioned it to Melissa during their last telephone conversation, and two days later her brother had called and said he was shipping her canopy bed from home.

She touched the lace covering that her mother had crocheted for her; it had taken her a year to complete it. Sierra remembered the joy she'd felt when she opened the big box on Christmas morning and found the lace folded in among sheets of lavender tissue paper. She'd been sixteen and madly in love with Alex.

Her eyes welled with tears. How many nights had she lain in this bed dreaming of what it would be like to be married to Alejandro Luís Madrid? He had been her Prince Charming. Ten years she'd known what it was like to be loved and fulfilled by a man of passion. Ten years of heaven, followed by three years of descending into hell.

God forgive her, she'd been the one to take the first step down.

The front doorbell rang. "Mom! Can you get it?" Carolyn called, unwilling to relinquish the phone.

When she opened the door, Sierra found Clanton covered with grass stains and dirt from head to foot and grinning from ear to ear. "I hit a home run, Mom! Man, you should've seen that ball fly!"

Dennis was behind him, looking pleased. "It wouldn't have been a home run if I hadn't tripped over my feet," he said in mock annoyance, "and you hadn't run like a rabbit."

"We're playing against the Baptist church on Saturday," Clanton said, entering the living room and tossing his dirty glove onto a pile of clean clothes that had yet to be put away. "I'm playing shortstop."

"You were supposed to ask your mother's permission," Dennis said, snatching Clanton's hat off. "Remember?"

"Mother may I?" Clanton grinned.

She laughed. "Yes, you *may.*"

Carolyn slid off the kitchen stool. "Daddy wants to talk to you," she said, holding the telephone receiver out to Clanton.

Clanton's expression changed immediately. He stared at the telephone as though it were a cockroach he wanted to squash. "Tell him I'm taking a shower!" he said loud enough for Alex to hear and stalked down the hall. He went into the bathroom and slammed the door. Sierra heard the click as he locked it.

Dennis gave her a grim look as Carolyn relayed the message. "I can see we have some work to do," he said softly. He tossed Clanton's hat onto a stool.

"A lot of work."

"I'd better get home before Noreen sends out a search party." Sierra walked with him to the door and thanked him for including Clanton in the adults' baseball practice.

"He's a great kid, Sierra," Dennis said.

"He's an angry kid."

"He's got reason. A lot of times it's not in our power to forgive someone who has hurt us. We have to ask God's help."

Words for her to think about as well, she thought as she closed the door.

She tried to talk to Clanton when he got into his bed. "Would you please talk to your father the next time he calls?"

"Why should I?"

"Because it'd make things easier on me," she said, hoping that would make some difference. "He thinks I've turned you against him."

"I'll talk to him," Clanton said, eyes blazing with the same fierce anger she'd seen in Alex's the last time he'd spoken to her face-to-face before walking out. "I'll tell him he's full of—"

She put her hand lightly over his lips to stop the flow of angry words. Clanton clearly had some of her faults as well as Alex's. "Please," she whispered. "I'm not without fault in all this, Clanton. Try to understand." She bit her lip, trying to find words to explain. If she cried, that would only make matters worse. She stroked his cheek tenderly. "Your father loves you very much."

His mouth worked. "If he loved me, he wouldn't have left," he said and turned over on his side so she couldn't see his face. She didn't have to. Her heart felt like a hot ball of pain inside her.

"His leaving had nothing to do with you, honey. I was angry for so long about having to move, and I took it out on Daddy. He got tired of it."

Clanton turned his head slightly and looked at her. "Do you still love him?"

Tears did come then, but she smiled, combing his hair back from his forehead. Dark hair just like Alex's. "He's your father, honey. How could I not?" She took his hand. "What he's done isn't right, Clanton, but I wasn't right either. Looking back, I can see so many things I did wrong."

"You never did anything wrong."

"Yes, I did. I wanted things to be *my* way." She stroked his cheek, aching for the pain she saw in his eyes. Hate and love were so closely linked. "If you can't forgive him for your sake, honey, will you forgive him for mine?"

Clanton rolled over again. He had always been stubborn. Just like her. Just like Alex.

Heart aching, she stood and straightened the covers over his shoulders. "I love you, Clanton." Leaning down, she kissed his temple. "So does your father."

We are at the top of the Rocky Mountains!

We did not even know it until we saw the water was running west. The climb was so slow and gradual and then this great expanse before you so you know you are on top of a great range. It is cool and dry and windy right now. But it was a long hard day of travel.

Kavanaugh and Joshua shot three antelope. They are good eating. I am so proud of him!

We crossed the Big Sandy and laid by to rest our oxen. I did wash. Artemesia joined me at the riverbank. She was a robust woman when we started and is now so thin a breeze could blow her over. She says she feels much better. She does not look it.

The last week has been hard going through dark hills and deep ravines and narrow passes. We have crossed creeks and fixed broken wagons. One of the oxen died last night and the wolves kept up a constant howling. I did not sleep much. Tonight is not much better with the mosquitoes buzzing and Henry and Matthew fighting with each other. I have to sit a while and write something or I will crack their heads together.

Beth was feeling poorly again today. The fever

comes and goes. I gave her some quinine and bedded her down for the night.

I am wearing new moccasins and pleased with the feel of them. My shoes were worn through and Henry is wearing my boots. Kavanaugh traded with a Cheyenne squaw and gave them to James to give to me. James offered him a dollar for them but he would not take it. He said it was payment for the suppers he has shared with us.

James has sent the boys to bed. The quiet is nice with the crickets chirping and the sky so starry. James is on first watch tonight.

Cal Chaffey is playing his mouth organ again. It is a mournful tune tonight. The wolves like it. They are joining in.

Paralee Sinnott has torn the sheets.

She was feeling poorly this morning, but Franklin made her drive the wagon just the same. She pulled out of line twice. By the end of the day she was at the back eating dust. We had made camp by the time she drove in. When she came in Franklin asked her where his son was and she said she shot him back in the road and left him for dead. Franklin Sinnott rode off fast as he could to go looking for him. As soon as he was out of sight, Paralee got down off her wagon calm as you please and set fire to his wagon full of goods to sell. It took flame so fast all we could do was pull the two wagons nearest out of the circle so they would not catch fire as well. Paralee just stood there with her arms crossed watching everything go up in smoke.

Franklin came back quick when he saw the smoke. When he saw what she had done, he come down off his horse like a wild man and hit her twice before MacLeod laid him out good and proper. Franklin lay there crying over his broken nose and dead son and calling her a crazy woman.

And right then young Frank rode in with a string of trout hanging off his saddle. He said Paralee sent him fishing.

We are laid by at Soda Springs and will stay over Sunday. Everyone has drunk from the springs. Some like it fine as it is. I did not like it much until I added sugar. Then it was tolerable good.

We are all in sore need of rest. It was hard pulling through mountains and crossing creeks. We have plenty of grass and wood here. Kavanaugh took Joshua hunting. James is annoyed. He needed Joshua to help him make repairs on the wagon but Joshua was off before we knew he was going. Joshua would rather ride point and hunt with Kavanaugh than drive our wagon or repair it. So Hank and Matthew are helping.

It is pretty here. I would be content to stop and sink in roots. James said I will like California better.

I am filled with sadness. When we pull out day after tomorrow, we will be taking the road to California. Most will be heading on to Oregon. I am thankful Wells and Nellie are going with us. Nellie is the closest thing I have to a sister and reminds me of Aunt Martha.

Oren McKenzie and Celia Banks have teamed up. Celia put the idea in Oren's head and he was agreeable. She has milk enough for baby David and her own little Hortense and she needs a man to help her work the land she is going to claim in Oregon. They will not marry until they have their allotments. Once they claim their 160 acres, they will tie the knot and have 320 acres together. She is a smart girl.

Winifred Holtz is grieving something awful. She loves little David as though he were her own. Celia wept with her and said she will not take him from her until all is settled in Oregon.

MacLeod led the wagons north toward the Snake River this morning. We and the Doanes, Stern Janssen, Ernst Holtz, and Binger Siddons pulled

out at the same time heading south. Nellie has
cried the whole day. She is crying still as I sit
and write in my journal. Wells keeps telling her
the going will be easier to California but I can
tell by Kavanaugh it will not. Robert and LeRoy
are glad to not be separated from Henry and
Matthew. Beth is mourning over not seeing baby
Hortense again. I almost told her I would be
having a baby in the spring but I thought it better
not to. I am feeling poorly and may lose it. And
I should tell James before anybody else.

Kavanaugh is going with us to California. I am
glad of his company. He said he has not been over
this land before but has heard much about it. He
said the next eight hundred miles will be harder
than anything we have traveled over before.

James says that means fewer people will come.

We crossed Raft River and have come as far as
a City of Rocks. We will rest here a day before
going on. Beth and I have made a game of seeing
things in the rock formations. Some are hundreds
of feet high. We have made out the shapes of
turtles and rabbits. Henry pointed out a group of
rocks that look like an eagle.

Joshua said he has no interest in childish games
and rode off. Now I see he has climbed up on one
section and is painting his name in axle grease
high up for all to see.

It has been hard pulling since we left the City of Rocks. Kavanaugh said Humboldt Wells is still a day away.

I wish we had gone on to Oregon.

We are nooning three hours during the hottest time of day and then traveling on until the sunset. The dust has been bad. We fan out, but the winds keep us from escaping it. Nellie is sick from the alkali dust. I am so sunburned I look like an Indian.

The children keep asking how long it will take to get to California. James lost his temper and said we will get there when we get there and if they ask again he will take his belt to them. He has no patience with this Heat and the Hard Labor. The roads are heavy.

I think he is wishing we had gone on to Oregon.

We came over mountainous roads today and reached Thousand Spring Valley. We are camped by good water. Joshua has taken the horses to good grass. Henry has gone with him to cut and bundle grass to take with us. I am too tired to write more.

We are laid by at Humboldt Wells. We will stay an extra day here. The animals need rest. So do we all. Grass and water are plentiful. It is pretty and there is shade.

Kavanaugh does not say much about what is ahead. His silence fills me with disquiet. If the going was easy he would tell us so. Summer has its heavy hand upon us.

Joshua asked me who his father is. I said James but he said he means his Real father. I asked him why he wanted to know and he said he had wondered about it for a long time. He said Clovis told him I had him with me when I came to live with Aunt Martha. I told him James was the only father he ever had. He was not satisfied. He said a man has to know where he comes from. So I told him my brother Matthew McMurray married Sally Mae Grayson and he is her child. He wanted to know what happened to her and I told him she died giving birth to him. Then he wanted to know what happened to his father. I said he died too. He wanted to know how and I said what difference does it make. He is dead. Joshua got mad and wanted to know why it was so hard for me to tell the truth. I said I had never lied to him or anyone. I said it was hard talking about people I loved who were gone. I said the past did not matter anyway because he is as much my son as Henry and Matthew. He said he is not. I did not think words could hurt so much. I told him I have loved him from the moment I helped bring him into the world.

317

He did not ask more after that. He just looked at me like he knew there was more than what I was telling him.

Joshua rode on ahead. I am afraid for him. James said he has common sense and Kavanaugh will watch out for him. I am afraid for other reasons.

Stern Janssen lost a wheel today. The wood had gotten so dry the spokes fell out. James is helping him fix it. They have taken the wheels off and are soaking them overnight in the Humboldt.

Joshua is not back. Kavanaugh said he saw him and he is well but not ready to come back.

We have fallen into the practice of gathering and supping together. Nellie has been feeling poorly and I have been cooking. The men give me what I need of their supplies to stretch the meal for all of us. While I cook, Nellie reads from her Bible and the men make what repairs need doing on the wagons. The children are too tired and cranky to get into much trouble.

Joshua killed two rattlesnakes before the oxen were even unyoked. Kavanaugh said they are good eating. I told him he could fry and eat them both with my good wishes. He did just that and Joshua joined him.

The oxen were too tired to be frightened by the snakes but Beth is in the wagon and will probably stay there until California. I may join her. The boys are bedded down under the wagon with James.

We had trout for supper. Binger caught enough for all of us.

Joshua is on guard tonight with Wells.

We passed more dead cattle today. We are using sage for fuel.

Kavanaugh said there is another company of wagons twelve or so miles ahead of us. I am glad to know there are others ahead and surviving.

Passed two dead oxen today.

The sand is deep and very heavy on our teams.

Wells got stuck and we had to use our oxen to pull him free. The grass is very poor but the water is plentiful. The skies are clouding up. I can hear the rumble of thunder in the distance.

It would be nice to have a break in the awful heat.

Our oxen scented water and went wild trying to get to it. We turned all but one and it drank from alkaline water. James and I doctored it. James held the animal while I poured grease down its throat. Beth is watching over it now and praying it will survive.

The milk cow has gone dry. We may have to use her to pull if we lose another ox. I expect we will because we have passed a dozen carcasses in the last four days.

We passed a grave today. Tobias Wentworth.
   Binger lost another ox.

Nellie said we are wandering like the Israelites in the desert. The land is cruel and the heat unrelenting. We are pulling out with first light and stopping when the sun is high. We wait a couple of hours in whatever shade we can find and then go on until sunset. But even then the going is so hard I sometimes want to lay down and die and have done with it.
   Maybe we are like the Israelites. God watched them die on the edge of the Promised Land.

The Humboldt has drained away into nothing. Kavanaugh just told us we got forty miles of desert ahead of us.
   I do not think I can make it.

Stern Janssen's wagon was so deep mired in sand he had to unharness the oxen and leave it. We

pulled three oxen out but the other just laid down
and died.

Nellie is so sick from the heat she is riding inside
their wagon. Wells is afraid she is going to die.

   If this desert does not kill us all, the mountains
I see ahead surely will.

———————————

18

SIERRA SWUNG THE BAT AND FELT THE HARD impact of the ball. Dropping the bat, she ran for first base.

"Go! Go!" the base coach said, urging her on.

"Run, Sierra! *Run!*" others shouted from the stands as she crossed second.

"Come on, Mom!" Clanton hollered, jumping up and down near third and waving her on. "Go for it! Go for it!"

She rounded third and headed for home. The second baseman caught the ball from the center fielder and was turning to zing it toward home plate. She knew she'd never make it before the ball did. "Oh, Lord, help!" she said. Clanton would never forgive her if she made the last out. Giving it everything she had, she charged ahead, dropping at the last second just as the catcher caught the ball. She plowed right into him, knocking him off his feet. The ball bounced off her helmet as he came down in a heap on top of her.

"Safe!" the umpire shouted amidst exuberant laughter.

"That's the way to do it!" Dennis was laughing as he ran over from his position as coach.

She and the catcher untangled themselves. "What do you think this is, Madrid? The World Series? Or professional wrestling, maybe?"

Rolling over, she made it to her hands and knees. "Sorry, Harry. You OK?"

"I will be in a minute," he said, flopping over onto his back, arms and legs splayed.

"Don't worry about Harry." Dennis grinned, giving her a hand up. "He's tougher than he looks. He just likes playing for sympathy."

Harry raised his head off the ground and scowled. "You taught her to slide, didn't you, O'Malley."

"My father taught me," Sierra informed him, laughing. She brushed herself off as her team surrounded her and began beating the dust off with their hats and pounding her back with congratulations.

Harry got up and pulled off his catcher's mask. "I tell you, there ought to be a regulation against plowing your elders down like bowling pins."

"Batter up!" the umpire shouted.

As Sierra headed for the bench with her teammates, she heard Carolyn calling her. "Mom! Mom!" Turning, she walked backward and waved. Her heart leaped as she saw Alex sitting in the grandstand next to Carolyn. Where had he come from?

The last inning of the game passed in a blur. She couldn't pay attention. She hadn't seen Alex in six months or talked to him in two. Her heart was hammering. Her palms were sweating.

Shame filled her. He couldn't stop by the condominium, could

he? No. Of course not. He had to come to a baseball game looking as if he'd stepped out of *Gentleman's Quarterly* and see her
wearing faded Levi's and covered in dirt and grass stains. No
makeup. Her hair tumbling down. Dirt under her fingernails and
in her teeth after sliding home. Perfect timing. She blew a strand
of hair out of her eyes.

"You OK?" Dennis said, putting his hand over hers.

"Alex is here."

"I wondered who that guy was sitting beside Carolyn."

"Did you happen to notice when he arrived?"

"About two minutes before you went up to bat."

"Great," she muttered, thinking of how she must have looked
plowing poor old Harry down at home plate.

Dennis glanced over at the stands. "Did Clanton know he was
coming?"

"*I* didn't know he was coming." She took a deep breath, blowing it out through pursed lips, trying to slow her ricocheting
pulse. "Kick me if I cry, Dennis. Kick me *hard.*"

"You cry and I'll haul you off to the slammer."

She laughed.

The team gathered in a circle and gave a cheer for the Lutherans
they'd been playing. "We only lost by two runs," Clanton said as
Sierra put her arm around his shoulders. "We'll get them—" She
knew the instant he spotted his father. His whole body went rigid.

"It's OK," she said softly.

Alex was holding Carolyn's hand as he walked toward them.
He was looking straight at his son. He didn't even spare a glance
at her.

Sierra noticed he'd lost weight, but then, so had she over the
past six months. Fifteen pounds, to be exact. Thankfully in all
the right places.

"I'm going to help Dennis put the gear away," Clanton said
and started to turn away.

She gripped his shirtsleeve. "You will not."

"I don't have anything to say to him."

"Then you'll listen."

Alex looked between them as he came closer. It was hard to miss the fact that she and her son were having a slight difference of opinion. He did look at her then, his eyes narrowed and suspicious. What did he think she was doing? When he stopped in front of them, his eyes flicked over her mussed hair, dusty T-shirt and pants, right down to her scuffed tennis shoes. Her face filled with heat. One side of his mouth tipped. "Good hit."

"Thanks," she managed, feeling dismissed.

Courtesy dispensed with, he looked at his son. "You played well out there, Son." When Clanton didn't say anything, she saw a muscle tighten in Alex's cheek. But it wasn't anger. It was hurt. He looked more vulnerable than she'd ever seen him.

God, please, don't let Clanton say anything cruel. Please.

Clanton didn't say anything. He just stood beside her, rigid and silent, her champion.

"What do you say I take you out for a hamburger?" Alex said.

Clanton uttered a soft laugh, glaring up at his father. "The team's going out for pizza," he said coldly and looked away.

"Why don't you join us?" Sierra said impulsively.

Clanton shot a look at her that would have withered an oak. "He doesn't play baseball," Clanton said. He looked at Alex again. "He plays around with other women."

Alex's face went dark red.

Sierra didn't know if he was embarrassed or ready to explode with rage.

"You're such a jerk, Clanton!" Carolyn said, her mouth trembling.

"Shut up! What d'you know?"

"I know more than you do!" she said, her blue eyes filling

with tears. "Elizabeth said—" She broke off, paling at the look on Clanton's face.

"You little Judas!"

Sierra could feel the blood draining out of her face. Was *that* where Alex took their daughter on Saturdays? On excursions with his mistress?

Clanton took a step toward his sister. "Why don't you move in with *them*, you little—"

"That's enough, Clanton," Alex said, steel in his voice. He barely spared a glance at Sierra, and she was glad of that. The last thing she wanted was for him to see how much it hurt to know Carolyn had been spending time with Elizabeth Longford. "You'd better learn to accept things as they are."

"I don't have to *accept* anything, least of all *you*. You're a cheat and a liar, and I wish you and your girlfriend were *dead!*" He took off across the baseball field toward Dennis and the other members of the team.

"Mom?" Carolyn said, tears running down her cheeks.

"I'll go after him," she said quietly, eager to escape before she made a fool of herself or said something she'd regret. She headed toward her teammates, swallowing the hot tears that were choking her.

"Mom!" Carolyn cried out. She made to follow Sierra, but Alex was holding her hand. "Let go!" she said, sobbing, and pulled free of her father to run to Sierra. "Are you mad at me, Mom?" Tears ran down her cheeks. "Do you hate me?"

"No," Sierra said, kneeling and pulling her close. She stroked her hair and kissed the top of her head. "I just wish things were different, that's all."

"I didn't mean to hurt you. I only talked to her the one time. I—"

"Shhh . . . I love you very much, and nothing will ever change that." She tipped her daughter's chin and gave her a shaky smile.

"You go have fun with your father while I talk to Clanton. I'll see you later at home." She kissed her.

"Clanton's so mean."

"No, honey. He's hurt. People say awful things when they're hurt." Just as she had. Just as Alex had. Poor Clanton. What chance did he have of being any better than they'd been? "You tell your father how much you love him. He needs to hear that. Now, go on."

"Sierra," Alex called. "Wait a minute." She recognized that tone and wished she could just keep walking. If not for what she'd just said to Carolyn, she'd run. She was reeling inside, her stomach quivering, her eyes hot with tears. She didn't need a lecture from Alex about what a lousy mother she was or what a lousy wife she'd been.

He looked at her, and she saw something flicker in his eyes. "Where's the team going? We'll meet you there."

No respite for the wicked. Not even privacy to have a good, long cry. "Three blocks down in the shopping center," she said, forcing herself to speak evenly. "I'll do what I can, Alex, but I can't promise. . . ." She shook her head and turned away, resigning herself to a painful evening.

Dennis did some long, hard talking to Clanton before they reached the pizza parlor. He knew how Clanton felt; his own father had left his family when he was in his teens.

"I saw him once after he left and told him I hated him. I never saw him again. He died when I was twenty-three."

Sierra saw how much that confession cost Dennis, as well as the impact it had on Clanton.

"He hurt my mother," Clanton said. "Every time he calls, he hurts her."

Sierra blinked back tears. "I hurt him, too, Clanton."

"Not like he did." Clanton struggled to contain his emotions, torn between love and loyalty to her and love for his father.

Dennis put his hand on Clanton's shoulder. "Your father's hurting himself most of all. He's cut off from you and your sister. Do you remember what we were talking about the other night at youth group? Everyone sins. No one is perfect. And no sin is greater than any other. When you believe in Jesus, you confess and repent, and he cleanses you. He puts you on the right track. What happens when you don't have that sustaining faith? You're cut off from love itself."

"He's not repentant," Clanton said.

"Are you?"

Clanton fought to hold his tears back. "He's still living with her!"

"And you're still hanging on to your anger against him. You just wished him dead."

Clanton hunched over and cried, muttering incoherent words. Dennis cupped the boy's head and pulled him against his chest. "Give it to the Lord, Clanton. Don't make the same mistake I did. It still haunts me." He looked at Sierra, and she saw the tears in his eyes. She also knew her son needed time alone with this man of God.

"I'll see you inside," she said, touching her son and then getting out of the van. She knew Clanton would open up more if she weren't present.

She spotted Alex as soon as she entered the pizza parlor; her instinctive homing device still worked. She could sense his presence anywhere. He was sitting with Carolyn in a booth back in the corner. She wanted to pretend she hadn't seen them and walk over to the others. The last thing she wanted to do was speak to Alex or think about Carolyn building a relationship with a future stepmother.

Alex was staring at her, and she knew she'd only gain his further ire if she left him to wonder where Clanton was.

Someone called her name. She glanced toward them, forced a smile, and waved. "Be there in a minute." First things first. She had to set Alex's mind at rest. She walked over to the table and smiled at Carolyn. "Did you order pizza yet?"

"Pepperoni!" She grinned and took a sip of her soda.

Sierra looked at Alex. "Dennis is talking with him. They'll be in soon." His eyes met hers, and she felt his pain. What a tangled mess they'd made of their lives—and dragged their children right into the quagmire with them. "If it doesn't happen tonight, Alex, we'll keep trying. All right? Don't give up on him. Please."

Again, that look she couldn't decipher. "I won't," he said bleakly.

Smiling tremulously, she left their table and joined the others.

When Clanton came in, Carolyn left the booth so her father could talk to him alone. She came straight to Sierra. "Daddy said he'll take us to the movies and then to dinner." She kept up a stream of chatter about her father while Sierra watched Dennis and Clanton sit down in the booth with Alex.

Dennis smiled and talked for a few minutes, undoubtedly trying to put his companions more at ease. Alex responded. She saw him smile. Odd how that hurt. When Dennis left them alone, Alex looked across at his son and started talking. He talked for a long time. Clanton just sat staring at Carolyn's empty soda glass. After a while, Alex didn't say anything more. He just sat looking at his son, grief and regret etched in the new lines around his eyes. He said a few more words. Clanton got up and left the booth. Alex raked a hand back through his hair and looked away.

For the first time since he'd left her, Sierra felt compassion for her husband.

Carolyn left with her father. Clanton spent most of the evening talking with Dennis. Noreen came and sat with Sierra. "Children see things in black and white," Noreen said. "Right and wrong. Good and evil. They're so sensitive to those things. The older we are, the more shades of gray we see."

"I don't know what to do. So much of this is my fault. He wants a divorce."

Noreen put her hand over hers. "Are you still in love with him?"

Sierra gave a mirthless laugh. "I've been in love with Alex for as long as I can remember, and I'll probably love him until I die. But that doesn't change anything, does it? He said he's sick of me and in love with someone else. He's done everything possible to get me to agree to a divorce. In the beginning, I think I refused because I wanted to hurt him as much as he was hurting me. Then it was pure cussed stubbornness. But now? I don't know anymore. I just don't know."

Noreen squeezed her hand. "I don't know if this will help you or not, but my parents fought all the time when I was growing up. I used to cry myself to sleep hearing them scream at each other. They said they were staying together for us, my brother and me. I used to wish they'd get a divorce."

"Did they?"

"No. Never. They're still together and they're still fighting. They have other excuses now, and they still embarrass anyone who comes within ten feet of them. I don't go home very often."

Sierra remembered the fights she'd had with Alex. They hadn't screamed at one another, but the cold war had gone on for months at a time. At what cost to their children? She'd been so caught up in her own pain, she'd been blind to theirs. And Alex's.

Audra's words came back again, haunting her. *"Three years I've watched you wallow in self-pity and keep your temper tantrum going. It's been something to watch, Sierra. A real show!"*

Sierra closed her eyes. *God, forgive me. She was right. I behaved so badly, Lord. What can I do to make things right again? How can I make amends?*

And the answer came, bringing with it a wave of pain.

Let him go.

Clanton said he had a stomachache, and they went home early. While he took a long, hot bath, she sat in the living room, praying. She knew what she had to do. When she tucked Clanton into bed, she stroked the black hair back from his forehead. "I love you so much, and I'm sorry I've made a mess of things."

"You didn't."

"Oh, Clanton, there's so much you don't understand. I pushed. I pushed so hard for so long for what *I* wanted. I never stopped to consider what your father needed. Please don't do the same thing. You'll end up losing him the same way I did. He *needs* you, Clanton. He needs to be able to love you."

"What about you, Mom?"

"I have you and Carolyn. I have Michael and his family. I have the Lord. What does your father have, Clanton? And I share the blame for it. I want to make things easier for all of us."

They talked for over an hour, and Clanton agreed he'd talk to his father the next time he called. Relieved, Sierra took a long shower and changed into black leggings and a long forest-green tunic. She was brushing her hair when the doorbell rang.

Alex stood under the porch light, their daughter sound asleep in his arms. "Where's her room?"

"Down the hall, second door on the right," she said and stepped back. She watched him carry Carolyn down the hall. She followed, switching on the light. She pulled the comforter back. Alex lay Carolyn down gently so she wouldn't awaken. Untying her tennis shoes, he slipped them off her feet. Sierra left the room as he drew the comforter up over his daughter and kissed her good night.

Her heart was hammering when Alex came into the living

room. He looked around. "You didn't bring any of the new furniture with you."

She could tell nothing from his tone, but it occurred to her
then he might have wanted some of the things Bruce Davies had
brought into the house they'd shared together. She saw another
glaring mistake, another selfish act on her part. "Roberta suggested I sell . . ." She shook her head, embarrassed. She couldn't
pass the blame onto Roberta. It had been her own decision,
another act of defiance. "I'm sorry, Alex. I never even considered
asking if you wanted the furniture Bruce Davies—"

"I didn't say I did," he said abruptly. He looked away from
her and around the living room. "Reminds me of the house in
Windsor."

His words came back to haunt her: *There's a right way and a wrong
way to decorate.* She looked around, trying to see things from his
perspective. She'd kept the sofa they'd bought during their first
year of marriage, though she'd recovered it last month with green
corduroy. She'd found the brightly colored throw pillows on sale
in an import shop. She still had the hatch-cover table. On it was
a lead crystal platter with rocks the children had collected from
a recent visit to the beach. The old brass lamps Alex had called
ridiculous sat on modern end tables on each end of the sofa. She'd
polished them to a golden glow and purchased new shades. In the
corner, near the front window, was a tall, healthy fern.

It was as far from Bruce Davies' kind of decorating as you
could get. Nothing went together, but somehow the mix made
everyone who walked in feel comfortable. At least, they said so.
Two had even asked her to help decorate their homes.

But how did it make Alex feel?

"Would you like me to make some coffee?" she said for want
of anything else.

"It's a little late for coffee."

It was a little late for everything. Conceding, she nodded

sadly. "I guess it is." She picked up the long white envelope from the kitchen counter. "I had a long talk with Clanton this evening after we got home. I think he understands things a little better now."

"Understands what?" Alex said, dark-eyed.

"That our marriage breaking up wasn't solely your fault. He'll talk with you the next time you call." Taking a breath, she took a few steps toward him and held out the envelope.

Eyes narrowed, he took it. "What's this?"

"The divorce papers you gave me. I signed them tonight. You can have your divorce, Alex. I won't fight you anymore." She hadn't realized the cost of those words, nor had she expected to see the look that came into his eyes. He wasn't relieved. As he searched her face intently, she used every ounce of her will to keep the tears back and to appear calm and accepting.

Oh, God, be with me. You are my hiding place. You are my shield, my ever-present help in times of trouble. And this hurts more than I ever thought possible.

"Why now?" Alex said roughly.

"Because it's time." A time for all things. A time to love. A time to let go. A time to move on with her life and allow Alex to move on with his. "It would've been easier on everyone if I'd done as you asked in the first place. I was hanging on to my anger. And false hopes. I know now it only made things worse. For everyone."

He looked at her for a long moment. "You've changed."

"I hope so."

He tucked the envelope inside his jacket pocket. She'd never seen him look so grim. He started to say something but shook his head. He walked to the door, opened it, and went out without a word. She closed the door quietly behind him and leaned her forehead against it.

I'll trust in you, Lord, no matter how much it hurts. I'll trust you.

When next Alex called, Clanton answered. Alex picked him up on Saturday and they spent the full day together, the first since Alex had left.

We are laid by in Ragtown with twenty other wagons.

There is water here and the animals have good grazing. James is letting me handle replenishing the supplies while he has the wagon refitted. And I am getting my wash done. The place is named for all the clothing hanging on bushes. Even unmentionables. It is a sight to see!

The Randolph party is heading out along the Truckee River tomorrow. They are eager to reach Sutter's Fort. They are answering Sutter's call for settlers. Several of the men here are Ohio farmers. The blacksmith with them fixed the rims on our wagon and sold us some spare bolts.

I was hoping we would be traveling on with the Randolph party. It seems to me the more people the less chance of trouble, but James thinks differently. He wants to wait and give the oxen time to fatten for the assault on the Sierras. The others agree. Kavanaugh gives no opinion one way or the other. I think he would speak up if it was a poor idea. So I am somewhat comforted. Joshua is angry. He is eager to see what is over the mountains. I suppose it is a good thing we are waiting another day or two.

Nellie should be stronger by then. Another day in
that desert and we would have been burying her.
Nellie asked me to pray for her. All I could do was
take her hand and say God help us. She seemed
satisfied with that. She keeps on reminding me God
has helped us this far. And I keep telling her we are
not at the end of the trail yet.

Our oxen have good grazing here. James is
cutting grass and bundling it for fodder. It was
good he did that along the Humboldt or the animals
never would have made the last forty miles.

I look up at the mountains and wonder if we can
make it before winter hits. The wagon master of
the Randolph party told us not to wait longer than
a week. He said a party went through two years
ago and got trapped in the winter snows. Most
of them died and those that did not were reduced
to eating their kin. After hearing that story, I was
ready to pack up our gear and set out right then.

Kavanaugh rode ahead to find an easier route
over the mountains.

Joshua went with him. They have been gone
four days. I am afraid something has happened to
them. James said we will follow the trail left by
the Randolph party until we hear otherwise.

It is hard going. We crossed the Truckee four
times and now have to dismantle the wagon and

haul it up the mountain. Binger cracked two ribs
when the windlass came loose, but we did not
lose his wagon. Plenty of wood for a fire. The air
is cold at night and the days are getting shorter.
Joshua is keeping us in fresh food. He shot a
deer. I have strips of meat drying on the wagon as
we travel.

I heard the most fearsome noise last night.
Kavanaugh said it was a puma. I asked him
what a puma was and he said it is a mountain
lion. James spotted a bear crossing the meadow
this morning. I knew something was in the wind
because the oxen were nervous. Kavanaugh put
himself between the wagons and the bear and had
his Sharps ready. That huge beast reared up on
its back legs and scented the wind. I am thankful
he knew better than to come closer.

Kavanaugh just told me to pack the drying
meat away or the bear will come in for it. I have
done so.

James is standing guard. Stern will take the
watch in another two hours. The children are
settled under the wagon and sound asleep. I can
not sleep a wink for fear of that bear.

It has been so long since I have felt safe. The
last time I can remember was when I was a child
and my mama was still alive and well. I never
knew the dangers that were around me while she

lived. She was not even much afraid when the Sioux and Fox Indians were warring. She always said God was with us. I can remember hearing people talk about Black Hawk, but I was never afraid. I knew Mama and Papa would take care of me. And I knew God would too. I remember thinking Papa was the strongest man alive. All that changed so fast when Mama died. The McMurray family unraveled.

Sometimes I find myself wondering how Mama felt about being so far from Galena and her dear sister. She lost three children on that homestead. I was too young to remember how they died or when. But I remember the markers. Mama never talked about them other than to say I would meet two sisters and a brother in heaven someday. I remember Mama talking about Aunt Martha, too, but I can not remember a single time when she talked about the life she led in Galena. And it must have been a charmed life with church socials and quilting parties and afternoon teas. She never talked much about my grandmother and grandfather either except to tell me they both believed in Jesus and were in heaven and I would meet them someday, too. Aunt Martha told me my grandfather made his money as a smelter and Grandma was a Good Christian Woman. She

died of consumption just like Mama did and my
grandfather died of brain fever.

I never thought to ask more. I was so young
and it never seemed to matter.

Now I have a hundred questions and will never
know the answers to the least of them.

The weather is turning cold. Beth is down with
fever again. I wish Doc was here to tell me what
to do. I dont want to lose her like I lost my little
Deborah.

Beth seems better. It snowed today. It did not stay
on the ground around us but was still worrisome.
We can see the mountains white above us. I have
never seen anything so majestic and beautiful
or terrifying. Kavanaugh said we have to push
harder and make the foothills before the snows
move down.

James is sick with mountain fever. Matthew and I
are driving the wagon while Hank tends what few
stock we have left and Beth sees after her father.
Nellie is weak with dysentery.

Kavanaugh has sent Joshua ahead with Binger
Siddons and Ernst Holtz. They can move faster
without us and bring us help.

I could not help but cry when Joshua rode out
of sight. He is slipping away from me a little more

every day and I do not know how to hold him.
James says I have to let go of the boy. My head
knows it, but my heart says different.

I was his age when Sally Mae pushed him into
the world. She died without ever looking at him.
All his life I have loved him. In a strange way he
is more part of me than my own babies. Maybe I
love him so much because I had to fight so hard to
keep him alive. I dream sometimes of him laying in
his mother's blood crying. I took him to my heart
then and will bear him there until my days end.
He clung to life when his mama did not care and
his father wanted him dead. Now he is hungry for
more of life and I am afraid to let him go and find
it. What I fear most is he will ride away and never
come back. Just like Matthew did.

Kavanaugh touched me last night. It was just a
brush of his hand over my hair as I was sitting
near the fire worrying about James. I know he
did not mean for me to know he touched me. But
I felt it just the same. Feelings came up inside me
I can't describe.

I did not look up at him afraid of what I would
see in his eyes or he would see in mine.

I have wondered on occasion why he agreed to
be scout for us and then why he said he decided
to come along to California. Now I know. Maybe
I knew the moment he looked at me in that

mercantile back in Independence and I have just been fooling myself.

And James knows too or he would not have said if he dies I will be safe with Kavanaugh.

James is sleeping better since his fever broke and I am much relieved though still worried about him. He is slow in getting his strength back. Beth is doing better than her father. The mountain air seems to agree with her. She gathered flowers today and made a wreath for me. She is a dear thoughtful child who always wants to please everyone. She watched over Deborah. Now she seems to watch over me.

Matthew likes to tell stories. He is good at it. He will be happy when we get our land and I can dig through the trunk Aunt Martha bought me. His books are in it.

Nellie lets me read from her Bible in the evening. It is noisy getting started because everyone wants to hear their favorite. Beth likes the story of Ruth best. Nellie's favorite is Esther. The boys would rather hear the battles of King David. Wells likes the story of Gideon. He says it shows how God can take a cowardly farmer and turn him into a mighty warrior able to save an entire nation from destruction. James says he just likes hearing me read.

A great valley stretches out before us and the land looks rich and green from fall rain. Joshua has come back to us and says we are three days from Sutter's Fort.

We are all thankful the journey is almost over.

We had happy surprises when we arrived at Sutter's Fort. Virgil Boon and Ruckel Buckeye are here. They had a falling out with MacLeod and left the train at Fort Hall. They followed the Snake south and followed the Humboldt by the same route we did, but they took the Carson River route over the mountains. They said they passed one of the most beautiful lakes in God's creation.

They reached the fort two days ahead of us.

Wells and Nellie are going to take land north of Sutter's Fort. They take the ferry across the river tomorrow.

I am much aggrieved. I thought we would live near the Doanes who have become such wonderful friends. But James told me this morning he has decided we will go clear to the Pacific. Sutter bought Fort Ross from the Russians and says the land is rich there for farming.

If there is a ship waiting, my husband will want to board and sail until we reach China! And if he does, he will be going on alone.

We said good-bye to the Doanes this morning.
I have been crying all day. James is not saying
much. He is wise to keep his silence.

   Joshua and Kavanaugh have gone ahead to see
the lay of the land.

We saw Indians today. They are of the same
kind we saw working at Sutter's Fort. They were
gathering grain and roots in the marshes.

The wind and rain is bitter cold. We have crossed
a range of hills and come into another valley.
Mexicans came upon us and said the land is taken
by Mariano Vallejo. They said we are welcome
to come and winter at his rancho. James assured
them we are only passing through and thanked
them for their kind invitation. He told them we
are heading north until we find the Russian River.
He asked where is a good crossing and they told
him. Sutter told us the river will be low enough
to cross easily if we reach it before the heavy
rainfall. Joshua has gone ahead to see if that is so.

The Russian River was wide but not too deep to
ford. A day after we crossed, the skies opened up
and it has been raining heavy upon us ever since.
The river swelled so fast I could scarce believe it.
Nellie would say God was with us and that's why
we made it across.

Matthew is sick with fever. I have a touch of it myself.

Each day gets harder.

We are wintering in a valley northwest of the Russian River. The Russian Fort is still days away, but I can go no further. I was sick in the wagon the day the decision was made to stay here. The cramps were hard upon me and I was sure I was going to lose the baby. We stopped mid day to let me rest. When we started out in the morning, there was a crack and the wagon dropped. When it did, two wheels split.

Our axle is broken and two bolts are missing. James and the children have looked all day for them and can not find them and we have no spares.

I have not said so, but I am relieved we can go no further. If the axle had not broken, we would still be westering. It is like a fever in James. He thinks what is over the next mountain will be better than what is here. This is good land with timber for building and plenty of water. What more does he want?

Kavanaugh is gone. He and James had a falling out. It almost came to blows. It all started because James wants to go on to Fort Ross. He was all for leaving the wagon and packing the

rest of the way but Kavanaugh would not let
him. He said — Mary Kathryn has gone as far
as she can go, man. Have you no eyes in your
head? And James got all red in the face and
told him I was none of his business. Kavanaugh
said that might be so, but it was time to build a
shelter and wait out winter. James accused him
of tampering with the wagon. Kavanaugh said
nothing to that. James ordered him to leave.
So he did. He got on his horse and rode away
without so much as a by your leave.

I wonder if he did do what James says. If so,
I am grateful to him. This child bears down upon
me as the others never did. Another day and
I would have lost it and maybe died as well.

James is talking about building a cabin. It will
be hard work, but I am eager to have a roof over
my head again. I do not want this baby born in a
covered wagon.

I am feeling much stronger. Staying in one place
does wonders for a body. James still talks of
moving on after the baby comes. I hope he will
change his mind.

I keep telling him this is good rich, dark soil,
with plenty of earthworms and few rocks. We will
not find better to build our home.

James has started breaking the wagon down.
He is going to rebuild it into two carts like the
Mormons use. He said we still have two good
wheels and not much left to carry. I guess I will
be walking again.

We ain't going anywhere. Looks like we are just
going to die right here. One by one.

James is dead.

I dont know what to do.

I can make no sense of anything. I can not even
think.

God, why do you hate me so much?

———————————

19

"I'M WAITING FOR SOMEONE," SIERRA TOLD the waitress. "A glass of water will be fine until she arrives." Providing Audra came at all.

It had taken the better part of two days for Sierra to gather enough nerve to call Audra and ask her to lunch. She'd expected Audra to refuse or say something painful. Instead, she had said simply, "Where?"

Sierra hadn't been prepared for that. "Wherever you'd like."

"The club. One o'clock on Thursday. Is that all right?"

"Eleven-thirty would be better for me, Audra. I'll be on my lunch hour."

"Fine," she said in a clipped voice. "I'll be there."

Sierra arrived early and saw Meredith sitting alone in the lounge. She joined her for a few minutes, reminiscing and catching up on news.

"That makes three of us," Meredith said when Sierra told her she and Alex were getting a divorce. "Eric dumped me for a younger, richer model, and Lorraine finally divorced Frank. Luckily, she got herself a first-cabin attorney. She's on a Caribbean cruise right now. And guess who's paying for it?"

"How's Ashley?" Sierra said, sorry to hear so many sad tidings.

"Bulimic. She collapsed a few weeks ago and is in counseling now. She looks like she's a survivor of the Holocaust."

A few minutes before Audra was due to arrive, Sierra wrote out her new address and telephone number. "Please call. I'd love to have you come for dinner. Mondays and Fridays are best for me. Pick a date and let me know."

Meredith looked at her with a bemused smile. "I might just surprise you and take up your invitation."

Sierra bent and kissed her cheek.

She was checking on her reservation when Audra arrived. Blushing, she extended her hand. "Hello, Audra."

After a brief hesitation, Audra took her hand. "It's good to see you again, Sierra."

"Your table is ready, Mrs. Madrid. Right this way."

They sat in a quiet alcove between some ferns. Sierra had asked for a private table and given the young man a healthy tip to ensure it. Audra didn't say anything after she ordered white wine. Sierra ordered a lemon-lime. Maybe it would settle her stomach.

Taking a breath, she blew it out slowly and lifted her head. "I've had a lot of time to think things over, Audra. You were right about everything. Not the least of which, you were right about the way I treated you. I wanted to apologize to you in person."

Audra stared at her for a long moment. "Well . . . ," she said slowly. "I came prepared to defend myself. I've gone over my side of our conversation a hundred times over the last few days. One word of condemnation and I could've nailed your ears to the wall. And here you go, taking the wind right out of my sails." She lifted her wine glass. "Congratulations."

Sierra didn't know what to make of her words. She'd known this meeting would be difficult. Clenching her hands together, she prepared herself for whatever Audra had to say. She'd keep silent and *listen* if it killed her.

Audra gave a soft mirthless laugh. "I *am* a snob, Sierra. I *am* a social climber. The one thing I've always wanted—and found absolutely impossible—is to fit in. The only person in this world who really loves me is Stephen. God knows why. From the time I was a child, I've had one great talent: alienating people."

She fumbled with her silverware and then, as though catching herself in a terrible faux pas, put her hands in her lap. She looked across the table, directly into Sierra's eyes, and tipped her chin. "Sometimes, I'd see a look on your face that made me cringe inside. That time on Rodeo Drive, for example, when I bought that ridiculously expensive dress and asked you why you didn't buy something, too. I don't even know why I did it. To put you in your place, I suppose. But you looked at me, and for just an instant I saw myself through your eyes. It wasn't pretty." Her hand shook slightly as she lifted the glass of white wine again. "So, for whatever it's worth to you, Sierra, I apologize, too. Truce?"

Sierra felt a sudden rush of warmth toward this woman she'd always seen as her enemy. She caught a glimpse of Audra's insecurities and loneliness and ached for her. Lifting her glass of lemon-lime, she smiled. "I think we can do better than that, Audra. We can be friends."

When Audra said Alex and Elizabeth didn't seem to be getting along, Sierra asked that Alex be considered a forbidden subject. "It's over, Audra. He's with someone else. It hurts to talk about him."

"It's not over until you're divorced."

"I signed the papers for him last week. It's only a matter of time."

An odd look crossed Audra's face. For a moment, she seemed desperate to offer some advice. Then, showing uncharacteristic sensitivity, she changed the subject.

They parted amicably. Audra said lunch would be on her next time. "I'll take you to La Serre."

"You will not," Sierra said with a laugh. "One of the things that used to bother me most was knowing I couldn't reciprocate. So you can treat me next time, if you like, but after that, we're going Dutch and someplace the average Joe can afford or we don't go anywhere at all."

"Oh, all right," Audra said, pretending to be annoyed.

Sierra returned to work feeling elated. She had gone to lunch expecting to face Audra's disdain and condemnation. Instead, she had come away with a new friend, one she might have had three years ago if she hadn't been so caught up in herself.

✳✳✳

When she arrived home, the children were already there, Clanton working on his math at the kitchen table while Carolyn talked on the telephone to Pamela. "Marcia says to say hi, Mom."

"Tell her hello back and remind her we're going shopping this Saturday." Alex was taking Clanton to Magic Mountain again. Friday afternoons, he always picked up Carolyn and spent the evening with her.

Dropping her purse on the counter, Sierra slid onto one of the kitchen stools and began opening the mail. In the pile was a course catalog from a local junior college. Scanning it, she saw several business courses that would help her at her job. While practical, they didn't look as interesting as one entitled "Creative Decorating on a Limited Budget."

She chuckled. Now, there was a course that sounded right up

her alley. But she'd already done all the decorating she could afford for the time being, and she had several projects that were yet to be completed. The old armoire that had belonged to Alex's parents was stripped and ready for staining, and she had the fabric she wanted to cover the wing chairs. She'd also bought the acrylics to start on the flower-and-leaf trim she'd drawn for Carolyn's bedroom.

Tossing the catalog aside, she picked up the bill for her car insurance. Since she had traded in the BMW for a Saturn, her rates had dropped drastically.

Carolyn hung up and slid off the stool, opening the refrigerator. "I'm hungry. What's for dinner?"

Sierra grinned. "How about hot dogs with macaroni and cheese for a change?"

"Aw, Mom. Can't we order Chinese tonight?"

"Not tonight, honey," she said, opening a letter from Alex's parents. She wrote to them once a week as she'd always done. They were inviting her and the children to spend Thanksgiving with them. María tactfully mentioned Alex had plans to go East this year. When she finished the letter, she left it out so the children could read it.

It was a long drive to Healdsburg, but it was time. She hadn't been home since her mother died.

The telephone rang again. "It's for you, Mom."

She took it. "Hello?"

"Marcia said you signed the divorce papers."

Her heart jumped at the sound of Ron's voice. "News travels fast," she said, keeping her tone light.

"I heard about it the day Marcia did. I waited this long so you'd have a chance to adjust."

Sliding off the stool, she put the kettle on. Audra claimed there was nothing like a cup of herbal tea to settle jumpy nerves. Ron asked about the children and her new home. She didn't have to ask where he'd gotten her telephone number. Marcia would have given it to him three weeks ago, along with the news of her divorce.

"Do you see Alex very often?"

"When he stops by to pick up one or both of the children," she said, sensing his caution with her. He was sensitive enough not to ask if Alex was planning to marry Elizabeth Longford.

Ron told her Judy's baby was crawling and Arlene had taken two weeks' vacation in Baja. "She came back tanned and sassy."

Sierra laughed. She'd forgotten how easy it was to talk to him. Relaxing, she asked about several of the teenagers she'd worked with while at Outreach. He told her one was back in high school and another had moved to Kansas to live with her grandmother. He filled her in about several others who had entered the program. They talked for over an hour before Ron said, "I'd like to take you to dinner Friday evening," and obliterated Sierra's sense of security and ease.

"I don't know, Ron. I'm not sure I'm ready."

"I'm asking you to dinner, Sierra. I'm not asking you to marry me."

"I know, but I have a feeling the one might lead to the other."

He gave a soft laugh. "That was frank. Am I that transparent?"

"You were open and honest, Ron. I was blind and stupid."

"You were trying to keep your life together."

"I'm still trying."

"Welcome to the human race," he said. "Look, what if I promise I won't even try to hold your hand for six months? Unless you give me permission to do so, of course."

She laughed. "It would be *such* a relief not to have to fight men off," she said dryly. He teased her for the next five minutes, making light of her concerns in order to alleviate them. "Give me some time to think about it," she said finally, noticing the way the children were looking at her. They knew it wasn't their father on the telephone.

"I'll call you Friday."

She had a feeling Ron knew Friday evenings and Saturdays were Alex's time with the children and her time alone to think. Marcia knew, and it seemed whatever she knew, Ron knew.

"Who was that?" Clanton said when she hung up the telephone.

"Ron Peirozo."

"Hey! Are we going sailing again?"

She looked at her two children and saw the idea didn't seem to bother them in the slightest.

"Maybe."

I have been going over it again and again in my mind.

I want to figure out what could have happened. James said he was going down to the stream to try to catch some fish for supper. When he did not come back by dusk, I sent Hank to fetch him. Hank came running back screaming Papa was in the creek and would not get up. He was dead when I got to him.

It took the two of us to pull James up onto the bank. He was white and bloated and had a cut on his forehead. He must have slipped on a rock, fallen, and hit his head. He must have been knocked senseless. How else could he have drowned in less than a foot of water.

Events are plaguing me. I can not think of anything but the Horrible Thing I did to James.

I had to use the horse to drag James's body home. I washed and dressed him in clean clothes to prepare him for burial. I was so tired by the time I finished, I could do no more until morning.

Joshua dug the grave, but it took all of us working together to half carry, half drag James to his resting place. I knew it would be a fearsome thing to get him in it and did not want the children to see. Worst of all, I could not leave the blanket on James. We have none to spare and winter upon us. So I told Joshua to take them back to the wagon.

I unrolled James out of the blanket and he went down into the earth with a terrible thud. And then I cursed him. I was so mad at him that I had to do it. I cursed him for dying and leaving us. I cursed and wept and covered him over with dirt.

And now I can't stop thinking about him down there in the cold.

How could you leave me like this, James? How could you bring me and our babies two thousand miles and then die at the end of the trail? I should have listened to Aunt Martha and married Thomas Atwood Houghton. I would have been living in a nice warm house with plenty of food. My children would be warm, fed, and safe.

You never even thought of building us a cabin and now we are left here in the wilderness

shivering in what is left of our wagon. You never
thought about how few supplies we have left
and winter on us. You just had to keep looking
west, didn't you, James? You just had to keep
on wondering what was over the hills. You never
had a single thought what would happen to us if
anything happened to you! And what will happen
to our children if I die having this baby you put
in me?

I hate you, James Addison Farr. I hope you rot
in hell for what you have done to us.

I don't mean it. I'm so scared, James. What am
I going to do without you? Where do I go to find
help? How are we going to survive in this wild
place?

There is this terrible silence without you, this
ache inside that gets heavier every day.

Better had it been me who died. You would
have known what to do to keep the rest alive.

I used the last of our salt pork and flour this
morning. The rain is heavy upon us. The cold
goes into my bones. Joshua says we should go on
to the Fort. I am too sick to make it. I told him to
take the children and go.

We ate the last of our beans tonight. Joshua
leaves in the morning for Fort Ross. Hank,

Matthew, and Beth will not leave me. Joshua
said he will ride west as far as the ocean and then
head north. He is riding James's horse and taking
his own for packing. I gave him what money we
had left for supplies. It was the last of what Aunt
Martha give me.

God, please, help him find his way there and
back to us.

Joshua has been gone four days. We have no
food and no ammunition. The fish are not biting.

God, I won't ask you to help me. But please
help my children.

You must be watching over us, God. I can think
of no other reason for the Strange Occurrence.

A grizzly came into our meadow. I called a
warning to the children. The boys made it to
the wagon, but Beth froze. I told her to run, but
she was too scared to move with that she-demon
coming straight for her and making a roar from
hell itself. I never even stopped to think. I just
started running for her and praying. Oh, God, did
I pray. Out loud. The words just came pouring
out of me in Pure Terror. I have not prayed so
hard since Mama was sick.

And You answered! You told me to sing
to that beast from hell and I did. Oh, I did. I
thought I must be going crazy with fear, but

I did it anyway. I remember now MacLeod
told the men guarding the stock once to sing
to the animals during a storm. And we were in
the midst of a storm, hard rain, thunder and
lightning and that Terrible beast coming from
the woods. I sang loud enough to wake James.
I sang whatever came into my head, mostly
hymns Aunt Martha used to play on the piano
and Mama taught me. Hymns I had not sung in
years. They come back. The bear was up on two
hind legs and only twenty some feet from us. I
thought we were dead for sure. That grizzly was
eager to tear us limb from limb and there I stood
with Beth tucked behind me singing like a crazy
woman.

But that bear stopped! Oh, Lord, she did. She
came down and cocked its head, and looked at
me. I did not look it in the eyes but up at heaven,
singing with all my might. The beast moved
its head back and forth. I was afraid my voice
would dry up, but it did not. The words kept
coming back to me, one hymn after another. The
bear stayed right there and listened for so long I
thought my hair was turning white! And then she
just lumbered off, calm and quiet as you please
and disappeared into the woods.

I sank down on my knees and laughed and
wept and held Beth to me. She said — Mama, it

was a Miracle. And all I could say was — Yes, A Blessed Miracle.

I feel changed inside myself. Something gave way or cracked open or something.

Oh, Jesus, You are there! Mama was right after all.

———————————

20

SIERRA HAD ALWAYS LOVED WALKING ALONG Mathesen Street in the fall. The trees were orange and gold, the light breeze crisp, the air clear. She'd taken the children down to the Plaza and bought them donuts from the deli while they wandered around, looking in shop windows.

Now, going up the steps of the old house, she felt the tug of grief again. When they drove up the drive last night, she'd expected to enter a cold, empty house. Instead, someone had turned on the furnace. A fire was going in the parlor, the screen in place and wood in the basket. In the kitchen was a Pyrex dish of warm enchiladas and a note from Alex's mother.

"We look forward to seeing you and our grandchildren tomorrow. Dinner at three. Love, María and Luís."

She called them to let them know she and the children had arrived safely and to thank them for their thoughtfulness. "Your brother gave us the key," María said. "We left it under the mat on the back porch."

She called her brother to let him and Melissa know she'd arrived. "We'll come by tomorrow morning," Mike said. "There's something I need to talk over with you. It's important."

"What time?"

"Eleven. We're supposed to go to Melissa's parents for turkey dinner. We'll have to leave by one to get there on time."

"Eleven it is."

She and the children had just shrugged out of their coats when Mike unlocked the door and his family poured in. For a few minutes, all Sierra could hear were the excited voices of reuniting cousins. She kissed her niece and nephews and announced she had brought back a bag of donuts from the deli.

Mike got right to the point. "A couple wants to buy the house and turn it into a bed-and-breakfast."

Sierra's stomach dropped. "Buy the house?"

"They've been looking for property in the area for over a year. They liked this house. Apparently they stopped by once, and Mom invited them in for coffee and cookies. She gave them the grand tour but said she wasn't interested in selling. She told them to check back in a year or two. They took her at her word and came by a week ago. When they found out Mom had passed away, they traced me through the church pastor."

"Did you tell them we don't want to sell?" Sierra said.

Mike exchanged a look with Melissa. He sat down and leaned forward, his hands clasped between his knees. "No, I didn't. I wanted to talk it over with you first."

"I thought you loved the house as much as I do."

"I do, Sis, but I've already got a home in Ukiah. My business is there. If I were to sell out and move, I'd want to go farther north to Garberville. Or Oregon. I haven't the money to hang on to this place for sentimental reasons."

Sierra got up and walked over to the fireplace. She ran her hand along the dusty mantle and looked at the old Seth Thomas mantle clock. It had run down months ago. Even with the furnace on, the house had a musty smell of disuse.

"The only other alternative is to rent the place out, and I don't want to do that either. I've heard nothing but horror stories from friends who've rented property and had their places destroyed. The law being what it is, someone can move in and wreck a place before you get them out."

Melissa rose. "I'll make some coffee," she said softly and left the room. Sierra knew her sister-in-law was making it clear to both of them that she had no say in their decision. It was up to them what they did about the house.

Her family had lived in Sonoma County for over a hundred years. Mary Kathryn McMurray had been the first one to put down roots in the fertile soil now covered by tract houses. Ah yes, Mary Kathryn McMurray, who had come with all the eagerness and joy that she herself had felt when Alex had moved her to Los Angeles!

"Do you want the house, Sis?"

Oh, God, do I have to give up my home? You know how much I love this old house. What do you want me to do?

Again, the answer was clear. *Let go.*

"Sierra?"

She leaned her head against the edge of the mantel. What choice was there? "No matter how much I want it, it's beyond possible. I don't have enough left of my inheritance to buy out your share in it, and then there are the taxes." She lowered her hands and turned. "And I just bought my condo. I'd take a loss if I tried to sell it now with the market being what it is. That's why I got it for such a good price in the first place. And then, if it did sell, I'd be out of work up here."

"Do you want the house?" he said again.

She knew her brother would bend over backward to make things easier on her, even at cost to his own family finances. "I want what's best for all of us," she said quietly.

"So what do you think that means?"

She forced a smile for his sake. "What's this couple like?"

A look of relief filled her brother's face so that she knew exactly what he wanted. No more burdens to bear. And could she blame him? She was the one living in Los Angeles, too far away to pitch in and help with maintaining the house. He had been taking care of everything since their mother had died.

"They're nice people, in their midforties, financially set. They've been living in San José for the past twenty-two years. They have two children, a boy and girl. The boy's off at Bible college studying to be a pastor. The daughter's married with a baby on the way. Jack's hobby is woodcrafting, and Reka's into gardening."

Sierra thought of her mother's backyard going wild. It would be nice having someone pour love back into it and make it bloom again. Hadn't Mom invited these people in for coffee and cookies and given them a grand tour? Hadn't she been the one to say come back in a year or two? She'd known she'd be gone by then. Full realization struck her, tightening her throat with tears. "It's just like Mom to tie up all the loose ends, isn't it?" she said with a smile.

"Yeah," Mike said, his voice husky with emotion.

"So," she said more lightly. "Do you have their number?"

He nodded.

"Why don't you call and ask if they'd like to come up on Saturday and we'll talk turkey."

He laughed, his eyes moist. "Sure."

She debated telling María and Luís the next day. They were upset enough over Alex's broken marriage, without adding to their worries of never seeing their grandchildren. One word about selling the Mathesen Street house and Thanksgiving would be ruined for María, who lived for her children and grandchildren.

There were a dozen running around when Sierra arrived. Clanton and Carolyn piled out of the Saturn and joined in the games. They remembered their Spanish, picking it up as though they'd been jabbering it nonstop at home.

Luís hugged her tightly when she came into the house and then kissed her on both cheeks. She hadn't seen him since Alex had left her, and his greeting brought a lump to her throat. María was right behind him, crying, and talking in rapid-fire Spanish.

Alex's brothers and sisters treated her with the warmth they always had. His older brother, Miguel, a vintner for one of the Sonoma wineries, even flirted outrageously with her. His sister, Alma, let it slip that Alex had brought Elizabeth Longford home for a few days to meet the family.

"Papa wouldn't let them stay here. He said Alex could take her to a motel room, but he wouldn't have them sleeping together under his roof. Alex rented a suite at the Doubletree. She refused to come back with him the next day. Alex and Papa had words. He's called and talked to Mama, but I don't think he and Papa have talked since."

Grandfather. Father. Son.

Sierra changed the subject, but Alex's name kept coming up. And then he called. He talked to his mother. Then he talked to Clanton and Carolyn. Papa went outside for a walk. When he came back, Alex had long since hung up. For the rest of the evening, she could feel Luís watching her. María, too.

God, how much we hurt others without even thinking about it. We think we can make a decision without it tearing other people's hearts in two.

Sierra took Clanton and Carolyn aside when she found an opportunity. "How would you feel about coming and spending a few weeks with your grandparents next summer?" From their eager responses, she knew she could approach Luís and María about the idea. She found the chance while helping María wash and put away dishes.

"Would you and Luís like to have Clanton and Carolyn spend a few weeks with you next summer?"

María started to cry. "*Sí, sí,*" she said. "As often as possible. What about Christmas?"

Sierra hugged her. "We can't come Christmas, Mama. We're in a pageant at the church. Easter. We'll come for Easter, if that's all right with you."

"*Sí.* You come home Easter."

Most of the relatives had already headed home to Santa Rosa or Cloverdale or the Bay Area where they lived. Clanton and Carolyn were the last of the younger generation lounging around in the small, neat country house on the edge of the vineyard.

"The family is scattering," María said, teary as each one left. "Alex off in Connecticut—"

"Mama!" Luís hissed and gave Sierra an apologetic look.

"It's all right, Papa," Sierra said, trying to ease their discomfort. "I know about it." The children reported everything, even when she wished they wouldn't.

Luís walked her to the car. "When are you and the *niños* leaving?"

"Sunday morning. Early. It's a long drive."

"I'm going to six o'clock Mass." He looked old—old and hurt—and she loved him unbearably.

She kissed his cheek. "We'll meet you there."

He cupped her cheek. "My son is a fool."

Sierra's eyes filled. "No, Papa. *I* was the fool."

Dear Lord, since that bear I have been thinking.

And I have been looking and seeing lots of things different from before. It is like something changed inside me. It seems to me everything around me now cries out You are here. You have put your stamp on every created thing. I can hear Mama from so long ago pointing out flowers and trees and birds and animals and saying how they are all gifts from You. She said to me once that You decorated the world from the depths of the sea to the heavens just for us.

Maybe I am wrong, but I do not think You did all that purely for our pleasure. I think now you did it so we could see You.

I see things differently now, Lord, and spent a good part of my day choked up with grief over the hard things I have said about You.

It rained today and I kept thinking how it washes everything clean and the earth drinks and becomes fertile. Aunt Martha used to talk so much about the Word being a double-edged sword revealing to us our sins so that we could confess and ask forgiveness and receive Your Mercy and Grace. The *so that* part always eluded me. Now it seems to ring in my ears day and night.

And I was thinking too about time. I suppose

You do not have need of it, being God and all, but I am glad I have more of it.

The fog last night reminded me of how clouded my thinking has been where You are concerned, Jesus. I could feel the oppressing Fears that have been my companion for so long closing in again like that misty gray blanket. I was awake most of the night worrying over so many things. And then Dawn came pink and orange and took my breath away and the fear with it. How could I think of dying and my children starving before such Glory?

A good night's sleep is a precious thing, Lord. Sometimes I am so tired I ache for rest and sink into a cottony place where even hard ground feels like a feather bed. Maybe tonight will be like that now that I have told You what has been on my mind.

I guess if You heard my prayer over that bear, Lord, You can hear me about this. We are hungry, Jesus. We made do with two fish Hank caught today, and I am thankful to You for them. But it is not enough to keep us going. So, I am asking You again to save us from death. Please, Lord, help us again or we will starve just like those poor folks who did not make it through the mountains.

21

"WHAT HAPPENED?" SIERRA SAID WHEN CLANTON unlocked the door and walked in at three in the afternoon on Saturday instead of ten in the evening when Alex usually brought him home.

"He dropped me off," he said, slinging his backpack onto the wing chair she'd just finished recovering.

"Did you have a fight?"

"Not with him."

The look of defiance on his face and swelling across his left eye made her stomach drop. Had Alex hit him? "Did you say something to Elizabeth?"

"Yeah, you could say that, but she said something to me first."

"What?"

"She told me to take out the garbage." He gave a defiant snort. "Yeah, right, like I'm the one living there all week. I told her she could take out her own trash. I'm not her personal servant. Then she launched into this lecture on how she had to give up every Saturday with *Alex* so he could be with his snarly, snot-nosed son."

She could feel the heat of anger rising and fought to remain calm. "Were those her exact words?" Elizabeth worked with Alex every day of the week. She spent every night in his bed. She had him all to herself on Sundays. And she was complaining about the *one* measly day a week he spent with his two children?

Didn't you?

"Close," Clanton said, giving her an odd look when she winced. "She called me a 'half-breed.' So I told her what she was."

"Oh, Lord," Sierra murmured and sat down on the couch. "What did you call her?"

"You know what I called her. I said it in Spanish, but I guess she got the point. What did you expect? She started in on *you*." His eyes glittered. "She said the reason Daddy left was because you were a dull housewife with no brains and no class. And it looked like I took after you. So I told her she wasn't any better than a common hooker, just a little more expensive on the upkeep. She slapped me across the face and called me a 'foul-mouthed, uncouth little wetback.'"

His eyes lost the heat of anger and glistened with hurt. "I didn't see Dad standing in the doorway. I've never seen him look so mad. He told me to get my things. He was taking me home. And she just stood there, smirking."

Sierra ached for him. She remembered the way Alex had looked at her the day he'd left. She'd never known a man whose eyes could be so hot and cold at the same time. "Did he say anything to you on the way home?"

"Nothing," he said softly. He turned away slightly, but she'd already seen his tears. "I'm going to my room."

Sierra wanted to call Alex and give him a piece of her mind about the fiasco. She wanted to take Elizabeth Longford into a ring and pulverize her.

A wetback?

A plague on her, Lord! Forgive my wrath, Father, but I'd like to rip her heart out!

If she didn't *do* something, she'd explode.

"Clanton? I'm going for a walk. I'll be back in a little while."

Her walk turned into a run, and by the time she returned, she was streaming sweat, her lungs heaving, her heart pounding like a kettledrum. She leaned over the kitchen sink, gasping for air, and splashed water on her hot face. She drank a few sips of water. The telephone rang.

Snatching the kitchen towel from the oven handle, she dried her hands. It rang again. If it was a telephone sales call, they were going to wish they'd picked another number. As it turned out, she barely said hello before Alex was making demands.

"Let me talk to Clanton."

God! Help! If you can cool me off, cool me off fast!

"Why?" she said tautly. She wasn't ready to hand her son over to Alex again. Not for a long, long time.

"Why're you breathing like that?"

"Because I went out for a run, OK? A hard run! It was either that or buy a shotgun and shoot *two* people!" She slammed the phone down.

It rang again. She gritted her teeth. Turning, she caught a glimpse of her face in the glass front of the cupboard-mounted microwave. Amazing! No steam coming out her ears, but she looked rabid enough to begin frothing at the mouth.

Clanton came out of his bedroom. "Aren't you going to answer it, Mom? It might be Dad."

"It *is* Dad. If you want to talk to him, you answer it, because if I do, I'm going to tell him what he can do with himself and that . . . that *broad* he's living with." She stalked off down the hallway and went into her bedroom.

The telephone stopped ringing. She could hear Clanton's voice, subdued, scared, his heart in Alex's hands. He didn't say much more than hello. Apparently, Alex wanted to do all the talking. She clenched her hands, wanting to pick up the extension and listen to the other end of the conversation. Instead, she sat on the bed and prayed through clenched teeth.

Strike them with lightning, Lord. Open the earth and swallow them.

Alex and Clanton didn't talk long.

Expecting to have to pick up the pieces, Sierra came out to find her son rummaging through the refrigerator. "What did he say?" she asked, surprised that he was hungry. She always lost her appetite after a big fight.

Clanton straightened, a carton of milk in one hand and a Tupperware container of cold homemade enchiladas in the other. "He said he wasn't mad at me, but it was going to be a week or two before he could see me again."

"And?"

"And, that's it." He shrugged, set the milk on the counter, and put the entire Tupperware container into the microwave.

Sierra heard from Audra before Alex called again.

"He left her."

"Excuse me?" Sierra said, startled. Audra hadn't even identified herself before blurting out the news.

"Alex left Elizabeth," she said. "He packed everything and walked out on her last Saturday. They had a huge brouhaha over something, and this after Vesuvius erupted in Connecticut."

What had happened in Connecticut? She didn't have a chance to ask before Audra rushed on.

"Alex came in Monday morning looking like thunder and told Steve to assign someone else to his work. He doesn't want her within ten feet of him. She came in an hour later. Steve talked with her briefly. He wouldn't tell me what was said, other than that she gave notice and left."

"Where's Alex living?"

"In a hotel in Beverly Hills, I think. Do you want his number? I could get it for you."

Sierra thought about it for a moment. "No. He'll call when he's ready. He told Clanton he'd be in touch with him and Carolyn in a week or two."

"You don't want to talk to him?"

"I've said enough already." As usual.

Alex didn't call. He came by. Not on a Friday evening, but on Saturday in the pouring rain. She heard the doorbell ring and Carolyn and Clanton talking to someone. They knew not to let strangers in, so she assumed it was one of their friends stopping by or her neighbor, Frances, with another delicious treat she'd concocted as an experiment for her gourmet cooking class.

"Nice."

Her heart jumped at the sound of his voice. Luckily, she was firmly planted on the ladder, where she was just dabbing the last touches of gold acrylic paint on the sunflower design she'd drawn along the wall of her bedroom. She'd completed half of it over the last two weeks.

She looked over her shoulder and saw Alex leaning against the doorjamb, watching her. "I wasn't expecting you." Amazing how calm she sounded.

"I know." His glance flickered over her.

Sighing inwardly, she looked away. The last thing she needed was his disdain. Why did he always have to catch her looking like someone who had crawled out of a bag of rummage-sale rejects? She brushed a strand of hair back from her eyes, wondering how much paint she had smudged on her face. She had at least a dozen stains on her paint shirt, and her cut-off Levi's should have been trashed years ago. There was a hole under the right back pocket big enough that he'd be able to see the cotton flowered underpants she wore underneath.

"Are you taking the children out?" she said, feigning indifference. Maybe someday her heart wouldn't leap into her throat at the sight of him.

When he didn't say anything, she looked back at him and found him staring at her canopy bed. She felt the heat come up into her cheeks when he looked up at her again.

"What happened to ours?"

"I sold it."

Had he winced, or was she just imagining it? He looked around the room. "I guess it wouldn't've fit in here anyway." His glance halted abruptly on the old armoire she'd refinished. He'd moved it into the garage when Bruce Davies had redone the house, intending to take it to the dump. He'd left before he had the chance.

Something flickered across his face as he looked up at her again, his eyes barely grazing hers. "I need to talk to you," he said grimly and went out.

She shut her eyes for a minute and then gathered her brushes, balanced her easel, and went down the ladder. She put everything down on the drop cloth and went into the bathroom to wash her hands. Glancing up into the mirror, she saw tendrils of sandy blonde hair curling in all directions. A smudge of green was across one cheek, some brown on her nose. Picking up the soap and washcloth, she scrubbed her face. That done, she debated changing into clean clothes and dismissed the idea. Raking her hands back through her hair, she French-braided it quickly.

When she came into the living room, she found Alex looking at Mary Kathryn's quilt, which she'd mounted on the wall. Audra had taken her to a museum a few weeks ago, and she'd seen a quilt mounted in the same way. Liking the effect, she'd promptly come home, purchased material to make a sleeve, and bought a wooden drapery rod. Audra had been impressed when she saw what Sierra had done. Even better, they'd spent the better part of an hour talking about the quilt.

"It belonged to Mary Kathryn McMurray," she said to Alex. "She was a relative of mine who came across the plains by wagon train. She settled in Sonoma County in 1848. That's her trunk at the end of the couch." It served as a side table. She winced, realizing the old brass lamps Alex hated so much sat on top of it. Naturally, she had to draw his attention to it.

He didn't say a word. The condo rang with silence. Frowning, she realized what was wrong. "Where are the children?"

"I asked them to make themselves scarce for a little while. Clanton said he'd play billiards at the clubhouse, and Carolyn said you wouldn't mind if she went to Susan's."

She was immediately filled with trepidation. Why would he send the children off unless he was going to say something to her he knew she wouldn't like? What could he want?

Oh, God, *the children!*

"Don't look at me like that, Sierra."

"Like what?"

"Like a deer caught in headlights. I'm not planning to run over you."

She turned away and went into the kitchen. "Would you like some coffee?" Her mind was racing. She didn't even notice if he answered yes or no. She wished she had read the divorce papers over more carefully. What had they said about custody of the children?

"I'm not living with Elizabeth anymore."

"Audra told me." She fumbled in the cabinet for coffee and filters.

"Audra? I didn't think you even spoke to her anymore."

"We get together for lunch every few weeks."

"Since when?" he said in surprise.

She measured coffee. "Since I took her to lunch and apologized."

Alex came over and sat on a stool on the other side of the breakfast counter. She could feel him looking at her. Like a bug under glass. She poured water into the coffeemaker, refusing to look back at him.

"What do you and Audra talk about?" he said carefully.

"We don't talk about you, Alex. That was one of the first ground rules I laid down." She shrugged. "She broke it last week."

"Did she tell you what happened?"

"She said Elizabeth quit and went back East."

"I moved out after the little altercation with Clanton."

"Can we talk about something else, please?" she said, uncomfortable. She didn't want to hear about his love affair with Elizabeth Longford. She didn't want to hear about his broken heart. She didn't want to hear about how difficult things were for him. She wanted him to get to the point and leave so she could breathe normally again.

"I want to spend more time with my children."

Here it comes, she thought.

"You're shaking," he said softly.

"I'm not giving you custody, Alex. Whatever it said in those papers I signed and gave you, I'm not—"

He lifted his hands. "Relax. I'm not asking for that. I wouldn't. They're happy with you. I just want . . ." His voice trailed off, and he uttered a soft curse, dragging his hands back through his hair. He looked at her again, and she noticed the lines around his eyes and mouth, the unveiled pain in his eyes. "I just want a chance to be a part of their lives again. A couple of hours on Friday with Carolyn and a few on Saturday with Clanton isn't enough."

She almost reminded him that was more than he'd spent with them *before* he left her and moved in with Elizabeth.

Lord, keep me silent. Make my words sweet. Help me see his side of things more clearly and with more compassion than I have in the past. Give me your eyes, Father.

Alex searched her face when she said nothing. Turning her back on him, she took two mugs down from the cupboard and filled them with coffee. She didn't invite him back into the living room. She liked having the breakfast bar between them.

"Thanks," he said flatly and put his hands around the mug as though to warm them. She couldn't remember ever seeing him nervous before.

"You can see the children whenever you want, Alex. As long as you don't prevent them from continuing what they're doing."

"Such as?" he said, eyes narrowed slightly.

"They both go to church youth group on Wednesday nights."

"Which church?"

The issue of religion had never been important to either of them. Now, it was of tantamount importance to her. "The church where we were playing baseball."

He thought about it for a minute, troubled. "Mama said you went to Mass with my father."

"The children went to catechism in Windsor."

"I know. Are they still going?"

O God, help me. I don't want to start a war with Alex, but I want my children to have a personal relationship with you. I don't want them to have to go through a priest or be bound by guilt or penitence.

"No," she said, clasping her own mug between both hands as he had done. "We're happy in this church, Alex."

"You don't think God's in a Catholic church?"

She felt the weight of Madrid family tradition behind his question. These were his children.

"I think God is wherever he chooses to be, Alex. Catholic or Protestant, it doesn't matter. When I sit with your father and mother, I know they love the Lord as much as I do. They've loved him longer and harder. But this church is where I found my way home, Alex. It's where the children are learning the meaning of Christ's love. These people aren't just friends. They're like family. Dennis especially. I'd be dead and Clanton still wouldn't be speaking to you if not for him."

He frowned heavily, eyes fixed on her. "What do you mean, *dead?*"

She smiled, shaking her head at the memory. "Let's just say I was driving a little fast one day when Dennis pulled me over. He's a highway patrolman. He gave me my first and, I hope, *last* speeding ticket."

He looked at her, his eyes intent, searching. "I'm sorry, Sierra."

She knew he meant he was sorry about everything. "Don't be. It's the best thing that ever happened to me." If she hadn't hit rock bottom, would she have ever seen how much she needed the Lord? Would she ever have been soft fertile soil for the seeds that had been scattered throughout her life by a dozen different people? Would she have ever understood Jesus' love for her?

Alex got up and left the breakfast bar. She watched him move around the living room. He paused before the quilt again and rubbed the back of his neck. He had always done that when he was past exhaustion or depressed about something. In their earlier years, she'd rubbed his back and told him how she loved him. Often, they ended up in bed together, forgetting everything but the pleasure they found in one another.

Her skin grew warm, remembering.

It was better not to think about those times.

"How would you feel if I leased a condo in this complex?"

Her heart stopped. "I beg your pardon?" she said weakly.

Alex turned around and looked at her. "I said, how would you feel if I leased a condo in this complex?"

She recognized that look. Double-barreled, point-blank determination. *"You* want to live in a *condo?"* She couldn't believe he would even suggest it. He wouldn't even marry her until he had found them a small house to rent. *"I don't want to share walls with someone else,"* he'd declared. She would have lived in a shack as long as she could be with him.

His eyes never left her as he said, "There's a condo available for lease. I wanted to talk it over with you before I signed the papers."

"You always swore you wouldn't live in an apartment or condo." Alex looked around the living room. "It's bigger than I expected, and I haven't heard any noise while I've been in here today."

"My neighbors are working." Not that they made all that much noise when they were home.

"Then you object."

"I didn't say that. I—" She closed her mouth, deciding she'd better think before she went further. She felt a hint of panic stir. It hurt every time she saw him. Was she going to have to see him *every* day? And what if he found some other woman to move in with him? Or he started dating any one of a dozen attractive single women living in the complex? Or . . .

A hundred painful possibilities leaped into her mind, sending shards of pain through her. What if . . . what if . . . what if . . . ?

Alex sat down on the stool again and clasped his hands loosely on the breakfast counter. "I want to share the responsibility of the children with you again. I could keep them when you wanted to go out."

"Out?" As in dating? Was he hoping to marry her off? Ron would be delighted to know that.

"Clanton said you wanted to take a college class but didn't want to leave them home alone any more than you have to already with work. If I was living within a few doors of you, you could leave the children with me."

"It was an afternoon class, Alex. I was working."

"You don't have to work."

"Yes, I do."

His eyes darkened. "Not if you'd start accepting the money I've been sending you, instead of doing whatever you've been doing with the checks."

"Live on alimony, you mean? No, thank you. Every time you send me a check like that, I'm going to tear it up and flush it down the toilet!"

"Why do you have to be so pigheaded stubborn?"

"Look who's talking." She tried to calm down. "Alex, I've seen what living on alimony does to other women. Some of them can't get along without it. Or they feel they deserve more and more. Cost-of-living increases. Petty vengeance. You want me hanging around your neck like a millstone for the rest of your life? Alimony is as bad as welfare, and I want some self-respect out of this whole mess. I may not be living in the fancy neighborhood we used to, but I'm making it on my own. I'm *happy* here, and I'm paying my *own* bills."

"I should be paying for your support. We've been married thirteen years."

"We *were* married, and you can consider the debt forgiven."

He started to say something and stopped. Letting out his breath, he raked his hand back through his hair. "Look, I know it's because of what I said to you that day I called after seeing the house in the real estate section. I hurt you. *Dios*, don't you think I know it?"

"Maybe it was that in the beginning," she said frankly, "but not anymore." Covering her face, she took a breath and released it slowly, trying to rein in her emotions. She lowered her hands to her lap and looked him in the eye. "You mention money, Alex, and I see red. It was one of the buttons you used to push all the time."

"I have a few buttons of my own," he said, eyes hot. "One of them is the fact you won't accept any kind of help from me. You used to lean on me, Sierra."

"Yes, I did. And look where that got us," she said, feeling the prick of tears. She swallowed and pressed her lips together, trying to think of words gentle enough, yet strong enough, to explain her position. "You've been very generous with the child support, Alex, and I'm thankful. Let's just leave it at that."

"Do you use any of it?" he said bitterly.

Heat filled her. Was he accusing her of misusing their money? "I put it in their savings accounts," she said, hurt and angry. "Some of it I use for clothes. I have records of every cent you've ever given them."

"No doubt, but what about that private school? Why aren't they going anymore?"

"Because they hated it! Because Clanton was suspended twice, and Carolyn was on the verge of ulcers trying to get straight A's."

"Why didn't you tell me what was going on?"

"And if I had? What would you have done?"

"Tried to help!"

She searched his eyes, wondering if he really would have.

"What did you think I'd do, Sierra?"

She bit her lip and said nothing. She'd been so convinced he would accuse her of being a rotten mother, the same way he'd accused her of being a rotten wife. She'd been afraid to tell him, ashamed she couldn't fix things on her own.

"Talk to me, Sierra."

"It doesn't matter now. You were busy at the time."

Color came into his face and a look of bleakness. "I'm not busy now. I'm going to be working a lot less at the office. I've already talked my plans over with Steve. He's putting up the money for the equipment. It's already ordered. All I need is a place to put it."

Why hadn't he made the same arrangements a year ago? It might have saved their marriage.

She caught the direction of her thinking and halted. If she condemned him, she'd have to condemn herself. Everybody has 20/20 hindsight. She could see her own mistakes with heart-wrenching clarity.

"I'll make it easy, Sierra. A simple yes or no. Yes: I sign the lease. No: I don't."

She wanted to say no. She wanted to avoid more pain. She wanted to avoid seeing him with other women. She wanted to avoid seeing him at all. She knew that was impossible. And if she said no, how would the children feel when they found out? Angry? Betrayed? They loved him. They wanted to see their father as often as possible. How could she be selfish and deny them that right? Besides, they *needed* him.

"I haven't said anything to the children," he said quietly, "and I won't if your answer is no."

She was touched by his sensitivity. It was one of the things that had made her fall in love with him in the first place, that and his male machismo, as her father once termed it.

"Go ahead and sign the lease."

His dark eyes took on a familiar glow before he looked away. "Can I use your telephone?"

She frowned slightly, uneasy. "It's over there."

Pulling a business card from his shirt pocket, he wasted no time punching the number. "Roberta Folse, please. Roberta? Alex Madrid. The answer is yes. How soon can you take care of the details? Good." He glanced at his watch. "I'll meet you there in about thirty minutes." He dropped the receiver lightly into its cradle.

Turning his head, he smiled at her. Her stomach dropped the

same way it had the first time he'd looked at her. *"Gracias,"* he said. *"Las cosas serán más fáciles."*

She forced a smile in return, thinking how wrong he was. Things would not be easier. At least, not for her.

"I'll give the children a call later this evening. In the meantime, you can tell them I'll be moving into one-sixteen early Wednesday morning."

When he left, she groaned aloud and buried her head in her arms. "Oh, Lord, it's going to be a hundred times worse than I thought."

Alex would be only three doors away.

I never expected You to send a heathen to answer my prayer.

But I reckon You do things however You please.

An Indian came to the edge of our meadow today. Beth saw him first and thought he was a mighty strange looking deer. Well, I saw he was not a deer at all, but a man dressed up in skins and a deerhead mask. He had a bow and arrows and stood watching us intently. Hank was all for getting the gun, but I said we would wait to see what he would do. Besides, what good is a gun with no ammunition.

I remembered what Kavanaugh told us about the land belonging to the Indians and how we should give back something for the privilege of traveling through. Well, we are going nowhere, Lord. So I wondered what that Indian was thinking while he stood there looking at us.

I wondered if he was angry that we settled in his pretty valley without asking first. So I told the children to stay by the wagon while I went to see if I could make peace with him. I know a few signs from having watched Kavanaugh.

I could not offer the Indian a bite of food to eat as we have no food for ourselves. The Indian was of small stature, muscular, and has dark eyes and hair. I could not guess his age. He did not know what I was waving about, so I offered him the only thing of real value I own—the pretty cross necklace Aunt Martha gave me when I left Galena. He was well pleased by the gift but did not know how to work the clasp. I helped him. He disappeared into the woods and I thought that was the end of it. It was not.

He came back again later carrying a small deer, fresh killed. He laid it at my feet and made it clear it was a gift. I wept as I thanked him. Before he left us, he made his name known to me. Koxoenis. From his gestures and pantomime, I think it means Bringer of Meat.

I am weeping again. I am so undeserving and yet You have provided food for me and my family. We will not starve after all. The children are at this moment asleep with full stomachs for the first time in many, many days, and I have You to thank. You sent Koxoenis.

All hope was lost and is now revived in me again.

Joshua returned today with beans, salt pork, flour, coffee and powder, shot and lead. We are living with abundance. I told him about Koxoenis. He is very eager to meet him. I asked if he had seen Kavanaugh. Joshua said no. One of the men said Kavanaugh headed north to Oregon.

Koxoenis came back today. I was pleased to see him. He stood at the edge of the meadow until we waved an invitation for him to come to us. I think he is shy. Joshua made signs that he was welcome to share our supper. He ate sparingly of our bread and would not accept even a small portion of the venison he brought to us. When we finished, he motioned for us to follow him. He did not go more than a hundred feet from our fire when he used a digging stick he was carrying to pull up some plants. He gave them to me and made signs that the roots and leaves are good to eat. With a shy smile, he ran off into the woods again.

All this time we were so hungry and food was growing within reach.

Lord, I am having Terrible Trouble with Joshua. He is Intent on Doing Something! He keeps talking about looking for Koxoenis or going to Sutter's Fort or down to Monterey. He wants to go his own way whatever way that might be. He is not the boy I know him to be and he is not the

man I think he can become. He is one huge pain
in my heart and gut.

It has gotten me thinking how much Trouble I
have been to You.

I am Truly Sorry, Lord.

I remember how full of Wrath You were at
those Israelites You brought out of Egypt. They
kept whining and fussing and complaining like
Joshua does now. And like I was doing before the
Day of the Bear. I remember too how You wanted
to wipe all those Israelites off the face of the
earth, but Moses begged You not to.

Well, Lord, I know just how You feel because
I wanted to wipe Joshua off the face of the earth
today. He made me so mad I was shaking with it.
I said things I should not have said. But maybe
that was better than what I wanted to do. Lord,
if I had had a cane I would have beat him with it.
He was none too happy with me either.

How can you love someone so much and still
get so mad you want to kill them? I saved his life
fourteen years ago. And today I was in the mood
to take it.

Joshua is not much help to us, Jesus. He
would rather be at Koxoenis village learning their
ways than staying here and helping us in ours.

Would You please Do Something with him,
Jesus?

I give him to You cause if I don't, I swear that boy won't live to spring.

Koxoenis came back today. He was curious about the wagon. I wonder what kind of house he lives in. I showed him inside our poor makeshift abode. Then I offered him fish stew, bread, and coffee. I said to the children it would be interesting seeing where and how he lived. Joshua said he will go with him and find out. I said if Koxoenis welcomed him, he was free to do so. Joshua made sign language with him and they went off together. They have been gone all day, but I have no fear my son will come to harm. You sent Koxoenis to us and he has proven to be a kind and generous friend. I think Joshua will have much of interest to tell us when he returns.

Joshua said Koxoenis lives in a village several miles southwest of us. He said the others were frightened when they got there and spoke harshly to Koxoenis for bringing him. I suppose there is good reason. When I think of the way the poor Indians were treated at Sutter's Fort, I shudder. Sutter fed them in troughs like animals and used them like slaves. Joshua said Koxoenis has a wife and two small children who run naked wherever they please. He said his house is made of bark, bound tules, and mud and is weather tight and warm inside.

His wife cooks a mush made of acorns in a basket by stirring hot stones! The chief has a great store of food stuffs and gives generously to the people.

Koxoenis showed Joshua other foods that grow around us. Joshua said he will teach Hank, Matthew, and Beth how to find these plants come daylight.

Joshua and Hank have been digging all day. Joshua said Koxoenis's people dig down two feet and build the dome house over the pit. He can build this house in a few days while it will take weeks of effort to build a cabin. Our duck cover is torn and leaking. We need shelter from the cold California rain.

Joshua has made a pole frame work over the pit and is covering it with tiers of bark and tules. He has the boys and Beth mixing mud. Thankfully, we have had two days of easier weather. The clouds lie over the ground like a blanket.

We are now living in a hut like Koxoenis and his people. I wonder what Aunt Martha would think of me living like a savage. I must admit living in this hut is far better than living in our wagon. We moved in as the rains started again, and we are dry and warm.

Thank You, Lord, for putting a roof over our heads again.

22

THE CHILDREN REPORTED EVERYTHING TO
Sierra whether she wanted to hear or not. "Dad rented some
furniture," Clanton said after his first visit. "He's got a new couch
and a couple of swivel rockers. He bought a whole wall setup
with a big- screen television and stereo, and you should see his
computers!"

Carolyn was more impressed with the white rats he'd purchased for her and kept at his place. "They're so cute, Mom. I
call them Peaches and Cream. They're both males, so we won't
have any babies."

"Well, that's nice."

"And he has an aquarium. Just a little one for some pretty
goldfish."

Lures.

Clanton and Carolyn began spending more and more time with Alex. They'd come home from school, scarf down snacks, rattle off some news, whiz through their homework, and take off for *his* condo. She began wishing she'd said *no*. She missed the sound of their voices, even the strident ones when they were fighting. Sometimes she resented how eager they were to be with him, and then she was always struck with guilt afterward. Sometimes she found herself aching with loneliness.

Is it a sin, Lord? You're supposed to be enough. I love you. I do. Help me to accept these changes and not be so jealous and needy. Help me to know in my heart you are sufficient. Help me rest in you.

Choir helped. On those evenings, she and the children walked to church together and then went out to a family café afterward for a late dessert. Sunday was the one precious day a week, for she had the children all to herself. They went to church early and didn't get home until almost one in the afternoon. After a late lunch, she walked back to church with them so they could take part in the youth activities and she could attend the evening Bible study.

Gradually, she felt less alone. She used the time the children were away to study and finish all the little projects she'd laid out for herself but never had time to do. She turned on the radio and listened to a Christian station that played contemporary rock, free to sing along without anyone listening to her but the Lord.

Christmas drew closer. Rather than be elated, she was depressed. All her shopping was done, the packages wrapped and hidden in her bedroom closet and under the bed. The children knew better than to go poking around in her room after Thanksgiving. She'd begun addressing Christmas cards the first week of December and had started her letters. She always wrote to everyone. It was the one time a year when she could catch up on all the news from friends and family.

Ron called again. "You sound a little down."

"I'm writing Christmas letters, and I get a little depressed every time I have to write, 'Mom died of cancer, and Alex and I got a divorce' over and over again. Just the sort of glad tidings friends like to read at Christmas time."

"Would a proposition help cheer you up?"

Her mouth twitched. "That depends."

"Strictly honorable, I assure you. I'm having a Christmas fund-raiser at the Hyatt Regency, and I'm in desperate need of a pretty hostess."

"To serve drinks and appetizers?"

"No. To stand beside me and greet guests, the kind of guests who have lots and lots of money and love giving it to good causes like Los Angeles Outreach."

"Are any movie stars going to be there?" she said, teasing.

"A few."

"You're kidding!"

"I take it you might be interested."

She feigned hesitation. "Well, I don't know. Is Mel Gibson attending?"

"No."

"Then I don't—"

"I'm begging."

She laughed. "I'd love to help out and you know it. How dressed up do I have to get?"

"Very. I'll be in a tux."

Ron gave her the details. He would pick her up early. The fund-raiser included a full-course dinner and dancing. "It'll go until the wee hours," he warned her.

Clanton was just going out the door when she hung up the telephone. "Honey, would you tell your dad I need to talk to him? It's important."

The telephone rang a few minutes later. "What's up?" Alex said.

"Can the children spend the night with you on December 21?"

"Spend the night? Where are you going to be?"

"At a fund-raiser with Ron. He said it'll be late before I get home."

"I haven't got any extra beds."

He sounded so cold. "Maybe I can borrow a couple of sleeping bags." Maybe he had made other plans, plans she didn't want to hear about. "Never mind, Alex. I should've thought it through before asking you. Carolyn's been wanting to spend the night with Susan, and Clanton can always go to—"

"I'll stay with them over there," he said firmly. "We'll do something fun for the evening, and I'll wait at your place until you get back."

"It's going to be very late, Alex."

"You've got a comfortable sofa."

"Are you sure?" He sounded less than pleased about the whole thing.

"Yeah, I'm sure."

Taking a deep breath, Sierra called Audra and told her she'd been invited to a formal fund-raiser and was going to be acting as hostess. "I need to find a dress."

"How much can you spend?"

"Don't even think about Rodeo Drive."

"What size are you?" When Sierra told her, she said, "Great. You can borrow one of my gowns. When can you come over?"

By the time Sierra got there, Audra had already picked out the dress she thought Sierra should wear. After seeing the others, Sierra had to admit she liked it the best. It was a deep red velvet that fit her perfectly. "I bought it for a Christmas party four years ago and never wore it," Audra said, admiring it on Sierra. "My feet are a little bigger than yours, but I know just where you can get some satin pumps and have them dyed to match," she said while snapping on a gorgeous necklace that glittered like diamonds.

"These aren't real, are they?" Sierra said, fingering it.

"Zirconia. Stop sweating." She handed her matching pierced

earrings and then helped her snap on the bracelet. Stepping back, she looked her over. "Perfect. It looks better on you than it did on me." She went back into her closet and came out with a fur coat.

"Not on your life!" Sierra said, backing up. "Absolutely not, Audra. If I damaged it or it got lost, I'd kill myself."

"I thought you were going to say something about all the little animals that lost their lives to make it."

"Well, that, too," Sierra said, making a quick calculation. It would take a lot of cute little minks to make that coat.

"That's what I told Steve, but men just don't think about those things when they're trying to show the world how successful they are." She carried it back into the closet. "I wear it to the opera once in a while just so he won't get upset about it. No one harangues me there. Oh, *good!* I knew I bought something to go with that dress." She came back out with a red velvet, satin-lined cape. She draped it over Sierra's shoulders and took a step back. "Take a look at yourself."

Sierra did, and her mouth dropped open. She looked like someone else, someone who'd stepped out of a fairy tale. "I remember feeling this delight as a little girl up in the attic dressing in grown-up clothes with my best friend." Laughing, she looked at Audra in the mirror. "What do you think?"

"I think you look fantastic. Does Alex know you're going to this affair with Ron Peirozo?"

"He's babysitting."

✳✳✳

Alex came early on the night of the fund-raiser. She'd told him Ron was picking her up at five, and he arrived an hour early.

"Mom, Daddy's here."

"Ask him if he'd like a soda, honey. I'll be down in a little while."

Nervous and excited, she had already bathed and was fixing her hair in a loose French braid. She put on a little makeup, then dabbed on Shalimar before she stepped into her dress. Slipping into the red satin shoes, she put on the jewelry. She was ready half an hour before Ron was expected.

"Mom, you look so *pretty!*" Carolyn said as she came into the living room.

Sierra smiled, gratified that at least one person in the room noticed the change in her. Alex just stared at her. He didn't say anything. What had she been hoping? That his mouth would fall open and his tongue loll out? She put the red cape carefully over the back of a chair.

"Where's Clanton?" she said as she laid her gloves and a red, beaded purse Audra had found on top of the cape.

"Brady's," Carolyn said. He was a friend Clanton had met at church who happened to live in the complex. "He said he'd be home in a few minutes. He's borrowing a video game. Are those diamonds, Mom?"

"No, honey. I wouldn't put my toe out the door if they were."

Carolyn looked at her father. "Don't you think she looks pretty, Daddy?"

Blushing, Sierra avoided Alex's eyes.

"*Sí, su mama está muy hermosa,*" he said softly.

Her heart tripped as she looked at him. She looked into his eyes and saw he meant every word.

Carolyn picked up her backpack and headed for her room. Sierra turned, tensing. "Where are you going, honey?"

Carolyn glanced at her dad. "I've got some homework to do."

"Tonight?"

"Just for a while. Daddy's taking Clanton and me to Magic Mountain. I guess I should take a bath, too."

Sierra looked back at Alex and saw the sad smile touch his mouth. "She was watching *Parent Trap* a few days ago."

She put her hand over her stomach. "Great," she said dully.

He noticed the gesture. "Are you nervous?"

"A little." Less about going out with Ron than she was seeing that look in Alex's eyes. She let out her breath and came around the chair to sit down. The hatch-cover table was between them. She liked having something between them.

Alex's eyes narrowed slightly. "How well do you like this guy?"

This guy? "Ron's one of my best friends."

"How does he feel about you?"

She blushed. "Why are you asking?"

"You quit working for him. I'm curious why."

She almost told him it was none of his business. Considering his own behavior, he had a lot of nerve to ask *any* questions. Instead, she curbed her anger and decided to be honest. "I left because I knew if I stayed, I could end up in an affair with him."

Alex's eyes darkened, not with anger, but pain. "The way I did."

"I don't want to talk about the whys and wherefores of you and Elizabeth, Alex."

"Neither do I. I want to talk about you."

"What about me?"

"You look . . . radiant," he said heavily. "Are you in love with this guy?"

There it was again, that tone. Was he baiting her? "I was *in love* with you, Alex," she said before she thought better of it. She paused, drawing in a steadying breath. This situation was impossible! "I don't think I'll ever feel like that again about anyone. And if I did, I think I'd run as fast as I could to get away from it."

"The way you ran from Peirozo."

She could feel the prick of tears and fought them. "Are you deliberately trying to spoil my evening, Alex? I *like* Ron. He's kind and fun. I'm looking forward to this evening. I've never been to anything like this. I just want to enjoy myself. Don't you think I have that right?"

"Don't cry," Alex said softly. "I wasn't asking to ruin your evening, Sierra."

"Why *are* you asking?"

"Because I don't want to see you hurt."

She gave a bleak laugh. She had never heard such a flimsy excuse in her life. Especially from him. *"You* hurt me, Alex. Ron doesn't have that kind of power over me."

He leaned toward her, eyes intent, searching. "Don't go out with him tonight."

Looking into those dark depths, she remembered everything from the past. She knew why he warned her. When they were young and deeply in love, when her emotions had crested over some crisis, real or imagined, Alex had been the one to catch the wave and ride the passion.

"I'm not your concern anymore, Alex. I haven't been for eight months." Why should those words bring that wounded worried look into his eyes? She felt compelled to set his mind at ease and gave him a tender smile. "Someone told me to grow up. I have."

The doorbell rang.

A muscle jerked in his cheek and he stood up. "I'll tell him you're not feeling well."

She stood as well. "No, you won't." Truth have it, she wasn't, but she had no intention of leaving Ron high and dry. This fundraiser was far too important to him and his work. "I feel fine, Alex."

"You're pale." He turned his head sharply as the door was unlocked. "What'd you do? Give him a key?"

"Hey, Mom!" Clanton said, barging in. "Aren't you going to let Ron in?" He stared at her. *"Wow!"*

"You can say that again," Ron said from right behind him. He didn't even notice Alex. He couldn't have been more open in his admiration, which went a long way to bolstering her spirits.

Clanton brushed past her in his hurry to dump his soccer gear in his bedroom.

"You take my breath away, Sierra," Ron said, leaning down to kiss her lightly on the cheek. She felt a touch of sadness that his compliment didn't have a fraction of the effect Alex's had. As Ron straightened, she saw his expression alter slightly and knew he had seen her ex-husband. She took his hand deliberately.

"Ron, this is Alex. Alex, I'd like you to meet Ron Peirozo, a dear friend of mine."

Ron held out his hand. Alex hesitated for a fraction of a second before taking it. Neither said anything. They were too busy measuring one another. Sierra knew under other circumstances they would get along very well. They might even be friends. Right now, she was the only common ground—and not one that would bring them together.

Letting go of Ron's hand, she picked up her purse and gloves. He took the red cape and laid it over her shoulders. His hands gripped her arms gently, drawing her a few inches closer to him. "Ready to go?"

Alex understood the gesture and shoved his hands into his pockets. "Have a nice evening."

Sierra walked with Ron to the door. Ron gave Alex a nod as he opened it for her. "Nice meeting you, Alex."

"Yeah, likewise."

She didn't look back. She didn't dare.

Ron didn't mention Alex, nor did she. He spent the drive to downtown Los Angeles filling her in on the programs at Los Angeles Outreach. "People are going to be asking you questions," he said and made sure she knew what was going on.

As she stood beside Ron and greeted guests as they arrived, she recognized numerous faces and names. Several lingered over her hand, making fulsome compliments. Ron teased her about it over a dinner of prime rib. "I should've brought a whip and chair to keep some of these animals back."

She was proud of Ron and impressed by him as he stood at the podium and gave a flawless and relaxed welcome and presentation. He was as at ease in front of this crowd of socially elite as he was with the children he found in the ghettos and beneath the freeways. She knew that those listening to him would be only too willing to support him and his work. He was sincere, zealous, and accomplishing a great deal. The young men and women serving were all "graduates" of the program. "Talk to them, and they'll tell you the difference Outreach has made in their lives. The Lord has blessed us that we might bless others. . . ."

When the band started playing, Ron led her out onto the dance floor. "I've already had several pledges that'll cover the next few months' expenses," he said, holding her close. She felt the warmth of his hand at the small of her back and the brush of his thighs. He was a good dancer, smooth and graceful, guiding her expertly. She felt safe and protected in his arms.

After the first dance, she had other partners, all interested in hearing about Los Angeles Outreach and Ron Peirozo. A few asked her about her relationship to him. A few just wanted to get close enough to ask her out. She was flattered but not interested.

Ron danced with her again several times and needled her unmercifully. "I thought you'd succumb to that actor's charms for certain," he said, inclining his head toward a movie star who'd danced with her several times.

"Are you kidding?"

"I saw you swooning when he took your hand."

"That was before I spent five minutes with him. The guy's no better than a neighborhood masher. He asked me to spend a weekend in Hawaii with him. Can you believe it?"

"I believe it. I've had a few licentious thoughts of my own about you this evening. Want to go sailing with me?"

"Knock it off, Peirozo."

He laughed. "See the gentleman over there talking with Arlene? He was just asking me if you were taken."

"Tell him *yes*."

"I already did." Leaning down, he kissed the curve of her neck. Alex used to kiss her in the same place. With him, it had always sent melting heat all through her body and made her knees weak. With Ron, she didn't feel anything but the pleasing warmth of his lips.

She talked with so many people she lost count. She danced until her feet ached, and she relished every minute of it. On the drive back to Northridge, Ron talked about the pledges he'd received and what it would mean to ongoing programs. They'd made enough money in one evening to cover foundation expenses for the next year.

He pulled into the Haven's parking lot and shut off the engine of his Mercedes. Turning to her, he smiled. "Did you have a good time?"

"Wonderful," she said, drowsy. She never stayed up past eleven-thirty, and it was almost two in the morning. She felt the light brush of his fingers and looked into his eyes. Warmth and desire were there, unhidden. For one brief moment, she wondered what it would be like to be loved by Ron. "I'd better go in," she said softly.

Sensitive to her feelings, Ron touched her cheek lightly and then got out of the car. He came around and opened her door, handing her out. They didn't say anything as they walked along the pathway to her condo. The porch light was on. She wondered if Alex was asleep on the couch.

Turning to Ron, she thanked him for the lovely evening. "Anytime," he said, leaning down to kiss her cheek. Thanking him again, she took her key from her beaded purse and opened the door. Glancing back, she smiled.

"Good night," Ron said and headed back along the pathway to his car.

Not looking into the living room, Sierra closed the door quietly.

"How was it?" Alex said, snapping Mary Kathryn's journal shut and tossing it heedlessly on the hatch-cover table.

The sound of his voice and thump of the book made her jump. "Wonderful," she said, turning to him. "How was your evening?"

"Bueno." He stood up. He didn't even look vaguely tired. His eyes were clear and sharp. "We went out to eat and then rented a couple of movies."

"Sounds like fun." Her stomach knotted with tension at the look on his face. He was angry, though about what she didn't know. And she had no intention of asking. "Well, thank you for watching the children for me. I appreciate it."

"Sure."

"I'm sorry it's so late."

"You said it would be." He crossed the living room and stood in front of her. A small frown briefly puckered his brow as he studied her face. "I guess I'd better go."

"Yes," she said, having difficulty breathing, "I guess you should." She looked around. "Did you bring a jacket with you?"

"No." His mouth tipped in the sensual smile that had turned her heart over at sixteen. It still had that same effect. "Worried about me getting cold between here and my condo? I'm only three doors away."

"I think you're warm enough." She opened the door. "Good night, Alex."

He paused in the doorway and looked back at her. "Did he kiss you good night?"

She blushed. "Not that it's any of your business, but *no*, he did *not* kiss me good night."

Stepping back inside, he cupped the back of her head and abruptly pulled her forward. Before she could gather her wits, he leaned down and planted his mouth firmly over hers in a hard, hot kiss. He released her as suddenly as he'd held her, smiling sardonically. "You looked like you needed kissing," he said roughly.

Sierra stepped back from him, her heart pounding in her ears.

His eyes went dark as they stared into hers. He took another step toward her. "You still do."

"Don't," she whispered desperately.

He wasn't listening. Kicking the door shut with his foot, Alex caught hold of her and pulled her against his hard chest. His head came down and he kissed her again, with the same devastating effect she'd experienced the first time on the Mathesen Street porch so many years ago. He kissed her as though he never intended to let her go. . . .

For a moment she struggled against him. He dug his hands into her hair until it was tumbling about her shoulders and down her back. He kept on kissing her until her insides began to melt and quake.

Her love and the long months of celibacy and loneliness worked against her. Physical hunger swept through her. Sweet memories pulsed.

Oh, God! Oh, God, this is what you meant it to be between a husband and wife!

Husband.

Wife.

Not anymore.

In the midst of the storm of wonderful sensation came the army of doubts marching through her fevered brain, armed with devastation weapons.

Had he held Elizabeth Longford like this? Had he whispered incoherent words of Spanish as he touched and caressed her the way he was touching and caressing her now? Was she just a substitute? Available. Easy. A quick fix now that Elizabeth was gone.

So convenient, too. Only three doors away.

"Don't cry, Sierra," Alex said raggedly. *"Por favor,* don't cry."

But she couldn't help it. Her body pulsated with need for him while her mind tore her heart to shreds. She drew back as far as she could, her hands clenched. She felt him loosening his hold on her and wept harder. When he stepped back, she covered her face and turned away in complete humiliation.

If he hadn't known how much she still loved him, he could have little doubt now. It must give him a lot of satisfaction to know how easy it was to break down her walls and storm the citadel.

God, I'm such a fool!

"Sierra, I'm sorry . . . ," he said bleakly. "I didn't mean to . . ."

When he put his hands on her shoulders and tried to draw her back against him, she jerked away from his touch. "Just *go,* Alex," she said, hiccuping. "Get out of my life."

The door opened quietly and closed again.

She went upstairs, crying, and removed the dress. She hung it up carefully, tears running down her cheeks. She removed the jewelry and put it back in the velvet box. She slipped out of the red satin shoes and stripped off her underwear, then turned on the shower and stepped in. She stood beneath the pounding stream of water and gave in to her grief.

✳✳✳

She was still crying when she went to bed. Curling on her side, she covered her head with her pillow. She'd just dozed off when the telephone rang. The clock glowed three forty-five. She wanted to ignore the intrusive ringing but was afraid it would awaken the children.

It was Alex, and he sounded strange. Had he been drinking?

"I don't want to talk to you," she said, starting to cry again.

He wasn't listening. He was talking in Spanish, making no sense at all. Usually she could understand Spanish well, but he was speaking so fast and she was so tired, the words were a blur. She did catch a couple of familiar words. One of which was *esposa.* Wife.

He had a lot of nerve.

"You divorced me, Alex. Remember? Leave me alone."

She hung up. When the phone rang again, she yanked the plug. Covering her head, she wept herself to sleep.

———————

Joshua has been to the village six times in the past month.

Koxoenis makes him welcome. During his last visit, Joshua saw Koxoenis's preparations for another hunt. Koxoenis does not live with his wife or even look at her, but spends most of his time in a sweathouse where he rubbed deer marrow into his bow and arrows. Joshua said Koxoenis spoke to his weapons. He also drank a foul smelling concoction that made him very sick. Perhaps it is some kind of purification rite. After the sickness passed, he rubbed angelica and other herbs over his body and his spear.

Joshua followed Koxoenis to watch. He said Koxoenis mimics the movement of a deer so perfectly he was able to become a member of a herd grazing in a meadow at dusk. The animals were not even aware he was among them until he made his kill. Before dressing the animal, Koxoenis knelt beside it and stroked it tenderly, speaking to it. When the meat was prepared for the people, he did not partake of any of it.

Joshua has learned many valuable things from Koxoenis and his people. He has taught Hank how to make a fish trap and Matthew how to make snares for rabbits. He dammed our creek and threw a root into the water. It stunned the fish so that they floated to the surface. We smoked enough in one of our barrels to last us several weeks.

Joshua also taught Hank and Matthew how to make bolas using the side ribs of wild iris leaves and tying bones to each end. Joshua says the Indians use these simple weapons to catch quail, cottontails, and squirrels. The boys have been practicing diligently. Joshua said the Indians are not as fussy about what they eat as we are, but will dine on wood rats, snakes, lizards, and grubs. He has tried them all and said they taste good. I am not so adventurous.

Beth pulls up cattails and peels them. The stalks are good eating. Other edible greens are in abundance. Come spring, we will have berries. They grow in profusion near us.

Lord, You have made this earth as bountiful as Eden. We do not even have to put a plow to the soil to have food to sustain us. But we will come spring.

———————————

23

"HE'S SICK, MOM," CAROLYN SAID.

Hungover, more likely, Sierra thought, but didn't say it aloud. Her own head was aching from lack of sleep.

"He didn't answer the doorbell, so I let myself in," Carolyn reported. "He's still in bed, Mom. Daddy's never in bed this late."

Clanton collaborated. "Couldn't you go check on him?"

"He was up late babysitting last night, remember? He just needs to sleep in."

"You're up," Clanton said.

"Couldn't you go see if he's all right, Mom?" Carolyn pleaded, worried.

"And do what?"

"Call a doctor or something," Clanton chimed in.

She'd like to *something* all right, but after last night, she was afraid to get within twenty feet of him.

"Please," Carolyn said.

She looked between her two children and realized if she didn't do something, they'd think she was a coldhearted, uncaring hypocrite of a Christian. Weren't you supposed to *love* your enemy? "I'll take him some chicken soup," she said and took a Tupperware container out of the refrigerator. Frances had given her a batch, swearing it could cure just about anything.

Maybe she should drink some and pray to be cured of Alejandro Luís Madrid.

Clanton gave her the key to Alex's condo. Her heart was in her throat as she unlocked the door and went inside. It was exactly the same layout as hers, but the decor was vastly different. The living room had a big black leather couch and glass coffee table. Modern lamps stood on each side of the room. The wall was solid with electronic equipment: a big-screen television set, VCR, radio, CD and tape deck, game systems, and a quartet of small, but undoubtedly powerful, mounted speakers. The kitchen was spartan, except for the coffeemaker near the sink and the rats in their cage on the end of the breakfast bar. There wasn't much in Alex's cabinets, and only a few pots and pans in the cupboards below. The stove and microwave were both so clean, Sierra knew Alex had never used them. Opening the Tupperware container of soup, she poured a portion of the contents into a big mug, added a little water, and put it in the microwave. Curious, she looked under the sink. The garbage bucket below was full of empty Mexican take-out food containers.

I am not *going to feel sorry for him!*

She went up the stairs to the master bedroom and found Alex sprawled on his back, only partially covered by the vibrant Aztec-design comforter. All she saw was muscle, bronze skin, and dark hair. Heart flip-flopping, she looked away and spotted the pullover shirt he'd worn the night before. It was inside out on the floor. Nearby were his Levi's, also inside out, the belt still in the loops. His shoes were on the far side of the room, two dents in the wall above them.

Setting the mug of hot soup down on his side table, she picked up an empty pint of whiskey. In all the years she'd known Alex, she'd never seen him have more than one drink of anything intoxicating. He liked to be in control. She went into the bathroom and tossed the bottle into the trash basket.

When she came back out, she picked up his shirt and pulled it right side out, folded it, and put it on his chair. She did the same with his pants, removing the belt and curling it on the top of his dresser.

Steeling herself, she turned and looked at him. Her stomach tightened as she came over to the bed and looked down at him. He was so beautiful, so perfectly made. He was wearing the gold crucifix his mother had given him. Her heart squeezed tight with pity and tenderness. Frowning slightly, she noticed he'd added something to the gold chain, something she'd returned to him with the divorce papers he'd wanted her to sign.

Why was he wearing her wedding ring around his neck?

"Alex?"

He groaned. Shifting his body, he muttered something in Spanish and opened his bloodshot eyes. He stared up at her as though he couldn't believe she was really there.

"The children think you're dying," she said dryly, crushing the urge to brush the dark hair back from his forehead.

Wincing, he pushed himself up onto his elbows. "I feel like it," he said in a raspy voice. He looked at her again.

She avoided the intensity she saw in his eyes. "I brought you some chicken soup," she said, nodding toward his side table as she moved away from his bed.

"I didn't mean to hurt you last night, Sierra. I swear —"

"I know. Let's just forget about it." He didn't need to do anything to hurt her. She hurt every time she looked at him. It came with loving someone, even after they'd betrayed you.

As she headed for the door, Alex shoved the comforter back. "Don't go." He groaned in pain as he sat up. Holding his head in his hands, he muttered softly in Spanish. "I've got to talk to you. Just give me a few minutes to take a shower."

"We can talk another time." She smiled faintly. "When you're feeling better."

Dropping his hands, he looked at her bleakly. "I'm not going to feel better, not until I talk things out with you."

She had thought she was finished with crying, but tears sprang to her eyes. "Maybe I don't want to hear what you have to say."

"Maybe you don't," he said, "but I'm asking you to listen anyway. *Por favor.*"

When he stood up, her stomach dropped. She'd forgotten he slept in his briefs. She'd forgotten a lot of things that came back with a rush. "All right." She would have agreed to anything at that moment just to get out of the bedroom and away from him and the feelings he could still arouse in her without even trying.

"Wait here."

"I'll wait downstairs."

She searched his cupboards until she found coffee. Her hands were shaking as she made it. She expected to have more time, but he came down the stairs a few minutes later, wearing sweats and raking his hand back through his wet hair. He looked handsome even with a hangover. Looking at him, she felt depressed. She was never going to get over him. Never.

"Gracias," he said when she slid a mug of hot coffee across the breakfast bar to him. She had to have something between them, something to fill his hands, something to fill hers. He took a sip.

She had the feeling he was bracing himself. He finished the whole cup of coffee before he looked at her. "You're still my wife."

She felt the blood drain out of her face as she stared into his dark eyes. Panic set in. "No, I'm not. I did what you asked. I signed the papers. I gave them to you so your attorney could —"

"We're still married, Sierra."

"Maybe. For a few more months, until the divorce is final."

"Nothing's final, and it won't be. There's not going to be a divorce unless you file against me."

"I don't understand," she said, confused. Hadn't he told her over and over how much he wanted a divorce? "I did what you asked."

"Yeah, but I changed my mind. I didn't give the divorce papers to my attorney. I put them through the shredder at the office."

"You what?" she said faintly.

"I shredded the divorce papers."

"I heard you the first time, but why? Just so we'd have to go through all this misery again?"

"I don't know why I did it at the time, but it turned out to be a good idea."

"A — a good idea?" Did he think he could waltz back into her life and pick up where he left off? Or leave her dangling while he enjoyed himself? She wanted to throw the hot coffee at him. Instead, she slammed her cup on the counter and headed for the front door.

Alex caught hold of her halfway across the living room and swung her around. "I never loved Elizabeth the way I love you, Sierra. I knew it'd lead to disaster the first time I touched her."

She hit him, a hard right hook square to his jaw, knocking him back two feet. Rage and hurt filled her. She lost control completely and attacked him again. Lunging at him, she pounded at his chest until she realized he was standing and taking it. With a sob, she gave him a hard shove over the back of his leather couch.

Grabbing the back of her sweater, he dragged her along with him. They bounced, arms and legs tangling, and rolled onto the floor.

"You *jerk!*" She clambered to her feet, trying to get to the front door again. Alex was faster. He swung himself over the couch and planted himself in her path.

Spreading his hands, he presented himself. "Go ahead. Hit me again. I deserve it."

"Get out of my way!"

"I'm not finished."

"I *am!*"

"You're still in love with me, Sierra."

"I'll get over it!"

"No, you won't. And neither will I. Not ever."

She drew in another ragged sob. "Do you think it makes me feel better to have you say you didn't even love her? Do you think it *helps* to know you threw our marriage away for a fling?"

"It wasn't a fling."

"I don't want to hear about it, Alex. Don't give me the gruesome details. Just get out of my way!"

"Sierra—"

"Let me out!"

He caught hold of her shoulders. "My affair with Elizabeth had a lot to do with what you said. I wanted to feel I'd *made it.* Education hadn't done it for me. Neither had money. Daughter of the American Revolution, you said. Remember? A trophy I could hold up to the world to show them Alejandro Luís Madrid was more than a wetback's son!" His eyes were wet, tormented. "You knew me better than I knew myself, Sierra. Until Connecticut. I got a good look at myself there, and I wanted to vomit."

"Don't you *dare* call your father a wetback!"

His face softened. *"Te amo."* He cupped her face. *"Te amo muchísimo."*

She used her knee this time and caught him low and hard.

Shoving him back, she made it to the door. "I'm not going to love you anymore, Alex," she said, sobbing. "It hurts too much!"

Yanking open the front door, she fled.

———

My lying in time is drawing near.

The weight of the baby presses down. I have made what preparations I can and have explained to Beth what she must do to help me. She is younger than I was when Joshua was born, but she is a calm and willing girl and a great comfort to me. I hope she will be strong for whatever happens.

Lord, I am afraid for all my children. Please bring this baby into the world without taking me from it.

I know you sent Kavanaugh to me, Lord, and I thank You that he was obedient and arrived in time. I am sure I would have died otherwise. Joshua had gone off to find Koxoenis and ask if his wife could help me. I was praying for deliverance when someone opened the tule mat cover over our doorway. I have never been so glad to see anyone as I was to see Kavanaugh. He put his knife in the fire and then cut me. When that was done, he pulled me up so I was squatting. The baby came quick and easy after that. By the time Koxoenis, his wife, and Joshua arrived, my new daughter and I were asleep.

Kavanaugh told me today he will not leave again unless I tell him to go. He did not say more than that, but his meaning was clear. I think I have known he wanted me since the day he looked at me in the mercantile back in Independence.

I have named my baby daughter America Farr. Beth is taken with her and a great help to me. I am slow in mending and still weak. Kavanaugh is tender with me and firm in organizing the children. They do not mind. They have always held Kavanaugh in awe. Especially Joshua, though I sense tension between them now.

Kavanaugh is building us a cabin. He has set the boys to gathering stones for the foundation while he cuts timber. Joshua has not had much to say about anything lately. Something is eating at him and he will not say what. Hank and Matthew and Beth do all the talking.

The rains have been coming down steady for a week, but Kavanaugh and the boys continue to work. The rock foundation is complete and the sills set. Kavanaugh and Joshua work on notching the logs to build the walls.

This evening, we are all sitting around the pit fire. Hank, Matthew, and Beth are about their lessons while Kavanaugh whittles. He will teach the boys when they finish their reading and exercises.

I am glad my boys do not fight learning like my
brothers did. They must take after Mama. They
can all read and write better than my father and
brothers ever could, but they are far from Educated
by Aunt Martha's standards. I wish I had not been
so foolish as to say I did not want to have a Bible in
my possession.

Kavanaugh and Joshua have had a Falling Out.
Joshua was swinging at Kavanaugh with all his
might, but Kavanaugh blocked aside each blow. I
kept screaming at them to stop, but Joshua would
not listen. Kavanaugh unbalanced Joshua and
took him down on the ground and held him there
while trying to talk reason to him. Joshua was
in no mood to be reasonable. When Kavanaugh
released him, Joshua jumped up and spit on
him. I could not believe he did such a thing and
thought Kavanaugh would kill him sure. He did
not have a chance to do anything because Joshua
got on his horse and rode off. I ran after him and
asked what had happened, but he would not say.
He was crying and said he would not come back
until Kavanaugh left.

Joshua has been gone for three days. My heart
aches so I can not even eat. It did not take five
minutes for me to find out what set Joshua on
such a rampage. Kavanaugh wants to marry me.

He asked Joshua for permission since he thought he was the firstborn son. Joshua said he saw the way of things and accused him of using him to get close to me.

Kavanaugh and I have had much time to talk about many things. I thought I would be with James all my life. I did not expect to lose him. Yet I know I can not manage on my own out here. A woman with small children can not build a homeplace and plant crops all by herself. And going back home to Illinois is impossible.

I know too that Joshua will not stay with us for long. His leaving us will have little to do with Kavanaugh and all to do with his own nature, though he may be contrary and stiff-necked enough to use Kavanaugh as an excuse. Each time Joshua goes away, he stays away a little longer. He has the same hunger to see the world that James had. I am afraid it is the kind of hunger that will drive him before the wind all his life unless he faces the Almighty and comes to himself. I grieve knowing James never did. It must be in the Farr and McMurray blood to contend with God and everything else. We either see the light or die looking for it.

I have peace now I never thought to have and wonder often why I fought so hard in receiving it. Coming to the light does not mean it is easy watching Joshua wandering in darkness. But

telling him about You does not seem to get his
Attention. I guess I can not expect words to do it.
Mama and Aunt Martha talked to me plenty and
I never saw the Truth in what they were saying.

I have learned a little more about Kavanaugh
over the past days. His full name is Hamlet
Bogan Kavanaugh. He is twenty-eight years old
and can read and write. He was born in Boston
to a blueblood father and an actress mother
who thought naming him after a Shakespearean
character might lend him some dignity. He
did not think much of the name she gave him.
Despite the fact his mother never married, she
made sure his father paid for an Education. His
father agreed to pay for tutors if she promised to
leave him alone. She kept her part of the bargain.
Kavanaugh is his mother's name. She died when
he was thirteen. He went to his father then, was
given fifty dollars and told to leave Boston and
never darken his father's threshold again. He did
and has never been back.

I told Kavanaugh he did not have to tell me
such Personal Business, but he said I should
know he was born on the wrong side of the sheets
before we get married and start bearing children
together. I became Flustered when he said that.
He seems to have things all worked out in his
mind about the way things will go between us. I
asked him what he would have done had James

not died of a Thursday. He said he would have
waited however long it took. I asked him how
many children he expects to have and he laughed
and said one at a time, Mary Kathryn, and gave
me such a look I felt it down to my toes.

He is gone now and I can breathe freely
without the wild drumming of my heart to get
in the way of my head. I sent him away so I
could think things through. I was surprised he
did not try to talk me out of my solitude. He is a
strong man, stronger than James in many ways.
But there is not the hardness in him I expected.
James ran roughshod over my heart. There was
a wildness in him that could never be tamed.
It seems so odd now I think about it. James,
the farmer, the wild one, and Kavanaugh, the
mountain man, so settled inside himself. For
all his buckskins and long hair, Kavanaugh is
a gentleman who will not take advantage.

I do not want him here when Joshua comes
home. My son and I have things to settle between
us before I say yes to Kavanaugh.

You do not make things easy, do You, Lord?

Joshua is gone and I sit here wondering if I will
ever see him again. My heart aches so, and yet
I knew this would come. I have been fighting
against it for two thousand miles and it is no use
fighting it anymore. He thinks he is a man and he

has made up his mind to go his own way. At least
he no longer believes Kavanaugh used him to get
close to me. Kavanaugh likes Joshua for himself
and understands the restlessness in him. Maybe
knowing that will bring him back again someday.
He made no promises.

He said he is going to ride back to Sutter's Fort
and then head north to see what Oregon is like.
After that, he does not know where he will go or
what he will do.

I wept when he rode away. I kept thinking
about those Israelites wandering forty years
in the wilderness and dying within sight of
the Promised Land because they were so
Contentious. If only they had trusted the Lord,
they would have lived out their lives in a land of
milk and honey.

I hope it will not take Joshua as long as it took
me to find his way through the wilderness to You.

I have been thinking about Aunt Martha so much
lately. Sometimes I wonder if our thoughts touch
one another across the miles. I wrote her a long
letter yesterday, but I do not know when I will
have the opportunity to send it.

I think Kavanaugh has changed his mind about
marrying a widow with four children. He has
been gone twenty-three days.

I have begun the plowing. Hank and Matthew are helping me while Beth minds America. Together we will get a small crop in.

It is Terrible Hard Work, but I think I can manage with the children. We have enough to eat. We have a cabin to keep us safe and dry. We have good land and seed to plant. And we have You, Jesus. Aunt Martha told me anything is possible with God. So I am asking You to help us in this Great Enterprise. We are stuck here, Lord. Help us make the best of it.

———————

24

SIERRA DIDN'T SEE ALEX THE NEXT DAY, AND he didn't call the children. She thought it was because of what had happened between them until Carolyn said, "I told Daddy we were in the church pageant tonight. He said he was going Christmas shopping."

Then Clanton hit her with, "Can Dad spend Christmas with us?"

Sierra rebelled. "No, he cannot spend Christmas with us."

"He'll be all alone," Carolyn said, clearly distressed by the idea. "He'll be lonely. Couldn't we ask him? Please?"

"We'll talk about it later," she said, hoping in the interim Alex would be run over by a truck or kidnapped by terrorists. "Right now, we have to get to church and into costume."

During the next few hours, she relished being caught up in stage jitters and the excitement of getting ready to perform. Once in costume, the choir members gathered together and prayed that their performance would do more than entertain. They prayed it would open the hearts of those listening to the music and the reenactment of the birth of the Messiah.

Once the program started, her nervousness cooled. She had practiced so much, her part all came back the moment she moved onto the platform some parishioners had built to extend the choir loft. She gave herself up to the music, singing from her heart, feeling the joy of the Christmas story and its meaning to the world.

Joseph traveled from the town of Nazareth in Galilee, on one side of the church, to Judea, the city of David called Bethlehem, on the platform, where he registered himself and his young wife, Mary, for the Roman census ordered by Quirinius, governor of Syria.

"And it came about that while they were there, the days were completed for her to give birth. And she gave birth to her first-born son; and she wrapped Him in cloths, and laid Him in a manger, because there was no room for them in the inn."

Clanton was one of the young shepherds who knelt before the angel Gabriel as he sang his solo announcing the good news of great joy: "For today in the city of David there has been born for you a Savior, who is Christ the Lord." The adult choir joined as tiny pinpricks of light shone on the ceiling, and then the new, bright star appeared in the "heavens."

"Glory to God in the highest, and on earth peace among men."

Joining Gabriel was the heavenly host of children in white, complete with wings and halos, their voices blending in sweet harmony. Among them was Carolyn. The music expanded again as the adult choir joined the children's voices. Sierra's heart beat fast as the crescendo came, filling the church to the rafters with praise-glory sounds for the newborn King. Jubilation!

Oh, Jesus, Jesus, would that I could feel this joy every day of the year.

Her whole body felt alive and warm with the love and excitement of the Lord's birthday. She forgot everything else, especially what the Lord expected of her.

The pastor gave a prayer following the pageant, and refreshments were served in the social hall. The last person she expected to see was Alex. When she spotted him standing on the far side of the room, looking handsome in black slacks, a gray silk designer shirt, and black sports jacket, her heart dropped into the pit of her stomach and bounced up into her throat. He was talking with Dennis; it didn't look like a casual conversation.

"Hey! Dad's here," Clanton said, still holding his shepherd's staff.

"Yes, I see him." The rat. The creep.

Deserting her, Clanton set his staff before him and parted the sea of choir members and guests to get to his father. Carolyn spotted Alex soon afterward and fluttered over in her angel costume.

Little traitors.

Sierra was still reeling from what Alex had said to her in his condo. *I never loved her the way I loved you.*

Yeah, right! If he loved her so much, why had he walked out? Why had he told her he despised her and couldn't wait for a divorce? Why had he looked at her as though he hated her?

The way you're looking at him right now, beloved?

She turned away, selecting a cookie from a large platter. Chocolate, her favorite. It tasted like dirt. All the joy she'd felt half an hour before while singing praises to the Lord evaporated, boiled away by resentment and anger.

He's ruining my Christmas, Lord. Couldn't you remove this ache I have when I see him? He cheated on me! The least you could do is give him some kind of awful disease.

"Daddy said he's flying to San Francisco tomorrow," Clanton said. "He's spending Christmas with *abuelo y abuela.*"

Bitterness surged through Sierra. He didn't even have the sensitivity to stay at home alone for Christmas and suffer! No.

He had to go to Healdsburg and enjoy a wonderful Christmas with Luís and María.

Of course, she completely disregarded the fact that they'd invited her to come, too.

Carolyn sighed expressively. "I wish we could go."

So did Sierra, but she wasn't about to admit it. "We'll go at Easter."

It was too expensive to fly three people north to San Francisco. Worse, she'd have to look at *him* over the dinner table and face the hopes of Luís and María on top of it.

Besides, she couldn't afford the time off work.

On top of that, it was too late to make reservations. All the flights would be booked solid over the holidays.

Excuses flooded her mind as she waited for Alex to come over and speak with her. Visions of him on his knees danced in her head, but he didn't come within twenty feet of her. Instead, he left quietly, unseen.

When she realized he was gone, she told herself she didn't care. But it galled her nevertheless.

The telephone rang as soon as she walked through the door. "Cooled off yet?" Alex said.

"Why would I be hot?"

"You tell me."

She banged the receiver down, hoping she'd burst his eardrum. The telephone rang again. Snatching it up, she snarled, "I don't want to talk to you. I don't want to see you. I don't want to hear about you. I want to forget you live on the same planet I do."

"Merry Christmas to you, too!" Ron laughed.

Her face went hot. Covering it, she plunked down on a breakfast bar stool. "I'm sorry. I thought . . ."

"I was Alex. I take it you two are talking again."

She gave an unladylike snort. "If that's what you call it." The doorbell rang. Carolyn *ran* to it. And guess who was standing under the porch light, his arms laden with Christmas packages, all professionally wrapped? He couldn't bother doing such menial labor himself. Wrapping had always been her job, along with the Christmas cards and shopping.

Sierra hissed when she inhaled. "I have to go, Ron. I need to find some Raid."

Alex didn't stay long, and after one brief glance at her face, he concentrated entirely on the children. "I'll be back December 28th," he said, kissing Carolyn. "Want to see me out?" he said to Clanton.

"Sure."

When the door closed behind father and son, Carolyn turned and looked at her. "This is going to be the *worst* Christmas of my life!" Tears streaming down her face, she ran to her room.

Sierra had a strong feeling it wasn't going to be very joyful for her either.

And she was right.

In years past, Alex had fixed the turkey. Her father had taught him how. "It's a Clanton tradition. The men cook the bird on Thanksgiving and Christmas." She fixed the bird this year and it was dry as a bone. Gravy helped, but not much. Clanton and Carolyn made no complaints, but she could tell they would have preferred a Mickey D to her festive efforts. The best thing about the turkey was the skin.

As soon as the dishes were in the dishwasher, presents were distributed. The children were clearly more excited about what Alex had given them than what she'd bought. Who could blame them? His gifts were frivolous, hers practical.

She played Christmas music on the radio, but it sounded flat and depressing. When she wasn't fuming, she ached with loneliness, thinking about Alex laughing and having fun with his father and mother, sisters and brothers, nephews and nieces, cousins, second cousins, *third* cousins. The neighbors would probably come to join in, for heaven's sake!

All through the evening, she kept remembering Christmases past. While the children played, she sat watching television. Dickens's *Christmas Carol* was on. She identified with Scrooge. Then, to cheer her up even more, she watched *It's a Wonderful Life*. She made it all the way to George Bailey jumping off the bridge before she turned it off.

I'm a new Christian, Lord, and this is the worst Christmas of my life!

Who do you say that I am, beloved?

Lord. You are Lord.

Then obey me.

"Do you have a headache, Mom?" Carolyn said, coming downstairs and seeing her rubbing her temples.

Headache, heartache, soul ache.

The last thing Sierra wanted to hear Sunday morning was a sermon on forgiveness. Peter's denial. Jesus had known his disciples' weaknesses. He had warned Peter. "The spirit is willing, but the flesh is weak." He had also known Peter would repent. "When you turn . . ."

Like Alex saying he was sorry, saying he loved her.

I can't, Lord. I can't forgive him and go through it again!

But the words from the pulpit kept hammering the wall around her heart. "If you love Me, you will keep My commandments . . . love does not take into account a wrong suffered . . . love bears all things, believes all things, hopes all things, endures all things."

Sierra kept remembering the look on Alex's face when she told him she didn't want to love him anymore. It hurt too much. It was true, but that didn't matter. She loved him whether she wanted to or not. Still, what kind of love tore people apart inside?

Nothing made sense to her anymore, least of all the war of emotions going on inside her. All the while she had thought there was no chance at all of reconciliation. She thought Alex hated her. She'd finally seen her part in the disintegration of her marriage. She had accepted blame.

Now, he wanted forgiveness . . . and she wanted revenge.

Unsettled, her conscience pricking at her, she shut her eyes tightly.

I'm not like you, Jesus.

"We can do all things through Christ who strengthens us," the pastor said.

I don't feel strong, Lord. The only solid things I feel are anger and hurt. How do I forget what he's done to me? How do I stop thinking about him with another woman? How do I ever trust him again?

". . . whatever is true, whatever is honorable, whatever is right, whatever is pure, whatever is lovely, whatever is of good repute, if there is any excellence and if anything worthy of praise, let your mind dwell on these things. . . ."

The way he did, Lord?

The way you're doing, beloved?

She wanted to leave the church. She didn't want to hear words that opened her eyes to her own sin; she wanted the finger pointed at Alex. She had come to be renewed, uplifted, enlightened. She hadn't come to be convicted.

If you love Me, you will keep My commandments. Love one another, just as I have loved you.

She wanted to cry out. *God, do you have to scrub an open wound? Do you have to pour salt on it?*

"Whatever you do, do your work heartily, as for the Lord," the pastor said, continuing his message.

She winced. What *was* she doing?

How could she hold a grudge against Alex and call herself a Christian? How could she expect to feel joy and peace in her life when she clung to past hurts and fears of future pain? The risk was what paralyzed her. Where were the guarantees of a happy ending?

I don't belong in your kingdom, Lord. I'm not like any of these good people sitting around me.

What would they think of her if they knew she'd punched Alex not once, but half a dozen times with everything she had? And then kneed him where it hurt most. Never mind what *they* would think. God had seen!

Humiliation set in, her face heating up.

O Lord, I lost control. All I could think about was the fact he walked out on me. He said he was sick of me. He said he wanted out of our marriage. It was hard, but I let him go. I gave him the papers he said he wanted. I listened to what Dennis and the others said about allowing a nonbeliever to leave a marriage. And now he tells me he never loved her the way he loved me. How do I believe him? How can I trust him? I'm not strong enough to go through this heartache again. I'm not strong enough to go through it now.

I'm not going to give you more than you can bear.

Why don't I feel comforted by that, Jesus?

She walked home with the children and fixed them bologna sandwiches and tomato soup for lunch. Alex was coming home in a few days. Her mind whirred with conflicting thoughts. She wanted to forgive and forget, but feared the cost of both.

"Maybe Daddy will call," Carolyn said.

"He never calls on Sundays," Clanton said between bites of sandwich.

Sierra knew he'd be at Mass with his parents today. But when he was here, what did he do?

And why was she allowing herself to think about that snake again?

She and the children walked back to church in the afternoon, and she was treated to another heart-wrenching lesson during the evening Bible study. The subject was self-righteousness. The

Word was a double-edged sword, and she was sliding right down the blade of it.

Couldn't you ease up on me a little, Lord? Do you have to use a jackhammer?

She left the class before it was over and found solitude in a cry room built for mothers who were nursing their babies. She sat nursing her grievances in the rocking chair, locked in the silence until youth group was over and it was time to meet Clanton and Carolyn.

Alex was walking down the path toward her condo when she and the children returned. She should have known.

"Daddy!" Carolyn cried and ran to him. Clanton wasn't far behind. The three talked briefly and walked toward her. She'd never felt so alone, so cut off.

"Have you eaten?" he said.

"Not yet," Clanton said. "I'm starved."

"Why don't I take all of you out to pizza?"

"Mom, too?" Carolyn said, excited about the idea.

"Mom, too," Alex said, looking at her.

She knew he would understand if she said no. He wouldn't argue or try to persuade. She knew the children would understand as well. That was the problem. She felt exposed and petty. They had such great hopes. Shouldn't she? "That would be nice," she said, lowering her gaze from his. She'd do it for the children.

He was still driving his Mercedes. He opened the door for her while Clanton and Carolyn piled in the back. When they reached the pizza parlor, Alex ordered a large combo and pitcher of soda while she and the children secured a booth. When Alex joined them, he handed the children a handful of quarters for the video games that lined the back wall. As they dashed off, he slid into the seat opposite her.

"Finally, we're alone together," he said, a rueful smile touching his lips. The place was packed with Sunday evening diners.

She smiled back, aching inside. Why was it so much easier to maintain her anger when there was distance between them? Now, sitting across the booth from him, she couldn't sustain it. It melted despite her determination, leaving behind a sense of vulnerability that frightened her more than anything else. "I thought you weren't coming back until the twenty-eighth."

"I couldn't wait."

She didn't ask for what. "Didn't things go well with your parents?"

"Papa's speaking to me again. We had a long talk. You paved the way for me." His eyes darkened. "I meant what I said the other day, Sierra. *Te amo.* I want us to get back together."

"Don't take my agreement for granted."

"I'm not. Don't you think I—"

"I don't want to talk here, Alex," she said, looking away, tears starting. "I can't."

"Yo comprendo," he said softly. "We'll eat and take the children home. Once they're settled for the night, we'll go back to my place."

"No way. I don't want to be alone with you."

"Don't you trust me?"

He meant the question to be light, seductive, but she looked him square in the eyes. "Should I?" She saw that the barb stuck and felt immediately ashamed. *Forgive,* the Lord said, and she had just stabbed Alex with a sharp blade. Looking down at her hands, she could almost see the blood on them and wanted to weep. The only way she could think to make amends was to be honest. "I know where we'd end up, Alex, and sex isn't going to help solve our problems."

"That cost you," he said huskily.

"It's true, isn't it?"

"It might ease the tension between us."

"And cloud the issues." She could see so clearly now how they'd often used sex to bypass issues that were causing fractures in their relationship rather than step back, look, listen, repair, and move on together. "If we're going to reconcile, we have to build a solid foundation this time."

"This time? Isn't love enough?"

"If it's the right kind."

Her words clearly hurt him but she couldn't weaken. When he searched her face, she felt he was looking for weakness.

Lord, help me stand firm. Show me what to do. I love him, but I don't want to give up my soul to him.

Alex frowned slightly, perplexed. "OK," he said softly. "We stay at your place."

"No. We'll begin by talking on the telephone."

She needed space between them. She had made too many decisions based on her emotions, and look where that had gotten her!

The Lord said to renew your mind, and she intended to do that. With distance between them, she would be able to keep her mind clear to *think*.

One thing she already knew. It was going to take God to get them back together again and make their marriage work.

———

Kavanaugh has returned.

I was so relieved to see him riding across the field. He was gone so long I thought he had come to his senses. He said he has not changed his mind about anything, but figured I needed time to adjust to the idea of having another husband. He said he rode to Yerba Buena and then Monterey. He bought a wedding ring there from a Mexican

jeweler. On the way north, he met other settlers.
Five families have taken land east of us near
the Russian River. While Kavanaugh was there
getting to know everyone, a man returned from
Sutter's Fort and said he heard a rumor gold
was discovered in the trace at the mill on the
American River. Two of the men have sons who
are going back to find out if it is true.

Kavanaugh said one of the men at the new
settlement said he could perform a marriage
ceremony for us. He has a Book of Common
Prayer and the wedding service is in it.

Kavanaugh and I are wed. Lester and Charlotte
Burrell held a party for us after the ceremony.
There were twenty-seven people there, all
strangers who have quickly become friends. We
had music! One man played a fiddle and another
a mouth organ. I danced until my feet ached.
They are good, hospitable people and were very
happy to give us a proper wedding celebration. I
feel at home in California for the first time since
crossing the Sierra Nevada mountains.

I thought to make Kavanaugh and I a wedding
quilt so that we would not have to share James's
blanket. So I went to the trunk to take out the
squares of fabric the ladies from the quilting club
gave me. Beneath them I found a thin wooden

tray and under it a Wonderful Surprise. Aunt
Martha packed her pretty yellow dress and white
lace shawl. When I took them out, I found her
Bible in the folds.

I sat weeping over it for the longest time, just
rubbing the black leather. The binding is worn from
her loving hands, and just touching it makes me feel
closer to her. I remember all the hours she spent
reading it. When I opened it, I found her note.

I read from Aunt Martha's Bible for the first time
this evening. We are starting at Genesis and will
read straight through to the end. After I finished
the story of creation, we all talked a long while.

The children are in bed now and Kavanaugh
has gone out to check on the stock and take a
bath in the creek before coming to bed. I have
paged through Aunt Martha's Bible. I feel close to
her with it in my hands. She has written prayers
and notes in the margins. Favorite Scriptures are
underlined. Pressed between the pages are other
surprises that remind me of spring and Mama and
days gone by in Galena—a golden Alexander, a
pink-lavender shooting star, white Indian plantain,
yellow-orange coreopsis, purple coneflower, black-
eyed Susans, buttercups, blue aster, a rose-purple
blazing star, and violet marsh phlox.

Lord, bless her and keep her always.

———————

4

The Reconciliation

25

ALEX CALLED EVERY EVENING AT TEN-FIFTEEN.
Carolyn was always in bed by nine, while Clanton dragged
his feet until ten. One conversation with his father made him
cooperate.

Each night the telephone would ring, and Sierra's heart would
jump. Taking a breath, she'd answer while sliding onto a stool in
the kitchen. Alex did most of the talking, while she doodled on the
notepad to keep from letting her nervousness come across the line.

As she contained her emotions, Alex opened up. The conversations became excruciating and confessional. The last thing she
wanted to hear about was his relationship with Elizabeth, but he
had a need to unburden himself.

"She left the East Coast in a bid for independence," he told her. "She was attracted to me because I was the opposite of the kind of man her father wanted her to marry. Not that she had marriage in mind."

Sierra could see how it had happened. Work had drawn them together. Elizabeth was assigned to work closely with Alex. Alex was a charismatic man, full of fire, brilliant and exciting. While Sierra was fighting with him at home, Elizabeth was waiting at the office, ready to console and sympathize, ready to build him up rather than tear him down. He'd spent progressively longer hours at the office. They started having lunch together, then dinner. A few drinks led to more. Then the guilt set in, and the only way to alleviate that was to cast blame. Sierra knew she'd become the perfect target. She had already set herself up for the fall by her own childish behavior months before Elizabeth Longford ever came on the scene. If it hadn't been Elizabeth, it would have been another woman.

"What happened when you went east with her?"

"What do you mean?"

"Audra said something about a fiasco in Connecticut."

"You could say that. Her father and I had words. The same kind your father and I had. You remember what happened?"

"Yes. You eventually became very good friends." It had taken a few years, but Alex and her dad had grown close. By the time her father passed away, he was Alex's champion, second only to herself and Luís.

"No," Alex said. "That's not what I mean. Do you remember what you did? You came down the stairs and stood beside me. You said you loved me. You made it a declaration, loud and clear. You were ready to fight for *us*, no matter what it cost you, even a break with your parents." He let out his breath derisively. "Elizabeth tossed me to the wolves and stood back to watch who'd win."

Rather than make her feel better, his words left her wondering if things might have turned out differently had Elizabeth been a little wiser or loved Alex a little more.

"Don't go quiet on me, Sierra. I'm trying to tell you I saw what she was. It took Connecticut for me to understand what she was doing. She didn't love me, and I didn't love her. We were using each other. She used me against her father. I used her against you."

"If you knew all that, why didn't you leave her sooner?"

He was quiet for a moment. "Pride."

"Be honest, Alex." She was tired of crucifying herself between two thieves: regret for yesterday and fear about tomorrow. She needed the truth from him, no matter how much it hurt. They couldn't build on anything less. "I promise I won't hang up on you, no matter what you say."

"All right," he said heavily, clearly not eager to impart what was coming. "I wasn't sure I wanted to come back to you."

Well, at least she knew he wasn't holding back anymore. Swallowing her hurt, she asked, "What changed your mind?"

"When you said you'd never take the children away from me, it stopped me cold. I'd expected you to fight dirty."

And why wouldn't he? She had been vindictive, carping and complaining over the move. After three years of that behavior, why should he have expected her to be fair when faced with divorce?

"Finally I realized *I* was the one playing dirty," he said. "And then there was the day I watched you play baseball." He gave a low laugh. "By the time the game was over, I was wondering why I'd ever left you in the first place."

"Because I hit a home run?" she said, smiling sadly as she made doodles on the notepad.

"No, because I hadn't seen you laugh in months. You looked young and happy again, the way you were when we first started out. You took my breath away. I sat there watching you and remembering the good times. I felt sick, wondering what happened to us."

And so it went. Alex called, she listened—and learned. As the days passed, she left the stool and sat on the sofa, feet propped up on the old hatch-cover table. "If we do get back together, what are you going to do with all that stereo and game equipment you have in your living room? And that horrible black couch," she said.

"What makes you think we'll be living in your condo?"

It got her to wondering. Where *would* they live? How would they meld their lifestyles? Sierra was beginning to realize how little they had in common.

Lord, how are we going to make this work?

She spent as much time as possible reading the Bible and thinking things over. Again, she learned: Be anxious about nothing. Be thankful. Work out the tangles of your life one by one before the Lord. She had to fix her eyes on Jesus constantly in order to live above it all with Christ, in him, rather than get caught up in the old resentments, hurts, and fears.

Her feelings changed as Alex talked. The anger got lost somewhere and compassion slipped in, not just for Alex, but for Elizabeth Longford as well. She knew from Audra that Elizabeth had moved back to Connecticut. When Alex left, her life fell apart. Her bid for independence from her father had blown up in her face.

"She called to tell us she's getting married," Audra said.

Sierra told Alex, testing his reaction she supposed, but better to know now rather than later if he wanted to change his mind about the direction they were going.

"I heard." His response was quiet, neutral.

"From Audra?"

"No. Elizabeth called while I was in the office last week. She told me."

Sierra's heart dropped. She hadn't realized he was still in contact with her.

"It's the only time we've talked since she left," Alex said, seeming to read her mind. "I met the man she's marrying when I was in Connecticut," he went on. "She was engaged to him once before and backed out. He's a Harvard grad, a lawyer. Rich. Family connections back to the founding fathers. Her father's choice." He gave a soft self-deprecating laugh. "I *liked* him. When I put all that other stuff aside, he was a pretty decent guy."

Sierra gathered her courage. "Maybe Elizabeth called to tell you hoping you'd change her mind."

"That occurred to me," he said gently. "That's why I told her I'm doing everything in my power to reconcile with my wife."

Sierra closed her eyes, imagining how much it would have hurt her if she was in Elizabeth's position. "What did she say to that, Alex?"

"She said she was sorry."

Sierra pitied Elizabeth. She had taken Dennis's advice and spent a few minutes each day praying for Elizabeth Longford. Doing so had erased her animosity. She prayed now, during the lull in conversation with her estranged husband.

"Sierra? Talk to me. Scream at me. Say something."

"We never realize how many people we hurt with our actions, do we, Alex? It's like a chain reaction. I was so angry with you when we moved down here. I never listened to what you wanted or needed. I was only interested in what I wanted. I hurt you so much, and out of that I hurt Elizabeth, too."

"You had nothing to do with Elizabeth."

"Yes, I did. If I'd been the wife I should've been, you never would've turned to her. So I share the blame with you for her pain, too."

He said something in Spanish. "You remind me of your mother."

She teared up and swallowed them down. He couldn't have

paid her a dearer compliment. "I still miss her. Sometimes I'll see something or read about something I know would make her laugh, and I pick up the phone to call. I'll get halfway through the number before I remember she isn't there anymore."

"I should've been with you," he said hoarsely.

He'd been with Elizabeth, instead. Blinking back tears, Sierra didn't say anything. Her throat ached. Would the hurt ever go away?

"I was trying to figure a way out . . . ," Alex said softly.

"Of our marriage."

"No. Out of what was happening between me and Elizabeth. The guilt was eating me alive. I knew you needed me, but I couldn't deal with it or face you. I couldn't face your mother. I was sure she'd know the minute she looked at me that something was wrong. Then Papa gave me that lecture on the telephone. I knew he was right, but I didn't like being told what to do. By the time I got there, I was uptight and ready for a fight. I had all kinds of excuses and reasons. Papa and I had words after the memorial service. He said he was ashamed of me for the way I treated you. Your mother's letter was the last straw. I had to get out of there."

"What did she say in the letter?"

"She wrote she knew the first time she saw us together that I was the right man for you." He didn't say anything for a moment, then added in a choked voice, "She said she loved me and was proud to have me as a son."

They talked past midnight, leaving Sierra bleary-eyed for work. After running errands, she came home, fixed dinner for the children, and stretched out on the sofa to read her Bible. The next thing she knew, Clanton and Carolyn woke her up at ten.

"We're going to bed, Mom," Clanton said.

Trying to focus through her exhaustion, Sierra pushed herself up. "I didn't mean to fall asleep. What time is it?"

"Daddy called earlier," Carolyn said. "He's going to call you at ten-thirty." They each kissed her good night and went downstairs.

As Sierra waited for the telephone to ring, she sat looking up at Mary Kathryn's quilt. It occurred to her that not only were her feelings changing, but so was the way she saw things. She thought about her first ecstatic months as a Christian. After having been told about Jesus from childhood, she'd finally understood for herself who Jesus was. Creator, Redeemer, Almighty God, King of kings, Lord of lords. Realization had struck like an atomic blast. Hot white light blinded her for a little while. She'd been so caught up in the sudden opening of her mind and heart to Christ, she hadn't seen anything else clearly. She hadn't looked. She had known only one thing: Jesus loved her. Alex didn't, but the Lord did. After months of turmoil and grief, she'd felt happy. She'd felt hopeful. In the midst of everything, she had felt safe.

Then Alex pushed back into her life, rocking her foundations again. She'd finally adjusted to being without him; Ron stood by in the wings waiting to walk out onto center stage. She was working, carrying her own weight, being responsible. The children were settled in their new school, involved in the church. Clanton had stopped fighting. Carolyn had stopped obsessing about grades.

Why now, God? she had cried. Why couldn't things stay the way they were? Why couldn't Alex just stay out of her life the way he'd said he wanted?

But her vision had been adjusting to the light. It seemed each day she could see life—herself—more clearly, through Scripture, prayer, and her daily walk with Jesus. She could see right into the dusty, dirty, secret corners of her life. Christ brought everything to light.

Painfully, vividly, she saw her part in the passion play.

Anguish filled her as she recognized past sins and present ones

441

she had fallen into out of habit, hidden ones she loathed to face. Alex wasn't the only guilty player. She stood stripped before a mirror, seeing herself as she had been: childish, self-centered, filled with self-pity, casting blame, complaining.

It is better to live in the corner of a roof than in a house shared with a contentious woman.

She was ashamed and grieved, yet oddly enough, a sense of peace followed her self-examination. She was reminded of her mother in the attic, the window open, the fresh air blowing in as she dusted, swept, and sorted out trash from the treasure.

Oh, Lord Jesus, do that for me. Please. You know me better than I know myself. Open my doors and windows and let the Holy Spirit move through me. You are welcome in my house. Come into me, into my foyer and my living room. Wander at will through my parlor and kitchen. Be with me in my bedroom and bathroom. Go through every closet and every drawer, from the basement to the attic of my life. I belong to you, Father. Stay with me forever. Jesus, please remove everything in me that doesn't glorify you. Make me your vessel.

Oh, God, you are my God. I seek you. My soul hungers and thirsts for you. My body longs for you as dry land beneath a heavy rain. Your love is better than life.

"Are you falling in love again?" Alex said softly late that night after they had talked for two hours.

Eyes closed, her head resting against the back of the sofa, she smiled. "Yes." But not with Alex—she'd never stopped loving him.

She was falling in love with Jesus.

We found our dear Koxoenis shot dead near the banks of our stream today.

Lord, who would murder such a gentle man who did nothing but show kindness and hospitality to others? Kavanaugh thinks Koxoenis was badly wounded and tried to reach us for help. Thinking of him suffering fills me with anguish. Oh, God, that we had found him sooner. Kavanaugh said the wound was mortal and we could not have saved him, but we could have at least comforted him in his last hours upon this earth. We could have held him close and prayed for him.

Kavanaugh carried Koxoenis to our home. We washed him and wrapped him in a blanket and buried him beside James.

Lord, I am so grieved. Please do not hold it against Koxoenis that I failed to explain You to him. I tried so hard each time he has come to visit, but sign language leaves so much unsaid. He did not understand me, and I did not know how to explain. And now he is lost forever.

Father, please let me speak on his behalf. Koxoenis was kind and generous, and obedient to Your will. He heard Your voice that day we were so hungry. He came to us and gave us meat. He showed us the food You had planted all around us. He taught Joshua how to build us a shelter so that we were warm and dry through the cold winter months. He was our first and dearest friend, and though he did not know You, Lord, I believe in my heart he was your child in spirit. I have never known a man more humble and loving.

Please, Lord, be merciful and bring Koxoenis
into Your kingdom.

Beth and I gathered flowers today and took them
to the small knoll where James and Koxoenis lie.
But when we reached it, we found Koxoenis's grave
empty. The cross we had made for him lay upon
the mound of fresh earth and on it was a Pomo gift
basket. It is the most beautiful thing I have ever
seen with designs woven with red, yellow, and
green feathers and small beads. Around the rim
are tiny black topknot quail feathers.

I have placed the basket upon our mantel and
will remember our beloved friend and his people
each time I look at it.

Kavanaugh brought supplies back from the
settlement near the river yesterday. Beth and
I walked to Koxoenis's village today to bring
apple pies to his wife and children, but when we
reached it, everyone was gone. No fires were
burning. No children were playing. No smoke
came from the sweathouse. No women sat
working with stone mortar and pestle crushing
acorns. The village was deserted and desolate.

Kavanaugh said Indians move where the
food is. He thinks this village site may be their
winter home. Spring and summer must be spent
elsewhere. The money beads the people wear are

made of clamshells. So I suppose the people must spend time each year near the ocean. Perhaps they are there.

We learned from Joshua that Koxoenis's people ate fish, acorns, pepperwood nuts, buckeyes, and a mixture of toasted seeds and grains ground in a stone mortar and sifted in a basket. They called it pinole. Now that spring is here, everything is green and growing. There must be a hundred different things to eat that we have not yet discovered. And come summer, the berries and wild apples will be ripe. They will taste better than the dried ones I soaked to make the pies.

I hope we will see Koxoenis's people again come fall, but my heart tells me we will not be so fortunate.

Lord, please be with them and protect them from harm.

———————————

26

"RED ROSES, MOM!" CAROLYN CALLED FROM the front door. "Come see!"

Sierra came down the stairs and gasped as she saw the arrangement being brought in. "Living-room table, ma'am?" the deliveryman said. He was young, sporting a T-shirt that said "God spoke and *BANG* it was," long black hair, and a single hoop earring.

"Yes, that'd be fine."

When he set the arrangement down, he gave her a saucy grin. "Someone's either smitten or in deeeep trouble."

She laughed. *Smitten* was such an antique word for such a modern young man. "Hang on a minute," she said and gave him a ten-dollar tip. She found the card tucked in among the baby's breath and ferns: *Happy Valentine's Day. I love you. Alex.* Twenty-four red roses in a crystal vase.

She called him. "Thank you for the roses."

"What do you say we take the children out tonight? Dinner and a movie."

She smiled. "I'd like that."

"How about letting them sit in the front row while we sit in a back corner and neck the way we used to?"

She laughed. "How about we all sit in the middle *together?*"

They had a wonderful evening together. As it turned out, Clanton and Carolyn pleaded to sit closer to the front, and she and Alex sat in the middle. At first Alex didn't touch her. They sat side by side, both staring up at the big screen with the animated Disney characters frolicking, both wound up like a couple of two-dollar clocks. Halfway through the movie, Alex took her hand. When she didn't try to withdraw, he finally relaxed.

"Aren't you going to invite him in?" Carolyn said when they reached the condo.

"I want to show him my new game," Clanton said as though on cue.

Sierra looked between them and knew what her children were hoping. How could she explain she wasn't ready?

"Another time," Alex said, coming to her rescue. He took a step back.

"Mom," Carolyn whined, her heart in her eyes.

"It's all right, Alex," she said. "Come on in. I'll fix us some hot cider while you take a look at Clanton's game."

She was in the kitchen putting cinnamon sticks in the cups of steaming cider when Alex came back. "Are the children coming down?" she said, glancing toward the stairwell.

"They're playing a video game."

"Carolyn?" She had never been interested before.

He shrugged. "You look nervous."

"I am a little," she said, giving a self-conscious laugh. "Why don't we sit in the living room?" She gave him a mug of hot cider, took one for herself, and led the way to the couch she'd recovered. She sat at the far end, curling her feet up beneath her.

Neither knew what to say to break the tension. She remembered other nights on this couch. The silence stretched along with her nerves.

"It does get in the way, doesn't it?" Alex said heavily.

"What?"

"Wanting you this much. Knowing you want me, too." He looked at her, hiding nothing.

Sierra's heart began to drum hard. Alex set his mug of hot cider on the hatch-cover table and stood up. She looked up at him, afraid he'd kiss her and start something she couldn't let him finish. Or worse, he would leave.

His expression softened. "As much as I'd like to, I'm not going to rush you."

"I'm not trying to be difficult, Alex."

"*Yo sé.* You've got to learn to trust me again."

She looked down into her cider. "So much has happened to me in the last year. I've changed in ways I don't think you understand." She looked at him again. "The Lord is the center of my life, now. I can't go back —"

"Dennis and I talked about it."

She was surprised. "You did?" She knew Dennis wouldn't hold back; he'd lay out salvation one, two, three.

"I go to Mass, Sierra. I have every Sunday since I moved here." He glanced away, rubbing the back of his neck. "I figured it was time I confessed and did penance. Dennis talks about grace, but there's justice, too."

She put her mug down and stood up. "I forgive you, Alex."

He looked at her, his eyes moist. "I knew that when you said you wanted to talk, but I can't let go of it. I said vows, *querida*. It doesn't matter that they were in Reno and not in a church. I could have been saying them in a parking lot and I still would've known I was speaking before God. The last thing I ever thought I'd do was commit adultery. And then I did. I never thought I'd be capable of hurting you. And then I did that, too. Deliberately. Every chance I got."

She wanted to put her arms around him, but he moved away slightly, putting distance between them. He was gripped with guilt. It was eating at him. She knew that look. She also knew he wanted to tell her something—something she wasn't going to like. The muscles in her stomach tightened.

No more, Lord. Please, no more.

"Father O'Shea asked if I'd had a blood test."

Sierra could feel the blood draining from her face. She blinked.

"Yeah, you look exactly the way I felt," he said bleakly. "That aspect never occurred to me, either. Not until a celibate priest brought it up. I called Elizabeth and asked some blunt questions. She wasn't very happy about them, but she was honest. I knew I wasn't her first. But I didn't know how many. Do you know what I'm saying, Sierra? Do you understand?"

"Yes."

"She's been with five other men, one in high school, two during college, one afterward, and the guy she's marrying. She said she didn't think there was a chance any of them were HIV-positive, but there's no way of knowing, is there?" His eyes were haunted. "I can't stop thinking about it." His eyes filled. "You came to me a virgin. You never even kissed another guy before me."

"Are you telling me you're—?" she couldn't finish the question.

"No. I've been tested four times over the past few months. All negative, but who knows? Are we hearing the truth about this thing?" He came to her and cupped her face. As he stroked her cheeks, his eyes welled with tears and torment. "How do I ever make love to you again without wondering if I'm killing you in the process?"

"Oh, Alex," she whispered, putting her hand against his chest. She felt his heart pick up speed; her own matched the rhythm.

He took her hand and removed it from him. "I almost didn't tell you," he said hoarsely, "but you've got a right to know. It's something else you're going to need to think about before you make any decisions, isn't it?" He moved away from her.

She knew he was heading for the door. "Alex . . ."

"I'll call you," he said hoarsely. Without looking back, he opened the door and went out.

It has been three years since I wrote anything in this journal.

We have spent our evenings reading Aunt Martha's Bible. I found out who killed our beloved Koxoenis and it near broke my heart. I might never have known had I not noticed the amethyst cross Charlotte Burrell wore to the Christmas gathering. My heart stopped when I saw it around her neck, and my throat closed so tight I did not think I could draw breath let alone speak. I was so full of anger I wanted to tear that necklace from her throat, but You held me from it. She asked me what was wrong. Soon as she did I knew I could speak.

I did not ask her about the cross. Instead, I did what You set in my mind. I told her about our first winter in California and how we would

surely have starved to death had it not been for
the kindness of a Pomo Indian named Koxoenis.
Lester joined us as I told Charlotte about our
dear friend. I told them how Koxoenis gave us
meat and taught us how to find food. I told them
how he welcomed Joshua into his own home and
village and taught him how to make fish traps
and build a shelter that kept us dry and warm
through the cold, wet winter months. I said he
was as near an example of God's love as I had
ever seen in my life and a true answer to a prayer
I had said in desperation. I told them the only gift
I was ever able to give him was an amethyst cross
on a gold chain exactly like the one Charlotte
was wearing.

Lester looked sick. His face got all white and
blotchy. I thought he was going to die right there
on the spot. He said he was sorry. He said when
he saw the Indian with his bow and arrows, he
thought he was a threat and shot him. He took
the cross because he thought Koxoenis must
have killed a white settler and stolen it. Charlotte
was too ashamed to say anything. She gave the
necklace back to me and could not say a word.

I grieve now more for Lester and Charlotte
than Koxoenis. They will live with this on their
hearts for years to come. I told them I forgive
them and You do, too. But I don't know that

it made them feel any the better for taking an innocent man's life.

Oh, Lord, how many things I have done without thinking of the cost to others.

Ham has a son of his own now. I have never seen a man so taken with a child. He sits by the crib and watches Micah, sometimes for an hour or more. When Micah awakens at night, Ham brings him to bed and watches me nurse him. It is disconcerting at times. He said just last night how blessed a woman is. When I asked him why, he said a woman gets to feel a child grow inside her and, once the babe is born, she provides sustenance with her own body. No man can ever experience that.

James never in all his days talked this way.

What manner of man have you given me, Lord?

I never thought I would love a man so much my heart would break every time I looked at him. And it is so. I fell in love with James the first time I saw him, yet it is this fierce and rugged man who has grown to be a part of me. I have wondered about it much of late. I think it is because James withheld a part of himself. Kavanaugh gives everything. James yearned for more than I could give. Kavanaugh is so filled up with love, it pours out of him onto me and

my children. James risked everything to reach
his dream. Kavanaugh would die for us. James
touched me and I burned. When Kavanaugh
touches me, I see heaven.

Lord, may I be a proper wife for him. He
deserves better.

The crops came in bountiful. As is everything.
I told Ham I am in a family way again. He was
distressed at first and asked if it was good for me
to be having another baby this soon. I could not
help but laugh. It is a little late to be worrying
about such things.

Lord, I thank You. And if You do not mind me
asking, I would like a girl this time.

Dear Lord, sometimes my heart swells so much
with love for You it closes my throat up with pain.
I am not much as children go, I know. I am not
like Mama or Aunt Martha.

Mama used to pray thank You prayers in the
meadows and sing to You. She said there are
earth psalms all around us singing praises to
You and it is nice to join in. Since I am not much
good at singing, I hope you will understand I am
grateful for so many things.

Tears, a balm, soothing and cleansing. Cups, of
plenty and sorrow. Cold to make me appreciate
warmth. Manure, though I do not know if you

will like me saying so. But Lord, when spread
over turned ground where new seeds have been
planted, it brings forth growth. Like my troubles
in my life, Lord. It was Affliction and Distress
that made me come to You and now I do not ever
want to leave.

I am thankful for the pieces of fabric the
quilting club gave me—woven and designed like
You wove and designed me in my mother's womb.
Like you designed my children. I am grateful
for our new fireplace that gives us warmth, light
drawing each of us together.

Dust! The small particles dance on the light.
Would that I could dance like that for You in
broad daylight instead of going off in the woods
because the last time I did it my children thought
I was out of my head.

I am glad for the candles so I can see to write.
You are my lamp, Lord, lighting my way out
of darkness. I am thankful for the gold nuggets
Kavanaugh brought home yesterday, pure and soft
the way my heart should be. Lord, make me so.

Thank You for the Good Water we have. It
quenches my body's thirst and reminds me that
You are Living Water for my soul.

Even the Air I breathe, Jesus. I cannot see it,
but it is there, moving and necessary to keep me
alive. Like You. And the Flowers. I have never
seen so many colors and kinds splashed across the

hillsides. Even Gray Skies are a good thing from
You because they make me yearn for sunlight.
Seeds show me death and resurrection.

I do not know if You approve of me saying this,
Lord, but I am grateful for the way I feel when
Kavanaugh knows me. Even with James I never
felt this explosion of fire and light inside me like a
rain of stars.

Is all this but a hint of what it will be like to
be in full communion with You, Jesus? Do You
show us the part so that we yearn for the Whole?
I remember Aunt Martha reading to me once that
to look upon the face of God would bring death.
Still, sometimes every bit of me yearns to be in
Heaven with You all the while I still want to stay
here and live to be an old dottering woman seeing
her children and grandchildren around her. I do
not understand all that is changing inside me.

Sierra held the worn journal tenderly, tears streaming down her
face. Mary Kathryn's beautiful letter to God was the last entry in her
journal. As she had turned the last page, she'd found an envelope
carefully glued inside the back binder. Inside it was a single sheet of
paper. She recognized her mother's clear, neat script.

Dear Sierra,
We have no other journals by Mary Kathryn McMurray
in our possession. If there were others after it, I'm sorry to
say they were lost or passed along to another branch of

the family with whom we have no contact. We do know through family records that Mary Kathryn and Hamlet Bogan Kavanaugh had eight children together and lived to a healthy old age. What records we do have come down to us through your father's ancestor, America Farr, Mary Kathryn's last child by James Addison Farr. James was your great-great-great grandfather.

Mike has all the family papers if you are interested in looking at the details.

I love you,

Mom

P.S. I went through everything carefully, but could find no further mention of Joshua.

27

SIERRA SAT STARING AT MARY KATHRYN'S quilt. Alex hadn't called in several days. She knew he was giving her time to digest what he'd told her. She *had* thought about it. She had taken a couple of days off work to be by herself in order to think things through. While the children had been in school, she had walked through the mall and sat at the coffee shop. Later, she sat in her breakfast nook, the sun streaming in through the window, and read her Bible and prayed. No solutions came.

I wish you would put answers in neon signs, Lord. What am I supposed to do?

When she'd crawled into bed earlier, she couldn't sleep, so now she sat on the couch and stared up at Mary Kathryn McMurray's quilt.

What would you do, Mary Kathryn? Shoot him? Forgive him and take him back?

Sierra's life had changed so much. She was happy with the changes, comfortable with them. Alex would only turn her life upside down again, not to mention the risks involved in trying to make their marriage work. She wasn't as worried about HIV as Alex was. She was more worried about the emotional risks, the fears inherent in loving him again the way she once did. Alex had been the center of her universe.

Jesus, you are my center now. Is Alex going to be happy with the changes in me?

They had barely brushed the subject of faith during their long evening discussions. Truly, she had been afraid to broach the subject with him. Church attendance had never been part of their routine other than to attend Mass with his parents on special occasions. Did Alex understand how important Jesus was to her now, that she needed the Lord more than she needed him? She *wanted* Alex. She wanted him to share her life completely. If she knew Christ had no place in his life, how could she reconcile with him without compromising her new faith?

I lived with him thirteen years, Lord, and I don't know what he believes. Truth to tell, I don't know much about the inner workings of his heart. It was always my own that mattered.

Oh, God, why are we so proud and foolish? We don't listen until we're faced with disaster, and then we come crying home to you, wanting you to fix us! I love him, Father, but is this kind of love enough to make our marriage work? We have so little in common. I never realized until now. We come from different cultures, different social backgrounds, different religions. He's brilliant and I'm average. He graduated from college with honors, and I managed to get out of high school and take a few business courses. He likes ultramodern, and I like antiques and sunflowers and lace. Lord, he likes '70s music, and I'm sick to death of it. When I think about all of this, my head reels. I wonder how we ever lasted as long as we did. Great sex. Was that it? Was it passion for one another that held us together, Lord?

A flush ran up her cheeks, and she caught her thoughts. Was it proper to talk with Jesus about such things? If not, she hoped he would forgive her, but there was no one else she could go to, no one who would understand her from the inside out. Who else could do that but the one who created her?

As she prayed and talked with God, she struggled with all the questions. Had she caused her own downfall by living in a fantasy world, never being willing to see who Alex really was? Was that why their marriage had worked as long as it had?

Was that it, Lord? I still ache when I see him. I'm a Christian now, and I still ache for him. I love you, Jesus. Everything's changed, not the least of which is me. And still I love him.

Lord, what do I do? What's your will for me in all this?

She leaned her head back against the sofa and looked up at the quilt.

And then it dawned on her. A flash of insight from out of nowhere, from within her. And with it, God's quiet loving voice.

Be still, beloved. And know that I am God.

She blinked, amazed, overwhelmed. It was right there before her eyes, only she had been blind to it. The message her mother had said would come had finally arrived. Sitting forward slowly, Sierra studied the quilt—and understood.

"One day it will come to you like a star bursting in the heavens. And what a day that will be!"

Sierra stood and went to the quilt, smiling in wonder, her fingers tracing the scarlet thread that held all the pieces together and made them a whole incredibly beautiful work of art. "Oh, Lord . . . ," she whispered brokenly. How could she have been so blind?

Who am I, beloved?

"You are God. Almighty God."

Sierra wept with joy as enlightenment sang in her very blood. Responding to an impulse, she called Alex.

"Sierra," he said hoarsely. "What's wrong, *querida?*"

She had awakened him. Glancing at the kitchen wall clock, she grimaced. She hadn't even thought about the time. "Nothing. The children are fine. I'm fine."

"Something's happened. What is it?"

Should she tell him to go back to sleep? Her heart was racing, her soul singing praises to the Lord. "Can you come over?"

"*Sí.*" He didn't even ask what time it was. After she hung up, she raked her hands through her hair. One-fifteen in the morning! What must he be thinking? Embarrassed, she called him back to apologize and tell him her discovery could wait until morning.

Maybe it should wait until she'd had more time to think. Would he understand if she even tried to explain now in the feverish excitement of discovery? Doubts crept in. Maybe she was overreacting. Maybe she was getting overemotional. Maybe her imagination was running rampant.

O Lord. O Lord.

Alex didn't answer. Before she hung up, there was a tap on the door.

Taking a deep breath, Sierra opened it. Her heart turned over at the sight of her husband. He had pulled on his old sweats and stood barefoot, his dark hair disheveled. He looked worried.

"I'm sorry, Alex. I didn't even look to see what time it was."

"I'm awake now," he said coming inside.

"You'll think I'm crazy, but there's something I want to show you."

O God, let him see. Let him understand. Help us! Be the glue that holds us together this time.

Alex followed her into the living room, looking around for something out of place. No earthquake had happened. No ceiling falling in on her. Nothing unusual. He looked at her, bemused, questioning.

She looked up at the quilt. "The question's never been *whether,* but *when,*" she said, more to herself than to him.

"When what?"

She smiled at him. "It says that every knee will bow and every tongue will confess that Jesus Christ is Lord. So the question is do we relinquish everything to the Lord, or do we make him strip us bare before we understand *he's* in control."

Alex shook his head. "I don't know what you're talking about, *querida.*"

"Sit down with me, please, Alex. I have something very important to ask you." She turned to face him as they sat together on the couch. "This is the most important question I'll ever ask you. Who is Jesus to you?"

Surprised, he searched her eyes. "God the Son, Creator, Father, Savior."

Her eyes welled with thankful tears. "So you do believe."

"*Sí, amor mío.* Since I was a little boy. I never wanted to make an issue of it with you. Your family . . . mine . . . *impossible . . . yo comprendo.* And then, when I walked away from you, I figured I'd walked away from him as well. I didn't think he would forgive me, that he could—"

His voice broke, and Sierra felt her throat tighten with tears at the depth of his despair. He met her eyes. "But he has, *querida.* Dennis helped me see that. God has forgiven me—he has restored me to himself. And that's why I won't give up on us. If he can forgive, he can help us to do the same."

Relief swept through her, and joy as well. She looked up at the quilt. "Almighty God, Creator, Master. He's the Alpha and Omega. Mary Kathryn McMurray came to understand. She made that quilt so others would see as well. I was just so blind."

Oh, the wonder of it all.

Alex touched her, a mere brush of his fingers, tentative, comforting. "Why are you crying?"

"Because he's *sovereign*, Alex. I guess I just didn't understand what it meant. I've been turning things over and around and inside out, trying to decide how to fix things, how to make them right, how to make sure everything would work the way it's supposed to work. And then tonight, as I was looking at the quilt, I realized I'm not in control at all. God is. He always has been. He is Almighty God."

She looked up at Mary Kathryn's quilt. "She knew, Alex. It took heartache and tragedy for her eyes to be finally opened, but in the end, she knew. And she put it there in her quilt for all to see who had the eyes to do so."

I am so much like her, Lord. Stubborn, stiff-necked, and you have loved me through everything. Thank you for your patience with me.

Alex looked at the quilt, frowning. When he looked back at her again, Sierra could see he wondered if she'd taken leave of her senses. She got up and went to the quilt.

"I noticed the scarlet thread the first time Mom and I took the quilt out of the old trunk in the attic. I just didn't understand until this evening why Mary Kathryn picked that color. Do you see how it stands out? Do you see how it holds all the pieces together, Alex? Mary Kathryn made each square separately over a period of years. Each shows something significant that happened to her: tragedies, births, changes in her life, upheavals. And here at the end, the stone wall with that red cord hanging from the window opening. I never understood that." She stood before the quilt, tracing a portion of embroidered grape leaves and grapes. Shaking her head, she turned and looked at him, her heart full of love.

"I read her journal, the whole thing, several times, and I never understood why she made that wall as her last square. There was never a mention of a wall in her journal. Tonight, I understood. It's Rahab's wall."

"Rahab?"

"Rahab, the prostitute who hid the Israelite spies who came to Jericho. Moses had died, and the Israelites entered Canaan to take possession of the Promised Land. Joshua sent spies to Jericho, and Rahab took them in. She was a prostitute who had lived a life of sin and disobedience, and yet, in that moment, she risked her life to protect those men and hide them from the ones looking for them because she believed in their God. She had faith, and she acted upon it. The spies told her to hang a scarlet cord in her window, and though everyone else in Jericho would be put to the sword, no one in her house would perish. And they kept their word. She married Salmon and is named in the lineage of Jesus Christ."

She looked up at the quilt again. "But it's more than that, too. Scarlet is for Jesus and his death on the cross. Scarlet is for the blood he shed for us so that we could be redeemed. He was there in the beginning of it all. Faith is the key."

"Scarlet for her faith, you mean?"

"No, not her faith. Mary Kathryn contended with God. Early in her journal, she was angry and rejected him. After that, she scarcely mentioned him in a good light—not until much later. She wasn't faithful at all. In a sense, she was like Rahab, prostituting herself to other gods in a foreign land. Her home and land mattered more than anything. Then it was her husband and her children. And with each loss she suffered, God was there with her. She didn't understand that until the end. That's what the scarlet thread signifies. That's why the wall is her last block. The window is open, and the scarlet cord flowing out and upward, tying it all together. God was there with her throughout her life. He brought her through."

She laughed softly, filled with relief and joy. "Look at the stitches, Alex. Grape leaves and grapes, chains, doves, crosses, olive branches—so much skill and beauty. When she quilted this

465

wall, she did it with a passionate love for her Savior. She realized everything that had happened to her was through God's will. She finally surrendered. She *believed*. And because she did, God opened her eyes so that she could look back and see how he had been intimately involved through everything. Death. Birth. Fire. Disinheritance. Love. Betrayal. Loss. God allowed her to go through all those things so that she would come to him. Once she did, she saw the wonder of all of it."

She came back and sat down with Alex again. "The things that happen in our lives are allowed to happen because the Lord wants to draw us to him. We make decisions and do things, thinking we're in control, but we never really are. God is. It's arrogance and pride to think we rule our lives. It's an illusion. We're never able to orchestrate a thing. God is in control."

She put her hand on his knee. "I thought you were in control of my life, Alex. When you moved me to Southern California, I felt powerless. I was angry and frightened. I rebelled. I didn't even think about turning to the Lord. I turned to friends, and their lives were in shambles. I turned to my mother, and then she was taken away from me. I wanted to turn back to you, but then you were gone, too. God finally got through to me on the Hollywood Freeway." She laughed through her tears. "Sacred ground for me was a strip of macadam in Los Angeles County."

He brushed the tears lightly from her cheek, his eyes tender. She wanted more than anything for him to understand. "Oh, Alex, don't you see? I never would've needed Jesus if I'd had any control at all. Everything that's happened — all the pain — he's turned to *good*. It's served his purpose. It brought me to him."

His dark eyes softened. "I saw the change in you." He cupped her cheek tenderly. "I was a fool to leave you."

She covered his hand with her own. "Had you not left me, Alex, the change would never have come. I thank God for all of it. I thank him with every ounce of my being, Alex. All the pain was blessing. I didn't fall in love with you by chance. It was God's design. I know now he draws us to him, all through our lives. If we let him. Some of us are just so stubborn it takes a long time to see his will at work." *Some never do, do they, Lord?*

She held his hand between hers and searched his eyes. "Jesus is at the very heart of who I am now, Alex. I can't go back."

"I wouldn't ask you to give him up, *querida*. I only ask you to allow me in."

Sierra's heart melted. God had given her this man for a purpose. She had married Alex as an untried girl, head over heels in love. She was still married to him, still in love with him. The difference now was that she was one with Christ, wed to Almighty God. And with God all things were possible.

"We haven't anything in common really, have we?" she said softly. "Except Jesus. He's our common ground, Alex. He brought us together, and he'll hold us together if we make him our foundation. I don't need to worry about the what-ifs anymore. I don't need to have an answer to everything. I don't have to have everything worked out perfectly in my mind before I can start over. Neither do you, beloved. We just need to draw closer to *Jesus*. We need to trust in his plan for us. We need to learn from him. And we need to step out in faith and begin."

She touched his cheek tenderly, feeling the firm line of his jaw. "Oh, my love, if we make drawing closer to Jesus our goal in life, how can we not draw closer to one another at the same time?"

Covering her hand, Alex turned his head and kissed her palm. *"Mi querida, te amo muchísimo.* You are so beautiful to me, *mi amor."* His dark eyes were flooded with tears. "I am sorry for the pain I caused you."

"And I you, Alejandro."

Oh, God, forgive me for the pain I caused you with my stubbornness. I love you, Jesus.

She went into Alex's arms naturally, leaning her head against his chest. She could hear the steady, rapid beat of his heart. "We still have a lot to work out."

"I'll get rid of the black couch."

She laughed and breathed in the beloved scent of his body, familiar and heady.

Oh, my love. Be like a gazelle on the mountains of spices. I have awakened. Be with us, Lord. Make this a love triangle, a sacred one to last a lifetime and beyond.

Alex drew back slightly. "First things first." Releasing her, he pulled the gold chain with the crucifix his mother had given him and her wedding ring from beneath his sweatshirt. Opening the clasp, he let the two slide into the palm of his hand. He looked at her then, the question clear in his eyes. He was taking nothing for granted this time.

Smiling, Sierra held out her left hand.

"*Dios, te doy mi gracias y mi vida,*" he whispered in relief and thanksgiving. The tension fell away, and joy leaped into his dark eyes as he slipped the gold wedding band back on her finger. Taking her hand, he stood.

Fourteen years ago, they had faced one another as they did now, the future before them. Cupping her face, Alejandro Luís Madrid kissed Sierra Clanton Madrid reverently, before the Lord.

"May no man or woman put asunder what God has joined together," he murmured.

Sliding her arms around his neck, she kissed him back.

Oh, Father, we rejoice in you. We praise your name!

Mold us and make us one with you.

Leota's Garden

FRANCINE RIVERS

Tyndale House Publishers, Inc.
Carol Stream, Illinois

To my grandmothers,
women of strength and faith—
MARTHA WULFF
MARGARET ELEANOR KING
ANNA TORESIA JOHNSON

ACKNOWLEDGMENTS

*No book is ever written without the help of many people.
I would like to thank:*

May Sandine for sharing her memories;

Jim Ruppert and Cyndi Perez of Exchange Bank in Windsor, for patiently answering my questions regarding banking;

Tim Moore and his assistant, Dianne Moore, at Edward D. Jones in Sebastopol for information about the stock market;

Rosie Sanchez Wagner at Fred Young and Company Funeral Directors for answering some delicate questions;

Patricia Rushford for sharing her expertise on home care for the elderly. Her book, *Caring for Your Elderly Parents*, was invaluable;

and Karen Ball for encouraging while editing.

1

CORBAN SOLSEK'S HEART DROPPED AND HIS STOMACH CLENCHED tight when he saw the B on his sociology proposal. The shock of it made heat pour into his face and then recede in the wake of cold anger. He'd worked hard on this outline for his term project! He'd checked his information and sources, reviewed the methods by which he planned to present his ideas, and proposed a program. He should've received an A! What gives? Opening the folder, he glanced through the perfectly typed pages, looking for corrections, comments, anything that might give an indication of why he hadn't received what he knew he deserved.

Not one red check anywhere. No comment. Nothing.

Stewing, Corban flipped open his notebook, wrote the date, and tried to concentrate on the lecture. Several times Professor Webster looked straight at him as he spoke, singling him out from the other hundred and twenty students inhabiting the tiers of desks. Each time Corban stared back for a few seconds before looking down and scribbling some more notes. He had great respect for Professor Webster, which made the grade even harder to take.

I'll challenge him. I don't have to accept this without a fight. It wasn't a *good* proposal. It was *excellent.* He wasn't a mediocre student. He poured his heart and soul into his work, and he intended to make sure he was treated fairly. Hadn't his father instilled that in him?

"You have to fight for yourself, Cory. Don't let anybody kick you around. They kick you, kick 'em back harder. Knock 'em down and make sure they don't get up again. I didn't bring up my son to take any guff from anybody."

His father had worked his way to the top of a trucking company through hard labor and fierce determination. He'd done it all, from truck driver to mechanic to sales to administration to CEO, and finally to part owner of the company. He was proud of his accomplishments while at the same time embarrassed by his lack of formal education. He'd never gotten further than the sophomore year of high school. He'd quit to help support his mother and younger siblings after his father died of a massive heart attack.

The same kind of heart attack that killed him the year after he retired, leaving a wealthy widow and two sons and a daughter with healthy trust funds.

"Focus on where you're going," his father had always said. "Get into a good college. The best, if possible. Stick it out. Don't let anything or anyone get in your way. Get yourself a sheepskin from a big-name college and you're halfway up the ladder before you have your first job."

No way was Corban going to accept this grade. He'd worked too hard. It wasn't fair.

"Did you have something to say, Mr. Solsek?" Professor Webster stood staring at him from his podium.

Corban heard several students laugh softly. There was the rustle of papers and the creak of seats as others turned and looked back at him where he sat in the center middle row.

"Sir?"

"Your pencil, Mr. Solsek," the professor said with an arched brow. "This isn't a percussion instrument class."

Corban's face flooded with heat as he realized he'd been tapping his pencil while his mind raced in agitation. "Sorry." He flipped it into the proper position for writing and aimed a quelling glance at two twittering coeds. How did those airheads make it into Berkeley anyway?

"Are we ready to proceed then, Mr. Solsek?" Professor Webster looked back at him with a faint smile.

Embarrassment melted into anger. *The jerk's enjoying this.* Now Corban had two reasons to feel indignant: the unfair grade and public humiliation. "Yes, sir, any time you are." He forced a dry smile and a pretense of calm disdain.

By the end of the lecture, the muscle in Corban's jaw ached from tension. He felt as though he had a two-ton elephant sitting on his chest. He took his time stuffing his notebook into the backpack already crammed with books and two small binders. Thankfully, the other students cleared out of the lecture hall in quick fashion. Only two or three paused to make any remarks to Professor Webster, who was now erasing the board. Corban kept the report folder in his hand as he walked down the steps toward the podium.

Professor Webster stacked his notes and tucked them into a file folder. "Did you have a question, Mr. Solsek?" he said, putting the folder into his briefcase and snapping it shut. He looked at Corban with those dark, shrewd eyes.

"Yes, sir." He held out his report. "I worked very hard on this."

"It showed."

"There wasn't a single correction."

"No need. What you had there was very well presented."

"Then why a B and not an A?"

Professor Webster rested his hand on the briefcase. "You have the makings of an excellent term paper from that proposal, Mr. Solsek, but you lacked one major ingredient."

How could that be? He and Ruth had both gone over the paper before he turned it in. He had covered everything. "Sir?"

"The human element."

"I beg your pardon?"

"The human element, Mr. Solsek."

"I heard you, sir. I just don't understand what you mean. The entire paper is *focused* on the human element."

"Is that so?"

Corban stifled his anger at Webster's sardonic tone. He forced himself to speak more calmly. "How would you suggest I make it more apparent, sir?" He wanted an A in this course; he wasn't going to accept less. Sociology was his major. He had maintained a 4.0 for three years. He wasn't going to break that perfect record now.

"A case study would help."

Corban flushed with anger. Obviously the professor hadn't read his paper carefully enough. "I incorporated case studies. Here. On page 5. And more here. Page 8." He had backed up everything he had proposed with case studies. What was Professor Webster talking about?

"Collected from various volumes. Yes, I know. I read your documentation, Mr. Solsek. What you lack is any *personal* contact with those who might be most affected by your proposed programs."

"You mean you want me to poll people on the street?" He couldn't keep the edge of disdain from creeping into his voice. How long would it take to develop a proper questionnaire? How many hundreds of people would he have to find to answer it? Wasn't that thesis work? He wasn't in graduate school. Not yet.

"No, Mr. Solsek. I'd like to see you develop your own case study. One would do."

"Just one, sir? But that—"

"One, Mr. Solsek. You won't have time for more. Add the human element and you'll earn the A you covet. I'm sure of it."

Corban wasn't quite sure what the professor was driving at, but he could sense an undercurrent of disapproval. Was it a personality clash? Did his ideas offend? How could that be? If the programs he proposed were ever put into practice, they'd solve a lot of current problems in government systems.

"Do you have anyone in your own family who might fit the lifestyle scenario you've presented, Mr. Solsek?"

"No, sir." His entire family lived in Connecticut and upstate New York, too far away to do the number of interviews he'd need for a paper. Besides that, his family had money. His father had broken the chain of middle-class mediocrity. Corban's paper zeroed in on those who were economically challenged. Nobody in his family depended on social security to survive. He thought of his mother living in Switzerland part of the year with her new investment-broker husband.

"Well, that presents a problem, doesn't it, Mr. Solsek?" Professor Webster lifted his briefcase from the table. "However, I'm quite sure you'll work it out."

"Quit grousing, Cory," Ruth said that afternoon in their shared apartment a few blocks off University Avenue. "It's simple. If you want an A, do what Professor Webster wants you to do. It's not like he's asking you to do something terrible." Raking her fingers through her straight, short black hair, she opened a cabinet in the kitchenette. "Are we out of coffee filters *again?*"

"No, there are plenty. Look in the cabinet to the left of the sink."

"I didn't put them there," she said, closing the cabinet where she'd been searching.

"I did. Made better sense. The coffeepot is right underneath where the outlet is. I moved the mugs too. They're on the shelf above the coffee and filters."

Ruth sighed. "If I'd realized how difficult you are, I would've had second thoughts about moving in with you." She took the can of coffee and pack of filters down from the cabinet.

"One case study." Cory tapped his pencil. "That's all I need."

"A woman."

He frowned. "Why a woman?"

"Because women are more ready to talk, that's why." She made a face. "And don't ever tell my advocacy friends I said that."

"A woman, then. Fine. What woman?"

"Someone with whom you can develop some rapport," Ruth said, adding a fifth heaping scoop of French roast to the basket.

"I don't need to get that personal."

"Sure you do. How do you suppose you'll get answers to the kind of questions you want if you don't make friends with your subject?"

"I haven't got time to develop a friendship, Ruth."

"It doesn't have to be *lifelong,* you know. Just long enough to finish your paper."

"I've got a few months. That's it. All I need is someone who meets my criteria and who'll be willing to cooperate."

"Oh, I'm sure *that'll* impress Professor Webster."

"So, what do you suggest?"

"Simple. Offer an incentive."

"Money, you mean?"

"No, not money. Don't be so dense, Cory."

It annoyed him when she spoke to him in that condescending way. He tapped his pencil again, saying nothing more. She glanced back at him and frowned slightly. "Don't look so ticked, Cory. All you have to do is offer services in exchange for information."

He gave a hard laugh. "Sure. What kind of services could I offer?"

She rolled her eyes. "I hate it when you're in one of these moods. You can't be such a perfectionist in this world. Good grief, Cory. Just use your imagination. You've got one, haven't you?"

Her tone grated. He leaned back in his chair, shoving his proposal away from him on the table, wishing he had taken a different avenue with his project. The prospect of having to talk with people made him nervous, although he wasn't about to admit hat to Ruth. She had a double major in marketing and telecommunications. She could talk to anybody, anytime, on any subject. Of course, it also helped to have a photographic memory.

"Quit stewing about it." Ruth shook her head as she poured herself a cup of black coffee. "Just go down to the supermarket and help some little old lady carry her groceries home."

"With my luck, she'll think I'm some mugger after her purse." He took up his pencil and started tapping it. "Better if I go through some community organization."

"There. You came up with a solution." She leaned down to kiss him on the lips, then took his pencil away and tucked it behind her ear as she straightened. "I knew you'd figure it out."

"What about dinner?" he said as she moved away from him. "It's your night to cook."

"Oh, Cory. I *can't.* I'm sorry, but you know how long it takes me to put a meal together. If I'm going to do it, I have to do it right, and I've got two hundred pages of reading and some materials to review before a test tomorrow."

No less than what he had to do most nights.

She paused in the doorway. Leaning against the jamb, she gave him a winsome smile, her dark hair framing her perfect, oval face. She had such beautiful dark eyes and the kind of smile toothpaste advertisers liked on billboards. Her skin was flawless, like an English lady's. Not to mention the rest of her from the neck down. Ruth Coldwell came in a very nice package, and underneath it all, she was smart. Not to mention ambitious.

One date was all it had taken for Cory to know she was a match for him. Even more so after the second date and a passionate night in his apartment. She made his head spin and sent his hormones into overdrive. A month after their first date, he was having trouble concentrating on his work and wondering what he was going to do about it. Then providence had smiled on him. Ruth had spilled out her money worries to him over coffee. In tears, she said she didn't know where she was going to get enough money to finish the semester. He suggested she move in with him.

"Really?" Her beautiful brown eyes had glistened with tears. "You're serious?" She'd made him feel like a knight in shining armor saving a lady in distress. Money was no problem for him.

"Sure."

"I don't know, Cory . . ."

"Why not?" Once he made up his mind, it was a matter of finding the best way to achieve his goal.

"Because we haven't known one another very long," she had said, troubled.

"What don't you know about me that you need to know?"

"Oh, Cory. I feel as though I've known you all my life, but it's a big step."

"I don't see that it would change much. We spend every spare minute together as it is. We're sleeping together. Save time if we lived together."

"It's sort of *serious*. Like getting married. And I'm not ready for that, Cory. I don't even want to think about marriage at this stage in my life. I have too many things I need to do first."

The word *marriage* had sent a chill through him. He wasn't ready for that kind of commitment either. "No strings," he had said and meant it. "We'll share expenses and chores right down the middle. How's that?" He grimaced now as he remembered saying it. But then, he'd said a lot of things to convince her. "It'd cut expenses for both of us." Although money was no problem for him, he had been worried about hurting her pride.

She'd moved in the next afternoon.

They'd been living together for six months, and sometimes he found himself wondering . . .

Ruth came back into the kitchen and leaned down to kiss him again. "You have that look again. I know it's my turn to cook. I can't help the way things fall sometimes, Cory. School comes first. Didn't we agree on that?" She raked her fingers lightly through the hair at the back of his neck. Her touch still made his blood warm. "Why don't you order some Chinese food?"

Last time she'd called in an order, it had cost him thirty bucks. It wasn't the money that bothered him. It was the principle. "I think I'll go out and have some pizza."

Straightening, she grimaced. "Whatever you want," she said with a shrug.

He knew she didn't like pizza. Whenever he ordered it, she ate it grudgingly, pressing a paper towel over her slice to soak up the grease. "I need my pencil," he said as she headed toward the doorway again.

"What a grouch." She took it from behind her ear and tossed it onto the table.

Sitting alone at the kitchen table, he wondered how it was possible to be so crazy about someone and still feel things weren't quite right.

Something was askew.

Raking a hand through his hair, he stood up. He didn't have time to think about his relationship with Ruth right now. He needed to figure out what he was going to do about his report. Snatching the telephone book, he slammed it on the table and flipped it open to the yellow pages. There was a long list of charity organizations offering services to seniors. He spent the rest of the afternoon calling them and asking questions until he found the one that might suit his purposes.

"It's wonderful that you're interested in volunteering, Mr. Solsek," the lady on the other end of the line said. "We have very few college students among our ranks. Of course, you'll need to come down for a personal interview, and we have forms for you to fill out. You'll also need to take a weekend orientation class. Do you have a CPR certificate?"

"No, ma'am," he said, stifling his irritation. Personal interview? Forms? Orientation classes? Just to volunteer to take some old lady to the bank or grocery store?

Jotting down the pertinent information, Cory gave a deep sigh. *A pox on you, Professor Webster, for getting me into this!*

"You will do no such thing, Anne-Lynn! What ever made you even consider anything so utterly ridiculous?" Nora was positively trembling. Just when she thought everything was perfect, her daughter threw a monkey wrench into the works. Well, she wouldn't have it! Everything was going to move forward as planned.

"I've tried to tell you how important—"

"I'm not going to listen, Annie." Nora rose from the table, picking up her cup and saucer. They rattled, revealing her lack of control. She forcefully steadied her hands and carried the dishes to the tile sink counter, setting them down carefully. "You can just call Susan and tell her you've come to your senses."

"Mom, please. I've thought it all through very carefully—"

"I said *no!*" Nora refused to look at her daughter. She didn't want to see how pale she was, how pleading her blue eyes could be. Emotional manipulation, that's all it was. She wouldn't fall for it. Striving for calm, she rinsed the cup and saucer, opened the dishwasher, and placed them carefully on the rack. "You're going to Wellesley. That's been decided."

"You decided, Mom, I didn't."

Nora slammed the dishwasher door at the quiet comment and turned to glare at her daughter. "Someone has to have a little common sense. For once, even your father agreed. Didn't he tell you a degree from a prestigious college like Wellesley will open doors for you?"

"He said Cal would do the same."

"Oh, *Cal.* Just because he went there."

"Dad said he wants me to do what will make me happy."

Nora's heart pounded in anger. How dare he undo all her work. Just once couldn't he think of someone besides himself? The only reason he wanted Annie to go to Cal was to keep her on the West Coast. "He wants your best, and I don't? Is that what he's implying? Well, he's wrong! Love means you want *the best* for someone."

"This is best, Mom. I have a job. I'll be able to make it on my own."

"As a waitress. Earning minimum wage. You're so naïve."

"I know I won't be living as comfortably as I do here with you and Fred, but I'll have a place of my own—"

"Shared by a hippie—"

". . . and food and—"

"Do you think I've sent you to the best private schools so you can wait tables? Do you have any idea how much it's cost to educate you? Music lessons, dancing lessons, gymnastics lessons, deportment classes, modeling classes, cheerleading camps. I've spent thousands of dollars, not to mention thousands of hours of *my* time, bringing you up with the best of everything so that you would have the opportunities I *never* had. I've sacrificed for you and your brother."

"Mom, that's not fair—"

"You're right. It's not fair. *To me.* You will not go off and live in San Francisco like a hippie in that cheap little flat of Susan's. You are not tossing your opportunity to go to Wellesley to the wind just so you can take some art classes. If you had any real talent, don't you think I would have sent you to Paris to study?"

She saw the wince of hurt flash across Annie's face. Good. Better to cut clean and make reality come clear. Better to hurt her a little now than see her daughter throw away all her chances for a bright, affluent future. She could continue her silly art classes as elective courses.

"Mom, please hear me out. I've prayed for a long time about this, and—"

"Anne-Lynn, don't you dare talk to me about God again! Do you hear me? The worst thing I ever did was send you to that church camp. You haven't been the same since!"

Tears welled in her daughter's eyes, but Nora refused to weaken. She couldn't if she were to see her daughter beyond these crossroads. Anne had to take the right path. Nora knew that if she gave in for one moment, every hope she had ever had for Anne would be lost.

"I love you very much, Anne-Lynn," she said, taking a soothing tone. "If I didn't, I'd let you do whatever you want. Trust me. I know what's right for you. Someday you'll thank me. Now go up to your room and think things over again." Seeing Anne open her mouth to speak, she raised one hand. "No more right now. You've hurt me enough as it is. Now please do as I've asked."

Anne rose slowly and stood at the table, her head down. Nora watched her, measuring whether she was going to have to fight more to make sure Anne didn't throw her life away. She was such a beautiful girl, tall enough to be a model, hands perfect for playing the piano, grades high enough to go to any college in the country, but not a bit of common sense. Nora's eyes burned with unshed tears she didn't bother to hide. What cruel irony was this? Did Anne now mean to strip her of all her dreams?

"Mom, I have to start making decisions for myself."

Nora clenched her teeth, sensing the gulf widening between them. "Since you're so fond of the Bible these days, perhaps you should look up the part about honoring your father and mother. Since you have an absentee father, you're to honor *me*. Now go to your room before I really lose my temper."

Anne left quietly.

Trembling again, Nora leaned back against the kitchen counter. Her heart was drumming a battle beat. It had never occurred to her that Anne would resist the plans made for her. Perhaps she shouldn't have been so pleased about Anne's graduating from high school early. That had given Anne too much time to think of other things to do.

Relaxing slightly, Nora sighed. She'd been so proud of Anne, eagerly telling her friends how she had graduated in January with a 4.0 GPA, actually higher than that with the few college classes she had completed. But how can you have a better-than-perfect average?

She should have gotten Anne into something to keep her mind occupied. Then Anne wouldn't have had time to go visiting Susan in her flat and thinking how grand and exciting an independent, poverty-stricken life would be.

"I'm going to move in with Susan. . . ."

Susan Carter! That girl would never amount to more than a hill of beans. The Carters were nice enough, but they lacked class. Tom and his blue-collar job, and Maryann with her low-paying nursing job. How they managed to feed and clothe six children was beyond Nora's understanding. It was a pity Tom Carter didn't have more ambition so Maryann could have stayed home and minded her children. Their son Sam had landed in jail, and Susan was trouble waiting to happen.

Nora went into the dining room and took a crystal-stemmed wineglass from the mahogany china cabinet. Returning to the kitchen, she opened the refrigerator and took out a bottle of chilled white Chablis. She needed something to calm her nerves. She filled her glass, then recorked the bottle and replaced it before going out into the sunroom. She sat on the white wicker chaise lounge with the plump flowered cushions and stretched out her slender legs.

The old resentments bubbled. What Nora would've given to have the opportunities she was giving Annie. And did her daughter appreciate them? No. Like a spoiled child, Anne-Lynn wanted her own way. She wanted to make her own choices. She hadn't yet said, "It's my life and I want to live it." But it all came down to the same thing.

"I won't allow it. She's not going to ruin her life."

Inhaling through her nose, she released her breath slowly to calm herself. Then she sipped her wine. She needed to think about Annie and what she would do if this pipe dream continued. There was the rest of spring and summer. Anne-Lynn had too much time on her hands. That was the problem. Well, that could be solved easily enough. Nora would make sure Anne was committed to something. Tutoring at the middle school through June and then helping during summer school would look good on her records.

Her head ached. She could feel another migraine coming on. If Anne came downstairs again, she'd have her make up a cold compress. Maybe that would make it clear to her how this stress affected her mother.

Oh, why did Anne-Lynn have to rebel now? Just because she had turned eighteen last week didn't mean she was ready to run her own life! It was Susan planting ideas in her head. Or Anne's father. Nora had a good mind to call him and tell him what she thought of his latest interference. Cal! Middle-class people go to Cal. Perhaps if he had suggested Stanford . . .

The last four years had been so wonderful. Anne had buckled down after the turbulent, emotionally charged preteen years when Nora had often wondered if her daughter was going to run away and live on the streets. Anne had excelled at everything, pleading only once to quit ballet and music. But when she was told no, she went along with the program laid out for her. She had studied and worked hard at school, was popular with the other students, and received more than her share of calls from male admirers. But there were only a few Nora had allowed her to date. After all, she didn't want Anne marrying some ordinary Joe from the Bay Area.

Wellesley. That's where Anne-Lynn would meet quality people, where she would mix with students from Ivy League colleges—and marry the right kind of person.

Why did Anne-Lynn want to throw it all away now?

"I've prayed . . ."

Those words grated more every time Nora heard them. She downed the rest of her wine and rose to pour herself another glass.

In the beginning, Nora hadn't thought much about Anne's "conversion." True, the word had rankled. It was like a slap in the face, an insult. What did the girl suppose Nora was? A heathen? Hadn't she made the family attend church services regularly? Anne's biological father had been a deacon once, and though Fred didn't have time, he gave generously to the church. Nora frowned in annoyance thinking about it again. She had served on women's committees many times and filled bags with canned goods whenever there was a food drive.

And then, all of a sudden, after one summer camp, Anne-Lynn comes home and says, "I've become a Christian, Mom. I accepted Christ Jesus as my Savior and Lord at camp. Pastor Rick baptized me. I'm so happy, and I want you to be happy, too."

She'd *become* a Christian? What did she think she'd always been? A pagan?

Nora had let it go. Although she viewed it as a silly proclamation, she did begin to notice some welcome changes taking place in her daughter's attitude and behavior. If Anne wanted to attribute it to Jesus, fine. As long as the rebelliousness and stubbornness ceased, that's all that mattered to Nora. Anne listened and did as she was told. She even said thank you, kept her room neat and clean, and offered to help around the house. A blessed change, indeed, after several years of fits of preadolescent moodiness. If Anne came home from camp a young lady willing to do what she was told, well, then, thank God for it.

Only occasionally did Nora see a look come into her daughter's eyes that indicated she was caught in some sort of inner battle.

Everything had been so wonderful over the past few years. Anne had become the daughter Nora had dreamed she could be. All of Nora's friends envied her such an accomplished, lovely girl—especially when their own daughters were talking back, experimenting with drugs, sneaking out with boys, running away, or getting pregnant and having to have an abortion.

Anne was perfect.

Anne was her pride and joy.

And she was *not* going to be allowed to make any foolish mistakes.

Upstairs in her sunny room, Annie sat cross-legged on her bed, beneath the lacy, crocheted canopy. Clutching a pink satin pillow against her chest, she fought the tears spilling down her cheeks. Why did her mother always have to make her feel so guilty? No matter how hard she tried, no matter how well she did, it was never enough. One mistake, one thought out of line with what her mother wanted, and Annie knew she'd be told again how ungrateful, rebellious, stubborn, and stupid she was. When words didn't prove strong enough to maintain control, a migraine came on with a vengeance. Her mother was probably downstairs right now tending herself with a glass of white wine and cold compresses while lying on the chaise lounge in the sunroom.

And it's my fault, Annie thought, feeling hopeless. *Every time I try to break away, this happens. When will it stop?*

Oh, Lord, You know how hard I try to take captive every thought and focus on You. Mom knows how to press every button. Why is she like this? Jesus, You know I've tried to understand my mother, tried to please her, but nothing is ever enough. Worse, nothing made sense anymore. Her mother complained about how much money and time she spent on Anne, but she wouldn't allow her to get a job or live on her own. *She's the one who insists I go to Wellesley. You know how much that costs, Lord. I can't go when I feel You nudging me toward studying art, but Mom won't even listen. Lord, she says she likes Susan, but now she's calling her a hippie and saying she's not good enough to be my roommate.* How could her mother say she was proud of Anne's scholastic achievements one minute and in the next breath tell her she was stupid and incapable of making decisions about her own life?

"Since you're so fond of the Bible these days, why don't you look up the part about honoring your father and mother?"

Did honoring mean to do everything you were told without question? Did it mean swift capitulation? Did it mean giving up yourself for the sake of living out someone else's dreams? No matter what that dream was?

Annie knew if she went to Wellesley as her mother wanted, the plans for her future wouldn't end there. Mom would be calling and asking whom she was dating, if the young man had "potential." Of course, what that meant was high test scores, excellent grades, and a major that would guarantee a financially healthy career. Law. Medicine. Business. Her mother would want to know if the young man came from a "good backgound." Someone descended from a passenger on the Mayflower. Someone with a family tree. Someone whose successful parents had lots of *old* money and high social standing.

She shook her head. Mom could be open-minded. She wouldn't mind it if her daughter dated a descendant of immigrants as long as the family was well respected and well known.

A Kennedy, perhaps?

Guilt gripped her. She was being irrational. Her mother wasn't *that* bad.

Am I becoming like her, Lord? When I tear loose, am I going to do to my children what she's doing to me? Or am I going to lose all reason and find myself saying to them someday, "I didn't have any freedom, so you can do whatever you want"? Oh, Father, forgive me, but I'm beginning to hate her.

The last thing Anne wanted was for anger and bitterness to take hold of her, but it was so frustrating! Her mother wouldn't even listen to her. And it was only getting worse. *I thought I could grow up and move out, be on my own, but it's as though she has her claws sunk into me. The harder I struggle, the deeper she wounds me.*

"God, help me . . . please."

Honor. What did it mean?

Maybe if she went to Wellesley . . .

No, that would just delay the inevitable. Even if she went to Wellesley, she would still hear how much her mother had sacrificed for her future. And if she didn't go to Wellesley, she would never hear the end of how ungrateful she was for the opportunity she had wasted.

Lord, I'm in a no-win situation. What do I do?

Every which way she turned, Annie felt blocked. Like a calf making a run from the herd only to have the drover ride her down and nail her with a lasso. The fire was burning and the iron red-hot, but it wasn't God's name her mother wanted branded into her flesh.

"Property of Nora Gaines," *that's* what she wanted. But would that be enough?

Nothing she did was right unless it was done her mother's way. *"Get back in the corral, Annie. I know what you were meant to be, and I'm going to make sure I drive you to it."* But did she know? What was it her mother really wanted?

I don't know what to do, Lord. I feel You drawing me one way, and Mom's dragging me back in the other. How do I break free to do Your will without hurting her? Why can't she let go?

Annie wanted to love her mother the way a daughter should, but it was getting harder. She could barely stand to be in the same room with her. If she hadn't come upstairs, she would've exploded with words she'd only regret later. She had kept her head down to hide her feelings from her mother. She had held her tongue because she knew it would be like a grass fire if she let loose one word. She had to clench her hands to keep from rising up and shouting, "Get out of my life, Mother! Nothing ever pleases you! I'm sick of living like this. Why don't *you* get a life, so I can have my *own?*"

The molten words would have come pouring out of her, burning away the landscape of her relationship with her mother, blackening everything. Some things Annie knew about her mother, things she wished she didn't. One of them was that Nora Gaines was good at holding grudges. She kept a list of the hurts she had suffered over her lifetime. And who had caused them. She never forgot anything, never forgave. The past was like ammunition, boxed and waiting. And she was quick to load and fire. Annie knew the name of every person who had ever hurt her mother and how they had accomplished it. Nora Gaines made sure of it.

Sometimes the blame from past transgressions spilled over onto Annie's head, and the litanies would begin.

"You're just like your father. He never had sense enough to think about the future either. . . . You're just like your father, dreaming all the time. You're just like him. . . ."

Or worse.

"You're just like your Grandma Leota. Always thinking about yourself. Never caring about anyone else's feelings. . . . My mother never had time for me. Look at all the time I've made for you. I was never loved the way you are. . . . My mother never gave me a thing. I had to go out on my own at eighteen and make my own way. . . . I've always wanted to make sure you had the best opportunities. I've made sure you had all the things I never had."

Not once could Annie remember ever hearing her mother say a nice thing about her own mother, Leota Reinhardt. And it made Annie wonder. Was Grandma Leota to blame for the way her mother was?

There was no way to measure cause and effect because Annie only knew her mother's side. She'd never heard Grandma Leota say much about anything. In fact, Annie had seldom *seen* Grandmother Leota. Though her grandmother lived right over the hills in Oakland, Annie could count on two hands the times she had been taken for a visit. And as soon as the family arrived, Annie and Michael were sent out to play in the backyard so the adults could talk.

She frowned. It had never been her grandmother who sent them out.

Her mother always developed a headache shortly after they arrived at Grandma Leota's, so they never stayed longer than an hour or two. On the way home, Mom would fume and catalogue Grandma's failings.

Once, when her parents were still married, Annie had overheard her father say he liked Leota. Only once. The words had been thrown down like a gauntlet. A battle royal had ensued, long and loud, with doors slamming, glass breaking. The memory of that night was etched permanently in Annie's brain. A memory of brutal accusations shouted back and forth. Six months later, Annie's parents filed for divorce. By the tender age of eight, Annie had known better than to mention or ask questions about Grandma Leota.

Lying back on her bed, Annie stared up through the crocheted canopy. It had been a present on her fourteenth birthday. Her mother had thrown a party for her, complete with friends from school, ballet, and gymnastics. The house had been full that day. Her mother had made sure her present was opened last, then proceeded to tell everyone how she'd seen the canopy covering in a home-design magazine and called the publisher who put her in contact with the company. "It came all the way from Belgium." Everyone had oohed and aahed over it. One friend had even leaned over to whisper, "I wish my mother would buy something like that for me."

Annie remembered wishing she could throw it back into its big professionally wrapped box with the massive silk ribbons and flowers and hand it to the girl with her best wishes. She wanted to scream, "I didn't ask for it! She's going to use it against me. The next time I dare disagree with her, she's going to say, 'How can you be so ungrateful? I bought you that beautiful canopy cover. I had to call long distance to that magazine and then stay on hold forever just to find out where it came from. And then I had to write to the company in Belgium. Do you have any idea how much that canopy cover cost? I would have died to have something so beautiful in my drab little room when I was a child. And now you won't do the simplest thing I ask of you.' "

Something shifted within Annie, a subtle warmth, the barest flicker of light. Just a spark, but it was like a match lit in a dark room. She could see clearly, and a chill went through her.

Oh, God . . . oh, God. I'm lying here on my bed the same way Mom is lying on her chaise lounge downstairs. I'm nursing my grievances the same way she nurses hers. I despise what she does, and I'm becoming just like her.

Annie sat up, heart pounding. *I can't stay here. I can't go on like this. If I do, I'm going to end up hating my mother the same way she hates hers. Lord, I can't live like that.*

Slipping off her bed, Annie headed for her closet. Sliding the mirrored doors open, she reached to the high shelf and pulled down her suitcase. Opening her dresser drawers, she took out only what she needed, packing hastily. She had enough to get by until she was settled with Susan. She took her Bible from her nightstand and put it on top of her clothes. Closing the suitcase, she locked it.

Should she speak with her mother? No, she didn't dare risk it. She knew the scene that would come if she confronted her. Sitting down at her desk, she opened a side drawer and took out a box with pretty stationery. She sat for a long moment, thinking. No matter what she said, it wasn't going to change her mother's mind. Wiping her eyes and rubbing her nose, Annie pressed her lips together. *Lord . . . Lord . . .* She didn't know what to pray. She didn't know if she was doing right or wrong.

Honor.

What did it mean anyway?

"Mom," she wrote, "I'm grateful for everything you've done for me." She sat for a long time, trying to think what else to say to make the blow easier on her mother. Nothing came to her. Nothing would help. All she could imagine was the anger. "I love you," she wrote finally and signed it simply, "Annie."

She placed the note in the middle of her bed.

Nora heard the stairs creak once and knew Annie was coming down. *That's good. She's had time to think things over.* Nora relaxed on the chaise lounge, pressed the warming compress over her eyes, and waited for her daughter to come and apologize.

The front door opened and closed.

Surprised and irritated, Nora sat up.

"Annie?"

Growing angry, she threw the compress down and rose. She went into the family room and called out to her again. Annie was probably just going out for a walk to sulk. She'd come back in a more pliable mood. She always did. But it was aggravating to be made to wait. Patience wasn't one of Nora's virtues. She liked to have things settled as quickly as possible—and she didn't like to worry and wonder about what Annie was thinking and doing. She liked to know where she was and what was running through her mind.

Why is she being so difficult? I'm only doing what's best for her!

As she entered the living room, she saw Annie through the satin sheers of the front plate-glass windows. Her daughter was tossing a suitcase into the trunk of the new Saturn her father had given her as a graduation gift. Shocked, Nora stood staring as Annie slammed the trunk, walked around to the driver's side of the car, unlocked it, and slid in.

Where does she think she's going? She's never to leave without asking permission.

As Annie drove down the street, two emotions struck Nora at once. White hot rage and cold panic. She ran for the door, throwing it open and hurrying outside. *"Annie!"*

Nora Gaines stood on her manicured front lawn and watched the taillights of her daughter's car flash once as she stopped briefly at the corner and then turned right and drove out of sight.

2

LEOTA REINHARDT WASHED AND RINSED HER CHEESE GLASS, GREEN
Fiesta plate, fork and knife and set them to air-dry in the plastic
stand on the sink counter. The house was silent, the windows all
closed. She used to leave them open all through springtime, loving
the sound of the birds and the smell of clean, flower-scented air
drifting in from her backyard garden. But her garden had gone to
seed over the past few years, her arthritis keeping her a prisoner
inside. Pulling the sink plug, she looked at her gnarled hands as the
warm, sudsy water drained away.

Just as time is draining away. At eighty-four, she knew she didn't
have much left. Sadness filled her, a loneliness that seemed to deepen
with the long days and nights of waiting.

A door slammed, and Leota raised her head and watched as three
children appeared just beyond her west-side, white, paint-chipped
fence. The house next door was close, so close she could talk to her
neighbors if she knew them, which she didn't anymore. All the neighbors she had known were gone. They'd moved away or died long ago.
The house west of hers was now occupied by a young black woman
with three children, a boy of about nine and two little girls perhaps
seven and five. Leota was the last one from the original families that

had purchased these houses just before World War II. Her husband's parents had bought this house when it was new. She thought back briefly to those troubled times when Bernard had gone off to war and she had moved in with "Mama and Papa," bringing her two babies with her. George had just turned three, and Eleanor was a toddler and into everything.

When Bernard came back home a changed man, Mama and Papa insisted they remain with them. They saw his brokenness, and Leota faced her lack of options. For a time they all lived together civilly, if not happily, until the garage was lengthened and converted by Papa and Bernard into a one-bedroom unit with a living area and windows that looked out into the garden. Oh, the bitterness of those years.

Things were better when Mama and Papa left the "big" house to them and lived in the smaller unit. Then Papa died a few weeks later of a heart attack, and Mama lived on thirteen more years. It wasn't until the last few years of Mama's life that Leota felt they had finally made peace.

"I misjudged you." Mama's accent was still evident, even after so many years in America. She had tried hard to lose it, but it had returned as death approached, as though, perhaps, her mind was wandering back to her childhood in Europe. When Leota had leaned down to tuck the quilt around her, Mama had touched her cheek, her blue eyes rheumy with tears. "You've been good to my family, Leota." Kind words after so many years of misunderstandings. Mama died a week later.

Leota found it odd that she should remember those words now while watching the three neighbor children file solemnly down their back steps and across the yard. The boy carried a small shovel, the older girl a shoe box. The smaller girl was crying in abject misery. No one spoke as the boy dug a hole. He had just set his shovel aside when their mother came out the back door. She went to them and spoke to them briefly, holding out a square of pretty, flowered cotton. The older girl took it and knelt down on the ground as her sister took something limp from the box. A dead sparrow. The mother took up the empty box and walked back to garbage can, tossing it in while the youngest girl folded the pretty cotton around the tiny bird, then placed it tenderly in its small grave. They sang a hymn, one that touched off Leota's memories of church services long ago: "Rock of Ages" . . .

But what were they doing to the song, adding notes and warbles? Why couldn't they just sing it as it was written?

As the first small scoop of dirt was carefully shaken into the hole, the little girl jumped up and fled to her mother, clinging to her long, zebra-print skirt. The woman lifted her and held her close, turning away to the house as the boy finished the burial.

So much pomp and ceremony, so many tears for a single sparrow.

Oh, Lord of mercy, will anyone care when I'm gone? Will anyone shed a single tear? Or will I lie dead in this house for so many days until the stench of my decaying body brings someone to check on me? She had tried so hard to keep her family together and had failed in all attempts.

The older girl stuck a hand through Leota's fence and broke off a few daffodils, volunteers that had naturalized from long-ago plantings. Leota wanted to slide the window up and shout at the child to keep her thieving hands off the few remaining flowers in her garden, but just as quickly as the anger came, it dissipated. What did it matter? Could the child reattach them to the broken stems? She watched the little girl place the flowers on the fresh grave, a last offering of love to the departed bird. As the child turned, she spotted Leota framed in her kitchen window. Uttering a startled cry, the child fled across the backyard, leaped up the few steps and disappeared inside, the door slamming behind her.

Leota blinked, hurt deeply. The look on that child's face had been like a slap on her own. It hadn't been guilt at being caught stealing two daffodils that had made that child run so fast. It had been fear.

Have I become the witch in a child's fairy tale? Why else would such a look come into a child's face unless the poor dear thought she'd seen an ugly old crone who meant to do her harm?

Tears prickled Leota's eyes, blurring her vision. Her heart ached.

God, what did I do to bring things to this sad end? I always loved children. I loved my children best. I love them still.

Yet Eleanor called infrequently and managed to visit only a couple of times a year. She never stayed longer than an hour and would spend most of it looking out the front window, fearing some hooligan would steal the hubcaps from her Lincoln. Or was it a Lexus? And George was just too busy to visit, too busy to call, too busy to write.

Turning away from the kitchen sink, Leota took a few steps to the table by the back window. Bracing herself, she sat down slowly, wincing at the pain in her knees. The glass was stained from years of rain pouring down, trailing dust and grime from the clogged roof gutters. The last time she'd climbed the ladder to clean them out was ten years ago; the last time she washed her windows was last spring. It rained the day after, and she hadn't done it again since.

Beyond that cloudy window was her long-abandoned garden, her place of retreat and renewal. She merely glanced at it now—it hurt too much to see the scraggly roses growing in a tangle, the undisciplined bushes that had once been so carefully shaped. Weeds poked up everywhere, choking out the flowers. The lawn was dead in places and overgrown in others. Pots still lined the brick restraining wall, but the precious plants she had purchased with hard-earned money were dead, some from thirst through the summer months and others drowned by winter rains. The cherries that had dropped last year had rotted on the small patio, leaving stains like drops of dried blood. Oh, and her lovely lavender-purple wisteria . . .

Leota closed her eyes against the grief. Her wisteria had gone wild, shoots twisting, twining, and thickening until they broke the overburdened lattice now sagging and blocking the gate to the vegetable garden—a garden that once yielded enough to feed her family and the neighbors. Now it produced nothing but mustard flowers and milkweed—and tiny apricot trees from the fruit that had dropped and rotted into the ground.

Flexing her fingers slowly, Leota reached for the newspaper, sliding the blue rubber band off and putting it into an empty plastic margarine container. All those silly rubber bands, one for every day of every year she'd been reading the *Oakland Tribune*. What was she going to do with all of them? What was she going to do with the dozens of plastic margarine containers stored in the pantry? or the pie tins? or the magazines? Thank the Lord the magazine subscriptions had run out and no more were coming. Now there was a bane from Satan called junk mail.

Though inclined to read the paper, Leota decided a glance was enough. What good would it do her to read the details of how the world-at-large was going to hell in a handbasket? Iraq and its madman. Soviet splinter-countries with their nuclear weapons and hot tempers. Japan and China with their ancient grudges. As for the local news, she already knew Oakland had more than its share of murder and mayhem and government corruption. Editorials? The same old stuff year after year. Why read about it? The last time she read the whole page, they were firing pros and cons about teaching inner-city children ebonics! What happened to learning proper English? She thought of how hard Mama Reinhardt had practiced the language, even though she never intended to work outside the home. And Papa, who did manage to learn English well, only worked until the war years, then fear and suspicion kept him unemployed.

No, she didn't need to read the front page to see that the world hadn't changed much in her lifetime. If she wanted details, she could watch them in living color on one of the news shows that ran between four in the afternoon and eleven at night. She had watched from time to time and seen the same carnage repeated hour after hour. No need for people to go out and rubberneck anymore. They could see actual footage from a police car window if they liked. As for wars, take a good long look on CNN. And nothing was too disgusting or perverse to be discussed openly on any number of talk shows.

"Don't even get me started on the sitcoms," she muttered to the silence. *Politically correct* was just another way of saying anything goes, no matter how deviant. And all this hoop-tee-la about celebrities, most of whom she didn't know.

Lord, why don't You just take me home? I'm tired. I hurt. I'm sick of seeing what's happening in the world. It's getting worse. I'm no good to anyone. I've become a cranky old hag who scares neighbor children half to death. Those I love have their own lives to live. Isn't that the name of a soap opera?

That was something she swore she would never do. Watch soap operas. But she was getting desperate. Sometimes she turned the television on for no other reason than to hear the sound of another human voice.

She found the newspaper sections she wanted: the comics and Dear Abby. She had read the advice columns for so long she knew exactly what kind of advice would be dispensed. She'd read all the problems anyone could imagine and quite a few she was sure people had made up.

There's nothing new under the sun. Sometimes she felt like a Peeping Tom or a voyeur getting a glimpse into the private lives of other people. Well, why not? She didn't have much of a life of her own anymore. Anyone looking through *her* window would be bored to death. She chuckled. She could just hear them now. "What's that old woman doing? Sitting at her nook table, sitting in front of her television, sitting in the bathroom, lying in bed sleepless because she slept most of the day in her chair?"

She'd heard on some talk show that people should exercise their minds. Since she couldn't exercise her body anymore, she figured she might as well try rolling the marbles around in her head. So she'd taken to working crossword puzzles and studying German from a book Bernard had bought for her shortly after they married. A pity she hadn't started earlier. It might have helped build a bridge between her and Mama Reinhardt. Anyway, she was still keeping her mind busy. The last thing she wanted was to develop senile dementia or Alzheimer's. Heaven help her if she wandered out her door one day and took off in Oakland, looking for who knew what. She'd get lost on the streets. End up sleeping in a doorway. Poor Eleanor and George would get a call that their crazy old mother had been found sleeping on a park bench.

Maybe that'd get their attention.

A friend of hers from working days had been moved by her children to Chicago. Cosma Lundstrom had written that she had gone out for a nice walk one bright, sunny day and had almost frozen to death in a doorway before her frantic children found her. She'd written Leota all about it.

> *The sun was out, but then the wind came up. They'd told me about the wind, of course—this being the "Windy City"—but I never expected it to get that cold. I sat down and couldn't get up. That stoop was so chilly it might as well have been a brass bench on the South Pole. I think my backside froze to the blasted thing. And then my false teeth stuck together so I couldn't even ask for help. I suppose everyone who passed thought I was having a gay old time, sitting there and smiling when all the while the fact was my lips were frozen to my gums!*

How she'd laughed over that letter. Cosma always wrote funny things. She'd taken a trip once to Arizona with some senior citizens and written back that it was 117 degrees with a windchill factor of 10.

> *They said it was cheaper going in the summertime. Now I know why! I was so hot I bought a bathing suit and didn't care who saw my ancient wrinkly legs. A lot of good it did me. Why in the blazes would anyone heat a pool in Arizona?*

One year, the Christmas card Leota sent Cosma had came back with a line drawn through the address. Someone had written "Deceased" in bold letters and ink-stamped a hand pointing back to the return address.

Deceased.

A fifty-year friendship was over. Just like that.

Deceased.

What a cold, unfeeling word. It just didn't fit the woman who had been so full of life and laughter and keen observations. Cosma had been a God-sent gift all those years ago when Leota was working and Mama and Papa were still alive. She and Cosma had the same boss, a kindly man who had two sons serving in the Pacific. He made a point of hiring the wives of servicemen. Both young, both with husbands off to war, Leota and her new friend had had much in common. Cosma had always been the one to listen to her woes and offer sound, often-followed advice concerning Mama Reinhardt.

Leota's eyes teared up. *Oh, Lord, how I miss Cosma. I've no one anymore. Emphysema must have gotten her. I always told her smoking wasn't good for anyone. But she had to start, thought it made her look so elegant.* She shook her head. Cosma hadn't been in Chicago more than a year when her children had to move her into a rest home. "Me and my oxygen bottle have new digs," she'd joked in a letter. "Remember how we used to walk around Lake Merritt after work and we'd be as fresh as daisies when we finished? Now, it's all I can do to walk from my chair to the bathroom. The most exercise I can manage is writing letters. As long as my fingers do the walking and talking, I can manage."

Oh, the fun they had had when they were young going to movies such as *Above Suspicion, Notorious,* and *Gilda* together. Several times they'd gone to the downtown USO and swung to Glenn Miller and Harry James with soldiers on liberty, crying on the way home because it seemed as though the war would never end and their own husbands would never come home.

And yet, while Leota had worried about what might happen if Bernard were killed in battle, Cosma took on life like a bullfighter. And life had gored her badly when soldiers came to her door with the news that her first husband, Jeremy, had been killed in action on Guadalcanal.

Cosma met her second husband, Alfred Lundstrom, a handsome, blue-eyed marine from Minnesota, when he was back in the States recuperating from a wound he'd gotten in the South Pacific. He and Cosma married within a month of their first date, shortly before he rejoined his unit. Al returned in one piece. He packed up Cosma and moved her northeast to Minnesota. "This city girl is milking cows!"

she had written. They had remained long enough to have their first child, a boy, and then moved back to California.

When Leota had heard their plans, she'd been filled with hope that they would end up living in the Bay Area. She'd longed to have her friend back. She'd been desperately unhappy then, working long hours, at odds with her mother-in-law, with whom her children were bonding in her place. Any time she told them to do something, Mama stepped in and said they didn't have to do it. And then there was Bernard, still at war within himself.

But her hopes didn't materialize. Al saw a lucrative future in the Southland, and, as it turned out, he was right. He arrived in time for the boom years of building and did so well in construction that he eventually opened his own business.

"This man lives to work," Cosma had grumbled once on the phone. Al died of a heart attack when he was sixty-five.

"I'm ashamed to say I'm mad at him," Cosma had written. "He just retired. We had all these plans of how we were going to enjoy our golden years together, and off he goes without me. Just like a man. Can't take time to meander. Just a straight shot to where he's going."

Thankfully, Al had been well insured and the sons had been trained in the family business. Cosma had gotten over being mad within a few months, but she mourned for several years. It was her daughter who blasted her out of the house with a cruise to Mexico. After that, Cosma started traveling on her own.

Leota had loved Cosma's letters and lived vicariously through her adventures, for no two lives could have been more different.

Bernard had never been ambitious or particularly industrious. He'd come home whole in body but wounded of heart and mind. He wasn't the beau she'd fallen in love with and married at twenty. He was like a tired old man, sitting in his easy chair and closing his eyes, not to sleep, but to shut the world out. She had tried all kinds of ways to bring him out of his depression, but he was mired in it. Then he started to drink to deaden the ache in his heart and drown the consuming guilt. He never allowed himself to get too drunk. He would drink just enough to make himself drowsy. Only once did he overdo it to the point of losing control. She managed then, briefly, to get past his barriers and close enough to his tormented thoughts to glimpse the pit he was in. He told her everything, and she had felt the darkness surround her, too. For a time afterward, he tried to keep her down there with him, but she fought free, finding the ways and means to climb out. *Oh, God, oh, God!* she'd cried out, and the Lord had put His hand down to her and drawn her up.

"It wasn't your fault, Bernard. It wasn't your doing!"

"You don't understand!" He was angry, frustrated. "How *can* you understand? You're not German!"

"Nor are you! For God's sake—and the sake of your children—rise above it!"

He was determined to remain where circumstances had placed him. He couldn't climb over them or go around them; he couldn't break out of the prison of his mind. After a while, he wouldn't listen to her.

Mama and Papa had asked him a few pointed questions when he first returned home from the war. "Were you able to find out anything?" Papa had asked, while Mama waited tensely.

"The city was destroyed," Bernard had said. "There was nothing left. Nothing." His voice was so hard and cold, it was clear the door on his wartime experiences had been slammed shut and locked from the inside. Mama and Papa never asked him anything about the war again.

It was left to her to pick up the pieces and try to put Bernard back together again.

Mama and Papa Reinhardt had waited for that to happen. They'd watched and noticed her every failure. Only Papa occasionally seemed to understand how hard she was trying; Mama understood nothing.

"A wife should be able to make her husband happy," Mama had said, and Leota had felt the full weight of blame for Bernard's unhappiness placed upon her shoulders. She had wanted so badly to lash out in self-defense, but she knew what would happen if she did. Knowing what Bernard had seen had been a trap. Leota possessed the terrible power to silence her tormentor at any time she wanted. All she had to do was tell the truth and watch the sword of it hack Helene Reinhardt down to size. Mama would never dare to look at her with that superior disdain and contempt again. At times the temptation was so great she had to leave the house, because Leota knew she could never speak of it—not without breaking trust with her husband. And that was something she would not do. She had promised never to tell his parents what he had told her that wine-soaked night.

How many evenings had she escaped into the garden, working by herself until night fell? She would sit in the darkness and weep, anger and frustration mingling with the wrenching love and grief she felt for Bernard. A desperate hope held Leota silent and where she was. She still loved him. If she used what she knew to defend herself, it would be at great cost.

Tears burned Leota's eyes as she stared down at the newspaper, remembering how hard she had struggled and how many years it had been before an angle of repose had been reached between her and Mama Helene. In the end, she had loved the old woman and been glad she had kept silent. Better that it had come from Papa and not her.

I kept the promise, Bernard. I never said a word, my darling.

Sadness gripped her. Bernard had died a few years after Al. Not from a heart attack but from complications brought on by alcoholism. Over the years, he'd stayed home while she went to church. "Why should I go? There's no God," he'd say. "How could there be a God with the world the way it is?" But she knew better. Without God, she would not have had the strength to stay. It wasn't until the end that he repented and wept for the wasted years.

And still she clung to hope. And waited.

She picked up her pencil, staring at the crossword puzzle. What was a four-letter word for gateway? *Arch.* What was a five-letter word for excellence—*worth? Merit.* She penciled in the letters carefully. A Keats' creation—*poetry;* wet spot—*swamp;* assumed name—*alias.*

The wall clock bonged softly from the living room. She'd been sitting at the table working on the puzzle for over an hour. Leaving her pencil on the newspaper, she pushed herself up. Her joints were so stiff and painful these days. Entering the small laundry room that had once been a back porch, she put a few clothes into the washing machine. She had only a little detergent left. Sprinkling a tablespoon of it over the clothes, she turned the dial to "small load." She stood for a moment, watching the water pour down. It was an old machine, like her, and it could be temperamental at times. Today it was working fine.

Thirsty for a glass of milk, she went to the refrigerator. There was enough milk left to fill half a cheese glass. She supposed she would have to go shopping again. She couldn't put it off much longer. She had two eggs left, half a loaf of bread, and canned goods. No meat. No fresh vegetables or fruit. No cookies either, though she supposed she had enough fixings to make some.

It was only a few blocks to the Dimond District, where she had shopped for more than sixty years. Up until a few weeks ago, she had had no problems walking and carrying back the few items she purchased at the supermarket. But the last time she went, a teenage boy on a skateboard had bumped into her. She had been crossing the parking lot when suddenly he was there.

In a frantic effort to keep from falling down, she had dropped her grocery bag, scattering things every which way. You'd think she was to blame the way the boy glared at her. Never in her life had she heard such cursing as came from that boy. Without shame, he spewed out a stream of four-letter words that brought heat surging into Leota's face. Then he jumped back onto his skateboard and rattled off, leaving her shaken, mortified, and flustered. It only took a minute for her temper to rise. What was the matter with young people today? Maybe that boy's parents had spared the rod and spoiled the child. And now he was a savage bent on running down little old ladies.

One of the supermarket baggers bringing carts back in from the parking lot happened to notice her gathering her scattered groceries and paused to help. "Looks like a heavy bag, ma'am. You want a taxi? I call 'em for a lot of old folks living round here all the time. Doesn't take more than fifteen minutes for one to get here."

Leota bristled. Maybe it was the way the girl said "old folks" that got her dander up even more. "I didn't drop these things! Some little hooligan on one of those roller boards almost knocked me down!" She straightened her dress and squared her shoulders with as much dignity as she could muster. "Customers aren't even safe in your parking lot anymore."

"He's got no business skating 'cross the lot. We got signs posted."

"Maybe he can't read." Considering the public education system, it wouldn't surprise her in the least.

"I'll tell the cab company to put a rush—"

"No, you won't. I'm not so old and decrepit that I can't manage to walk home."

"Sorry," the girl muttered, taken aback. "Didn't mean no offense."

"Any."

"Any what?"

"*Any* offense." Mama Reinhardt had spoken better English.

The girl muttered something and went back to her carts, banging them together and shoving them toward the store.

That had been a week ago.

Leota jotted "detergent" on her list. At the rate it was growing, she would need two trips in order to tote everything back up the hill.

She'd seen a little old man pulling a red wagon behind him and thought at the time that he was out of his mind. Now she thought he was probably being very practical. She could put two full shopping bags of groceries in a wagon and pull it home much more easily than she could carry them in her arms. And if she had to stop and rest, she wouldn't have to put the loaded bags on the ground and then stoop over and try to heft them back up again and risk wrenching her back.

A red wagon.

Good idea, but where was she going to get one?

She washed out the milk carton, filled it with water, and put it back in the refrigerator. Water would have to do until she gathered the courage to walk to the store again. She stood gazing at her supplies. A jar of bread-and-butter pickle chips, a half-pound of butter, an almost-empty jar of mayonnaise, four plastic-wrapped cheese slices, and one small mason jar of apricots. It was the last one of the hundreds she had put up over the years. For two years it had sat like an orphan on the pantry shelf before she gave in yesterday and tucked it in her refrigerator. How many apricots and cherries and plums had rotted on the ground over the last few years? What a crying, shameful waste it was!

Fruit trees needed tending. They didn't live the long lives of oaks or redwoods. They needed pruning and care. Ignored, they declined into scraggly, woody trees that produced less and less fruit. Insects infested them and they became diseased. Winds came up and branches broke off. After a few years, a tree that had once produced enough fruit for an entire neighborhood wouldn't produce enough for the birds and one little old lady.

Leota slammed the refrigerator door and walked into the living room. Weary, she sank down into Bernard's old easy chair. It fit her perfectly. After Bernard died, she'd spent the better part of three weeks covering it with a thick, pretty, aqua fabric. The work had been good therapy. Now, after thirty years of widowhood, she had worn down the nap, leaving the chair arms, headrest, and seat cushions almost bare—as well as permanently indented. But it fit her the way it had fit Bernard after all those nights of sitting and staring.

She was becoming like him. Sitting. Staring. Waiting.

Thinking about the past.

Her thoughts were often on the good times she had had over the years. Sometimes just getting old was the hardest cross to bear. She used to walk around Lake Merritt just for the pure pleasure of hearing the birds sing, seeing the children sailing their boats, feeling the sunshine on her shoulders. And all those years she had worked, she had stood on city corners waiting for a bus to bring her within four blocks of home. She had worked hours in the garden, sometimes until the sun went down, and still had enough energy left over to go to a dance hall with a friend and do a fast lindy. She had been a strong woman, full of energy.

Now . . . now all she did was walk from her kitchen to the living room to the bathroom to the living room to the bedroom. She had worn a path into her carpet. Only her mind wandered now, traveling wherever it would. From past to present. Across the city. Across a nation. Around the world. Sometimes into the heavens. Or down to hell.

Oh, Lord, I used to dream of going to Europe. I wanted to see London, Rome, Paris, Vienna. I still do, but I'm old, so old just thinking about walking four blocks to the grocery store and back again wears me out.

Maybe if I had company it wouldn't be so bad.

Someone.

Anyone.

She thought about calling George and discarded the idea. It was just past noon. He would be working. No two-hour lunches for her son. He had given her his office number, but she knew by the expression on his face as he did so that the last thing he wanted was his mother calling. "In case of emergency," he'd said. But even then . . .

No. She could wait until later. Seven maybe, if she was still in the mood. She'd called at five-thirty once, thinking he would be home. She had heard cars and trucks in the background. When she asked where he was, he said he was in his car, a convertible at the time. It scared her half to death thinking of him holding a telephone in one hand and driving down the freeway with the other. She'd told him to put both hands on the steering wheel and hung up. She'd waited for him to call her back when he got home. When he didn't, she called his house thinking he'd been killed on the freeway. His wife, Jeanne, had answered. Yes, he'd made it home safely. No, he hadn't mentioned she had called. He was in his den working on a project. She'd put the phone down and gone to get him. A few minutes later, she'd come back on the line. Sounding embarrassed, she said George couldn't talk to her right then. He was in the middle of something. Was there something she needed? Leota said no. How are you, Mother? Fine. Everything is fine. As fine as it ever was.

George never called back. He wasn't one to talk on the telephone unless it had to do with making money.

Leota didn't want to call Eleanor. She didn't want to hear her daughter's excuses for not calling or coming by once in a blue moon or inviting her mother to her own house just over the hill. Leota didn't want to pretend she believed the lies Eleanor spoke—lies that were never quite veiled enough to keep from stabbing at her heart.

"Oh, I'm so sorry, Mother. I should've called before this, I know. Time just gets away from me. You know how it is. We have so many things going on. I just returned from taking Anne-Lynn down to see Fred's family in Newport Beach. We stayed for ten days. It was wonderful. We had such a good time together. They always stop everything when Anne-Lynn and I come to visit. I thought Anne-Lynn might enjoy the beaches, but all she wanted to do was see the museums. She fancies herself an artist, you know. Oh, you didn't. Well, I suppose she has some talent, but it's just a passing phase. She's going to Wellesley in the fall. On scholarship. Oh, yes, Michael is doing very well at Columbia. He's on the dean's list. We just sent him a check for the new semester."

Eleanor and her subtle reminders of her own mother's failures. Eleanor and her grudges. Eleanor and her wounds and endless whining.

I'm sick of it, Lord. You know I don't want to become a burden to my children. Sometimes I just wish You'd take me home.

The silence closed in around her. She waited, motionless in her chair, for the still, small voice . . . for some sign . . .

For a stroke.

Nothing happened. No voice from the heavens. No flash of light in her dim living room. And she was still breathing. She could still feel her heart beating. She had a strong heart. She would probably live to be a hundred. What joy. *Thanks a bunch.* Tears pricked and anger bloomed.

Everything I've done is meaningless. What did I get for all my hard work? The sun rises and sets and rises again, the same as it's always done, the same as it always will. Not that I thought the world would stop, mind You, Lord. Just a little thank-you would have been nice. But no. The seasons come and go. The days pass. And what difference will any of what I did make to anyone when I'm gone? Did they even know? Did they understand?

All I have will fall to my two children, Lord, and what will they do? Sell the house to strangers. Have a garage sale and collect a few coins for things I've held precious over the years. My clothing will end up in a ragbag, my garden will get torn out, the letters from loving friends will go in a trash can.

It would have been better had I died long ago than live to see how pointless it all is.

Was it ever thus?

Oh, God, what is the point of life?

Leota leaned her head back and closed her eyes. Waiting. Thinking.

It might be better if I got Alzheimer's, Lord. I had a happy childhood. It'd be nice to go back and live in it and forget what came later. What if I did forget everything? And everyone? Haven't they forgotten me? But what if . . .

Her thoughts galloped, leaping over hedges, tearing down hillsides, splashing through streams of water without even getting wet, and brought her back to her chair again, heart pounding as panic stirred. What would the future hold?

Leota pressed her lips together. *You know what else, Lord? I'm tired of one-sided conversations with You!*

She got up and turned on the television. Canned noise was better than none at all.

It was early afternoon and the soap operas were on in full force. Oh, joy. Bold, restless youths, lecherous doctors chasing nurses (and patients) through hospital corridors, ladies moonlighting as prostitutes, psychotic neighbors visiting with toxic cookies. She kept turning the knob, clicking through channels. Her options were less than stellar: news bulletins on the latest wacko wanting to start a war, infomercials hawking the latest and greatest to improve your life or make you a millionaire, talk shows spotlighting pain and degradation while audiences hooted and brawled. . . . She couldn't click through the channels fast enough. There had to be something, *anything* that might be enlightening as well as entertaining. Reruns of old ladies enjoying the golden years in the Florida sunshine . . .

My mind is turning to tapioca pudding, Lord. I am going to end up just like poor Mrs. Abernathy. Remember her, Jesus? The little old lady who lived on the corner back in '45. I'd see her when I was coming home from work. I'd ask her how she was doing, and she would give me the gory details of her bodily functions. Am I coming to that? First visitor through the door will know what happened on my last trip to the bathroom.

I'll swallow that whole bottle of aspirin before I let that happen. So far, I haven't told anyone whether my plumbing is working all right. Not that they've asked me. But I promise You, Lord, if it comes to that, I'll go down and buy myself a couple of packs of sleeping pills and chase them with a bottle of gin!

"Service organizations for the elderly . . ." she heard in passing and clicked back to hear more. "We have Nancy Decker here with us today to tell us what her volunteers are doing and how the program is going."

Companions. On call. No cost. Volunteers delighted to accompany the elderly to stores and on errands. Just call . . .

Just call, eh? Well, why not? What choice had she? On her own, she might get hurt and become a burden to her children. She could avoid going out of her house, but the idea of death by slow starvation was less than appealing.

She looked at the number on the television screen. *So it comes to this,* does it, Lord? She waited another long moment, hoping for a better answer. When none came, she lifted her telephone receiver.

"I wonder what kind of do-gooder they'll send me," she muttered to herself in disgust as she dialed.

3

GREAT NEIGHBORHOOD. CORBAN LOOKED AROUND WARILY AS HE
parked his jet-black Trans Am in front of the small, graying, stucco
house. Irritated and tense, he looked around at the run-down houses
and unkempt yards. An old, blue Chevy was parked across the street
from him, one side dented, black spray paint decorating the driver's
door with *N14*. The house where the car was parked looked as bad as
all the others, except for a decorative touch of fancy black iron bars
over all the windows.

What am I doing here?

He thought of a few choice names for Professor Webster and his
ideas about the necessity of adding the "human element."

Mouth tight, Corban checked the interior of his car to make sure
nothing of value was in sight. Nancy Decker had warned him what
to expect in this part of Oakland. "Your best protection is to be
completely aware of your surroundings. The people who get mugged
are generally the ones who aren't paying any attention to what's going
on around them. Oh, and don't leave anything valuable visible in
your car."

Too bad he hadn't invested in a car stereo system that could be
unhooked and carried. Gritting his teeth, Corban installed The Club

on his steering wheel before getting out and locking the door with his keyless remote. He'd feel less vulnerable if he was driving an old, beat-up Chevy. One with dents in it. The kind no one would bother stealing.

Tucking his keys into his front Levi's pocket, Corban came around his car and stood on the sidewalk looking at the house where his assignment lived. The lawn was overgrown, except for the brown spots where it was diseased or dying. Bushes crowded the front stairwell. Water stains ran down the front corner, where a roof gutter had broken loose—probably overweighted by leaves from the winter-barren tree that was pulling up part of the concrete curb. The place looked dirty, as though the pollution of decades lay over it like a coat of dust, washed down periodically by winter rains.

Clearing his throat, he set his mind on getting this interview over and done with and started up the walkway. *She lives in a dump.* Weeds sprouted from the concrete stress lines on the sidewalk. From appearances, the old lady had little or no money. She was probably living on social security and whatever meager savings she had. Obviously it wasn't enough to hire help to keep her garden neat or do anything about her grimy house and hanging gutters. Not enough to sell out and move into a residential care facility.

She met his criteria for the report: poor but not destitute.

A low white fence that acted as a property line leaned beneath the weight of a tangle of bloomless rose vines. He could see down the driveway to a carport. Just beyond it was a garage barely large enough to park anything bigger than a Model T. The windows along the side boasted ugly, faded, green-and-white metal awnings.

The front steps had been painted at one time. Green and red, no less! The outside of the front windows was thick with grit. The old lady probably couldn't even see through to the outside world. An old rocker on the small porch was occupied by a large garden spider. The hanging pots contained the brown, scraggly remains of whatever greenery had once grown there. The front door looked solid enough to hold back a battering ram, not that any would be needed. A would-be robber would have easy access through the two side windows. Break one pane, reach inside and unlock the door, and voila, a criminal would have access to anything he wanted. Assuming, of course, the old woman had anything worth stealing, which Corban highly doubted.

The only thing to impede entry were the thin curtains that maintained some privacy. Rather than a peephole, which wouldn't be necessary with the two side windows anyway, a small leaded glass window was strategically built into the center of the heavy door. For dignity, he supposed, if that was possible in such impoverished surroundings.

Corban rang the doorbell. He stood in front of the little security window so the old lady inside could get a good look at him. Raking his fingers through his hair, he put a smile on his face.

No answer.

Faintly annoyed, he wondered if she was deaf. He put his thumb to it and pressed harder this time, paying closer attention. He heard the bell ring inside. It wasn't a hard buzz, but a melodious *ding-dong*. He waited another minute. When there was still no response, he debated pounding on the door. Dismissing that idea, he glanced at the narrow, side window. The curtain covering it was sheer enough that he might be able to see into the living room. He tried but could see nothing through the layer of dirt. Grimacing, he dug in his pocket and found his laundered and ironed monogrammed handkerchief.

Leota heard the bell from her kitchen, dried her hands on a dish towel, and headed for the front door. It rang again before she passed by her dining-room table. She was in the middle of her living room when she saw a stranger rubbing the window beside her front door. What in the world did he think he was doing? She stopped and watched, growing angrier by the second. It was bad enough she hadn't the strength or energy to wash her windows without some stranger coming and rubbing a spot right smack dab in the middle of one. She'd have to look at that clean spot now and be reminded of her failings as a housekeeper.

The man peered in, trying to see past the sheer curtains. Heat came up inside Leota like lava up a volcano shoot. Anger galvanized her past the arthritic pain in her hips, knees, and ankles. She marched the last few steps, threw the bolt, and opened the door. "What do you think you're doing peeping into my house?"

The young man drew back sharply, his face going dark red. "I-I'm sorry. I'm Corban Solsek, ma'am. Nancy Decker sent me from—"

"I don't care who you are!" So what if he was sent. That didn't excuse him! "Fine thing! Did she send you over here to peep through my windows?"

"No, ma'am! I rang the bell twice. I didn't know if . . ." He stopped, his color deepening to purple.

"I was dead?"

He looked aghast. "That wasn't what I meant to say."

"Wasn't it?" She could almost see the wheels in his brain working and spinning, trying to find some reasonable answer.

"Deaf, ma'am. I didn't know if—"

"I'm neither deaf nor dead as you can well see." She was beginning to enjoy herself.

"I'm s-sorry . . ."

Leota saw the hint of annoyance in his hazel eyes. He didn't like being reprimanded. She supposed he would rather be rude and get away with it. She decided not to show pity. "You *ought* to be sorry." She pushed the door wide open. "Well, don't just stand there like *you* have rigor mortis. Come on in here!" She stepped back, allowing him plenty of room. He was *big*. Probably one of those athletes doing a good deed for the day to make up for raising Cain the rest of the week. "Go on into my kitchen. Under the sink you'll find some glass cleaner."

"I beg your pardon?" A look of utter consternation spread across his handsome young face.

Leota lifted her chin a little higher and stared him straight in the eye. He might be a foot taller and more than twice her weight, but she was not going to be intimidated. She'd seen enough television and read enough in the newspapers to know she'd better not let him get away with anything. "You messed up my window, young man. You can clean it." He opened his mouth, but she didn't give him the chance to argue. "Either that or go back and tell Miss Decker to send someone else! Someone who isn't rude enough to be sticking his nose against my front window."

Pressing his lips together, he marched through her living room, past her dinner table, and into her kitchen. Didn't take him more than six steps. "Where did you say to look?"

Leota had to restrain a smile. He sounded positively huffy. "Under the sink! Where else do you suppose people keep glass cleaner? Or do *you* have a hearing problem?"

"There aren't any paper towels under here," he grumbled loud enough for her to hear.

"Stand up! The paper towels are right there in front of your nose, hanging from the rack on the dish cabinet. If the roll were a snake, it'd bite you!" She stepped to the middle of her living room, watching him like a hawk. "Two won't do the job." When he gave the roll a good yank, she put her hands on her hips. "I didn't say the *whole* roll! Four or five. That's enough. Those things cost money, you know. Now roll the rest back up neatly the way they were. *Neatly,* Mr. Solsek."

A muscle was twitching in his cheek when he came back. He didn't even glance down at her as he went out the front door, sprayed window cleaner from the top of the window to the bottom, and started rubbing hard and fast. She could see his lips moving. Cursing her, no doubt.

Her own lips twitched. She could see those towels were getting soggy, and the job wasn't half done. Turning, she went back into her kitchen and took a washcloth from a drawer. She ran warm water over it, wrung it out, and brought it back, along with four more paper towels.

"Here." She thrust the cloth at him. "Use this first. And then the rest of these." She took the damp, blackened paper towels from him and stepped back to watch him work. After a few minutes, the front window pane was as clear as it could be with the film of dust on the inside. Even at that, there was a world of difference between the half-clean pane and the matching window to the right of the door.

Suddenly, looking at the windows, all she wanted to do was climb back into bed and pull the covers over her head.

Corban had done his best to control his anger as he went outside and scrubbed the windows. Now he came back in and looked at the window from the inside. "How's that?"

The old woman didn't say anything. She just stood looking from one window to the other. Before she could enlist him to clean the rest of her dirty windows, he held out the filthy cloth. "Where do you want me to put this?"

"In the laundry basket on the back porch. The paper towels go in the trash under the sink." She held out the wad she had taken from him.

Corban took them and headed for the kitchen, thankful that the old bat hadn't ordered him to get a bucket and do the whole house. Not that it couldn't use it. The whole place, from the greasy ceiling to the old yellow-and-gray linoleum on the kitchen floor could stand a cleaning. At least the metal and yellow-and-brown-flecked Formica dinette table was clean, though the ancient gas range and rounded-front refrigerator could use a scouring.

"And be sure you put the Windex back where you got it!"

Did she think he meant to steal it? He tucked it under the counter, deposited the sodden paper towels in the paper trash bag diapered with a plastic grocery sack, and slammed the cabinet. He found the washer and dryer tucked in the tiny back porch; both machines looked older than he was! He spotted the laundry basket containing one faded pink towel, a washcloth and a pastel, flowered polyester dress similar to the one the woman was wearing. He tossed the dirty washcloth on top.

The house depressed Corban. It was dusty, dimly lit, and grim. And there was a smell. He couldn't define it . . . it wasn't just the house but the peculiar, indescribable scent of the old woman herself. Corban was faintly repulsed by it. He was equally repulsed by his surroundings. Worse, he was repulsed by the frizzy, white-haired old woman in her cheap dress, bubbly crocheted cardigan, and old pink, fuzzy, matted slippers. She stood there in her seedy living room looking like an old banty hen ready to peck at him. She stared at him with those rheumy blue eyes, and from the look in them, he could see she didn't much care for him either.

That annoyed him. He was volunteering his time to help, wasn't he? She should show a little gratitude.

We're off to a bad start. He shouldn't have looked through her window, but how was he supposed to know it would take her five minutes to get to the front door? Regardless, he had to do something to salvage the situation. How was he going to get the information he needed if he wasn't in her good graces? He forced a smile. "Nancy said you needed to go to the grocery store. I'll take you."

There. That should bring a smile to the old crone's face.

Leota pursed her lips. He was looking at her, waiting. For what? A pat on the head. A big kiss? She didn't want to go anywhere with this arrogant young whelp. She'd seen him glance around her house with a look of distaste. No doubt he came from grander environs. Bully for him. She didn't move and she didn't say anything. She looked him over in his faded blue Levi's. Whoever heard of wearing a tan suede coat over a white *T-shirt*. His hair was cut short, crop-ped like a Roman caesar. And oh, did he have the airs. King of the world, was he?

"I've got arthritis. I'm not much good at kneeling."

"Ma'am?" He tilted his head slightly.

"Nothing. Just thinking out loud."

He looked perplexed, then faintly irritated. Like he had places to go and people to see. And she was wasting his precious time.

"Would you like me to get your shoes for you?"

Oh, so polite.

Just because she was old didn't mean she was senile. She knew she was wearing her slippers. Why *shouldn't* she be wearing them? It was her house. People didn't sit around all day in their walking shoes, did they? If she wasn't in such dire need of groceries, she'd tell him to go back to wherever he came from. However, she had enough sense left to know she didn't have much choice. The idea of pandering to this twerp went against her grain. But so did going hungry. She was down to living on canned vegetables. She couldn't wait another three days for that Decker woman to find and send another volunteer. Volunteer? He looked as though he'd been drafted!

"I know where my shoes are, young man. You can sit right there and wait while I get them." She pointed at the couch. When he didn't move, she shrugged and headed for the bedroom. Fine. Let him stand there. Not only did she not care whether he was comfortable or not, she just might take an extra long time with her shoes, just to spite the Prince Charming!

Corban glanced at the couch again. It looked about as comfortable as a bed of nails. He'd made the right decision to stand. He sighed as the woman shuffled away. As slowly as she was moving, he might as well take the opportunity to look around.

The living room and dining room were all one room with thick wood molding up one wall and over the ceiling as the dividing line. The dining-room table was old-fashioned, made of solid dark wood with claw feet. On top was a crocheted doily and a vase containing dusty plastic flowers. There was a china hutch against the back wall that was overcrowded with dishes and glassware. No Wedgwood. No Royal Doulton.

The rug was faded. Whatever color it had been, it was gray and worn now. A path to the kitchen. A path to the hall where she'd disappeared. The brightest spot of color in the two rooms was the knitted afghan thrown over the back of the ugly sofa. A big over-stuffed chair sat squat and lumpy beside a step-style end table that was overloaded with books and magazines. Another equally burdened and dusty end table was at the other end of the couch. The matching lamps looked like imitation Greek urns with yellow-ing shades. Over the mantel hung a landscape print—one of those reprints like a hundred thousand others anyone can buy, complete with its tacky, ornate, gold-painted frame. A half-dozen pictures and a few figurines stood on the mantel. One was of a little girl with three geese. Another was of a boy sitting on a fence. Here and there on the walls around the room were framed pictures, mostly handmade. The biggest was an embroidered sampler of blooming morning glories and bold, black, ornate lettering proclaiming "As for me and my family, we will serve the Lord. Joshua 24:15."

A braided, half-circle rug lay in front of a fireplace that probably hadn't been lit in a decade. On the small, brick hearth were a big, dust-covered seashell, a tarnished brass cricket, and a pair of big old black boots.

Everything she had was old, faded, broken-down junk. The most expensive pieces the old woman owned appeared to be the big, brown Naugahyde recliner and large, box-style television set in the front corner of her living room. There'd be no estate sale here. A rummage sale, more likely.

Corban could hear the old woman's shuffling footsteps coming closer. He glanced toward the doorway and noticed the old, iron-grate floor heater smack dab in front of the open doorway to her bathroom. The entire room, from the floor to the middle of the wall, was a nightmare of pink, black, and green tile.

When the old woman returned, he cringed inwardly. She was wearing a long brown coat with a collar and big, black, plastic buttons and thick-soled, brown slip-on shoes. Ignoring him, she walked over to her recliner and leaned down. When she straightened, she held an old black purse by its handle, looking for all the world as though she had a rat by the throat. She held it in front of her with both hands and looked at him dolefully. "I'll need my grocery list. It's on the counter to the right of the kitchen sink."

Imperious old hag. "Yes, ma'am."

As they went out, she locked the front door carefully. When Corban offered her his arm before they went down the front steps, she took it. Grudgingly. He could feel her trembling. A case of the nerves? Or just old age? Not that he cared. He drew the keys from his pocket and pressed the remote. "I'll get the door for you." He patted her hand and stepped away.

She stared, jaw set. "I am not getting into that sports car!"

She sounded as though he meant to enter her in the Indianapolis 500. "It's not a sports car, ma'am. It's just a—"

"I don't care *what* it is, I'm not getting into it. It's only five blocks to the market. We'll walk."

"Walk?" Five blocks through one of the worst neighborhoods he'd ever seen? Would his car even be here when they got back?

"Of course. I've been walking to the market for more than fifty years."

"Five blocks down and five blocks back makes *ten* blocks, ma'am," he said, trying to make a point of the distance.

"Congratulations. You can add. It's gratifying to know, since I've read that most students who graduate from high school these days can't even read."

He steamed. Hadn't she called for help because she couldn't make it on her own? He tried to think of something, *anything*, to talk her out of it.

She fixed him with a glare. "You look like a strapping young man, Mr. Solsek. I think you can make it ten blocks."

Corban muttered an expletive under his breath as she started off without him. He looked at his car, looked around the neighborhood, and felt a bubble of panic. "Would you give me a minute so I can park my car in your driveway?" He tried to soften his tone. "I wouldn't want it in anyone's way."

Leota stopped. She turned and looked at him. What a crock of horse manure! She knew exactly what was worrying him—and she acknowledged it was a reasonable concern. He would just have to learn the hard way there was nothing he could do about it. Maybe next time he'd have sense enough to borrow someone's beat-up VW or come by bus.

"Go right ahead. Be my guest."

She watched him practically leap over the back of his car, slip into the driver's seat, remove whatever that red gadget was from the steering wheel, and start the engine. A nice, purring roar sounded. That car must have cost his folks a pretty penny. He backed it expertly into the middle of the street, swung around, and roared up her narrow driveway.

Smiling slightly, Leota waited.

One minute.

Two.

Three.

She knew what was happening without even looking, though it was a great temptation to walk over and stand at the end of her driveway where she could watch the show. Instead, she stood there in the middle of the sidewalk, content to imagine.

She heard his voice once. Rather loud, replete with frustration. One word only, but it certainly clarified his feelings. The shiny bumper appeared as he inched his car backward. He parked it on the driveway just above the sidewalk so that his front door opened toward her front steps. She watched his power window go up. She pursed her lips. It wouldn't do to laugh at someone so proud. He reinstalled that red thingamajiggy and got out. She heard the click as he locked the doors with his little magic twanger. Pocketing his keys, he walked across her poor, miserable, weed-infested lawn. By the time he reached her, he appeared to have regained his composure. "I couldn't open either door," he said with a bleak smile. "Your driveway's too narrow."

"Your car is too wide." She smiled up at him innocently. "If it was six inches smaller, you could've made it out your window."

Corban felt the heat climb up his neck and fill his face to his hairline. "You could've warned me."

"I've learned experience is a far better teacher." She lifted one hand. "Your arm, if you please. I'm old, as you've noticed. I need support in my dotage."

It was on the tip of his tongue to tell her he'd buy her a cane. Any kind she wanted. One with a dragon head! However, the lure of acing Professor Webster's class gripped him, nailing his tongue to the roof of his mouth. He had to keep on track. He breathed in slowly and managed a stiff, "My pleasure, ma'am."

"Oh, drivel," he thought he heard her say.

Neither spoke another word for five blocks, and when they got to the store, Leota Reinhardt did all the talking.

"I've never been so embarrassed in my life!" Corban heaved his sports coat into a chair. "I wanted to buy duct tape and use it on that old hag by the time we were halfway through the grocery store!"

"You're in a fine state." Ruth laughed. "What happened?"

"What *didn't* happen! First off, she made me wash her front window. You should have seen this dump, Ruth. Then she insisted on walking five blocks down to the market. When we got there, she took an hour poking through the vegetables and fruit, complaining to the produce manager how nothing tastes real anymore. 'You might as well eat plastic!' she said, and you should've seen the guy's face. And then she pushes the cart over to the meat section and points out how everything is packaged for families. 'You have to buy ten pork chops to get a decent price. Do you know how long it would take me to eat ten pork chops?' she says. And all that was *nothing* compared to what she had to say to the poor checker. That old woman was telling the girl how she used to buy pork chops for five cents apiece and the price of a single tomato is worse than highway robbery."

"Calm down, Cory. It couldn't have been that bad."

"Three bags of groceries, Ruth. *Heaping* bags! I had to carry two of them *five blocks uphill*. She stopped a couple of times, but just when I thought I'd have the chance to put them down and rest a minute, she'd start off again. She put her bag on the porch wall and dug around in her purse for five minutes trying to find her key. My arms were aching. I was just about ready to dump her stuff and go when she opens the door and tells me to take the sacks into her kitchen. I came back and carried in the other one, too, because I knew if I didn't, I'd have to wait another half an hour for her to walk from the front door to the kitchen with it. I offered to put her things away, and she said she could do it herself. And then, to top it all off, she hands me a quarter!"

Ruth laughed. "Well, I suppose in her day, that would be considered a good tip."

Corban knew better. "She did it to be nasty."

"Oh, come on! Why would she do that?"

"You'd have to meet her to understand." He yanked open the refrigerator and looked around. With a mumbled curse, he pulled out a bottle of red wine. Setting it on the counter, he opened the cabinet, looking for a clean glass. Finding none, he glanced at the sink. "Did you have friends over or what?"

"The women's advocacy meeting was here this afternoon," she said, distracted by her studies. "Sorry. I haven't gotten around to doing the dishes."

Stifling his irritation, he slammed the cabinet and opened another. He took out a mug. "This isn't going to be as easy and quick as I thought."

"What?"

"The old woman."

"Well, did she answer any of your questions? Were you about to get any information?"

"Are you kidding? I didn't get the chance to ask her a single question. I wasn't there ten minutes before I knew I wasn't going to be able to get anything useful out of her until I've established some kind of rapport with her. And God knows how long that will take." He downed half the mug of wine. His head was pounding. Nothing like a tension headache to make one want to drink. After a few hours with Leota Reinhardt, he felt like taking the bottle by the neck and draining it.

Ruth wrote something in her notebook and glanced at him briefly before returning her attention to the text propped against two stacked books. "So why don't you find another way to fulfill the requirements for the class? See about going to a senior gab group or something."

"Professor Webster doesn't want a dozen opinions. He wants *one* case study. I've already invested three hours in this old woman. I'm not throwing that time away on the off-chance I might have better luck with someone else."

Ruth's eyes narrowed at his tone. "It's your report." She shrugged. "Do what you want."

Corban was irritated by her indifference. He needed to vent, and she was making it clear she had neither the time nor inclination to listen. She was bent over her textbook again, highlighting one line with yellow before writing down the important point in her notebook. She might as well have put up a sign that said "Get lost. I'm studying."

He finished the wine and left the mug in the sink. He didn't have time to nurse grudges. He had to calm down and get busy on the reading assignments that piled up after every class. Ruth had the right idea. Focus.

Leaving her alone at the kitchen table, he went into the living room. His desk was next to the window that overlooked the neat apartment courtyard pool. He liked being able to look outside. Ruth had teased him about watching the coeds sunbathe and swim, but that hadn't been it. He didn't like the feeling of being closed in. Ruth didn't care about having a window in front of her. She said she studied better with walls around her and privacy. He also noticed she liked being close to the refrigerator and the coffeepot.

Whatever their idiosyncrasies, things seemed to be working okay. He had his space, and she had hers.

So why was he still steaming?

Sitting at his desk, he stacked some papers from Ruth's meeting and tossed them onto the floor. Someone had opened one of his notebooks and doodled all over a page. Gritting his teeth, he tore it out, wadded it up, and tossed it into the garbage can. Opening the center drawer of his desk, he found one pen left in the plastic tray. He bought them by the dozen. "Do me a favor, Ruth. Tell your friends to stay away from my desk!"

"Sorry," she called back. "What's missing?"

"Pens. Again."

"I'll get you some more when I go to the store."

"When are you going?"

"Not right now." There was an edge to her voice. "Why don't you have some coffee?"

Anything to shut him up. The last thing he needed right now was a jolt of caffeine. He felt ready to explode as it was. It wasn't just Leota Reinhardt. It was school. It was Professor Webster and his ridiculous demands. It was Ruth. It was her friends using his apartment for their meetings. It was his whole, stinking life.

He looked around the apartment, now in shambles after Ruth's friends had come by to talk about how the world mistreated women. Since affirmative action had been cast aside, they believed women were getting a raw deal. Yeah, well, he'd like to know who was getting the raw deal here? He had straightened things up this morning. Now the cushions were tossed helter-skelter, half-empty bowls of chips left on the coffee table with a bowl of congealing ranch dip. The carpet needed another vacuuming. Newspapers were turned inside out and left on the floor. It ticked him off. These women were so fixed on equal rights they forgot all about common courtesy.

Shoving his chair back, he went back into the kitchen. "I haven't complained about your friends coming over, Ruth, but I've just about had it. They can straighten the place up before they leave or they can meet somewhere else."

Her eyes flickered briefly as she looked about to argue; then her expression changed from faintly annoyed to heavily resigned. "All right. I'll take care of it." She stood and set her books aside. "I should've done it before you got home. Just try to chill out, will you? You get so uptight about nothing."

She went into the living room. In the space of a few minutes, she picked up the newspapers, leaflets, and napkins and shoved them in the trash can beside his desk. Corban pitched in, carrying the chips and dip into the kitchen while she hauled the vacuum out of the closet and plugged it in. He dumped everything into the garbage bag.

"Just leave the dishes, Cory. I'll do them!" Ruth called above the hum of the vacuum she was running back and forth. She was quick and careless, yanking the plug, looping the cord several times around the handle before shoving the machine back into the closet.

She came back into the kitchen. "I said I'd do the dishes." She brushed him aside. "I can't do everything at once, you know."

He stepped back from her resentment, wanting her to understand. "I don't like chaos."

"Well, good luck. Chaos abounds."

"It doesn't have to abound in my apartment."

She tossed the washrag down and faced him, eyes bright with temper and the hint of tears. "Look! I'm *sorry* you had a rotten day, but don't take it out on me." She turned her back on him and went back to washing the dishes. "You can be so unreasonable. I was going to clean up. I just wanted to get some work done first. You act as though I've never done my share."

"I didn't say that."

"Didn't you? What's more important, Cory? Having a spotless apartment or graduating with honors? Sometimes I think the only reason you asked me to move in with you was so you'd have a maid!"

Far from it, considering the countless times he'd picked up after her. But he saw the mood she was in now—a mood she made perfectly clear had come on because of his ill temper—and he clamped his mouth shut.

Maybe he *was* being unreasonable. Maybe he was making a big deal out of nothing. There were more important things in the world than having the dishes washed and put away, and the cushions on the couch where they belonged. A little chaos never killed anyone, did it? Why did he let it get to him? She'd warned him up front, before moving in, that she wasn't the neatest person in the world.

Maybe it was just seeing how that old woman lived in a house coated with grime and caked with dust that had triggered him.

He watched Ruth. She was seething. She barely washed and rinsed the glasses. Another word out of him, and he was sure she'd pack and leave. He'd make peace with her later. Chinese takeout. A red rose. It'd all blow over.

Frustrated and restless, he went back into the living room and sat down at his desk and jotted down a few notes:

> *Leota Reinhardt. Cantankerous. Demanding. Suffers from arthritis. Needs caregiver. Senile (?) No mention of family. Lives in squalor. Only financial support social security (?) Education (?)*

He didn't know much considering the time he'd spent with her. Next time he'd get her talking.

Turning on his computer, Corban opened a file and wrote in everything he'd observed about the old woman and her surroundings. The more he thought about her, the more she suited his case study. Maybe the day hadn't been a complete waste after all.

When he finished, he felt a little more satisfied. He'd be better prepared next time. At least he'd know what to expect. He'd take her a little something, too. Maybe if he poured on the charm, he'd be able to wring a little information out of her.

Reading over his page of notes, he smiled, then crumpled up his handwritten notes and tossed them into the trash can. He hit the save button on the computer and exited the document, then went on to more important and pressing matters, leaving Leota Reinhardt filed and forgotten in cyberspace.

4

"I'M NOT SURPRISED YOU LEFT, PRINCESS. I knew it would happen someday. You know you can come and live with me and Monica in San Diego anytime you want. We'd love to have you."

Annie sighed. "I know, Daddy, but I can't do that. You know how Mom would see it." Her mother would cast all the blame for rebellion on her second husband, Annie's father, Dean Gardner. He'd been a convenient scapegoat over the years for a variety of things.

"What *is* that noise in the background, Annie?" her dad said. "Are you having a party?" He sounded as though he approved.

"No, Dad. It's a parrot. Susan's bird-sitting. He can get a little loud at times."

"Sounds like he carries on a conversation."

"He spouts things from television. His owner left it on for him while he was at work. So he'd have company."

"Back to your mom, honey. She sees things exactly the way she wants to see them." There was a distinct and familiar edge in his voice. "You have to start living your own life and stop living it for her."

"I understand that, Daddy, but I don't want to burn bridges. I love her. I want to be able to see her and talk to her without—"

"Good luck."

Annie sighed. She rubbed her forehead. She knew there were bitter feelings between her mother and father. It was exhausting sometimes, feeling like the base on a teeter-totter of resentments and grudges nurtured on vitriol. Back and forth, up and down. Would it never end? Why couldn't they understand that she loved them both? They each had their own agenda in winning her confidence. She knew that. She understood it. And it hurt because, whether they realized it or not, her mother and father each used her as a weapon against the other.

Maybe calling him hadn't been such a good idea. Maybe she should have waited until her own feelings were clearer.

"I'm sorry, honey. Look. Give me the address of where you're staying and I'll send you some money to get you started."

"I have money, Daddy. I'm living with Susan Carter. You remember her, don't you?" She gave him the address.

"San Francisco? Are you sure you want to live in the city?"

She could hear the apprehension in his tone. "There's a security system where we live. We have to buzz people in. It's a nice little apartment with a Murphy bed. I'm using a futon."

"A Murphy bed? When was this place built?"

She laughed. "Quit worrying, Daddy. I'm a big girl, remember?"

"Are you sure you don't want to come down to San Diego? I'm sure you could get into UC without any problems, considering your grades and SAT scores. You got the okay for Berkeley, didn't you? Even if you had to wait until next semester—"

"I'm not going to college, Daddy."

"Not at all?"

"I'm going to school, but it's not anything like Wellesley or Cal. I'm registered for two classes at the Institute of Fine Arts." When he didn't say anything, she knew she had surprised him. Did his silence denote displeasure as well? It was one thing to tell your daughter to do whatever her heart told her to do and another to hear she had tossed aside sizable scholarships to prestigious universities and colleges in favor of taking a couple of art classes. "Try not to worry, Daddy. I feel led to do this. I don't know why yet, but I have to go where I sense God is directing me."

"Honey . . ."

She had tried to speak openly with her father, but it was difficult. What she said simply did not compute for him because he wasn't a believer. Telling him God was leading her always made him nervous. Yet she couldn't lie about it. It was hard to make him see that she needed to be where God wanted her to be. And she felt His unmistakable presence in her artwork. When she was drawing or painting, she felt a rightness about it, a closeness to the Creator who was opening her eyes and ears and heart to the world around her.

A world that included family members ripped apart by divorce and dysfunction.

And perhaps a grandmother who held some key to understanding her mother and herself.

"The whole point is for me to be on my own, Daddy. Isn't that what you said? I won't be living in the lap of luxury, but Susan's flat is nice and spacious. We're close enough that I can jog to the zoo or the beach. There was an opening where Susan works, so I've already lined up a job."

"What sort of job?"

"Waiting on tables. It's a top-rated restaurant. I'll earn enough to pay my share of the rent and expenses."

"What's it called?"

"The Smelly Clove."

"Who would want to eat in a place called the Smelly Clove?"

She laughed. "Anyone who likes garlic. This restaurant is very well known, Daddy. Garlic is the *in* thing. It's very good for you."

"I'll send you the checks I've been sending your mother."

Her father had his own ways of voicing his disapproval. "I didn't call to ask for money, Daddy. I'm eighteen. I'm an adult now. Remember? Keep your money."

"In the eyes of the law, maybe, you're an adult," he said ruefully, "but you're still my little girl."

Her eyes filled with quick tears. "I need to stand on my own."

He was quiet for a moment. "So you didn't call for money or advice."

"No."

"You know I love you, don't you?" he said tenderly.

"Yes." She pressed her lips together. Her heart ached.

"What's up, honey? What did your mother say to you before you left?"

Annie closed her eyes. The hurtful things her mother had said kept coming up and filling her head like so much flotsam. Her father was far too perceptive, but she was not about to regale him with her mother's hurtful remarks. Why add fuel to the fires of bitterness?

Her mother might have expectations far and above what any human could manage to fulfill, but her father wasn't perfect either.

Monica was the second woman he had lived with in the past four years, and she was less than half his age. Annie's mother said her father had a Peter Pan complex; her father said one taste of marriage with Nora was enough to cure any man for life.

"Can you tell me about Grandma Leota, Daddy?"

"Leota? What brought her up?"

"I was just curious. She's my only surviving grandparent, and I don't even really know her." He didn't say anything for a moment, and Annie sensed he was weighing his words carefully.

"She must be in her eighties," he said. "I only met her a couple of times."

"What was she like?"

"Oh, I don't know. Ordinary, I guess. I liked her."

"Can you be more specific?"

He gave a dry laugh. "I don't mean to imply I liked her just because your mother holds some deep-seated grudge against her. I mean I *liked* her. She made me feel welcome the few times we visited her. The last time I saw her, she made German chocolate cake and homemade meat-and-potato sausage and sauerkraut. I was looking forward to enjoying a feast. Of course, we weren't there long enough to taste any of it. Your mother launched into some diatribe about the past."

Oh, Daddy, let's not go down that path again. "Did Grandma say anything?"

"No. She listened. She didn't say a word that I can remember, not that she had a chance or that anything she could have said would have made a difference. Your mother was in high form that day. I was embarrassed, really embarrassed. Nora gathered you and Michael from the backyard and went out to the car. I didn't have much choice but to apologize to Leota and leave."

"Why didn't Grandma ever come to our house?"

"She wasn't invited. Any invitations extended always came from her. No, I take that back. Your mother invited her to our wedding."

"Did she come?"

"Yes. She came to the reception, too. And she came to your christening."

"Then she drives a car."

"I don't think so. I don't remember seeing a car when we were at her place. And I doubt it. She worked in an office somewhere near Lake Merritt. I think she had the same job for years, though I couldn't tell you what she did. Whatever it was, your mother said she loved her work more than her family."

Annie frowned. Was that what her mother had meant about her being like Leota Reinhardt? Annie wanted to study art, and she had to turn away from her mother's hopes for her in order to do so?

Why does it have to be a choice between what my mother wants and what I feel led to do?

"Why the sudden interest in your grandmother, Annie?"

"I've always wondered about her, Daddy. I was just afraid to talk about her with Mom."

"And no wonder. She's not exactly reasonable when it comes to her mother. Why don't you go see Leota and decide for yourself?"

"I've considered it, but . . ."

"Let me guess. Your mother would take it the wrong way. Right?"

"Well . . ." If her mother found out, she would be hurt. She would feel betrayed. But why did it have to be that way? What had happened to cause such animosity on her mother's part? Was that animosity returned? Her father made it sound otherwise, but he had his own agenda. Still, Annie wondered. Could the estrangement between her mother and grandmother simply be a difference in personalities? Or was there something far deeper going on?

"You're just like Leota!"

What did that really mean?

Who *was* Leota Reinhardt? What had she done that made her so persona non grata?

"Look, honey. If you live the rest of your life trying to please your mother, you're in for a lot of heartache."

"Daddy . . ."

He sighed heavily. "Okay. I'll leave it alone. It's your decision." He hesitated. "What do you hear from your brother?" His tone was so dry, Annie winced. He had never gotten along very well with his stepson. Michael was the product of Nora's first marriage to Bryan Taggart. Taggart had bowed out of his son's life as soon as the divorce was final. Michael had been three at the time. Annie's father had once told her that her mother had made several efforts to extract money from Michael's father for child support. However, the legal expenses and emotional upheaval hadn't been worth what her mother called "the paltry amount of guilt money."

Taggart had moved to another state, remarried, and had other children. When Michael was sixteen, he found out where his father was and contacted him. Somehow, his mother had gotten wind of it. She had a sixth sense about such things. That single telephone call had been like a foul stench in her nostrils. Sometimes she was like a bloodhound on matters that she deemed against her authority. That time, she caught the faint scent, followed the trail, and treed poor Michael, baying at him until he confessed. Annie would never forget her verbal evisceration.

"How could you do this to me? After all I've sacrificed for you! I've loved you and been there for you all your life, and this is the thanks I get!" Not that Taggart had opened the door for Michael. In fact, from what little Annie remembered from that terrible fight between her half brother and her mother, Taggart had made it clear that he wasn't interested in pursuing a relationship with his son.

Would the same thing happen to her when she talked with her grandmother? Would the door be forever closed to her? And what if her mother found out she had gone to see her grandmother?

"Annie?" Her father's voice drew her back to the present.

"Oh, Michael's fine, last I heard."

"When was that?"

"Christmas. He sent a note." She hurried on rather than tell him it was addressed to her mother only. While she had idolized Michael, he had never cared much for her. The note had been just that, short and to the point. He had earned a promotion and was making more money, both bits of news to cheer her mother and give her excuses for why he never had the time to come home for a visit. "I called and left a message on his answering machine just to let him know I've moved out."

"Uh-huh."

"He's busy, Daddy. You know how hard he works."

Her father didn't say anything to that, which was just as well. Nothing he could say would ease the hurt Annie felt. The truth was her half brother didn't seem to care about anyone but himself. He certainly had little time to spare for the mother who doted on him and bragged about him at every opportunity. *"My son who graduated with honors from Columbia. . . . My son who was courted and hired by a Fortune 500 company. . . . My son who is so handsome he could have been a model for GQ. . . ."* Nora Gaines enjoyed the reflected glory of being Michael Taggart's mother.

"If you do decide to go see your grandmother, tell her hello from me, would you?"

"I haven't decided whether to go or not, Daddy."

"I hope you will, honey. Something's eating you. And it never pays to let someone else do your thinking for you. Not even your doting father."

Annie thought about her grandmother over the next few days. She couldn't seem to get Leota Reinhardt out of her mind. She thought over everything she remembered about her, which was not very much, and everything her mother had ever said about her, none of which was good. She couldn't shake the feeling that she should go and see her grandmother, no matter what the cost.

And the cost would be high. She could count on that. Still, some little seed of unrest was taking root and growing inside her.

Why, after all these years, should this plague her so? Just because her mother had accused her of being like her grandmother? It hadn't been the first time that shot had been fired. Why had it hit the target now? Why should it hurt so much to be compared to someone she didn't even know? Maybe it was the implication that wanting to take a path other than the one planned for her was somehow wrong and bad. What had Leota done? And why?

Annie prayed about the situation and all that was bothering her. She prayed for release, but it didn't come. If anything, the gentle nudging became a push. Even during her devotional time in the Word, her grandmother would come to mind. *"I am the vine, you are the branches. . . ."* Annie knew very well that Scripture referred to Jesus, so why did Leota Reinhardt come to mind every time she read it?

Was it because Grandma Leota was the last of the vine from her mother's side of the family? Her grandfather had died before she was born. She had only heard about Great-Grandma and Great-Grandpa Reinhardt. Everything her mother said about them was in rosy contrast to the dark hues of Grandma Leota. "They were the dearest people I ever knew," her mother had said once, "and so giving. Why they put up with my mother, I'll never know. She never had time for anyone but herself."

"Unless you be born again . . ."

Lord, I don't know what You're trying to tell me. Are You saying Leota Reinhardt doesn't believe in You? I don't know anything about her other than if I go to see her, it'll hurt Mom if she finds out.

And what about Leota Reinhardt? What if she didn't know Jesus Christ as her Savior and Lord? What then?

That concern began to outweigh all the rest. What if no one had ever cared enough to tell Leota Reinhardt the good news about Jesus Christ? What if she was unsaved? Annie was plagued by guilt. Every which way she turned, she faced it. She felt guilty about not going to Wellesley; she felt guilty about disappointing her mother; she felt guilty about calling her father and trying to learn something from him about Leota Reinhardt, because it had merely given him more fuel to fire his hate for her mother; she felt guilty about doing nothing.

What made it worse was what it told her about her depth of faith. If she could stay where she was, safe and silent, she might as well cast her faith aside. If she wasn't willing to risk anything—everything—to bring the word of the Lord to her own grandmother, she might as well close her Bible and go to Wellesley or Cal or wherever the stronger of her two parents deemed she should go.

Lord, I can't go on like this. I can't. I'm weak. I'm stumbling. What good is my faith or my witness if my family is in a shambles?

The more she reflected on how little she knew about the old woman, the more she knew she had to go and find out for herself where her grandmother stood before the Lord. And maybe, in the process, she would learn something about what had happened to erect the high, thick walls between her grandmother and her mother.

"I put before you the blessings and cursings . . ."

Which was Leota Reinhardt?

Oh, Mom, what is it in me that makes you see the mother you despise?

Leota sat staring at the television. She had already figured out the words in the saying and was waiting for the statuesque blonde in the green satin dress to turn the next square. *"Y,"* Leota said aloud. *"Y!"* How much easier could it be? _N_L_ _ _M WAN_S _ _U. She could read it as plainly as if the rest of the letters were turned already. *Uncle Sam wants you.* She could even see the poster with the old bearded gentleman in the top hat pointing at her.

"I'd like to buy another vowel," the contestant said and named an *O*.

Disgusted, Leota got up and went to the television. Bending down, she turned the knob, clicking through the channels, desperate for something interesting or challenging—anything that might while away the hours without making her want to put her foot through the square of glass.

Dallas reruns. *Click.* News. *Click.* A television talk show on mothers who had stolen their daughters' boyfriends.

Grand.

Click. A movie about a mother who had plotted the murder of a high school cheerleading contestant so that her daughter could win. The advertisement assured her it was a docudrama!

Trash is trash, no matter what fancy name you call it.

Click. Music straight from hades, complete with the demons dancing around. *Click.* An old movie. Leota had seen it before, back in 1947 or thereabouts. It hadn't been much good then. She doubted if the years had improved it. *Click.* Boxing. Fit her mood, but not her sensibilities. *Click.* Real-life cops in action. Oh, that ought to be about as fun as reruns of the Clinton hearings.

Why would anyone want to watch these shows? People were depressed enough. Did the networks want people to become suicidal? Maybe that was it. It was a government conspiracy. Oliver Stone was probably working on a movie. *If I'm lucky, I'll be dead before it's on television.*

Click. Home shopping network. What on earth are they selling this evening? Jade jewelry from the Orient. China. Japan. Our new best friends. Amazing how quickly people forgot history when cheap commodities were made available.

"Oh, to blazes with it!" Leota punched the power button. She straightened in the silence and looked out her murky front window. It was dark outside, except for the faltering streetlight. Her mantel clock chimed eleven. She wasn't the least bit tired. Why should she be after dozing in her chair throughout the afternoon? She knew she had slept because her neck was stiff. She could look forward to a long, sleepless night.

She looked at the pictures on the mantel. The most recent one she had of Eleanor was five years old. It was a Christmas portrait of the family. Very professional. Very polished. Eleanor was wearing a red satin blouse with a string of pearls. Real ones, of course. Her husband, Fred, looked attractive with his thick, white hair and expensive dark suit jacket. Michael stared at the camera with those dark, arrogant eyes, and little Annie looked so pretty with her long strawberry blonde hair. Naturally curly, just like her father's.

What a handsome man Dean Gardner had been. And what a pity that marriage had broken up. She'd liked him. Dean hadn't been wild like Eleanor's first husband, Bryan Taggart, nor as focused and successful as Fred Gaines. It just seemed a crying shame the problems hadn't been ironed out in the beginning. Problems not dealt with had a way of growing like weeds in a garden. If given full freedom, problems became a lifestyle that choked out all the good memories, lessons learned, goals, or clear insights. Eventually it killed love itself.

God, how can a child I loved so dearly hold me in such contempt? Answer me that, Lord. Where did I go wrong?

It grieved Leota just thinking about Eleanor. What was the matter with her girl? Three marriages, two children who excelled at everything they did, a house behind an iron gate, fancy cars, vacations to Europe, and still Eleanor wasn't happy.

I've been praying for her for years, and what good's it done? I give up, Lord. You deal with her.

She closed her eyes, her heart aching. *Just once, I'd like to hear one of my own flesh and blood say they love me just as I am. Just once I'd like my daughter to come visit me and say thank you for all the sacrifices instead of cataloging all my failures. Just once, I'd like to hear Eleanor or George say, "Thank you, Mama. I appreciate all you did."*

Fat chance.

Oh, God, why can't I come home to You now? What are You waiting for anyway? I've done all I can do on this earth. I'm old. I'm useless. I ache all over, inside and out. I stand here in my living room looking at pictures of my family. They make me want to weep. Each one has his or her own life now, and there's no room in those lives for an old woman. I'm tired of listening to Eleanor tell me what a lousy mother I was. I'm tired of turning the other cheek. I'm tired of turning on the television set just so I can hear another human voice. I'm tired of sitting in the nook gazing out at my dying garden. I'm tired of living! Oh, God, I want to come home!

"I set you free so that you might live and have life abundant."

Leota's heart pounded; anger poured through her. Life *abundant?* In the next world maybe, but not here. Not now. *Why are You doing this to me? What did I ever do to deserve this kind of treatment? I'd like to know.*

"Where were you when I laid the foundations of the earth? Have you ever commanded the morning to appear? Can you hold back the movements of the stars? Are you able to restrain the Pleiades or Orion?"

Weeping, Leota sat in her worn chair. *I know who You are. I know You can do all things. Haven't I worshiped You alone for as long as I can remember? Didn't I meet with You daily in my garden and lean on You through all those years of . . . Oh, God, don't You understand? I'm tired of being misunderstood. I'm tired of the pain of living. I'm tired of being alone.*

"I want to come home. Please let me come home." She leaned her head back against the rest and let the tears flow unchecked down her cheeks. Why was He waiting?

Quit whining.

An image drifted into her mind . . . a cauldron filled with gold.

The gold was boiling, and black impurities rose, wraithlike, to the surface of the golden liquid.

Is it I, Lord?

"Wait upon the Lord and see what I will do."

As if she had a choice . . .

Corban sat at his desk, jotting down ideas of how to get on Leota Reinhardt's good side and make his assignment easier. "Bring wire cart for carrying groceries. Get her a cane. Clean her windows." He grimaced. The last thing he wanted to do was wash the old woman's windows, but if it would get her to talk to him, he'd do it. He tapped his pencil. Something easy. Something that wouldn't take much time or effort. Chocolates, maybe? Flowers? He dismissed both ideas. He'd only known the woman for a couple of hours, but he was sure if he brought candy and flowers, she'd nail his ears to the wall and then throw darts at his head for kissing up to her.

Glancing at his Rolex, he saw if he didn't start for the campus now he was going to be late for Professor Webster's class. Tossing his pencil down, he grabbed his backpack. Shouldering it, he went out the door, letting it lock behind him. As he strode toward the university, he tried to think of some way to talk the professor out of requiring him to do a case study. There had to be some way to avoid spending any more time with that old bat.

While in the library checking out books on Monet and van Gogh, Annie checked at the reference desk for an Oakland telephone directory. Leota Reinhardt was listed, along with her street. Maybe if Annie saw the house, she would remember it. On the way home, she stopped at a big chain bookstore and purchased a map of Oakland.

Susan unlocked the door and came in with a bag of groceries. "Call the cops!" squawked the rainbow lory on a stand by the window.

"I live here, Barnaby. Naughty bird. Did you make another mess?"

"I vacuumed a little while ago," Annie said with a grin.

Susan set the bag of groceries on the counter. "Won't do a bit of good. He just starts flinging seed again. I think he figures he has to plant a crop so he'll have seed next year. You're a dumb bird, Barnaby. Dumb bird!"

Barnaby opened his wings and fluffed them as though he were indignant at such an insult, then smoothed them down again, staring at her with disdain. "Whatcha gonna do?"

Susan and Annie laughed. "You have the most appalling manners,

Barnaby. Why a policeman would have a pet at all is beyond me. Of course, Raoul didn't have to take you out for a walk, did he? All he had to do to keep you happy was turn on the television and leave you plenty of food. Unfortunately, we don't have a television."

"Somewhere everybody knows your name," the bird sang out.

"We won't be stuck with you forever, you know." Susan started putting things away.

"I think you may have him longer than you planned," Annie said.

"Raoul said he'd be back from Los Angeles in a week or so." Susan peered at the bird. "Hear that, Barnaby? In a week, you're outta here, buddy."

Annie grinned. "There's a message for you on the answering machine. From Raoul."

Susan rolled her eyes. "Oh no. Bad news?"

"Depends on how you look at it." Her grin widened. "He's been hired. He's already put a deposit on a furnished apartment. Problem is the management won't allow pets."

"That is *not* a pet—" Susan pointed at the bird—"What about his stuff? He has to come back. . . ."

"He boxed it up before he left."

"He *knew.* Why didn't he just sell the bird?"

"Here Kitty Kitty!" the parrot squawked at her.

Annie grinned. "Raoul said he knows you'll take good care of Barnaby. He couldn't trust him to anyone but someone who was a bird person."

"Birdbrain, you mean!" She eyed the parrot. "Great. Just great."

"911!" Barnaby said in a perfect imitation of William Shatner, and made the sound of a siren. "911!"

"Another word out of you and you'll be plucked, packaged, and frozen like this chicken!" She tossed the package of poultry into the small freezer.

Annie laughed. "She doesn't mean it, Barnaby."

"You don't think so? The only reason I agreed to bird-sit is because I missed my canary. He was so cute. *That* is a feathered piranha!" She looked at Annie's map spread out on the floor. "Planning a trip?"

"A short one." Annie smoothed it a little and finished tracing the route with the yellow highlighter.

"Who's in Oakland?"

"My grandmother." Annie smiled self-consciously. "I'm not even sure what I'm going to say to her."

"You'll think of something." Susan flopped down on the old sofa she'd purchased at a garage sale. Her father and two brothers had hauled it over the Bay Bridge in their pickup truck and lugged it into the building. When it wouldn't fit into the ancient Otis elevator, they muscled it up four flights of stairs to the small flat, where Susan had sandwiches, freshly baked cookies, and sodas waiting. "When do you think you'll go?" Susan popped the top of her soda.

"Tomorrow. I'm not scheduled to work until four, and I haven't got a class."

"How long has it been since you've seen her?"

Annie blushed. "Four years, I think. I can't remember for sure."

"Four *years?*" Susan drank some of her soda and then shook her head. "I've never gone longer than a couple of weeks without seeing some relative or another. We've got family coming out of our ears."

Annie had met at least three of Susan's uncles and a dozen cousins during her visits at Susan's house. She always felt a little overwhelmed when standing in the Carter's small house, packed from stem to stern with relatives. Everyone talked at once and they were loud. The men gathered around the television to watch whatever sport was in season, while the women gathered in the kitchen to cook and talk and laugh. "Have any of them ever gotten mad at each other?"

"Oh, sure! Someone's always ticked off about something. Hottest fights are around the dinner table when Uncle Bob and Uncle Chet get going on politics or when Maggie starts in on equal rights. Daddy'll jump right in on anything."

Annie had met Susan's older sister only a few times and found her quick-witted and very likable. "Is Maggie a women's activist?"

"Only when the situation calls for it, which is every time she comes over for a visit with the folks." Susan grinned. "Daddy says the only reason married women with children are working is because people are so greedy they want too much. Of course, Mom is working, but that doesn't count because she has a calling. You never know who will throw the bait first. Maggie'll come right back at him and say some people would like to have a nice house and live in a decent neighborhood that's safe for their children, and the only way to afford it is to have two people working. Then Daddy'll come back and say the neighborhoods would be a lot nicer if the mothers were all home taking care of their children like they're supposed to. They go round and round about it." She laughed. "They can get pretty steamed up sometimes."

"Do they stay mad at each other?"

"Not for more than an hour. Funny thing is Maggie told me she and Andy have already decided that when they get pregnant, she'll stay home. Listening to her talk, you'd think she was for zero population control and government-run day-care centers. Truth is she takes after Daddy. They both like nothing better than a good, rousing debate. Daddy loves to play devil's advocate at the dinner table. Whatever side you're on, he'll take the opposite. He says it's a good way to learn to think. Mental fencing, he calls it." Susan took a long swig on her soda. "No one gets hurt."

Annie couldn't even imagine what it would be like to debate with her mother just for the fun of it. The combatants would have to wear emotional body armor because any verbal fencing around her house would have been done without the safety guards. Two minutes into it, and her mother would turn it into blood sport. *"Sticks and stones will break my bones, but words will never hurt me."* Whoever came up with that little cliché didn't know her mother. Nora Gaines could dismember people with her tongue.

Annie felt almost sick with guilt. What sort of a daughter was she?

Susan got up. "I'd better put the rest of the stuff away." She opened the refrigerator, took out a container, and opened it. "Gross! I should take this home for my little brother and let him turn it in as a science project."

Distracted, Annie wasn't listening.

It was a relatively short distance between Black Hawk on the east side of the hills and Oakland on the San Francisco Bay. There was a tunnel right through the hills at one point. Easy driving, easy distance. Thirty minutes max? Yet Grandmother Leota might as well have lived in New York State for all the time the family had spent together.

Susan's voice came from behind the door of the fridge. "What did you do today?"

"I called my mother." Annie was embarrassed the minute she said it. She made it sound like it was the biggest chore of the year.

Susan paused in her hunt for food. "And?"

And her mother had had a fit. *"Have you come to your senses yet, Anne? Do you have any idea how much you've hurt and disappointed me?"*

Annie didn't look up at Susan. "I told her I have a job. I started to tell her about my art classes, but she hung up."

"Oh, Annie . . ." A glint of anger stirred in her friend's dark eyes. "Anytime you want to be adopted, just let me know. My parents love you."

Annie blinked back tears and looked down at the map. She adored Susan's parents, but no one could replace her mother. She wished things were different. She wished her mother could love her as unconditionally as the Carters loved their children. None of them were perfect. Two had been in and out of trouble through their teen years. Susan's older brother, Sam, had even spent a couple of months in juvenile hall. Tough love and patience had turned him around. Susan had been talking about him yesterday.

"He's graduating this June. Can you believe it? He was such a reprobate! We'd all given up on him, but Mom and Dad said he'd come around in God's own time. And he sure did. Not that he doesn't still like to rock the boat . . ." Sam. The wild one. "James Dean's reincarnation," Susan had once said. "The raging bull of the family, and full of it, too . . ."

Annie looked at the map again, going over the route she had traced with her Hi-Liter. "My mother's all right, Suzie. She just wants what she thinks is best for me." But did her mother *love* her? Annie realized part of her own drive to do well had been the hope that she would please her mother. What if she hadn't gotten a 4.0 GPA? What if she hadn't played piano for the Lady's Guild as her mother had promised she would?

And yet every time she did well at something, there was always another task set before her, something a little higher, a little harder. High school honors classes. Peer counseling. Summers of community service. SAT tests. The first set hadn't been high enough, so her mother had had her tutored before retaking them. Finally scholarship and college applications. And then the pot at the end of the rainbow her mother had been chasing for her: Wellesley. *All those rich girls from all those important families. Think of what your future could be, Annie!*

Annie knew she had panicked. Just the thought of what lay ahead had scared her enough to make her run. She felt she couldn't breathe anymore. The pressure of her mother's expectations had been crushing her. Each time she pleased her mother, the situation had grown worse, not better. Her mother would view the success with pride and see "the possibilities," leading to further demands and expectations.

"Think how much more you could've done, Annie, if only you'd tried a little harder. If I'd had your opportunities . . ."

Annie knew no matter what she did, it would never be enough.

Or was she just trying to excuse herself for running out?

Dropping her Hi-Liter, she rested her head on her crossed arms.

*Lord, am I a quitter like my mother said? Am I a coward? Am I afraid
I wouldn't be able to make it at a real college?*

"You're just like Leota!"

She could still see the look in her mother's eyes when she had
said it.

"Annie?" Susan said softly. "You okay?"

"I'm okay." She rubbed her forehead. "I'm just trying to put all the
pieces together."

"Maybe you should just walk away. Give her time."

Annie looked up, stricken. She knew Susan didn't care much for
her mother. Nora Gaines had never done anything to make Susan
feel welcome. Sometimes she wouldn't even take the message when
Susan called. *"That* girl," she always said in that certain tone she
could take on, as though Susan carried some kind of social disease.
*"Why don't you cultivate a friendship with Laura Danvers. She comes
from a* good *family."* Which, of course, meant a family with wealth
and social standing . . . someone else who lived inside the gates.

Her mother didn't understand. Things had probably changed a lot
since her mother's days in high school. Maybe then things were the
way they appeared. Not anymore. Laura Danvers was pretty and
dressed nicely, but she also had a cocaine addiction.

*"Her mother says Laura goes to parties all the time and has a
wonderful time. Why won't you go when you're invited?"*

Because Annie knew what went on at the parties. She wasn't into
that scene. She didn't want to fit in when it meant smoking pot,
drinking, or having sex. Sure, Laura was popular. When she was
high, she went along with any guy who happened to be with her.
Everyone in school knew she had had two abortions before she was
seventeen. And just before graduation practices had started, one of
the girls in gym said Laura had tested positive for HIV.

Annie's mother knew none of that, and Annie didn't feel it was her
place to talk about Laura's private life. She also didn't want to get
involved with Laura's crowd. They all thought they were being so cool,
but all they were doing was throwing away their lives with both hands.

Besides, even if Annie told her mother everything that went on in
the corridors of the high school or at the parties, it wouldn't matter.
Her mother probably wouldn't believe her. Nora saw only what she
wanted to see. She looked at Susan with her long, dyed, black hair
and nose ring and saw trouble. She looked at Laura Danvers with her
eighty-dollar haircut and Saks Fifth Avenue clothes and saw class.
And that was that. Her mind was set.

I'm guilty, too, Lord. I'm not what people see. I've worn a mask. I've pretended everything was fine because I haven't wanted to witness to my mother. I've just obeyed her, Lord. I've tried so hard. And I was afraid, too. I admit it. I've been afraid to face my mother's wrath. And now that I've left home, I'm afraid if I go one step further and see my grandmother, my mother will never forgive me.

"Love the Lord your God . . ."

"Annie?"

She felt Susan's hand on her back. She let out a shaky sigh and sat up. Raking a hand back through her hair, she crossed her legs Indian fashion and looked at her dearest friend. "Suzie, I don't know if I'm doing the right thing."

Susan sat down on the rug with her. "What can be wrong with seeing your grandmother?"

"You don't understand. My family isn't like yours. Everything's complicated." So complicated she couldn't see the beginning, middle, or end of the mess. Just a thread, that's all she wanted—just a slender thread so she could grasp what had happened to make her mother so bitter. Maybe then she could begin the process of untangling some small part of the jumble of knots.

Oh, Lord, I want to understand my mother. I don't want to end up hating her the way she hates her mother. "Love one another," *You said. Help me do that. Please help me.*

"I'm so nervous." Annie held out her hands. They were shaking.

Susan reached out and took hold of them. "It'll be okay."

"Suzie, I don't even know where to start. What do you talk about with your grandparents?"

"Everything! They love talking about the past. Grandma Addie talks about her father all the time. I never met my great-grandfather, but I feel as though I know him because she's told me so much about him. He jumped ship in San Francisco in 1905 and was there during the 1906 earthquake. And he was still alive when Neil Armstrong walked on the moon. Isn't that cool? Grandma and Grandpa both grew up during the Great Depression and lived through World War II. You just ask a couple of questions and they're off and running with a dozen stories. Some I've heard a hundred times, but it's still fun. Especially when they're telling us tidbits about the folks when they were little and into things. It's a kick."

"My mother says all my grandmother cared about was her job."

Susan frowned. "What did she do?"

Annie shrugged. "I don't know. My mother's never said."

"Well, that's a start right there, Annie. Ask your grandmother about her work."

"There are so many things I want to ask her." She looked down at the map and the yellow line tracing the route to the neighborhood in Oakland. Leota Reinhardt lived a couple of blocks off the MacArthur Freeway. The house should be easy enough to find.

"Do you want me to go with you? I could call and see if Hank could switch me with one of the other girls."

"Thanks, Suzie, but I'll go by myself this time."

"Call 911," Barnaby squawked.

Annie and Susan laughed.

5

ANNIE TOOK THE FRUITVALE EXIT OFF MACARTHUR FREEWAY. She turned right at the bottom of the hill, drove another block, and turned left. An old brick church stood majestically on the corner at the base of a hilly, tree-lined avenue. The street was narrow and lined with charming little wood-and-stucco cottages. Each one had a front porch, and though some of the homes looked run down, with yard work and a fresh coat of paint they would be enchanting. Great-Grandma and Great-Grandpa Reinhardt had probably lived here during a time when people sat outside in the fading evening light, visiting with their neighbors and watching their children play together.

Annie made a U-turn at the end of the block, in front of an old brick elementary school. She drove back slowly and pulled up in front of the house that bore the numbers of her grandmother's address. Two little black girls were playing hopscotch on the sidewalk next door. They were dressed alike in blue jeans and bright pink sweaters, their hair in beaded cornrows. As Annie got out of her car, the girls paused in their game to watch her warily.

She smiled. "Hello!"

They smiled back, though they didn't say anything. Their parents had probably told them never to talk to strangers.

Leaning back inside her car, Annie reached for her purse and the present she had brought for her grandmother. She looped her purse strap onto her shoulder and pushed the door shut. Studying the small house before her, she thought it must at one time have been one of the prettiest on the street. Rhododendrons and azaleas grew along the front of the house. There were no blooms now, but in a few months, the bushes would be covered. The lawn was in poor shape, but proper mowing, a weed treatment, and some fertilizing would bring it back in no time. The barren tree in front looked like it could be a winter-dormant flowering plum, beautiful in blossom. There were several such trees in her mother and stepfather's backyard, all carefully tended by Marvin Tikado's gardening service.

The border alongside her grandmother's house was entangled with climbing rosebushes. Pink roses, Annie remembered. The white picket fence would be glorious when the vines leafed up and covered it with red blossoms. She saw the wisteria overhanging the carport at the end of the drive. Soon, its lavender blooms would hang like over-ripe bunches of grapes, mingling with the scent of roses.

This home must be simply glorious in spring.

Brightly painted front steps greeted her, and there was an old rocking chair pushed back in the corner of the front porch, its seat so worn, Annie thought, her grandmother must have spent count-less hours sitting outside. It was dusty and cobwebbed now, but perhaps when the colder weather passed, Grandma Leota would sit outside again. The rhododendrons were too high in front to see over them to the street, but that could be quickly remedied. Annie also noticed the hanging pots and thought how pretty they would be filled with fuchsias dripping hot pink and purple comet-shaped blossoms.

Her heart thumping, Annie rang the bell. She thought she could hear the television playing inside. Grandma Leota must be home. The question was, Would she open the door to someone she hadn't seen in years . . . someone she probably wouldn't even recognize?

Lord, please let my grandmother invite me in. Help me not to say anything that will upset her and close any lines of communication between us. Help me see things clearly from all sides. Lord, help.

She waited, hoping, excited, her stomach trembling with niggling fears and uncertainties. Why should she expect any kind of welcome? Had she even bothered to write? She thought of a dozen ways she had slighted her grandmother without even thinking about it. She didn't even know when Leota's birthday was.

The door opened a crack. "If you're selling something, I'm not interested."

"Grandma Leota? I'm Annie. Annie Gardner."

The old woman looked at her oddly. "Annie?"

She must not remember. Why should she? "Annie Gardner," she said again, hoping to jog her grandmother's memory. It had been such a long time. Her mother and father had divorced when Anne was five, and she could count on one hand the number of times she had been brought over here. "Nora's daughter."

She looked into her grandmother's brown eyes but couldn't read her expression. Did her grandmother remember anything? Maybe she had even forgotten she had grandchildren.

Annie's heart sank.

Leota remembered. Oh, indeed, she remembered. She just couldn't speak past the lump in her throat as she looked at the beautiful young girl standing on her porch. How many years had it been since she last saw her granddaughter? Anne-Lynn Gardner wasn't a little girl anymore. She was tall and slender, with that lovely fall of strawberry blonde hair. She was holding an African violet with lovely purple blooms. How did Annie know violets were her favorite flowers? The plant was in a little pink ceramic pot.

"Nora's daughter, Grandma Leota," the girl said again, clearly distressed.

"I know who you are." Leota was dismayed that she sounded so gruff and impatient. She opened the door a little wider to show the girl she was welcome. After all these years, little Annie was a young woman. *Oh, God, all those lost years.* Leota's throat closed tight.

Annie stepped inside and glanced to where the television was still on. "I hope I'm not interrupting."

Leota stepped over and punched the power button. "Geraldo can live without me."

The room fell into silence. She turned and looked at her granddaughter again, studying her. She could see Eleanor in the girl. She had her mouth and nose, with some of her father in her as well. Those beautiful blue eyes. Leota drank in the sight of her, wondering what to say, wondering why she had come. She must have some reason after all these years. She looked nervous and embarrassed. "Are those violets for me?" Leota smiled at her, hoping to put her at ease.

"Oh! Yes. Of course." She held them out in both hands, as though it were an offering.

"My favorite flowers," Leota said as she took them and admired the soft, velvety, purple petals. "How did you know?"

"I didn't," Annie said softly. "I thought they were pretty and that you might like them."

"I do. Very much. Thank you." She thought of the violets she had planted in her yard and how lovely they had looked peeping up from the feather moss. She looked at Annie, wondering again why she had come, yet too afraid to ask. Why spoil the moment? "Would you like something to drink? Tea? Coffee?"

"Anything would be fine."

"Come into the kitchen then. I'll fix us some tea."

Tea. With her granddaughter.

I wonder when I'll wake up from this lovely, lovely dream?

Annie followed her grandmother. She hadn't expected Leota to be so small. She was only about five feet tall and thin. Her hair was white and pinned up in a French roll with wisps here and there. She was wearing an old-fashioned, white cardigan, a blue flower-print dress, and pink slippers. Annie thought she looked adorable. Her grandmother held the pot of violets as though it were her most cherished possession. She looked at it for a long moment and then set it carefully on a small table by the windows. A newspaper was spread out, and Annie noticed the half-worked crossword puzzle. Then she noticed the backyard. *Oh, how sad . . .*

"I remember your garden. I thought it was wonderland."

Leota glanced up. "Wonderland?" That description seemed to please her; then a sadness filled her expression as she followed her granddaughter's gaze. "Well, it's not a wonderland anymore. It's a jungle. I haven't done any gardening in a long time."

"Are the elves still there?"

"Elves?" Leota thought for a moment, but she couldn't remember.

"In the rose lattice back by the vegetable garden. There were green, porcelain elves sitting on the slats. Three of them, I think. Just big enough to fit in the palm of your hand."

"Oh, my, I'd forgotten all about them." She had put those little figurines out years ago when Michael was just a child, hoping he would take delight in them and they might spark some sense of surprise in him. When he never mentioned them, she forgot all about them.

"There was a big green frog, too," Annie said, smiling as she looked out the window. "Over there in the far corner where those calla lilies are growing."

Leota warmed at the way Annie remembered details about the garden. "I imagine he's still there. I haven't moved him." She had put those silly things in the garden to bring joy to her grandchildren, but they had never been around long enough for her to know if they'd even noticed them. She'd dreamed once, long ago, of having Easter egg hunts and . . .

She turned her thoughts from going down that rocky path again. What good was it, going over past hurts and disappointments? Thinking about what might have been never made things better.

Annie looked around the kitchen, and Leota wondered what her granddaughter thought about it. It was small and cozy. At one time, it had been very cheerful, with its canary yellow walls and white cabinets. The window over the kitchen sink looked straight across into the neighbor's kitchen. Annie wouldn't know it could be pushed up so ladies could talk back and forth while they did their dishes and their children played in the backyard.

"What would you like?" Leota watched Annie's face as she looked around the room. She had such a sweet expression. What a contrast to that young man who had come to "volunteer."

"Whatever you're having, Grandma Leota. Could we sit in here?"

"You sit anywhere you want, dear," Leota said and watched her granddaughter sit in the chair opposite her own. Annie gazed again out the window at the backyard, and she didn't look the least bit put off by the lack of care. Might the girl be seeing what had been, not what was? Leota wished she hadn't let things go, but her arthritis made it difficult to get around. Of course, that wasn't the full reason. She might as well admit it. She had let things go because she had given up. Why spend all those hours in the garden when there was no one but her to enjoy it? She was sorry now. She shouldn't have done that. She should've kept it up. Now it was too late. She couldn't undo the destruction of the last few years. She was too old.

This was no time to count her regrets. Her granddaughter had come to visit. *Praise God.*

Leota felt like having something special, something to celebrate this occasion. Opening a drawer, she poked around and found a few packets of Constant Comment tea she had tucked away after Mama Reinhardt had died. Mama had loved Constant Comment tea, and the two of them would sit together in the afternoons and sip it together. Did she have any cookies stashed away? If so, they would be as old as the tea and stale and hard enough to set with mortar. Crackers? None. Oh, how she wished she had known Annie was coming. She could have bought the fixings and made some Toll House or peanut butter cookies. Maybe next time.

Would there be a next time?

Oh, God . . . please.

Her hand trembled as she filled the teakettle. She carried it to the stove and turned on the gas burner. "It won't take long." Would Annie get tired of waiting and leave? Young people these days seemed to be in such a rush about everything. Places to go. Things to do. She had heard about all that from Cosma. *"Maybe it's those video games they play all the time. Everything moves so fast. Like gnats on a screen door, battering away and driving you crazy."*

"I'm not in any hurry," Annie said, returning her attention to her grandmother.

"Are you hungry? I don't have any cookies, but I could fix you a . . ." A what? She didn't have any lunch meat. She hadn't fixed any tuna. She didn't even have peanut butter on hand. ". . . an egg sandwich? Would you like that?"

"I'm not hungry. I just wanted to see you and talk with you."

Leota came and eased herself into the chair opposite Annie. "How's your mother?" The girl's eyes flickered slightly, and she lowered her head. The tension was back. Leota watched as Annie clasped her hands on the table. Something was wrong. "Is Eleanor ill?"

"No, Grandma Leota. Mother's fine. It's just that . . ." She looked out at the yard again, and Leota saw the sheen of tears in her eyes. *Oh, dear. Something's wrong again. Isn't that always the way of it?* Leota waited, wondering why Annie had come to her. She had never been included in the family circle before. Why now?

"We're not on the best of terms right now," Annie said after a long pause.

Leota felt the girl's pain. Did she dare pry? What if she asked the wrong question and her granddaughter left? She wanted to offer some comfort, but what could she say that wouldn't be misconstrued? *"Things will blow over in time?"* That wasn't necessarily true. Things had never blown over between Leota and Eleanor. "Would you like to talk about it?" she said cautiously.

Annie looked at her again, her blue eyes so troubled and filled with pain that Leota's heart squeezed tight. *Oh, Eleanor, what have you done to our little Annie?*

"Mother says I'm like you."

"Oh, dear," Leota said ruefully, and Annie's face turned pink. The poor girl looked so embarrassed and distressed, Leota was sorry she had said anything. She knew where she stood with Eleanor. The why was not as easily understood. "Why would she say a thing like that?"

Annie looked down at her clasped hands. "I decided to study art in San Francisco instead of going east to Wellesley."

"Are you good at art?"

She raised her head and looked at Leota, letting out her breath softly. "Mother said if I had any real talent, she would've sent me to Paris to study."

Leota heard no bitterness, nor did she see any resentment as Annie repeated her mother's assessment. *Oh, Eleanor. Ever the judge and jury.* A spark of anger lit inside Leota. "What do *you* think, Annie?"

She smiled bleakly. "I may not be as good as I think, but I love it."

"What sort of art do you do?"

"I've tried all kinds. I'm not sure where my strengths are yet, if I have any. I did a lot of pencil sketching through high school. The budgets were cut so much, though, that our school could offer only two courses. Art wasn't a high priority."

"What are you going to study?"

"I've registered for a course in art appreciation and another in form. I'd like to try watercolors and acrylics. Maybe in time I'll know what I'm supposed to do."

"It's not out of the blue. You have a relative who was a commercial artist."

"Really? I didn't know that."

Did Eleanor even know? She couldn't remember if they'd ever talked about relatives long past. "She would've been your Great-Great-Aunt Joyce. She was from my side of the family. She died before your mother was born. A few of Aunt Joyce's things were passed on to me when my mother died. I might have a few of her pictures tucked away somewhere. She made a good living drawing ladies' fashions and stoves and farm machinery. Things like that. Nothing very exciting. She did a few greeting cards, too, if I remember correctly."

"I'd love to see them."

"I'll see if I can find them." She hadn't thought about them in years. Where might they be? In her hope chest, perhaps? Or in a box in the attic? How could she get up there to look for them?

The teakettle whistled. Leota rose and turned the gas off. She poured hot water over the tea bags and set the kettle back on the stove. "Do you like your tea strong?"

"Any way you're having yours will be fine," Annie said.

Leota dipped the tea bags up and down until the tea was a rich amber. "Sugar?"

"Plain is fine."

A people pleaser. Leota had a feeling Annie liked sugar in her tea, but didn't want to be a bother. The teacups rattled slightly as she put them on the table, one before Annie and the other on her crossword puzzle. She opened a cabinet and took out a cobalt blue sugar bowl. Removing the lid, she loosened the sugar inside and set the bowl on the table close to Annie. Opening a drawer, she took out a spoon and set it on the table as well. She couldn't offer cream—she didn't have any. Nor did she have any milk. She needed to make another trip to the grocery store.

When was that young college student coming back? What was his name? Corban. That was it. Corban Solsek. He was supposed to come on Wednesday. Would he? She hadn't been very nice to him. Stuck-up little twerp. What day was this? Maybe she'd call that nice Decker woman and ask her if she could send someone else.

"It smells good, Grandma," Annie said. "Thank you."

Leota sat at the table with her granddaughter. She smiled to herself as she watched Annie sprinkle two teaspoons of sugar into her tea. Either she had a sweet tooth or she didn't like tea. Leota decided the next time she went to the store she would buy a can of that fancy instant coffee, the kind they advertised on television. Whatever the cost. French vanilla. Cappacino. Double Dutch chocolate. Something special. And she'd buy the fixings for cookies, too. She wanted to have something nice to offer the next time her granddaughter came to visit.

Assuming there would be a next visit.

Leota began to worry. This visit hadn't even gotten under way and all she could think about was how little time she might have to get to know this girl before she left. She had the feeling that when Annie walked out the front door, that would be the end of everything important. *Oh, Lord. Help me! Is she as sensitive as Eleanor? One wrong word and off she'll go and I'll never get to see her again?*

God . . . help!

Annie sat in silence, fighting the fears that were suddenly plaguing her. Had she been right to come? What did her grandmother think of her? Of what she'd said about her mother?

It was Grandmother who finally broke the silence. "So you're old enough to be on your own."

"Yes. I moved in with a friend from high school. Susan Carter. She graduated a year ahead of me. She's a lot of fun."

"Fun."

"Not in a bad way," Annie said quickly, thinking about the way her mother viewed Susan. Annie didn't want to give her grandmother the wrong impression. "Susan's very responsible. She's taking classes at San Francisco State, and she's paying all of her own expenses."

"What's she studying?"

"Right now, she's classified as 'undecided,' but she'll probably major in nursing. Her mother's a nurse." Annie told her about the apartment and the advantages of its location. "I like to run."

So that's why she looks so thin, Leota thought.

"It's not that far to the zoo and only a mile or so to the beach," Annie said. "There's a jogging path there."

Leota seemed to remember something about Annie being involved in sports. Eleanor must have said so, but Leota was embarrassed she didn't know more. "Were you on the track team?"

"No. Mother didn't think it was a good idea for a girl to be a runner, so I was in gymnastics until I was fifteen."

"Why did you stop?"

"I broke my arm in a fall. The injury prevented me from continuing with it."

"Ladies didn't jog in my day," Leota said, "but I used to walk around Lake Merritt on my lunch hour. I could keep up quite a clip in those days. And I loved being out in the open for a while. I kept my walking shoes in the bottom drawer of my desk at work. It raised a few eyebrows, I can tell you. Not that it stopped me. Things have changed since then. I've heard it's not unusual these days for women to wear tennis shoes to work. Is that so?"

Annie smiled. "I see ladies in business suits and tennis shoes downtown all the time. Lots of women change into heels when they get to their offices."

"Putting all those poor podiatrists out of work," Leota said with a chuckle.

Annie relaxed. Something about her grandmother made Annie feel quite at home with her in this small house. The soft gleam of humor in her grandmother's eyes gave Annie courage . . . made her decide to risk asking personal questions.

"What did you do for a living, Grandma?" What was the career that had been more interesting than her family?

"I was a secretary. Just an ordinary secretary."

"Did you enjoy it?"

"I was good at it."

"How long did you work?"

"Thirty years."

That would have been long after her mother left home. Perhaps there was something to her mother's supposition. "Did you work for the same company all that time?"

"Oh, no. I worked for four different companies all together. They were all in the same office building, just two blocks away from the lake. One went out of business, but I was hired right away by one of their competitors. When that boss retired, I worked for the gentleman who bought his company. Then that company merged with another. I stayed on and worked for them as well."

"Why did you finally leave?"

Leota smiled slightly. "I turned sixty-five."

"Oh. Did they let you go because of your age?"

"No. I gave them notice two weeks before my birthday."

She made it sound as though she couldn't wait to leave. Was that so? "Did you find the work fulfilling?"

"Fulfilling? No, I wouldn't say secretarial work was particularly fulfilling. It paid the bills. And I liked the people."

Annie frowned. How was it that someone who was supposed to have loved her work so much would not seem the least interested in talking about it when the opportunity arose? Perhaps it had been the people she had worked for who had been the draw. Had she been involved with someone? Was that what had caused the rift between her grandmother and her mother? It didn't seem likely. Had Nora known of anything clandestine, she would have said something about it. There had never been any indication that her mother would care about protecting Grandma Leota's reputation. If anything, her mother would've used that kind of information to nail Grandma Leota's coffin shut.

"You look so troubled," her grandmother said quietly. "Is it something I've said?"

"No. I was just thinking . . ." Annie blushed, realizing the track of her thoughts. She was condemning her mother exactly the way her mother had condemned Grandma Leota all these years. What right had she to criticize her mother, even in her own mind? Had she walked in her shoes? Had she seen through her eyes?

Dwell on what is true and right and lovely.

She rubbed her temple. *What is true? What is right?*

"Do you have a headache? I have some aspirin."

"No. I'm fine, Grandma Leota. Really. There are just so many things . . ." She pressed her lips together, afraid she would cry. She expected her grandmother to start asking questions the way her mother always did. What could she say?

Leota sat still and quiet, as though she was waiting.

Annie felt uncomfortable. She was far more used to her mother's verbally pounding at her for an answer.

"*Tell me what's wrong now.*"

"*Nothing, Mother.*"

"*I suppose you want to quit piano again. Well, I'm not going to let you. Do you hear me? Someday you'll thank me for making you keep up your lessons. If I left it up to you, you'd quit everything.*"

"*Mother, I just need a little time—*"

"*You can have all the time you want, right over there on that bench. You can sulk just as well at the piano as you can sulk in your room. Now, go practice! I promised the ladies you'd play at the luncheon. . . .*"

Annie closed her eyes against the voices that wouldn't leave her alone.

Leota could see the girl's struggle. Annie was terribly upset about something. "Why did you come, Annie?" What could she do to help her granddaughter?

Annie lowered her hands. They were trembling. She put them around her teacup. "I hardly know you, Grandma Leota."

Leota longed to respond, to blurt out that she would have had it otherwise. Yet she didn't dare utter such provocative words. They could be too easily misconstrued. She would not be party to casting blame on anyone, not even on Eleanor, who was at fault. Leota had been the victim of her daughter's grievances for too many years. Instead, she said very cautiously, "We can remedy that."

Annie raised her head and looked at her. Her blue eyes were glassy with tears and misery. She looked so vulnerable, not like a young woman at all, but rather like a little girl who had been badly hurt by someone she loved. Leota recognized that look. Hadn't she seen it on Eleanor's face countless times as a small child? Her heart squeezed so tight, she could hardly breathe, let alone say any words of comfort.

"I've missed you, Grandma."

Leota gave the softest gasp. She couldn't speak. It wasn't that she didn't have any words; it was that she had too many. Words of love collected over the lonely years. Years before Annie was even born. All the way back to the day she had placed Eleanor in the arms of Helene Reinhardt. Eleanor had cried. Oh, how she had cried.

And so had Leota as she sat on the bus going downtown and doing what she had to do.

Oh, Lord, are You giving me a second chance?

Something of Leota's inner struggle must have shown on her face because Annie reached across the small table and touched her hand. Once. Gently. A tentative exploration. Leota wanted to grasp that young, slender, strong hand and hold on and never let go. Instead, she sat silent, unmoving, afraid if she made one sound there would be an unleashing of the frightful grief and hope inside her. It hurt so much. Oh, what a burden hope could be, especially to one so young and obviously encumbered with her own pain.

"I guess that doesn't make any sense, does it?" Annie said softly, her voice breaking slightly.

It made all the sense in the world to Leota. "I've missed you, too," she said finally. It was a terrible understatement, but to say any more and give a hint to the depth of her true feelings might send the girl running. *Oh, Lord, she has no idea who I am. She has no idea of the undercurrents and undertows of the past.* Poor Eleanor had been in the vortex and never understood. *I didn't want to explain. How could I without destroying all her illusions about her family? Oh, Jesus, let these mild words be enough, but not too much.*

And so they must have been, for Annie raised her head and looked into Leota's eyes, searching. Then Annie's eyes warmed and glowed. Closing them, the girl lowered her head, almost as though saying a silent prayer.

Corban couldn't believe what the old woman was asking. He'd taken her to the grocery store, where she had purchased brown and granulated sugar, soda, eggs, chocolate chips, and a five-pound sack of flour. Five pounds he had to carry, along with the pound of sugar and other items. She had gone on a real spree this time. She bought a gallon of milk, instead of her usual quart, and a carton of flavored cream. French vanilla. She bought a small box of Constant Comment tea and another of Orange Spice. She even bought two tins of fancy instant coffee, although she almost threw a fit when she saw how much they would cost her. She didn't let the price go unnoticed by the poor checker. "Three dollars and eighty-five cents for that *little* can?" she had harped. "That's robbery! Six ounces, it says right here. What's the stuff made of? Gold?"

Corban hadn't said a word. In fact, he had been touched, thinking she was going to offer him some instant cappuccino after all he was doing for her. He'd even decided to forgive her for the quarter insult from the first visit. He should've known better. When they reached the house, she told him she had some ice water in the refrigerator— he looked like he needed some. She even told him he could dampen a paper towel and dab his face. "You're a little red."

Yeah, well, toting two twenty-pound sacks of groceries up the hill could do that to anyone.

She still wouldn't ride in his car.

And then she hit him up for one more chore. "Before you leave, I'd like you to get something down from the attic for me."

"Attic?"

"Yes. Attic. You know, the space builders leave between a ceiling and a roof. The house is small, I grant you, but it's still big enough for an attic."

Gritting his teeth, he suffered through her sarcastic little lecture. "Sure. Whatever." The sooner he did as she asked, the sooner he could ask if they could sit down and talk for a while. He had some questions to ask her.

She took a flashlight out of a kitchen drawer and marched into the living room. Was it just his imagination, or did she actually have more pep in her step today? Standing in the small corridor facing the horrible pink-and-green-tiled bathroom and the two small bedrooms in either direction, Leota Reinhardt pointed up imperiously. She reminded him of the Statue of Liberty with a flashlight in her hand.

"There's the door." She gave him a disgusted look. "Well, for heaven's sake, why didn't you bring the chair? Did you think you could leap up there like Superman?"

He wanted to throw her up through the trapdoor to the attic. She could join the other bats that were probably hanging from the rafters. "I thought there might be a ladder," he said, striving for reason. He knew it was a stupid thing to say even as he said it. She jumped on it like a cat on a mouse.

"Oh. You want a ladder. Well, you might find one out in the storage shed back behind the garden gate. I used a ladder when I pruned the trees. If you want to use it, go get it. Might not be in the best of shape, but it'll make the climb easier, I suppose. If you can get it into the house."

"I'll get a chair," he said through gritted teeth.

Setting it carefully in the little hallway, he made sure it was on solid wood and not on the grated floor heater. It wobbled slightly when he stepped up. He opened the small trapdoor to the attic and stared into the darkness. It smelled of dust and old wood.

"There might be rats."

His heart jumped into his throat. "Have you heard any up here?" He looked down at her.

"I've heard things scurrying around up there at night," she said calmly. From where she was standing, she was safe from whatever rodent might come leaping from the dark corners. He was the one who would be toast. "But I wouldn't worry too much, Mr. Solsek. They're probably more scared of you than you are of them."

Was that a gleam in those eyes? Was she making fun of him? His temper rose another notch. Were *all* old people this difficult?

"And it could be my imagination," she said sweetly. "You know how an old lady gets when she's lived by herself for a long time. A little soft in the head. Isn't that right? But there are spiders. Of that, I'm sure."

So was he and that was exactly why he wasn't eager to go climbing into that infernal space. What else inhabited the darkness up here?

She rapped him on the thigh with the flashlight. "You'll need this if you plan on seeing anything."

"Thanks." Stewing, he snapped the light on and moved the beam around the small space. He would hardly call this an attic. He saw a stack of boxes, an old wooden cradle, a wooden apple crate with some empty mason jars, and an old birdcage big enough for something the size of a parakeet or a canary.

"I'd like the boxes brought down."

"All of them?"

"How many are there?"

"Three."

"Only three? I thought there were more. Turn around and look behind you."

Corban turned and felt a web across his face. He uttered a single, foul word and made a quick swipe across his face, hoping the eight-legged occupant hadn't gotten into his hair or fallen into his shirt. No, there it was, racing toward the boxes he was supposed to retrieve. He squashed it.

"What on earth are you doing up there?" Leota Reinhardt cried out from below.

"Killing a spider."

"How big is it? The size of my dining-room table? You're going to pound a hole right through my ceiling."

The flashlight flickered. He swore again as he shook it.

"Is that the only word you know, Mr. Solsek?"

"Sorry," he muttered, realizing what he had said.

"For someone who attends one of the best schools in the country, you have a very limited vocabulary."

"I apologize, Mrs. Reinhardt." Enough already!

"That's all very well and good, young man, but if you've broken my flashlight, you're going to buy me another one!"

The beam came back on. "It's still working."

"It had better be. Just get the boxes and get down from there before you wreck my house."

Corban made six trips up and down. He was panting and sweating worse than he had from the walk up the hill. His leg muscles were beginning to cramp before she finally said, "That's the one I want." It had better be. It was the last one.

He hated even to suggest it. "Do you want the other ones put back up there?"

She looked him over. "No. I think I'll look through them first. When I'm done, I'll just push them into the guest room."

"Good idea," he said, appreciating the reprieve.

"You can put them away again next Wednesday."

"You know what really ticks me off?" Corban told Ruth that evening. "I've been over there three times already, and I don't know bo-diddly about her."

"What's the problem? She won't answer your questions?"

"I haven't asked any! I'm so tired by the time she's finished using me for slave labor, I forget why I came."

"So, what are you going to do?" Ruth said, continuing her exercises. She was sitting on a mat with her legs in Chinese splits and touching her head to her knee. Bounce, bounce, bounce and then swing across to the other leg, touching her head to her knee. Bounce, bounce, bounce.

"I'm going to go back this weekend and tell her about my report."

"Do you think she'll cooperate?"

"If not, I won't waste any more time on her."

Over the next two days, Leota opened all six boxes. Each brought memories flooding back. Some were good; some were better off locked away in the recesses of her heart.

The first box was filled with Christmas decorations. It was a box with twelve dividers, designed for shipping bottles of wine. Over the next two hours, Leota removed the tissue paper from every carefully wrapped ornament and took out the shiny, beaded garland and strings of lights wound around tissue-paper rolls. She hadn't put up a Christmas tree in ten years. Christmas trees were expensive these days. One cost as much as her electric bill for a month! Even if she'd had the money, she'd had no way to bring one home.

The best Christmases had been the earliest ones, when she and Bernard were alone with their children in their own little apartment. What joy to see the bright-eyed wonder in the children's eyes as they stared at the tree. She remembered evenings when Eleanor would be snuggled in her lap and George cuddled against her as she read stories to them. Those were her most precious memories, for after moving into this house, there had been little time for anything but work. Mama Reinhardt had been quick to take responsibility for her grandchildren.

Leota carefully rewrapped each ornament and replaced it in the box. She tucked the garland and lights back in their slots and pushed the box to one side.

The second box was filled with old clothing, and each item made her remember why she had saved it. Her wedding suit; a beautiful, satiny robe Bernard had given her for their first Christmas together; a red dress she had purchased for her birthday while Bernard was in the army. He had sent the money and told her to buy something nice for herself. Mama Reinhardt had been scandalized that she had spent all the money on herself rather than use some of it for her children. Papa had come to her defense, but it hadn't taken the sting from Mama's opinion of her.

Running her hand over the dress now, Leota remembered how angry she had been. Mama Reinhardt had been so resentful of her. Nothing she could do in those days had been good enough. Papa said she didn't understand, and indeed, she hadn't. Leota had worn the dress the evening she bought it. She had been so angry, so defi-ant. When she came home, Mama had been waiting up. It hadn't been that late—only ten o'clock—but the children should have been in bed long ago. Mama told her that they had stayed up because they were worried about their mama. She said she told them there was no need to worry about someone so selfish. Their mother certainly knew how to take care of herself.

That had been the last straw. She had tucked her children into bed and then come back to have it out with Helene Reinhardt. But as it turned out, her mother-in-law was the one who poured out all her frustration and resentments before Leota even had the chance to open her mouth. Papa Reinhardt intervened and said enough to silence his wife.

Even then, Mama hadn't understood everything.

Leota hadn't thought the children knew anything about that night. Not until a few years ago, when Eleanor had told her she had discussed it with her psychologist. She had flung that bit of information like a grenade. It had exploded in the living room, its shrapnel wounding both of them terribly. Eleanor thought she knew everything. Oh, how wrong she was, but it would do no good to explain that she had heard only one side of things. What good would it do to remind Eleanor she had been five at the time and couldn't have understood all of what she heard, let alone the intensity of the anguish involved? Once Eleanor got an idea in her head, there was no changing it. She was like a pit bull, jaws clamped shut, shaking the life out of something.

"That was the night you hurt Grandma Helene so badly she never got over it," Eleanor had accused.

In a sense, it was true. Once Mama understood why Papa had invited Leota to live with them, she never got over it. Poor Papa. Even after that evening, he continued to walk down to Dimond Park and spend hours there, rain or shine. In the later years, Mama had gone with him.

Leota looked at the red dress that had caused such a ruckus. It was still brand-new. She had only worn it that one evening. After that night, she folded it up and put it away.

Next she pulled out an old wool shirt Bernard had worn. She had given it to him for his birthday the first year he had come home from the war. He had worn it for Sunday dinners. She could still see him sitting at the foot of the table, facing Papa. They loved and understood one another. It was Mama who had never completely understood. She didn't want to face the fullness of what life had dished out to them. Bitter herbs and sorrow. So much sorrow.

In the bottom of the box was Bernard's army uniform. Pinned to it were the medals he had received: the Silver Star, the Bronze Star, and the Purple Heart. He had told her to burn the uniform, but she had tucked it away. She had been proud of him. He had made his stand, not counting the cost. And, oh, what a cost it had been! The memory of what he had told her in a moment of weakness made her shudder. She had asked him once if he had talked about everything with Papa.

He said no. Yet over the years Leota had wondered if Papa hadn't known everything already.

Some things were better left unsaid.

As for Leota, she had chosen to close her mind to the things she couldn't change and move forward. There were too many good things in life to allow things beyond your control to destroy you.

If only Bernard had been able to think the same way.

The next two boxes were filled with children's toys, games, and books. She set the items out one by one: a cigar box full of cowboys and Indians; a denim sack of Lincoln Logs; a homemade doll in a flour-sack dress with embroidered hem and sleeves; an envelope full of jacks and the ball, a checkerboard and box of checkers; a tin of used watercolor paints; a can of used crayons; and a number of old, worn books—including George's favorite, *Kidnapped.* She had put these things away as George and Eleanor had outgrown them, hoping one day she would take them out once again for her grand-children to enjoy. She had imagined holding her grandchildren in her lap and reading to them.

She looked through the books, the first edition of *Curious George;* an old discolored booklet from Montgomery Wards entitled *Rudolph, the Red-Nosed Reindeer; Tales of Peter Rabbit;* a dog-eared collection of fairy tales; Robert Louis Stevenson's *A Child's Garden of Verses;* and *The Wizard of Oz.* Stacking them again, she placed them back in the box, once more packing away the lost hopes and broken dreams.

Doesn't every young wife imagine a life of fulfillment and joy? And then reality comes barging in, and she has to do what's neces-sary and right for the time. No one can see ahead to what comes from circumstances. Life is filled with trials and tribulations.

"Take heart, beloved. I have overcome the world."

I know, Lord, but You're up there in heaven, and I'm still down here. You lived thirty-three years on this earth. You know what it's like. And here I am, over eighty. I'm tired of it. The first twenty were wonderful, and I thank You. If I didn't have good times to remember, what state would I be in? But You must know, Lord, the last sixty-plus haven't been much fun.

She thought of the Old Testament people who had lived hundreds of years. What a daunting thought.

The fifth box held a jumble of personal mementos from Mama and Papa Reinhardt and the children. Mama had been good about helping Eleanor keep special mementos from her school years in the home-made scrapbooks. She used cardboard from the heavy boxes she got for free from the grocery store. Papa would cut them for her, and she and Eleanor would glue magazine pictures over them. The front of one was a collage of Hollywood movie stars. Inside it were essays Eleanor had written, party favors from school dances, programs from events she had attended, and school pictures. Another album was papered with pictures of places to see, such as the Grand Canyon, the California redwoods, Oregon beaches, the Rocky Mountains. Inside the scrap-book were mementos from George's school years.

There had once been pictures of relatives, but they were all gone now. The few pictures left were of the children during their school years. All the remaining pictures Leota had of her family were sitting on the mantel. She only had three pictures of Bernard. The one taken on their wedding day hung in her bedroom. The second was of her and Bernard with George as a toddler and Eleanor as a baby. The third was of Bernard in his uniform. It had been taken and sent home to her when he graduated from boot camp. She had given it to his parents, and they had displayed it proudly on the mantel until he came home and told them he wanted no reminders of the war. Mama had put it away after that. She didn't even hang it on the wall in the little apartment behind the carport. When Bernard died, Mama had placed the picture on top of her television set where she could see it every morning, noon, and night of her last ten years of life.

Tucked in the box among the collection of mementos was an old shoe box. Leota untied the pink ribbons and lifted the lid. Inside were letters from the old country that Mama Reinhardt had saved. They were written in German and beyond Leota's comprehension. Yet, when Mama Reinhardt had died, she couldn't bear to burn them or throw them away. If Mama Reinhardt had cherished them enough to save them all those years, who was she to discard them? They were neatly organized in small bundles and tied with slender pink silk ribbons. One bundle for each year, starting in 1924—the year after Mama and Papa Reinhardt had immigrated to the United States. There were no letters after 1940.

Leota wondered what the letters said. Perhaps she should destroy them, yet the thought bothered her. The shoe box of letters only took up a little space. Maybe someday a relative would learn to read German and decipher them. Then again, maybe that wouldn't be such a good idea.

She knew what Bernard would have wanted.

She weighed the box in her hands. *Lord, what should I do? Our family history may not be pristine, but it's ours nonetheless. What*

*risks are involved in saving them? Who might be hurt by what they
contain? And if I did burn them, how much of who we are would go
up in smoke?*

Sighing, Leota set the box aside. She didn't know what to do about
the letters. She would think about it for a few days and then make up
her mind; if she couldn't decide, it would be left to someone else to
figure out. Let Eleanor or George burn the past if they so chose.

Before she put the lid back, she noticed one long, brown envelope
tucked lengthwise in the box. She took it out and turned it over in
her hands. It had no markings on it and was unsealed. Opening it,
Leota took out some official-looking documents. Spreading them
out, she read them. Mama and Papa Reinhardt's naturalization
papers! Both had passed their test before a judge and become American citizens in May of 1934.

It was no accident that these papers were in with the letters from
Germany. "Oh, Mama, you were pulled between two worlds, weren't
you?" Yet, it was a message, too.

Leota folded the papers carefully and tucked them back into the
envelope. She wrote on top, "Naturalization Papers for Gottlieb and
Helene Reinhardt." She placed the envelope on top of the letters, so
anyone opening the box would see it first. Then she replaced the lid,
retied the ribbons, and set the box aside. She didn't need a few days
to decide after all. She would keep the letters.

The last box was filled with her own keepsakes. She had weeded
them out the last time she went through this box. It had been the
month after Mama Reinhardt had died and she had tucked some
of her things away in the attic. She held a bundle of letters from
Bernard while he was away at war, and took out another of cards he
had bought for her over the years for her birthday and Mother's
Day.

For the rest of the day, she read them. Some made her weep,
especially the ones from the war. Bernard had been so full of life
and fun when she met him, but the youthful optimism and enthusiasm had quickly given way to the realities of war. She read until
midnight, when she became too tired to continue, and left the
remaining letters and cards on the dining-room table to finish the
next day.

There were fifty-three letters in all. She could hear Bernard speaking
to her as she read them, the young Bernard, so full of passion and
hope for the future. She read every single one of the eighty-nine

greeting cards. Each had a note written at the bottom. *"All my love, always, Your Bernard . . . I couldn't have made it a day without you. . . . You are the light of my life. . . . Ever yours by the mercy of God . . . all my love . . . all my love . . . all my love . . ."*

Someday perhaps her children would read them. Perhaps then they would understand. These were her proof that Bernard Reinhardt had always loved her, even through the years of heavy drinking and the bouts of deep depression and silence.

Oh, Lord, in that day, let the accusations against me be put to rest. Let my children's eyes be opened so they will see and finally understand some small part of why things were the way they were. They don't have to know everything, Lord. Not so much that their lives will be shattered. Just let them know enough to put their sour feelings about me aside and count their blessings. I did the best I could with what I had.

Carefully stacking the letters in order, she bundled them again.

For now, she supposed Eleanor would continue to cling to her own view of the past. She would hold on to the tattered crazy quilt of experiences stitched together by her own fertile imagination. Bits and pieces of conversations, things she had been told or overheard—fragments of truth, but never the whole of it.

Stand back, Eleanor. Stand back and take a good look.

Leota stacked the letters, retied the ribbons, and went through the rest of the things in the last box. What other treasures might she find? She took out a beaded evening bag; a lace collar with pearl buttons; a prayer book with a worn, leather cover; and the portfolio of Great-Aunt Joyce's drawings. She would go through them later with Annie.

Near the bottom of the box, she found three white hankies wrapped in tissue paper. One was edged with lace, another with tatting, and the third was beautifully embroidered with forget-me-nots. Her mother's work. So fine. She had never been able to bring herself to blow her nose in one of them, the mere thought seeming almost sacrilegious. Leota thought about Annie as she took each hanky out and admired it. As an artist, her granddaughter would appreciate the time and effort that had gone into making these lovely things. It was right that she have them.

On the bottom of the box were two sets of clothing. One set had belonged to George when he was a toddler: a pair of worn jeans with holes in the knees; a blue, red, and green striped shirt; a cowboy hat; and a pair of boots. The other set belonged to Eleanor: a blue dress with tucks and gathers, pink ribbons stitched around the bodice, and white embroidered flowers on the collar and hem. Mama Reinhardt had made it.

Along with the dress was a pair of white, scuffed, Mary Jane shoes for a baby.

Leota held the items of clothing in her lap and wept.

6

LEOTA PEERED THROUGH THE PEEPHOLE IN THE FRONT DOOR and saw Corban Solsek standing on her front porch. Why was he back? Was it Wednesday already? Couldn't be. Annie said she was coming for another visit on Monday. Her classes were on Tuesdays and Thursday and Friday evenings.

She opened the door and noticed the spiral notebook he was holding. "You're a few days early, aren't you?"

"I wanted to talk with you, Mrs. Reinhardt. If you have a few minutes."

"I think I have a few to spare." She opened the door for him. "Well, come on in," she said when he hesitated. She could tell how much he was looking forward to this visit. His mouth was a hard, flat line. He didn't look nervous; he looked annoyed. "Get it off your chest, whatever it is." He was probably going to tell her she was an old coot and he didn't have time for her folderol. A pity. He might have learned something from her if he'd been willing. Then again, she had to admit she might have learned something from him as well if he didn't irritate her so much with his know-it-all attitude. Every time she looked at his sanctimonious face, she wanted to box his ears.

"Can we sit down?" he said when he was standing in the living room.

Apparently whatever was on his mind wasn't going to take just a minute or two to sort out. She looked at the notebook again. "Are you planning to take notes?"

"If you don't mind."

"What if I said I did?"

His jaw clenched and unclenched. "I wouldn't do it."

"No. I imagine you'd wait until you got back to wherever it is you live and then write it all down the way you want it to be."

His eyes darkened. "Look, you've made it more than clear you don't like me. I've never been able to figure out what's the problem."

"Haven't you? I'll give you a hint. You have the manners of a goat in a produce market."

He stared at her, mouth agape. "I wouldn't call *you* Miss Manners."

Leota laughed. She closed the front door and looked at him. She laughed some more.

"What's so funny?"

The poor boy was practically snarling. She continued to chortle as she walked past him to her chair and sat down. Pulling a Kleenex from its box, she wiped her eyes. "Well, now, I'd say that's the first honest thing you've said to me since you darkened my doorstep."

Corban stared at the woman, not knowing what to say.

"At least you have the good graces to blush," she said, merciless.

He shook his head and sat on the edge of the sofa. "Maybe it would help if I told you a little about myself."

"It'd be better if you told me what you wanted in the first place."

He felt oddly ashamed, but what for? He was trying to help the elderly, wasn't he? He frowned slightly, unable to hold her gaze. Her calm troubled him. She was looking at him, and he had the uncomfortable feeling she was seeing deeper into him than anyone ever had, seeing things even he wasn't aware of.

"Get to the point, Mr. Solsek."

"I'm a student at UC Berkeley. I'm working on a term paper for a sociology class. I need a case study."

"Just one?"

He nodded. "My professor's made it a requirement."

"What's the subject of your paper?"

"It's on some ideas I have about caring for the increased number of elderly in our nation."

"Extermination, perhaps?"

He tried not to be insulted. She sure knew how to push his buttons.

"All right." She smiled wryly. "So, what is this idea of yours?"

"An expansion of residential-care facilities in high-density popula-tion areas. The idea is twofold: care for the elderly and renewed life to the inner core of our cities. The government could subsidize the takeover of some of the old office buildings and hotels in the inner cities, refurbish them and convert them into residential-care facili-ties. Occupants would pay a lump sum in order to live at the care facility for the rest of their lives. One floor could be a medical facil-ity. Another could be for recreational activity. Of course, this is just a quick summary. There would be all kinds of services offered under this kind of system."

He looked at her again, watching, hoping for some sign of affirma-tion. What he got was a deadpan stare.

Leota leaned back, all humor gone. How could someone bright enough to get into Berkeley be so naïve? "Would occupants have visitation rights?"

His mouth flattened. "I'm not designing a prison system, Mrs. Reinhardt. Of course, visitors would be welcome. There'd be guest accommodations available for a limited time and for a small fee."

"What if someone wanted to move out of the facility?"

"It'd be unlikely anyone would want to leave."

"Especially if the initial investment was nonrefundable. Or used up." Or if the attendants put sedatives in the food!

He frowned. "The point is all occupants would be given the high-est level of care during the latter part of their lives. They would have a safe environment, the security of good care, comfortable surround-ings, communal interaction. Many don't have that now."

"Someone like me, you mean. Someone in an inner-city neighbor-hood, living on social security. Someone old, with declining health and little, if any, family support."

Corban sat back on the sofa and smiled. "Yes, someone like you."

"How old is your professor, Mr. Solsek?"

"Why are you asking?"

"I think he has something else in mind for you to learn. If I could hazard a guess, I would say he's in his sixties."

"Close, I guess. Why?"

"The poor fellow is looking ahead to retirement and his declining years. He's probably horrified at the thought of someone like you deciding what will happen to him."

Corban's face went red; his eyes blazed with temper. "That's a cheap shot! I'm wasting my time here. What do you know about the way things are now? You're locked up in this decaying house all day watching game shows and *Brady Bunch* reruns! The most fun you have is tormenting the checkers at the supermarket." He stood up, tucked his spiral notebook under his arm, and headed for the door.

"Where *are* you going?"

"I'm leaving. What does it look like? I've wasted three weeks coming over here, hoping to get to know you. I'll call Nancy and tell her to find you another volunteer."

"Well, now, *there's* an attitude to open minds and hearts."

The fire in his eyes died, and Leota almost felt sorry for him. Almost.

"I've got eight weeks to write this report, Mrs. Reinhardt." He sounded weary and depressed. "I need someone who's willing to give and take."

She knew what part of that he thought she was. He was blind as a mole in a tunnel. And troubled about it. That was a good sign. Was his despair merely because of his report, or was there more going on in his life than a sociology class? Maybe he didn't even know what was bothering him. He was barely out of adolescence. How could he? "If you'll sit, I'll give my opinion on what you've told me so far."

He frowned, looking decidedly wary. "I can guess."

When she didn't say anything, he slowly returned to the sofa and sat. "Okay. Go ahead."

He had all the enthusiasm of a man with an apple on his head with her in possession of the bow and arrows. "I'm speaking my opinion now. It can't be taken as gospel on the general geriatric population, you know."

He nodded, grim-faced.

"I would find it daunting to live in a building inhabited solely by old folks."

He leaned forward. "Not everyone in the building would be old, Mrs. Reinhardt. There would be nurses and doctors, maids and cooks, recreation directors—"

She held up her hand to stop the flow. "Let's put it this way, Mr. Solsek. I would find it daunting if the only young people I ever saw were those who were paid by the government to attend to my needs."

He looked confused. "I'll leave you to think about that one. Before you leave, I have a question for you, and I don't want an answer today. I want you to think about it and tell me on Wednesday. That is, if you decide to come back."

"Go ahead," he said cautiously.

"Why do you want to house old people like me in a government-funded facility and keep us away from the rest of society?"

"*Partially* funded, Mrs.—"

"Wednesday, Mr. Solsek. *Think* about it."

Corban stood up slowly. Leota saw the struggle going on in his face. No less a struggle than what was going on inside herself at that moment. His ideas troubled her. She recognized the foundation he was building from. Clearly, he didn't. Telling him would do no good. He wouldn't believe it if she did. Could she make him see it for himself? Probably not. He was far too sure of himself. The young were always on fire to make a better world.

Oh, God, is this the way it starts?

"I'll make a deal with you," she said. "If you're willing to give me an honest answer on Wednesday, I'll answer whatever questions you intended to ask me the first day you came here."

Corban studied her. He didn't look happy with her proposition. Maybe he thought she just wanted to keep him coming around for her convenience. Of course, there was something to that.

"I haven't got a lot of time to waste, Mrs. Reinhardt."

"Neither have I, Mr. Solsek." She had never suffered fools gladly, but she felt an inner nudging where this one was concerned. How much did he know about the way the world really was? Maybe it was compassion that drove him. All the more reason to light the lamps and let some light shine into that dark mind of his. A little at a time so he wouldn't be blinded by it.

And it's up to You anyway, isn't it, Lord?

Corban let out his breath slowly and rose. Calmly, this time. Tucking his spiral notebook under his arm again, he went to the door and opened it. Pausing, he looked back at her. "I'll think it over and talk to you on Wednesday."

"God willing, I'll still be here."

Leota worried all day Sunday. Despite what her granddaughter had said, Leota didn't think Annie was coming back.

Over the years, she had invited Eleanor numerous times to Thanksgiving dinner, Christmas, Easter, her birthday. Sometimes Eleanor would say that sounded nice and she'd bring the family; then she'd call later and say she couldn't make it after all. She always had a reason:

One of the children was sick; her husband had to work; unexpected friends had called and would be arriving for the weekend. The underlying message had always been loud as a trumpet: *You weren't there for me, so why should I be there for you?* When Eleanor did come, she spent the entire time looking for anything she could seize upon to dredge up the past and point out yet again her mother's many faults.

Lord, I know I wasn't perfect, but I tried so hard.

Time hadn't helped Eleanor see the truth about anything. Leota had even hoped the arrival of children might open Eleanor's eyes so she could see the wider scope of how life is less than perfect. No such luck. Eleanor was a master at controlling her life and those of her loved ones. She made sure she was always home when the children were. She made sure they had everything they needed. No thrift-store clothing for *her* children. Macy's and Capwell's. No day-old bread. Three square meals a day, apportioned so that there wouldn't be weight or skin problems. No home remedies when tummy aches hit. Only a medical doctor would do, and a professional counselor if things became difficult emotionally.

Leota wanted desperately to believe all the lame excuses. She wanted to ignore the slights and pretend she hadn't heard the words designed to cut. The few times she had attempted to defend herself, Eleanor had left without hearing her out.

Leota had finally wearied of it. She hadn't called Eleanor once last year. She had received four perfunctory calls: one for Christmas, one for Easter, one for her birthday, and one for Thanksgiving. Mother's Day came and went without a card or call.

A card had come each holiday from her son. "Love, George and Jeanne"—it was Jeanne who signed the cards and addressed them. Those few times Leota saw George, there was no bitterness in his attitude. He was just caught in his own world and his own worries.

He was more like Bernard than he would ever realize.

Lord, I have to believe or I'll know there's no hope of reconciliation. I've dreamed for so long of a close relationship with my children and grandchildren, but did Annie come and just stir up hope? It hurts. I just keep thinking about all the lost years.

Would Annie call and say she was sorry but she wouldn't be coming? Young people had such busy lives these days. Places to go. Things to see. Interesting people to meet. Why would a beautiful eighteen-year-old girl want to spend time with an old woman?

Leota tried to read her Bible to take her mind off her worries, but she couldn't concentrate. The telephone rang once at six o'clock. The sound always startled her. She received so few calls. This time the ringing of the telephone filled her with a sense of dread and despair as never before. She let it ring four times before she answered, and it was several seconds before she realized the voice on the telephone wasn't her granddaughter but some saleswoman. She was so relieved, she listened. Usually, she hung up before they finished the first sentence of their spiel. This evening, she couldn't stop thinking about Annie. What if her granddaughter had to make a living doing telephone solicitations?

When the woman finally ran down on her memorized sales pitch, given in double time, and asked whether she was interested in this wonderful offer, Leota said, "You did that very nicely, dear, but I'm an old lady living on social security. I don't even have a CD player."

"Oh." She sighed. "I'm sorry I took up your time, ma'am."

"I hope you'll have more luck with your next call."

"Thank you, ma'am." The poor girl sounded almost teary. "You know, you're the first person tonight who's been polite to me."

"Don't give me too much credit, dear. I usually hang up."

The saleswoman gave a soft laugh. "Most people do. I've had ten people hang up so hard they left my ear ringing, and several others who've cussed me out. Comes with the territory. Anyway, thanks for listening, ma'am. I hope you have a pleasant evening."

"I hope you find another job."

The woman laughed. "So do I!"

Leota hung up gently and let out her breath. She read her Bible for another half an hour before putting it aside and giving up on it. She knew what it said, but it was hard to dwell on the good sometimes. She turned on the television, checked every channel, and shut it off.

What was she going to do with all those Toll House cookies if Annie didn't come? She had baked three dozen. They tasted pretty good, too. She had tried one just to make sure she hadn't botched the recipe. After all, it had been three years since she last baked them.

The telephone rang again at seven-thirty. She let it ring and ring before answering, sensing this time it would be Annie.

"Grandma Leota? I hope I didn't wake you."

"I don't usually go to bed until after the ten o'clock news."

"Oh. Good. What time do you get up?"

Leota had awakened at five-thirty every morning for years. She had hoped to get over the habit, but years of rising early to have enough time to get ready and catch a bus to work had set a routine. Her alarm clock had broken years ago, but her eyes still popped open at the same time every day. Her routine never varied. Awake at five-thirty, up at six, take a bath, get dressed, fix breakfast and sit down to read her Bible, read the newspaper and do her crossword puzzle for the day. Always in that order. Since having to give up her gardening, Leota found that the rest of her day was an agony of boredom.

I'm waiting to die, Lord. That's all I'm doing.

"Grandma?"

"I'm dressed and about by seven-thirty."

"Oh. Good. Would it be all right if I came earlier?"

"Earlier?"

"Well, I thought about coming over around the same time I did before, around one, but I'd rather come in the morning and stay for the day. Would that be all right? I'll bring lunch."

Leota didn't know what to say. All day? *Oh, my, all day!*

"Grandma? If you'd rather I waited until later, it's all right."

"Oh, no. The earlier, the better. And you don't have to bring anything. Just yourself."

Annie gave a soft laugh filled with apparent relief. "I'm so glad, Grandma Leota. I've been looking forward to this for days."

Leota put her hand against her heart. *Oh, my dear, I've been looking forward to this for years!* "I made cookies."

"Did you?" Annie's voice sounded husky when she continued. "How long since you've had Chinese food, Grandma Leota?"

"Oh, I don't know. Years and years."

"There's a great deli on the corner not far from us, and they have the best Chinese food in the world. I'll bring lunch. I promise, you'll love it." She sounded so excited. "I'll see you tomorrow morning."

Leota sat for a long time in her chair, relishing the feelings. Then the little worries started up again. What if Annie got into an accident? What if she got mugged going to the deli? What if . . .

Oh, Lord, keep her safe. I hear San Francisco is like Sodom and Gomorrah these days. It's not the same city it used to be when Cosma and I would have to dress up to go there. We even wore hats and gloves. From what she'd heard at the grocery store, the traffic was awful these days. Drug addicts were everywhere, looking for easy prey to steal money. Leota frowned. Was it just yesterday she'd read that there were fourteen thousand homeless in San Francisco, and many were addicts of one sort or another? *God, please, keep Annie safe. Don't let any harm come to her. Put angels around her.*

When she finally went to bed at eleven o'clock, she lay awake another hour or more, her mind whirring with all the dire possibilities of what could happen to a beautiful girl in an evil world.

Annie arrived safely at nine. She was wearing jeans and a white T-shirt with a tan jacket. Her hair was loose and curly, framing her pretty face and flowing over her shoulders and down her back. Leota thought she was the most charming girl she had ever seen. Prettier by far than any of those anorexic models on the covers of magazines.

"I hope you haven't eaten yet," Annie said as she came in, two bags in her hands and her purse looped over her shoulder. "I couldn't resist the Danish rolls."

Leota had been too worried to eat breakfast. She'd kept looking at the clock, wondering if Annie was all right. "Did you have any problems getting here?"

"None at all. Traffic was going the other direction. It was clear sailing through San Francisco and across the bridge, and you're just a hop-skip off the freeway. Shall I put the Chinese food in the fridge?"

"Put it anywhere you want." The house felt different with Annie here. She filled it with life. "Would you like some coffee to go with the rolls?" Leota said, following at her slower pace.

Annie put the bag of Chinese food in the old refrigerator and closed the door. "That would be perfect."

"Plain or fancy?" Leota smiled, filled with the assurance that she was stocked for any possibility. Whatever her granddaughter wanted, she had.

"Whatever you're having, Grandma."

Leota was dismayed by her lack of interest in libation. She thought of the outrageous price of that fancy coffee—and suddenly wanted to tell Annie how much it cost for no other reason than to let her know how much this visit meant. However, she thought better of saying anything. She hardly knew her granddaughter. What if Annie misunderstood and was offended?

Instead, she said, "How has your week gone?" She was eager for any information.

Annie told her about her two classes, one in art history and the other in sketching. Both sounded interesting, as well as time-consuming. Lots of reading for one and projects for the other, but Annie seemed excited about all of it. Leota sat, enchanted, at the kitchen table, just listening to her talk. The room fairly hummed with the girl's youthful enthusiasm. Leota decided that Annie was a levelheaded young lady who intended to make the most of life. How refreshing! Instead of seeing the foibles of those she served at the restaurant as faults, she found everything about her customers interesting. No doubt they liked her equally as well. How could they not?

Leota rose once to spoon the sweetened powdered coffee into the cups she had taken from the china hutch yesterday. She poured hot water; then, with the coffee ready, she stood undecided. Perhaps it would be more polite to serve Annie elsewhere than in her small, cluttered kitchen.

"Would you like to have the coffee and rolls in the dining room?"

"Could we just stay here?" Annie's smile was sweet. "It's so nice to look out at the garden."

Leota's defenses came down completely. "I like it in here, too. I always have preferred this room to the front." She folded up the newspaper and set it aside. So what if it was a little untidy? Annie didn't seem to mind. "Though it's been a bit depressing the past few years." She put the two cups on the table.

"Why, Grandma?"

"I can't work in the garden anymore. I haven't the strength to do the work. There's a lot to properly keeping up a garden." Remembering the Danish rolls, she added two of the plates Cosma had given her years ago. They were hand painted with gold rims and so lovely she had never dared use them. Just the thought of breaking one kept her from taking the risk. She had few precious things, even fewer from loved ones. Well, it was high time she used them. Though Annie didn't know it, this was a celebration day. Only the best would do, and if anything was broken, so be it. What good would pretty china do when the owner was dead and buried?

"These plates are beautiful, Grandma."

"A friend gave them to me years ago. She brought them back from one of her trips. France, I think." She told Annie about Cosma. They sat at the tiny kitchen table sipping coffee and eating sweet rolls.

As Annie sat in the little kitchen, she found herself thinking about her mother's hands as she looked at her grandmother's. Her mother kept her nails perfectly manicured, often going to the salon to have them tipped with acrylics and painted some pretty shade. Grandma Leota's nails were neatly trimmed and natural. Her fingers were slender and graceful despite the effects of arthritis. She still wore a wedding ring. It was a simple gold band, worn so long it appeared to be part of her finger.

"Mom doesn't like gardening." Annie sighed. "She likes having a beautiful yard, but she prefers to hire someone to look after it." Marvin Tikado's gardening service came once a week to mow the lawn around the house, trim the bushes, and make sure there were no weeds anywhere. Periodically he replanted new border flowers along the cobblestone walk to the front door.

"I loved gardening," Grandma Leota said, gazing out at the back. "I spent hours out there." It had been a place of refuge. She had started when she first moved into this house with Mama Reinhardt. Mama didn't want her in the kitchen, and she hadn't felt comfortable sitting in the living room with Papa Reinhardt, reading the paper or some book. So she had taken on the responsibility of the Victory garden. She had gleaned knowledge from neighbors who would give her cuttings to start in jars or seeds to start in egg cartons. She had loved watching things grow and had been surprised and delighted to find she had a green thumb.

"Now, you can't tell that anyone ever spent time out there." Enough of that, Leota told herself. The last thing a young person wanted was to visit an old person who did nothing but complain. "I found Great-Aunt Joyce's drawings. Some of them are just advertisements . . ."

They went into the front room where Leota had left the portfolio on the dining-room table. Annie untied it carefully and opened it. The first picture was an advertisement of a coffee grinder. There was another of a cast-iron woodstove for the kitchen. Another was of a farm wagon, still another of some kind of farm machinery. There were advertisements of lawn chairs and china cabinets, tooling and buggies, lanterns and sleds. Pretty soon the table was covered with pen-and-ink drawings on paper yellowed by aging.

"These are wonderful!" Annie said, looking from an advertisement of a man's watch with its chain to a book cover. *Fairy Tales and Funny Frolics* proclaimed the sheet with a girl sitting beneath a gnarled tree trunk watching a grasshopper dressed in a tuxedo and holding a lantern. Setting it aside, Annie lifted another drawing of swirling leaves and flowers and shapes with *Menu* printed in black, Gothic letters.

"Look at these beautiful borders, Grandma Leota," Annie said, admiring several large sheets that had samples ranging from grape leaves and grapes to intricate Celtic knots and Moorish designs. One looked like latticework with climbing roses. One sheet was a drawing of a lady in Victorian dress, standing amidst sunflowers. The picture was bordered by trumpet vines and flowers with *Sensible Holiday Gifts* printed almost primly beneath. Annie studied a page with the letter *H* in all sorts of styles, from the simplest block to the most ornate style.

There was an advertisement of a rocking chair with elaborate arms, a wooden frame, and cushions that looked like tapestry. Great-Aunt Joyce had experimented with people as well, doing numerous drawings of men and women wearing everything from work clothes to wedding attire.

"I love this one." Annie held up an ink drawing of a woman sitting on a piano stool. She was wearing a high-waisted, floor-length dress with puffed sleeves. Her back was turned so that you could see the elegant curve of her neck and her hair drawn up into a bun. Soft curls escaped at her temple. Her hands were poised as though she were about to play a piano that was not there.

There were sheets of animals. One page was a study of a work-horse wearing blinders—front right, front left, straight on. Another was a study of a milk cow—standing, walking, grazing. Annie lifted and observed page after page of machinery.

"Her bread and butter, I think," Leota said, thinking they were probably not very interesting. But Annie's eyes widened.

"They're amazing, Grandma. Look at the detail! Every nut and bolt. I could never draw like this."

"Never say never."

"Oh, my . . ." Annie said, lifting one from the dozens. It was a pen-and-ink drawing of a flowered rug, so detailed it looked like a black-and-white photograph.

"Her real interest comes through in the pictures toward the back." Leota sat at the end of the table and watched her granddaughter's face. Annie loved everything she was seeing. Her pleasure gave Leota pleasure as well.

Annie lifted the thin sheets of paper carefully and found page after page of buildings: a simple country church, a cathedral, a three-story Victorian house with veranda, a four-story brick office build-ing, a tree-lined street with quaint shops, an adobe mission, a Queen Anne cottage with rose arbor and picket fence, a log cabin, a lean-to in the redwoods with a fire blazing. All in pen and ink. All drawn with the finest details. Roses on a lattice. An upstairs stained-glass window. A bird on the porch rail. The cross on the steeple.

"Mother never mentioned Great-Aunt Joyce at all," Annie said.

"Eleanor probably—" She stopped and then corrected herself.

"Your mother probably didn't know anything about her. We never talked about my side of the family."

Annie glanced up in surprise. "Why not?"

Leota shrugged.

"Were you close to your mother, Grandma Leota?"

She thought it a strange question. Close in terms of proximity or affinity? What did it matter? "My mother died when I was twelve. I remember very little about her other than she was ill for a long time."

"What about your father?"

"I didn't see very much of him. He was in the merchant marines."

Annie forgot all about the drawings. "What happened to you after your mother died? Where did you go? Did you have any brothers or sisters? Any relations?"

The questions came so quickly, Leota didn't know where to start. Or whether to talk about it at all. She thought for a moment.

Annie blushed, looking uncomfortable for the first time since her arrival. "I'm sorry, Grandma. I didn't mean it to sound like an interrogation. It's just that I know so little about you."

"I don't wonder," Leota said sadly, then added quickly, "but there's not much to tell. I had an older sister. She died of consumption in her early twenties. And I had a brother who went to sea like my father. He was fifteen when he left. I never heard from him after that." She frowned slightly. "Strange. I haven't thought about him in so many years . . ."

"What happened when your mother died?"

"One of the ladies from the church took me in. Her name was Miss Mary O'Leary. Irish as Irish comes." She gave a soft laugh, closing her eyes as the memories surged sweet. "Oh, I haven't thought about her in years."

"Were you happy with her?"

"Oh, yes. She was very robust, very healthy. She loved to take long hikes in the hills on Saturdays. I think she did it at times to wear me out. She kept me too tired to get into mischief."

Annie laughed. "Were you prone to it?"

"On occasion. I pulled a few pranks in my day. Miss O'Leary taught at the high school. She made sure I settled down enough to complete my education. I did very well under her tutelage." She smiled. "Or else."

"Did you go to college?"

"Oh, mercy, no. There was no money for a venture like that, and very few women went to college in those days anyway."

"Do you wish you could've gone?"

Leota felt pulled back to those days when her future had stretched out like dawn on the horizon. Life was full of possibilities. It was an unfolding adventure, something new around every bend in the road. "I wished for many things. I wished for more education. I wished for home and family. I wished for travel." She smiled at Annie. "Wishing doesn't cost anything."

"Do you still wish for things?"

"Not as much. What I wish for now is far different than what I wished for when I was young." Reconciliation. *Oh, yes, Lord, I wish for that with all my heart.* Yet, Leota knew she might as well be wishing for the moon where Eleanor was concerned. Reconciliation wasn't in her daughter's vocabulary. She had all the stubborn pride of her German ancestry. God help her.

Leota didn't want to follow those thoughts further and decided to change direction again. "Maybe you have Great-Aunt Joyce's talent."

"I can only dream of such a thing." Annie gazed at the drawings she had spread across the table. "They're so good."

"Of course, they are. These are the drawings she kept in her portfolio. These are the best of her work, probably the pictures she was most proud of doing. Keep in mind there's no way of knowing how many she threw away. She must have had years of practice."

Annie smiled at her. "I hadn't thought about that."

"People don't usually think about those things. They look at a van Gogh and stand in awe. Most people never know about the years and years of painting he did, and that he never sold a single painting while he lived. They read about the millions a museum will pay for one of his paintings, and yet van Gogh died a poor man."

"You know some art history."

Leota chuckled softly. "I know a little about a lot of things." She tapped a drawing. "Besides that, Annie, this may not even be the kind of artwork you'll do."

Annie looked dejected. "I have no idea what kind of work I'll do."

"Why should you know? You're only eighteen."

"I should have some idea."

"Well, you do. You're going to study art. You've just started down that road. Enjoy the landscape while you're going. The signposts will come soon enough."

They talked about the pictures. Leota favored the drawings of people, while Annie was fascinated by the elaborate designs and borders. She said she wanted to sketch them so that she could experiment with colors later. She said she could imagine swirls of vibrant colors, reds flowing into oranges and yellows, deep indigo blues to purple and lavenders streaked with sparks of gold.

Leota watched her face and saw the wonder there. *Oh, she's so young, Lord. Don't let life stamp out that light in her eyes.*

"You can tell a lot about a person by what they draw," Annie said. "She loved people and architecture."

"What would you draw?"

"Flowers." Annie smiled up at her. "I'd love to paint an English garden someday."

Leota sighed, stricken with regret. No wonder Annie remembered the backyard.

"What's the matter, Grandma? Did I say something wrong?"

"Not at all. It's just that I wish you'd seen the garden a few years ago when it was all I had hoped it would be." Afraid her granddaughter would see the sheen of tears building, she rose stiffly and headed for the kitchen. "I'll warm up our lunch."

They ate Chinese food together at the kitchen table, with the sounds of children playing in the backyard next door. Leota thought about the swallow the children had buried and the flower plucked between the slats of her fence. Maybe Annie would come and put a flower on her grave. There was some solace in that thought, for it carried the hope that someone would care when she passed on.

Annie picked at her food and gazed out at the backyard. Leota wished she hadn't said anything about the garden. Yet she couldn't help thinking about how Annie would have loved it a few years ago when it had been in its glory. Everything had come together in a blaze of color that was a wonder to behold. But Leota had been the only one there to enjoy it.

Was that when she lost her desire to work in the sunshine? Had it been the grief that no one cared enough to come and see the work she had done and how it had turned out? It was the last Easter she had invited her children to come for dinner. It was the last time they had told her they had other plans.

The sorrow came up inside her, and it took all her determination to press it down again where it wouldn't break through and show. If it did, Annie might never come back. Why would she want to spend time with a maudlin old woman who couldn't let go of the hurts of the past?

"Mother never let me work in the garden," Annie was saying. "She didn't want me interfering with Mr. Tikado's work. She said he had planned everything to have a certain effect and planting other things would only spoil it. And with piano lessons and gymnastics and school, I really didn't have much time left over." She turned her gaze from the window.

Leota looked into those clear, blue eyes and saw the hurt in them. "I've spoiled your visit. I'm sorry, dear." What more could she say?

Annie's eyes filled with tears. "You didn't spoil anything, Grandma. I was just thinking of all the times we could have come to see you and didn't. It wasn't right. It *isn't* right. Mother is . . ." She pressed her lips together and looked away again. Leota saw her swallow and felt the girl's pain as though it was her own. "So unforgiving," Annie said finally.

Leota caught a glimpse of Annie's fears. She wanted to be able to reassure her that Eleanor would forgive her for her rebellion, but she couldn't be sure. She didn't want to offer false hopes to this hurting child. Eleanor had proven intractable where her mother was concerned. Might she be the same way with her own daughter? What a terrible loss that would be.

"I wish I understood my mother."

And I, my daughter.

Annie put trembling hands around the coffee cup and stared into it for a moment. When she raised her head, Leota saw the desperate unhappiness there. Had she been covering it up for her sake? "I need to know," Annie said softly. "What does Mother hold against you?"

Leota sighed. "I've thought that over for years, Annie. She's always said I didn't care about her or her brother and that I was a bad mother."

"Did . . . did you care?"

Annie spoke so tentatively, Leota pitied her more than she pitied herself. "I cared very much, and I was the best mother I could be under the circumstances."

"What circumstances, Grandma?"

"What life hands you." She didn't want to talk about it. She couldn't give all the details without putting others in a bad light. And she didn't want to be put in the position of defending herself against her own daughter. What good would that do? It would only put Annie in the middle of something she couldn't fully understand. It might make Annie feel ashamed, too. There were so many things that came into it, things Leota had never told Eleanor. Some things were best left unspoken.

Weren't they?

If only Mama Reinhardt had known everything from the beginning, then things might have worked out differently. She hadn't known, and her careless words had cost so dearly. Leota thought of the poor old woman in her later years, wanting to make up for earlier mistakes and knowing it was too late. The darkness had triumphed, it seemed, and no amount of light had been able to dispel it. So far.

"*I didn't know. He didn't tell me . . .*"

"*I know, Mama. And I couldn't. It's done now. Let's put it behind us.*"

This is the way it would always be. She had accepted that.

Eleanor was descended from strong German stock. Her blood was a blessing and a curse. *Oh, God, why couldn't her strength have been channeled elsewhere than into her resentments and endless disappointments?* What would it take for Eleanor to see the truth—all of it—and finally purge herself of bitterness? Leota was weary of the battle. Too much time had passed for things to be undone and put to rights.

Leota had almost given up hope of anything changing until Annie came. But she couldn't burden her granddaughter with her dreams. She had the hope of her salvation and that was enough. Death would come, and the pain would stop.

Annie reached over the table and took her hands, startling her from her grim reverie. "What if we brought it back?"

"Brought what back?" Leota's thoughts were stumbling over the past, searching for other avenues she might have taken. Why? It was too late. You couldn't relive your life or change the course of it.

"The garden, Grandma. What if we worked together and made the garden what it was?"

Leota's heart leaped, but only for a moment. It was sweet of Annie to suggest it, but the girl had no idea what she was saying. Leota had been cast out of the garden five years ago by old age. Her joints had ached horribly from arthritis. She had become dizzy in the warmth of the afternoon sun. On fall days, even two sweaters hadn't been enough to ward off the chill that seemed to set into her bones. She had finally come into the house one day, taken off her work gloves, and thrown them away. What was the point of all that toil when she was the only one around to see the result. And it made her sick anyway . . .

No, it was too late. She shook her head at the impossibility of the task. Annie couldn't know. She couldn't even guess the work that went into making a garden flourish.

And yet . . .

Hadn't that been her dream over the years? To work in the garden with her children and grandchildren?

No, she must be sensible. It was only kindness that had made Annie offer. "I'm too old." She couldn't climb a ladder to prune trees or turn the soil. She couldn't work on her knees anymore. If she got down on them, she'd never get up again.

"You have the knowledge, Grandma, and I have the strength. You could tell me what to do."

She saw the eagerness in Annie's eyes, an eagerness no doubt born of ignorance. "It takes *time,* Annie. You have school and work and friends. You have your own life."

"I want to spend time with you."

"You're welcome here anytime, dear. Don't think for a minute you have to work to be welcome."

Annie searched her eyes. "Couldn't we try, Grandma?"

"Well, I don't . . ."

"Please."

Leota weakened. She looked out the window, remembering how the garden had once looked. Then her vision cleared and she saw all that needed to be done. "Not today," she said finally, weary and depressed. "We'll talk about it next time."

Next time Annie would have had time to think things over more carefully and realize she had better things to do.

7

"Where did you say Anne was?" Nora's hand gripped the phone tightly, her face going hot.

"She's gone to visit with her grandmother in Oakland," Susan repeated.

The adrenaline of anger pumped through Nora's veins. Her daughter wouldn't do this to her. She couldn't. Susan Carter was lying. She had to be. Anne-Lynn wouldn't dare betray her like this.

"Mrs. Gaines?"

"You must have misunderstood, Susan."

"Leota Reinhardt. Isn't that her grandmother's name?"

Nora's heart pounded.

"Would you like to leave a message, Mrs. Gaines?"

"Did Anne-Lynn say what time she would return?" Her hand gripped the phone so hard her fingers hurt. She had no intention of leaving a message with Susan Carter. It was sure to be forgotten or given incorrectly.

"Later this afternoon."

"Could you be more specific, Susan?"

"No, ma'am. I'm sorry. I can't." She sounded anything but sorry.

"But I can tell you Annie and I are both on the same schedule at the restaurant this week. I'm sure she will be home in time to get ready for work."

Nora fumed. How dare the cheap little no-account call some hole-in-the-wall flat Annie's *home*. Nora could hear someone talking in the background! "You have a male visitor." Some hooligan, probably on drugs. Any self-respecting man would be working at this time of day. Or going to college.

"There's no one in my apartment, Mrs. Gaines. I'm all by myself."

"You needn't lie, Susan. I can hear him."

"What if I told you he wasn't a man?"

"A television, I assume."

"We don't own one."

Cheeky girl. Nora had never liked her. She liked her even less now that her daughter was living with her. She could just imagine the sort of influence Susan Carter was going to be on Anne. The man continued talking in the background, and what he said raised the hair on the back of Nora's neck. "What's he telling you? To call the police? What's going on, Susan?"

"Oh, nothing much. He's talking about another mugging, I suppose," Susan said with airy indifference.

"He's telling you to dial 911!"

"Good old Barnaby. Always the one to overreact."

"I knew there'd be trouble if my daughter lived with you."

"I'll tell Annie you called, Mrs. Gaines."

The sharp click in her ear made Nora wince. Furious, Nora grabbed her personal directory, slapped through the pages until she found the number she needed, and punched the numbers. The telephone rang four times before she heard an answering-machine message. "This is the Carters' residence." The calm, sweet voice made Nora feel she was listening to fingernails raking down a blackboard. "We're sorry, but we can't come to the telephone right now. Please leave a message at the sound of the beep."

"This is Nora Gaines. I suggest you look into what's going on in your daughter's apartment before she gets *arrested* for indecent behavior! One of the men she's entertaining was screaming for 911 when I called." She slammed the telephone down and stood up. She was so angry she was shaking.

How could Anne-Lynn do this to her? Nora was meeting two friends for lunch in half an hour. What was she going to say to them? If she didn't have her emotions under control by then, they'd be like sharks in bloody water. They'd want to know what was wrong. They would want to know what had happened to make her so upset. What could she tell them? That her perfect daughter had run away? That Anne-Lynn, with her straight A's and sky-high SAT scores, had thrown away the opportunity to go to a prestigious eastern college? That Anne-Lynn preferred living in some cheap little dump with some cheap little tramp in San Francisco rather than live another day in Black Hawk with her own mother?

"Stupid! She's stupid!" Nora went into the kitchen, opening and slamming cupboards as she took down the coffee grinder, a cup, and some sugar. Her heart pounded hard and fast as she stuffed a filter into the coffeemaker. Beans scattered as she poured them too quickly into the grinder. She shook the machine as it hummed. Taking the top off, she poured the grounds carelessly, spilling half over the sides of the filter and some onto the tile counter. Cursing, she hurled the basket into the sink, leaving a trail of grounds across the floor in its wake. The maid was coming this afternoon. Let her clean up the mess!

She didn't want coffee anyway—and she certainly didn't need it when her heart felt as though it would burst any second. One cup of coffee and the caffeine would push her over the edge into a heart attack.

And it'll be your fault, Anne-Lynn Gardner. All your fault. You'll be sorry for hurting me like this. You'll come to the hospital and stand by my bed and hold my hand and beg me to forgive you. You'll say, "I'm sorry, Mother. You were right. I should've gone to Wellesley. I should've listened to you." Nora uttered a ragged sob and bit her lower lip.

She deserts me *and goes to visit my* mother!

Nora itched to grab her car keys and drive to Oakland. She wanted to tell her daughter what she thought and how she felt. The hot words were already bubbling, the steam building. Oh, the sacrifices she had made. And did Anne even appreciate them? No! It was bad enough that Anne refused to go to college. It was bad enough that she had run out on all of the wonderful, painstaking plans made for her. It was bad enough that she had gone off to live like some bohemian in the City. But *this* . . .

"She's gone to visit with her grandmother in Oakland."

It was nothing short of betrayal.

Annie drove across the Bay Bridge, the portfolio of Great-Aunt Joyce's work on the seat beside her. Grandma Leota had insisted she take it home with her. "It's been up in the attic all these years, dear. You take it home with you. It's part of your heritage. Maybe looking at those pictures will encourage you with your art."

And she had given her a thin box that contained an exquisite hand-embroidered handkerchief with lace edging. "Your great-grandmother made it. She sold things like that. She wasn't able to do anything else because of her poor health. Just hankies and embroidered pillowcases and the like. She made crocheted lace, but I don't have any of that left to show you. She'd send me down to a fancy millinery shop a few blocks from where we lived and have me sell it to the lady there. I can remember my mother sitting by the front window where the sunlight would spill in on her. All day she would sit there and do needlework."

Annie had never seen such beautiful work and said so. Her grandmother had been so pleased. "It is beautiful, isn't it? I knew you'd appreciate it."

It would look wonderful pinned to black velvet and put in an antique frame. The next time she went down to the art-supply store on Market, she would buy what she needed.

When she entered the flat, Barnaby let out a screech. "Call 911! Call 911!"

"Oh, hush, you dumb bird!" Susan said from the bathroom, where she was brushing her hair. "You've gotten us into enough trouble today!"

"What happened?"

"You don't want to know."

Annie laughed. "That bad?"

"Worse than bad. Catastrophic." She stuck her head out the door. "But there's no time to tell you about it now. We have to leave for work in fifteen minutes. Are you going to have something to eat?"

"I took Chinese to my grandmother's." She added some bits of fruit to Barnaby's bowl. "Here you go, my fine, feathered friend."

"Polly wants a cracker."

"Dumb bird," Susan said, coming out of the bathroom. "Your name is Barnaby, and you don't eat crackers!"

"Polly wants a cracker."

"Tough," Susan said. "Fruit it is, buddy."

"Call 911!"

Annie laughed and headed for the bathroom to change her clothes, while Susan stood glaring at the rainbow lory. "What is it with this bird?" Susan said. "It's getting so I say anything and he's calling for the police."

"He doesn't think you like him."

"Oh, now, where would he get an idea like that?" Susan glowered at the bird pacing back and forth on his perch.

"Call the cops! Murder she wrote."

"Maybe we should put a hood on him when the telephone rings. You know, the kind they put on a falcon. That might shut him up."

"911!"

"If you were a dog, Barnaby, I'd have you in a choke collar so fast your head would spin!"

"Polly wants a cracker!"

"Starve, you mangy buzzard!"

"She doesn't mean it, Barnaby," Annie crooned, coming out of the bathroom in her straight, black skirt and white blouse. She'd brushed her hair quickly and was doing a French braid. "I'll be ready in just a minute, Suzie." She came over and stood near the bird as she finished her hair. "You're a pretty bird, Barnaby. A very pretty bird."

"You might not think so after I tell you what he did today. Your mother called."

Annie turned and looked at her. The rueful look on her friend's face was warning enough. "What happened?" she asked as they left the apartment.

"She heard Barnaby calling for the police. So she called my mother, and my mother called me. She wanted to know if it was true I was about to be arrested."

"Oh, Suzie." Annie closed her eyes.

Susan laughed. "Still think Barnaby's a pretty bird? Want to go back in and wring his neck?"

"I'm sorry." She was always apologizing to someone about something her mother said.

"Why're you apologizing? You're always doing that, Annie. It's not your fault." She came down the stairs.

"What did you tell your mother?"

She shrugged. "I told her we were throwing beer busts and orgies and running track lighting so we can grow pot in our living room. What else?"

"You didn't!" Annie went cold inside at the thought of what *her* mother would make of such a statement.

Susan laughed. "Of course, I did. She knows me better than that, Annie. She didn't believe me for a second. In fact, she laughed. Especially when I told her about our bird." Her smile turned rueful. "A pity *your* mother doesn't know us as well."

The mailman came shortly after Annie left. Leota opened the door and reached out, pulling the sparse bundle from the metal box mounted on her wall. She closed the door and locked it again.

Well, well. She had won one million dollars from some publishing clearing house, and they were sending it to her bulk mail. What did they think? She was born yesterday? She walked into the kitchen as she sifted through the rest of the mail. A mailer advertised carpet cleaning. Forty-nine dollars to shampoo the rugs in two rooms. Highway robbery. She'd rented a machine five years ago for less than ten dollars and done the whole house.

Of course, it had been days before the rugs were completely dry, and the work had almost killed her.

She looked at the gray rug. Was it five years? Maybe it was longer than that. Six? Seven? Too long.

On the other side of the advertisement for carpet cleaning was a notice about a missing girl. Stranger abduction. Missing since 12-15-97. Not a day went by that Leota didn't find one of these depressing notices in her mailbox. What was happening to the world that so many children were missing?

Two envelopes were from charities, undoubtedly looking for donations. One of them was from the organization that had sent Corban Solsek. She should have known she would end up on their mailing list. Maybe she'd send them a check for ten dollars, rent that rug-cleaning machine at the grocery store again, and have Corban Solsek shampoo carpets for her. Oh, wouldn't he greet that idea with a happy smile. She couldn't help but chuckle at the idea. She would suggest it the next time he came just to see the look on his face.

If he came back . . .

Dumping most of the mail into the recycling bin, she tore open her bank statement and sat down at the kitchen table to study it. Everything looked in order. Social security had deposited her monthly check. A dividend had been added. Twice a year, enough to pay taxes, plus some. She was saving in case the house needed repairs. But not this year. She wrote so few checks, balancing the statement was always easy. She was even making interest, enough to buy stamps to send in the few bills she had. Utilities. Water. Telephone. Fire and theft insurance.

Pushing the statement aside, she gazed out at the garden again. Time would tell if Annie had been serious about bringing the garden back the way it was. Whatever happened, it had been a sweet thought, sweet enough to spark something inside Leota for the first time in a long time. Her mouth curved.

"And there isn't much spark left in this old gal, Lord." But what a day. Perfect, in fact. *Annie's wonderful, isn't she, Lord? It makes me feel good knowing a little of my blood runs in her veins.*

The telephone rang. Who would be calling her this time of day? Annie, perhaps, just to let her know she had arrived home safely. Leota made it to the telephone by the seventh ring.

"Mother, is Anne-Lynn with you?"

Leota blinked. "Eleanor?" When was the last time she had called?

"Nora, Mother. Remember? *Nora.* I *hate* the name Eleanor. That's why I never use it." She huffed as though striving for calm. "I'm calling for Anne-Lynn. Is she there?"

"No. She isn't here." Leota tried to push down the hurt feelings that rose again. Her daughter had never understood, never even tried . . .

"*Was* she there this afternoon?" Eleanor spoke as though talking to a retarded child.

"Yes. She left over an hour ago. What's wrong?"

"Nothing I can't take care of."

"How have you been, dear? It's been a long time since—"

"Just hunky-dory." Eleanor's tone was filled with mockery. Her anger radiated through the telephone lines. "I've been busy, very busy."

"You've raised a wonderful daughter. You should be—"

"I can imagine what you two talked about today."

Anger rose through the pain. "No, I don't think you can."

"Well, I'm sorry, Mother, but I don't have time to talk with you right now. I need to talk with my daughter."

Leota had no doubt in her mind what that meant. "Try not to say anything you'll regret, Eleanor."

Her daughter hung up.

Leota put the receiver back slowly and sat down in her recliner. She should have held her tongue. Eleanor never would listen to anything she had to say. Why had she even made the attempt? She put her head back and closed her eyes, all the joy from the day with Annie dissipating.

I didn't need that, Lord. I didn't need that one bit.

Corban thought about Leota Reinhardt's question for several days. In fact, he couldn't get it out of his head. Why did he want the elderly singled out and settled in one area? He thought of all kinds of practical reasons. Medical care would be more readily available. More services at lower costs could be provided. He couldn't think of one negative about his idea for facilities financed by private money and assisted by government funding. What had she seen in it that he was missing? Why had she made that crack about Professor Webster? Why should anyone be horrified by his ideas? They were sound. They were compassionate.

She abhorred the ideas he had presented. Why?

He obsessed about it so much, he finally called Leota Reinhardt and told her yes, he'd like to come by on Wednesday to talk with her again. She sounded surprised to hear from him and said he could come as long as he would walk with her to the bank. "They open at nine. Come early."

"All right." He was unable to keep the annoyance from his tone. He'd been hoping to sit down, talk for an hour or so, and leave. Now, it seemed he would be making another trek to Dimond.

"I think we can walk and talk at the same time, Mr. Solsek. Be here at ten. Anytime after that and I'll already be on my way."

The next morning, he rang her doorbell at nine-thirty sharp, sure that if he got there any later, she'd have left just to irritate him.

"Good morning," she said, letting him in. "You look bright-eyed and bushy-tailed."

He knew how he looked. He had been so bleary-eyed this morning, he'd nicked himself while shaving. "I was up late working."

"On your paper?"

"No. Another class. Philosophy."

She smiled sardonically. "It's that interesting, is it?"

"After one in the morning, it's a little hard to make any sense out of anything." Everything about this old woman made him feel he had to defend himself.

"Are you a slow reader?"

"*No,* I'm not a slow reader. You try getting through two hundred pages of reading in a night." He saw the flicker in her eyes.

"It was a simple question, Mr. Solsek, not an accusation."

"I'm sorry. I didn't mean to sound insolent."

She gave a cool laugh and headed into her kitchen. Stifling his annoyance, Corban followed. Standing in the doorway, he watched her turn the handle on the stove. There was a click as the flame caught on the front burner.

"Read enough and you'll learn there's nothing new under the sun," she said and set a kettle firmly upon the burner. "Take a seat, Mr. Solsek. Would you like coffee or tea?"

Something about the way she said *Mr. Solsek* made him uncomfortable. He wanted to start over. He wanted to like her and have her like him. And he knew he was making a mess of everything. "Why don't you call me Corban, Mrs. Reinhardt?"

She looked at him then, studying him briefly. "Corban, it will be. Coffee or tea?"

Was she mocking him again? "Coffee. Please."

"Plain or fancy?"

He almost rolled his eyes. What was going on here? He felt like a turkey facing Thanksgiving. "Are you having any?"

"I'm not the one who needs to wake up."

"I'm awake."

"Barely. Sit. You haven't eaten, either, have you?"

"No." He never ate breakfast. He guzzled black coffee and went to classes. He never ate until afternoon.

"I think I might even have a sweet roll left for you."

Suspicious, he watched her bustle around her small kitchen, taking a mug from the cabinet, then a brown bag from a breadbox. She wanted something from him, that was for sure, something more than a walk to the bank.

"So," she said, pouring hot water into a mug. "Did you come up with an answer to my question yet?" She spooned in instant double-chocolate mocha coffee.

"No."

"Have you been thinking about it?" she said, setting the cup in front of him.

Corban stared down at it grimly, the aroma of the steaming chocolate-coffee combination assaulting his senses. He remembered how she had complained about the cost. He didn't dare tell her now that he hated sweetened coffee. He always made his strong and black. During finals, he lived on Mad Maxes: three shots of espresso in a cup of black coffee.

Shuddering inwardly, Corban turned the cup between his hands, determined not to blow this interview no matter what he had to swallow. "I've been thinking about your question. In fact, I've been thinking about little else."

"That's good." She eased herself into the chair opposite him. Folding her hands on her newspaper, she waited.

He sipped the coffee and tried not to grimace. "I'd appreciate it if you'd just spell out your objections to what I proposed, Mrs. Reinhardt. It'd make it easier."

"Easier, perhaps, but it wouldn't sink in as deeply."

"That's just it. I don't know what you want to sink in."

She was silent for a long moment, looking at him. He could almost see her wheels turning. There was such sadness in her eyes, Corban felt uncomfortable. He had disappointed her in some way, and he couldn't stop the twinge of conscience.

"I want to help people like you, Mrs. Reinhardt." He meant it.

"Corban, I'll put it simply. What begins in mercy can end in destruction. I have objections, but some of them I can't put to words. It's a—" she thought for a moment again, frowning—"a sense of impending doom."

He should've been insulted, but something in the way she said it made him pause. "Maybe you just don't understand what I want to do."

"Corban, you think you're blazing a new trail, but you're just going down the same worn path. Where do you think it'll end up?"

"Better off than we are now. There are already facilities similar to what I'm writing about, but they're all privately funded. People have to be loaded to get into them. You'd have to come up with one to two hundred thousand dollars just to get in the door of some of these places. Once you've signed, you'd have complete care until you died. What I'm trying to work out is a program for people who've worked all their lives but don't have a big estate to show for it."

She shook her head sadly. "You don't see it, do you? The dangers. Maybe you haven't got it in you to see what I do." Her eyes looked moist and troubled. "Then again, I've probably overstated my concerns. I'm just an old woman. What do I know?"

He felt the subtle rebuke, but before he could comment, she went on. "Let's leave it alone a while, shall we? Let the idea perk. After a while, you'll get the real taste of it." She looked down at his cup. "You don't like the coffee?"

Corban thought about lying but knew he'd have to finish the whole cup if he did. He still had the cloying aftertaste of the first sip. "I'm sorry, but it's a little too sweet for me." Seeing her mouth tighten, he added, "I'll buy you another tin of it." He hoped that would stave off any complaints about how much she had spent on the stuff.

She took the cup and poured the contents into the sink. "Thank you, but I think the tin I bought will be around long after I'm gone." She rinsed the mug and set it upside down on a towel on the sink board. "I'll get my sweater and we can go to the bank." She sounded as though she was marshaling her troops. She went into the front room.

On the way down the hill, her hand tightened on his arm. Corban could tell the walk to the market and bank was not an easy one for her. He couldn't understand her stubborn refusal to ride in comfort. "Why won't you let me drive you, Mrs. Reinhardt?" He spoke gently, remembering the last time and how tired she had been. Worn out, in fact.

She kept walking, looking straight ahead again. "This is the only time I get outside anymore. I used to walk all the way around Lake Merritt on my lunch hour, and now my world has narrowed down to the few blocks between my home and the market." She glanced up at him. "Would you have my world narrowed even more?"

He knew where she was going with that question and was gratified the subject wasn't closed. "The facilities wouldn't have to narrow your life. There would be activities."

"That sounds ominous."

"Why should it?"

"Well, you tell me. What sort of activities do you have in mind for us old folks? Maybe I'll change my mind about where this idea of yours is heading."

He dove in, hoping to sway her. "Arts and crafts?"

"Oh." Leota Reinhardt said nothing more.

They turned the corner and walked a block, then stood at the stoplight, waiting for the pedestrian sign to go on. He held his silence all the way across the street, down another block, under the freeway overpass, and to the next light before he surrendered, knowing she wouldn't say anything until he pressed. "I take it you don't like that idea."

"Oh, I suppose it would depend on the arts and crafts. Were you thinking about gluing Popsicle sticks together and making birdcages? Things like that?"

Kindergarten stuff? "Not exactly." What exactly? He hadn't thought about it.

"Paint by numbers, perhaps? That's real challenging."

"Okay," he said dismally, "I haven't thought about all that in detail. Would you like to make a few suggestions?"

"How about a class on how to work a computer?"

He laughed. He couldn't help himself. "A computer? You've got to be kidding."

"Why? You don't think someone my age could learn?"

"Maybe. But why would you want to?"

"That's the sort of question they ask someone intent on climbing Mount Everest. Because it's there. Why else?"

"It'd drive you nuts."

"Push me over the edge into complete senility, hmm? Is that what it does to you?"

He grinned. "On occasion."

"You have the idea locked in your head that you can't teach an old dog new tricks. What if the old dog wanted to learn?"

He had the feeling she was baiting him. "I suppose you could learn the elementary stuff. A class could be pared down to the bare basics."

"Meaning what? I'd be dead before I could figure out any more than that?"

Was she determined to tick him off? "I didn't say that."

"You think it would be better to offer classes that require no thinking, is that it? What do they call them these days? No-brainers? Something that won't challenge us poor old folks too much. God forbid, we couldn't take anything too mentally challenging. Put us under any kind of stress, and poof, we'll croak. And then who's responsible?"

She was warming to the subject, he thought grimly. She wasn't walking anymore. She was marching, and dragging him along with her. Cantankerous old broad! He groped for reason.

"Why would you want to learn how to use a computer?"

"I didn't say I would."

"You just suggested it!"

"I was thinking out loud. I suppose you don't do that sort of thing."

"I talk to myself on occasion." Especially after a visit with her! "Fine. Computer classes. Why not?"

"Consider it preventive medicine." She slowed down. "I've read articles that say maintaining an active mind could ward off Alzheimer's."

"Are you worried about developing that?"

She glowered up at him. "I don't know. I can't remember."

He had no doubt this old lady was of sound mind. Right now, at least. "Did the article suggest what kind of activities?"

"Games like chess. Learning a foreign language. Putting complex puzzles together. Studying music. That sort of thing."

"Do you do any of those things?"

"Well, I don't play chess. You need two people for that." She looked up at him. "Do you play?"

"No. It never appealed to me."

"A pity. Music is out. I don't have a piano. A foreign language might be something, but I can't get very excited about that. It's one thing to learn French if you're planning on going to France. Since I'm not going anywhere, it seems a sorry waste of time. Ebonics, perhaps. That would make more sense."

He laughed, imagining this little, old lady learning to speak street lingo.

"Or I could just stick to what I do," she went on. "Work crossword puzzles. Read the newspaper. Read my Bible."

"I noticed you have a lot of books around."

"They belonged to my husband. I never had much time for reading."

He sensed an undercurrent and decided to go with it. "Why not?" Maybe he would get some family history.

"I preferred spending what spare time I had in my garden." She glanced up at him again. "I don't imagine there'd be much gardening in one of those facilities of yours, would there? Potted plants only. Did you know that plants grown in hothouses have barely any scent at all? Might as well have one of those silk things that fade in the sunlight."

He sighed inwardly. He was beginning to understand that Leota Reinhardt's mind didn't wander. It was fixed, steady as you go. "I think I get your point." The only way anyone would get Leota Reinhardt into the kind of facility he thought would be the wave of the future would be doped and tied, gagged and dragged.

Shaking his head, he opened the door of the bank for her and followed her inside. Why was she so set in her thinking? Why did she find his ideas so repugnant? She'd already made it clear she wasn't going to spell it out for him. She wanted him to "get the real taste of it" for himself.

He felt as though he'd just been enrolled in kindergarten and was learning by tactile experiences.

He needed to figure out what she was thinking. He needed to see from her perspective. The only way he was going to get what he needed from her was by spending more time with her. Oddly enough, his decision didn't fill him with the grim despair he knew he would've felt a week ago. The more time he spent with her, the more he wondered what she was thinking. And why she was thinking it.

Leota Reinhardt was turning into an interesting challenge.

8

ANNIE SAT AT THE KITCHEN COUNTER, READING HER ART HISTORY
book, a binder open beside her so that she could write notes. So far
she had been to only three classes, but all had proven fascinating.
The instructor was an artist who knew art history inside and outside
and upside down. His passion for the subject came through, firing
her imagination as well.

The telephone rang, causing her pulse to shoot up. It rang a
second time and she started to reach for it, then held off. After four
rings, the machine picked up the call. "This is 555-7836. No one is
available to take your call. Please leave your name and number at the
sound of the beep."

She listened, thankful Susan hadn't played any more pranks and
changed the message again. The last message was, "In jail. Need bail.
Unless you have bond, don't respond." Though Annie's father had
laughed and left a message, her mother had not seen the humor in it.
"I suppose you think that's funny, Susan. It isn't! Anne, this is your
mother. Call home."

Annie had done so and suffered through a fifteen-minute, one-
sided diatribe in which her mother had called her to task for not
having the courtesy to call home sooner. *Do you have any idea how
much I worry about you? I had to take a sleeping pill last night . . ."*

"Just erase the message, Annie," Susan advised. "For crying out loud, you know what she's going to say. She's been giving you a guilt trip for as long as I've known you."

"She's my mother. I can't just ignore her." No matter how much she wished she could. But her conscience wouldn't allow it. Over the past few days, her mother had called no fewer than ten times. Each time she turned up the guilt even higher.

"I love you so much. . . . Every time I see the news, I wonder . . ." Her mother didn't have to say the rest. Annie knew it already. Her mother wouldn't worry so much if she were attending Wellesley. After all, she would be in a women's dormitory; there would be supervision; she would be mingling with girls from *good* homes.

The answering machine beeped. She heard a man laughing. "What happened to the other message? You make parole? This is your big bro, in case you've forgotten the sound of my voice. I'm driving up to the big city this weekend. Whaddya say to a ritzy dinner someplace? Someplace other than that garlic joint where you work. Give me a call back, Suzie Q."

"Bad boys . . . bad boys . . . whatcha gonna do . . . ," Barnaby belted out, bobbing his head as he stood on his perch.

Annie chuckled before returning her attention to her textbook, thankful the call hadn't been from her mother. She hadn't responded to the last two calls, one from last night and one from this morning, although she knew she'd have to call her mother soon or hear the telephone ringing again. The date had come and gone for Annie to change her mind and go east to college. Why wouldn't her mother let it go? She was like a pit bull with her teeth sunk into an idea.

Susan came in an hour later. Annie had just finished reading the last section assigned and was going over her notes. "Mom and Dad send their love," she said, flinging her purse onto the sofa. "Any calls?"

"Sam."

Susan pushed the button and stood listening to her brother's voice. "Awesome!" She grinned. "Let's give him a heart attack and ask him to take us to the Carnelian Room!"

"You ask him. I won't be here."

Susan frowned. "You're going to see your mother?"

"I'm scheduled to work Thursday and Friday this week, so I asked my grandmother if I could spend Saturday with her. I'd like to spend the night, too, but I don't want to put her out. Would you mind if I borrowed your sleeping bag?"

"It's yours."

"Thanks, Suzie."

Now if she could just get Grandma Leota to let her work in the garden.

"You're really getting into this volunteer business, aren't you?" Ruth said, a mocking smile on her face as she continued her stretching exercises on the floor. She was wearing black sweatpants and a white tank top. "Wednesday and now Saturday, too."

"We didn't have anything planned, did we?"

"Not that I've heard about." Not missing a beat of the music, she touched her forehead to her right knee and then walked her hands across in front of her, took hold of her left heel and touched her forehead to her left knee. "I'll probably be studying all day."

Corban watched, annoyed. She had the exercise video on the television, the volume turned up. He'd seen her go through this often enough to know she had another forty-five minutes to go before completing the routine. "Feel the burn," the too-perky exercise leader droned on. "Hold it. That's it. One. Two. Three. Four . . ."

It was hard for him to concentrate when Ruth did her workout in the living room. The music wasn't bad the first dozen times, but after that, it began to wear on his nerves. He wanted to put his foot through the television screen and send the image of Jane Fonda into oblivion. "I thought we agreed you'd do this in the morning," he said evenly.

"I know, but I wasn't in the mood today. I thought about skipping it all together and decided I'd better not. Skip one day and pretty soon I'd skip another."

The way he was supposed to skip studying for the next hour? "I have two hours to study before I have to leave, and I can't concentrate with that music going."

"It won't kill you to wait half an hour!"

Her tone lit his fuse. He punched the VCR power button, shutting it off. "And it wouldn't kill *you* to hold to the schedule we agreed on."

Her face was flushed, whether from the workout or temper, he didn't know. Nor at that moment did he particularly care. Her dark eyes were hot. He met her glare, waiting. He was beginning to think he'd made a terrible mistake when he asked her to move in with him.

A frown flickered across her face as she looked into his eyes. She glanced away, then straightened into a sitting position and stood in one smooth movement. "I'm sorry. You're right." She pushed another button and took the ejected video from the VCR. She slipped it into its case and snapped it shut. "I'll go out for a run instead." She dropped the box lightly on the coffee table, rather than onto the shelf where it belonged, and went into the bedroom.

Corban sat on the couch and flipped his philosophy book open. His teeth were clenched so tight his jaw was beginning to ache. He didn't want to think about what might be going on in Ruth's head right then. But he figured he knew anyway: She always knew when to capitulate—right at the last moment.

She came out of the bedroom wearing red satin running shorts and a white sports bra. She slipped a white band around her head, adjusting her short hair while looking at him. He recognized the expression she wore. She knew she looked good, so good she thought she could take his breath away anytime she wanted. It had been true the first couple of months of their cohabitation. His eyes flickered over her from head to running-shoe-clad feet, but it wasn't desire that flared this time.

"Maybe we could do something together when I get back from my run." She gave him her cat smile. "I shouldn't be too long."

"Take your time," he said, returning his gaze to the book in his lap.

She stood a moment longer. He could feel her staring at him but didn't give her the satisfaction of looking at her again. Her ploy had worked before, but not this time. He wasn't a puppet she could work by pulling a few strings. He cared about her. More deeply than he wanted to admit. He also knew if he looked at her again, he was going to say what was running through his mind, and he'd regret it later. Sometimes, though, he wondered if she cared for him at all.

She went to the door. Opening it, she turned back to face him again. "You know, Cory, sometimes I wonder why you invited me to live with you. I thought you loved me. Isn't that silly? You make me feel *used*."

He looked up from his book. "In that case, I'd say our relationship is strictly symbiotic."

She slammed the door on her way out.

Nora pulled up in front of her mother's house. Heart drumming, she sat still for a few seconds, trying to calm her nerves. She needed a cigarette. She needed a glass of wine. She closed her eyes and drew in a slow breath, holding it and expelling it slowly. Her yoga instructor had once told her that would calm her. So had her psychologist.

Still trembling, Nora got out of the car, pressed the remote to lock the door, and headed for the house. She hated coming back to this neighborhood, feeling so torn with memories each time she did. Tucking her red, leather clutch bag under her arm, she punched the doorbell. How long had it been since she last saw her mother? A twinge of guilt stirred, but she quickly smothered it with resentment.

Why should *she* feel guilty? So what if she had turned down several invitations her mother had extended over the past years? Had her mother been there for her when she was growing up? No. Her mother had moved her and George in with Grandma and Grandpa Reinhardt, then danced off to live her own life. Had her mother been with her the first day she went to school? No. Grandma Helene held her hand and walked her to school. In fact, it had been Grandma Helene who had walked her to school every day until she was in second grade and sent off by herself.

Had her mother gone on any of the school outings? No. Grandma Helene had gone. Once. Nora felt a twinge remembering how embarrassed she had been when other students commented on her grandmother's thick German accent.

Had her mother been the one to make her a dress for her high school prom? Of course not. She'd made it herself!

What good had all her mother's work ever done anyone other than herself? There had never been money for any extras. While other girls had shiny Mary Jane shoes with chic straps, she had worn oxfords. When other girls took piano and dancing lessons, she had to take clarinet because the school taught it for free. When other girls went on family outings and vacations, her family stayed home.

She remembered Grandma and Grandpa bickering, always in German so she couldn't understand what they were saying. She remembered her father drinking and sitting for hours in his chair— silent, morose, alone—while fear roamed rampant within her.

And where was her mother through all those years?

Living her own life just as she pleased. Working!

She deserves to be left alone. Then she'll know what it feels like to be deserted.

Nora was swimming in the high tide of her emotions when her mother finally opened the door. "What took you so long, Mother?" Had she looked through the peephole and seen who it was—and hoped she'd go away?

"I was in the kitchen. I don't move as quickly as I used to." She lifted the chain and stepped back.

Nora entered and stood in the living room, looking around. The smell of the house made memories come flooding back. Few were good. "Nothing's changed, has it?"

"Why would it?" Her mother closed the door quietly. She left the chain off. "Would you like some tea or coffee?"

"No, thank you." Tea would have been nice, but Nora didn't want to accept anything from her mother. Not now. Her mother could offer her the moon, and she wouldn't take it. It was too late. "I won't be staying very long, Mother. I just felt there was a need to clarify some things regarding Anne."

Her mother eased herself into her recliner and folded her hands in her lap. She seemed to be in pain, and she had aged a great deal since the last time Nora had seen her.

I'm not going to feel sorry for her. Not after the way she ignored me most of my life!

Sitting on the edge of the sofa, Nora put her clutch bag beside her and held her knees. "Anne is at a very impressionable age. She needs guidance. Up to a few weeks ago, she'd always been the model daughter. Now, she's taken it in her head to throw away college, live with a hippie friend in San Francisco, and become an artist, of all things. But maybe you know all this since she's been here visiting with *you*."

Her mother's eyes narrowed slightly, but she said nothing one way or the other. Nora had expected as much. No cooperation. "She's a gifted student, Mother. She graduated with top grades, had very high scores on the SAT. She had immaculate references and recommendations. She was offered a wonderful scholarship to a prestigious college in the East. Then one day she just snapped and said she didn't want to go. She got in her car and drove off without thinking things through." Nora smoothed her skirt and rested her hands on her knees again.

"Now I've fixed things temporarily so that she can still go. I've spoken with the dean of admissions and told him Anne has taken ill and couldn't come. They've agreed to hold her scholarship until next semester."

"You lied to them?"

Nora's face went hot. Anger surged, making her feel on fire. Leave it to her mother to see the negative side of anything! *"Do the right thing,"* she had always said. Do the right thing! Had *she?* "She *is* sick, Mother! She must be sick in the head to throw this opportunity away!"

"Because it's what you want?"

"Yes," she said through her teeth, rising. "Yes, it's what I want for her. It's what *anyone* with half an ounce of sense would want. She's groomed herself for years for this chance, and suddenly she runs. Well, I'm not going to let her be such a little coward. I'm not going to allow her to throw it all away."

"What if it's not what she wants?"

"It *is* what she wants. It's what she's *always* wanted. We've been talking about colleges from the time she entered kindergarten."

Her mother sighed softly, looking weary and old. "Maybe if you would just hold off for a time and allow her to find her own way—"

"You mean the way *you* did. Back away completely." Nora should have expected as much. "I should be like you?" She saw the flicker of hurt in her mother's eyes at her sarcasm, but anger took hold of her. "Is that it, Mother? Have nothing to do with making some kind of future for my children?" She saw the sheen of tears in her mother's eyes and felt ashamed. In the wake of her shame came another wave of anger. How dare her mother try to make her feel guilty? "I should've known you wouldn't help me or even try to understand. You never did."

"I understand. Only too well." She sounded so sad, so worn down and hopeless.

Nora's eyes also filled with tears. She fought them, not even sure why they had come welling up, making her want to cry out. Part of her wanted desperately to reach out to her mother, to say she was sorry, to cling to her. Another part wanted to lacerate her for all the times Nora had desperately needed her and she hadn't been there. "I want what's best for my daughter!"

"I know you do, dear. But your best may not be God's best."

Nora stiffened at the gentle words, for they were a firm rebuke. "What would you know of God's best for my daughter? When was the last time you went to church, Mother? Ten years ago? I go *every* Sunday. Anne-Lynn should honor my plans for her. Instead she's decided to be stubborn and rebellious. And you're helping her!"

Her mother closed her eyes as though she couldn't bear to look at her.

"I should've known better than to come and talk to you," Nora said, voice cracking. "You were never there for me before. I was foolish to hope you'd be here for me now." She snatched her clutch bag from the sofa and headed for the door.

"I've always been there for you," her mother said in a choked voice. "Every day of my life, only you never understood. You never even tried."

Nora turned on her furiously. "When were you *ever* there for me? Name once!"

Her mother didn't respond to her attack. Instead, she spoke in a quiet tone. "You've always said I destroyed your dreams. Why would you enlist me to do the same to your own daughter?"

Trembling, Nora stared at her. She drew in a shaky breath. "You always twist everything I say just so you can make me feel guilty."

"I can't make you feel anything."

"Oh, yes, you can." The resentment and bitterness filled her to overflowing. "I want you to know the *only* reason Anne-Lynn spends any time with you at all is because she knows it hurts me. She's using you to get back at me. You just don't understand."

"I understand you perfectly, Eleanor."

Trembling violently, Nora yanked the front door open. "That's how much you care, Mother. You still persist in calling me *that* name when you know I hate it!"

"You've always been Eleanor to me, and you always will be."

"There's no talking to you! You always have to have your way in everything. Well, enjoy your solitude!" She hurled the door shut. Her heels clicked on the steps. Two black children had drawn a colored-chalk hopscotch on the sidewalk. No child would be allowed to make a mess like that in Black Hawk. They paused in their play to look at her. Averting her eyes, Nora got into her car and started the engine. Pulling away from the curb, she drove quickly down the street, turned right, and headed for the freeway on-ramp.

She wept all the way home.

Despite Ruth's apology after her run, Corban remained depressed. He always felt an emotional backlash when he let his emotions get the better of him. For the first time since she'd moved in with him, he refused to take back what he had said. She noticed, of course, but said nothing.

It seemed to him that she made more effort over the next two days. She did her share of household chores and kept her bargain about maintaining quiet during his study hours.

Yet, he knew he was living in the eye of a tornado.

Her attitude would change when she met with her friends again. It always did. The storm clouds were building overhead, and he and

Ruth would end up in the twister before she settled down again. If she did.

Having overheard some of the conversations as well as what Ruth had told him, Corban had gleaned that most of these young women with whom she hung out were from broken families, as was she. Two girls had been sexually abused by male relatives. He could understand how they might hate the men who had abused them, but did that group all males in the brutal category? Or give due cause for becoming lesbian? Three of the ten who met had "come out of the closet." Two of those were "comfortable" with their alternative lifestyle, their families having come to terms with them; the third was an emotional mess, swinging from frothing hostility to despair.

"Someday she'll kill herself," Ruth had said flatly after one particularly distressing evening in which the girl had monopolized the meeting in venting her anger. "And it'll be her parents' fault for not allowing her to be herself. They should be forced to see it's perfectly natural for some people to be homosexual. She was born that way."

"Hogwash! She's the one who isn't accepting things."

Ruth's eyes had flashed. "She's happy as what she is."

"Happy? You call that happy?"

"Well, if you had people calling you terrible names, maybe you wouldn't be happy either!"

"The only names I heard this evening were the ones coming out of her mouth."

"You're so closed-minded, Cory. It's pathetic. If I didn't know better, I'd say you were homophobic."

"*I'm* closed-minded? Well, maybe they ought to meet somewhere else since it's my apartment they're coming to in order to vent their spleens against all males."

They had digressed from there. It had been one of their worst arguments ever. After they finally shouted themselves out and spent the night sleeping apart, they had agreed to let the subject drop. For two weeks, Ruth had gone elsewhere to meet with her friends. And then they were back again, his digs apparently being more comfortable than wherever else they'd been.

They made him nervous, these women who sat around talking about intolerant men and patriarchal society and equal rights for women. *Equal* to them meant women should get the first chance at the best jobs. Another case of affirmative action gone awry. More militants who wanted to use discrimination to end discrimination.

"We're just going to meet for an hour or two on Saturday morning,"

Ruth said, serving him the dinner she had prepared, Prego poured over boiled noodles with some parmesan sprinkled on top.

"Any Tabasco?"

She set the bottle down in front of him. "There's going to be a march in San Francisco in a couple of weeks, and we want to prepare for it."

"What's it about this time?"

"Funding for AIDS research. We thought we'd make a banner."

Sloshing Tabasco over his spaghetti, Corban decided to be elsewhere on Saturday.

The bell rang on Friday afternoon shortly after Annie finished getting ready for work. She pressed the intercom. "Who is it?"

"Sam."

"Come on up." She pushed another button, releasing the lock on the front door of the building. "Suz. Your brother's here."

"Tonight? He wasn't supposed to get here until tomorrow."

"Well, he's here." Annie plumped the pillows and tossed them onto the couch, gathered up some of Susan's clothing, and quickly folded and stuffed the items into a dresser. Hurrying across to the kitchen-ette, she gathered glasses and plates and put them in the sink, squirting in liquid soap and running water over them. They'd have to soak for now. It was Susan's turn to do them, and they were both on their way to work.

Susan appeared from the bathroom, dressed in her black, straight skirt and white blouse. The doorbell buzzed as she frantically brushed her hair on the way to answer. "What are you doing here? It's Friday. You said Saturday."

"Chill out, Suzie Q. I just came by to let you know I'm checked in . . ."

Annie turned from the sink and felt his gaze fixed on her. Susan laughed, looking from him to her. She winked. "You remember Annie Gardner, don't you, Sam?"

"This is *Annie*? What happened to the Pippi Longstocking replication?"

Annie blushed. "Nice to see you, too, Sam." She was embarrassed at the reminder of how she had worn her carrot-red hair in pigtails. The red had faded some, along with the freckles that had once dotted her nose.

His eyes warmed, and a wolfish smile spread across his handsome face. "All grown up . . ."

"But she's got someplace to go."

"Bad boys, bad boys," Barnaby sang out loudly, and they all laughed.

"We're on our way to work, Sam, but you're welcome to hang out here if you'd like."

"No way. I came to the City to have some fun."

"Whatcha gonna do . . . whatcha gonna do . . . ," Barnaby sang loudly, bobbing his head.

"Sounds like the bird'd like to go with me." Sam grinned.

"You want him?" Susan said brightly. "You can have him with my blessings."

Sam laughed. "No way."

Annie took her jacket from the back of a chair. "I hate to break up the family reunion," she said with a smile, "but we'd better go, Suzie. We're going to be late."

"You know, I haven't eaten yet," Sam said, following them out. "Why don't I come to the Smelly Clove?"

"You hate garlic."

"Hate's a strong word. Besides, it has medicinal value, I hear."

"It does."

"Well, I think I might be developing a cold. I need a little preventive medicine. What do you say?"

Susan gave him the address and directions as they went down the stairs and out to Annie's car.

"See you there." Sam lifted his hand in a casual wave, then crossed the street to his van.

Susan slid into the bucket seat and snapped on the seat belt. "Well, well. I've got the feeling we're going to see a lot more of my brother." She looked at Annie and grinned.

Annie figured Sam had changed his mind when he didn't follow them to the restaurant. She was more relieved than disappointed. Though his obvious flirtation had been heady and a decided boost to her self-confidence, she knew he was dangerous in more ways than one.

At fifteen, she had thought Samuel James Carter, rebellious and delinquent, was some kind of romantic hero. She had fantasized about being like the heroine in a Harlequin novel, whose love and purity would melt the arrogance and cynicism of the hero.

But she had grown up over the last three years. She had learned how devastating and heartbreaking Sam's rebellion had been to his family. They could joke about it now, but she remembered Suzie's anger and Mrs. Carter's tears. He'd had to crash and burn before his life turned around. Sam was deep water, and where the world was concerned, Annie didn't know how to swim.

"He must've tipped Hal," Susan said in passing.

"Pardon me?"

"Sam. He's being seated in your area."

Annie collected several dishes of food and delivered them to patrons, asking if there was anything else they needed. She saw Sam sitting at a small table in the corner, where he could watch everything going on in the room. The bar waitress had just left his table, and several young women seated nearby were looking at him. He didn't appear to notice them. All his attention seemed fixed on her. His smile was roguish and challenging.

She passed him by once. "I'll be with you in just a moment, sir."

"I'm not going anywhere, *ma'am*."

She replenished coffee for several tables and then went back to his. "Have you decided what you'd like this evening, sir? Or would you like a little more time?"

"I've decided." His eyes twinkled in amusement.

Taking the leather pad with pencil from the pocket of her short, black apron, Annie flipped it open.

"Why don't you tell me what the specials are anyway." He leaned back, studying her at his leisure.

There were six dishes posted on the chalkboard at the restaurant entrance. Part of her job was to memorize them. She described each with all the succulent adjectives the management provided, aware of Sam's amused perusal throughout her recitation.

He grinned. "Very nicely done."

"So, what'll it be?" She spoke to him as though he were a perfect stranger who had just come into the restaurant for the first time.

"The twenty-clove rabbit."

"A good choice," she said, jotting down his order. "Soup or salad?"

"What kind of soup?"

"Gazpacho garlic."

"Salad. Ranch dressing. Plenty of pepper."

"I'll bring you some bread."

"Bring plenty of water, too, please, while you're about it."

She gave a soft laugh and flipped her order book closed and tucked it into her pocket.

Friday was always busy. She was working eight tables and moving fast to make sure everyone had what they wanted. One table would no sooner empty and be bused than another party would be seated. After two hours she had made enough in tips to buy groceries for a week.

And Sam was still there.

Replenishing his water glass for the third time, Annie noticed his plate. "You don't like the rabbit?"

He grimaced. "Let's just say I don't think I'm going to have any trouble with vampires. I'm going to have garlic coming out my pores for the next week."

She managed to fight off a grin. "You won't get a cold."

"No, but I'm getting the cold shoulder." His brows lifted in a teasing question.

"I don't think you'll have a problem about that. There are three ladies at the table just behind me who have been trying all evening to get your attention."

"Is that a brush-off, Annie? I'm wounded."

"You have the skin of an armadillo, Sam."

"And I thought you used to have a crush on me."

"Before I knew any better."

He grinned. "I'll try anything at this point." When she started to turn away, he said, "By the way, what's your sign?"

It was the oldest line in the book, and he knew it. Obviously it was time a few things were clarified. Perhaps when they were, he wouldn't waste his time. "The fish."

"Pisces." The roguish grin was back, along with a decidedly wicked gleam in his eyes. "Good sign."

"Yes, it is. But not Pisces."

He frowned. "No?"

"Nope. Ichthus. Jesus Christ, Son of God, Savior."

The teasing demeanor evaporated, and he looked straight into her eyes with an intensity she hadn't expected. "There's a message for me in those words, I take it."

"I hope so."

His mouth curved ruefully. "Worried the lion wants to lie down with the lamb?"

Heat surged into her cheeks. She expected him to laugh, but he didn't. His expression grew serious, contemplative. She felt the pull of his charm, the stirring inside at his intense look. With slow deliberation, she placed his check on the table, closed her order pad, and tucked it in its place. "Have a nice evening, Sam. Try to stay out of trouble."

Nora sat in her family room, a white throw wrapped around herself. She stared at the television but could make no sense of the movie. Her mind kept drifting.

It was ten o'clock, and Fred wasn't home yet. He'd left a message on the answering machine that he was taking clients out to dinner. Surely it didn't take this long, unless he'd gone to the City.

Thinking about dinner in the City made her think about Anne working in a restaurant. Maybe Fred had taken his clients where she worked and would put in a word to her about the distress she was causing her mother. No, Fred wouldn't do that. He had left Anne's upbringing entirely to her. He had felt his position as stepfather left him out of the loop where Annie was concerned. As long as she didn't interfere with his life, he would stay out of hers. They had a congenial relationship.

Sometimes it bothered Nora that Fred refused to become more involved. "It's up to you how you handle things," he would say. "She's your daughter, Nora, not mine."

She needed an ally this time. She needed someone strong to back her up.

Why wouldn't Anne listen to her anymore? Why was her daughter turning against her now and running to her grandmother?

When eleven rolled around, Nora began to feel unease in the pit of her stomach. The past reared its ugly head once more, haunting her as it always had with people's previous mistakes. She'd fallen in love with Bryan Taggart when she was sixteen. He was four years older, had a job, and was going to college. He was handsome, bright, and charming. She had been convinced he would fulfill all her hopes for a better life.

What had started as a romantic adventure had quickly turned into a nightmare of fights, bills, sleepless nights, and broken dreams.

She had been so desperate to make the marriage work and thought a baby would force Bryan to keep the job that seemed to offer the most promising future. However, her announcement that she was pregnant hadn't held the marriage together; it had shattered it. Bryan had been furious, calling her deceitful and selfish. He'd said she had done everything to ruin his life and he was sick of her. He deserted her before Michael was born, leaving her with no other choice than to move back in with her mother and father.

She still remembered what her mother had said to her the first evening she had come home. It had been the greatest cruelty of all after all she had been through in over two years of marriage. "You expected too much too soon." Crushed and feeling dismissed, she'd sought solace from Grandma Helene, who had agreed with her about everything. Bryan Taggart hadn't been good enough for her.

At least she had finished high school during those torturous months.

Her second marriage hadn't been much better than the first. Dean Gardner had all the markings of her Prince Charming. A graduate of Stanford with a major in business and accounting, he was already starting up the ladder in banking. As Dean's wife, she would have security and the opportunities she had lacked before. And so would Michael. She registered for college classes during the hours that Michael was in school. She took her son to all kinds of cultural events. She poured everything she could into developing her son and herself into people who could mingle in the best of society.

And all the while she was bettering herself, Dean was cheating on her. She hadn't learned about his affair with one of the secretaries in his office until several years later. She had only known something was wrong, but when she became pregnant with Anne, Dean had once again become the doting husband he'd been in the beginning. He'd been an even more doting father when Anne was born.

As soon as Anne was old enough, Nora resumed her efforts to see that Michael was given the best education possible. She began making plans for Anne as well. She played classical music during her daughter's crib time to increase her intelligence. Even the games she played with Annie were designed to develop mental skills and physical abilities.

Her children were going to have every opportunity she missed; their potential was going to be developed.

Dean came to resent the attention she poured on the children. Most of all he resented her love for Michael. "You never discipline the boy!" She'd never been able to understand that accusation when it seemed Michael's every moment was regulated. His *life* was one of discipline. Wasn't she seeing to that?

And yet, despite all her efforts, Michael had betrayed her too. He had searched for Bryan Taggart. Though they had met, no real relationship had grown from it. Yet it seemed something had broken between her and her son anyway. The more successful Michael became, the more distant he was. She had poured out so much love and effort on him, but he had no time for her.

Dean had never understood how torn she was, how wounded. She'd taken him at his word to do whatever she needed to find what it was she wanted. Unlike her mother, she took Anne everywhere, even to the college classes she took. When that became impossible, she gave up her own dreams to make sure Anne would have the opportunities she had missed. Wasn't she doing as much for Michael?

And then Dean stunned her by saying he was quitting a job that paid six figures a year and starting his own business. She saw all her security going up in flames. The fights had started then and hadn't ended until he filed for divorce. Her lawyer had insisted that Dean was being more than generous, giving her the house and savings. Alimony would have been asking too much, especially since his only income then was the pittance he was making in his new business enterprise. The one good thing she could say about Dean Gardner was that he never quibbled about sending child support. The checks always arrived at the first of the month.

The year they divorced, she heard from Anne—then six—that he had moved in with the woman who had been his secretary at the bank. When he relocated his business to southern California, the woman had stayed behind. Anne told her after a holiday visit that they were still friends. Nora could make no sense of her ex-husband's life, nor did she want to have anything to do with him, other than to receive her monthly checks. However, by court order, Nora had been forced to send Anne to spend the summer with Dean.

When she returned, Nora learned that he was living with another woman. He lived with that woman for several years before she apparently accepted a lucrative job in New York and left. Amicably, again. Now Dean was living with yet another woman, younger this time.

It had been fourteen years since their divorce, and still Nora would sometimes feel the hurt that he hadn't loved her enough to make their marriage work. The things he had said were so cruel, so demeaning, so completely untrue. And still, even after all this time, she felt jealous every time she heard he was with someone else.

What sense was there in that when she loved Fred?

The third time is the charm, so they say. And thus far, she had thought her third marriage was perfect.

Until tonight.

Where was Fred? It was after two in the morning, and he still wasn't home.

Was he betraying her, too, just like everyone she loved had betrayed her?

God, why do they do it? Why do they all turn away from me? I pour out my life on them, and they turn away. My mother didn't love me enough to spend time with me. My father hardly ever said a word to me. Bryan deserted me. Dean cheated on me. Michael never has time for me. Anne wants to have everything her own way. And now Fred . . .

The garage door hummed. Her heart thumped crazily, mingling relief with anger. How dare Fred stay out this late? She sat in the wing chair facing the hall. He would see the light was still on and come in to check on her. She heard the door from the garage open. He appeared, his suit coat still on, his raincoat draped over one shoulder, a briefcase in his hand. He looked tired.

"Where have you been, Fred? I've been worried sick about you. It's half past two."

"I've been at Scoma's in San Francisco. The gentlemen from Japan arrived this morning. Remember?" His mouth was tight with irritation.

She frowned slightly, her anger seeping away. Something was wrong.

"You don't even remember, do you, Nora?" Fred said quietly. He just looked at her, waiting. She was at a complete loss of words. His smile was bleak. "You're so caught up in Anne's insurrection that everything else has gone bye-bye." His eyes darkened slightly. "I told you a month ago these men were coming. I told you how important this contract could be to the business. They'll be here through Saturday."

She saw accusation in his eyes. "Why are you angry with me? What did I do wrong?"

"Yesterday morning I told you I'd call and let you know where we were having dinner tonight. You were supposed to meet me there, Nora."

She felt cold, suddenly remembering everything. How could she have forgotten?

"Where were *you,* Nora?"

"I was at my mother's," she said in a shaky voice, horrified that she had let him down so badly. It was Anne's fault this had happened! If Anne hadn't run off and put her through an emotional wringer, she would have done her duty by Fred.

His expression altered. "Is your mother sick?"

"She looks worse than I've ever seen her." It was true. She had been shocked at how her mother had aged since the last time she saw her.

"Did she call you?"

"No. I just . . . I just had a feeling something was wrong." Thinking about Anne's betrayal, she put her hands over her face and started to cry. "I had to see her. Everything else just went out of my head. I've just had the worst day of my life. And now, to top it off, you're angry with me."

In the past, Fred had always been quick to comfort her. Tonight he stayed where he was. With a sigh, he dropped his raincoat over the back of the sofa and set his briefcase down. "I need a drink." He went behind the wet bar, took a bottle of scotch from the lower cabinet, and poured himself half a glass.

Sniffling and dabbing her nose with a lace hanky, Nora couldn't stop the twinge of resentment that Fred hadn't even thought to offer her one.

"It's going to take some doing for me to save face." Fred's tone was grim. He took a swallow of scotch and put the glass down on the bar. He looked across at her enigmatically. "Face matters with the Japanese. Since Mr. Yamamoto's wife was there and anxious to meet you, the fact that my wife didn't show up said more to them than the hundred pages of documents I've been working on for six months."

It wasn't just anger in his eyes. It was hurt and disappointment. She had let him down badly. Fear curled in the pit of her stomach. Would he leave her like all the rest? She tried so hard and nothing ever worked out the way she planned. "I'm sorry, Fred."

"It's a little late to be sorry." He took up the glass again, swallowing the rest of the scotch. He put the glass on the counter. He looked at her again and shook his head slowly as though trying to make sense of everything. "Nora, sometimes I wonder . . ."

"Wonder what?" she said softly when he didn't continue.

He looked weary and older than his fifty-seven years. "It's better if I don't say anything more right now. I'm tired. I'm going to bed."

What was *that* supposed to mean? That it was all her fault? Why couldn't he try to understand how horrible her day had been? He would understand then how the dinner this evening had slipped her mind. Despite all her efforts, all her sacrifices for those she loved, no one seemed to care what she suffered.

Fred took up his raincoat from the back of the sofa and bent for his briefcase. "We'll talk more in the morning."

Somehow those few words held an ominous sound.

When he walked out of the room, Nora wept, this time in fear of what the morrow would bring.

9

CORBAN PULLED INTO LEOTA REINHARDT'S DRIVEWAY, NOTICING
There was a car with a Christian fish symbol on it parked in front of
her house. He noticed other things as well. The lawn was freshly
mowed, and the bushes in front of the house were pruned neatly and
low enough now that the front porch was visible. The hanging pots
had been removed.

As he went up the front steps, he saw that the rocking chair had
been washed. The seat was still wet, as was the entire front porch. No
spiderwebs, no dust, just the smell of dampness and fresh-cut grass.

Had another volunteer come over? He felt a twinge of irritation
that someone was intruding. Ringing the bell, he waited. On the
third ring, he became worried that something might have happened
to Mrs. Reinhardt. Why wasn't she answering her door? Hearing no
sounds from inside, he moved to peer through the window beside
her front door, but remembered her remarks upon their first meeting. If she didn't want to answer, she didn't have to answer.

Resigned, he went down the steps, wondering what to do next.
Just as he was opening his car door, he heard voices at the back of the
house. Squeezing past the hood, he strode up the narrow driveway.

"Mrs. Reinhardt?" he called out as he came around the back

corner. She was standing in the garden above the small patio area outside the back door; she was wearing a flowered, polyester dress and a white sweater. A girl was with her.

A very pretty girl.

"Corban, what are you doing here? It's Saturday."

"Just thought I'd drop by," he said, trying not to stare at the old woman's companion.

"This is my granddaughter, Anne-Lynn Gardner. Annie, this is Corban Solsek. He's from a charity that sends volunteers to help old people."

The girl was not much taller than the old lady. She had a trim, athletic figure and long, strawberry blonde hair held back carelessly by a denim scrunchy. She was wearing a soiled, white T-shirt, faded blue jeans, and dirty tennis shoes. She removed a gardening glove and stepped forward, hand extended. "I'm pleased to meet you, Corban." Sweat dampened her forehead and dirt smudged her cheek. Despite her disheveled appearance, she glowed with innocence and an open friendliness that made him smile back.

"Likewise," he said.

"You've arrived just in time," Leota said, a gleam in her eyes.

That remark was enough to snap him back to full attention. Raising a brow, he looked at her. "Dare I ask?"

She chuckled. "We were about to prune the trees in back. It's not the best time of year for it, but they're in dire need. And you're just the man for the job."

"I seem to be the *only* man around."

"Don't spoil the compliment."

He laughed. She looked better than he had ever seen her. Being outdoors seemed to agree with her.

"We're going to bring the garden back," Anne said, smiling.

What was he getting himself into? "I don't know the first thing about gardening."

"I don't either." Anne sounded positively delighted. She pulled the glove back on. "We're about to learn. Grandma supplies the brains. We supply the brawn."

"Corban will take exception to that, Annie." Leota smiled straight at him. "He's a senior at the university, and you know how smart they all think they are."

While Anne laughed, Corban glowered at the old lady, feigning annoyance with her. "I don't suppose it would hurt me to get my hands dirty just this once."

"Good boy. Rise to the challenge. Tools are in the shed to the right of the gate."

He could care less about gardening, but he could see that today Leota Reinhardt was in the mood to talk. Maybe it was the presence of the little dish walking along the cobblestone pathway ahead of him. Whatever it was, he intended to hang around and take mental notes.

"There's a ladder on the back wall," Leota called, following at a much slower pace. She had her hands out slightly as though to balance herself better. "And a saw. It should be hanging on the wall to the right of the door. And a can of latex paint and a brush."

Corban wondered why she was talking about paint. They were going to prune trees, not touch up the stucco.

"Watch for black widows in there," Leota called, standing at the open gate beneath the sagging arbor. "They like dark places."

"We will, Grandma."

Groaning inwardly, Corban hung back, hoping the girl wouldn't expect him to brave the arachnids. She didn't even bat an eye in his direction. Without the least hesitation, she picked up a broken branch and opened the door. She attacked the webs like a warrior with a sword—upward, downward, forward, moving fearlessly into the dim, dusty environs. She banged around briefly and handed the saw out to him, then came out carrying a ladder.

"Don't just stand there, Corban," the old lady said. "There's an extension pruner mounted on the wall. And we'll need the can of latex paint and a brush. Should be on the shelf."

"What's an extension pruner look like?" He looked around cautiously before going inside the dusty, shadow-filled shed.

"Two poles that fit together after you get them outside. On the end of one are clippers."

He found the pieces and became entangled in the rope attached to the lower part of the clippers. Winding the rope quickly around his hand, he picked up the two poles and brought them outside, thankful to be in the sunlight again. He didn't feel anything crawling on him.

Anne had already set up the ladder near the biggest tree in the center of the walled-off garden in back. "What kind of tree is it, Grandma?"

"Apricot. The one over there is a cherry tree. The other one is a plum." She shook her head. "What a tangled mess . . ."

Corban couldn't have agreed with her more. The trees had

branches pointing in all directions; the ground was covered with weeds, some knee-high, though those toward the back were higher than that. Worst of all was the layer of shriveled and rotted fruit beneath the tree—several years' worth by the looks of it. Small trees had sprouted here and there.

"Okay, Grandma. We've got all the tools. Now where do we start?" Anne stood there, saw in hand, looking ready for almost anything.

Leota Reinhardt made her way carefully toward them. She reached up to one of the branches sagging down and snapped off a portion. She looked at it and then around and up through the tree. "First thing you have to do is remove all the dead, broken, and diseased branches. That one and that one—" she pointed—"start up there and work your way down and out. Find a growth bud and cut just above it." She glanced at him. "Corban, put that pruner together and use it. Annie can't do it all by her lonesome."

"Watch out below," Annie said as the first branch swung down.

"Easy," Mrs. Reinhardt said. "You don't want the branches banging into each other. Hand the can up to her, Corban. Annie, you need to paint over the cut so no germs can get in and the sap won't bleed too long. Use the pocketknife I gave you."

Annie took the knife from her back pocket, pried open the small can, and tucked the knife away again. Corban watched her dab paint onto the cut branch. Setting the can into a joining of branches, she leaned down for the saw she had put on the ladder tray.

"The pruner, Corban. The pruner!"

The old woman was like a general mustering her troops! She stood on guard at the gate, watching the battle. "Leave that one, Annie. Cut the one to the right. We want to thin the tree so that air will circulate and there'll be more light to all the branches."

"This one, Grandma?"

"Yes, that's it. That's the one. Corban, see if you can get the one over there. Pull. Don't be afraid of it. See how that limb is rubbing on the bigger branch? It's doing damage. There's probably a wound there. Annie, you'll need to paint over it so there won't be any decay. There's a branch right there that needs cutting. The wind must have snapped it. See it? The one with the brown leaves. Can you climb, honey?"

Anne laughed. "You betcha." Stepping off the ladder into the tree, the saw dangling from a hook on her belt, she moved through the tree with grace and ease. She paused briefly to get the can of paint and hook it to her waist along with the saw. She didn't seem to care that some paint was getting on her Levi's. Corban worked below, glancing up at her. She was like a kid at a picnic.

"Heads up!" Annie called as another branch took flight.

As the old woman tutored her minions, the tree took shape. It began to open from within, light filtering through the green leaves making the edges shine gold. The branches no longer spread in all directions, unwieldy and out of control, but were contained, rounded upward, flat on top like a wineglass.

"Now," Mrs. Reinhardt said with a sigh of satisfaction, "there she is. That looks just right."

Anne came down from the ladder. She stepped back almost to the gate, where her grandmother stood, and looked up. The smile the old woman wore was childlike in its pleasure.

"The tree will bear fruit this year," Mrs. Reinhardt said. "Lots of it."

Corban frowned. "I'd think with fewer branches, you'd get less fruit."

"A good pruning stimulates the right kind of growth. Same holds true with people."

He was about to ask her what she meant by that when Anne said, "What should we do with the prunings, Grandma? Too bad we don't have a chipper. I've seen crews working on the trees that line the streets. They feed the branches in, and they're chewed up into a fine mulch that they spread under the tree, all in a matter of minutes."

"We have something better than a chipper." Leota Reinhardt's grin was pure mischief. "We have Corban." She looked at him and waved her hand in command. "Just cut the bigger branches into two-foot lengths. I'll get some string and you can make small bundles and stack them by the back door. I'll burn the branches a few at a time during the cold spots ahead."

"While Corban's doing that, Grandma, I'll start on the cherry tree," Anne said, folding the ladder.

Corban stifled his irritation. Little Miss Eager Beaver and the Slave Driver. What did these two women think he was? Part of the Conservation Corps? Breaking a dead branch over his knee, he tossed it aside, then picked up another branch. It would be easier to do the work as quickly as possible than to try to get out of it.

Pretty little Anne-Lynn Gardner was already perched on the ladder beneath the cherry tree. Corban broke another branch over his knee and tossed it aside. If he could get some information out of her, the whole day wouldn't be shot. "I take it you and your grandmother are close?"

"Not as close as I'd like us to be." She peered down at him, the saw poised. "Our family didn't come often, but when we did visit, my mother relegated me to the backyard. I hardly know my grandmother, Corban." She began sawing the dead limb. "But I'm going to remedy that."

Leota found the ball of twine in the laundry cabinet on the back porch. She was already exhausted. Just standing at the garden gate wore her out. The sunshine felt so good, but it also drained her of what little energy she had. Too many months of sitting inside in artificial light, she guessed. She had become as pale as a moldering corpse. Well, she wasn't sitting inside anymore!

She took her sun hat from the wall, where it had been hanging for two years and went back outside. Her legs felt like lead as she went up the four brick steps to the cobblestone walkway that ran in front of the living unit Bernard had built for his parents.

Everywhere she looked, things needed pruning, thinning, tying up, and removing. Hours of work. For her, it had always been a labor of love. Would it be so for Annie? Poor Corban looked so grim. She had no illusions about why he had agreed to help: He was after information; probably interrogating Annie right now. Not that Annie could tell him much. The little darling wouldn't even realize she was being interviewed. It wouldn't enter her head that someone might want to use her.

Then again, maybe she was being unfair to Corban. It wasn't entirely his fault he was so puffed up with knowledge that he didn't have a lick of sense. Education was no less an idol these days than it was in the past. Corban didn't have her advantages. Sometimes the school of hard knocks taught more than the best universities in the land.

And You, Lord. You teach the heart as well as the mind. Sometimes the truth is hard to bear, but it's better to walk in the light of truth than to live in the darkness of lies.

She was panting slightly when she reached the gate. "You work quickly," she said to Corban.

His gaze flickered from Annie to her. She stumbled over one of the cobblestones. Keeping her balance, she gripped an arbor post.

"Are you all right, Mrs. Reinhardt?" Corban looked worried. What did he think? She'd keel over and die at his feet and his paper would go up in smoke? "I'm fine. Just old and clumsy."

"I'll get you one of those garden chairs."

"Buttering me up, are you?"

He paused and gave her a sardonic smile. "It's easier talking to you when you're conscious."

She chuckled. The lad lacked good manners, but he had spunk. She admired that. "So, have you been asking Annie all kinds of questions about the old lady while I was in the house?"

"I tried."

At least he was learning to tell the truth and not be pretentious.

Annie parted two branches and grinned down at her. "You are a great mystery, Grandma."

"It's good to be a mystery. Piques the interest. If I told Corban everything about myself, he wouldn't bother coming around, and I'd have to break in another volunteer." Corban returned with the American steel chair and plunked it down on the small, weedy lawn. He was clearly annoyed. "Well? Isn't it the truth?"

"You shouldn't tease him, Grandma. I'm sure he won't forget all about you after getting the information he needs for his report."

"You must be seeing sides of him I've missed." Corban's face turned red, whether from temper or embarrassment she didn't know. She looked him in the eyes. "If I'm wrong, tell me."

"I'm thinking about leaving right now."

"Oh, stop pouting. Before you go, move the chair over there in the sunshine. I'll be able to see better what Annie's doing to that cherry tree."

Corban snatched up the chair, maneuvered it through the gate, and slammed it down again. He came back and offered his arm for support.

"And I didn't even have to ask," she said, smiling up at him. She eld firmly to his arm as she made her way over the rough ground of the back section. "Such a good boy, seeing to an old lady's needs." She settled herself comfortably in the chair. "Thank you, dear."

"You're welcome, *ma'am*," he said through his teeth.

She took the ball of twine out of her sweater pocket and held it out to him. "In case you change your mind about leaving." When he just looked at it, she said, "For the branches. Two-foot lengths. Did you forget already?"

"I was hoping you had." He took the ball of twine and went back to work.

Leota was warming to him. He was stiff and stuffy and self-seeking, but he might just be reachable. She leaned back, enjoying the feel of sunshine on her face. "Did you know an apricot tree can live up to a hundred years?"

"How old is yours, Grandma?"

"Sixty-five years old, or close to it. It was just starting to bear fruit when I came to live with Mama and Papa Reinhardt back in 1939. I planted two cherry trees in 1942. One died. I never knew what killed it. One day it was healthy and the next the leaves were withering. I was worried some blight had gotten it and would spread to the other tree, so I cut it down quick and burned it. I did a lot of working and praying on that soil before I planted that plum tree to replace it."

"Sounds like a lot of worry expended on a tree." Corban tossed one tied bundle aside and started to put together another.

"It was 1944. Worry was part of breathing. The war was going strong. My husband was in the army, fighting in Europe. Seeing that tree die made me worry all the more about him."

Corban paused in his work and looked at her with a frown. "I don't get it. What does a tree dying have to do with your husband in Europe?"

"Nothing, I suppose, except that this was my Victory garden. It's hard to believe everything will turn out right when your fruit tree dies overnight."

"Oh." He still looked confused. His smile was polite, but his expression said it all. He thought she was losing her marbles. "Did your husband come home?"

"Yes, he came home." Corban looked at her, waiting for more. She looked back and smiled. He could wait awhile longer. He wouldn't appreciate what she had to tell him. Not yet, at least.

"What was Grandpa like?" Annie said, still perched on the ladder. She snipped another branch, lowering it carefully through the others before dropping it.

"What has your mother told you?"

Annie went still on the ladder. "Nothing much," she said after a moment and started working again.

Poor Eleanor. So much anger, so much shame. All because she was too blind and too stubborn to want to see the truth. *Lord, sometimes I wish I could shake that girl until the walls around her heart crumble. I imagine You know exactly how I feel.*

"He was a good man, Annie," Leota said firmly. "He had a good heart. He cared deeply about many things. He was just . . . quiet."

Bernard hadn't always had the drawbridges up. There had been a time when he was like a knight mounted on a great steed ready to go into any battle. Hadn't he stormed her citadel and claimed her heart? She had agreed to marry him after four dates, the announcement coming as such a shock to his parents that they never quite got over it. Papa almost had, perhaps, but Mama hadn't fully accepted her until the end, and by then, it was too late to undo the years of damage.

For three years she and Bernard had been blessed with happiness. Then the Japanese had bombed Pearl Harbor and turned their world upside down. Bernard had joined the army rather than wait to be drafted. She had understood his reasons, but that didn't stop the fear from almost eating her alive all the time he was gone. She had loved him so much she thought she would die without him. It wasn't until later that she came to understand that there were things worse than death.

Bernard Gottlieb Reinhardt had gone off to war young and proud of who he was: a loyal American willing to put his life on the line to bring Hitler down. His parents were as eager for Hitler's regime to be destroyed as he, for they followed the news of what the ego-mad dictator was doing in Europe. They prayed for their relatives living in Germany, agonizing over what might be happening to them. What they did hear was soul-wrenching. Why couldn't others see what was really happening and get out of Germany before it was too late? They could come to America, the land of freedom and opportunity.

Freedom and opportunity . . .

Opportunities dwindled quickly for those who still retained thick German accents. Distrust abounded.

Poor Bernard had carried so much responsibility on his shoulders. He had gone off, not just to fight a war but to seek out two uncles and their families and find out what happened to them. If he could find them.

And, as God would have it, he did.

The Bernard Gottlieb Reinhardt who came home was not the same man who had marched proudly off to war. The veteran was a stranger, broken and filled with an anguish so deep that nothing had ever lifted him fully from the depths of his depression. Not even alcohol could deaden the pain he lived with until the day he died.

Corban said something to her and, shaken from her memories, she looked at him, confused, still lost in the mire of memories.

"Your husband, Mrs. Reinhardt. What did he do for a living?"

"Oh, he did lots of things. He painted houses for a while. Then he did drywall work. He was employed by a roofer. I guess you could say

Bernard had so many different jobs that he became a jack-of-all-trades. You'll have to take a look inside the apartment behind the carport. Bernard built that for his parents. He did everything, even the plumbing."

She didn't see any reason to tell them that after the war Bernard couldn't seem to hold a job longer than a year. Something always happened: hurt feelings, a fight, poor pay, layoffs, firing.

"He became a handyman after a while. People would call him to do odd jobs. A little of this, a little of that. Whatever he did, he did well."

Annie was looking at her from her perch. When Annie smiled, Leota saw something in her expression that made her want to weep. Perhaps Eleanor had said more than Annie was willing to share.

"With that kind of occupation, it'd be impossible to save enough for retirement years," Corban said.

Leota's mouth tightened. She supposed he meant Bernard had left her without resources. That was true, but not something she liked to dwell upon. "There are more things to life than money, young man." She had no intention of going over Bernard's shortcomings as a husband or father. He had done the best he could.

"I didn't mean any slight against your husband, Mrs. Reinhardt."

The foolish boy was still fixed on his project, gathering facts, making suppositions. All wrong. "The fact is, we never talked about retirement," she said. "There wasn't time. In our generation, most people worked until they were sixty-five or seventy or were wheeled out the door feetfirst. Some got tossed out a month before retirement benefits were scheduled to start. Bernard died in 1970. And don't ask me how he died. I didn't request an autopsy."

When Corban winced, she closed her eyes, sorry she had been so abrupt. She sighed and opened her eyes to look into his. "There are things you can never understand, Corban, and I haven't the heart left to explain."

He frowned, searching her face. For the first time, she saw compassion. She smiled slightly. "It's not going to be as easy as you thought, is it? This project of yours."

"No, it isn't."

"What happened to you?" Ruth said when Corban entered the apartment.

"I've been doing manual labor," he said dryly, collapsing onto the battered sofa. He was exhausted, dirty, and annoyed. Glancing around the apartment, he felt slightly better. He had expected to come home to a mess, but Ruth had been busy. The rug was vacuumed, the pillows on the sofa plumped, the coffee table clear of its usual debris after one of her gatherings. "What happened? Was the meeting canceled?"

"No," she said in annoyance. "I just finished cleaning up. Everyone left hours ago. Where have you been, Cory?"

"At Mrs. Reinhardt's helping her granddaughter prune fruit trees."

"Granddaughter?"

Corban heard the edge in her voice. Jealousy? Nice to know he was appreciated. "Her name's Anne. Eighteen or so. She's going to some art school in San Francisco."

Ruth leaned her shoulder against the kitchen door frame and crossed her ankles. She smiled, her expression enigmatic. "Pretty?"

"Very. Petite. Hair to her waist. Blonde."

"Natural blonde?"

"Nasty question."

She laughed. "Oh, forget it. People who live in the City and fancy themselves artists are a dime a dozen. Sounds like a ditz to me."

"You're being pretty cavalier, considering you just had a meeting with your women's activists."

Eyes flashing, she pushed away from the door frame and went back into the kitchen. "Do you want some dinner? I made a tuna casserole."

"I already ate at Mrs. Reinhardt's. Pork chops at $3.59 a pound." He laughed. Mrs. Reinhardt had made sure he knew how much his meal had cost her.

"Why are you laughing?" Ruth came back and stood in the doorway, a kitchen towel over her shoulder. "She sounds like a rude old biddy."

"Yeah, she is," he said, head back against the sofa. "Disagreeable. Snarls every other word at me. Orders me around like a personal servant. She hasn't an ounce of respect for my person."

"Does she know you're studying at the university?"

"She knows. That's just another strike against me."

"Why?"

He leaned forward, raking his fingers through his hair in frustration. "Why do you think? She knows she's part of my project."

"You told her?"

"She didn't give me much choice. She nailed my ears to the wall the last time I was over there. It was either be up-front with her or get tossed out the front door. Figuratively speaking, of course."

"So are you getting what you need from her?"

"I'm getting bits and pieces. She feeds facts to me like dog treats. Sit up, Corban. Fetch, Corban." He thought of the dozen bundles of cut branches stacked neatly on her back porch. How many morsels of information had he eked out of her today? Every time he learned something about that old woman, more questions loomed.

Leota Reinhardt wasn't as simple as she seemed.

"Kiss her off, then, Cory. Just go to one of the senior centers and interview some people. Or go to one of those residential-care facilities. For heaven's sake, don't make such a big deal out of one old lady."

Easy for her to say. "I've gone this far with Mrs. Reinhardt; I'm not throwing in the towel now." Things she had said today had stirred a deeper interest. Talking to her, though, was like pulling up strings from a tapestry when what he was after was the whole picture. "She was different today. I saw sides to her I hadn't seen before."

"For example."

"She has a sense of humor. She can take a hunk out of you and then stitch you up in the same sentence."

"Nice," Ruth said dryly. "Are these new sides going to get your paper written?"

That wasn't what was bothering her, and they both knew it. Corban stood up and went to his computer. Pushing the power button, he sat down. "I've got to write some notes while the information is fresh in my head." He moved the mouse and clicked the word-processing icon. He knew Ruth was still standing in the doorway; he could feel her looking at him. The air crackled with tension.

"Why don't we do something tomorrow, Cory? Go to a movie or take the ferry to Angel Island. *Something.* I've been worrying lately. Don't you think we're getting in a rut?"

They were in a rut, all right. One *she* had dug. Funny she should notice that now. Maybe she was feeling a little less secure about him and her situation. Well, let her. "We'll see." Pulling up the file, he started typing.

> *R's granddaughter was visiting today. Noticed a difference in R's attitude. Cheerful. Focused. Sharp sense of humor. Made numerous jokes at my expense. She talked more than usual. Talked some about her husband.*
>
> ***Look for information on Bernard Reinhardt.*
>
> *Anne said she didn't know much about her grandmother. Family didn't visit often.*

"Maybe I'll go without you," Ruth said.

He heard the faint threat behind her declaration of independence: *Absent yourself and I might find someone more attractive out there, buddy-boy.* Angry, he looked her. "Do what you want, Ruth. Only be careful." He hoped she saw the rest. *Don't think you can make me dance to any tune you play. The spell you cast is weakening.*

Her eyes flickered, then quickly steeled over. "It's nice to know you'll worry about my well-being." Turning her back on him, she went into the kitchen.

Corban turned his thoughts back to Leota Reinhardt.

A cabinet door banged in the kitchen.

> *What caused family estrangement?*
> **Get to know Anne-Lynn Gardner.*

Hadn't Anne said she was staying over tonight with her grandmother? Maybe he would go by again tomorrow and get her telephone number.

10

LEOTA SAT IN THE MIDDLE OF THE CHURCH, IN THE MIDDLE OF A PEW, with Annie. Hands folded in her lap, Leota gazed at the stained-glass windows along the east side. Early morning sunlight came through, making the rainbow hues glow with color bolder than life. At the front was an old, rugged cross mounted on the wall. Banners hung to the left and right proclaiming King of Kings and Lord of Lords in exquisite, silken designs of gold and purple.

Men and women of various ages and skin colors all garbed in maroon, white-collared robes sat in the choir just below the cross. The pastor, not the one she remembered, sat off by himself to the left of the pulpit in a thronelike chair. He looked solemn, dressed as he was in a long, black robe and embroidered stole.

How many years had it been since she had stepped foot in this old church with its grand edifice and beautiful windows? How long had it been since she was surrounded by fellow parishioners? Six years? Ten? It wasn't even the same denomination—not that she was bothered much by that. There was a good feeling in this place, a warmth that permeated the people. In addition to the two greeters at the door, a dozen or more people had smiled or said hello to Leota and Annie.

627

The last time Leota had come here, she'd been so tired and depressed, she'd known it was her last time attending church. Old age—and its limitations—had caught up with her. The walk to the bus stop had been fatiguing. The wait had been stressful, especially when several young hoodlums eyed her purse, seemingly waiting for possible witnesses to walk away and leave her vulnerable. Luckily, the bus had arrived before she was mugged.

The ride had gone smoothly, but by the time she reached the church, she had been in dire need of using the rest room, which was downstairs. Two or three steps were easy enough to manage, but a flight of stairs in a narrow, curving passageway was risky. She had been bumped several times by children racing down to Sunday school. Holding tightly to the railing, she had moved slowly, afraid of falling and breaking bones. The younger, more able-bodied folks had to squeeze around her.

By the time she went down the stairs, into the rest room, and back up those stairs to the sanctuary, she was exhausted. She'd sat in the back of the church, distressed and unnoticed, barely able to hear the sermon. In her sad state, the services had passed in a blur. All she could think about was the long journey home. How long would she have to wait for a bus? Who might be waiting at the bus stop to threaten her? She'd been so tired at that point, she sat fearful of how she would make the four-block walk on the flat section before coming to the hill on which her little house was built.

It had all been too much for her. Life was stressful enough without adding to it. After that day, she hadn't gone back to church. The first few Sundays she'd stayed home from church, she'd tried to console herself with services on television. Surely the Lord wouldn't mind. Yet breaking the long habit of attending church every Sunday had been heart wrenching. And what a lonely proposition those television evangelists were, with their dramatic presentations, professional singers, glitzy environment, and guilt-grinding appeals for money. They'd made her feel so bad at times that she'd thought about sending a big chunk of her social security check.

Instead, she turned her television off.

The saddest part was that no one missed her. She'd been attending the same church for years, and when she stopped going not one person called to find out why. She supposed if she had been more involved, perhaps her absence would have been noticed. As it was, she hadn't been involved in anything. When she left, no one cared.

For a time, she had met God in the garden. And then that precious time was stripped away as well. She wondered if it was the same with Him as it had been with the church. God certainly didn't need her. With all the thousands out there serving Him mightily, what did one uncommitted little old lady matter?

She stopped speaking to Him for a while. Then she started in again. Who else could she talk with on long, lonely days?

Leota looked around surreptitiously, searching for familiar faces. None that she could see. The congregation was mixed now, more black than white, a few Asians and Hispanics scattered about. Just like her neighborhood. Some people were dressed in fine suits and dresses, while others were in jeans and T-shirts.

She felt comfortable, far more comfortable than in past times. Maybe it was having Annie sitting next to her. Yet, she felt it was something more than that . . . there was a spirit in this church that seemed to bind the people together. It didn't matter what race or cultural background. They all seemed to know one another and greet one another with affection.

Wasn't that the way it was supposed to be? Where else could one go in this world to find such a sense of peace among all peoples but before Jesus Christ? This was the first time she'd been in a church that felt that way. It seemed a silent proclamation: We are one in Christ, brothers and sisters all.

Lord, I don't know any of my neighbors anymore, but I sure feel I know everyone in this church. Not by name, but by Name. Jesus is shining right out of them. Most of them anyway. That pastor could sure use a smile on his face, but maybe he's talking with You before he talks to us.

Everyone stood and sang "Amazing Grace," and the tears flowed unexpectedly down Leota's cheeks. She hoped Annie wouldn't notice and be embarrassed. The poor child would wonder why her foolish old granny was crying.

Oh, but Lord, I can't help it. It feels so good. It feels like I've come home. Hearing that old hymn is like a taste of heaven. And yet, it's a mixed feeling, Jesus, because I know Annie and I will walk out of here in a little while, and it might be a long time before I stand and sit and pray and sing in a church again. Oh, Lord, maybe this will be the last time. Period. Unless Annie comes back for another weekend visit. But I can't count on that, can I, Lord? I can't count on anyone or anything. It's not my right to do so. She has her own life.

Leota's throat closed so that she couldn't sing at all. She continued to mouth the words so no one would notice her lapse should they happen to look. She could hear Annie singing; her voice was clear and lovely. Eleanor had probably had her in voice lessons. Eleanor had desperately wanted voice lessons when she was a teenager, but there had been no money. Leota had suggested Eleanor join a church choir, but her daughter had thought that was the cruelest thing anyone had ever said to her.

Others were noticing how well Annie sang, too. A young black woman turned and looked back at Annie, smiling as she did so. Pleased, Leota looked at her granddaughter with pride. Annie wasn't noticing a thing because she sang with her eyes closed.

Oh, Lord, she's lovely, isn't she? And such a blessing. I know I ought to be thankful for the little time I have with her. I shouldn't expect more. And I am grateful, Lord, I am. But You have to know how much this hurts. She'll go back across the Bay in a few hours, and it might be a long time before I see her again. I know I should relish the moment, enjoy it for what it is. Help me not to think about tomorrow . . .

There were times, though she hated to admit it, when she wondered if it wouldn't have been better had Annie never come. *It's just like when the feeling comes back into your foot when it's been numb. Hurts so much. Oh, God, life hurts. I forgot how much.*

She and Annie sat again. The pastor began his sermon. " 'There is a time . . .' " As he read from the Bible, Leota's mind raced ahead of him, remembering the Scriptures: *"There is a time for everything, a season for every activity under heaven."* Ecclesiastes. Written by an old king who had squandered his years in vain pursuits. The pastor read only a portion of the passage before starting to build his point about Christians becoming involved in the community, making their voices heard about the way the government was run, being active rather than passive.

Leota tried to concentrate, but her mind wandered. She would hear a few words and off her mind would go again, into the past, wandering down tunnels like a rabbit racing through its warren. She was familiar with the book of Ecclesiastes. She knew the passage very well. Yet none of what the pastor said seemed to apply to her. She wished he had stuck to the Scripture instead of going off on what everyone ought to be doing to change the world. If she had learned one thing in her long life it was to put less stock in what the world was doing and more in getting right with the Lord. It took God to change a heart. A changed heart meant a changed life. Enough of them and then, maybe, God willing, the world would change.

Yet it seemed unlikely. From all she had read in the Bible over the past years, the world was winding down. Nothing was going to get better. It was going to get a whole lot worse. And then it would end in fire.

She supposed this young pastor was talking about the meantime. He wanted everyone to work hard to try to change things for the better while the world waited for Jesus to come back.

The thought exhausted her.

She was past the age of being involved, being active, making any difference in the world. The truth was, she didn't care anymore. Let the fire come. She was closer to a time to die than anything else. She didn't fault the young pastor for his zeal, for his great hope of seeing a cleaner, safer, more loving community. But hadn't he read Revelation?

" 'There is a time . . .' " he quoted again. He used the words like a bell tolling. As indeed it was.

Leota's mind wandered again. *"A time to plant and a time to harvest . . ."* The trees were pruned now, for the first time in years. There would be fruit when summer came, fruit in abundance to be canned and given away. Would Annie want to learn how? Would Anne turn the soil in the Victory garden and plant vegetables? And what about the flowering shrubs and perennials? Leota let her mind drift in memories of color—pink, blue, red, purple, yellow. *Oh, the yard around the house was lovely, Lord. Wasn't it? You remember.* Leota could see it all again in her mind's eye, the way it had been, the way it could be again. The garden had burned bright in a blaze of rainbow colors. Fiery bright color . . . colors more beautiful than any stained-glass window.

Will Annie see it as I did, Lord? Will she feel Your presence there as I did? Or will it be boring work, as it was for Eleanor?

Hurtful words came flooding back in the echo of Eleanor's angry voice, bringing a wash of pain with them.

"You'd rather garden than spend time with your own daughter!"

"Join me, Eleanor. Come outside with me and see through my eyes, if only for an hour . . ."

"I hate gardening. I don't want to have ugly hands like yours, with dirt under my nails and calluses. I want to have hands like Grandma Helene's. . . . I hate being on my knees. Grandma said you can't make me . . ."

Oh, God, why couldn't Eleanor see? Why couldn't she feel the joy I felt? Why did she hate everything I loved?

"A time to tear down and a time to rebuild . . ."

Leota's family was torn down. Destroyed. *Can I rebuild what I had with my children when they were small, Lord? Is there any chance for me and Eleanor? And what about George? Would that I could tear down the walls around him with my bare hands! He's so much like Bernard I want to shake him out of himself, but he won't let me get close enough. He doesn't even realize how much like his father he is.*

Oh, God . . . was that it? George was like Bernard. *Father, why is my son hiding? What is he afraid to face?* Failure, perhaps?

"A time to cry and a time to laugh . . ."

Leota had cried enough tears for a lifetime. She wanted to laugh again. She wanted to stop grieving over the might-have-beens. . . .

I want to dance before I die, God. I want to embrace life the way I used to. What happened to all that strength I used to have? I was so sure of You, so certain everything would turn out fine. "God will take care of me." I always told myself that. Isn't that what they always say in church? God will make it turn out right. I have felt forsaken.

There was a stirring within her, like a soft whispered kiss.

Yes, I know. Now, there's Annie. Thank You, Jesus, for Annie. I don't mean to be ungrateful. But I still yearn for my daughter and my son, Lord . . .

Images flooded her mind, pictures of the days when Eleanor and George were little and she could hold them close and kiss them and love them freely. It was so long ago, before surviving got in the way. Her children had never understood why she'd had to work, and she couldn't explain without hurting others. She'd thought in time . . .

"There is a time . . ."

Leota closed her eyes against the tears. *I thought when they grew up, they would see more clearly. They would finally comprehend the sacrifices. They would ask questions . . . Why? What happened? How?*

It hadn't happened. They'd never cared enough to ask. Not to this day. And still they don't know.

When will they ever know the truth, Lord? When will they ask why things were the way they were? When will they see through my eyes? Or is it Your will that the truth die with me? Is that it, Jesus? Surely that wasn't God's way.

"I am the truth . . . truth sets you free . . ."

The truth would hurt. Eleanor was so wrapped up in herself, and George had closed himself off from Leota. Could it be . . . ? Was he doing the same thing to his wife and children? The same thing

Bernard did so many years ago? Was George's pain as great? Was his heart broken?

Over what, Father? Oh, Lord God, I ache for my children. I love them so much. I want them back. I know I ask too much. I've always asked too much, Lord. I wanted so much for them. I wanted them to receive all You have to offer. Why wouldn't they accept anything? Was it because it was offered with my hands? Is that what I did wrong, Lord?

Her throat choked; tears burned her eyes. She'd failed them.

"A time to search and a time to lose . . ."

Leota closed her eyes. *Oh, Lord, my lambs are lost. Will they even recognize Your voice when You call to them? Will they cry out in relief and run to You? Or will they turn a deaf ear? Will they hear, but run away in fear? Will they go on slapping away the hand that reaches out to rescue them?*

She had tried so hard, and yet it had all come to nothing. And here was this exuberant, young pastor saying "Do . . . do . . . do . . ." Well, she'd done all she could do, and nothing good had come of it. She never had enough time. Days, weeks, years slipped away.

Annie took her hand. Startled, Leota looked at her. Her granddaughter smiled, a tender look of concern in her eyes. Blinking back tears, Leota smiled back, hoping none of the anguish she was feeling showed. Annie's eyes filled with tears, too, and she took Leota's hand in both of hers, holding it tenderly on her lap.

Leota closed her eyes again. *I have done nothing good, Lord, and yet, here I sit seeing what You have done. Maybe there is hope yet.* If she could let go. If she spoke truth. If they would listen . . .

"A time to keep and a time to throw away . . ."

The gentle words filled her.

Oh, Lord, I will hold tight to my love and not let go. I will throw away all the cruel words flung at me. I will cast away anger and hurt and despair. I won't think on the false accusations, the slights, the long silences, and the rejection. I will think about You. I will think about Annie. I will think about the flowering fruit trees. I will think about the perennials and annuals that will come even without care. Flowers don't grow if it doesn't rain, and it's been raining, Lord. Oh, it had been raining such a long, long time.

"A time to tear and a time to mend . . . a time to be quiet and a time to speak up . . . a time to love and a time to hate . . . a time for war and a time for peace."

Leota pressed her lips together. She would tear down the walls and mend the fences. She would be silent no more. *Oh, Father, it is time, isn't it? It's time to speak of the past, to make the truth known. I have loved long and hard, but it's time to hate the evil that has held my children away from me. I will go to war for Eleanor and George, whether they like it or not. The battle is not over until I draw my last breath. I have waited and waited, and I will wait no more. I will shake them with what I have to tell. I will shake them to their very souls. Maybe that will be enough to tear down their altars and smash their idols and turn them once and for all to the living God who made them to be His children.*

"Glory be to the Father," the congregation sang out suddenly, and the rafters seemed to ring with the sound, "and to the Son and to the Holy Ghost. As it was in the beginning, so let it be again . . ."

As Leota stood again with the rest of the congregation, she didn't remember a word the pastor had said, but she felt refreshed. She made no attempt to join in the singing, but let the words rain down upon her. *Lord, cleanse me again. Wash me with Your living water and hyssop. By Your blood I am made white as snow. Heal my wounded heart and make me whole. And then, Lord, give me Your sword.*

Four men went forward, and a prayer was said before the offering plates were taken up. A young black woman sang. Leota recognized the name of the hymn printed in the program, but what the girl was singing didn't much resemble what Leota remembered. The melody was almost lost in the fancy scales up and down, the warbles and trills. She supposed this is what people called *soul* music, but it made her want to shout, "Just sing it plain like it was written! Sing it plain!"

Annie was smiling. She and everyone else in the pew seemed to be enjoying the music. That was plain enough to see. Leota could see for herself the young woman was putting her entire heart into that hymn. The girl reached a high note, and Leota felt goose bumps. It reminded her of the day she had watched the children next door bury that bird. They'd all sung a hymn in the same style. Quieter, because they were burying a bird . . .

By heaven, it wasn't the same woman, was it? She did look vaguely familiar.

Leota noticed the offering plate coming closer and felt acutely distressed. She dug in her purse, trying not to think about how many days it would be before another social security check arrived. All she could find was nine dollars. Nine dollars! What a pittance that was to offer the Lord of the universe, the Creator of all. Embarrassed, she folded the bills and kept them in the palm of her hand. When the plate was passed to her, she tucked the bills beneath the white offertory envelopes already filling it and passed it on.

The old familiar doxology was sung as the men carried the plates forward and placed them on the altar. The pastor said one last prayer, asking that the Lord would empower all present to go out and *do something* bold for Jesus. As he left the pulpit, everyone began singing again, one last rousing song with a Jewish-sounding melody accompanied by much hand clapping. Shocked, Leota stood limp and silent. This display of zeal was far from the solemnity of past services. And these people were nothing like the placid-faced parishioners who used to fill these pews.

When the song ended, everybody started talking and moving about. Some crowded into the center aisle and headed for the door, where the pastor was waiting to greet them, but the rest seemed in no hurry to depart. They clustered together in small groups, smiling and talking and laughing.

Things had certainly changed.

She and Annie hadn't taken two steps when the young black woman in the row in front of them turned around to greet them. Her name went right in Leota's right ear and out the left.

"This is my grandmother," Annie said, "Mrs. Leota Reinhardt."

"Well, I'm pleased to meet you, Mrs. Reinhardt," the young woman said. "Are you and Anne from out of town?"

"No. I attended this church for over twenty years."

The woman looked confused. "Now, *I'm* embarrassed. I thought I'd met everyone who attends here."

"I haven't come for a few years. Too hard to get here from where I live. I used to ride the bus." She slipped her hand beneath Annie's, needing support. So many people milling around made her nervous. She moved stiffly. She didn't want to get bumped and fall on her face and make a fool of herself. Anne put her hand over hers.

"Where do you live, Mrs. Reinhardt?"

"In the Dimond District."

"I'm familiar with the area. What street?"

Annie told her.

"Well, you don't say. Arba Wilson lives on the same street. You must know her."

"I don't know anyone on my street anymore." Leota wished they could leave and save her further embarrassment. Arba Wilson. Well, she finally had a name to put to the face of her next-door neighbor.

Annie looked at her, perplexed. Her granddaughter must have felt

635

the discomfort radiating from her because she started to move. Besides that, it was clear the lady greeting them didn't know what to say. Extending her hand, Annie shook the lady's hand and said they were very pleased to meet her, but they had better be going.

Others said hello as they made their way to the door. The pastor shook Leota's hand as Annie made swift introductions. His grip was strong enough to make Leota wince. "I hope you put a visitor's card into the offering plate," he said.

"No, I didn't." She had noticed it upon sitting down but hadn't thought to fill it out.

"Oh, well, I hope you enjoyed the service, Mrs. Reinhardt."

"It was different from what I'm used to." In fact, everything had been different. And refreshing.

"You liked it though, didn't you, Grandma?" Annie said with a smile.

"I didn't say I didn't," Leota told them both.

"Well, that's good," the pastor said.

"I thought that young woman was going to sing the roof right off." The pastor smiled, eyes shining this time. "She surely does sing in the Spirit, ma'am."

"You look much better when you do that," she said without thinking.

"Do what, ma'am?"

"Smile."

"Grandma!" Annie said with a laugh. "I think we'd better go."

The pastor laughed. "Just be sure you bring her back, Miss Gardner." He turned to greet another behind them.

Annie was chuckling all the way to the car. "What?" Leota said, faintly annoyed.

"You are really something, Grandma." Annie laughed as she tucked her into the front seat and strapped the seat belt on her. She kissed her cheek and then shut the door, making sure it was locked.

A familiar black car was parked in Leota's driveway when Annie drove up the hill. What on earth was Corban Solsek doing here on a Sunday? He came down the front steps and waited on the sidewalk as Annie parked in front of the house.

"Hi, Corban," Annie said as she got out of the car and came around to help her grandmother.

Leota fumbled with the seat belt, trying to find the release button herself and having no luck.

"I'll get it, Grandma," Annie said, leaning into the car and over her. The belt snapped free, and Annie drew it carefully around her, allowing it to retract.

"Back for more yard work, are you?" Leota said to Corban as Annie helped her out of the car. She could tell by the look on his face that he thought she was serious.

Annie laughed softly. "Be good, Grandma," she said under her breath. "If you give him a rest today, maybe we can get him to help next weekend."

Leota chuckled. Here was a girl after her own heart.

"I just stopped by for a few minutes," Corban said.

So he was making his excuses before he stated his purposes. "Well then, hello and good-bye." Her hand firm on Annie's arm, Leota passed him by. He had to step onto the lawn to get out of their way.

"I guess I've worn out my welcome," he said wryly. "Annie, can I get your phone number?"

Leota stopped and looked back at him. "What for? I thought you already had a girlfriend." She had never seen red flood a face faster.

"I do, and I'm not asking Annie for her number to ask her out."

"Well, then why do you want her number?"

"Because I thought if anything happened to you, it would be good to have the phone number of a close relative."

She looked him in the eye and saw him shift uncomfortably. By now, he should know better than lie to her or think she would let him get away with it. "Are you planning on knocking me down my front steps any time soon?"

His eyes flashed, and the blush receded. "Any day now."

She chuckled. "Well, then come on along. If you've got more than a minute, you can come inside. I'm tired and I have to use the bath-room."

"She's different when you're around, Anne. More open," Corban said while the old woman was out of hearing. He explained his project quickly. "I learned more about your grandmother yesterday than I've learned in weeks."

"Does she know you're doing this report?"

"She knows. I didn't tell her about it to begin with. Big mistake."

"I can understand that, can't you? It would seem to her you came on false pretenses."

He thought that a hard remark but conceded. "I suppose."

"She must've forgiven you."

"I'm glad you think so."

Anne smiled up at him. "She likes you."

"Yeah, right. Me and the black plague."

Annie laughed. "I haven't known my grandmother very long, Corban, but I know she says what she thinks. If she didn't want you here, she'd tell you to leave."

"Maybe she's just being polite."

Annie chuckled. "She's frank. We were at church this morning, and she raised a few eyebrows."

"She didn't like it?"

"I think she loved it, but the service wasn't what she expected."

"I didn't know she was religious." He made a mental note. "What denomination is she?"

Annie sighed. "May I make a suggestion?"

"Sure. Shoot."

"Forget about interviewing Grandma and get to know her as a person."

"That's what I'm trying to do, Anne."

"Are you? Really?" There was something in her eyes that reminded him strongly of Leota Reinhardt. She was looking beyond everything he said to something deeper. Did she know what motivated him? Sometimes he wondered if he knew himself. Unlike the old lady, however, there wasn't the least hint of unkindness in her expression.

"I'm trying to do good with what I learn from her." He wanted Anne to understand. Her clear blue eyes held his in an unwavering, uncompromising look, and his conscience twisted. Anne Gardner might as well have said, *Please don't use her.*

"Okay." He nodded. "No more notes, mental or otherwise." Maybe if Anne knew what his ideas entailed, she would be more sympathetic to his cause and give him some assistance. "I'd like to take you to coffee and explain . . ."

"We can have coffee right here," Leota said from the doorway. "It might be good for you to spill all your beans on the table and let Annie examine them. Let's see what she has to say about the government projects you want to see come into fruition for us poor old folks."

Corban took the challenge. Mrs. Reinhardt had made him think a few things over, and he now had more concrete ideas about what kinds of recreational activities might be available in the elder-care facility. Maybe the amendments would be more to her liking.

Anne sat listening without comment.

Mrs. Reinhardt heated water and mixed fancy cappuccino for her granddaughter, then brewed a pot of regular coffee for him. The old lady said nothing during the half an hour he talked, though he expected her to jump in and make her objections known. She served them both and then sat in the chair nearest the windows, gazing out at her garden while he talked.

When Corban finished, he waited for Anne's approval, knowing it would carry weight with her grandmother.

"It sounds as though you have very admirable intentions," she said.

He waited for more, but she just looked at him with a perplexed frown. Her gaze moved to her grandmother and back to him.

Her placid neutrality annoyed him. "What's wrong with the plan?"

"I don't know." She shook her head. "There's just something about it that troubles me."

"Explain what you mean."

"I can't explain. It's . . ." She shrugged.

"It's *what*?"

"Visceral." She sighed. "I'm sorry, Corban."

The old woman turned from the window and patted her granddaughter's hand. When Mrs. Reinhardt looked at Corban, he saw tears in her eyes. She smiled at him, and it was the tenderest of smiles, one like he had never seen before in all his life. "Why don't I make us some lunch?" She put her hands flat on the table and pushed herself up.

"Oh, Grandma, I'll do that."

"I'll take out the fixings."

The doorbell rang as Mrs. Reinhardt moved to the cabinets. "See who that is, honey, would you please?" Corban had never heard her use that tone before. *"Honey."* Sweet, warm, a melting fondness.

Anne left the kitchen. A moment later, Corban could hear voices and laughter in the living room. Company, he thought, annoyed. So much for his afternoon alone with Mrs. Reinhardt and her granddaughter. So much for getting into their reasons for not liking his ideas. The day was going to be a complete waste.

Anne came back into the kitchen followed by a punk-looking girl and a man a few years older than Corban. "Grandma," Anne said, "this is Susan Carter, my best friend and roommate . . ."

Roommate? Corban looked the girl over. She was looking back at him with one eyebrow up and a half smile curving her mouth. Anne was oddly matched to this hip girl with her dangling earrings, black-dyed hair, tight jeans, black spandex top, and come-hither look.

". . . and her brother, Sam. He's a student at San Jose State University. Criminology." Sam had his sister's dark hair and eyes. He looked like half a million other college students that Corban saw every day: Levi's, brown sports coat, white T-shirt, deck shoes, and no socks. Grinning, Sam extended his hand to the old lady. As Mrs. Reinhardt placed her hand in his, he lifted it with great ceremony and kissed it like a European count. Corban sneered inwardly.

"This one's a rascal." The old woman actually sounded pleased! Susan laughed. "She's already got you pegged, Sam."

Corban rose as Anne introduced him to the two. "Corban is a friend of my grandmother's."

Corban stepped forward to shake hands. "Pleased to meet you both."

Sam's eyes were cool and assessing as they shook hands. His grip was slightly harder than necessary. Corban smiled slightly. He could guess whom this joker wanted to impress, and it sure wasn't Mrs. Reinhardt.

"Corban's a student at Berkeley," Mrs. Reinhardt said. "He comes by and walks with me to the supermarket once a week." She gave him a mischievous look. "And he has some bright ideas about how to manage the elderly."

"We were just going to make some lunch," Anne said quickly.

"Good. We arrived just in time," Sam said.

A look of distress filled Mrs. Reinhardt's face. "I don't know if—"

Susan grinned. "No need to worry, Mrs. Reinhardt. We didn't come to mooch. We stopped by the deli on the way. Sam bought enough to feed an army. Sandwiches, potato salad, coleslaw, dill pickles, chips, and carrot cake."

"Oh, well, in that case, you're welcome," Mrs. Reinhardt said, and they all laughed.

All but Corban. "I wish I could stay," he said drolly. He looked between Sam and Susan. "My girlfriend and I had plans for later this afternoon." He saw the hard gleam leave Sam Carter's eyes.

Susan gave a dramatic sigh and rolled her eyes. "Well, my goodness, that was certainly to the point." She put her hands up and drew back as though his announcement had just made him a pariah. "No need to worry."

He gave a humorless laugh and held his hand out to Mrs. Reinhardt. When she placed hers in his, he didn't kiss it. He put his other hand over it. "I'll see you on Wednesday, Mrs. Reinhardt. Thanks for the coffee." Releasing her, he looked at Anne. "Can I talk to you for a minute alone?"

She followed him into the living room, where he lowered his voice so the others couldn't hear. "Watch out for that guy."

"Sam's harmless."

"Yeah, right. Do you think you'll be spending weekends with your grandmother?"

"It'll depend on my work schedule."

"Where do you work?"

She told him. "I'll be over to see her as often as I can."

"Would you mind giving me your phone number?"

"Not at all." She looked around and spotted a notepad beside her grandmother's chair, then jotted her number on a slip of paper. Tearing it off, she handed it to him. "I just hope you won't have to use it."

Corban could feel the heat coming up in his face. He felt as though he had just been slapped.

She frowned slightly, searching his face. "I'm hoping I can get to know Arba Wilson."

"Who?"

"The lady next door. We saw her at church this morning. It's kind of you to want to keep an eye on Grandma Leota, Corban, but it really would be better if she got to know her neighbors. Besides, you only come on Wednesdays. If anything happened . . ."

So she had believed his reason for wanting her phone number. "I think you're right."

As he turned away, she put her hand on his arm. "I appreciate what you've done for my grandmother, Corban. She was alone until you came to help her."

He heard laughter in the kitchen. "She's not alone anymore." The house was too full for his comfort.

"I think there's room for one more. Or even two if you'd like to bring your girlfriend by sometime."

His mouth tipped. Now *there* was an idea. "Maybe."

"He's good-looking," Susan said when Annie came back into the kitchen.

Annie laughed. "I'm not surprised you noticed, Suzie."

"And he's taken," Sam said pointedly. "He made that clear."

"So what?" Susan said. "Men change their minds, too, you know. How many girlfriends have you had and dumped?"

Sam's eyes darkened. *"Dumped* isn't the word I'd use."

"Discarded? Left mooning for the sun, moon, and stars."

Annie could see Sam didn't appreciate Susan's ribbing. "It's a pretty afternoon. Why don't we have a picnic in the backyard? Would that be all right, Grandma?"

"I think that would be a splendid idea. There's more room to fight out there." Her dry comment drew a surprised chuckle from both Carters. "You'll find an army blanket in the guest-room closet, honey."

Sam carried one of the old, American steel chairs out to the lawn for Leota. "Where do you want to be, ma'am?"

"Right there is just fine."

Annie thought her grandmother looked darling sitting in the sunshine wearing a battered straw hat. Flapping open the army blanket, Annie spread it on the grass. Sam caught the other side and smoothed it for her while Suzie set out the cellophane-wrapped sandwiches and plastic deli containers. They'd even thought to bring a package of paper plates and packets with napkin; plastic fork, spoon, knife; salt and pepper; and a wetwipe.

Sam surprised Annie and said a blessing. When he raised his head, she looked into his eyes, hoping he hadn't done it just to make a good impression on her. Suzie reached for a plate. "What would you like, Mrs. Reinhardt?"

"A little of everything, except a sandwich. Those big rolls are too hard for me to eat."

Suzie grinned. "My grandmother can't eat them this way either. She says she's worried her store-bought teeth would come out."

"It happens."

"Not to worry." Suzie opened a sandwich and forked the fixings onto a plate. She cut half of the roll into bite-sized pieces. "There you go, Mrs. Reinhardt. You can't beat the taste of San Francisco sourdough." She handed the plate to Annie.

Annie added salads, garnishes, and chips and gave it to her grandmother. Sam's hand brushed hers as she reached for a sandwich of her own. "Sorry," she murmured, withdrawing her hand.

"Don't be." Sam held the sandwich out to her, a sultry look in his eyes.

"Sam said he couldn't get anywhere with you Friday night," Suzie said, dark eyes dancing at them over an open soda can. "So he thought he'd give it another try today."

Annie blushed. "You didn't have to go to such lengths, Sam."

"You mean, all I'd have to do is ask and you'd go out with me?" His mouth tipped.

Annie could feel her grandmother watching them. "No, I didn't say that."

Sam gave his sister a rueful look. "She doesn't trust me."

"Probably because she's been hearing about your antics since we were in grade school."

Sam looked at Annie. "People change."

She could see he was in earnest. "I know they do." She had no doubt his life was much different from his wilder days, but that didn't change her mind about becoming involved with him. She didn't want to become involved with *anyone* right now. She didn't know enough about herself to move into any kind of relationship. She was vulnerable. It would be too easy to make a serious mistake.

"I'm cute, aren't I?" A hint of devilry was back in his eyes.

"Yes, you're cute."

"Entirely *too* cute," her grandmother said, drawing laughter from brother and sister.

When Sam looked at Annie again, she lowered her head. He was attractive, disturbingly so, especially when his attention was focused on her. She had things to work out, things to think about deeply. If Sam's life could change so much, perhaps other lives could as well. Starting with her own.

Sam leaned toward her, reaching for a sandwich. "Relax, Annie. I'm not as bad as you might think."

"This yard must have been beautiful," Suzie said, looking around.

"Nice thing to say," Sam said under his breath.

Suzie grimaced. "Sorry. I didn't mean that the way it came out, Mrs. Reinhardt."

"Don't apologize. You're exactly right. A pity you two didn't come by yesterday."

"Why?" Sam said.

"We would have put you to work. So far, Annie's trimmed the front bushes, mowed my lawn, and pruned the fruit trees."

"Corban helped a lot," Annie said and took a bite of her sandwich.

"Yes, he did, but he's gone now, and there's a lot more to be done. I think this young gentleman is so eager to woo you, we could enlist his help."

Annie gulped down the bite of deli sandwich. "Grandma!" Her face was hot.

Sam laughed. "Consider me enlisted, your ladyship."

"All right, young man. We'll see if there's more to you than charm and good looks. Eat your sandwich. You're going to need your strength. As soon as you're finished, Annie will show you where to find the tools. And then I'm going to tell you what to do and where to do it."

11

NORA SAT IN PASTOR BURNIE'S OFFICE, WAITING. She realized she should've called before coming. Perhaps if she had, she wouldn't be left sitting where anyone might see her and wonder what she was doing here. She'd forgotten there was a Bible study today. Women were milling around in the great room waiting to begin their class. She'd also forgotten Pastor Burnie taught the class.

If she hadn't been so upset, she would've stopped to think what others might say about her coming to church for counseling. Now she felt exposed, humiliated, and angry. There was no privacy in this big church. Everyone knew everything about everybody. Maybe the Catholics had the right idea about going into a confessional. At least there people had privacy. Why hadn't she realized when she saw all the cars in the parking lot that the women's Bible study was meeting this morning? Half a dozen women had seen her come in. She recognized two, and they were probably talking about her right now. She'd had lunch with them. She knew what they were like. How they delighted in knowing and discussing everyone's business!

Uncrossing her legs, Nora crossed her ankles and folded her hands in her lap. Her palms were sweating. Her heart was pounding. She was trembling. She wouldn't be in this miserable situation if her psychologist, Dr. Leeds, had been willing to speak with her for longer than one minute! She'd been completely undone when his secretary told her the doctor's schedule was full for the next two weeks. Two weeks! She'd told the woman she needed to speak with him right away, but the woman insisted he was with a patient and did not want to be disturbed. The patronizing tone of her voice had made Nora want to scream. Instead, she simply told the secretary she would not be put off. She'd insisted the secretary get Dr. Leeds on the line immediately; it was an emergency.

He came on the line shortly after that, as she knew he would. She'd had to insist before. This time, however, he didn't seem to care that she was in crisis. She could tell by his tone that he was angry with her. When she'd tried to explain, he said it was old territory and he would call her back at *his* convenience. When she said she couldn't wait, he told her to take a Valium! He said he wanted her calm when he spoke with her. She told him she could be calm if he would speak to her right then, but he said, "I will speak with you later, Nora" and hung up.

After the thousands she had paid Dr. Leeds over the past three years, that's all he had to say? Take a Valium and wait? If he'd given her five minutes of his precious time, she wouldn't be sitting in the church office in front of God and everyone waiting for Pastor Burnie to be free enough to speak with her. This was all Annie's fault! If she'd gone off to college where she belonged, there would be no reason to worry.

Nora trembled with agitation. Seeing her mother always upset her. That's what was wrong. A few minutes in the company of Leota Reinhardt was enough to undo a month of sessions with Dr. Leeds. Nora never remembered the breathing and meditation exercises the doctor had taught her until after she left her mother's house. Dr. Leeds had told her to be honest with her mother. And say what? Tell her mother how much she despised her for abandoning her children, how she couldn't stand to go back to that house, how her childhood had been miserable? She'd said all that a hundred times. Her mother *knew,* not that she cared.

Nora raised a hand and pressed trembling fingers to her throbbing temples. It never failed. All she had to do was think of her mother and her head started to pound.

What was taking Pastor Burnie so long?

Nora crossed her legs again. She started thinking about Fred and how angry he was with her for not showing up for dinner with his clients. She had tried to apologize, but he wouldn't even look at her. He scorned the omelet she had cooked for him. "When have you ever seen me eat breakfast, Nora?"

He had never been rude before, and it had stunned her. Then there were his eyes . . . they had been darker than she had ever seen them. She poured him some coffee, but he didn't touch that either. It was as though anything she offered him was tainted and untouchable. Nothing she did was good enough.

It was like living with Grandma Helene. Nothing was ever good enough. . . .

Nora didn't want to think about the past. She didn't want to talk about it. She wanted to figure out how to get Annie home again and how to make Fred forgive her.

Fred's words rang in her ears. "You're always sorry, Nora, but nothing ever changes. Just once, I'd like to see you think about someone other than yourself. I'd like to see some effort . . ." He had started to say more, but she had been so distraught, she had fled into the living room and flung herself into the swivel rocker. She thought he would follow her and say he was sorry for upsetting her. That's what he usually did. But last night, Fred went upstairs and closed the bedroom door. When she went up and asked him whether he cared how she felt, all he said was, "I'm going to bed. I'm tired."

Tired? Of what?

Of her?

No one understood her. No one cared.

Fighting tears, Nora glanced around Pastor Burnie's office. Three walls were covered with bookcases laden with volumes neatly arranged in categories: family, Bible studies, commentaries, devotionals, prayer, biographies. Two entire shelves behind Pastor Burnie's desk held various versions and editions of the Bible: King James, New International, *The Living Bible,* New American Standard, Phillips, New Living Translation, *The Jerusalem Bible, TouchPoint.* Nora frowned. *How many Bibles does one man need? Of course,* the man was a pastor . . . perhaps he collected them. One Bible was enough for normal people. More than enough. She had tried reading it once—after all, it was supposed to be classic literature—but it was boring.

What was taking Pastor Burnie so long? Nora stood up and paced. The wall behind the couch on which she was sitting had family pictures on it. The beatific face of Sally Burnie annoyed her, as did the laughing faces of the Burnies' son and daughter. Here and there about the room were mementos from trips Pastor Burnie and his family had taken to Israel, Africa, Greece, an Indian reservation in New Mexico, an orphanage in Honduras. They stood there, in every picture, smiling, always smiling.

How did they manage to be so happy? She knew their lives hadn't always been easy. Sally had multiple sclerosis. Pastor Burnie's salary was a fraction of what Fred made, yet they got by. The Burnies' son had learning disabilities, and though their daughter was quite intelligent—Nora studied the girl's features in the photo on the wall—well, she would need her brains. Nora didn't understand it. How could the Burnies all be so happy when so many things were so clearly wrong?

Why can't I be happy? What have I ever done to deserve the misery I live with on a daily basis?

She heard Pastor Burnie in the outer office. It was about time. He entered his office. "Hello, Nora." He closed the door quietly behind him. "I'm sorry for the delay. We needed to have one of the deaconesses take over the class this morning. I had to give her a quick outline of what I was going to cover. Now, how can I help you?"

She burst into tears. She hadn't meant to cry, but what could she do when she was so unhappy? Dr. Leeds sometimes put his arms around her and let her cry it out.

"Has something happened to Fred?" Pastor Burnie's tone was concerned, though he kept his distance.

Nora clenched her hands in her lap. "Fred is just fine. Everything is business as usual. Annie left home. Had you heard that yet? Her father spent a ridiculous amount of money on a car for her, and she just got in it and drove away without so much as a backward glance. She's living with a hippie in San Francisco, of all places. I'm so disappointed. I thought my daughter had a conscience."

"She's living with Susan Carter," he said quietly. "I know her. And her family. Susan's been well grounded."

Nora looked at him. "So was her brother Sam. Do you remember him? He's caused that family nothing but grief. Did you know he was in jail for a while?"

Pastor Burnie's expression made Nora's face go hot. She wasn't gossiping! It was the truth about Sam Carter. How could the pastor look at her as though she was carrying tales he didn't want to hear? He went around his desk and sat down. Nora felt as though a wall had gone up between them. She was on one side; he was on the other.

She had never felt so uncomfortable and confused in her life. She couldn't look him straight in the eyes.

What had *she* done to feel so ashamed? She dabbed at her nose delicately with her lace hanky. Maybe Pastor Burnie didn't understand the whole picture. He'd be more sympathetic when he did. "Anne had a scholarship to Wellesley. All those years of hard work, and she threw it away."

"College isn't for everyone."

"It is most certainly for Anne-Lynn."

"You seem very certain of that."

His neutral tone irritated her. "Of course, I'm certain! It's what she's always wanted. It's why we worked so hard. She's always had outstanding grades. And when she didn't, I made sure she had a tutor. She's belonged to the best clubs. What girl wouldn't want an opportunity to go to a prestigious school like Wellesley? Any girl with an ounce of sense would jump at the chance. Anne-Lynn said she'd go."

"Do you think Annie might have said that to please you, Nora?"

What was he driving at? "If she wanted to please me, she wouldn't be taking art classes in San Francisco. *That* certainly doesn't please me. What use is that going to be to her? Besides, she hasn't any talent." The words came out before she had time to think how they would sound. She saw the pastor's eyes flicker. Her face heated once more. "I didn't mean it that way. I'm just upset. That's all. Sometimes things come out badly when I'm upset."

She dabbed her eyes and blew her nose delicately. "I suppose some might say Anne can draw a little, but you can't make a living at it. She's only opening herself up to rejection. I don't want to see her hurt. I want to see her *succeed*."

Pastor Burnie put one hand over the other on his desk blotter and closed his eyes. Was he praying? Nora cleared her throat nervously. He raised his head slightly and looked at her. "Nora, all the answers to your problems are found in a new relationship with God."

What was *that* supposed to mean? "I know God."

"Do you?"

"Of course, I do! I've been going to this church for five years. Have you any idea how much money Fred and I have given? And I've been on all the most important committees."

"People come to church for all kinds of reasons. It would help if you could tell me what you believe."

"Believe about what?"

"About Jesus Christ."

"This is ridiculous." Nora felt cold with shock at the implications. "You know what I believe. I believe what everyone else who goes here believes." She was completely at a loss as to what more she could say. And yet Pastor Burnie sat, waiting. Hadn't she said enough? Was this a trick question? Furious, she glared at him. She wasn't a Sunday school child to be tested on her recitation of the Apostle's Creed or the Ten Commandments. She was an adult, for heaven's sake! "I don't know what you want me to say."

"I'm not asking you to recite anything, Nora." His smile seemed almost tender. "What I do need is some idea of where you stand with the Lord."

She gave a bitter laugh. "Considering how my life is going, I would say I don't count with God at all. He certainly hasn't shown me any favors lately. No matter what I do, it's never enough to change anything." She stood up and moved to the window overlooking the street.

"What brought you here?"

"Desperation." Why not tell him the truth? Maybe he wouldn't be so holier-than-thou if he knew he was her last choice. "My therapist didn't have time for me today, and I needed help. That's why I came to you. I don't mean to sound insulting, but that's the truth." Why should she apologize for it, especially after he'd left her waiting for twenty minutes?

"Can you tell me what your problem is?"

She turned and saw the compassion in his eyes. Finally, someone willing to listen, someone willing to help her solve everything. Dr. Leeds hadn't been able to do it. Maybe Pastor Burnie could. "There are so many, starting with my own miserable childhood."

"Were you abused?"

"I wasn't beaten or molested, if that's what you mean, but I was most certainly neglected." She turned away and looked out the window. "My mother was gone early every morning and came home about the time my grandmother and I were making supper. And then she'd go out in her garden. My mother was never interested in me or my brother, you see. She just handed us over to my grandmother and went off to live her own life as she pleased."

She faced him again. "Anne-Lynn takes after her. What's worse, she is now spending weekends with my mother, who is undoubtedly poisoning her mind with lies. I know because Anne-Lynn hardly ever returns my telephone calls." Her heart ached.

"Is that why you're here today?"

"No. Partly. It's *her* fault . . ." She shook her head and swallowed convulsively. Pastor Burnie looked utterly confused. "It's my mother's fault," she said, hoping that would make it clear for him. "Fred's angry with me over some silly business function I missed. I went to speak to my mother about Anne-Lynn and was so upset afterward that I forgot all about the dinner. Now Fred hardly speaks to me. He's being so unreasonable. Everything is falling apart. No matter how much I do for everyone, no one seems to care about *me!*"

"What do you want me to do, Nora?"

He looked and sounded so sincere, but hadn't he been listening? She wanted him to tell her how to fix everything! She wanted him to say he would come to the house and talk to Fred and make him behave like a loving husband again. She wanted her pastor to talk to Anne-Lynn and make her come home and behave like a loving and dutiful daughter. But when she looked into Pastor Burnie's eyes, she couldn't say all that because she had the feeling he wouldn't even consider doing it.

Oh, why had she come at all?

Maybe all she really wanted was the chance to talk about how miserable she was. She wanted an empathetic listener. She wanted someone to understand her and stand with her against those hurting her. At least Dr. Leeds agreed it had all started with her mother.

She rubbed at her temples. When had her life gotten so out of control? Why did everyone she loved turn away from her? Husbands, children . . . her own mother had been the first one to reject her.

"Nora?"

"I don't know, Pastor Burnie. I just don't know anything anymore."

"That's a beginning."

She turned and looked at him. "What do you mean?"

"Sometimes we have to be knocked down before we look up."

She frowned. What was he saying to her?

"I can give you one certainty, Nora. God loves you. I can assure you the answers to all your problems are found in a personal relationship with Jesus Christ. Until the center of your life changes from you to the Lord Jesus, you're only going to repeat the same mistakes and have the same heartache over and over again. It's the condition of all flesh. But God loves you. He wants a personal relationship with you. He's made that possible through Jesus Christ's death on the cross. And by His resurrection, He's shown you have nothing to fear from Him when you come for His love and guidance."

There it was again: the insinuation that *she* was selfish. And what did Pastor Burnie mean about repeating the same mistakes? What was he talking about? She hadn't come to hear a Sunday school lesson. She didn't need him preaching at her. Was he so stupid he didn't know she was already a Christian? She had been sitting in the pews of this church for five years! Hadn't Pastor Burnie heard what she told him? Wasn't he listening at all?

"God doesn't want part of you now and then, Nora. He wants all of you all the time. That's what it means to ask Jesus into your heart."

"Meaning what? I'm supposed to spend every day at a women's Bible study or involved in some kind of missions work?"

He gave her *that* look again. Sad. Enlightened. It was as though he saw something in her of which she was not the least aware. "I didn't say that, Nora. I'm not speaking about works but about a relationship."

"A relationship you don't think I have. Isn't that right?" She allowed her anger to build. She was safe and strong inside her anger. She felt in control. How dare the pastor speak to her like this? She thought about all the times other people had said hurtful things to her, and the anger grew even more—burning coals that she fanned into flame.

People had always persecuted her. Her own pastor didn't even try to understand her pain and sorrow. Where was his *Christian* compassion? Where was the support? Shouldn't he feel some righteous indignation over how meanly she was being treated by her daughter and husband? Didn't it say in the Bible to honor thy mother?

Her mouth trembled. "I come to you in desperate need of help and all you can say is I need a relationship with Jesus? How *dare* you question my faith?" Her voice rose slightly. "After all I've done for this church over the years, how dare you question me about *anything* to do with religion?" Clenching her hands, she pressed down the urge to curse him.

"I'm a pastor, Nora. It's my calling to try and draw a lost lamb back into the flock."

"*I'm* not the one who's lost! You should be talking to Anne-Lynn. But then, you haven't listened to a word I've said, have you?"

"On the contrary."

Trembling violently, Nora snatched up her purse from the couch. "I should've known better than to come here. What do you know about counseling?"

Pastor Burnie's secretary glanced up as Nora yanked the door open. The woman's hands froze over the computer keyboard as Nora came out of the office. Ignoring her, Nora kept walking. Going out the doors of the church, she marched across the parking lot to her Lexus. Slipping into the driver's seat, she slammed the door and jammed the key into the ignition. The car roared to life. The tires screeched as she pulled out of the parking lot onto the main street. Someone pulled off a side street in front of her so that she had to slam on her brakes. Blasting her horn, Nora cursed as she pulled around the old Ford. "Stupid old fool! They should get these people off the road!"

She drove around for over an hour before deciding to go to the mall. She would walk and give herself time to think. Maybe she'd feel better if she bought a new dress. Something green. Fred liked green. Better yet, something blue. *She* liked blue.

She wandered through the stores, looking at the merchandise. Nothing appealed to her. Finally, weary and depressed, she stopped at the food court and bought a sweet roll and a cup of coffee. Sitting by herself, she watched the beehive activities of mothers with their children, groups of teenage girls giggling and watching the boys, boys watching the girls, older women sitting together and talking, a new mother nursing her baby in a quiet corner.

Hands trembling, she lifted her Styrofoam cup to her lips and sipped the hot fluid cautiously. She had never felt so alone before.

You can tell a tree by its fruit.

Where had she heard that? It sounded like something her mother would have said. She had always tossed out foolish little comments that didn't seem to go with the conversation.

"Good soil helps develop strong roots. . . ."

"Without proper pruning, these bushes won't bear healthy blossoms. . . ."

"Things grow stronger with some manure."

Nora had never cared about gardening.

"Come out in the garden with me, Eleanor. I want to teach you . . ."

Teach her what? How to dig in the dirt? How to tie up vines and plant vegetables she wouldn't eat? How to graft? How to transplant seedlings from the apricot or plum tree? Who wanted sprouts when they could buy a small tree from a nursery for a couple of bucks?

Her mother had never bothered to find out what interests she had. Not once had she taken Nora to a concert or a ballet, nor did her mother even consider the fact that Nora longed to go to college.

Interesting that the garden flourished while there had never been enough money for anything Nora wanted. As soon as she was old enough, Nora had gone to work at a fabric store and spent every break watching the woman who demonstrated the sewing machines. Grandma Reinhardt had already taught Nora the rudiments of dressmaking. In home-economics classes in high school, Nora had learned most of what she needed to make her own clothing. No ragged edges for her. She finished every seam, lined up plaids, and picked the best and most adaptable patterns. Thankfully, she had had enough talent that she could make dresses that looked as though they had been purchased off the racks at Macy's or Capwell's. By the time she was a junior in high school, she had achieved enough skill that not one of her friends suspected that the stylish clothes she wore were homemade.

Nora remembered one high moment in her life when Miss Wentworth, her home-economics teacher, had told her that she had the talent to be a designer. Nora had warmed at such praise, though she'd had no illusions about going to school in New York or even to a local college.

She had sworn to herself then that someday she would shop for herself and her children at the best stores. She would make sure no one in her family ever wanted for all the things she had missed during her childhood. They would live in a nice home in a nice neighborhood, have nice store-bought clothes, dancing lessons, season tickets to concerts and ballets, trips to museums, poolside parties at a country club, and a bachelor of arts from a prestigious college. No child of hers would go without *anything* money could buy.

It had cost her dearly, but she had kept that promise. Her first husband had run from the responsibility; her second had rebelled. But she had never wavered. Not that her children had an ounce of gratitude for all she had sacrificed for them. She had put them ahead of everyone and everything else in her life, hadn't she? Wasn't Fred angry because she had put Anne before him? She was so stressed over her daughter's mutiny that she hadn't thought about her own duties to her husband. And did Anne care what anguish she was causing? No, of course not. Anne didn't care about anyone but herself. She just waltzed away without so much as a "Thank you, Mother" for all the years of driving her to gymnastics and dancing and music classes, drilling her with lessons, typing out applications, and getting records in order. Not to mention the money! Thousands of dollars wasted. Nora could have gone around the world on what she had spent on her ungrateful daughter!

You can tell a tree by its fruit.
Why did those words hurt so much?
And why couldn't she get them out of her mind?

Susan sat on the couch crying. "Raoul never should've left Barnaby in my care! I think he's going to die. Just look at him, Annie."

Annie tossed her purse on the coffee table and went to the bird. "Hello, Barnie. Hello, sweetie." Barnaby didn't do his usual dance back and forth. He didn't say anything outrageous. He didn't move at all. His feet were clenched around the perch, his feathers puffed more than Annie had ever seen them. It was true. He didn't look himself. "I wonder what's the matter with him?"

"I know what's the matter with him. I'm such an idiot! I should be shot!"

Annie glanced at her.

Susan blew her nose and looked at her with red puffy eyes. "I borrowed that shop vac Howard has. You know, the guy across the hall? The handyman? I was so steamed because Barnaby had made such a mess. I was vacuuming up all the seeds and dried-up chunks of fruit and vegetables and bird guano. Well, the phone rang."

"And?"

"I bent over to answer. It was Sam and I was distracted for a second. Just a second, mind you. But it was long enough. I heard this big . . . *slurp*. Sam heard it, too, because he asked what it was. I looked and Barnaby was *gone*. He must've gone through the hose headfirst." She sniffed and blew her nose.

"Maybe he broke some bones," Annie said, worried. She touched him. He didn't move.

"I guarantee he didn't break anything. Just look at my hand." She held it out. "I shut off the machine and opened it, and he was flapping and pecking and scratching. He drew blood! He was covered with seeds and bits of dried and rotten fruit and whatever Howard had been vacuuming. Dog hair, I think. I had to clean him up." She cried harder. "I gave him a shower in the sink. I tested the water, Annie. It was lukewarm. He didn't like it very much. And he looked so pathetic all wet. I didn't want him to get pneumonia or whatever birds can get, so I dried him. With your blow dryer."

"Poor Barnaby." Annie stroked his feathers gently. "What a day you've had."

"Forget it. He's comatose. He just sits there like he's stuffed. He hasn't made a sound all day. Not a peep. He just *stares*." Susan buried her face in her hands and sobbed. "I keep waiting for him to keel over and croak."

"Come on, Barnaby. Perk up, sweetie," Annie said softly. The bird didn't respond. It didn't even bat an eyelash, if it had one.

"I've never liked him much, Annie, but I don't want him to die." Her eyes were red-rimmed. "Do you hear that, Barnaby? Don't you dare die!"

The telephone rang. The bird twitched once and froze again. "Poor baby," Annie said and leaned over to answer before the second ring.

"Annie, darlin'. I knew if I called often enough, you'd eventually answer."

"Hi, Sam." She smiled at his teasing.

"How's Barnaby?"

"In shock, I think."

"And no wonder. Imagine being sucked into a tornado only to land in a flood and then be dried in a desert whirlwind. Is he on his back with his feet up yet?"

"It's not funny, Sam."

"Don't worry, honey. He'll live. That bird is too mean to die."

"You should see him . . ."

"As a matter of fact, I was thinking I should drive up and check on Suzie Q."

"Uh-huh," she said dryly.

He chuckled. "You gonna be around this evening?"

"I think I'll take a jaunt to the beach."

He sighed. "Are you avoiding me?"

"I'm running for dear life."

"You've got me pegged all wrong, Annie."

She laughed. "It was nice talking with you, Sam." She handed the telephone to her roommate. "He's checking on you." Shrugging her backpack off, she set it on the floor beside the couch. She took an orange from the bowl on the counter and peeled it. Eating one section, she held another out for Barnaby. "Come on, Barnie. She didn't mean to scare you." He opened his beak, but she had the feeling it was a warning to leave him alone rather than readiness to take a bite of fruit.

"No," Suzie said to Sam. "Yes. Maybe. I don't know. I suppose I could try. All right. All right!"

Annie looked at Suzie. Her roommate was not usually so cryptic on the telephone, and Suzie's smile was faintly smug. Her good spirits seemed to be returning. The smile turned to a broad grin with a decidedly wicked gleam in her eyes.

"Right now? Oh, she's trying to tempt Barnaby with a wedge of orange." She laughed. "I'll tell her you said that, Sam. Now, she's frowning at me. Oh, really? Why doesn't that surprise me? Okay. Okay! Bye." She clicked the phone off and set it back on the coffee table with a *thunk*. "I have strict instructions to keep you on the premises this evening. Don't even think about leaving." She waggled her brows up and down. "My daring-and-do-well brother is bringing a friend with him, someone he says is the man of my dreams."

"That's blackmail, Suzie."

She shrugged, unrepentant, eyes twinkling. "So be it. Besides, you know how much I'd love to have you for a sister-in-law."

"You've got to be kidding. I'm eighteen!"

"Maybe it runs in the family. You told me once your mother was married at seventeen."

"And divorced by twenty."

She grimaced. "Oh. I forgot. Well, that doesn't mean it'll happen to you. When Carter men fall in love once, it lasts a lifetime."

"Suzie, your brother is not in love with me."

"The heck he isn't. I've seen him through crushes before. This is different, entirely different. He's gone completely gaga over you. I can feel the heat coming off of him whenever he's around you."

Annie felt the heat surge into her cheeks.

Susan's expression softened. "Annie, it wasn't that long ago that you had a crush on him."

"I know." She sank onto the couch and propped her feet up on the coffee table.

"So what's the problem?"

"Why does there have to be a problem?"

"I know you. You've never been free enough to enjoy your own life. This is your chance."

"I *am* enjoying life."

"In a restrained, inhibited sort of way. With your grandmother, no less. How safe can you get?"

Annie laughed. "And you think Sam is the cure for my ho-hum life? Yeah, right." She got up and headed for the kitchen. She hadn't eaten since this morning, and she was hungry.

Susan got up and followed her, lounging on the stool and leaning her elbows on the counter as Annie took out eggs, cheese, mushrooms, half a green pepper, and a small tomato. "I'll admit Sam was pretty wild, Annie. Is that what's bothering you?"

"No. I like him just the way he is. I like him very, very much. I always have." She rinsed the vegetables and put them on the cutting board. "I don't know if I can explain, Suzie."

"Try, would you please? Annie, I promise I won't tell Sam anything you tell me. If that's worrying you . . ."

"You can tell him if you think it might help him back off a little." She smiled at her friend. "Most girls, you included, seem to have a burning desire to get married." She shrugged. "I don't."

"Because your mother hasn't been able to make a marriage work?"

Annie paused from dicing the bell pepper. "Please don't talk about her that way, Susan."

"Sorry."

"No, it's my fault. I told you too much of what went on whenever I was upset."

"You had to talk to someone."

"But don't you see? You've only gotten my side of the story. She wanted me to do well. There's nothing wrong with that."

"She *drove* you to do well, and that's not right."

"I don't know." She started cutting again. "I've been thinking about my mother, trying to put everything together and make sense of why she's the way she is. There's a history between her and Grandma Leota that isn't clear yet. I want to find out what happened to make my mother so bitter and resentful."

"You can't make excuses for her, Annie."

"I'm not trying to make excuses. I'm trying to understand. Maybe if I can see things from both sides, I can help build a bridge between them."

"Good luck."

Annie knew it didn't make sense to others, but the Lord was speaking to her heart. If she let her head rule her life, she would walk away and seldom, if ever, look back. The way Michael was doing. Maybe it was just protection; maybe it was selfishness. She didn't know, and it wasn't her right to judge her brother. Yet, sometimes she worried that she was doing the same thing. She knew her brother held no deep affection for her—no deep affection for *anyone*, especially not for the mother who had paved the way for his success. Annie didn't want to become like that. Yet part of her saw the draw of not having to worry about anyone else's feelings or needs, especially her mother's.

During the first month away from her mother, the litany had

played in her head: *I want my own life! If I make mistakes, they'll be my mistakes. It's my life. Let me live it my way!*

But freedom didn't bring serenity. She hadn't been able to find any peace until she contacted her grandmother that first time. Since then, things were changing. Like the seasons, the heat of summer was giving way to the cooling fall. She relished the time spent with Grandma Leota. She was learning so much from her, absorbing vignettes on life. All the while they were in the garden, Anne felt Grandma was talking to her on two levels.

"You need to open up the tree so that the air can circulate and the light can reach into it."

Those words had struck something deep within her. Air and light. Good soil. Living water. Her heart ached, and she knew God was speaking to her though her grandmother.

No matter what Susan thought, Annie knew she was doing exactly what she was supposed to be doing. There was a rightness to it, a sense of homecoming. She couldn't allow anything to get in the way of going forward on this path.

Sam wanted to draw her another way. Not that he meant to pull her away from God. She knew he didn't. He loved the Lord, too, she had learned. He credited Jesus with pulling him up out of the pit he had dug for himself. And yet . . .

Annie sighed. Sam was handsome and charming and intelligent. He had a spirit of fun about him, a boyish delight in tackling life. He was attractive enough to set her pulse racing, but that didn't mean she should allow herself to be swayed. She knew he was not part of the plan God was unfolding to her. She couldn't explain *how* she knew, not even to herself, let alone to Susan. She just *knew*. If she went against that knowledge, she would miss the wonder that awaited her. Whatever it was . . .

Pruning.

She smiled to herself as she prepared the omelet. A simple thing like pruning. "You need to open up the tree so that the air can circulate and the light can reach into it," Grandma had said, and all the while Annie was up in that old apricot tree, she kept thinking that people were the same way. God would cut away His people's dead-end ideas, diseased philosophies, broken promises, and twisted dreams. Why couldn't people allow the Creator of the universe to have His will with them so that He could prune and shape them into the people they were meant to be? For then, what a harvest of good fruit there would be come summer!

Oh, God, that's what I want. Oh, Holy Father of life, You who cause things to grow, prune me. Cut and trim as You will. Lord, let Your spirit come up within me like the living sap of a tree. Let it be Your heart that beats within my breast. Let the fruit of my life be a reflection of Your love, peace, patience, kindness, goodness, faithfulness, and gentleness. Father, I can't do anything without You. I don't even want to try. Be the gardener . . .

"That looks pretty good." Susan was watching Annie fold the omelet in the pan.

"Are you hungry?" Annie slid the omelet onto a plate and offered it to Susan. "I can make another."

"See what I mean?" Susan took the plate. "You should be telling me to make my own omelet."

Annie laughed. "And have the whole apartment smell like burned eggs? I think not." She handed Susan a fork and cracked two more eggs into the bowl. "You can do the dishes."

Susan ate a bite and waved the fork at Annie. "You can't undo years of animosity, Annie. You know your mother. And don't give me that look. You can't change people. You're only going to get yourself hurt. It's been three months, and she still hasn't forgiven you for stepping out on your own. How do you think you're ever going to get her to forgive her mother after decades of hating her for whatever it was she supposedly did? How?"

"I don't know." But one thing she did know: Nothing was impossible for God. For some reason, He had put it in her heart to establish a relationship with her grandmother. Why would He do that unless He had plans? And His plans were always for a good purpose. "I know the Lord is working in all this, Suzie. And I want to be there to see what happens."

Susan chuckled. "Leota is pretty cool. I was a little worried what she'd say about us showing up on her doorstep and taking over the afternoon. Not Sam. He figured he'd waltz in and take charge. Next thing he knows, he's turning the soil in the back forty while I'm transplanting apricot and plum sprouts. That sure taught him a lesson! He told me he ached for a week. I'll bet Grandma Leota was really something when she was young."

Annie rolled the frying pan and the melting butter hissed as it coated the bottom. She poured in the omelet mixture. "I'm hoping she'll tell me more about herself." She cast Susan a rueful smile. "My mother always said I was a lot like Grandma Leota. I'd sure like to find out what that means."

Sam showed up at six o'clock with the promised friend. Annie noticed Susan's eyes light up when she was introduced. Chuck Hauge seemed to think Susan was all he had hoped for as well. "Sam's told me a lot about you."

"Believe everything you heard," she said with a cheeky grin. However, within half an hour, her mood was clearly dampened.

"What on earth is Sam thinking?" Susan said under her breath as she nudged Annie out of the way in the small kitchen and took ice from the freezer. "We have zilch in common. He's got a master's degree in business, for crying out loud. He's been working for some computer company in Silicon Valley for the past year. He doesn't say much about what he does, but he's probably on his way to being a CEO. And here I am, a waitress. He reads the *Wall Street Journal*. I read the funny papers. He likes sushi. I like steak, well done. He likes classical music."

"You like classical music." Annie barely suppressed a smile.

"Yeah, when I have insomnia."

Annie put the vegetable dip on a tray with crackers. "Classical music is supposed to raise the IQ."

"He doesn't *need* a higher IQ, and I'm a lost cause." Susan rolled her eyes and shook the ice into a bowl. Scooping a handful of cubes into her soda, she glanced over her shoulder. "Can I get you anything to drink, Chuck?"

Annie grinned at her while putting more crackers on the tray. "There's enough sugar in your voice to draw bees."

"Shut up," Susan said sotto voce. She fixed another soda then headed back into the living room. "Sam's days are numbered for getting me into this."

Annie followed her and put the tray on the coffee table. Sam glanced at her from where he was standing near the windows, where Barnaby resided silently on his perch. "Pretty morose bird. No change, I take it."

Annie shook her head. "Not a peep."

Susan looked up sharply, her eyes darting flames at her brother. "Not a word."

At Sam's slow, taunting grin, Susan stood. "Why don't we take a walk, Chuck? It's only six blocks to the ocean."

As soon as the door closed behind them, Sam left the window and sat on the couch, one arm resting along the back. "That couldn't have worked out any better if I'd planned it." He gave Annie a slow, teasing smile.

Annie swallowed. "Maybe we should take a walk, too. The air is nice and cool this time of the evening."

"I like it right here, where it's warm." He patted the sofa. "Why don't you sit by me?"

Annie settled in the worn, overstuffed, orange chair Susan had bought from an upstairs neighbor, who had moved the week before. Crossing her jeans-clad legs, she rested her arms on the flat velvet. "This is nice."

Sam just looked at her and shook his head, a rueful smile on his face. "I don't bite, Annie."

"That's not what I heard."

His eyes flickered and his gaze grew serious. "Let's back up and regroup here. I'm not on the make, Annie. I'm not coming on to you so I can sow wild oats."

"I know that."

"No, you don't. You've known me too long. Unfortunately. I wouldn't blame you for thinking I was a complete jerk, considering some of the harebrained schemes I pulled a few years back. You were around enough to hear the fallout." He leaned forward, his hands clasped loosely between his knees. "Look, Annie. I'll put it plain and simple. If your father were anywhere around, I'd feel perfectly at ease telling him my intentions."

Embarrassed, she looked away from the intensity in his eyes. "I'm flattered."

"Flattery isn't what I had in mind. Trust is a little closer to the mark."

She looked at him again, dismayed. "I don't distrust you, Sam."

"Is that so? Then why am I sitting here, and you're sitting way over there?"

If frankness was what he wanted, she would give it to him. "You still move as fast as you ever did, and I'd like you to put the brakes on. Right now."

He sat back slowly. "Okay," he said after a long moment. "So maybe I am in overdrive. The engine is a little heated. I'll drop it down to first. Is that better?"

"Think about driving down a different road. I'm not going to get involved with you, Sam."

"*Involved.*" His mouth tipped. "What a nineties word."

"We're friends. I don't want to do anything to spoil that."

He grinned. "Now there's an age-old kiss-off if ever I've heard one. I've used it a few times myself." His expression softened. "Okay.

Friends, it is. Which means we can go out and have some fun instead of deciding on plate patterns. What would you like to do?"

"I haven't the foggiest idea."

"We'll just go and see what looks interesting. Late supper. Some swing dancing. A walk on Pier 39. Whatever."

"What about Suzie and Chuck?"

"We'll leave them a note."

"I don't know, Sam . . ."

"All right. We'll stay here. Fine by me. Just the two of us. No television. I'll try not to make a pass at you, but I can't guarantee anything."

She laughed. "You are incorrigible."

He grinned. "That's what all my teachers said. Now what'll it be?"

She softened at the look in his eyes. Poor Sam. She hoped he wasn't hurting as much as she had when her crush on him was in full bloom. "I'll get my jacket."

The Lord always left a way to escape temptation, and she intended to take it.

12

LEOTA SWEPT THE SMALL BRICK PATIO. IT HAD BEEN MONTHS SINCE it had been done. The air was fall-brisk and made her bones ache, but she wanted the small area cleaned up before Annie arrived. It wouldn't do to sit around like an old woman all the time and let Annie and her friends do everything.

Pausing, Leota straightened, admiring the work that had been done over the past month. The garden no longer looked unkempt and abandoned. The trees were pruned, bushes trimmed and shaped, vines thinned and tied to frames and trellises. And with one smile from Annie, that handsome young fellow who'd come with his sister had turned soil in the Victory garden. He'd even mulched, and then repaired the broken slats in the lattice.

Smiling to herself, Leota leaned on the broom, resting while she looked over the potted plants set here and there on the small patio and retaining wall. Some desperately needed repotting—another lesson for Annie, if the girl was so inclined.

"Grandma!" Annie came around the corner. "There you are. When you didn't answer your doorbell, I figured you'd be out here."

Leota felt warmth return to her bones as she looked at her grand-daughter. Annie's blue eyes shone with love, and her smile lit Leota's heart. "You're early." *Thank You, Lord. Oh, thank You.*

"You don't mind, do you?"

"Of course not." Leota looked at what Annie had brought—a pipe with twisting metal curling out in various directions. "What on earth is that?" As soon as she said it, she worried she had hurt Annie's feelings. What if it was an art project she had completed? Annie laughed. "Whatever you'd like to think it is. Heat rays. Sound. It's a metal sculpture. I bought it at a garage sale."

Thank heavens. Someone's white elephant, no doubt. "What are you going to do with it?"

Annie bit her lip. "Well, I thought it would look interesting in the garden. I have some rust-proof spray paints—yellows, oranges, and reds. It'll look like sun rays."

Leota looked it over again, trying to rouse some enthusiasm. It was the ugliest thing she had ever seen.

"Oh, Grandma, I'm sorry. I should've asked first. I can take it home."

Leota laughed. Well, why not put it in the yard? The garden was no longer just hers anyway. It was Annie's as well. Why not let her play in it? "I think it has potential. You plant it in the middle of the lawn, if you want." She'd been curious to see what Annie would do when given a free hand. If this was the first hint, Leota knew she was going to be in for quite a show.

Arba Wilson's children were playing in their backyard. One paused to peer over the fence. "What's that thing?"

"A garden sculpture," Annie said happily. "Would you like to come over and help me set it up?"

Leota felt a flicker of irritation. She didn't want to share Annie.

"Could I?" The little girl jumped off the fence and ran up the back steps. "Mama! Mama! The lady asked me over. No, not the old one, the . . ."

In less than two minutes, the little girl, her older sister, and her brother showed up in the backyard. Leota stood holding her broom and watching. After a few minutes, her irritation wore off. Their enthusiasm amused her. How long since she had had children in this yard? Wasn't that why she had planted the garden in the first place? To draw her children out of the house?

Arba came down the steps and stood by the fence, watching while her children chattered away and helped Annie dig a hole and set the pipe into it. "How're you, Mrs. Reinhardt?" Arba smiled at Leota pensively. The expression on Arba's face made Leota wonder if the younger woman thought she might sprout horns and breathe fire and smoke.

"Still breathing."

Arba seemed nonplussed. "Well, that's good."

Leota shivered. The cooling air had sunk into her arthritic joints. "I think I'll go inside."

"They aren't bothering you, are they?"

"Who?"

"My children."

"Land sakes, no. Not as long as they're with Annie. They can come through the gate next time."

"What gate?"

Leota walked closer and pointed. "Back there. Of course, you wouldn't know. Can't see it for all those overgrown privet bushes. Should've been cut back ages ago. My husband put the gate in twenty years ago. I had a good friend who lived in your house. She died back in '64. Her children sold the place."

"Has anyone else used the gate since your friend died?"

"No. The next family had a baby and spent most of the time in the house. The couple stayed to themselves. Never saw much of them. Heard 'em though. They screamed at each other night and day. Even had the police over there once to keep them from killing each other. There've been a dozen families in and out of that house over the years, and most didn't even bother keeping the place up any more than you do. I guess they figured since they were renting, it was the landlord's responsibility, but he never bothered, either. That's why your lawn is all weeds now and the rest of the garden looks the way it does."

Arba's smile had disappeared. "I *work*, Mrs. Reinhardt. I work very hard. By the time I get home I'm too tired to spend time weeding and cleaning up a yard."

"An hour a day, and you'd feel the better for it. There's something about working with the earth that pours the energy you used up in an office back into you." Leota leaned on the broom for support and looked at Arba squarely. "At least, it did for me. I worked in an office for years. Took a bus *and* walked." Her joints were beginning to ache more deeply. "And I know you work, Arba Wilson. Your children are always on their own, except on weekends."

Arba's shoulders stiffened. "If they're bothering you, just tell me, Mrs. Reinhardt. I'll make sure they don't do so again."

"Someone could bother *them*."

Arba stilled, a worried look filling her face. "Has someone been bothering my children?"

"Not that I've noticed, and I've been watching them. They play very nicely by themselves, but they're out front where anyone could see they're not supervised. There are some bad elements around these days."

Arba looked distressed. "I don't have any choice, Mrs. Reinhardt. I wish I did. Every dime I make goes to rent, food, utilities, car expenses, and medical insurance. I don't have anything left over."

"Their father should help with expenses."

"Their father!" Arba gave a hard laugh. "The court's gotta find him first."

"Did he run off?"

"He's probably in L.A. Unless he's in jail again. I'd rather scrape by like I am than have him back in our lives. We don't need his kind of help, Mrs. Reinhardt. He put me in the hospital once and broke Nile's arm because he got in front of the television while his father was watching some sorry football game."

"Oh." No wonder Arba had such strong feelings against the man. Who could blame her? "Got any relatives who could help you?"

"A sister on welfare. I don't want my kids growing up thinking it's all right to sit back and let the government take care of you."

"Good for you. What about a baby-sitter?"

"Costs too much. I'd need financial assistance, and I don't want to start down that road."

"Then tell them to play in the backyard. They'll be safer there." Leota couldn't take the cold anymore. "Or they could come over sometimes and watch my television. As long as it's not that MTV." She turned and started up the back steps. Each step was agony, her knees aching clear through the joints. She started to open the door and stopped. "By the way, what are their names?"

"Kenya, Tunisha, and Nile."

"Well, for heaven's sake, why on earth did you name them after African countries and a river in Egypt?"

"So they'd be proud of their heritage. That's why."

"You want 'em proud the Africans were selling their own people to slave traders? Some heritages are best laid aside."

"I beg your *pardon?*"

"You heard me clear enough. My husband went off to war and ended up in Germany where his folks came from. He carried that ugly baggage for the rest of his life. Would've been better for every-one if he'd moved on in his life instead." The old impatience filled her. "When your children are over here on my place, I'm going to call them Carolina, Indiana, and Vermont! They're free, same as the Israelites. And they're Americans. You make them proud of it!" She slammed the screen door behind her.

"That grandma of yours is something," Arba said to Annie. "I haven't figured out what. Is she always like that?"

Annie held the pipe while the children filled in the hole around it. "I don't think she meant to offend you." It was the first time she had heard Grandma say anything about her grandfather that gave her some insight into him. She hoped she could encourage her to talk more.

"Oh, don't you worry about it." Arba laughed. "Old folks just get cantankerous sometimes." She looked toward the house. "I like her."

"So do I." Annie barely got the words out around the sudden constriction in her throat. Was she crying? But why? And why this sense of impending doom?

The children finished pounding down the soil around the pipe. "Is it gonna hold, Annie?" Nile gazed up at her, wide-eyed.

"I think so." She tested it with a gentle push, then a harder one. It held fast. She stood back, looking at the metal sculpture now secured in the flower garden. "Good work, you guys." The children scrambled to their feet and stood back with her.

"Come on home now," Arba said, stepping back from the fence. "Maybe we'll see Anne and her granny in church Sunday."

"Thanks for your help, you three," Annie called after them. Smiling, she gave Arba a wave as she headed for her car. She took out the small overnight bag, two plastic bags of groceries, and the large covered birdcage. She came up the driveway and in the back door. Setting the cage on the kitchen table, she left her overnight case on the floor and put the groceries on the counter. She opened the refrigerator and put away cheese, eggs, hamburger, zucchini, mushrooms, red-jacket potatoes, and two quarts of milk. She left a loaf of bread, a package of bear claws, a tin of sweetened coffee, a small box with twenty bags of sampler teas, and a tin of cocoa on the counter and headed into the living room to check on her grandmother.

She was sitting in her easy chair, a knitted afghan over her legs. She looked pale. "Are you all right, Grandma?"

"I'm fine. Just cold."

Annie took one of her hands. It was icy. She rubbed it. "What do you say I fix you some hot chocolate?"

"That would be nice, but I don't have any."

"I brought some." Annie hesitated when she saw her grandmother was shivering. "Why don't I build a fire first?"

"I haven't had a fire in years."

"If you'd rather I didn't . . ."

"Oh, no, I'd love it if you did. I always enjoyed a fire, but it got to be too much trouble setting it up and cleaning out the fireplace all the time. And I ran out of wood. The matches are there on the mantel behind your grandfather's picture."

Annie looked at the old picture. Her grandfather had been a very distinguished-looking man. "He must have had blue eyes." They were so pale in the picture.

"The bluest I'd ever seen. And blond hair. Like gold."

Striking the match, Annie drew aside the screen and lit the yellowing newspaper crumpled beneath cut branches and an old presto log. Everything was so dry, the fire caught quickly. "I don't know anything about him. Mother never said much of anything about him." When her grandmother didn't say anything, Annie decided not to press. "I'll put the water on."

"I made some tuna salad this morning," her grandma called to her. "If you're hungry, it's there on the top shelf of the refrigerator. Help yourself. There's a can of chilled peaches, too."

"Did Corban come by this week?"

"On Wednesday. I imagine he'll show up tomorrow again. He figures he'll get more information out of me when you're around."

Annie laughed. "He thought he was being subtle."

"As a steamroller. Anyone with half a brain could see through that cock-and-bull story. If something happened to me, they'd be looking through my little telephone book under 'in case of emergency' numbers and calling your mother or your uncle. Or you. By the way, did you bring that parrot with you? The one you said had a nervous breakdown?"

"He's in here."

"Is he any better? Let's have a look at him."

"He's eating again." She took the cover off Barnaby's cage and carried him into the living room. "I'm glad you said I could bring him over, Grandma. Susan's totally freaked out about him. She's convinced now that he's eating that he's punishing her with the silent treatment."

"Oh, my, he's a pretty thing."

"He's a rainbow lory."

"Some birds are gregarious. Maybe he'd get better with a mate."

"Raoul paid five hundred dollars for Barnaby, Grandma. At that price, I'm afraid he's destined to be single."

"Five hundred dollars for a bird! That's more than I was ever paid in a month! What did this fellow do for a living? Sell dope?"

Annie laughed. "He's a policeman."

"Well, he should've gotten himself a German shepherd. Would've been cheaper and he could've taken him along on the job. Why don't you put Barnaby on that table by the front window, to the left of the door? There's plenty of light there. Maybe he'll like that."

Annie set the cage down carefully. Barnaby twitched once and remained still. "He used to pace back and forth on his perch and talk all the time. Raoul used to leave the television on day and night to keep Barnaby company."

Her grandmother got up and turned the television on. "Any particular station?"

Annie grinned at the bird. "He doesn't say."

Her grandmother smiled and selected a PBS concert. "That might soothe his ruffled feathers."

Annie went back into the kitchen. She had wondered how her grandmother would take to Barnaby, but she could hear her grandmother talking to him and smiled to herself. She had hoped Grandma Leota would keep Barnaby when they offered him. Annie had read that pets added years to a person's life, and she wanted her grandmother around for a long time to come. Who knew? Barnaby might be just what her grandmother needed.

She brought the mug of hot chocolate into the living room and set it beside Leota. The fire was crackling. "Are you warming up?"

"Yes, thank you. I shouldn't've stayed outside so long. Work used to keep me warm enough, but standing around leaning on a broom doesn't get the blood moving. Why don't you go and paint that metal sculpture while I take a little nap."

Grandmother Leota's eyes drifted shut as she finished talking, and with a worried glance at her still-white face, Annie headed for the backyard.

When Annie finished, she stood back, admiring the effect. The red, orange, and yellow streamers of metal flowed out of the gray pipe like a starburst of color in the fall garden. Some of the leaves on the fruit trees were beginning to turn as well. A clematis was growing close by, and Annie curled several tendrils around the base of the pipe, thinking how pretty it would look if the vine grew to partially conceal the metal.

She put the cans of spray paint back into the plastic carrier, then set it on the floor just inside the back door. Grandma Leota was asleep, her recliner tipped back just enough to elevate her feet and not interfere with her view of the television set. The concert was over, and actors spoke with English accents. Annie guessed the program to be an Agatha Christie murder mystery. Barnaby was picking at the food in his bowl. He had become very neat since "the incident," as Susan called it. If her grandmother liked Barnaby enough, Annie had decided she would take the stand from the trunk of her car and set it up so that the cage top could be removed.

Annie carried her case into the spare bedroom. She hung up the dress she planned to wear to Sunday worship services, and took out her sketchpad and pencils. For the rest of the evening, she made studies in black and white. Serenaded by the droning white noise of the television, she drew her grandmother's face as she slept in the big chair. She drew her veined and delicate hands. Later, she made quick sketches of the fireplace and mantel, Barnaby on the table by the window, the lamp on her grandmother's side table with the doily, Bible, and reading glasses.

When her hand began to cramp, Annie set her sketchbook and pencils aside and went into the kitchen to start supper. She found a bowl in one cabinet and seasonings in another. She mixed a meat loaf. After washing her hands, she turned on the oven and searched through the lower cabinets for a baking dish. Pressing the meat loaf into it, she slid it into the oven. Washing two red-jacket potatoes, she put them in a pot of water and set them on the stove to be turned on later. She would slice and steam the zucchini while the potatoes were boiling.

The telephone rang. Annie stepped into the doorway as her grandmother answered. Turning away, she took two plates and silverware out and set the small kitchen table for two.

"Annie!" her grandmother called. "Would you mind if Corban came by for a while this evening?"

"Supper will be ready in an hour, Grandma. There's plenty for one more." She waited a moment and stepped into the doorway. "Did he say yes?"

"He's on his way."

Annie added one more setting to the table, two more potatoes to the pot, and went to join her grandmother in the living room. She sat cross-legged on the couch and set her sketchpad and box of pencils on the side table.

"I didn't intend to sleep so long." Her grandmother moved as though to work the kinks out of her shoulders and back. "I'm not much company for you."

"I enjoy your company, Grandmother, awake or asleep."

Leota lowered the chair so that her feet were on the floor again. She pushed herself up, stood for a moment, then began stepping from one foot to the other.

"Are you all right, Grandma?"

She marched slowly in place. "I'm at that age when I have to get the circulation going before I take any long treks."

"Where are you going?"

"To the bathroom. Then to the bedroom for a sweater."

"I can get your sweater for you."

"I know you can, but I'll get it. If I don't move around a little bit, I'll grow right into this chair and have to be buried in it."

The thought made Annie shudder, and she pushed it away quickly. No point in getting morose. Grandma was going to be around for a long time.

Annie greeted Corban at the door when he arrived. "Good evening, Mrs. Reinhardt," he said formally as he entered the living room.

"I think we've known each other long enough now that you can call me Leota," she said from her chair. "Where's your notepad?"

"I left it in the car." His mouth tipped ruefully. "You seem to clam up when I have it in my hand."

"How does your girlfriend feel about you spending your Friday evening over here with me and my beautiful granddaughter?"

"Grandma—"

"Ruth's in the City with some of her friends."

"Girls' night out?"

"There's a march tomorrow morning. A political demonstration. They'll be in the front lines." He didn't look happy about it.

"Dinner's ready, Grandma," Annie said, hoping to save him explaining further. Corban helped her grandmother from her recliner.

"You're learning," Leota said, smiling up at him. Annie saw he was put off by the compliment. *So defensive. Lord, what can we do to soften his heart and help him relax enough to show himself? He's like a box turtle, pulling in tight, waiting for the hammer to fall.* Annie followed them into the kitchen. When they were seated together, Leota looked at him. "Would you like to do the honors?"

"Honors?"

"Pray."

He blushed to the roots of his hair. "I don't pray."

"Don't or won't?"

"Religion's never been a part of my life."

"It hasn't played a big part in mine, either. Faith, on the other hand, is everything." Grandma held out her hands. Annie reached across the table to Corban so that they joined hands in a circle. Corban looked decidedly uncomfortable but resigned. Grandma Leota lowered her head. Annie did likewise, closing her eyes.

"Father," her grandmother said solemnly, "bless this food to our bodies' use and bless the hands that have prepared it for us. And help us, Lord Jesus, to minister to this poor heathen boy. Amen."

Annie pressed her lips together, trying not to laugh. Her gaze flickered to Corban whose face was even redder.

"Thanks," he said grimly.

"You're welcome." Her grandmother spoke without the least hint of humor. She offered him a bowl. "Squash?"

Rain pattered the roof as the three of them ate together. Grandma Leota paused and looked out at the backyard. "That thing looks good out there. It'll be the only color until spring."

Corban glanced over. His brows flickered. "Well, that's certainly . . . different."

Annie didn't know whether that meant he liked it or not, but it didn't worry her. "More meat loaf, Grandma?"

"No, thank you, dear. I don't usually eat this much. I have to watch my girlish figure, you know." She gazed out the rain-slicked window. "There are quite a few bare spots left for you to fill, Annie." She smiled at Corban. "And you, too, if you've the imagination for it."

"Fill with what?" he said.

"Whatever you have to offer."

Corban looked out at the yard and back at them, obviously at a total loss.

"I was thinking about bowling balls," Annie said.

"What are you talking about?" Corban sounded faintly frustrated.

"Bowling balls," Annie repeated. "They come in all colors. I bought two a few weeks ago at a garage sale. One yellow, one marbled pink and red."

"What for?"

She shrugged. "Oh, I don't know. They were pretty and didn't cost much."

He gave a gruff laugh and speared a piece of potato. "Sounds like shifting junk from one place to another."

"For heaven's sake, Corban!" Grandma scowled at him. "Weren't you ever a little boy?"

Annie sensed her grandmother was coming to her defense and was touched. "I've been thinking they might look interesting in the garden. Are you game?"

"You do whatever you want out there, honey. That garden is more yours than mine now."

Alarmed, Annie put her hand over her grandmother's. "It'll never be mine, Grandma. That's your garden. I won't change anything if you don't want—"

"Nonsense. Hush now, and listen. A garden is only yours as long as you seed, weed, cultivate, water, and prune. A garden needs lots of tender, loving care. You go out there and enjoy it. The Lord knows it's been neglected too long. Just watching you work and put yourself into it gives me pleasure past describing. So you go ahead and bring the bowling balls and anything else you want."

Annie bit her lip, feeling the ache grow. Was her grandmother giving up? She didn't want to take over the garden. She wanted to come alongside her grandmother so they could enjoy it together. She had so much to learn. There were so many things her grandmother could teach her. *Oh, Lord, give us time. Please give us time.*

Grandma Leota patted her hand. "Don't look so distressed, Annie." She gazed out the window once more. "It never belonged to me anyway. I had so many hopes and dreams while I was out there." Her hand tightened slightly. "It's lots of work. You don't realize at first. You have to soften the soil with hoeing and fertilizing. Then you plant the seed and water and weed, all the while watching and hoping for growth. Then you have to protect the seedlings from vermin, and prune when things grow too fast and wild. Sometimes they get away from you altogether. Sometimes they die, and you don't know why. But then others flourish, so that everyone can partake. That's the whole point, don't you see? Bearing fruit. Carrying the sweet aroma . . ."

Her eyes grew moist. "Those trees back there that you two worked on should bear fruit this year." She let go of Annie's hand. "If they don't, cut them down."

Annie's heart ached. There it was again, the feeling that her grandmother was speaking less about what was outside the window and more about what had gone on inside the house. The tears pricked, hot and heavy. She felt Corban looking at her, perplexed. Did he feel nothing about what Grandma had just said? Or was it that he just didn't understand? "Did Grandpa like gardening, too?"

Her grandmother blinked and looked down at her plate. "There wasn't much of a garden when he went away to war. Mama and Papa Reinhardt started it, but everything Mama planted withered and died. After I came to live with them, the outside chores fell to me. And it seemed I had a knack for gardening. After a short while, it was no chore at all because I loved being out there in the open air and sunshine. Right from the beginning, that garden became my place. I worked all day, you see, and when I'd get home . . . well, the garden was a refuge where I could work out my sorrows and frustrations and have joy poured back into me."

"Did Mother help you?"

"Sometimes Eleanor would come outside. I hoped she'd love it the way I did, but she never seemed to take to it. She became very close to your great-grandmother, you see, so she stayed inside most of the time. Eleanor was just a baby when I moved in here, and Mama Reinhardt took over rearing her and your uncle George when I went to work. Mama Reinhardt never approved."

Corban pushed his plate aside and leaned forward on the table. "Approved of you, or of you working?"

"Both, I suppose. She didn't understand. Those were hard times. Our country was at war against Japan and Germany. Papa and Mama Reinhardt were German immigrants, both with thick accents. It didn't matter so much with Mama—she wouldn't have worked outside of the home. But no one would hire Gottlieb Reinhardt. He was a professional man, an engineer, and it hurt his pride terribly to be looked upon with suspicion. He never talked about the discrimination. It's not like today when everyone is shouting about being discriminated against, but it was a blow to his honor and integrity. He wasn't angry; he was ashamed. Mama didn't know about any of this until years later."

"How could she not know, Grandma?"

"He was a very quiet man, honey. He didn't whine or complain. Every morning he left the house and stayed away all day, dipping into savings when no paychecks were forthcoming. She thought he was going to work. For months he would look for a job, pounding the pavement, knocking on doors, offering his experience and knowledge. After a while, he gave up. He would go down to Dimond Park and sit on a bench and read."

Annie saw the tears in her grandmother's eyes.

"He was too proud to tell Mama Reinhardt no one wanted to hire a German. They were both naturalized citizens, not that that mattered. People were afraid and suspicious." She smiled sadly. "I didn't know until a few weeks ago that they had their citizenship. I found their papers with some old letters."

"So you moved in with Great-Grandma and Grandpa to help them out financially?"

"Oh, I wasn't so high-minded and altruistic as that. I needed help myself. Papa was worried they were going to lose the house. He wrote to Bernard about the situation, hoping his son could help him. Bernard wrote to me. I was barely making ends meet by myself, and Bernard thought this was an answer from heaven for all of us. He thought it would be a good way for me to get to know Mama better, too. And I would have someone to watch over George and Eleanor so that I could get a job and help out until Papa found something. There were plenty of jobs with so many men gone. Just none for Germans, you see. So I came to Papa and talked with him about it. Papa said to move in with them, and I did. I found employment that same week."

"And that didn't hurt his pride?" Corban looked skeptical.

"Papa knew I'd worked before marrying Bernard. In fact, I'd worked much of my life, just as most people did back then. He didn't tell Mama the full situation, and it wasn't my place to do so. Things were bad enough between Mama and me without my rubbing her nose in the fact that I was the one paying for the roof over her head. She had been against Bernard marrying me in the first place. I was trying to keep peace, not declare war. Mama Reinhardt didn't know what was really going on until Bernard came home from the war. And by then, it was too late."

"Too late?" Corban frowned. The words hung in the air.

"For the children. I've had a lot of years to think things over, and I know most of our troubles go back to that time."

Annie felt her grandmother's pain. She took her hand between her own.

Her grandmother looked at her sadly. "It was unfair, really. You have to see Mama Reinhardt's side of it. All during those war years while I was working, Mama Reinhardt didn't know I was turning the money over to Papa. She just thought I didn't care about my children. She thought I was just looking for a way to pass George and Eleanor off on her so I could have a carefree, fun-filled life of my own while Bernard was off fighting the war. Papa never told her otherwise. He was too proud, I guess. Too hurt. Too ashamed. The damage was being done to the children more than anyone, and I didn't fully understand. I was caught up in my own resentments and frustrations. Mama Reinhardt loved George and Eleanor in her own way, but she said things, hurtful things about me. And being so young, they believed everything."

She sighed. "I look back now and see that all my actions seemed to make it look like I didn't care about them. I did work all day—five, sometimes six, days a week. Then I'd go to church on Sunday. It wasn't the denomination Mama and Papa had belonged to in Germany, so Mama would stand in the bedroom doorway and tell me I was going against everything Bernard would want."

"Was that true?"

"Of course not, but it was what she thought and it made things difficult on the children. They were spending so much time with Mama, their loyalties were being pulled toward her. And I made it worse. I held my tongue most of the time and nursed my grievances against her. Thankfully, I had a good friend. Cosma. She was a dear. We worked together. Her husband was in the service, too. Sometimes she and I would volunteer at the USO. We'd serve coffee and cookies and dance with the soldiers."

She shook her head. "I'll never forget one night when Mama Reinhardt waited up for me. She called me names in German. I didn't know what they meant, but I saw the look on her face and heard the tone of her voice." She gave a soft, humorless laugh. "I lost my temper and called her an old battle-ax. She said she was going to tell her son everything about me when he got home, and then I would be out of her house. Papa was up from bed by then and got between us. I thought he'd tell her the situation then. I hoped and prayed he would."

"But he didn't," Corban said, his eyes dark.

"Not entirely, and I didn't dare."

"Why not? She deserved it."

She shook her head slowly. "When you smash someone's pride, Corban, you make an enemy, not a friend."

He shrugged. "She was already your enemy."

"Papa wasn't. He was on my side. That might have been part of Mama's animosity. He said he couldn't tell her yet, but he would. I knew it was best to leave it to him and wait."

"Did he tell her?" Annie's heart ached for all her grandmother had endured.

"Eventually." She pushed her plate away. Annie saw that her hands were trembling. "This is so difficult. You're only hearing things from my side, and I can see you taking offense for me, but things are never so simple. You must try to understand and not hold anything against Mama Reinhardt." She reached out to pat Annie's hand. "She's family, you know. Her blood runs in you, as well as mine. Think of it from her side. I was unlike anyone she knew. I was very independent. Very modern. Very American." She smiled sadly. "She was against your grandfather marrying me because of that. She thought Bernard would be happier married to a girl more like those from their homeland."

Leota laid her supper utensils on her plate. "I think when I moved into her house, she was convinced I would try to take over everything. So she fought me from the start. She didn't want me cooking or cleaning or doing anything in the house. When I went off to work, that just verified what she thought about me. I didn't understand her any more than she understood me. She had difficulty with English. In fact, she and Papa spoke German to one another most of the time. I just stayed out of her way as much as I could. It's pretty hard to do in a small house, so I worked in the garden. I thought it would give them time alone together, and I hoped it would give me time alone with my children."

"But it didn't work out that way." Annie knew her mother hated gardening more than anything else. And now she knew why. Mother had never understood that Grandma Leota was extending an invitation to her. She'd always referred to the garden as a place of labor rather than a labor of love.

"No, it didn't work out that way. Things seldom happen the way we plan."

"What happened when your husband came home from the war?" Corban said. "Did he get everything straightened out?"

"We had a whole new set of problems." She held out her hand for his plate. "You're finished?"

Annie saw how her grandmother's expression changed subtly. Grandma Leota didn't want to talk about Grandpa Bernard. The pain was all too clear in her eyes. Memories too painful for tears.

Corban must have seen it, too. "Yes," he said slowly and handed her his empty plate. "Best meal I've had in a long time."

Annie was thankful he didn't press her grandmother with more questions. She smiled at him when he glanced at her.

Grandma Leota took his utensils and put them on her plate. Then she carefully slid his plate underneath her own. She held out her hand to Annie. Annie didn't want her to stop talking about the past; he needed to know everything in order to understand her mother. "Were you ever able to make peace with Mama Reinhardt, Grandma?"

"Years later." She sighed, her hands resting on the table. "It's hard to explain. I think she knew it was my salary that saved the house, because Papa signed it over to Bernard as soon as he came home from the war. But it wasn't until years later, when Papa was dying, that he told her everything." Her eyes had grown moist. "That's when she changed toward me."

She blinked and was silent and still a moment. "I knew she was sorry. I understood her better by then, too. We reached an understanding. We loved one another as best we could. Toward the end, I think we both put the past completely behind us." Taking a deep breath, she let it out and pushed her chair back from the table. "After all was said and done, she was the only company I had after your grandpa died."

Annie felt the anguish of that quiet statement. Both women had been alone in the end. She knew the fullness of that, for her mother had wept bitter tears when Great-Grandma Reinhardt had died.

I would've gone to see her if my mother hadn't still been there. . . ."

Filled with pity and a sense of shame she couldn't define, Annie rose. "I'll do the dishes, Grandma."

"You can put them in the sink for me, but I'll wash them. I need to stand up for a while and *do* something."

Annie relented. She knew it was her own nature to step in and try to take over the chores, but doing everything for her grandmother wasn't merciful or kind. Grandma did need to get up and move around and do things for herself. More important, she needed to know she was useful. There would come a time when more care would be needed, but this wasn't it. Not yet. Not now. Setting the plates and utensils in the sink, Annie stepped aside. "The dishes are all yours, my dear. Would you like me to dry?"

"No. We'll leave them in the rack. It's supposed to be healthier. Corban, why don't you get another bundle of wood and stoke the fire. I'll join you two in the living room when I'm finished."

Annie understood. Her grandmother was asking for a few moments to be by herself. She glanced at Corban and saw he, too, understood. He rose and headed into the other room. Annie put her arm around her grandmother's shoulder and kissed her cheek. "I love you, Grandma," she said, embarrassed by the thickness in her voice. "I love you very much."

Her grandmother looked up at her, her blue eyes full of tears. "I love you, too. And whatever your mama may have told you, I love her, too. Always have. Always will."

Corban put cut branches on the fire. Annie was behind him, stroking the small parrot. "I didn't know your grandmother had a bird."

"Barnaby belongs to my roommate's friend, but she's hoping Grandma Leota will adopt him. And you're hoping, too, aren't you, Barnaby?" Turning her head, she smiled at Corban again. The sweetness of it caught him off-guard. "Susan and I haven't enough time to spend with Barnaby—" she stroked the parrot again—"and birds need company."

Corban was disturbed by his reaction to Annie. Looking for a distraction, he picked up her sketchpad. "Is this yours?"

She glanced at him and her eyes flickered with embarrassment. "Yes," she said simply and looked away again. He wondered if she was worried at what he might say. Surely she didn't think him such an ogre that he would slam her work?

"Do you mind if I look them over?" He was determined to show her he could be kind.

"I suppose not. I was practicing."

The first sketch surprised him. "These are very good, Anne." He was amazed how good.

"You really think so?"

She looked so vulnerable. Did she really have so little self-esteem? He caught himself, remembering a similar look on Ruth's face when they were first dating, though he hadn't seen that look on her face since she moved in with him. There were times when he wondered if Ruth had ever really been vulnerable or if it had all been a ruse. Even as the thought came, he felt guilty for it. Ruth had been trying harder lately, though he had sensed a hardening beneath the surface smiles. Was it his attraction to Anne-Lynn Gardner that made him see Ruth Coldwell in a different light and question her feelings for him?

What about his own motives and feelings? Did he dare scrutinize his own behavior? Mouth tight, he sat on the old sofa and flipped through more pages. "How long have you been studying?"

"I just started classes at the Art Institute, but I've always loved to draw."

He studied one page. "Do you know what you're going to do with it? As a livelihood, I mean?"

She straightened slowly, whispering to the bird before answering him. "Oh, I don't know yet. Right now, I'm learning the fundamentals."

"What's your passion?"

"The Lord."

He glanced at her. There hadn't been the least hesitation or embarrassment in her response. Had he heard her rightly? "I beg your pardon?" Was she some kind of religious zealot? She didn't look the part.

She seemed to consider for a moment. She smiled and shrugged. "I want to paint things that will glorify God."

"Landscapes? That sort of thing?"

"And metal sculptures I buy at garage sales. Or walls." She laughed at herself. "Whatever. The Lord will let me know in His time."

She wasn't a ditz. She was just plain weird. Her face was lit up, her blue eyes shining as though lit from the inside. He thought she was the most beautiful girl he'd ever seen, including Ruth. Even if she was a little nuts.

He couldn't help but smile. Unlike Ruth, who kept him off-center all the time, this girl made him feel comfortable. And curious. "You weren't kidding about the bowling balls, were you?"

"No, I wasn't." She laughed. "Visitors could imagine them to be dinosaur eggs, don't you think?"

Her laughter wasn't forced or flighty. It was full of warmth and spilling out of her—and it was contagious. He grinned. "I hadn't thought of that. If I spot one at a garage sale, I'll buy it for you. How's that?"

"You go to garage sales?"

"Not often."

She gave him a dubious look. "Ever? Come on, Corban. Be honest."

She reminded him of her grandmother, nailing him on every white lie. "Okay. Once or twice. Out of curiosity. But I'll start looking around. I promise. I mean, I didn't realize people sold such valuable items as bowling balls. Anything else on your wish list? An old tennis racket maybe? Some golf clubs?"

She grinned. "Well, let me think about it for a minute." She sat on the other end of the sofa and crossed her legs Indian-fashion. "Yes to the tennis racket and golf clubs. I have some ideas how I could use them. But I'm more interested in old wash buckets and watering cans, birdhouses, ceramic animals, pots, and big rocks . . . that sort of thing. How's that for a start?"

"Do you think I'm a Rockefeller?"

"Bargain. Keep track. I'll pay you back. Just don't go whole hog."

"I was kidding, Anne." His mouth tipped. "Money's no problem for me."

She tilted her head slightly, looking at him with a strange expression. "I think it must be more of a problem than you realize."

Frowning slightly, he looked away from her intense scrutiny. He flipped another page in her sketchpad and tapped the drawing. "This is really good, Anne." The sketch of Leota Reinhardt's hands was so real he could see the paper-thin quality of her skin, the veins, the wedding ring that had become part of her finger, the short nails. They were hands that had worked hard, yet held a quality of grace.

"I'm sorry if I was out of line." The apology was quiet and utterly sincere.

He let out his breath and looked at her again. "Having money has its drawbacks." He thought of Ruth again. It would be nice to know where he really stood with her. He never remembered her being so offensive and defensive before they started living together. Or was it when they started sleeping together that things began to change? He wasn't sure anymore. He just knew something wasn't right. Something dark was working beneath the surface, something deadly that was eating away at the relationship he had hoped to have with her.

He stared at Anne's drawing and marveled at the detail.

Anne leaned over to look at what he was studying. "Her hands have always struck me as beautiful. Don't you think so? There are so many women now who have soft hands with long, silk-wrap nails painted in pretty pinks and reds. But my grandma's hands have such . . . character."

She was right. He thought of Ruth and the time she spent on her hands and nails. And her hair, and her body . . . even her feet. She'd sit and sand her heels and rub in expensive lotions. Everything about Ruth was practiced, right down to the voice lessons. Ruth was a work in the making. The sound of the workout video played in his head. He laughed under his breath as a thought came to him.

"What?" Anne glanced at his face, curious.

"I was just trying to imagine your grandmother doing a Jane Fonda workout in front of the television set."

Anne laughed. Oh, how she laughed. He loved the sound of it. He loved watching her face. She made him laugh, too. Oh, man, it felt good not to have to worry whether she would take offense at his mirth.

"What are you two cackling about?" Leota said from the doorway, a dish towel over her shoulder.

"I thought you were going to let the dishes air-dry, Grandma. You just wanted to be rid of us."

"This old mare is not completely out to pasture."

He grinned at the old woman, enjoying the moment. "Do you work out, Leota?"

"With barbells, you mean?" She gave him a droll look. "Not lately."

Anne laughed harder. "Add barbells to the list, Corban. Wouldn't they look great in the yard, Grandma? We could lean one upright against the fence and train a baby rose vine around it. Most people buy exercise equipment and let it gather dust in a corner anyway."

"If you find some barbells, you can bring them over and plant them." With that, Leota went back into the kitchen.

Corban turned another page in Anne's sketchbook. "Where'd you get these designs?" He studied the intricate swirls and curls, the sort of patterns he imagined he could find in a Moorish palace.

"Oh, that's just doodling." She got up and headed for the kitchen.

Just doodling? Corban watched her, his gaze starting at the thick fall of long, curly, strawberry blonde hair tied back at the nape of her neck and dropping down over her lithe form. She was thinner than Ruth, but definitely curved in all the right places. She dressed carelessly—a short-waisted pink sweater, worn blue jeans, and old tennis shoes. Ruth wore Levi's, too, usually with a white T-shirt, black leather belt, and tan blazer with a gold pin on the lapel. She wouldn't be caught dead in jeans with grass and dirt stains on the knees and a torn back pocket.

He turned the last few pages of the sketchbook, admiring Anne's work, and then set it aside as the two women joined him again. Leota settled herself. Gripping the arms of her chair, she pushed so that the chair tilted back and the footrest was raised. She looked tired and pensive. She caught him studying her, sighed, and closed her eyes. Did she think he was going to start an interview?

Anne sat on the sofa and took up her sketchpad. Corban hoped she would start drawing again so that he could watch how she worked. Instead, she put it aside and focused on him. "How long have you been doing volunteer work?"

"Couple of months." He glanced at Leota and saw she had one eye open and trained on him. "Okay. Okay. Your grandmother is my first assignment."

"Corban has such altruism. He's going to change the world for the better. Just ask him."

He blushed. Leota was smiling at him. Resigned, he looked at Anne and confessed. "I needed a subject for a paper I'm writing. Your grandmother is it, much to her disgust."

Leota chuckled. "In the beginning, that was true, but I'm beginning to enjoy your august presence."

"Thanks a bunch."

She closed her eye. "Doesn't take much to get your dander up, does it?"

"Look who's talking."

"Good for you." She folded her hands on her lap. "Don't let me get away with anything."

Corban decided to take up the challenge. "I'd like to hear more about your husband." He saw the muscles of her face tense slightly. Or had it been a wince? "You said there was a whole new set of problems when he came home. What sort of problems did you mean? Delayed stress? Family? Job?"

Leota sat silent.

He was sorry he had said anything. What an idiot he was. He could *feel* her silence. She was so still, he wondered if she was gathering strength for a blast of temper. She was probably going to tell him to march himself right out of her home and not darken her doorstep again. But when she slowly opened her eyes, she looked at Annie, not him.

"Bernard Gottlieb Reinhardt had the tenderest heart of any man I ever knew. And that is why life became so difficult for him. He felt responsibility for things he had no control over." A look of anguish filled her face. She closed her eyes again.

Why had she made such a point of her husband's tenderness?

Corban looked at Anne and saw tears trickling down her cheeks. Did she know what her grandmother was talking about? He looked back at Leota and grimaced inwardly. He really *was* a jerk. He was beginning to hate the whole idea of doing a term paper and using Leota Reinhardt as part of his research.

Leota tipped the chair up so she was sitting with her back straight, hands on the armrests, feet flat on the floor. "I suppose it's time," she said softly. Corban sensed from her expression that she had made a decision and was now determined to go forward with it, no matter how much it hurt.

Oh, *why* couldn't he have kept his mouth shut?

"The first time I saw Bernard, I was with a friend at one of the dance halls downtown. Bernard came in with several of his friends. He was the sort of young man that young ladies notice right away. Tall, handsome . . . he was blond and had beautiful blue eyes. He wasn't three feet inside the door of that hall before he was surrounded by women. He paid them no attention." She smiled. "I loved to dance, especially the swing, and I never lacked for partners. Bernard just stood and watched me all evening."

"He never asked you to dance, Grandma?"

She chuckled. "He didn't know how, and he had too much dignity to want to learn in front of everyone."

"So how did you meet him?"

"The band took a break. I was out of breath and hot from dancing. Bernard was standing near the refreshment table. The evening was more than half over, and all he had done was stand and watch me. He had a glass of punch in his hand and was sipping out of it. He smiled at me and lifted his glass. So I took the bull by the horns. I walked right up to him, said I was thirsty, and held out my hand. He blushed when he gave me his glass. I drained it, handed it back, and asked him for more."

"Grandma!" Anne said, laughing. "I'd never have courage enough to do something like that!"

"Most ladies wouldn't think to do such a thing. I was always one to go after what I wanted. Besides, I figured if I waited for him, I'd be old and gray before he said a word to me. There were rumors of war, and life didn't seem so certain. Then again, maybe that was just my excuse for being so brazen. I didn't want to miss the opportunity. I had never seen Bernard at the dance hall before. Seeing as he didn't dance, I figured it was unlikely I'd ever see him there again. Nothing ventured, nothing gained, as they say. One look at your grandfather and I thought the risk of complete public humiliation was worth the chance he might ask me out."

"Obviously, he did."

"Oh, he did better than that. He asked me to marry him."

"Right there in the dance hall? That *night?*"

"Well, later. In the rumble seat."

Corban laughed. He couldn't help himself. It was a side of Leota Reinhardt he would never have imagined in a million years. She turned her gaze upon him like a marksman ready to fire. He fought to regain control. "Sorry." A rumble seat!

"Of course you are," she said dryly. "I can guess what improper notions stampeded through your dirty little mind. Have you ever been in the rumble seat of a car?"

"No, ma'am." His lips twitched.

"Obviously not. It's a small space—a *very* small space—too small to carry on anything improper, I assure you. Especially when the car is in motion with the wind blowing in your face and the car bouncing over every bump in the road. And don't give me that cheeky grin of yours."

"Just getting even. Whose car was it?"

"One of Bernard's friends. Can't remember his name, but he knew my friend and asked if we needed a ride home. The dance ended late, and we were waiting for the bus when they drove up. I wasn't in that seat two seconds when Bernard put his arm around me, leaned down, and said someday he was going to marry me."

"What'd you say, Grandma?"

"I said, 'How about next Wednesday? It's my day off.' Of course, I thought he was joking. When he took me out the next evening, I realized he wasn't."

"It gives a new definition to whirlwind romance." Corban grinned even more broadly. "One week."

"Actually, it was almost a year, and most of that time was spent trying to change his mother's opinion of me. You see, Bernard went home that first night. His folks had been worried and waiting up for him. He told them he had met the girl he was going to marry. By the time he spilled out the whole story, they were convinced I was . . . well, not the sort of girl anyone would want for their only son. A girl who danced with all the young men at a public hall and drank from a stranger's glass and accepted a proposal in the back of a car." She smiled sadly. "A Jezebel."

She rubbed her thighs as though she ached. "I didn't understand them, and they didn't understand me. Until Bernard went away to war, we had very little to do with Mama and Papa. Bernard would visit them on Sunday afternoons after church. I fixed dinner for them a few times, but . . . well, Mama Reinhardt was a very good cook, and I was a new bride who had lived on tuna casseroles, corned beef and cabbage, and potatoes." She smiled in amusement. "Mama Reinhardt was not impressed."

Corban felt anger stirring inside him at the hurt Leota must have felt. "Sounds like an old bat to me."

"I think that's probably what you thought of me in the beginning." Leota gave him a pointed look. "Wasn't it?"

"Now that you mention it," he conceded with a wry grin.

"Maybe you still do. Didn't anyone ever teach you to respect your elders?"

"Yes, ma'am."

"Now that's one of the things I like about you, Corban. Your impertinence." Leota's eyes were twinkling, and Corban found himself liking her—really liking her—for the first time. She must have been something when she was young.

"So you didn't have them over for dinner often," he said, hoping to get her back on track.

"Once a month we suffered one another's company. I liked Papa right from the beginning, but Mama would sit and watch and not say anything. When she did, she spoke German to Papa, and he would translate."

"Didn't she speak English?"

"Not very well. Language was another barrier between us. English isn't any easier to learn than German, but over the years, we learned to talk to one another. More toward the end."

"Did Mother learn to speak German?"

"Your mother and Uncle George spoke German at home until their father returned from the war. After that, German was never spoken in the house again."

Annie's eyes widened. "Not even by Papa and Mama Reinhardt?"

"Not in Bernard's presence."

Corban waited, knowing whatever Leota had to say wouldn't come easily. He could see the tears welling in her eyes as she sat silent, gathering her thoughts. She blinked, her hands rubbing and rubbing at her thighs. She looked gray and old. Vulnerable. As though she were drowning in painful memories.

"Mama's loyalties were put to the test when Bernard joined the army," she said finally. "She and Papa both had brothers and sisters with families still in Germany. I remember both of them saying what a madman Hitler was. They would read the daily newspapers and grieve over every word that was said about Germany. Some editorials called them 'bloody Huns.' The Reinhardts had been receiving letters ever since leaving Europe, and the later ones were filled with glowing praise for the *fuhrer*. Of course, Mama and Papa wrote right back with the truth. Then the letters stopped coming."

She leaned back, her hands still. "I was with Bernard when he told them he had enlisted. Mama Reinhardt wept. I'd never heard crying like that before. Wailing like her heart was being torn from her. Papa told Bernard if the war turned in America's favor and he ended up in Germany, to try to find and save whatever kin he could."

She fell silent then. Corban bit his lip, giving her the chance to begin again. When she stayed silent, though, he couldn't hold back the question. "Did he make it into Germany?"

"Yes."

So much pain in a single word. Corban had never realized it was possible to communicate so much in one word. Annie sat still and silent, eyes flooded with tears, seeming to feel her grandmother's suffering as though it were her own.

"Bernard made it to the town where Mama and Papa Reinhardt had lived. The unit he was with destroyed it." She blinked, not looking at either of them. "He awakened one night after a recurring nightmare. He told me the men had gone mad, he among them. They killed everyone they saw. They wanted to wipe that town off the face of the earth."

Corban couldn't believe he'd heard right. He leaned forward. *"Why?"*

She looked at him bleakly. "Just before they came to the town, they had freed a concentration camp. Bernard said the smell was beyond describing, dead bodies stacked up like cordwood. The town was close by, close enough to have known what was happening, close enough to have been supplying the soldiers there. Bernard never got over what he saw and what he did about it." She closed her eyes. She was trembling.

Annie started to weep. She left the couch, knelt at her grandmother's feet, and put her head in her lap. Leota stroked her hair slowly. "Your grandfather said when the rage in him died, all that was left was shame. Shame for what he had done, but more shame for the blood that ran in his veins."

"Did Mama and Papa Reinhardt ever know?" Annie said tearfully.

"Bernard never spoke a word about it to anyone but me, and he only spoke to me about it one time, when it poured out of him against his will. It was like a cancer eating him up inside. Oh, his parents both knew something horrible had happened in Germany, something so terrible their son could never speak of the war. Perhaps if he had talked about it, he wouldn't have suffered so."

Corban couldn't imagine what the man must have felt. "How— how did he cope with what happened?"

"He came home, went back to work, and tried to get on with his life. Papa signed the house over to him, and he and Bernard built the apartment behind the garage. Mama moved in grudgingly, feeling I had stolen her house from her. She was filled to overflowing with resentment. She blamed Bernard's depression on me, saying in no uncertain terms that a good wife would be able to bring her husband out of it. She just didn't understand. And neither did I at that time."

She sighed. "Our squabbling must have made things worse on your grandpa. And your mother and George were afraid of their father. They didn't remember him, of course, since they were so young when he went away. After he returned, Bernard was given to bursts of anger in the beginning. He was a fine craftsman, but he'd work for a while, then lose his temper and get fired. He lost one job after another the first five years he was home. After word spread, he couldn't get full-time work. That just made him feel worse because then it had to be me working to pay the bills. He'd lapse into long silences. He always did such wonderful work. He built the lattice in the backyard. And he did those cabinets in the kitchen and that built-in china hutch back there. Beautiful work, but all he could get were odd jobs."

Eyes moist, Leota went on quietly. "In the evenings he would sit in front of the television and drink until he fell asleep."

"Oh, Grandma," Annie murmured, holding her grandmother's hand between her own and rubbing it gently as though to bring warmth into it.

"He was a good man, but broken up inside." Leota's mouth trembled. "And I never knew how to put him back together." Her lips curved in a humorless smile. "Like Humpty-Dumpty. Shattered."

Corban didn't know what to say or do to ease her suffering. The long silence made him uncomfortable, pointing out his ineptitude. The silence of ten minutes was unbearable to him. How had she borne the silence of years, especially knowing the cause of it?

"It's not just Germans," Leota said as though he had spoken aloud. "That's the thing of it. I tried to tell Bernard that, but he'd never listen. Look what the Japanese did to the Chinese during the rape of Nanking and to anyone who ever fell into their hands during the war. Look at what the white man has done to Native Americans. Look what the Africans do to one another. We have the holy wars in the Middle East, *jihad* against us, the genocide in Southeast Asia, and the Soviets splintering and aiming warheads every which way. Here in our own country right now, you feel the tide turning against Christians. They're being maligned and blamed for all kinds of things. No. There's nothing new under the sun. I remember thinking back in the sixties, when the Watts riots were going on, that what happened in Germany could happen here. And then the AIDS epidemic hit. It'd be so easy for the tide to turn against those who're poor and sick."

She shook her head. "No, it's not Germans. It's *mankind*. It's our own sin nature growing and taking control and ravaging the world. But Bernard would never listen. He would never accept God's grace and mercy. He knew there wasn't a way on this earth to undo what he'd done, and he wasn't willing to let God wash it all away with the blood of Christ. Not until the very end. So he suffered. And he made everyone around him suffer right along with him."

Annie shook her head, her expression filled with a sorrow that pierced Corban's gut. When she spoke, her voice was choked with tears. "I don't think Mother knows any of this, Grandma."

"You're right. She doesn't. She and George were too young to understand what was going on. They believed what they were told. I always thought to keep to myself what I knew until I died. But lately . . ." She looked at Corban, her eyes clear and bright, pensive. "Sometimes you have to tell the truth, no matter how hard it is. Even when it doesn't change anything. People seem to make the same mistakes over and over again."

Corban felt a heaviness in the pit of his stomach. Leota Reinhardt was trying to teach him something, and for the life of him he wasn't sure what it was.

"It helps me understand Mother a little better, Grandma. There's so much she doesn't know. Maybe if she did . . ."

"She has to *want* to know, sweetheart. The soil has to be softened before planting. Watering has to be done before a seed takes root." She touched Annie's cheek tenderly. "My, how an old woman rambles on when she has such a kind audience. Now, how about some of that herbal tea?"

Annie rose, leaned down to kiss her grandmother's cheek, and went into the kitchen.

Leota looked straight at Corban then, challenging him in some way. He sensed that she was trying to make him see past himself. *What is it, old woman?* he wanted to cry out. *Say it straight out. Tell me! I want to know. I want to see. I want to understand.*

She smiled, an irritating little smile that told him she wasn't going to make things easy for him.

All she said was, "I have hope for you, Corban Solsek." She waited another moment; then she rose stiffly from her chair, turned the television on to a game show, sat again, and leaned her head back. With that, she closed her eyes and said not another word for the rest of the evening.

13

NORA WALKED THE MALL. THE CHRISTMAS STORE WAS OPEN, BUT SHE walked past, disgusted. It wasn't even Halloween, Thanksgiving a distant six weeks away, and yet soon the holly and Santas would be cropping up like weeds in every store window. Every year Christmas came earlier, bringing with it an inner sadness. Why was it Christmas always depressed her? No matter how big the tree, how bright the decorations, how frenetic the festivities, she felt alone and lonely.

Pausing by a toy store, Nora remembered the excitement of buying presents for her children when she was younger. Michael had loved Lego toys from the time he was old enough to stack blocks. Over the years, she had purchased more and more complicated—and expensive—collections of the connecting plastic blocks. Where were they now? Stored in the garage in case a grandchild might someday want them? Or had Michael taken them with him when he moved away? She couldn't remember.

The dolls in the store window reminded her of shopping for Anne . . . and the frustration that went along with it. One Christmas she had stood in line to buy a Cabbage Patch doll for her precious daughter. When the store announced there was no more stock available, she had forked over two hundred dollars to a lady who had purchased three. Greedy witch. When Annie had opened the pretty package and seen the doll, she had said a quiet thank you, nestled it back in the box, and placed it under the tree.

"Don't you like it? Every little girl wants one of these dolls. You have no idea how difficult it was to get one for you."

"It's nice, Mommy."

Nora hated being called Mommy. She had reminded Anne-Lynn over and over to call her "Mom" or "Mother." "Mommy" was for babies.

Anne had taken the doll to school with her. When she returned without it, Nora had been angry. She had been so certain Anne had lost it and wondered how she could be so careless. "Do you have any idea how much that doll cost me? Two hundred dollars! I should've just bought you one of those cheap Raggedy Ann dolls!" Then, to make matters worse, Anne-Lynn had cried and confessed she hadn't lost it. She had given it away to a little girl who had received only a puzzle for Christmas. Standing at the toy store window now, Nora remembered how furious she had been over that. And why shouldn't she have been? She had waited for hours, paid a ridiculous price for something every normal little girl wanted . . . and what did her daughter do? She gave the gift away as though it meant nothing to her.

Just as I *mean nothing to her.* Tears pricked Nora's eyes as she stood gazing through the glass into the toy store. *All the things I've done for my children, and do they appreciate it? They don't care one iota about me or my feelings. All they care about is themselves. When did Michael last call me? On Mother's Day last year? Oh, Anne calls, but always from Leota's. Why does she keep asking if I'd like to come over for tea? Just to hurt my feelings? Just to let me know how much time and love she's expending on my mother? Mother and Anne both know I don't want to go over there for tea or anything else!*

She bit her lip, the tears welling, her throat tight and hot. Her children were both so selfish! Did they know how cruel they were? *I should cut them right out of my will. That would wake them up! And it would serve them right, too. They've abandoned me. I should abandon them. In fact, I should leave a letter to them and have the attorney read it aloud, telling them why I've cut them off.* That would make them sorry . . . that would make them writhe with guilt over how mean they'd been to her. If she had some fatal disease, like cancer, and she suffered for months . . .

Maybe they'd feel sorry then. Maybe Fred would be sorry, too.

She drew in a shaky breath and let it out slowly. Problem was, she was healthy. Physically. She had kept her weight down, exercised, eaten right. And yet she had just been to the doctor, wanting to know about the palpitations and stomachaches and headaches.

She was dying. She knew it. Even her bones ached. She must have cancer or something worse. She had gone through a battery of tests. Medical technicians had taken blood, made her drink barium, and done X rays. When nothing was found, she insisted the doctor order an MRI. Today she had gotten the results.

"I can find nothing wrong with you, Nora." His diagnosis: stress, which was causing psychosomatic symptoms. He suggested a psychiatrist. Furious, she told him she had been in counseling for years and it had done no good. Her life was worse now than it had ever been before. She'd burst into tears and said she wished she *were* dying. She wished she *did* have cancer. "Then they'd all be sorry for the way they've treated me!"

The doctor had talked with her for some time, encouraging her to check herself into some kind of care facility in the Santa Cruz mountains, where she could rest, talk with a counselor, and reevaluate her life.

He thinks I'm crazy. She pressed a hand to her temples. Well, maybe she was. Maybe she was headed for a nervous breakdown. Well, if she was, it certainly wasn't her fault. Nobody loved her. Nobody had ever really loved her. Not even her own mother . . .

God, why? I don't understand. I've tried so hard. I've done everything right, and it's all gone wrong. Nothing I do turns out the way I want. Two men I loved ended up hating me. Two children I've borne don't even want to talk to me.

Maybe I've always loved others too much. I should've been loving myself more instead of pouring time and money into my husbands and children. I should've been taking care of myself.

She turned from the store window and walked on, passing other ladies wandering in the mall. Some had children in strollers, some were walking with friends, and others sat on the pretty benches watching people pass. Nora paused again, looking in another window crowded with gift items.

Why shouldn't she shop for herself? Why shouldn't she buy something if it would make her feel better? Hadn't she always purchased little gifts to cheer others up? It was time she cheered herself up. Entering the store, she wandered among the displays, picking things up and setting them down. She spotted something in a distant corner. It made her smile. The item was cute and utterly impractical. It was also expensive, considering what it was, but she liked it and that was all that mattered today. It was time to pamper Nora instead of Nora pampering others. She had plenty of cash, but she decided to put the item on a credit card. Fred always gave her an allowance, but she figured he owed her this much after his reticence of late. She made her purchase and left.

The warm, fuzzy feeling passed quickly. By the time Nora reached the parking lot, she wondered why she had wasted fifty dollars on a stuffed bear. What would Fred say when he saw the bill? Of course, it wouldn't say *bear* on the debits. It would just list the store.

Sitting in her car, Nora took the bear from the bag and stared at it, hoping to resurrect the faint pleasure she had felt when she saw it in the first place. Maybe she had been thinking about future grandchildren. Her eyes welled, and tears spilled over. If her children ever did have babies of their own, maybe then they'd understand how she felt. They would know what a good mother she had been. They would know how she'd sacrificed for them. Maybe then—

A sudden picture filled her mind: Leota on her knees in the garden. Leota looking toward the house, tears running down her cheeks.

Where was I? Why didn't I go out to her?

Nora shut her eyes tightly.

I was helping Grandma Reinhardt. That's what I was doing. I was always helping Grandma. She said she didn't know what she'd do without me. Anger stirred again. *My mother never helped. All she ever did was take care of her own needs and wants. She never cared about anyone but herself.*

Yet the picture remained. Along with it, another memory flickered. She could almost feel Grandma Reinhardt's hand on her arm. "Nein. Your mama thinks it is fine to waste time planting flowers, but I have work to be done. You be a good girl and help with supper."

Nora's anger seeped away, leaving confusion and anguish. Stuffing the teddy bear into the shopping bag, she tossed it into the backseat. Jamming her key in the ignition, she started the car.

And then it surfaced again, the loneliness she had tried all her life to escape, the loneliness she wanted so desperately to press down where it wouldn't be recognized. It welled up so strongly that she gripped the steering wheel. She could hardly breathe through the pain of realization. Tears blinded her.

I have a husband.
I have children.
And still, I'm alone.

Fred was home. His car was parked in the garage when Nora pulled in. She was filled with dismay and guilt at the sight of it. She had wasted the entire afternoon wandering in malls, window shopping. All for what? To feel better? She felt worse. Now Fred was home early, and she had no idea what to fix for dinner. Had she taken anything out of the freezer this morning? Probably not. Who thought about dinner when the doctor was going to tell you that you were dying of some dreaded disease?

Taking the bag with the bear in it, she got out of the car. She unlocked the side door from the garage into the house, letting out her breath slowly, trying to prepare herself for anything. As she entered the kitchen, she saw an open box of pizza on the counter. Two slices missing. Fred was sitting in the family room, watching the evening news, a glass of wine on the side table. He'd changed from his suit and was wearing khaki slacks and a navy blue sweater. He always dressed nicely, even when lounging around the house. He was one of those men who grew more handsome with the years.

Please, God, don't let him stop loving me the way Bryan and Dean did. Please.

Fred looked at her, eyes troubled. "What did the doctor say?"

"Is that why you're home early?"

"I was worried about you. It's pretty late."

She set her purse on the counter. "I had some shopping to do." Her mouth trembled. "A gift." She didn't tell him it was for herself.

"What's the diagnosis?"

"Oh, I'm fine. Nothing wrong. I'm healthy as a horse. The doctor thinks I should be committed."

His mouth tipped. "You might think about it."

Nora burst into tears. Covering her face, she stood in the kitchen sobbing. She wished she were dead. She should drive into a tree or off a cliff into the ocean. Then her children would be sorry for treating her so badly.

She felt Fred's arms slide around her. He drew her close. "I love you," he said softly. "You drive me crazy, Nora, but I love you."

She clung to him and sobbed harder, thinking of all the ways she had neglected him lately. "I don't deserve you."

"No, you don't," he said with a hint of humor. "Just got lucky, I guess."

She drew back slightly and smiled up at him through her tears. What would she do without him? She remembered the harsh words she had spoken only yesterday. She thought of the account he had lost because of her forgetfulness. "You forgive me everything." He was the kindest man she had ever met. His gentle spirit had been one of the things that attracted her to him.

"We need help, Nora. We can't go on this way."

A niggling fear coursed through her. She could hear some inner bell tolling the death of another marriage. Kindness before the killing blow.

"You were the first woman I ever loved," Bryan had said the night before he walked out on her. The note he left behind was the last thing he ever wrote to her. Including child-support checks. How a man could manage to disappear so quickly and completely, she had never been able to understand.

Dean hadn't been so nice about it. "If you have anything to say to me, do it through your lawyer."

Nora shriveled inside. *I can't go through it again. God, help me. I can't.*

Whatever Fred wanted, she would do. She couldn't bear to fail again. She was so weary of the fight, sick of life, sick of herself. "Maybe you're right," she said meekly. "What do you think we should do?"

"Start by meeting with the pastor."

"He doesn't like me." She withdrew from his arms and turned away. "I went to him a couple of weeks ago asking for help."

"And?"

She put her arms around herself. "He said I wasn't a Christian."

"Why would he say a thing like that?"

Didn't he believe her? "Well, he didn't say it straight out. He implied it."

"What did you say to him?"

"I reminded him how long I've been going to that church and how much money we've given and then I left."

"I meant before," Fred said quietly. "To give him that impression."

"I don't remember."

Fred didn't say anything. He didn't have to utter a word. She felt ashamed and embarrassed and defensive. Her emotions were so muddled. She didn't want to think about Pastor Burnie. She didn't want to think about what he said, what she said . . .

She turned back to Fred. "Maybe if we go away for a weekend. To San Francisco. Or better yet, Carmel. We could get off by ourselves. Just the two of us."

"It's just the two of us now, Nora."

Hurt spread through her, gripping her heart. "You needn't remind me that Annie's left home without so much as a kiss good-bye." She turned away. "That was cruel, Fred, and after I've had such a horrid day." She rubbed her temple, feeling the beginning of another headache coming on. "I called Anne-Lynn this morning. She said she was on her way to art class when what she really meant was she didn't want to talk to me for even one minute," she said bitterly. "She didn't even give me the chance to tell her how sick I've been and all the tests I've endured."

All to find out there was nothing wrong with her. That it was all in her head. Stress. And who was to blame for that?

Fred took her shoulders. "Annie's grown up, Nora. You can't make her come home and be your little girl again."

"I wasn't trying to do that!"

He let go of her. "Weren't you? As long as she was here, you could tell her what to do. She has to learn to stand on her own."

She turned. "That's not true. I've never tried to run her life."

"You didn't try, Nora. You *did.* The poor girl couldn't breathe without you telling her how much air she could take in."

"How can you say such a thing? All I've ever done is love—"

"For as long as I've known you and Annie, you've been running her life. Control, Nora. That's what it's all about with you, isn't it? I have to tell you I was proud of her when she finally stood up to you and left."

Nora stared up at him, stunned. "Proud?"

"Yes, proud!"

Defensive anger welled up inside her. "You just didn't want her around anymore, isn't that what you really mean? You were jealous of our relationship. You never did understand how close we were. She wasn't *your* child. She was *mine.*" She saw the look on his face and knew her words were like daggers in his heart. Let them be. He had hurt her first. "The sooner Annie was out of here, the sooner you thought you'd have me all to yourself to do whatever you want whenever you want."

As the torrent of angry words poured from her mouth, part of her was screaming. *Why are you doing this to him? Stop it. Stop it!* Yet the flood came pouring down, drowning them both in her bitterness.

How many words does it take to do irrevocable damage?

Silence reigned between them for a full minute before Fred spoke in a weary voice. "When have you ever done anything someone else wanted, Nora?"

"I'm always doing for others. I've done everything for them from the time they were babies. You can't understand how I feel because you've never had children of your own."

"I wanted them, Nora, but you weren't willing."

"Don't throw that in my face now, Fred. How could I think about having a baby when Michael was in college and Anne-Lynn was consuming so much of my time." She heard her own words echo and saw the expression on his face. "I *love* Annie."

"That may be, Nora, but you love yourself more. You love yourself above everyone and everything."

She stared, bereft. "How can you *say* that to me after all I've done for them? When Annie left, I was devastated. You know I was."

"Oh, I know. Everyone knows. But the truth is you were devastated for all the wrong reasons. You thought you were in control. You had her future all laid out, years ahead."

"She *wanted* to go to college!"

"No, Nora. *You* wanted her to go to college! All I've ever heard is how much *you* wanted to go and never had the chance. I always wanted to ask. What stopped you?"

"What are you saying? That I should go to school *now*? I'm forty-five."

"It takes guts to live your own life, doesn't it, Nora? All you've ever done is tell others how to run theirs. All you've ever done is bully your children into living for you."

She was furious. "How can you say such cruel things to me?"

He sighed. "I'm saying it because it's the sorry truth, and it's about time you hear it from someone who loves you."

"Love? Is that what you call this? You don't know the first thing about love!"

He went back into the empty family room and sat down, eyes straight ahead on the droning television. "Have you ever asked yourself why your son never calls or comes home? Michael was the first one you drove away. No, I take that back. Maybe it was Bryan Taggart."

Pain swept through her. "I hate you." She was weeping again.

"You've never faced the truth about anything."

"It's *not* the truth. Michael cares."

"About what?" Picking up the remote, Fred changed the channel.

Himself, came the betraying thought. She rebelled against it. "You don't know my son the way I do."

"I know his mother. That's enough." Fred turned up the volume.

Trembling, Nora snatched up her purse and went upstairs. Tossing her purse into a wing chair, she yanked off her camel-hair blazer and went into her closet to hang it up. She was still shaking violently. She sat on the edge of the bed. Fred's words kept ringing in her ears: *"It takes guts to live your own life . . . you thought you had control . . ."*

"He's wrong."

Look around you.

Raising her head, Nora looked at the elegant Ethan Allen furnishings, the expensive draperies, the faint, peach-colored walls with original oil paintings and signed prints she had purchased from an exclusive San Francisco gallery. She had picked out everything herself, sparing no expense. How many thousands of dollars had she spent doing this room exactly the way she wanted it? Had she ever asked Fred what he might like?

She had done every room in this house the same way, including Michael's and Annie's. She had poured blessings lavishly upon her children. They had only the best. The best schools, the best neighborhood, the best clothing, the best toys, the best lessons, the most affluent church, the right friends.

To what purpose? To what end?

"It takes guts to live your own life . . ."

I sacrificed for them!

She heard a still, small voice questioning her. *Did you, beloved?*

I did. I did! I wanted Michael and Anne-Lynn to have a better life than the one I had. I wanted to be there for them the way my mother never was for me. I wanted to give them everything I ever wanted. I wanted . . . I wanted . . . love.

Nora covered her face with her hands, and her bitter weeping drowned out the quiet, beckoning voice of the very thing she sought.

Ruth came out of the bathroom and stared at Corban, her face ashen, her eyes red. "Guess what?" She held out a white, plastic object.

"What?" He peered at it, baffled. Her eyes were burning with anger, boring into him with dark accusation. "What is it?"

"A pregnancy test! What do you think it is?" She thrust it in front of him. "It's blue. See? Positive!" She uttered a foul expletive.

He could feel the blood running out of his face. His body was going cold, then hot. "I thought you were on the pill."

"I *am* on the pill. Not that birth control should be my sole responsibility!"

"That's not what I meant." He tried to stay calm. He tried to think. "How far along?"

"Two months. Three. I don't know! I didn't even think about it until I started throwing up a few days ago." She threw the test into the trash beside his desk and cursed again. "Jessie said I might be pregnant. So I thought I'd better find out."

Corban didn't know what to say. A baby! The first thought that came to him was how had he managed to get himself into this mess and how was he going to get himself out of it. Over the past few weeks, he had come to realize he wasn't in love with Ruth Coldwell. In fact, he wasn't sure he liked her all that much. Their affair had started in lust, pure and simple. Well, maybe not so pure. He had begun to wonder about Ruth's feelings within the first few months of living with her. Her motives had become pretty clear. She had needed someone to bankroll her living expenses while she went through school on scholarships. She liked his apartment, his car, his bank account. Pretty simple to figure out once ego was out of the way.

Well, now things weren't so simple.

"Stop looking at me that way!" she said, angry and distressed.

"What way?"

"Like I *planned* this pregnancy."

"I know you didn't."

"Darn right I didn't. The last thing I wanted was to get pregnant." She looked down as though she couldn't even bear to touch herself. "I've already gained two pounds." She burst into tears. "Why did this have to happen? Everything was so perfect!"

Perfect?

He could feel the perspiration beading on his forehead. His heart was pounding. His stomach was in a knot. Ruth was pregnant with his child. He looked at the plastic test in the trash and felt a rush of heat through him. Was it shame? Fear? Wonder? He couldn't even begin to assess the feelings stirring in him. He had to think, but she was pacing like a caged animal. He wanted to quiet her, to calm her. "We'll work it out, Ruth."

She stopped and glared. "Work what out?"

"What we're going to do." He stood up and went to her. "This isn't just your problem, you know. We're in it together."

Her shoulders hunched slightly. "I can't believe this is happening," she said bleakly. "I've been so careful." Corban drew her close when she began to cry. He had never seen or heard Ruth cry. He didn't think she could.

"It'll be all right." He rubbed her back, as though she were a frightened child, he the adult. He took on his new role of comforter willingly, if not eagerly. The panic was passing, the possibilities rising. He felt strangely protective. "People have had babies before us and made it through school."

She went rigid in his arms. "You're not suggesting I have it, are you?" She drew back from him. "Don't even go down that road, Cory."

He went cold inside at the look on her face. "Why not? You'd be done with the school year before—"

"No way!" Her eyes were hot. "Are you out of your mind?"

He frowned. "I graduate in June."

"Well, I *don't*." She turned and walked away, sitting in the chair on the other side of the room. Crossing her legs Indian-fashion, she gripped her knees and looked at him coolly. "What about grad school, Cory? You're going to graduate magna cum laude. You've already had an interview at Stanford. I still have another year . . ."

"You could transfer."

"Yeah, right. And who's going to pay *my* tuition? Santa Claus? My scholarship is *here*. I can't go off to whatever college I want. I don't have a trust fund."

She was firing all her guns at him, and he didn't like it. A coldness seeped into him. How had he ever gotten involved with this girl? Her eyes flickered. Could she see what he was feeling? Was it written on his face? She looked away again and bit her lip. It was a little late to hold her tongue. She looked at him again, troubled. "We always agreed, Cory. First things first. Graduate from college, then . . ."

Then what? He wondered now. Had they ever really discussed the after part? He felt sick inside. He knew he couldn't make any promises about financing her education, especially at Stanford.

A baby. His baby. He thought about the choices before them.

"Look," he said cautiously, "I haven't decided to go to Stanford. There's nothing wrong with staying here in Berkeley."

"You *want* to go to Stanford and you know it. Don't tell me you don't. If you stayed here, you'd resent having to change your plans."

"No, I wouldn't."

"Get real, Cory." Her face was rigid and pale. "I've missed two classes this week because I was too sick to go. I think they call it morning sickness. Only I'm sick until past noon. How many classes do you think I can miss and still keep my grades up enough to hold on to my scholarship?"

He knew what she was thinking. He had listened to all the

arguments for abortion and agreed with every one of them. Up until this moment, he had been pro-choice. Now he wasn't so sure. This was *his* child she was talking about. Something on the elemental level had shifted inside him. All the rhetoric didn't seem to matter. All the rationale, the justifications, the excuses.

Plain and simple, he felt sick at the thought of her having an abortion.

"I know it's not the best time—" he chose his words carefully— "but we can figure things out. If you don't want to keep the baby, we can give it up for adoption."

"I can't believe it. You're really suggesting I have it!" She sprang up and paced again. "This isn't a trophy we're talking about, Cory. This is *my* life!"

"I know, Ruth, but it's *my* child."

She stopped and glared at him. "I can't believe you said that. It's not a child yet. Don't call it a child."

"Spare me the feminist manure, Ruth. We've both had physiology and anatomy. I swear I'll take care of you. I'll pay for everything. I'll take responsibility. I'll even marry you, if you want."

"Thanks for the romantic proposal." She turned away, hugging herself.

Shame gripped him. Crossing the room, he put his hands on her arms. "I didn't mean for it to come out that way." He caressed her arms. "Ruth, I'm sorry. If I could undo things, I would. I know this wasn't planned. I know how much your education matters to you. I wouldn't ask you to give up on it. Just sit tight for a few days, all right? Let's think things over. Let's weigh all the options. Isn't that what choice is all about? Knowing there are options."

He felt her muscles relaxing. She let out a shaky breath. "I'm scared. I'm so scared, Cory."

Corban leaned down and kissed the curve of her neck. "So am I."

He wondered if they were afraid for the same reasons.

"You there!" Leota shouted from her front door. "Leave those children alone or I'm calling the police."

The two teenagers bullying Arba Wilson's children shouted obscenities at her and took off down the street. She came out onto her porch. "Come on inside, you three. You're sitting ducks for any little hoodlums out there on the sidewalk. Didn't your mother tell you to play in the backyard?" She held the door wide open for them. "Go on into the bathroom and clean yourself up, Vermont."

"My name ain't Vermont."

"It is when you're in my house. Now, get going." The two little girls were crying. She closed the screen door, latched it, closed the front door, and double locked it. "You two come into the kitchen with me." She took two dish towels from a drawer and wet them with tap water. She gave one to each and told them to wipe their faces. "What did those two boys want, anyway?"

"They wanted Nile to let 'em in the house."

Nile stood in the doorway, a wet cloth pressed over his eye.

"You're a brave boy."

"Don't call me *boy*."

"Oh, for heaven's sake. Fine. You're a brave young man. Do you like that better? Now plant your tailbone in that chair and cool off."

"Why should I?"

"Keep standing in the doorway, and I'll give your cookies and milk to the girls."

Nile sat.

"Mama'll wonder where we are." Kenya wiped tears from her cheeks.

Leota patted her shoulder. "She'll know, honey. I told her you three were welcome here. You can consider this a safe house. Carolina, you sit there. Indiana, you can have my chair. What time does your mama get home?"

"Six," Indiana said. "She's picking up Kentucky Fried Chicken tonight."

"It's her favorite," Nile said with a jerk of his head toward Kenya-Carolina. "She gets it 'cause it's her birthday today."

"Your birthday, is it? How old are you?"

"Seven."

"Well, I'm twelve times seven. So what does that make me?"

"Eighty-four," Nile said in a split second, adding, "Old."

"Brave and good at math. Looks like you have a fine future ahead of you, unless you let your lips start moving before your brain's in gear."

Indiana giggled. "You talk funny."

"It's called English, honey. I don't know ebonics." Leota put the icing-covered animal crackers on a pretty porcelain plate. By the time she poured three glasses of milk and set them down, the cookies were gone. Tunisha-Indiana had saved three for her. The Wilson children were polite. They said thank you. Even Nile-Vermont, who had put the wet rag aside. His eye was going to be swollen shut by the time his mama arrived.

She took the three cookies from Tunisha's hand and gave one to each of the children. One bag of cookies cost three dollars and eighty-nine cents. On sale. No wonder Arba Wilson had to work such long hours. Leota couldn't help wondering how many buckets of chicken the poor woman would have to buy in order to fill up these growing children.

Six o'clock was still two-and-a-half hours away. Resigned, Leota went to her pantry.

The three children ate two cans of fruit cocktail, six slices of bread, and three slices of American cheese before they were full. Leota stopped counting up the cost. The truth was, she enjoyed having them in her kitchen. They relaxed and chattered like little magpies. She had the feeling that now that they were refueled, they'd be running like Energizer bunnies.

"Would you like to watch television?" Anything to keep them calm and quiet. And inside where they were safe.

The children followed her into the living room. Unfortunately, talk shows and soap operas seemed to dominate the schedule. "Too bad I don't have any children's books. I could read to you."

"I have a book," Tunisha said. "I got it from the school library. It's in my backpack." She was out the front door and gone before Leota could call her back. Concerned those bullies might still be around, she went out on the front porch and waited. Tunisha ran up the driveway and around to the back of their house. Leota heard the screen door slam. A minute later it slammed again, and the girl came running back down the driveway with a book in her hand.

Leota watched her come up the steps. "Did you lock the back door?"

"Yes, ma'am." Panting, she handed Leota the book she had checked out.

"*The Wind in the Willows.*" Leota smiled. "Well, we'll see how far we get before your mama comes home."

A few minutes after six, the doorbell rang. Leota couldn't help feeling a little disappointed. Before their mother was even in the door, the girls were recounting the trouble on the sidewalk; the snack of animal crackers, fruit cocktail, bread, and cheese; and the adventures of Mole. Arba tried to shush them, looking embarrassed and uncomfortable. Worse, she looked scared. She tipped Nile's face up and inspected his eye. Then she looked at Leota. "Thank you for stepping in, Mrs. Reinhardt. I hope they haven't been too much of a bother."

"You can call me Leota, and they've been perfect ladies and gentleman." As soon as she had started reading, they had gone quiet as little mice. A pity she wouldn't get to finish reading the story. She'd been enjoying it. Resigned, she took a piece of junk mail from her side table, tucked it into the book and closed it. "Don't forget your book, Indiana."

Tunisha took it and held it against her chest. "Would you read some more tomorrow?"

Arba Wilson winced. "No, Tuny." She ran her hand tenderly over her daughter's neat cornrows. "Mrs. Reinhardt has more important things to do."

"Like what?" Leota said bluntly.

Arba's eyes widened. "You wouldn't mind?"

"I'd like to hear the end of the story."

Indiana grinned broadly at Leota and then up at her mother. "Can we, Mama? Please?"

Carolina snuggled against her mother. "Please? Can we? Can we?"

"A smart woman knows when she's defeated." Leota managed to restrain her smile. Tomorrow was Wednesday. Corban Solsek would be coming over to take her shopping again. She had better write up a new grocery list. She needed to lay in supplies.

14

ANNIE FLEW UP THE STAIRS, UNLOCKED THE APARTMENT DOOR, and tossed her backpack onto the sofa. Grinning, she picked up the telephone and punched in her grandmother's phone number. She paced as she waited for her to answer. "Hello," came the mellow greeting.

"Grandma! I've got the greatest news!"

"You won the lottery, and you're going on an around-the-world cruise."

Annie laughed. "Something better than that. My art professor has a friend with a gallery here in San Francisco. One of my paintings is going to be hung."

"Hung?"

"In his gallery. On a wall. For sale. My picture, I mean. Oh, Grandma, I didn't expect something like this to happen in a million years!"

"Well, for heaven's sake, why not? Anyone with half a brain can see you have talent."

How she adored her grandmother. "You've never even seen my paintings, Grandma. You have no idea whether I have talent or not."

"Of course, I know. I don't have to see anything to know. It's in the genes. Your great-aunt did those wonderful renderings. Great-

Grandma Reinhardt was an artist with her embroidery needles. And your mother was a master seamstress by the time she was sixteen."

"Mother? You're kidding, aren't you?" She had never known her mother to pick up a needle.

"No, I'm not."

"I didn't even know she sewed." Any mending that needed doing went to the French laundry.

"Oh my, yes. She started sewing her own clothes when she was thirteen. She made the most beautiful things. She'd go down to the most expensive stores and see what was popular. Then she'd buy remnants at one of the big fabric stores downtown and make copies with her own ideas added. She even finished the edges on all the seams, just like those exclusive shops do. She had a real knack for it. She got so good at it she was making her own patterns from tissue paper she bought at the five-and-dime." Grandma Leota didn't say anything for a few seconds and then added quietly, "I wonder why she stopped sewing."

Annie wondered as well. "I've never seen Mother make anything."

"If that isn't the strangest thing. Why would she quit doing something she enjoyed so much?"

"She probably didn't enjoy it, Grandma." Truth to tell, Annie couldn't think of one thing her mother had ever enjoyed. According to her mother, even shopping was a chore. Everything in life seemed to be just another burden. Why did she feel that way?

"Eleanor spent hours on that old treadle machine in the bedroom," Grandma Leota said. "It belonged to Grandma Reinhardt. She used it for mending. She showed your mother how it worked. In fact, I think that's how your mother started, by doing the family mending. When she was sixteen, she said she wanted a brand-new sewing machine. I would've given anything to get her one, but there wasn't money at the time . . ."

Grandma Leota was rambling again, but Annie liked it when her grandmother remembered the past aloud. Annie had learned more about her mother in the past few months than she had in her entire life of living with her. It was hard to picture Nora as an eager teenager designing her own clothes.

"Eleanor always seemed to be enjoying herself when she was sewing on that ancient machine, but then again, you can't judge by me. I've been told I don't know anything about anyone. Except myself, of course." She made a little sound like she was clearing her throat. "How much is that painting going to be?"

"Painting?"

"Your painting in the gallery. The one you called to tell me about. How much are they going to ask for it?"

"Oh . . . I don't know, Grandma. I was so excited, I didn't even think to ask."

"Any chance I could see it before you sell it?"

"I could ask for it back for a few days and bring it over this weekend. Unless you have other plans."

"Not unless you count plucking the hairs from my upper lip as plans. But don't get it back. Take a picture of it. You should keep an album of pictures of your work, noting who buys each piece. Oh, and Annie, before I forget, do you have any books around your place? Children's books?"

"I have a box of things I brought from home. There might be a few in there. Why?"

"Arba's children have been over here the past few afternoons. They come after school, and I read to them. They've even started bringing their homework here so they can do it at the breakfast-nook table. And now they're bringing friends. Two little Mexican boys from down the block and a Vietnamese boy from across the street. Can't remember their names. Tom, Dick, and Harry, I call them."

"You're reading to *six* children?"

"I'm halfway through *Robinson Crusoe,* but they don't seem much interested. The language is too old-fashioned for them. Carolina brought me some books yesterday. Children's horror stories, if you can imagine. I've never seen such book covers. Horrible things. She said all the kids are reading them. No wonder the world is going mad."

"I'll stop by the library."

"Just bring anything that will keep them interested until Arba gets home. I don't want the children getting restless and tearing my house down around my ears. At least they're bringing their own snacks now. I thought they'd be eating me out of house and home after the first day. I've never seen children put so much food away as those three Wilson children."

Annie could imagine. Three growing children were undoubtedly hungry after a long day at school, and her grandmother's social security check probably didn't stretch beyond feeding herself. Annie smiled at the picture of her grandmother reading stories to six children under the age of nine. No small task. She could help her grandmother's literacy efforts by picking up some peanut butter, jelly, and a few loaves of bread. And a couple of gallons of milk. Maybe a bag of apples and a bunch of bananas as well.

"I have some good news, too," Grandma Leota said. "Barnaby's eating just fine. Even tossed some seed on the floor today. Still hasn't made a peep."

"Great! I'll tell Susan. She'll be relieved. Do the children like him?"

"They leave him alone. Anyone even approaches that bird and he has his beak open and ready for attack. Arba calls him Jaws. Now, listen, honey. We'd better hang up. This is costing you."

"Only a couple of cents, Grandma."

"A penny saved is a penny earned."

Laughing to herself, Annie shook her head. "I'll see you Saturday morning, Grandma."

"Not Friday this time. Do you have a date with that Sam fellow on Friday?"

"Nope. I'm working at the restaurant."

"A pity. Such a nice young man. And handsome, too."

Annie laughed. "And dangerous. I love you, Grandma."

"I love you, too, honey."

Annie called her father with the good news, but he wasn't available, so she had to leave the message with Monica. She knew it was unlikely her father would receive it. Monica always seemed to forget to pass messages along. Annie punched in the numbers for home, then pressed the off button before the telephone had time to ring.

She sat with the telephone pressed against her forehead for a moment, praying silently that her mother would rejoice with her. She knew it was a lot to expect, but she wanted to share her good tidings with all those she loved. Besides, if her mother heard the news from someone else, it would just give cause for more hurt feelings.

Taking a deep breath, Annie pressed the numbers again and waited, counting the rings. She was trembling slightly, hoping—just this once—that their conversation would be pleasant. Someday her mother was going to have to accept the fact that Annie was no longer a child. She had to find her own way in life.

Oh, Mother, please just this once . . .

"Gaines's residence."

"Mother, it's Annie. I just called to share some wonderful news with you."

"The only good news I need to hear is that you've decided to be sensible and come home."

Annie steeled her resolve. "One of my paintings is going to be in a San Francisco gallery. For sale."

"How did that happen?"

Annie hesitated. "Well, my professor told me he was so impressed with it, he showed it to a friend."

"How nice for you." Her voice was so dry, Annie wished she hadn't called. "How old is this professor of yours?"

What tack was this? "Forty, forty-five. I don't really know. What does that matter, Mother?"

"All you have to do is think about it, Anne-Lynn. Do you really think a first-year art student is going to have a painting shown in a San Francisco gallery? Those galleries show paintings of well-known artists. I should know. I've been in them often enough buying paintings for this house. If you ask me, that professor wants something from you, and I can guess what it is."

Annie hadn't asked. All the excitement and joy she had felt was gone, along with the heady taste of confidence. "He's married, Mother."

"Do you think that makes a difference?"

"He's *happily* married."

"Oh, is that what *he* told you? You're intimate enough with him already that he's telling you about his personal relationship with his wife."

"Why do you twist things—"

"I'm not twisting anything. I was young once. Men in power positions are always hitting on stupid girls who are so starry-eyed they can't think straight. Use your head, Anne-Lynn."

Annie wiped the dampness from her cheek.

"Aren't you going to say anything?"

"What would you have me say, Mother?"

"You want the truth, don't you? I've always told you the truth about everything."

"You've never even seen my painting, and yet—"

Her mother sighed dramatically. "Well, I suppose now you're going to feel sorry for yourself."

Something inside Annie ruptured, leaving anger and sorrow in its wake. "I'll leave that to you, Mother." She pressed the off button and put the telephone back into its cradle. Within seconds, it rang again. Annie ignored it. The answering machine clicked in.

"Stop pouting and pick up the telephone, Anne. I've really had enough of this childishness. . . ." She kept talking until the machine clicked off. Annie leaned over and turned the machine off. The telephone started ringing again. It rang ten times before it stopped. Within a minute, it started ringing again. Fifteen this time. When it finally stopped, Annie sat down and wept. It would take a miracle for her to have the kind of relationship with her mother that she longed to have. She was battle-weary.

The telephone started ringing again and went on and on. Her mother wouldn't stop until she answered. Picking up her jacket, Annie went out the door.

Nora fumed. The longer the telephone rang, the angrier she felt. How dare Anne-Lynn not answer? Leota was to blame for this. Nora's nails pressed painfully into her right palm as she waited for her mother to answer.

One, two, three, four . . .

The click sounded and she didn't even wait to hear Leota's voice. "What have you said to my daughter to turn her so against me?"

"Excuse me?"

It was a man's voice. Heat flooded Nora's face. Had she dialed a wrong number? She slammed the phone down. Trying to calm herself, she took a deep breath and pressed the numbers carefully. It was answered on the first ring by the same male voice, belligerent this time. "Who is this?"

"Is this Leota Reinhardt's number?"

"Yes, it is. Who's calling?"

"Who are *you?*"

"Corban Solsek, if it's any of your business. Now I'll ask you the same question. Again."

What impertinence! "Nora Gaines. And it *is* my business. I'm Leota Reinhardt's daughter."

"Pleased to meet you, I guess. Hold on. I'll see if Leota wants to talk to you." Nora went hot all over while he muffled the receiver. She couldn't hear anything and wondered at the pause before her mother came on the line. "Eleanor? What's wrong?"

"Don't *Eleanor* me, Mother. What lies have you been telling Anne-Lynn?"

Silence reigned for several seconds. "I haven't been telling her any lies. What are you talking about?"

"She hates me! That's what I'm talking about."

"Of course, she doesn't."

"Oh, yes, she does. And it's all your fault. I know it. She spends all her time with you and never comes home where she's wanted."

"She's wanted here, Eleanor. Just as you are."

"There's a lie right there. You *never* wanted me, and you're just using my daughter to hurt me!"

"Is this the same old territory, Eleanor? Because if it is, I'll tell you once and for all, it's *hogwash!*"

Nora felt herself blushing hotly at the rebuke. "What did you say to me?" Only once in all her years had she ever heard that cold, steely tone in her mother's voice. And that had been aimed at Grandma Reinhardt.

"You heard me, Eleanor. I said *hogwash!* I should've said it to you a long time ago instead of letting you go on like a spoiled brat. If you want to have things straightened out and put right between us, you should come for tea sometime. You've been invited often enough!"

Nora jerked as the telephone was slammed down in her ear. She stared at it. The line was dead. She couldn't believe it! Her mother had hung up on her. She'd never done that before.

Fear gripped her.

How does it feel to be alone?

I am here, beloved. Turn to Me.

Voices warred in her head. Sometimes there was a chorus of them, ranting, raving, fanning her pain and anger. And then the quiet one would prod at her conscience, making her twist in discomfort, impelling her to cry out for help.

Come to Me, beloved . . .

What help have you ever gotten? She let the louder voice drown out the other. You've never been able to depend on anyone but yourself.

"I'm not to blame."

"Eleanor," her mother had once said, *"someday you're going to have to stop laying the blame for everything at someone else's door."*

Quick tears came at the memory. Her mother had said it to her the day she had come to tell her Dean Gardner had filed for divorce.

Shutting her eyes tightly, Nora remembered Dean's parting words: *"The only good thing that ever came out of our marriage was Annie!"* She had gotten back at him for that by winning custody when the court supported her charges of abuse. She'd dedicated herself to making sure Anne-Lynn didn't grow up to be a dreamer like her father. She had sacrificed.

You lied.

She had given up her own dreams . . .

You took vengeance.

Like your mother is taking vengeance?

Nora remembered her mother standing in her bedroom doorway. Nora remembered being angry about something. She had gotten up from the sewing machine, come over, and slammed the door in her mother's face. She could still remember the look on Leota's face. Stunned, hurt, confused.

Why was she remembering that now when her own pain was so great?

So that you might know . . .

Know *what?* Know that nothing had been right between her and her mother in years? She didn't want to listen to the voice whispering that she was the one in the wrong, not just about her mother but about everything. Yet it was that voice she was beginning to hear more loudly than her own, like a steady rain upon her head, impelling her to find shelter from the harder storm to come.

"If I had a daughter like that, I'd disown her." Corban felt his anger deepen at the sheen of tears in the old woman's eyes. He was so mad, he was shaking. If Nora Gaines had been standing in the middle of the room, he would have told her in no uncertain terms what he thought of her. He had a five-letter word that fit her to a tee.

"Don't judge." Leota gave him a hard look.

How could Leota defend her? "What gives with her, anyway?"

"She thinks I was a lousy mother." Leota sounded so weary. "And in some ways, I suppose she's right."

Corban sat on the sofa and leaned back. He thought about Ruth, so quick in wanting to end her pregnancy. What sort of mother would she be when she wanted no part of the baby she was carrying? *His* baby. Leota Reinhardt hadn't been that kind of mother, he'd bet. "What did you do that was so wrong?"

"I worked." Closing her eyes, she put her head back. "And when I was home . . ." She fell silent.

Corban wished he knew what he could say to make her feel better, but no words came.

"Would you mind going to the grocery store without me?" she said quietly, her voice quaking slightly. "I don't feel up to it today."

"No problem." She looked ready to cry. He supposed she just wanted time to herself without him sitting in her living room and being a witness to her shame and grief.

"The list is on the kitchen counter." She reached down for her purse, tucked in a pocket on the recliner. Unsnapping the old metal clasp, she took out her wallet. When he came back, she handed him two twenty-dollar bills. "Will that be enough?"

"Should be." He tucked the bills into the front pocket of his jeans.

She opened the coin purse and took out her front-door key. "I had two copies made. One for Annie and one for you."

He took it, knowing full well the trust she had just placed in his hands. He never expected to be so touched by a gesture. He gave a nod and held the key in his fist.

"Put it on your key chain before you lose it," she said and snapped the purse shut. She kept it in her lap, both hands on the top.

Taking his keys out, he did as she said. "Are you going to be all right, Leota?"

"I'll be fine." She rubbed her right arm as though it were aching. "I'm just a little tired is all."

"I won't be long."

"Don't hurry. And while you're out and about, you might think kind thoughts regarding my daughter."

"That's not going to be easy."

"Easier if you remember she's Annie's mother, and Annie has grown up to be someone very special."

Corban smiled wryly. "Touché."

It was the first time since coming to Leota's house as a volunteer that he'd done her errands on his own. He gathered all the items on the list, pausing to feel and smell the tomato and thump the honeydew melon the same way Leota did. On his way to the checkout, he had an impulse to buy her a little something. And he knew exactly what it would be. Backtracking to the produce area, he added one more item to the basket and paid for it out of his own money.

When he let himself into the house, Leota wasn't in the living room.

"Leota? Where are you? Are you all right?"

The bathroom door opened and she appeared, her hair damp around her forehead and temples. "I'm fine. I was just washing my face." Her eyes were puffy and red.

"I'll put these things away for you." He headed for the kitchen with two laden, paper sacks and one small, plastic-bagged item dangling from his arm.

When he finished putting Leota's groceries away in the refrigerator and cabinets, he folded the paper bags and tucked them neatly into the box Leota had set on a back-porch shelf. He shoved the wadded plastic bag into a five-gallon, blue-and-white-speckled soup pot next to it. Leota liked to "diaper" the paper bags she used for garbage. "Keeps them from leaking." Ruth had made fun of him when he started doing the same thing at the apartment.

Digging in his pocket, Corban pulled out the receipt and change due Leota, and then picked up the item he had purchased. "Your change, ma'am," he said with ceremony, "and a little something from me to you." He leaned down and presented her with the small flowering plant in a pretty, porcelain teacup on a saucer. Her soft word of surprised pleasure put a smile on his face.

She put the change on her side table without counting it and took the gift from him. The cup rattled and she nestled it tenderly in her lap. "Oh, my . . . African violets. Thank you, Corban. They've lovely."

"My pleasure, Leota." Never had his money been better spent. He liked the warm, fuzzy feel.

"Bernard gave me violets once. It was such a long time ago."

When she looked up at him again, he saw a little-girl-lost look in her eyes. It surprised him, as did the empathy that seized him. He felt close to tears and embarrassed by the inexplicable, heightened emotions. He didn't welcome these feelings. Maybe they had more to do with Ruth and the baby. Whatever it was, he felt Leota's pain. He couldn't get away from it.

He couldn't get around it or past it. For the first time in his life, Corban felt someone else's anguish as though it were his own. He had heard of people dying when they lost hope, and Leota looked like she was losing hope where her children were concerned. If not for Annie, her life might as well be over. Her hand was trembling as she touched the petals of the pretty, lavender flowers—and he hurt for her.

Is this what it feels like to care about someone? It was the pits. It made him uncomfortable. It made him feel vulnerable and ineffective. Worse, he didn't know how to stop it. He didn't even know when it began to happen. Sometime in the past month, he had stopped thinking of Leota Reinhardt as a subject for his project and had begun to see her as a friend. Feisty, straight-shooting, funny, irritating, enigmatic, challenging, endearing . . .

"Don't you have a class this afternoon?" she said.

His mouth curved ruefully. "At two."

She looked pointedly at the mantel clock. "Well, you'd better get moving now or you'll be late."

So much for warm, fuzzy feelings. If he stayed, she'd lecture. "Is Annie coming over Friday?" He hoped so. Leota always came to life when Annie was around . . . sweet, uncomplicated little Annie. She definitely had a way about her.

Unlike Ruth. She was deep, treacherous water.

"Saturday," Leota said. "She has to work on Friday."

"Maybe I'll drop by."

"Why don't you bring your girlfriend this time? I'd like to meet her." She tilted her chin slightly. "I'm sure Annie would, too."

"I'll ask her."

"What's her name, by the way?"

"Ruth." As if he needed the reminder.

Sam was waiting on the stoop of the apartment building when Annie returned from her walk. She went hot from the top of her head to the soles of her feet. They had had a date at six. He stood as she came closer. "Oh, Sam, I'm sorry!" To add to her embarrassment, she burst into tears.

"Hey, I'm not mad. I was just worried. Are you okay?"

No, she wasn't okay. She was miserable. "Why didn't Susan let you in?"

"She did and then left for work. I came out to get something out of my car, and the door swung shut behind me." He picked up a bouquet of flowers wrapped in pink cellophane. They were wilted.

How long had he been waiting for her? "What time is it?" She dashed tears from her cheeks and dug in her jacket pocket for her keys.

"Eight-thirty."

"Oh, Sam . . ." She unlocked the door and pushed it open. "Why did you wait so long?"

"I'll give you three guesses, and the first two don't count."

She glanced back over her shoulder and wanted to cry harder at the look in his eyes. He was making no secret of the depth of his feelings. She liked him so much, but she couldn't seem to get through to him that the Lord had other plans for her.

"I drove all the way up here from San Jose, Annie. I've been working extra hours, saving my money for weeks, just so I could take you out to a fancy dinner at the Top of the Mark. Seven courses at least. I even borrowed this great suit from a friend. I swear the guy models for *GQ*. I buy flowers, just the right mix of red for passion and white for purity so you won't think I'm out to ruin you." He wagged the bedraggled flowers at her. "And then I get here, ringing the doorbell with my heart throbbing in my throat, and what do I find? My *sister*." He put a hand to his heart. "You forgot all about me. I'm mortally wounded, Annie. I should sue for damages."

"I'm sorry." She sounded like a broken record. She couldn't stop thinking about her mother. *Lord, I don't want to be cut off from her, but it's so hard to walk Your path and please her at the same time.*

He tipped her chin, his eyes tender. "When are you going to stop feeling guilty about everything, Annie? Like anything you do is going to change people from the inside out." He took out his hand-kerchief. "Here."

"Thanks."

"Anytime. You'll notice that handkerchief is monogrammed. Christmas gift from my mother. Keep it. Every time you blow your nose, you'll think of me."

Annie laughed. She couldn't help it.

"That's better. Come on. Let's go upstairs. It's the least you can do after standing me up."

She opened the apartment door and let him in. "I'm going to wash my face, Sam. Make yourself comfortable."

Annie went into the bathroom and turned on the tap. Leaning down, she cupped her hands and scrubbed her face several times with cold water. Blindly reaching for the towel, she pressed it over her eyes. She glanced in the mirror and saw her hair was a wind-blown mess from her long beach walk. Hanging the towel back in its place, she raked her fingers several times through the mass of straw-berry blonde curls. Grimacing, she gave up and went back into the living room.

Sam's jacket was folded over a bar stool. He was standing at the window, his hands shoved into his pockets.

"Can I fix you some dinner, Sam?"

"Dinner should be here in forty-five minutes. Salad, French bread, eggplant Parmesan. How does that sound?"

"I love eggplant Parmesan."

"I know. Susan told me." He turned around and faced her. "So. Are you going to tell me what happened?"

She raked her fingers through her hair again. "Nothing. Every-thing." She let out her breath and sank into the overstuffed chair. She drew her knees up against her chest. "This was the best day of my life. And one of the worst."

"Your mother called."

She looked up.

His eyes were hot. She could see the tension in his shoulders, and she knew his anger wasn't aimed at her.

"I don't know what to do about her," she said softly.

"I could tell you."

"Oh, I know." She rested her forehead on her knees. "Everyone has an idea what I ought to do about her. Tell her off. Cut her out of my life." She raised her head and looked at him. "She's my *mother,* Sam. I love her. I'd like to know what made her the way she is."

"So you can fix her?" His tone was flat. "Forget it, Annie. It's a God-sized job." He came closer. "Take it from someone who was just as egotistical and self-centered and destructive as your mother is. The harder you try to make things right with her, the worse they're going to get." He gave a sardonic laugh. "Honey, my parents had to give up and throw me out of the house before I came to my senses. If they hadn't had the guts to do it, I don't even want to think where I'd be right now. Dead, probably."

She knew what he was talking about. She had lived through that time with Susan's family. She had seen his mother cry and his father pace in frustration. Susan had given her a daily, blow-by-blow report. "Your family prayed for you, Sam. All the time. And I prayed for you, too."

His eyes grew moist. "Maybe that's all you can do for your mother." He came over and sat on the couch. Leaning forward, he clasped his hands between his knees. "You've got to have boundaries, Annie, or people will walk all over you. Even Jesus had boundaries. He didn't let anyone stop Him from doing what He came to do. He had to get away from the hordes of people who were always demanding things of Him. They thought they could tell Him what they needed and what they wanted. Everyone had his own agenda. Left to ourselves, we're hellbound. Right from the first breath, our agenda is in opposition to God. The only one you can work on is you."

The tears came again. "Sam, I know that. That's why I left home. I knew if I stayed one more day, I'd end up giving in and giving up. If I'd stayed, I'd be back east at Wellesley right now, majoring in business or political science or something that would give me something in common with some future CEO or senator. I'd settle for Mom's dreams for me instead of finding out what God's plan is." She unfolded herself from the chair and rose. She was restless. "I suppose to most people, I made the biggest mistake of my life."

"You did what you had to do. You left. If you went back now, you'd find nothing changed. You can't make people change, Annie."

"I know that in my head, but every time my mother and I talk, my heart breaks for her. I know I'm where I'm supposed to be. It's not just a matter of being happy. I feel sure of being on a path God made for me. I don't know where exactly it'll lead, but sometimes I have this feeling of wanting to run down it, knowing Jesus is at the end of it. I wanted to tell Mom that today, but she wouldn't have understood. I was so excited about what happened, but she couldn't understand."

He leaned back. "Wouldn't, you mean."

"Couldn't, wouldn't, what's the difference?"

"There's a big difference, and you know it."

She looked at him in defeat. "One of my paintings is going to be offered for sale at a well-known gallery. It was like a reaffirmation from God."

"Susan told me. You're on your way, and your mother isn't happy about it."

"She thinks the professor is coming on to me."

His brows rose. "Is he?" He gave her a slow, predatory grin. "Would you recognize the warning signs if he were?"

She gave him a dry smile. "Sam, I knew *your* libido was in overdrive when I was twelve."

He grinned wickedly. "And I knew you had a major crush on me."

He loved teasing her about it. Her heart had raced every time he was around. Her insides would go all fluttery whenever he looked in her direction, even if his expression had been one of utter disdain. Little sister Susan's pesky friend, Annie. He still made her heart race a little too fast for comfort. "I've grown up, Sam."

He sighed dramatically. "Oh, for the good old days when Annie Gardner carried a torch for me. What goes around comes around, as they say. Now I've got a major crush on you, and you forget all about me and leave me cooling my heels on your front stoop."

"Serves you right. You were less than kind in the *old* days."

"I was stupid." He rose, and her heart did a flip. She hoped he wouldn't make a pass at her. Not now, when she was feeling vulnerable. He must have sensed her need for distance because he paused, studying her face, the devilish smile gone from his. "So where's this painting that's going to make you rich and famous?"

"Hardly rich or famous," she said, standing and heading for the kitchen. She told him the name of the gallery near Union Square. When he asked about the painting, she described it briefly.

The buzzer sounded. "Saved by the bell, hmmm, Annie?" She

could tell he was trying to read what she was thinking. "I'll take care of it." He opened the door and went out.

Annie opened a kitchen cabinet and took out plates and glasses. The silverware was in a drawer in the counter. Since she and Susan had no dining table, she set the coffee table and tossed a pillow on either side so they could sit comfortably on the floor. Sam returned and set out the Styrofoam containers while Annie filled two tall glasses with ice water. The small apartment was quickly filled with the mouth-watering smells of good Italian cooking. She breathed in the wonderful fragrance of basil, tomato, and garlic. "I'm glad you didn't leave, Sam."

"The way to a woman's heart is through her stomach." They sat down, and he held his hands out to her. "Shall I do the honors?" She put her hands in his and bowed her head. He said nothing for a long moment, his thumb lightly brushing the back of her hand, sending tingles up her arms. "Lord, for what we're about to receive, we thank You. And, Father, keep my thoughts pure, would You, please? And put up hedgerows of thorns around me if I even look like I'm going to step out of line. In Jesus' name, amen." He raised his head and shrugged. "I thought I should mention the last part to the Lord, just as a safety precaution."

She waited. He leaned forward slightly, just looking at her. She could feel the heat come up in her cheeks again. She cleared her throat softly. "The thing is to obey, Sam."

"I'm trying," he said softly.

"It would help if you let go of my hands. I can't use my fork otherwise."

"Spoilsport. What do you say you recline on the couch and I peel grapes for you."

"Not on your life." He loosened his hands enough for her to gently pull away.

The food was delicious, the company exactly what she needed. Sam told her about his week. He made her relax and laugh again.

"You've got me hooked on garage sales," he said dolefully. "My apartment is beginning to look like *Sanford and Son* with all the junk I've been picking up for Leota's garden. Sorry. Junk to me, treasure to you. You'll be delighted to know you are now the proud owner of an old wheelbarrow, a washtub, a watering can, and another bowling ball for your growing collection. It's just an ordinary black one this time, but I'm on the lookout for the unusual. All in my car, even as we speak. I spotted a hedgehog yesterday. Couldn't resist the little guy."

"A hedgehog?" She laughed as she gathered their dishes and took them into the little kitchen.

"Sure." He rose to follow her. "You know, one of those metal dudes with a brush on his back. You sit him on your back porch and use him to scrape the mud off your boots. Or that's what the old gentleman said. His house had a sold sign on it. Said he was downsizing. Must've been a CEO at one time. Knew all the lingo. I almost bought you a skiff, but I couldn't fit it in my car. It was only ten bucks because there was a hole in the bottom of it big enough for a shark to swim through." He picked up the dish towel. "You wash, I'll dry."

"I'll do the dishes later." She took the towel from him and tossed it on the counter. "Put a hold on all future purchases, would you, please? Unless you plan to keep them for yourself. What do I owe you for the loot you have now?"

His mouth curved slowly as he ran a finger lightly over her cheek. She pinched him on the underside of his arm. "Ouch!" He drew back in surprise. "I was only going to suggest a little kiss."

"Fine." She stretched up on tiptoes and gave him a sisterly peck on the cheek. She felt Sam's hands at her waist and put her hands against his chest. She could feel his heart pounding. "Sam," she said with a catch of her breath. She leaned back slightly, but he didn't let her escape. His eyes were so dark.

"Don't be afraid of me, Annie. I'm not playing your feelings. I swear I'm not."

"I'm not afraid of you."

"You're afraid of something." He cupped her face tenderly. "Is it this?" He leaned down to kiss her. It was the lightest of kisses, almost chaste except for the look in his eyes when he drew back and the quick response she felt. "Oh, Annie." He didn't hold back the second time. She felt his hands in her hair, then gliding down her back, pressing her closer and closer into dangerous territory . . . territory she knew she wasn't to enter.

"Sam, stop." She was trembling.

"I love you."

"If you love me, *stop.*"

"Annie . . ."

She held the distance strongly enough that he let her go. When he reached out to touch her face, she drew back another step and shook her head.

"Tell me you don't feel something, Annie."

"You know I do."

"You can trust me."

"I trust God, Sam, and this isn't part of His plan for me."

"How do you know that for sure? Your heart's racing as fast as mine. Tell me it isn't."

How could she explain to him when she didn't fully understand herself? "It'd be so easy to give in, Sam. To forget everything for a little while and just let it happen between us." Like so many girls she'd known from high school. Friends who'd lived fast and loose, thinking they'd never bear the consequences. Girls who lived for the moment and would pay for a lifetime. But it wasn't just that. There was something more to it, something beyond her comprehension.

"I'm not asking you to go to bed with me, Annie."

Feeling her face going hot again, she started to turn away.

Sam stopped her, reaching out to tip her chin back so their eyes met. "I wouldn't let it go that far."

Better to be frank. "You wouldn't mean to."

He searched her eyes. His gaze dropped to her mouth; he shut his eyes, then let out his breath softly. "Okay. You're right." He opened his eyes and looked at her for a long moment. "I can't help wondering . . ." He seemed to shake himself inwardly. Turning away, he went around the kitchen counter and took his jacket from the back of the stool. "I'll drop the loot off at your grandmother's Saturday afternoon. Is that all right?"

Her throat tightened. "Sam . . ."

"Don't you dare say you're sorry, Annie!" His eyes blazed with the intensity of his feelings. "If you do, I'm going to throw patience to the wind and carry you into that bedroom . . ."

She could see he was hurt and troubled. The old Sam was struggling with the new Sam. Tension filled the air for a few seconds, then he sighed and gave her a self-deprecating smile. "You were right to put the brakes on. If you'd given me an inch, I would have wanted to go the whole mile."

He closed the door softly on his way out.

Jesus, keep him strong, Annie prayed, *and me, too.*

15

THE DOORBELL RANG WHILE ANNIE WAS IN HER GRANDMOTHER'S kitchen. She had a tray of just-baked Toll House cookies in each hand and couldn't run to answer it. "I'll be there in a second, Grandma!" She closed the oven door with her foot and dashed for the counter.

"I've got it, honey."

Annie heard children's voices at the front door. "Trick or treat!" Leaning back, she looked through the doorway in time to see her grandmother raise both her hands and give a shriek. Annie laughed at the pretense, fully aware her grandmother wasn't the least surprised by the ghosts and goblins on her front steps. She and Grandma Leota had been preparing for the children all day.

Giggles came from the flock of children clustered on the steps. "So now you've done your tricking—," Grandma said, unlatching the screen door and pushing it open—"come on in and have a treat."

Annie heard the screen door slam and the front door shut firmly.

"Smells like heaven in here." Arba was standing in the kitchen doorway while the children's voices jabbered excitedly in the front room. "Carmel apples, popcorn, cookies, hot chocolate. I think you've thought of everything, girlfriend."

"I hope so." Annie grinned. "You can help serve." She slid the last of the cookies onto a cooling rack.

"No need." Arba pressed herself against the doorjamb as Nile squeezed past her, followed by his sisters and "Tom, Dick, and Harry"—or, as their mothers called them, Do Weon, Jorge, and Raoul. The children paused long enough to receive Annie's nod and then descended on the treats like ants over a mound of brown sugar.

"Nothing like Halloween to bring out the greed in children," Arba said. "One of Tunisha's friends called this afternoon. Her parents were taking a vanload of children up to the hills where the rich folk live." She smiled sardonically. "They figured they'd get better pickings up there. Some of them go to several neighborhoods and use pillowcases. They end up with enough candy to last an entire family for a year."

"I'm glad your children decided to spend the evening with me and Grandma Leota."

"Well, I'm sorry to say, not without persuading," Arba said sotto voce. "I'm warning you, girlfriend, they want ghost stories. You start telling them some nice, little, honky fairy tale and they're going to turn mean. Real mean." Her dark eyes twinkled merrily. "And there are more of them than there are of us."

Annie leaned close. "Don't worry, Arba. I've got a story that beats anything they've seen or heard on television or in the movies." She could hear her grandmother talking with the other ladies in the next room. Grandma Leota always raised her voice when she was speaking with Juanita Alcala and Lin Sansan Ng, as though speaking louder would help the two women understand English better.

Arba ladled hot chocolate into mugs and set them on a tray. Annie sprinkled marshmallows on top and recruited the children to help. "Come on, you guys. Grab some of the napkins, Nile. Raoul, you bring the tray of apples. Tunisha, bring in the cookies, please. Jorge, there's a Tupperware container full of damp washcloths over there on the table. You can carry that while Kenya takes care of that bowl of popcorn. Storytime is about to start! Hustle!"

Grandma Leota settled comfortably into her recliner while Juanita and Lin Sansan sat on the sofa. Arba took the overstuffed chair near the hallway that led to the bathroom and two bedrooms.

"Put all the goodies close enough to reach," Annie said, smiling as the children scurried into position. They settled down quickly. "Sit close together because it's going to be very dark in here in a minute." She gave little Kenya time enough to scoot back so that she was against her mother's knees; then she went into the kitchen and turned out the lights. Squeezing around Grandma Leota's recliner, she stood in front of the fireplace. "Ladies, please turn off the lamps beside you."

The only illumination came from a small light left on in the bathroom and the glow of the streetlight through the front curtains. "Everyone ready to listen to a true story?"

"A horror story?" Nile's eyes were wide and eager.

"I'm going to tell you how evil came to be in the world and who brought it." Annie stood in front of the fireplace. The mantel was lined with carved, unlit pumpkins. No fire had been set in the fireplace. That would come later, as the story was told. As would time for roasting marshmallows.

"In the beginning, before the earth and heavens were made, there was only God. Everything was formless. There was no day or night. There was no sun or moon, no stars in the sky. There were no flowers or trees or birds. There were no fish or animals. There weren't any people. Everything was darkness. Everything was stillness and silence."

She waited for several seconds. Too bad the sound of the freeway could be heard from a block away. Oh, well. It was as quiet as it was going to be. "And then the Lord said, 'Let there be light,' and there was light!" She lit a long match and touched the candlewick inside the first pumpkin. "God separated the light from the darkness and made day and night. He separated the waters so that there were seas and there was an atmosphere around the earth. He spoke and the waters rolled back and dry land appeared and mountains rose. He made the sun and the moon and the stars so that we would have seasons and signs in the heavens to tell us when something very important was happening."

The candlelight glowed through the carvings of sun, moon, and stars on the pumpkin.

"God spoke again, and there were fruit trees and every kind of vegetation. He spoke and the oceans teemed with living creatures from the smallest plankton to the great sea monsters that live in the deepest parts of the ocean. He spoke and there were beasts upon the earth—tigers and bears and rabbits and mice, elephants and lizards and frogs and grasshoppers and ants. And everything was good and perfect and beautiful."

She lit another pumpkin that had animals, fish, and birds carved around it. They looked as though they were running, swimming, and flying round and round.

"When all was ready, when plants were making air to breathe, and animals and birds and fish were bringing sound and movement, the

Lord bent down and took dust from the earth and formed a man. He made the man in the image of Himself, and then He breathed into the man's nostrils the breath of life. He took this man and placed him in a garden He had prepared. God brought all the creatures He had made before the man and let him name them. They belonged to the man in the same way you belong to your mothers and fathers who named you. But there wasn't a creature anywhere suitable to be a helper to the man, so the Lord made him fall asleep. He took a rib from the man's side and made a woman for him. She was bone of his bone and flesh of his flesh, and they were perfect for one another."

She lit the third pumpkin, and a man and woman holding hands were illumined. "The man's name was Adam, and his wife's name was Eve, and they lived together with God in the Garden of Eden. Life was perfect."

"What's so scary about this?" Nile snorted in disgust. "I've heard this story a hundred times in Sunday school. It's boring!"

Annie hunkered down. She lowered her voice and continued. "God also made other creatures called angels and seraphim and cherubim. These creatures were to serve the Lord God, to worship and praise Him, and to minister to all the men and women who would come from Adam and Eve. One was very beautiful. In fact, he was the most beautiful creature God created. His name was Lucifer, and he became so proud of his beauty that he thought he was as good as God. Not only that, he thought he should also have the power of God. So he fought a war in heaven and God cast him out, along with those angels who sided with Lucifer. One third of the angels in heaven fell to the earth."

She lit another candle and falling angels shone. "They're still here. And they are still warring against God. Lucifer goes by other names. Terrible names. Names you know and fear: Satan, Beelzebub, Serpent of Old. And his helpers are called . . . demons."

Kenya scooted back until she could lean against her mother's chair. Arba patted her shoulder.

"Satan, appearing as a serpent, slithered into the garden God had made for Adam and Eve. The serpent spoke to Eve, saying, 'Has God said you shall not eat of any tree in the garden?' Now God had told them they could eat of any tree in the garden but one, the tree of the knowledge of good and evil. Eve was confused by Satan's question and said God had told them they could eat from any of the trees except that one, and they weren't even to touch it or they would die. The evil one said, 'Surely you won't die.' Satan lied to Eve and told her if she ate from the tree, she would be just like God. Eve thought that sounded wonderful, so she went and looked at the forbidden tree. It was very beautiful, as was everything in God's garden, and she wanted what Satan said she could have. So she took the fruit and ate it."

"She was stupid," Nile said.

Annie turned the pumpkin around so they could see the candle-light shining through the carvings on the other side—a woman holding something out to the man. "Then she gave the fruit to her husband, and he ate as well. Adam knew better, but he did it anyway, and with that single act of disobedience, sin entered the world and brought death with it."

Leota watched the faces of the children as Annie wove Bible stories together in one long stream of God's love from the beginning. Annie changed her voice and expressions and gestured dramatically to bring the stories to life. Her granddaughter held the children's attention like the Pied Piper.

"Is Satan real?" Little Harry's almond-shaped eyes were uncertain.

Annie nodded solemnly. "Yes, he is real. I'm not making any of this up, Do Weon. Everything I'm telling you is the truth. Satan isn't a devil with horns wearing a red suit and carrying a pitchfork. He's a real spirit being, who roams the world like a roaring lion looking for someone to devour. And his demons help him. Satan is the father of lies and a murderer. No good comes from him."

Lin Sansan looked distressed, and poor little Kim, her daughter, looked ready to cry. She got up from the floor and crawled into her mother's lap. Lin Sansan glanced at Juanita and Arba and then at Leota, clearly uncertain as to what she should do—stay and listen, or leave. Leota figured it was the constraints of politeness that kept her in her seat. The woman seemed very shy, and Leota doubted the little lady could stand to bring attention to herself. So she sat, clutching her daughter to her, listening to Annie talk about things that clearly frightened the woman.

Do Weon leaned forward. "What happened when God found out?"

"He was very sad and very angry. But He still loved Adam and Eve. So He made the first blood sacrifice. He killed an animal and made clothing from its skin for Adam and Eve. Then He made them leave the Garden. Ever since that time people have had to work very hard to make a living. We have pain and sorrow. We're afraid. We hurt one another in all kinds of terrible ways. We're all just like Adam and Eve.

We have a sin nature now. Even when we know what's right, sometimes we do wrong. And it only takes one little sin to make you a sinner. Adam and Eve couldn't be with God anymore, not like they had been in the Garden when He walked and talked with them face-to-face."

Kim snuggled closer to her mother. "Does God hate us, too?"

"Oh, no, sweetheart. God loved them still and He loves us, too. He's our Father, and He wants us back again very much. Right from the beginning, God knew we would make bad choices. So He had already made a plan to provide us with a way back to Him. And He promised that to Adam and Eve after they sinned. He would give us a messiah."

Leota loved the way Annie said the word *messiah.* She made it sound mysterious and wondrous. With Annie's encouragement, the children repeated it. "Messiah," they said in the same tone as Annie. The clock chimed seven, but none of the children noticed. They edged closer, listening as Annie told them about Cain murdering his brother, Abel . . . how evil became rampant in the world until God decided to destroy everyone but Noah and his family. She told them about Abraham and his sons, then about Joseph in Egypt. They sat quietly through Moses and the deliverance of the Israelites and the giving of the law.

"The law was good and perfect and given by God, but it was also a terrible burden. People needed the law to learn to obey God again, but the law also taught the men, women, and children they couldn't obey every one of them. There were so many laws about so many things, no one, not a single person, could keep them all. Some didn't care, but others wanted to please God. The problem was, if you broke one law, that made you a lawbreaker and a sinner. And the punishment for sin is . . ."

"Death," the children said when she pointed to the pumpkin she had lit illuminating the skull and crossbones.

"And the people cried out, 'Oh, Lord, when will the Messiah come?' " She smiled at the children. "Say that with me . . ."

"Oh, Lord, when will the Messiah come?" the children echoed, following her lead as she pointed to another pumpkin illuminating her carving of a man with his hands raised to the heavens.

"Hundreds of years passed by, and there were terrible wars and famines and droughts. Death and Satan never take a holiday. The people would follow the laws and try to be good, and then they would forget again and be very, very bad. God would send men called prophets to call them back to Him. *I am your Father. I love you. Come to Me. Come to Me.* Sometimes the people would listen and repent. When they didn't, their enemies would come and take them captive and drag them away from their homes and make them slaves. And then the people would cry out again."

"Oh, Lord, when will the Messiah come?"

Leota noticed Lin Sansan was even saying it now, right along with her daughter, and Arba and Juanita.

"A thousand years passed. And another thousand. And more. When God knew it was exactly the right time, He sent an angel named Gabriel to a young girl named Mary and told her she was going to have a baby and that baby was going to be God's only begotten Son, Jesus, the *Messiah*."

"What's *begotten* mean?" Kim peered out at Annie from the safety of her mother's arms.

"It means that God was going to place that child inside Mary. Instead of a man being the father of Jesus, God was going to be His Father. Mary was confused, too, Kim. She asked Gabriel how she could have a child when she had never been with a man, and Gabriel told her that God Himself, the Holy Spirit, was going to overshadow her, and she would become pregnant. And that's what happened. God saw to everything, even to providing Mary with a godly husband named Joseph. He was a carpenter."

Leota leaned her head back and closed her eyes. She was exhausted. Maybe it was helping Annie carve so many pumpkins, or the excitement of having company fill the house. Still, it felt good to have the house full of children. Children had seldom come to the house when Eleanor and George were young. Mother Reinhardt had never encouraged it, feeling two were enough for her to handle. This was the way Leota had dreamed her house would be. Filled with friends and neighbors.

"When Joseph and Mary reached Bethlehem, Mary was ready to have Jesus," Annie went on. "They couldn't find a place to stay. They finally had to go out to a stable, which was probably nothing more than a cave in a hillside outside the town. Mary and Joseph were so poor all they could do when Jesus was born was wrap Him in some cloths and tuck Him into some hay in an animal's feeding trough."

She lit another pumpkin. "But an amazing thing happened as soon as Jesus was born. A new star shone in the heavens. It was a sign from God, who had made everything in the universe, that He had sent the Messiah at last. Sadly, not very many people even noticed that star.

Maybe they were inside their houses and didn't pay any attention. But men who studied the stars noticed it in the heavens. In fact, some of them followed that star right out of their own country. They knew it meant that someone of great significance had been born, a king or a god, and they wanted to find him and worship him. They didn't know Jesus was the King of kings and *the* God, the only God, the one who had created everything that ever was or ever would be. . . ."

Leota leaned back, listening to Annie's voice as she talked about the angel's visit, about King Herod butchering babies, about Mary and Joseph fleeing to Egypt . . .

Egypt. The land of sorrows.

"Out of Egypt God would call the Messiah."

Is Egypt only a country, Lord? Or a state of mind? How long was I in Egypt before You sent Annie to bring me over the rivers of self-pity into the promised land of plenty? I am so full, Jesus. Too full some days with the house overrun by children. And yet, I still crave more. I long for my own children to come home to me. Is this how You've felt all through the centuries since the beginning of time? I want to cry out to Eleanor and George and weep. Why are they so stubborn? Why won't they turn to me? Why won't they seek the truth about anything?

Sometimes—though she hated to admit it—Leota wished she'd never had children. *Do You ever feel like that, Lord? And yet, if I hadn't had Eleanor, I wouldn't have this sweet, unsullied young woman in my life now. I wouldn't be able to sit and hear Your story told all over again from the lips of someone who adores You. I'd be all alone, waiting to die.* Maybe all the sorrow was worth this bit of precious time. Leota had a daughter who despised her, but from Eleanor came this granddaughter who had become the apple of Leota's eye, her comfort in her old age.

But for how long, Lord? She's so young and so beautiful. I've seen the way Sam looks at her. And even Corban is beginning to have that look in his eyes, despite his attachment to another. How long before Annie becomes bored with an old lady who is getting more decrepit by the day?

" 'Crucify Him!' they all shouted." Annie's raised voice made Leota start. "The disciples ran away in fear for their lives. The Jewish leaders were afraid of losing their positions of power in the church. The Jewish people were angry because Jesus wasn't the warrior messiah they wanted. The Romans were afraid they would lose control of the world they had conquered. They wanted to keep peace at any price, even if it meant killing an innocent man. Everyone took part. Even you and me, though we weren't there. We sin just as they all sinned. Satan must have thought he had won the battle when Jesus died on the cross that day. He must've celebrated when they took Jesus' body down and took Him away to be buried. Jesus was a young man, only thirty-three, and He didn't have a tomb prepared for Him. They had to lay the only begotten Son of God in a borrowed tomb. And those who had loved Him lost all hope. They hid themselves away and wept. Oh, how Satan must have danced at Jesus' grave."

Leota closed her eyes against sudden tears. *Is that what's happened to me, Lord? Have I lost hope? Have I lost sight of who You are? Was I beguiled away from believing that You love me and all Your promises remain? I have felt so abandoned, but did that mean I was? I look at Annie now and know You heard every prayer I ever said. Not that You answered many. At least, not where Eleanor is concerned. Then again, I suppose she has something to say about how she lives her life.*

Lord, why did You curse us with free will? Why didn't You strike down Adam and Eve and start over with another perfect pair? Or would it have ended the same way yet again? We always seem to make wrong choices, then have to live with the misery of them. I tried to do what was right. Oh, God, I did. You know how hard I tried. Was I wrong? If I was right, why can't my children see it? And if I was wrong, why can't I?

The old clock on the mantel chimed once. Eight-thirty. Annie was acting out a lament, her voice filled with all the desolation of an old prophet: "When, oh Lord, when will You send us a Savior?"

Leota's heart echoed the cry. *I know You are the Savior, Lord. But, oh, Father, the enemy is so strong. He chips away at my armor, looking for chinks, for just enough space for a fiery dart to slip through and send me crashing down again into the pit of despair. He tore my family asunder before I was aware, and by the time I was, their hearts were so hardened I couldn't reach them.* Maybe if she'd fought harder and longer, but she was hurt and angry and withdrew, like a dog licking its wounds. Just like the disciples before God breathed the Holy Spirit on them. *Oh, God, that You would give me the confidence to speak truth! Maybe if they knew the whys and wherefores of my choices, they might have compassion. Eleanor is caught in a web of lies. And I'm sick of it, sick unto death of the recriminations. It was Bernard's story to tell, but he was too ashamed to speak. Or was it pride that kept him silent, Lord? Is that what binds us tighter than chains? Cursed pride. My own most of all.*

"Jesus arose!" Annie's voice was infused with joyful excitement, and the children clapped. "Death could not hold Him in the grave. Satan and all his demons could not destroy Him. He arose! And He is still alive to this very day! Anyone who believes in Jesus will never perish, but have everlasting life with Him. Those who believe will shed their bodies and join Him in paradise."

Death, the grand adventure. Easy for the young to think that when the years stretched out ahead of them. The young felt they had all the time in the world. They felt immortal. Leota turned her face away. Death drew closer each day. She could feel it approaching. Sometimes she was so afraid, her heart would pound. Other times, she felt perfectly at peace with it. Not that there was much she could do to stop its arrival. The unknown was so disturbing; it was all well and good to know the promises, but the uncertainty remained. What would it be like to die?

It reminded Leota of being pregnant with George. She knew the inevitable end: She would have a baby. There was no escaping. She was on a train going full speed ahead. Waiting and wondering about the destination had frightened her. Bernard had reminded her of how many millions of babies had been born before theirs was conceived. What good was that sort of comfort? *She* had never had a baby. Would she suffer terribly and scream and cry and make a complete fool of herself? Would she die?

And so it was now in her old age, with time speeding on. Maybe she would go to sleep in her bed one night and wake up somewhere else come morning. Wouldn't that be nice? To die in her sleep, unaware of what was happening.

Yet she knew that kind of death wasn't for her. She sensed it. Was it the increasing pain that warned her death wasn't going to be so easy? Or was it the result of all the wasted years of waiting and hoping? She had the feeling God was going to make her face the grim reaper head-on.

She let her mind drift back to the day when George was placed in her arms. Oh, how her breasts had hurt those first weeks he had nursed and she had bonded with him. The mere sound of his cry would bring her milk in. She would hold him close and gaze at him as his small mouth worked, drawing his nourishment from her body. And it had been the same with Eleanor. How Leota had loved dressing her daughter up and showing her off to the world. Before Bernard went off to war, they'd bring the children into bed with them in the morning. Oh, how they'd all played and laughed, snuggling close together.

"Papa needs your help," Bernard had written. Would she have done differently if she had known how four words could change her life forever?

I wanted to do the right thing, Lord. I went in with rosy glasses, thinking we would all work together for the common good.

"Mommy! Mommy!"

The voice was as clear as the day Leota had heard it. It was Eleanor crying out, struggling in Mama Reinhardt's arms. Her little arms stretched out to Leota, her eyes wide with fear. Mama Reinhardt had held little Eleanor firmly, glaring. She said something in German. Leota never knew what the words meant, but it had been enough to see the look in her mother-in-law's eyes and be held to silence for the sake of Papa's pride.

"I'll be back this evening, Eleanor. Grandma Reinhardt will take good care of you." Eleanor's cries still rang in her ears.

"Mommy!"

Anguish had filled her until she thought the weight would crush her heart. She had wept all the way to work that morning—and every morning after that for the first month.

"Grandma?" Gentle fingers brushed her hair. Leota opened her eyes. The lamp was on. The room was empty.

Leota shifted in her chair. "The children are gone." *Oh, God, I've lost them. I lost them years ago, but it feels like yesterday.*

"Yes. They left about an hour ago. They'll be by tomorrow to say thank you. I think the evening was successful. Don't you, Grandma?"

Tears blurred her vision. "I missed it all." *I missed all the important things in their lives because I had to work. I had to keep a roof over our heads and bread on the table. I missed going to my children's school plays and baseball games and parents' nights. I didn't get to chaperone dances or sit in the auditorium for the band performance or stand on the street corner and watch them in the parade. I didn't get to watch them grow up. Oh, Father, I missed everything.*

You sacrificed out of love for them.

Annie knelt beside her chair and took her hand. "Are you feeling all right, Grandma?"

"I miss the children," she said in a choked voice.

"They'll be back tomorrow."

"I miss them so . . ."

Annie looked so worried. Leota was annoyed with herself. She must sound like a demented old woman. Better to keep silent than concern her sweet granddaughter with things the dear girl couldn't change. Better to push the pain down deep inside again and try to keep it where it wouldn't show. Who wanted to be around someone who moaned and grieved over the past? Yet the anguish was so close beneath the surface. And she had so little time left.

Time enough to be alone again. Time enough to be abandoned one last time.

With a shuddering sigh, she sat up. "Well, now that I've had my nap, I guess I'd better transfer my old bones to bed." She brought the recliner fully upright and allowed Annie to help her stand. "I'll be fine now, dear. I can manage. I'll see you in the morning." She leaned heavily on the cane Annie had given her, trying not to wince as she walked slowly toward the hallway to the bathroom and her bedroom.

"Grandma?" Annie came to her. She put her arms around Leota and held her close for a long moment. When she drew back, there were tears in her eyes. "I love you, Grandma. You know that, don't you? I love you very, very much."

Oh, the sweet balm of those words. Grateful, Leota cupped Annie's cheek and looked into her eyes for a long moment. Blue eyes, beautiful, baby blue eyes, just like Eleanor's. "I love you, too, my darling."

"I'm sorry I didn't come sooner."

Leota knew what she meant. "God sent you to me at just the right time." She kissed her cheek.

"Everything will work out Grandma. I know it. God won't let us down."

"No, He won't." Leota wanted to give back the same comfort Annie was trying to give her. Annie needed to know her words had made her feel better and that her grandmother's faith was strong enough to withstand anything, whatever was to come. Leota did believe God wouldn't let her down. For the time it took her to use the bathroom, change her clothes, and slip into her bed, she held tight to that promise. Then the darkness closed in, and the doubts danced on her heart, and the old sorrows welled up as she faced the truth.

God never lets you down.

But people do.

Corban entered the apartment, wondering why all the lights were out. Where was Ruth? She was always home by this time of the evening. He flicked the switch and crossed the room, putting his book bag beside his computer. He had a lot of reading to do if he was going to catch up. He had become so focused on reworking his paper on elder care that he was behind in philosophy. He'd have to work harder and stay up later for the next week to get back on track.

He thought he heard a cat mewling softly and realized the muffled sound was coming from the bedroom. Frowning, he went to the doorway and peered in. The light from the living room shone in enough to show him someone was in bed. "Ruth?" He clicked the lamp on.

"Turn off the light!" Her voice was filled with tears. "Turn it off . . ."

He did as she asked. "What's wrong? Are you sick?" He came into the room and sat on the edge of the bed they shared. When he touched her leg, she drew both up close against her chest, weeping harder. "Ruth? What's happened?" Fear gripped him. "Is it the baby?"

"There is no baby," she choked.

His stomach tightened until he hurt. "Did you . . . have a miscarriage?" he said slowly, his heart pounding.

She pulled the blankets closer around her. "I told you I couldn't have it, Cory. I told you, but you wouldn't listen to reason."

He stood slowly and stepped back from the bed.

She began to sob. "They lied to me. They said it wouldn't hurt. It hurt so much I passed out. When I came to, I was in a room with six other women. I asked for something for the pain, but the woman said it would cost another fifty bucks. Can you believe anyone could be that insensitive?"

Emotions surged up inside him, hot, violent. He had to get out of the room. He had to get away from her. He went out into the living room and stood with his eyes tightly shut. He wanted to smash something. He could hear Ruth. No quiet weeping anymore, but loud, choking, anguished sobs. For whom? The child she had killed? *His* child? Or for herself because it wasn't as easy as she wanted it to be.

"Cory, I need you."

Grabbing his jacket, he went out the door, slamming it behind him. He walked down the block, passing the corner coffee shop where he liked to sit with friends. Someone called his name, but he kept walking. He didn't care which direction he went. He wanted to run. He wanted to get as far away from Ruth Coldwell as he could.

He found himself on the campus. He kept walking, passing by buildings where he had taken classes over the past three years. He saw the stadium and went around it, continuing upward until he found himself on Tightwad Hill, where people who wouldn't pay the price of admission sat to watch university football games.

Body-weary and spirit-spent, Corban paused, staring out over Berkeley and across the bay to San Francisco. The lights were beautiful.

Everything looked crisp and clean up here. Nevertheless, he felt tears gathering in the back of his eyes, his throat closing tight and hot.

Annie lived over there somewhere. He wished he could call and talk to her. He wished he could ask her what he should do now. He'd get arrested and hauled off to jail if he did what he wanted. He hunkered down and raked his hands through his hair. Why had Ruth done it? He had told her he would take care of her. He told her they could work things out. Weaving his fingers tightly at the back of his neck, he kept his head down and his eyes closed.

"Jesus," he whispered. Beyond that, he didn't know what to say. Up to a few weeks ago, he had been pro-choice. Funny how things could change so fast. He hadn't understood what it would mean when he had no say in whether his own flesh and blood had a right to live or not.

"I have a right to my own life," Ruth had said. Even if it cost the life of his child?

He dredged up all the philosophical discussions he had had over the past few years. None comforted him.

"Jesus," he whispered again, and the tears came.

Ruth was wrapped in a blanket and lying on the sofa when Corban unlocked and opened the door.

"Where did you go?" She peered at him.

"For a walk."

"It's eleven o'clock. You've been gone four hours." Her face was white, her eyes puffy from crying. Her hair was matted on one side as though she had spent most of the time curled into the fetal position on their bed, just as he'd left her. He couldn't look into her eyes.

"I needed to think."

"Don't you think *I* thought about it? That's all I've done for *weeks*. I had to do it, Cory. Try to understand!"

"I'm trying, but I'd rather not talk about it right now, if you don't mind."

She turned her face away, and he saw her swallow convulsively. "I've worked too hard to throw it all away, Cory." She looked back at him again, eyes glistening with tears. "And so have you."

She could cry an ocean of tears and not touch his heart. Not now.

"I have a right to my own life." She pulled the blankets tighter. "And so do you. One of us would have had to give up our dreams. And I knew it would be me in the end. That's always the way it is. The woman has to give up everything."

"Is that what your friends have been telling you? I would've been giving up plenty," he said tightly.

"And you never would have let me forget it either, would you?"

"We could have worked it out."

"Not in this lifetime."

Her bitterness fed his wrath. "You never gave yourself a chance to find out."

"I didn't have to wait. I *knew* what would happen. It's what's always happened to women. You agreed with me a few months ago."

"I was wrong."

She sat up slowly and waited. Corban knew she wanted him to look her in the face, but he couldn't. She let her breath out slowly. "Even if I wanted to undo it, Cory, I couldn't. It's too late."

She had seen to that. His child was dead. He looked at her then, in loathing, and saw her emotions flickering across her features: shame, sorrow, confusion, a desperate appeal. She buried her face in her hands and cried again. Pity stirred within him. Who was he to cast stones? Hadn't he been all for abortion up until a few weeks ago?

Sighing heavily, accepting his share of the guilt, Cory went to her. "I'm sorry, Ruth." *I'm sorry you did this terrible thing. I'm sorry my child is dead. I'm sorry we're both going to have to live with what you've done.* He touched her hair and sat down beside her on the sofa. "I should've given you more support." Maybe if he'd been around more, making plans for their future instead of trying to finish his classes . . .

"It would've been easier," she said, misunderstanding him completely. She turned to him weeping, her fingers clinging to his shirt. He could feel her whole body shaking violently against him.

It took all his will to put his arms around her and give her comfort.

16

"Anne-Lynn called me last night and said she's planning to have Thanksgiving in Oakland," Nora said, pouring coffee for Fred. "She's spending the holiday with my mother instead of with her family." She set the cup down hard, annoyed that he hadn't looked up from his morning newspaper. "Did you hear what I said?"

"I heard, Nora. I know about it already."

"What do you mean, you know?"

"Annie called last Wednesday and mentioned the idea to me. It sounded like a good one."

Nora steamed. "Where was I while this was going on?"

"As I remember, you were shopping." He lowered the newspaper enough to look her in the eye. "You said you were going to get a head start on Christmas this year."

She remembered now. She had purchased a power suit in cornflower blue silk for her daughter. It had cost three hundred dollars, not counting all the accessories—shoes, purse, scarf, gold pin with pearls—she had purchased to go with it. She kept imagining how stunning Anne-Lynn would look in the ensemble. Blue to match her eyes. Now Nora wanted to take everything back! Why should she give

Anne-Lynn anything when the ungrateful little wretch betrayed her at every turn?

She glared at the newspaper Fred had raised like a shield. "Why didn't you say anything to me about this before now?" She wanted to rip that paper out of his hands and tear it to shreds.

Sighing, Fred folded the newspaper abruptly and glanced at her, his brows drawing together in irritation. "Because Annie said she would call you back and talk to you herself, which she has now done." He spoke through tight lips. "Besides that, I have no intention of getting into the middle of this ridiculous situation between you and your daughter and your mother."

"*Ridiculous?*" She controlled her urge to scream at him. "I could use some support, Fred." She was proud of the cool timbre of her voice.

"You're the one who declared war, Nora, long before I was in the territory. I've chosen to remain neutral."

"That's as good as saying you're on Anne-Lynn's side. Or my mother's."

He closed the newspaper and tossed it on the table the same way he would toss a gauntlet. His eyes sparked. "What's wrong with Annie doing Thanksgiving at your mother's this year? It's an act of kindness."

"Kindness? Is that what you think?" She gave a brittle laugh. "She knows very well I want to have Thanksgiving *here,* in *our* home. My mother knows that, too."

"Why? So you can complain again about how much work it is for you and how no one ever appreciates what you do? Or so you can exclude your mother for another year?"

She caught her breath, and heat rose into her cheeks. "My mother can come if she wants."

"How magnanimous of you," he said dryly.

"That's not fair! I've invited her before. She's the one who's always chosen to stay away."

"Last I heard, your mother didn't have a driver's license. Has that changed? Did you ever once offer to pick her up or arrange a ride for her?"

Her skin went cold. "She can arrange her own ride."

He shook his head, gazing at her sadly. "Michael treats you the same way you treat your mother. Did you ever think about that, Nora? You taught him well, didn't you?"

Quick tears came to her eyes. "Michael *loves* me."

"Not so anyone would notice."

"What a cruel thing to say to me!" Her mouth jerked.

"I've been married to you for five years, Nora, and I've never heard you say one kind thing about your mother. And the few times I've had the opportunity to meet Leota, I've found her to be charming."

"Yes, *charming*. Charm is deceitful."

"And beauty is vain." He stood up. "I'm going to work." He took his jacket from the back of the chair and picked up his briefcase. "When you and Annie figure out where we're having Thanksgiving, let me know and I'll be there. Unless, of course, I've been *un*invited."

She held back tears of resentment. "Maybe I'll just go away for that weekend and have Thanksgiving all by myself! That'd make everyone happy, wouldn't it?"

"There's a thought." He left the room without a backward glance.

The quaking started inside her. *Would* her family be happier if she went off by herself and left them alone to celebrate Thanksgiving any way they wanted and with whomever they wanted?

Thanksgiving at her mother's! Thanksgiving in a cramped, prewar cottage surrounded by run-down houses in the middle of a ghetto. How delightful! Nora picked up Fred's coffee cup and carried it to the sink, dumping the contents before she put it and the saucer into the dishwasher. She ran water to wash away the coffee. What did Anne-Lynn know about stuffing and baking a turkey? Nothing! The only thing Nora had ever had her do for Thanksgiving was go to the florist and pick up the centerpiece, then set the table and help with cleaning up the dishes later. Last year George and his family had come for dinner. His wife, Jeanne, had brought two homemade pies, one pumpkin and the other mincemeat. The pies had been so-so, certainly not of the quality Nora could have made. The scoops of whipping cream she had put on each slice had helped. Annie had spent most of the day baby-sitting Mitzi and Marshall, while Jeanne got in Nora's way in the kitchen. Typically male, George and Fred hadn't lifted a finger to help. They'd been too busy watching a football game.

Anne-Lynn fixing Thanksgiving dinner. What a fiasco that would be!

Fred's words made her conscience squirm. It was true she hadn't made any arrangements for her mother in the past. Then again, George could have offered to swing by in his fancy Mercedes and pick her up. Even if it was out of his way. Was she supposed to do *everything* herself?

Thanksgiving would be so much better here.

She knew she'd get nowhere talking with Anne-Lynn. Picking up the telephone, she pressed in her mother's number and waited, breathing deeply to calm her emotions.

"Hello?"

"Mother, this is Nora. I think it'd be much better if I had Thanksgiving here again this year. You're invited, of course."

"I'm sorry, I can't hear you very well."

"Maybe you'd hear better if you turned the television off!"

"Whatever you're selling, I'm not buying." She hung up.

Nora let out her breath sharply. It was the second time her mother had hung up on her. Was Leota losing her mind as well as her hearing? She pressed in the number again, striving for control over her temper.

"Mother, it's Nora!"

"Eleanor? Oh, hello, dear. How are you?"

Nora gritted her teeth. Did her mother use that name just to irritate her? "I've called about Thanksgiving."

"Oh, Annie and I will be delighted you can make it."

"I didn't say—"

"It'll be wonderful! Just like old times! She has everything planned."

Old times? What good was there in having it like old times? "Mother! I want to have Thanksgiving here, at *my* house."

There was a pause. "Then we have a problem, don't we? Why don't you come over and we can talk about it?"

"I don't want to come over there."

"I know you don't. You never want to come here. Why is that, Eleanor?"

"I think you know."

"Why don't you come over and tell me?"

"Why are you making things so difficult?" she cried out in frustration.

"I don't have a long time left to live, Eleanor. I'm tired of waiting for things to get better between us. I'm in my eighties, and I'm not feeling up to snuff. I'd like to see us sort things out before I'm gone."

"There's nothing for me to sort out." Did she want absolution? Fat chance! "Besides you'll live to be a hundred." She couldn't keep the bitterness from her voice. When there was no response, she frowned, annoyed by the twinge of shame she felt. Fred's words came back to haunt and anger her: *"Michael treats you the same way you treat your mother.*" Why should she think of that now? And why should she feel guilty when her mother had been the one to dump her children on others while she chose to work? "Mother, why won't you be reason-able? You know very well there isn't enough room over there to have Thanksgiving dinner."

"Come on over and we'll talk about it."

"I have better things to do than argue with you."

"Have it your way, but if we don't talk it over, Annie will be here for Thanksgiving. We'll miss you." The line went dead again.

Nora said a foul word and slammed the telephone back onto the charge cradle. "All right, Mother. You asked for it. I'll come. And I'll give you a good piece of my mind when I get there!"

Leota had forgotten it was Wednesday. She might not have been so set on firing up Eleanor's dander had she remembered Corban was coming by to take her shopping. She didn't remember until he rang the doorbell and she saw him through the sheer curtains. "Oh, dear," she said, annoyed with herself. Eleanor would be in her car by now, winging her way over for battle.

Thankfully, he had learned to give her plenty of time to get out of her chair and make it to the door. Leota was all ready to apologize and send him home when she got a look at his face. "What's the matter with you?"

"Nothing."

"Did somebody die?" She unlatched the screen door and let him in.

"Everything's just fine, Leota."

"You know better than to lie to me. I thought we had that under-stood a long time ago." He looked like he hadn't slept since she had seen him last. He was pale, with dark shadows under his eyes—and more tense than she'd ever seen him.

"I don't want to talk about it," he said. "Is that okay with you?"

"Pretty good indication it's something that needs talking out."

"Lay off, Leota. I'm not in the mood today. Are you ready to go shopping or not?"

"I forgot it was Wednesday."

"You want me to come back another day?"

"No. I need some things for Thanksgiving." She couldn't leave and risk Eleanor showing up while she was gone, nor did she want to send Corban home when he clearly needed to get something off his chest whether he thought he did or not. "I'll write up the list and give you the money. You can take care of shopping for me today. How will that be?"

"Fine."

"You've still got the key to my house, haven't you?"

"Yes. Are you sure you want me to keep it?"

"I think I can trust you not to come back in the dead of night and rob me blind. Besides, it's a safety precaution. What if I collapse sometime and you can't get in to get me up off the floor?"

He didn't look amused.

Corban hadn't been gone thirty minutes when Nora arrived on Leota's doorstep.

Oh, Lord, oh, Lord, help me get through to my daughter. Help me . . .

Leota opened the door. "Hello, Eleanor. I'm glad you could come."

"Did I have a choice?" she said before the door was even unlatched. "We could've settled this over the telephone." She stepped into the house. She didn't look into Leota's eyes, but made a sweeping glance of the room, her face tightening as though everything about it brought back unwelcome memories. She noticed Barnaby and grimaced. "A parrot?"

"A rainbow lory, Annie tells me. Barnaby belongs to Susan Carter, but he's had a nervous breakdown and needs quiet and rest. That bird cost five hundred dollars. Can you believe that? A policeman gave him to Susan. Why don't you sit down and I'll fix us some coffee?"

"I don't want coffee."

"Tea?"

"Not tea, not water, not *anything*. I don't have time."

Leota eased herself back into her recliner. She looked at her daughter where she sat on the edge of the sofa. She was dressed in elegant gray slacks, a white silk shirt, and a charcoal tweed blazer. She wore gold earrings and necklace, and dark gray leather pumps with an edge of brown across the top to match the bag she hadn't unlooped from her shoulder. Her hands, nails perfectly manicured and painted red, gripped her knees.

One false word. Leota knew that was all it would take and her daughter would be on her feet and out the front door in a huff. "It's nice to see you, dear. You had your hair cut since I saw you last." It was shorter, just below her ears, layered and in soft frosted curls.

"I suppose you don't like it."

"I like it very much. It frames your face very nicely." Her daughter always did have a wonderful sense of style.

"Thank you," Eleanor said, a sour twist to her lips. "I came to discuss the arrangements for Thanksgiving dinner."

"We've invited George and Jeanne and the children. Jeanne says she's sure they can make it. She's going to bring a couple of pies. You can bring something, too, if you like, though it's not necessary. Annie plans to have the food on the sideboard back there. Everyone can serve him- or herself that way. We'll set the nook table for Mitzi and Marshall, and the adults can sit at the dining-room table."

"There's not enough room around your table."

"There will be when we put the table leaves in. They've been stored in the bedroom closet."

"You haven't the money for a nice centerpiece."

"I have a garden."

"Yes. You have a garden. *How* could I forget?" She pressed her lips together when her mother said nothing. "It'd be easier and much better if we had Thanksgiving at my house."

"I haven't had Thanksgiving here in years, Eleanor."

"You *never* fixed Thanksgiving dinner, Mother. Not once, that I can remember. Grandma Reinhardt is the one who had it because this was *her* home and not ours. And she did all the work."

"Just the way you do."

Eleanor lifted her chin slightly. "It's one of the things I *enjoy* doing for my family."

"About as much as Mama Reinhardt did, I would imagine."

Eleanor said nothing for a couple of seconds. Leota could feel the undercurrent and was afraid of being sucked under.

"Annie can't cook," Eleanor said finally.

"You might be surprised what Annie can do."

"Shocked, more likely. It'll be a disaster and you know it. Is that what you want? To see her humiliated?"

"It'll only be a disaster if you make it so."

"If it all goes wrong, you'll blame me. Is that it?"

"No one has ever cast blame on you, Eleanor." She held her breath for two seconds and then said it straight out once and for all: "I was always the scapegoat."

"Oh, that's rich, Mother. You *escaped* every bit of responsibility you ever had! Two children. Remember us? You moved into Grandpa Reinhardt's house and dumped us on Grandma so that you could go off and live the high life. Even when you came home, you were more interested in that garden than in me or George!"

"You had no idea of the circumstances—"

"No circumstances would make *me* dump *my* children. I've always been there for them. From the time they were babies I managed to be at home with them. I'm still at home for them."

"And you think that makes you a better mother than I was?"

"Yes!" Nora's eyes glittered with angry tears. "I do. I don't think you ever had any idea of what being a mother was all about."

Leota's heart broke as she looked into her daughter's eyes. How had they come to this impasse? Surely all that fury hid a sea of hurt, but how could Leota get through to her daughter and convince her she had always been loved? Leota had done what she thought was best . . . what she'd had to do. Eleanor looked away from Leota's scrutiny and closed her eyes as though she couldn't bear it.

"You have no idea how awful it was, do you, Mother?"

"No, I don't." She only knew how awful it had been for her. "Tell me."

Eleanor looked back at her in despair. "Why should I? So you can make more excuses?"

Leota had no more time to waste playing who-was-right-and-who-was-wrong. "How many years will it be before you decide to move on with your life instead of blaming everything on the past?" She saw the flush pour into her daughter's cheeks. Not from conviction, but from temper. So much for getting to the heart of things.

The sound of a key in the door drew their attention. Corban unlocked the front door.

Eleanor rose. "Who is *this,* and what's he doing with a key to the house?" she said heatedly as Corban stepped into the room. He looked at Eleanor in surprise and then glanced at Leota.

"This is Corban Solsek. Corban, meet Eleanor Gaines, my daughter."

"Nice to meet you." His tone of voice said the opposite.

Leota nodded at him. "You can put those groceries in the kitchen and join us if you would like."

"I've got another bag in the car."

"Did I give you enough money?"

"More than enough. I'll give you the change as soon as I put these things away."

Eleanor sat rigidly on the sofa, watching and listening. Corban glanced at her again. "If you'll excuse me, Ms. Gaines," he said and headed for the kitchen.

"Are you completely out of your mind giving a stranger a key?" Eleanor said in an angry whisper. "Who is this person, and what do you know about him?"

"Corban's been coming over to help me for several months now. Every Wednesday like clockwork."

"How did you meet him?"

"I called an agency after seeing an ad on television."

"Oh, *Mother.*"

Leota had had just about enough. "I need groceries. It's a long walk to the market, uphill all the way home. I don't drive. What would you have me do, Eleanor? Starve?"

"You can call in an order to a grocery store and they'll deliver it."

That would be nice and impersonal. And expensive. "I prefer this arrangement. Besides, Corban is good company." Nothing like a discussion with him to get her blood up. "Sometimes he even drops by on the weekend and helps in the garden." Not that he liked it much. She suspected he was becoming more interested in her grand-daughter than in horticulture.

"What does George have to say about this?"

"Why should George have anything to say about it? He hasn't called in months. I doubt he knows. He's too busy with his business and family to have time to run over here and help me."

"That's just an excuse," Eleanor said, clearly annoyed.

"Oh, you know how it is, Eleanor. I'm sure Michael is just as busy with his life, too."

Eleanor's eyes sparked. "What is that supposed to mean?"

"Nothing other than what I said. Why are you always so defensive about everything I say? All I mean is it's nice to have company once in a while. Corban is welcome here anytime he wants to drop by. I'm not sending him away."

"Just like you won't send Anne-Lynn home, even when you know it's where she belongs."

"If you wanted Annie at home, why were you going to send her off to Wellesley?"

Eleanor blushed dark red. "It would've been better for her future than *art* school."

"She's very gifted, Eleanor. Just as you were."

"Oh. You're an art expert now?"

"I know what I like."

"Leota!" Corban called from the kitchen. "Where do you want your Metamucil?"

"Above the sink! Cabinet to the left with the water glasses. You can put it on the bottom shelf with the vitamins and aspirin."

"He calls you *Leota?*" Eleanor was clearly scandalized.

"What would you have him call me? Grandma Moses?"

"Mrs. Reinhardt would be more appropriate."

"He's a friend. I told him to call me Leota."

"How do you know he isn't just worming his way in here in hopes you'll leave him something in your will?"

That gave Leota pause. Was that what worried Eleanor? Not concern for her mother's safety or fear that someone might be taking advantage of an old lady? It was her inheritance, such as it was. "What would I leave him that matters to you, Eleanor? You hate everything about this house. There isn't a thing I have that you want." At least, that was what Eleanor had always said. Had she changed her mind?

"Are you saying you're going to put him in your will?"

"We aren't discussing my will. I'm asking you what *you* want!"

Eleanor's eyes flickered. She looked embarrassed and ashamed, then angry.

Would Eleanor ever understand that she was the daughter of her mother's heart? What more could Leota do to make it clear? "If there's anything in this house that means anything to you, Eleanor, anything at all, all you've got to do is tell me and I'll make sure you have it."

Face pinched, Eleanor got up and went to the front window, drawing the curtain aside. Was she checking to make sure the hubcaps were still on her car?

Corban came back into the living room. Leota saw by the look on his face that he was ready to go. "Why don't you heat some water, and we can have some of that cappuccino Annie brought last week?"

Eleanor let the curtain drop back into place. Barnaby moved to the far end of his perch, as far away from her as he could get. She turned and glanced pointedly at her wristwatch. "I said I don't want any coffee, Mother. I'm late enough as it is."

"You wouldn't mind if Leota had cappuccino, would you?" Corban's tone was pure ice.

"Excuse me?"

He made a point of ignoring Eleanor as he looked at Leota. "Would you like some cappuccino, Leota?"

She tried not to smile at his defensive manner. Who would have known . . . ? "Yes, I would."

"I'll fix it then." He went back into the kitchen.

Eleanor stared after him in consternation. "I've never met anyone so rude."

"He's just being protective of me. Oh, I know he could use a bit of polishing, but then, so could we all."

Eleanor shifted the strap of her shoulder bag and straightened her jacket. "Are we settled now about Thanksgiving?"

"Absolutely. Annie and I will have Thanksgiving dinner here. I hope you'll join us."

Eleanor's cheeks flushed. "We'll talk about it more later." Yanking the front door open, she walked out, banging it shut behind her.

Corban came out of the kitchen a few minutes later with a cup of steaming cappuccino. He set it carefully on her side table. "Careful. It's hot."

"Thank you, Corban. What about you?"

"No, thanks," he said glumly. "Sorry if I was rude, Leota." He nodded toward the closed front door. "Annie's mother, right? Boy, is she a piece of work."

She looked up at him. "You could both do with some tenderizer. Sit down, Corban."

"I'd better get going."

"Not yet." She nodded toward the sofa. "Sit and tell me what's troubling you."

He sat, looking pale and strained. Leaning forward, he raked his hands back through his hair. When he raised his head again, she saw he was struggling not to cry. He shook his head. "I can't."

Leota watched the struggle. She could feel his grief as though it were her own, even not knowing the cause. He reminded her of Bernard. "Confession's good for the soul, Corban. Have you ever heard that?"

"I'm not a religious man."

"I'm talking about faith, not religion."

"I'm not a man of faith either." A muscle jerked in his cheek. "Besides, I'm not the one who needs to be confessing."

"If you talk about it, get it out in the open, it'll lose its power over you."

He shook his head again. "It's too soon," he said in a choked voice. He rose and looked at her in apology. "I'd better go. I wouldn't be good company today."

"You're right. I would miss your usually sunny personality."

He gave her a rueful smile. "Say hi to Annie when she calls you."

"You know her number. If it's easier to talk to her, give her a call. But get it off your chest, whatever it is." As he turned away, she said his name and waited until he was looking at her again. "Don't let the root of bitterness take hold, Corban. If you do, you'll spend the rest of your life trying to pull it out."

He closed the door quietly behind him. Leota heard his car roar to life. As the sound of it faded, despair came down over her like a suffocating blanket. She was all alone again. Her chest ached so terribly. She thought of Eleanor and George.

Nothing is ever going to change, she realized. *All right, old woman. Accept it. Just get up and go into the kitchen and take those pills you've been hoarding for the past year. If one is supposed to keep your blood pressure down, the whole bottle ought to give you a peaceful passing.*

"I love you, Grandma."

The words startled her. "Annie?" Had her granddaughter come in quietly, without Leota noticing? How could that happen when she'd been sitting in her recliner facing the front door? Had Annie parked in the driveway and come in the back door? Leota looked around her chair, but didn't see her. Maybe she'd fallen asleep and dreamed about taking all those pills and leaving the anguish of living behind her.

"I love you, Grandma."

Leota stared in amazement. It was Barnaby, speaking in Annie's voice. Clear. Sweet. Full of tenderness.

"Now you talk." She was filled with disappointment. "Lord, did You ever stop to think that I've had enough? I've done all I can think to do. And I'm done. Finished. I'd rather be up there with You than down here in the middle of this mess. And if I have to do it myself . . ."

"I love you, Grandma."

Annie. What would it do to Annie to find her grandmother's body crumpled on the floor and then learn she'd swallowed a whole bottle of pills? Leota knew what it would do.

"I love you, Grandma."

"Shut up. I heard you the first time." She supposed this was His answer, too. *I love you.* Was He telling her to stop feeling sorry for herself and keep up the good fight?

"Most people get to retire . . ."

"I love you, Grandma."

Fine, Lord. All right, all right! She knew very well if she went into the kitchen and swallowed all those pills, it would hurt Annie. No telling where she would pass out. She would hardly be a pretty sight, crumpled and dead and discovered several days later. *Far* from dignified.

"I love you, Grandma."

"I heard you already. Now, eat some birdseed!"

But Barnaby kept it up all afternoon, until Leota's fighting spirit was back in full measure—and she was ready to wring his scrawny neck.

17

THE LAST PERSON LEOTA EXPECTED TO CALL HER WAS HER SON. BUT call her he did. She was pleasantly surprised by George's voice on the telephone . . . until she understood the point of his call.

"Mother, Nora mentioned she met a young man at your house the other day."

"Corban," Leota said after a brief hesitation. Disappointment filled her, making her heart ache. "Corban Solsek. He's a volunteer for an elder-care agency I called. I suppose Nora also told you I got the number from a television ad."

"What do you know about this young man, Mother?"

"He came with a reference and he's willing to help. What more should I know?"

"He could be anything, Mother. I don't think it's wise to allow a stranger access to your house."

To the house. Not his mother. "A better question might be why it's necessary for an old woman to call and ask for help from strangers." She regretted the words as soon as they passed her lips. She was pouring on the mother guilt and building the walls higher. She could feel them going up, brick by brick. The mortar dried in the silence.

"If I had more time, I'd be over there helping you out," George said tautly. "But I've got a business to run, and it's all I can do to keep my head above water with the competition the way it is. You know that."

"Of course, I know." He had told her that every time they talked. Usually when she called and interrupted him. "Just don't begrudge me getting help where and when I can. Annie visits several times a month. She's met Corban. She likes him. If you and Nora have questions about his character, maybe you should talk with her. Or the agency." She gave him the name and telephone number. She hoped he wasn't talking to her with his cell phone while driving on a freeway. "He's a university student, George. Dean's list, I'm sure. Sociology, I think. Does that set your mind at ease, dear?"

"I didn't call to get a lecture."

She sighed. No matter what she said to make peace, it always backfired. Better if she said nothing and just went on with her life the way it was. "I know why you called, George." *Lord, I wish I didn't.* "Did you have anything else you wanted to say to me?"

"No, nothing else."

"We can talk more about it when you come for Thanksgiving."

"Nora said she's having Thanksgiving at her house."

So that was the way Nora intended to get her way. "Then I suppose you'll have to make a choice where you're going to be. Annie and I are still planning on having Thanksgiving dinner here."

"It'd be less work for you if Nora did it."

Poor Annie. She'd be in the middle of the mess. Pressured on all sides. "Go where you want, George. I'll be here." He said nothing to that, but at least he didn't hang up on her the way Nora did whenever she was thwarted. Leota let her breath out, hoping it would ease the ache in her chest. It didn't. "I have something to ask you, George."

"Go ahead." Clearly, he was not enthusiastic about it.

"Is there anything in this house that you want? Anything at all? You've only to tell me."

"I can't think of anything offhand."

"Well, think about it and let me know."

"Why are you asking me a question like that? Are you planning on giving things away?"

She could tell he was still thinking about Corban, the interloper. "I'm asking because I won't be here forever. I need to know so that I can give you what you want."

"I suppose I'd like half of what the house and property are worth."

She swallowed hard. So there it was. Cut and dried. Money. That's all he wanted.

"Mother?"

Leota supposed Nora felt exactly the same way. She could imagine her children sticking a For Sale sign in her front lawn and holding a garage sale within a few days of her death. They'd put all of her possessions out on the sidewalk with little price tags attached. Everything marked down for quick sale. Good riddance to bad rubbish.

She glanced around the living room, trying to see things through their eyes. She supposed most of what she possessed was junk by their standards. They didn't know that every knickknack, stitchery picture, and stick of furniture meant something to her. Everything in her house held special meaning and sparked a memory. These were not just things to gather dust. Her house held a library of stories, most of them private, some heartbreaking, some lovely, some tender. She would have been more than willing to share those memories had her children been interested in listening.

"Mother?"

Lord, I could become bitter. It would be so easy to give in to anger right now and curse George and Eleanor for the pain they've caused me over the years by their neglect and indifference. But then, they don't see it that way at all, do they? They've abandoned me because they felt abandoned by me.

She knew it was true. They'd been hurt and now they wanted to hurt her back. They'd wanted their mother at home, waiting, at their beck and call—fixing every situation, soothing every fear, and fulfilling every dream. And when she couldn't be, they'd set their hearts against her. They had chosen to cling to the lies they were taught by others rather than listen to the voice of their mother. Not once had they sought the truth.

Oh, God, why will they not turn to me and ask why things had to be the way they were? How much of the way they are is my fault because I wasn't willing to tell Bernard's secrets or crush Papa Reinhardt's pride? Or Mama Reinhardt's, for that matter. How many years did it take before Mama realized the truth and then had to grieve over poisoning the children against me? Better had she confessed to them than leave me with uncovering her shame. Would they even believe me now if I told them the truth? Oh, Jesus, blessed Savior, Lord God, still my beating heart and bring me home! I'm sick of this life! I'm sick of waiting and hoping and grieving! I'm sick of the disappointment. When will this life end?

"Mother!"

"I'm here, dear." *But not for much longer, I hope.*

"What did you want me to say?" His voice was quiet, defensive.

What did she want him to say? "I love you . . ." "I'd like to come for Thanksgiving. Thank you for the invitation . . ." "I've missed you, too. I look forward to sitting down and hearing about your life . . ." "Show me the past through your eyes, Mother."

They're so sanctimonious, so self-righteous, so independent. They've lived their whole lives in denial. They've never been willing to look at or hear the truth. Eleanor casts blame; George hides. Every time I've tried to tell them what really went on during those early years, I've failed. They've concertina wire around them, and every time I try to get through to them I end up lacerated.

Leota couldn't speak a word past the lump in her throat. *Take me home, Lord. Take me right now while he's on the telephone. Maybe then . . . oh, blast, what good is this stinking self-pity!*

"Mother?" Impatience this time. "Look, I'm sorry, but I haven't got the time for this right now. I'll call back later." He hung up.

She supposed he would have the time to call Annie and the elder-care agency and check up on Corban. She supposed he would have time to call Nora and report. She put the telephone back in its cradle and sat thinking for a long time. She thought about George and Nora and Annie. Michael Taggart, her grandson, didn't even come into the equation. He had deserted the sinking ship long ago. She wished him well. A pity she couldn't even remember what the boy looked like. The picture on her mantel was ten years old.

Opening a drawer in her side table, she found her personal address book and the number she needed. She pressed in the numbers carefully and listened to the telephone ring.

"Dryer, Shaffer, Pulaski, and Rooks," came the greeting. "How may I direct your call, please?"

"I'd like to speak with my attorney, Dexter Lane Rooks, please."

There was a pause. "I'm sorry, ma'am, but Dexter Rooks died several years ago."

"Well, what do I do now? He was my lawyer," she said, annoyed. "I need him to change my will."

"His son took over most of his father's clients, Mrs. . . ."

"Reinhardt. Leota Reinhardt. Well, then, let me talk to his son. I hope my file is still there."

"I'm sure it is, ma'am. I'll connect you with Charles Rooks's office. I'm sure they can help you. One moment please."

Leota tried to calm her frayed nerves and explain everything to Charles Rooks's secretary. Then she was placed on hold for so long she was certain she had been forgotten. Maybe they were hoping she'd die in the meantime and save them trouble. Just when she was about to hang up and try again, the secretary came back on the line. "Mr. Rooks will speak with you, Mrs. Reinhardt."

Sure enough, a cultured male voice came on the line. "Mrs. Reinhardt, how may I help you?"

Oh, Lord, do I have to go through it all over again? "I've decided to change my will, and I need it done as soon as possible. I have some papers here I'd like you to look over. I don't know whether to transfer ownership now or have that done after I'm gone."

"When can you bring these documents to the office?"

"I can't bring them to the office, young man. I'm eighty-four. I don't drive, I haven't the money for a taxi, and I'm too old to ride a bus. I need *you* to come *here*. If you need witnesses to the transaction, come on Wednesday. I can ask a friend to come in the afternoon instead of in the morning. Or there's my neighbor, Arba Wilson."

"Well, ma'am, I'm very busy, and leaving the office is—"

"Something your father would've done."

He hesitated. "Yes, he would've. Wednesday afternoon, you say? Would it be possible for me to come after five? I'll be in court all morning, and I have appointments in the afternoon."

"You can come for dinner if you like."

He chuckled. "Thank you, ma'am, but that won't be necessary. Give your address and telephone number to my secretary. Between now and Wednesday, write down the changes you want to make in your will and have the documents ready for me to look over. That'll expedite matters."

"I'll do that." She'd start this afternoon—if she could find her will. Hadn't she put it in the top drawer of her sideboard? Or was it in the safety-deposit box? Had she paid the rent on that box? Maybe her will was in the bottom drawer of her dresser with the few special pieces of jewelry Bernard had given her before he went away to war.

The secretary came back on the line and verified her address and telephone number. As soon as Leota ended that call, she dialed Annie's number. The answering machine was on. "It's Grandma Leota, Annie. Call me when you have time, dear. I'd like to discuss

Thanksgiving with you. And a few other things." Next, she dialed Corban. A young woman answered. "Ruth?"

"Yes, this is Ruth. Who is this?"

What a curt, cold voice. "Leota Reinhardt. Corban has—"

"Cory's not here. I'll leave him a message that you called."

The telephone clicked in Leota's ear before she could utter another word. Frowning, Leota put the telephone back in its cradle.

"What's all this?" Corban said, entering his apartment and finding several boxes piled near the front door. He could see two more open on the table in the kitchen and Ruth rummaging through cabinets.

"I'm leaving you," Ruth said, her back to him.

He shrugged off his book-laden backpack and heaved it onto the sofa beside two more boxes. "I thought we were going to try to work things out between us."

"What's to work out, Cory? You've already made up your mind how you feel."

"I'd say you were the one who'd already made up her mind."

She turned sharply. "What did you expect me to do? Stay and put up with your condemning, judgmental attitude?"

"I haven't said one word—"

"You don't have to *say* anything. I can see it in your eyes every time you look at me!" She turned her back again.

Corban's anger rose. "Those dishes were in the apartment before you moved in."

"Fine!" Opening her hands, she let two dinner plates crash to the floor. "You can have them. And the glasses, too." She swept six out of the cabinet onto the Formica counter.

Corban called her a foul name. "Go ahead and break everything if you think it'll make you feel better!"

Her eyes glistened with tears. "Do you think I care what you think?"

He wanted to throw her out of his apartment and toss her boxes after her. "I'm the one who's always compromised." He wished she'd died in that clinic.

"Give me a break, Cory. When did you ever compromise about anything?"

"What else are you trying to steal from me?" He flipped open one of the boxes by the front door.

"Go ahead. Go through them. Take whatever you want! You know what? I finally see you for what you are." She stood in the kitchen doorway, flushed with rage. "You're a *hypocrite!* It shouldn't have taken me six months to realize."

"What opened your eyes, Ruth? Killing our baby?"

She flinched, her face going pale. She called him a name fouler than the one he had called her. "It wasn't *your* life at stake, Cory. Or your education. I was always the one who had to take responsibility. Right from the beginning!"

"What are you talking about?"

"I'm the one who had to take precautions. Never, not *once* did you bother with birth control. Let the woman do it. Isn't that it, Cory? Let the woman take responsibility for the man's fun and games. Let the woman give up *everything!* She's just a vessel anyway, isn't she, Cory? You jerk! You were relieved when I took care of the problem. You just didn't want to know about it. That was my mistake. Better had I lied and said I miscarried. Everything would've been hunky-dory then. Isn't that right? You wouldn't have to share the guilt!" Tears poured down her white cheeks, hate poured from her eyes. "I deserved compassion after going through what I did, but that's too much to expect from you, isn't it?"

"*Compassion?* You knew how I felt!"

"Did I? Words are cheap, Cory. Actions speak louder than words! Haven't you ever heard that? You helped me paint the placards! You let me hold the meetings! You were pro-choice all the way. Or so you said until *I* got pregnant. Then there was a major paradigm shift. All of a sudden all the rules changed." Her lip curled in a feral smile. "You know what, Cory? You're a small-minded, male chauvinist *pig*. For all your intellectual posturing, you're just a right-wing funda-mentalist in disguise."

"And what are you, Ruth? Trading sex for a place to live. Trading sex so I'll pay your way. All that high talk about liberation! All that talk about equal rights! You're nothing but a prostitute living off a man."

"I hate you."

"You hate the truth!"

It got worse after that.

Sticks and stones break bones, but words destroy the heart and spirit. Both of them were annihilated by the time Ruth's two girl-friends came to pick her up and take her and her things to her new home.

Cory sat on the sofa after she was gone and wept bitterly. He didn't care that Ruth had left him. In fact, he was relieved she was gone and he wouldn't have to look at her face every day or tread carefully with every word he spoke lest he hurt her feelings.

When had she ever considered *his* feelings?

Grief overwhelmed him. Not an ounce of it was for Ruth. He grieved the loss of the one good thing that might have come from their sordid relationship: the child he was responsible for making. The child he should have been able to protect. The child who haunted his dreams at night.

Leota served Charles Rooks coffee while he read through her will and looked over the documents she had kept in a manila envelope for the past forty years. "Cream or sugar, Mr. Rooks?"

"Black, thank you. Please, call me Charles."

He looked very much like his father: blue eyes, bushy gray brows, bald on top with steel-gray around the sides, dressed in an expensive dark gray suit. This visit was going to cost her plenty.

"Arba, my neighbor, said she'd come over and sign whatever you need her to sign. I'll call her when we're ready."

"We won't be ready this evening, Mrs. Reinhardt. I'll need to take everything back to my office and have it typed in proper form."

"How long will that take, and how much will it cost?"

He told her the cost first, which made her heart flutter a little in shock, then said, "I'll have everything ready by the end of the month."

"At that price, I want it sooner. I'll give you a check before you leave."

He took his glasses off and laid them on the table. "This isn't something to rush into, ma'am. Sometimes it's better to think things over before you make major changes like this. Especially if there's been a family argument." He raised his brows in question.

"There's been no argument. I know what I'm doing. I've been thinking about this for a long time. I want everything fixed exactly the way I've said. I may be old, Mr. Rooks, but I'm not senile."

He smiled slightly. "No, ma'am. I don't think you are. But you do sound angry."

"Hurt, Mr. Rooks. And fed up."

"There's another way to handle all this that wouldn't cost you nearly as much money. You can have joint tenancy on your house. When you . . ."

"Pass on. Go ahead, you can say it."

He inclined his head. "Pass on, then. Your part will fall to your joint tenant or tenants. As to the other documents, you can fill in the back now and then sign them over when you're ready. If you do that, the will is fine as it is. Just the names changed. One last word of advice, ma'am. You shouldn't leave papers like these lying around your house."

"They weren't lying around. They were tucked away in a safe place."

"Mrs. Reinhardt," he said patiently, "do you have any idea what these are worth?"

"No, and I don't care." She sat down across the table from him, weary and heartsick. "I wanted to give my children an important inheritance, Mr. Rooks, something that would carry them through life and fill them to overflowing with joy." She put her hand on the papers. "Unfortunately, this is all they want."

"I'm sorry, ma'am."

He looked sincere, and despite all the awful things said about lawyers, she believed he spoke from the heart. She smiled sadly. "So am I, Mr. Rooks. So am I. Now, let's get down to business."

"Mother said she and Fred will come for a little while," Annie said that evening. "She called this afternoon. I think Uncle George talked with her."

No doubt. Thanksgiving would give them another opportunity to corner their mother and find out where their inheritance stood. It was a good thing everything would be settled long before everyone arrived for turkey dinner. "Should be a jolly Thanksgiving."

"Are you changing your mind, Grandma? Is this going to be too much for you?"

Yes. It would be too much for her. All the activity, all the excitement, all the tension. But she was not about to surrender to Eleanor. She'd make it through Thanksgiving if it killed her. "You'll be the one doing the cooking, Annie. I'll be your cheering section. Are you changing *your* mind?"

"No. Oh, Grandma, I'm so excited about it. We can do it. I know we can. It'll be wonderful. I'll come over this weekend and start on the house like you said, though it's perfect the way it is."

"A little painting here and there will brighten it up."

"I already have some ideas."

Leota chuckled. "I thought you might. You do whatever you like. I want you to consider this house as much yours as it is mine."

"I promise not to do anything without your full approval."

"You already have it, dear. By the way, I was thinking about inviting Corban. How would you feel about that? He's been a little blue lately, and I think his family is on the East Coast somewhere. He won't be able to go home."

"That'd be great, Grandma. Invite him and his girlfriend. And Arba and the children, too, if you like. And Juanita and Lin Sansan . . ."

"The more, the merrier." Leota intended to draft as many allies as she could for Annie.

The cold war was over. The real war was about to begin.

18

CORBAN WAS THE FIRST GUEST TO ARRIVE ON THANKSGIVING DAY. He fidgeted nervously, glad he'd brought with him two bottles of sparkling cider and another African violet.

"Dear boy," Leota said, taking the flowering plant in its small blue pot and smiling in such a way that his nervous tension eased slightly. "Annie's in the kitchen. Why don't you put those bottles into the refrigerator to chill? After that, would you please move Barnaby into my bedroom? I don't want him having a relapse today."

"Hi!" Annie said brightly, grinning at him as she put the foil back on the turkey she was checking. "We're getting there. I hope you're hungry. We have a twenty-pounder."

"I'll do my part when the time comes."

"Good. You can mash the potatoes. I'm hoping Uncle George will carve the turkey. Grandma said she'd do the gravy. We've got green peas and mushrooms, cranberry sauce, black olives. Arba's bringing candied yams and Aunt Jeanne is bringing pies—apple, mincemeat, and pumpkin."

"What about stuffing?"

"Of course, there's stuffing. It's in the turkey. Grandma's recipe. Plain and simple seasoned bread, celery, onions, and the giblets all ground together. Took us a good part of this morning, but it'll be worth it."

The doorbell rang, and Corban saw a flicker of tension in Annie's face. "Why don't you be the greeter?" she said. "I don't want Grandma to have to get up and down every few minutes. She should be presiding over festivities in the living room."

Leota was already at the door. "George, Jeanne. Come in! Come in!"

"Mama." The woman leaned down to kiss Leota's cheek. "How are you?"

"Fine, just fine. Come in, come in." She turned, her eyes shining. "Corban, this is my son, George, and his wife, Jeanne. And my grandchildren, Marshall and Mitzi. This is Corban, a good friend of mine." The children were staring at Barnaby, who was staring back, beak open and ready for attack.

Jeanne was the only one who seemed openly friendly. She smiled and greeted him warmly, while her husband stood silent and assessing. What did the guy think he was? A felon on parole? "I'd better get Barnaby out of here." The children trooped after him, asking questions about the bird that Corban couldn't answer. "You'll have to ask Annie. All I know is he's crazy and he bites." When he returned to the living room, he saw Jeanne was still holding the box she had brought in. "Let me take that for you," Corban said.

"Oh, I'll take it. You men sit and get to know one another." With that, Jeanne headed for the kitchen, the two children in her wake.

Corban turned to face the somber-faced George.

"My mother's told me you've been a big help to her."

"It's been my pleasure."

"When it hasn't been a royal pain in your backside," Leota said, settling back into her recliner. The three of them spent the next fifteen minutes in small talk—highly pained small talk. Corban had never felt so uncomfortable. Leota made a valiant attempt to get a conversation going with her son, but good old George wasn't cooperating.

"How is business going these days?"

"Fine."

"Still expanding?"

"Trying to."

"I suppose Marshall is still in soccer."

"I think so."

"You think so?"

"Jeanne handles the children's schedules."

"Don't you attend his games?"

"When I can." George shifted, glanced at Corban, then back at Leota. "Do you mind if I turn on the television, Mother? There's a good football game starting."

"If that's what you want to do."

How, Corban wondered, *could the man miss the look of sadness in his mother's eyes?* Maybe his presence was the cause of George Reinhardt's reticence? Maybe if he were out of the way, George would feel more free to talk.

"I'm going to go see if I can help Annie in the kitchen, Leota." At least the women were talking.

"It's so much brighter in here," Jeanne was saying when he joined her and Annie. "And the flowers you painted are wonderful, Annie. I had no idea you were so talented!"

Annie blushed. "Grandma said to do whatever I liked, and I've been having the best time, Aunt Jeanne. She'll sit in here, and we'll visit while I paint. She says she enjoys watching me."

"I don't doubt it," Jeanne said. "I'd like to watch. I'd love it if you'd do some of this in my house. I'd even pay you."

"Oh, I wouldn't ask you to pay me."

"Nonsense. You're a working artist, aren't you? You have to eat." She glanced out the window at the children playing. "You've been working in the garden, too, I see. Everything was so overgrown the last time I was here."

"Corban's been a big help." Annie grinned at him. "And Susan and Sam and some of the neighbor children. We've had plenty of helping hands."

"It used to be so beautiful." Jeanne sighed. "The first time I came here, the lilacs were in bloom. It smelled like heaven standing out there. I'm glad you're bringing it back."

The doorbell rang again. Corban turned in the doorway, but George was already on his feet. Seeing who had arrived, Corban steeled himself for a long, miserable day. The Ice Queen, consort in tow. Corban met Eleanor Gaines's cool look with a slight nod while her husband, Fred, greeted Leota with a kiss and compliment. The regal Eleanor barely said hello to her mother before she sailed toward the kitchen. He stepped back out of her way so she wouldn't ram him.

"Is everything going all right in here, Anne-Lynn? The turkey smells done." She nodded toward her sister-in-law. "Jeanne. Nice to see you."

Not much warmth between the sisters-in law, Corban thought, playing a fly on the wall.

"Everything's fine, Mother. I just checked the turkey a few minutes ago," Annie said, coming to her mother, who turned her face so Annie could kiss her cheek. Annie drew back slightly, eyes flickering. "I'm glad you were able to make it, Mom."

"I don't see any yams. Didn't you make yams?"

"Arba is bringing them."

"Who's Arba?"

"Grandma's next-door neighbor. She and the children will be over in a little while."

Clearly, that was an announcement that didn't please Annie's mother.

"I think I'd better check on my children." Jeanne headed for the back door. Corban was trapped between the living room and the kitchen.

"I thought this was to be a *family* gathering."

Annie blushed, her eyes flickering to him. He decided to rescue himself.

"Leota took pity on a poor, starving, college student," he said ruefully.

"Oh, of course, I didn't mean you," Eleanor said.

Liar. He looked her straight in the eye. "That's okay, Mrs. Gaines. I understand what you meant."

Annie gave him a pained look.

Eleanor turned her back on him. "Anne-Lynn, I really think you should take another look at that turkey . . ."

Corban thought about excusing himself and going into the bathroom. Maybe he could squeeze through the window and escape.

Somehow, Annie managed to get her mother back into the living room and sitting down. The television was blaring and those talking had to raise their voices. Adding to the confusion, Arba arrived, bearing gifts of candied yams and a sweet-potato pie. "The children are coming through the back gate, Leota. I think they already met your grandchildren over the fence."

"The back gate?" Eleanor's perfectly shaped eyebrows arched. "For heaven's sake, George, turn the television down." When he did, Eleanor looked at her mother. "What gate?"

"The one that's been there for years," Leota said. "Sam fixed the hinges a couple of weekends ago when he came over to see Annie."

"Sam?" Eleanor's lips tightened.

"Sam Carter. He's a very nice young man," Leota said.

"He's an ex-con, Mother." She rose, heading for the kitchen again.

"Oh, dear," Leota said softly. "Now, I've done it."

Corban could hear Eleanor's voice from the kitchen, not that she was speaking loudly. Everyone seemed to be holding their breath. "I didn't know you were seeing Sam Carter," Eleanor was saying, "though I don't know why I should be surprised by anything you do these days."

"I'm not seeing him in the way you mean, Mother." Annie's tone was calm and patient. "He's just a friend."

"Oh, of course. That's the vernacular for sordid relationships these days, isn't it?"

Fred rose, his face pale and tight. "Excuse me." He headed for the kitchen. He spoke softly, but the regal Eleanor was having none of it.

"This is between me and my daughter, Fred. Please stay out of it."

"Mother, please . . ."

"I knew this day would be a fiasco from the start. I just *knew* it! Didn't I tell you?"

"Shut up, Nora."

"*What* did you say to me?"

"You heard me, and so did everyone in the house. If the day turns into a disaster, it'll be *your* fault. Now, come back and sit down!"

Corban looked at Leota and saw tears welling in her eyes. In a moment they would be spilling down her cheeks. He glanced at Arba and saw mixed pity and anger. George's jaw was set, his eyes glued to the television set. Jeanne sat there, forcing a smile. The voices in the kitchen dropped lower, but they were just as angry, just as intense, just as intrusive. Corban rose. "I think I'll go outside and have a breath of fresh air." They wouldn't miss him if he snuck away.

"Don't even think about it," Leota said, keen eyed.

"What?"

"You know exactly what, Corban Solsek. You're staying."

George looked between them, frowning. When Corban looked back at him, a muscle jerked in George's jawline and he looked at the television again. "Let him leave if he wants to, Mother."

That was all it took to make up Corban's mind. "I'm not going far, Leota. Only as far as the front porch."

"Promise?"

"I promise."

He didn't come back inside until dinner was announced. The turkey was cooked to perfection, not that Eleanor Gaines could admit it. She sat at the dining-room table, back rigid, face pale, lips tight, eyes down while Jeanne, Arba, Annie, and Leota talked.

"Let's have the blessing, shall we?" Leota said, having been seated in the place of honor at the head of the table. Annie's eyes were shining again, and she held out her hands—one to her grandmother, one to her mother. Everyone joined hands, some less eagerly than others. Corban felt uncomfortable and embarrassed, but that didn't stop Arba from grasping his hand and giving him an encouraging smile.

"This is a day of Your making, Lord, for my family is under one roof again after so many years. Thank You, Jesus." Leota's voice was husky. She hesitated, then spoke again. "Open our minds, Father, and open our hearts as well. Come, join us at the table. In the name of Your precious Son, Jesus, we pray. Amen."

Platters of food were passed.

"There are no chestnuts in the stuffing." Eleanor glanced at Annie after a taste. "Did you put oysters in it?"

"Not this time."

"This is the best stuffing I've ever tasted," Jeanne said with enthusiasm. "Everything is wonderful, Annie."

Eleanor glanced at Jeanne, her mouth tight, and went back to eating in silence. The tension kept everyone cautious.

The children were laughing in the kitchen. "What're they doing in there?" Eleanor was clearly annoyed.

"Having fun," Fred said tersely.

Corban thought about his own family. He could remember the tension on Thanksgiving Day, his mother slaving away in the kitchen while his father worked in the den. Thanksgiving had been nothing more than a day when vendors and customers didn't call the office. It gave his father a day of rest from the telephone, but not from his obsession. Even when he had made it big, he couldn't rest in his success. He was driven by the memory of a childhood of deprivation, driven to overcome the stigma of having grown up on the "wrong side of the tracks," driven by his own feelings of inadequacy.

Corban's parents had lived in a big house in an exclusive neighborhood with a guard at the gates, but that hadn't changed his father. The man had always been driven before a strong wind. Then one day he was gone, blown away by a massive heart attack.

He died at his desk. His mother grieved for a few years, then remarried. She was making new traditions now. Thanksgiving in Paris. Christmas in Geneva.

Someone else always cooked.

A cold thought suddenly went through his mind, unbidden, making his chest tighten. *Am I like my father? Driven to prove myself? For what? And for whom? What am I doing? Where am I going?*

"Good dinner, Annie," George said, rising. He left his plate on the table and didn't bother pushing in his chair.

"George," Jeanne said, clearly annoyed.

"I'm just going to check the score." He turned the television on and made himself comfortable on the sofa.

"Where's a blackout when you need one?" Jeanne's mouth was tight.

"We had blackouts all the time back during the war years," Leota said. "The siren would go off and we'd pull down all the shades and turn out the lights. Frightened the children half to death sometimes. Melba was our block captain. She lived two doors down. She'd go out and walk up and down the street and make sure there were no lights on. Your grandmother—"

"No one ever bombed us," Eleanor said impatiently.

"Not if you don't count Pearl Harbor, dear."

Eleanor's face reddened. "Pearl Harbor is an ocean away, Mother. And the war's been over for decades."

Corban wanted to lean over the table and slap her. Where did she get off talking to Leota in that nasty tone? Gritting his teeth, he reminded himself he wasn't part of this family, and it wasn't his business.

Annie glanced at her grandmother. "I'd like to hear about the war years."

"Why?" Eleanor said sharply. "We were dirt-poor. Mother was never home. And Grandma and Grandpa Reinhardt were always bickering."

"They were?" Leota frowned.

"Usually over you. And money. Or rather the lack of it. We were a strain on their budget, in case it never occurred to you. Three extra mouths to feed. Grandma Helene was *not* pleased to be left with the responsibility of two children, and she made no secret of it to either of us."

"Mother!" Annie's face was white.

"Let it go," Leota said, putting a hand over Annie's. Leota didn't say much about anything after that. She sat quietly, picking at her Thanksgiving dinner while Annie and Jeanne tried to move the conversation through safer channels. No matter where they went, though, they found themselves in a minefield of Eleanor's making. As soon as Eleanor finished eating, she began stacking dishes. The clattering of porcelain and silverware seemed to announce the meal was over, whether they were finished or not. "I'll clean up," Eleanor said and pushed her chair back.

Annie's eyes welled with tears.

"I'll help you," Arba said, starting to rise.

"No, thank you. I'll take care of it myself."

Arba hovered halfway out of her seat until Leota smiled at her. "Stay put, dear. It's nothing personal. Eleanor just likes to do things her way."

Fred looked down the table. "I'm sorry, Leota. Annie . . ."

"It's not your fault, Fred," Annie said quietly and bowed her head.

As soon as the football game was over, George stood and announced it was time for his family to leave. Although Mitzi and Marshall protested, one look from their father silenced them. Eleanor, the grand martyr, had just come from the kitchen.

"What about dessert, George?" Jeanne's eyes flashed anger. "We haven't served the pies yet."

"Fine. We'll have pie and then leave."

"We'd better be going, too, Fred." Eleanor didn't even bother to take a seat. "I'm exhausted."

An embarrassed silence fell. Arba rose from the stuffed chair near the corridor. "Why don't you sit and rest a bit, Mrs. Gaines? Take the weight off your feet."

Annie stood ready to serve. "What will you have? Apple, mincemeat, pumpkin, or sweet potato?"

"Sweet potato!" Arba's children said in unison.

"Apple! Pumpkin!" Mitzi and Marshall joined in exuberantly.

Eleanor grimaced. "Must they shout like that?"

"How about a little slice of each?" Leota said.

"There you go, girl." Arba grinned.

Eleanor rolled her eyes. "None for me, Anne-Lynn. I'm too tired to be hungry. When everyone's done, I'll wash the plates."

"Apple," George said, stone-faced. Maybe his team wasn't winning.

"Corban, what will you have?" Annie said.

"If it's okay with you, I'll wait until later." With luck, the Ice Queen would leave and his appetite would return. Nothing like a contentious woman to sour a man's stomach.

When Annie went into the kitchen to serve the pies, she saw the roasting pan sitting on the nook table. It was scrubbed so clean it looked sandblasted. Annie opened the refrigerator for a look. What had her mother done with the turkey and leftovers? Heart sinking, she opened the cabinet beneath the sink. Sure enough, her mother had stuffed the meaty carcass into the garbage can, along with the candied yams, mashed potatoes, and peas. So much for turkey sandwiches, turkey casseroles, and turkey soup.

Arba, who had come out to help cut and serve pie, stood behind her. Annie swallowed hard and quietly closed the cabinet door, fighting the hurt and humiliation that wanted to overwhelm her. Her eyes burned hot with tears. "I'm so sorry, Arba." How could her mother scrape everything into the trash like that?

"What're you sorry about, girl? This isn't your doing." She stood, hands on her hips, and looked around. "Well, at least the kitchen's clean."

Annie gave a soft, broken laugh. "Oh . . ." She covered her face. How would Grandma feel when she found out?

Arba put her arm around her. "Honey, that was the best Thanksgiving dinner I've had since my mama went home to the Lord. Don't let anyone take your joy away, not even your mother!"

Still trembling slightly, Annie nodded. "Thanks, Arba."

"I'll make the coffee," Arba said.

Annie cut the pies in silence. When all the plates had the slices requested, she carried them into the living room two by two and delivered them. She wouldn't look her mother in the face. The hurt had given way to anger. She prayed her mother would keep silent until she left.

"Coffee would be nice," her mother said.

"Arba is making it."

"I'll help her." She started to rise from the sofa.

"No, you will not. You've done enough already, Mother."

"You needn't be so rude, Anne-Lynn. All I did was wash the dishes."

Annie looked at her then. She lowered her voice. "That's *not* all you did, Mother. You did a lot more than that."

Her mother blushed, her gaze skittering away. Fred looked up at Annie, his expression troubled and questioning. "Your pie." She forced a smile and handed him a plate with sweet-potato pie. Her mother kept her head down.

As Annie left the room, she imagined what was going on in her mother's mind. She was probably mulling over the words, chewing on them, ruminating until she could find some way to spit them back in her own defense. Annie refused to feel guilty this time. Whatever her mother decided to say, she was not going to allow the words to pierce her heart and spoil this day.

Corban came into the kitchen. "I'm on my way out. Thanks for dinner, Annie. It was great."

"Are you sure you can't stay longer?" She knew her grandmother enjoyed sparring with him, and she had the feeling the others would soon be on their way.

"I have to study."

She looked at him. "I know this isn't the time, Corban, but I'd like to know what's troubling you."

"No, you wouldn't." His eyes were dark with anger.

"I wouldn't say it if I didn't mean it. Friends help one another."

He smiled slightly. "So I might give you a call sometime."

"I'll be here all weekend. You know you're always welcome."

He gave a nod and left without another word.

Arba served coffee while Annie gathered empty dessert plates. She could feel her mother's gaze following her, willing her to look in her direction. She went back into the kitchen, stacking the dishes carefully in the sink. Time enough to wash them later after everyone left.

"We'd better be on our way," Arba said, gathering her children. She leaned down and kissed Leota's cheek, whispering something in her ear. Leota smiled and patted Arba's cheek tenderly. "You're a sweet girl," she said, then sat obviously pleased as she received kisses from Tunisha and Kenya and a handshake from Nile. "I'll see you at three on Monday," Leota said.

George took Arba's departure as a sign for his own. He went for the coats Annie had hung in the guest room. Marshall and Mitzi thanked Grandma Leota for the nice day, though they were too shy to kiss her good-bye. Leota made an effort to rise from her chair when George came back into the room.

"Don't get up, Mother. We'll show ourselves out. Thank you for the fine day." He grazed her cheek with a quick kiss and put his hand at Jeanne's elbow, nodding toward the door.

"You don't mind if I say good-bye to your mother, do you?" Jeanne stepped around him and leaned down, smiling. "This is the best Thanksgiving we've had in years, Mama. I hope we do it again."

Annie's eyes smarted with tears as she heard her grandmother's mumbled reply. "I've prayed for years to have the family together again."

"Me too," Jeanne said in a husky voice. When she straightened, her eyes were moist. She came around Leota's chair to Annie and hugged her tightly, whispering in her ear. "Good job, honey. And don't give up the ship." She patted her cheek and then joined George as their family went out the front door.

Annie looked at her mother then. She met her gaze and remained on her feet, waiting.

"I guess it's time we left, too." Her mother stood, chin high. "Fred?"

He stood and came to Annie, hugging her tightly. "I don't know what your mother did to hurt you, Annie," he whispered, "but I'm sorry about it."

"I'll get over it."

"I know." He kissed her cheek.

Her mother had gone for the coats. She came back into the room and held Fred's out to him. He shrugged into it and took hers, opening it and holding it for her so she could slip her arms into the sleeves and draw it on. Annie stood next to Grandma Leota's chair, her arm resting on top of it. Her mother gave her a hard-eyed look of displeasure. Then she looked at Grandma Leota. "Thank you for the nice day, Mother," she said coolly. "Anne-Lynn, I'll call and speak with you later."

"Give me a day or two, please."

Her mother's eyes flashed, and then she went out the door, Fred following at a slower pace.

"What was that all about?" Grandma Leota said when the front door was closed and they were alone.

"Nothing for you to worry about, Grandma." She hoped her mother would give her time enough to pray and let go of the anger and hurt. If she didn't, they would both regret it.

Her grandmother sighed. "The house is so quiet now. I'm glad you're still here."

Annie knelt down beside the chair. "We're going to have the whole weekend together. Remember? I'm not leaving until Monday morning."

"We can have leftovers for the next few days."

"I'm afraid not, Grandma. They're all gone." She had quietly taken the garbage out back so that her grandmother wouldn't see what her mother had done. "Except some mincemeat pie."

Grandma Leota smiled and leaned closer. "Thank you, dear. Thank you for all you did today. It was as close to a perfect day as I've had in years."

Annie almost wept. "We did get them all under one roof again, didn't we, Grandma?" All except for Michael.

"Yes, we did. And no one killed any of the others." Grandma Leota's eyes sparkled with mischief. "Though there were a few moments . . ."

Annie gave a soft, broken laugh. "I love you, Grandma."

"I love you, Grandma." Barnaby said from the front bedroom. "I love you, Grandma."

"Oh, dear," Grandma said in disgust. "That bird is at it again."

Annie laughed, all the tension of preparing and surviving Thanksgiving burst like a dam. Tears ran down her cheeks.

"I love you, Grandma!" Barnaby was demanding attention. It was as though he was saying, "Hello in there. Don't forget about me!"

"I'll get him, Grandma," Annie said. "As soon as his cage is draped, he'll quiet down."

Grandma Leota tipped her recliner back. "If not, just put the vacuum cleaner in the middle of the room. It shut him up the last time!"

"Well, I'm glad that's over," Nora said as they drove down the street. She expected Fred to say something to that, but he didn't. He drove in silence, mouth set, eyes straight ahead. Annoyed, she turned on the radio. When she heard his sixties music, she punched the seek button and let it sift through stations until it came to one with classical music. She stopped it there, hoping Beethoven or whoever it was would soothe her frayed nerves.

"What'd you do, Nora?"

Her heart gave a flip. "What do you mean, what did I do?"

"In the kitchen."

"I washed dishes all by myself."

"Arba offered to help."

"I was hoping for a little time alone with my daughter."

"Hogwash." He looked at her then, one brief, hard look that made her feel suddenly vulnerable. Exposed.

Guilt assaulted her. Resenting it, she crossed her arms and looked out the window.

"Out with it, Nora. What did you do?"

"I threw away the leftovers." Shame filled her, but only for an instant before her instincts for self-defense took over. "That's *all* I did. No one likes to have leftovers for days after Thanksgiving."

"That depends on who did the cooking!"

Her head snapped around as she glared at him. "Meaning what? Annie's a better cook than I am?"

"You've fixed me many wonderful meals over the years, Nora, but until today, I didn't know how moist and delicious turkey could be." Then he looked at her again. "Admit it. You were jealous."

"I was not."

"No? What other excuse could there be for your rotten behavior?"

She could feel her cheeks filling with heat. When she looked at him again, she saw the hard glint in his eyes before he stared at the road again.

"I wonder if you'll ever change, Nora." He turned off at their exit. "If you don't, you're going to end up a bitter old woman."

"Like my mother?"

He slowed the car and stopped at the light. "She's lonely, maybe, though I expect Annie, Corban, Arba, and the children fill in the gaps you and George have left. But you know something, Nora? I didn't see one hint of bitterness in your mother, not like I see in you. I find that amazing, considering the way she's been treated by her own children."

The light changed to green. Fred applied the gas calmly and turned onto a busy boulevard.

"I have reason to be bitter," Nora said quietly, blinking back tears. "You just don't understand. You don't know what it was like."

"Then why don't you tell me?"

"She moved us in with Grandma Helene and Grandpa and went to work. She'd leave early in the morning and not come home until late afternoon. After a while, I felt as though I didn't even have a mother!"

"What about Grandma Helene?"

She closed her eyes. "We were a burden to her. I don't know how many times I heard her say she was too old to have the responsibility of two small children. And it was true. It wasn't fair to her. She'd get terrible headaches and lie on the couch with a cold

779

cloth on her forehead. And she'd say she was sure she was going to die. I lived in fear she would and it would be our fault."

"What about your grandfather?"

"He was away all day at work. He'd read the newspaper and then write letters at the dining-room table. He and Grandma would talk to one another in German. I learned to understand after a while and knew she was always complaining about my mother. Grandpa would listen to her for a while and then go out for a walk. Sometimes he would take George and me. He was shy, I guess. He never said much of anything." The only thing Nora could remember him saying was, *"Your mama is a good woman."* He would say that time and again. She'd never been able to understand how he could feel that way toward a woman who could dump her children and go off to live her own life as she pleased.

Fred took the garage remote and pressed it. She fell silent, feeling overwhelmed by sadness. As soon as he parked the car and turned off the ignition, he turned to her. "Keep talking."

She took a shaky breath. "My grandmother loathed my mother. She would tell us how my mother went to dances and movies while she had to take care of us. She would tell us how my mother kept all her money for herself and never even pitched in to pay for the food we ate. I don't remember Grandma Helene ever saying a nice thing about my mother when she was away working. And when Mother was home, Grandma Helene would criticize her to her face, and my mother would just stand and take it. Or go out in her garden. I used to hate her for that. I used to wish my mother would fight back and fight for us, and then when she did . . ."

Fred took her hand and squeezed it gently. "Go on."

"I woke up one night and heard them screaming at one another. Grandma Helene in German, and Mother, hysterical and crying and raging. Then I heard Grandpa crying. And Grandma Helene, too. I hated them both for hurting Grandpa. He was such a gentle man, and I could hear him sobbing and speaking in this. . . . this *broken* voice. I didn't understand anything he said, but I knew how much they'd hurt him and I . . . I couldn't forgive them for it."

"What about your father?"

"It was worse when he came home. I was so afraid of him. Mother stayed home with us for a little while and then went right back to work again. It was as though we weren't enough for her. My father would sit in his chair and drink."

"Didn't he have a job?"

"Oh, he worked. He had his own business for a while, but nothing ever lasted. I remember his coming home in a rage once after he'd been fired. George and I hid under our bed while he broke things in the living room. It was Grandpa who talked to us about it all later. He told us the war had changed my father. He said my father had been a master carpenter before he went away to fight for his country, but I only saw him finish two things: the apartment he built behind the garage for Grandma and Grandpa and the cases of beer he'd down day after day."

She looked at Fred, wanting him to understand, to empathize. "Can you imagine how Grandma Helene must have felt, giving up her house to my mother? Grandma Helene seldom set foot in the house after that, not unless my father gave her a personal invitation. I hated Thanksgiving, Grandma sitting there and never saying a word to anyone. She'd eat in silence and keep her eyes on the plate, and my mother would pretend to be so happy." She'd taken one bite of her mother's dressing recipe today, and the memories came flooding back. She hadn't meant to hurt Anne-Lynn's feelings when she stuffed that turkey into the garbage. All she'd wanted to do was throw the past—and all the pain that went with it—away. She could still see Anne-Lynn's face when she'd come out of the kitchen: white, pinched, hurt, angry.

"Didn't your mother take care of your grandmother until she died?"

Nora nodded. She swallowed hard. "I've wondered about that over the years. I don't know how they could stand to live together, feeling about one another the way they did. It must've been hell on earth." She put her head back against the seat and closed her eyes. "I suppose Mother felt guilty for stealing my grandparents' home. Taking care of Grandma would have been penance."

"What were they like together when you went to visit them?"

"Visit?" She gave a brittle laugh. "Are you kidding? Why would I go back when I couldn't wait to get out of that house and away from all of them? I married Bryan Taggart just to get out." She gave another brittle laugh. "Not that he made my life any better. The only good thing that came out of that marriage was Michael." She pressed her lips together and turned her face away so Fred wouldn't see the tears of hurt welling. Had her son even bothered to call home today? She covered her mouth with her hand, her shoulders shaking.

Fred's thumb caressed the back of her hand. "You've got to let it go, Nora. You can't change the past. You've got to let it go and move on."

"It's not that easy. I've tried."

Fred sighed heavily. "You still miss her, don't you? Even after all this time. You withhold your love because you feel it's been withheld from you. And you've never been able to kill it completely, have you, Nora? That's why you haven't been able to forgive her."

She took her hand from his and rummaged in her purse for a Kleenex. He made it sound as though her daughter had been gone for years instead of months. "I could forgive Anne-Lynn if she came home where she belonged."

He took the keys from the ignition. "I wasn't talking about Annie, Nora. I meant your mother." Opening his door, he got out and left her alone in the car.

19

Annie left early Monday morning, but not before Leota was able to take care of business. Leota felt relieved and faintly smug that she had managed to get Annie's signatures on several documents without her granddaughter being the least bit suspicious. One set was for the bank, the other for Charles Rooks, who had prepared everything as swiftly as though she were about to die.

Her greatest worry had been how she would convince Annie to sign everything prepared for her. If Annie realized what she was doing, she might protest. However, all the worrying had been wasted. All Leota had needed to do was tell Annie the truth: She wanted to be sure there was someone who could step in to help if the need arose. With Eleanor still angry and George so distant, it made perfect sense to have Annie as her executor and give her power of attorney.

That was all Annie had needed to hear. She signed on the dotted line. She didn't even read anything. She obeyed Leota's wishes. It wouldn't have mattered to the girl if she was signing her life away. Of course, she had no idea what all she had signed. Leota had only told her half the truth, not all of it . . .

For the first time in months, Leota walked alone to do her errands. She registered and posted the envelope to Charles Rooks. He would keep everything secure in his office files and safe, as they'd agreed. She sat on a bench to rest for a few minutes, then went into the grocery store to buy a roasted chicken, ready-made salad with dressing in the package, and two eclairs. Why not celebrate? Everything was settled.

Exhausted when she got home, she fed Barnaby and sat down to rest. She settled into her chair, her eyes drifting shut. *Thank You, Jesus, for my precious granddaughter. She has been better to me than ten daughters and sons. Please watch over her and protect her in the days ahead, for they will be rocky. Give her wisdom when she makes her decision. I don't even know what to pray for Eleanor and George anymore, Lord. Am I wrong to wish?*

With a sigh, she drifted to sleep.

Arba's children came after school. Leota served them peanut butter and jelly sandwiches. They'd been hoping for turkey, but she said it was all gone. She read two chapters from *The Secret Garden*. They wanted more, but she said it was time to buckle down to homework. Arba arrived at five and asked Leota to dinner. "I bought a pizza on the way home." Much to the children's noisy delight.

"Not this evening, dear, but thank you."

Arba studied her. "Are you all right, Leota?"

"I'm fine, just worn out after all the festivities." And she was, bone tired, weaker than usual.

"I'll check on you later."

"If you do, you'll likely wake me up and I won't thank you for it."

Arba had long since gotten used to Leota's brisk manner and grinned. "Yes, ma'am."

"There's nothing wrong with me that a good, long rest won't cure."

"The children won't be coming over tomorrow, Leota. I'm picking them up early and taking them in for dental checkups." There was an immediate protest at her announcement.

"We're right in a good part of the story!"

"Ah, Mama."

"I don't need to go to the dentist."

Arba hushed them again. "Thank Grandma Leota and head for home." They said their sad good-byes and filed out of Leota's house, following Arba like little ducklings. Leota chuckled and closed the door. No doubt they'd feel better when Arba opened that box of pizza.

Annie called half an hour later.

Leota frowned. "Did Arba call you?"

"She said you were looking tired."

"I am tired. And since I answered the telephone, you know I'm not sick or dead."

"I've been thinking . . ."

Leota could imagine. With Annie's soft heart, she was probably worrying about those papers she'd signed and what they might mean. The poor dear probably thought her grandmother had covered all the bases and now intended to zing off like a fly ball, right over the center fielder's head and out of the park. Home run, straight into the Lord's arms. Well, not a chance. Not now. Not when she had a faint glimmer of hope. Thanksgiving had given her that.

"Sometimes thinking too much can get you into trouble, honey. What you did will help me sleep nights, Annie. Now, don't feel you have to call me every single day. Spend more time painting something wonderful and stop worrying about this old hag."

For all she said to Annie, she couldn't sleep. Tired as she was, her mind was whirring. There was a constant buzzing in her ears, like a hive of busy bees. She finally gave up and got out of bed. She still needed to write letters to Eleanor and George, explaining why she had done things as she had.

She sat at the nook table, wrapped snugly in her bathrobe. Her feet were cold, despite her slippers. She didn't want to turn the heat up yet. She never turned it up until seven in the morning. It was barely three.

The note to Annie was easy . . . precious Annie, open and free of all resentment, a breath of fresh air in this house of stale memories. George's letter was a little harder. He reminded her so much of Bernard, holding all his troubles inside. What could it be? Business? Thank God he anesthetized himself with television sports rather than alcohol. Or was that any better? She hoped Jeanne would break through to him before his children were grown and gone.

Eleanor was another matter. Leota drafted three letters and discarded them all. Every time she tried to think of ways to explain herself to Eleanor, she felt deeper despair. No amount of explaining would get through to someone who had already made up her mind, and Eleanor's was set in stone. Finally, Leota wrote simply what was in her heart. The only thing she could do was state the truth. Simple, brief, heartfelt. Let Eleanor do with it as she would.

Folding the letter, she tucked it in an envelope. Then she put the letters where she hoped they would one day be found.

She felt strange. She sat on the edge of her bed, troubled. The buzzing in her ears had grown worse. She felt an odd sensation . . . then a *ping* in her head, one small stab of pain, and finally a strange warmth—like someone's hand cupping her ear. Her right arm was numb. When she stood to go into the bathroom, she had no feeling or strength in her right leg. There was just dead weight, pulling her down, down, down . . .

She heard a thud, but could make no sense of it. How had she ended up on the cold, wood floor?

Corban noticed two newspapers on the porch when he came up the steps. The mailbox attached to the side of the house next to the front door was jammed full. Frowning, he rang the doorbell and waited. No response. Usually, Leota was watching television on Wednesday morning. He didn't hear a sound coming from inside the house. Frowning, he went around to the back. Sometimes she sat at the nook table and worked crossword puzzles while waiting for him.

The shade was down. It was never down during the day.

He uttered a curse and ran around to the front door again. "Leota!" He pounded on the door. Still no response, not a single sound. He dug in his pocket for his keys, jingling through them until he found the one she had given him. He jammed it in the lock and opened the door.

"Leota?" He stepped into the house for the first time uninvited, leaving the door slightly ajar behind him. The stench assaulted his senses, as if the toilet had overflowed. Breathing through his mouth, he called her name again. When he stepped into the corridor, he saw her lying crumpled beside her bed. She looked dead.

Sick at heart, he went down on one knee. He took her wrist. Her skin was paper thin and she was cold. Her eyes were open and seemed blank until he put his hand gently over them, intending to close them. She made a grunting sound, and his body jerked back in surprise.

"I'll get help," he said. He didn't want to leave her on the floor, but he was afraid to lift her and put her on the bed. What if she'd broken bones when she fell? Moving her could hurt her even more. Standing, he yanked the spread off the bed and covered her carefully. "Hang on, Leota. Don't you die on me!"

After making the call, Corban opened the front door and went back into the bedroom to sit on the floor beside Leota. "Just hang on." He held her hand and rubbed it. "Hang on." He kept saying it like a mantra. "Hang on. Hang on." While his mind was screaming *hurry, hurry!* It took ten minutes for the fire truck and paramedics to arrive, the longest ten minutes of Corban's life. He stood and moved back out of the way, feeling helpless while the EMTs worked. They were swift and efficient, but it was clear things didn't look too good.

"Too dehydrated to get a line in her," one said.

"Pulse reedy . . ."

"Let's get a move on!"

"Are you a relative?"

"A friend. I'll notify the family. Where will you take her?"

The technician gave him the name of the hospital.

"Wait a minute!" Corban stepped over before they wheeled Leota out the door. He was afraid they were wheeling her right out of his life for good. He took her hand, his own shaking. "Leota." Her gaze wandered to him, dazed, confused. He wondered if she could understand anything. "I'll call Annie, Leota. Then I'll come to the hospital." He squeezed her hand gently. "Hang on!"

Annie knew something was wrong the moment the classroom door opened and Susan came in. "Corban called. Your grandmother collapsed. They've taken her to the hospital in an ambulance."

Scrambling to put her art supplies away, Annie tried not to cry. "Is she going to be all right?"

"I don't know, Annie."

Everyone was staring, some with sympathy, others annoyed at the interruption. The instructor came over. "Go ahead, Miss Gardner. I'll gather up your things and leave them at the office for you."

"Which hospital?" Annie said, racing down the hallway with Susan. She started to cry. "Oh, Suzie. I *knew* something was wrong when Arba called me Monday night. I should've gone back then."

"Your grandmother told you herself she was fine."

"I shouldn't have believed her. I should've gone to check on her. I should've called her last night."

"Annie, you can't be everywhere at once. Besides, no one ever knows when their time comes." She grimaced. "Sorry." They went out the doors into the misting afternoon air. The sky was overcast with a heavy chance of rain.

"I'd better drive," Susan said when they reached the parking lot. "You're in no condition to get behind the wheel."

"You're on the schedule to work."

"Let them fire me!"

Annie took a deep breath, forcing herself to calm down. *Lord, You're in control. I know You're in control. No matter what happens, I know my grandmother's life is in Your hands.* "I'll be okay, Suzie. I knew this would happen someday." *Oh, God, not so soon. I've only had a little time with her. I want more!*

"Give me your hands." Susan planted herself in front of the car door and held hers out, a determined glint in her eyes. "I'm not letting you go until you stop shaking." Annie did as she asked. Susan held her hands lightly for a moment. "Okay." She kissed Annie's cheek. "Just go slowly, would you? It won't do any good if you have a wreck getting to the hospital."

"I'll be careful. I promise." She opened the car door and slid in.

"Safety belt." Susan was holding onto the door and watching her.

"Yes, mother," she said dryly. "Oh! Did you call my mother?"

"I'll call her as soon as I get to work. That'll give you enough time to get to the hospital before she does."

If she does. Annie couldn't help the thought. Would her mother even bother to come?

Oh, God, if Mother doesn't come now, I'll go and drag her by the hair to the hospital!

Fighting back tears, Annie started the car and backed out of the space. Aware of Susan's watchful gaze, she shifted carefully and drove slowly from the lot. As soon as the traffic cleared, she pulled out and was on her way.

Hang on, Grandma. Oh, Lord, don't take her yet. Please, don't take her!

When he arrived at the hospital, Corban couldn't get much information on Leota's condition. The first question was always "Are you a member of the family?" As soon as he said he was just a friend, they refused to tell him anything. Even when he said he was the one who had found her and called 911, they were hesitant to reveal anything.

Frustrated and worried, he decided to sit it out in the waiting room. When Annie arrived, she would tell him what was going on and how Leota was doing. He wasn't going home until he knew.

She arrived, racing down the corridor, her face ashen. "My grandmother was brought in. Leota Reinhardt. Where is she please?" When he touched her arm, she turned. "Oh, Corban!" She flung herself into his arms. "Thank God you found her!" The nurse gave him an apologetic look and told Annie her grandmother was still undergoing tests. She would notify the doctor that Mrs. Reinhardt's granddaughter had arrived.

They sat in the waiting room together, but Annie couldn't sit still for very long. She paced, sat, got up and looked out the window, paced some more, sat. Corban saw Eleanor and Fred before Annie did. Eleanor Gaines looked pale and stressed, her eyes dark but not red-rimmed from crying, as Annie's were.

"Mother!" Annie said. Corban noticed she didn't fling herself into her mother's arms, but kept a safe distance from the cold front. "Thank God you've come."

"What's *he* doing here?"

At Annie's quick blush, Corban clenched his hands. How had a woman like Eleanor Gaines *ever* produce a daughter like Annie?

"Corban found Grandma. He's the one who called 911." Annie gave him a grateful smile. "He's been waiting to find out how Grandma Leota's doing."

"How is she doing?"

"Nice of you to ask," Corban said before he could stop himself.

"That's uncalled for," Fred said quietly, his hand firm beneath his wife's elbow.

"Sorry." Corban ran a hand back through his hair. He conceded he had spoken too quickly, but Eleanor Gaines's attitude made him boil.

Annie was crying again. She turned away from her mother and stepfather and sat down on the sofa, burying her face in her hands. Eleanor looked uncomfortable.

"Anne-Lynn." She approached hesitantly, her hand hovering over Annie's hair, then sat down slowly on the sofa beside her daughter. "This wasn't unexpected."

"It was to me," Annie said, hiccuping a sob.

"Get ahold of yourself, dear." Eleanor glanced quickly around at the others sitting in the waiting room. Her eyes grazed Corban's with dislike.

The feeling is mutual, lady.

She took a fancy handkerchief from her leather purse and offered it to Annie. "Your grandmother is very old. Things are bound to go wrong with her health. We all go sometime, dear."

Annie looked at her mother, drawing back slightly. "She's your *mother!* Don't you even care that you might lose her?"

Eleanor went white at Annie's words. She sat frozen when Annie jumped up and paced again.

"Of course, I care about her," Eleanor said belatedly, her eyes dark with some indefinable emotion.

Annie turned and stared at her. "Since when have you cared, Mother? Did you care about making Thanksgiving special for your mother? Not on your life. You only came to Thanksgiving dinner because you couldn't convince Uncle George to stay away, and I wouldn't come home!"

"Don't you *dare* speak to me like that!" Eleanor rose from the sofa.

"Why, Mother? Because it's the truth?" Tears ran down Annie's cheeks, and Corban had to fight off the strong urge to go to her and hold her close. "You did everything you could to ruin the day for Grandma and make everyone else miserable. You even threw the turkey away!"

Eleanor's face turned deep red. She glanced around, clearly aware that everyone in the waiting room had stopped watching Annie and was now looking at her. "Stop this tantrum right now, Anne-Lynn."

Corban's eyes widened. Mrs. Gaines's voice was actually trembling.

Annie's voice, on the other hand, was firm. "Why? Because you're embarrassed? You should be."

"You're making a fool of yourself."

"So *what?* Do you think I care if I look foolish? I'm just taking after my mother!"

"Annie . . . ," Fred said gently.

She turned on him. "Don't defend her! Maybe if someone had bothered to tell her the truth a long time ago, she wouldn't be so hard-hearted."

"How can you accuse me of that?" Eleanor was crying now. "After all I've sacrificed for you."

"You *sacrificed,* Mother. And you never let Michael and me forget it. You reminded us every step of the way. But what was it all about? All you ever cared about was making Michael and me into your little trophies. Look at what Eleanor accomplished! Not once did you ever make a sacrifice of *love.* Not the way Grandma Leota did for you and Uncle George."

"You don't know anything about the way it was!"

"*You're* the one who doesn't know, Mother! You never knew! You never *cared* to know!"

Face agonized, Eleanor grabbed her purse and tucked it beneath her arm. "I won't stay and listen to this!" She sailed from the room like the *Titanic*, full steam ahead, straight for the iceberg.

"That's right, Mother! Run away!" Annie called after her. "That's what you always do when things don't go your way, isn't it? Go ahead. Leave!" With that, she sat again, weeping.

"There are things you don't know, Annie."

At Fred's quiet comment, Annie's eyes flashed at him. "Don't you *dare* say a word against my grandmother, Fred. All you know about her is what my mother's told you." She clasped her hands tightly as though trying to hold in the violence of her emotions.

His face was filled with compassion. "I wasn't going to speak against Leota." He sat down beside Annie and put his hand over hers. "Your mother loves Leota more deeply than you can understand, honey. She's just afraid of showing it."

"Well, she better hurry up and learn how!"

Corban couldn't listen any longer. He needed to get out of the room and walk. Somewhere. Anywhere. All the emotions pouring out of Annie and Eleanor had his own in riot. He'd had to grit his teeth not to leap up and join in the fray, so instead he went down the corridor and stopped at the emergency counter. "Any word?"

"We'll let the family know as soon as we hear anything, Mr. Solsek."

"Thanks. Thanks a lot." He stalked away, banging the doors open and striding outside.

Eleanor Gaines was hunched against the wall, her coat drawn tightly around her, her face ravaged by tears. When she saw it was Corban, she turned her face away.

Mouth tight, he walked on.

Leota tried not to let fear reign, but that was difficult in an unfamiliar environment surrounded by strangers. Lights and sounds . . . a tunnel. What on earth were they doing to her? She faded in and out, dreaming peacefully of her garden for a while. Then someone would move her and she'd wake up, confused and annoyed at so rude an interruption. Finally, she roused from sleep, found light coming in a window, and saw Annie sitting in a chair beside her bed.

"Hi, Grandma." She leaned closer, smiling. "You're going to be all right."

"Where am I, dear? What's happened?"

Annie frowned. "I don't understand, Grandma." She looked frightened.

Well, no more than Leota was frightened, hearing the garbled sounds coming from her own mouth. What was wrong with her tongue? Frustrated, she tried again, but only confused words came out.

Leota started to cry.

Annie's blue eyes welled with tears as well. She stroked Leota's arm—at least Leota could see her doing it, but she couldn't feel a thing.

"Am I dying?"

Annie glanced up at someone out of Leota's range of vision. "Does she understand me?"

"There's no way to know," a woman said. "Just keep talking to her. She's responding. That's a good sign."

"Can I tell her what's going on?" Annie said in a quieter voice.

"It can't hurt. It might make her less restless."

Leota could hear the sound of wheels rattling softly.

"Corban found you, Grandma. He called the paramedics. You're in the hospital. You've had a slight stroke. Your right side is affected; that's why you can't move very much. And it affected your speech, I guess. Do you understand, Grandma?" She wiped the tears from her cheeks. "They've given you medication that will help. And you're on an IV drip. You were dehydrated, so they want to get your fluids up to normal again."

Leota listened, taking it all in. Though her body wasn't working, her mind grasped the situation. She didn't know whether to thank God she was alive or ask Him why. Why hadn't He let her go? What use was she now?

Lord, is this why You put it in my head to get everything sorted out when I did? This is a dirty trick. I am not *pleased. Not— one—bit.*

She must have dozed off, because when she opened her eyes again, Annie was gone. Time passed, though how much she didn't know for sure. People came and went. Once she opened her eyes to see Eleanor standing above her, pale and drawn. She looked every year of her age, which made Leota sad.

"Eleanor . . ." It didn't come out right, and her daughter looked even more distressed. "Eleanor . . ."

Mouth trembling, Eleanor looked away. "What do we do now, Mother? What do we do?"

Until that moment, Leota hadn't thought much about what lay ahead for her. She closed her eyes, afraid of what she might see in

Eleanor's when she looked at her again. The words *convalescent hospital* loomed in her mind, bringing with them all the dire possibilities. Fear swept through her like wildfire. *This is not the way I want it to end, Lord. Don't let them toss me in a care facility and forget I ever lived. What will happen to me now? Oh, God, I'm so afraid.* No one could understand her, not even Annie who loved her so. Did they all think she'd lost her mind?

She could hear people talking around her, over her, about her. The doctor and nurses discussed her condition together. The only one who thought to talk to her about it was Annie. And it wasn't good news.

The daily routine frustrated Leota. She was examined, turned, washed, exercised, fed, turned again and again and again. Once she cursed, mortified when that one word came out clear as a bell. She looked into the nurse's eyes in apology, wondering what the young woman thought of an old lady swearing.

The nurse smiled. "I know it's frustrating, Mrs. Reinhardt. It's slow going, but you're improving. Swearing is a good sign in this case."

Grand. In a week, I'll be cursing like a sailor.

"The doctor is pleased with your progress."

That makes one of us.

The nurse gently rolled Leota onto her side while she remade the bed beneath her. Finishing one side, she gently rolled Leota onto her other side to complete the task. *Clean sheets every day, just like Jackie O.* Though Leota doubted Jackie had soiled hers. The nurse changed the top sheet and replaced the blankets, snugging them down and tucking them beneath the mattress.

"There you go, Mrs. Reinhardt. Clean and neat as a whistle." Leota heard a clang as the nurse brought up the bars on one side of the bed, and then on the other.

Lord, is this what life comes down to at the end? I've been washed, diapered, and tucked into my crib like a baby. I'm even toothless again, my dentures in that glass on the side table. It's humiliating to be so helpless. And so useless.

The nurse pushed the curtain back so that Leota could be seen from the hallway by any passerby. *So much for privacy.* Leota tried not to let it bother her. She supposed it was easier for the nurses to check on her that way, see if she was still breathing.

There was no use wasting time. Determined to get better, Leota tried to practice speaking. She worked at it until the woman in the bed next to her buzzed the nurse. "Can you give that old lady something to make her sleep? She hasn't shut up all afternoon. She gives me the heebie-jeebies."

The nurse spoke softly, soothing the other patient who had had a gallbladder surgery. The poor woman was in pain and asking for more medication. "I'm sorry," the nurse told her, "I can't give you anything for another hour." The poor dear began to cry, and the nurse drew the curtain between the two beds. Leota felt as though a door had been slammed in her face.

Someone turned on the television. Probably hoping to distract the other patient and get her mind off her pain and troubles for a little while. Leota thought of Bernard, sitting in his chair, listening to radio programs, ball games, news, and later watching television. Milton Berle. *I Love Lucy.* Dinah Shore. "See the U.S.A., in your Chevrolet . . ."

After Bernard died, she turned off the television and left it unplugged for two years.

She thought of George on Thanksgiving Day. *"I just want to check the score . . ."* And Jeanne, eyes filled with hurt and frustration, saying, *"Where's a blackout when you need one?"*

Oh, Lord. Tears ran down into Leota's ears and hair.

Oh, Jesus, does nothing ever change in this world? Is it always like this? The sins of the father visited upon the sons? Where are the blessings You promised? She could feel the despair settling into her bones, bearing down on her spirit, crushing her.

What use am I to anyone now, Lord?

God, what purpose have You in this suffering?

"Suzie, I know I'll be letting you down, but I have to do this. I've thought about nothing else over the last few days, and I can't bear the thought of my grandmother going into one of those convalescent hospitals. And that's what the doctor is saying will have to happen. I want to take her home."

"You don't have to explain, Annie." Susan's eyes were compassionate as she listened, her hands clasped between her knees. "Don't worry about the rent. I can make it okay. There's a girl at the restaurant who's been looking for another place to live. She was just talking to me about it yesterday. Her roommates are partying all the time and she's not into drugs. She wants out. She'd move in tomorrow if she could."

Annie sat down, relieved. "Oh, good. Then you're not upset with me?"

"Sad, yes. Disappointed, sure. You're my best friend, and I'll miss you. But upset? No." She leaned back on the couch and crossed her legs, lotus fashion. "Have you thought this over really well, Annie? This isn't a small task you're thinking about taking on."

"I know. I'll have to take things as they come. I don't mind admitting I'm scared. I'm not sure I even know how to begin."

"My mother could help, you know. She's done a lot of practical nursing in homes."

Annie had forgotten all about Susan's mother going back to school when all the children were in junior high. Maryann Carter had gotten her degree in nursing two years before Susan had graduated from high school. She'd worked as a licensed practical nurse for years. Now she was a registered nurse. "I don't think Grandma has the money to pay a private nurse, Suzie. And I know I don't."

She shook her head. "I didn't mean that. Mom could tell you how to make sure the house is safe. She would give you some fast training and resources. She knows a lot about taking care of the elderly. She should. Remember, she's been taking care of Granny Addie for the past few years. Granny hasn't had a stroke, but she's had her share of health problems. Diabetes. Hypertension. Arthritis. She can't do a lot on her own anymore. She's lucky to be in a big family."

"And a loving one."

Annie served Susan's mother coffee in Leota's kitchen. Maryann Carter had agreed to meet her at Grandma's house as soon as Annie explained the situation.

"This is such a pretty kitchen," Maryann said, looking around. "Sunny yellow-and-white trim, and those lovely flowers."

"Grandma said I could do whatever I liked in the house. I had a lot of fun doing this."

"I wish you'd make my kitchen look like this." She laughed. "I might want to spend more time in it." She lifted the pretty porcelain teacup and took a sip of coffee. She grew pensive, gazing out at the garden for a long moment before she looked at Annie again. "Before we begin, set my mind at ease. Have you considered how this will change your life, Annie?"

Annie didn't answer right away. She knew Susan's mother wasn't looking for a quick, altruistic answer. She had thought about the changes she would have to make, the things she would have to give up . . . but she hadn't been able to stop thinking about what would happen to her grandmother if she didn't step in. "Yes, I have."

"You'll have to put your own goals on hold for an indefinite period of time. It could be a long time."

"I already have. I quit school yesterday." Her instructor had heard her out and said he was sorry to see her leave, but he understood. He also gave her some good news. Her painting had sold, and a check would be coming in the mail. She had almost wept when he told her. She had wondered how she could possibly move in with her grandmother without a job to carry her expenses. The last thing she wanted to do was be a financial burden. She knew her grandmother was living on social security and that it was barely enough to take care of her expenses without adding Annie's to them. Though the painting hadn't sold for a great deal of money, it was enough to pay her share of expenses for some time to come.

Susan's mother nodded. "I know you're committed to this. And I can tell you love your grandmother very much. But . . . do you know what you're getting into as far as your grandmother's physical care?"

"I think I do."

"Well, let's see if you do." Maryann pushed the cup and saucer aside and folded her hands on the table. "You'll need to exercise every joint and every muscle of your grandmother's body so that her limbs and muscles don't waste away or draw up and thicken. You'll need to have a routine so that you can do these range-of-motion exercises four times a day. Ulcers can form over bony areas where constant pressure breaks down tissue and blood flow slows. That means you'll need to turn your grandmother every two hours, day and night. She'll need good nutrition, which means you must plan menus and cook three meals a day, every day. Besides that, there's the very personal side of care. Hygiene is extremely important. Bathing, brushing her teeth, combing her hair, taking care of her fingernails and toenails, washing her after she urinates or has a bowel movement . . ."

Annie blushed.

Susan's mother smiled. "If you're going to take this task on, Annie, the first thing you're going to have to do is put aside your feelings of embarrassment about bodily functions. There's no room for modesty. You'll need to concentrate on making your grandmother feel less self-conscious and more comfortable about all these things. If you're embarrassed, she'll be embarrassed."

Annie nodded.

"Your grandmother will need a social life, but not so much of one that she's overstimulated. You're going to need to plan for time off."

"I can handle this. I know I can."

"No, you can't. You have to be realistic, Annie. I know you're young and strong, but you cannot do this all on your own. We're talking about twenty-four hours a day, seven days a week, thirty days a month for however long your grandmother lives. No human being can do that alone. You need a care plan. You need *help*."

"I've prayed about all this, Mrs. Carter."

"I think you're old enough now to call me Maryann, honey. And I know you've prayed about all this. So have I. So has Susan." She looked at her. "So has Sam."

Sam. Oh, dear.

"I don't have to tell you how my son feels about you, do I?" Maryann's eyes glistened. "Tom and I have always looked upon you as a daughter. We even prayed Sam would notice you someday, and now that he has . . ." She gave a slight shrug. "Well, Sam, like the rest of us, is going to have to learn to wait upon the Lord." She searched Annie's eyes.

Annie looked back at her. "I love Sam, but . . ."

"He's like a brother."

"Not exactly." Annie looked down at her coffee cup. A brother wouldn't make her pulse race the way Sam did. "I don't know how to explain it." Or if she should.

"Sam will be coming around, and he'll be trying to change your mind about all this."

"He can try, but it won't change anything. I've prayed about it. I've prayed long and hard."

Maryann nodded. "Prayer is a good start. Now we have to take action." She stood. "Let's go have a look at your grandmother's bedroom. We'll start there." She looked around as she went. "Good," she said, standing in the corridor. "There's room enough for a wheel-chair to get through these doorways." Standing in the bedroom, she looked around. "Do you think your grandmother would mind if you repainted this room?"

"I don't think so."

"Use warm, bright, contrasting colors. What you did in the kitch-en would be wonderful. You'll need to remove some of the furnish-ings. It's too crowded. And those pretty porcelain figurines will have to be moved. Too easy to knock over and break. Maybe you can pull these heavy curtains back during the day." She waved her hand as dust billowed out. "And have them cleaned."

Maryann looked at the ceiling. "We can have a pole put in beside the bed. Tom knows how to do that. Medicare will pay for it. The pole will be something your grandmother can hold on to when she's getting up. With help, of course."

And so it went. Annie spent the rest of the afternoon following Maryann around the house and taking copious notes on what needed to be changed, added, or taken away in the bedroom, bathroom, living room, dining room, and kitchen. By the time they finished, Annie felt overwhelmed by details. "I had no idea . . ."

"You can always change your mind, Annie."

"Oh, no, I don't want to do that. I just see what needs to be done now." She laughed. "I'm going to have to call in the cavalry." Susan. Arba. Corban. And Sam, too, if he'd be willing to pitch in time and labor. She felt feverish with excitement. One day at a time, one task at a time.

"Do you think your mother would help you?"

Annie shook her head.

Maryann took her hand and squeezed it. "I'm sorry, Annie."

Her eyes burned hot with tears. "I can't think about my mother right now or what she wants. Grandma Leota takes precedence. I can't stand the thought of seeing Grandma put away somewhere."

"There are some very good care facilities in the area."

"Maybe so, but it wouldn't be the same as Grandma being in her own home with someone who loves her taking care of her. I know you understand. You have Granny Addie."

Maryann nodded. "Even when you love someone, it's not always easy. Granny Addie can be a very trying old soul at times. Your mother . . . well, maybe . . ."

"My mother doesn't care about Grandma Leota. They've been estranged for years. Mother thinks I've taken sides, but I haven't. I just want more time with Grandma Leota. I want all the time I can get, and I don't think there's much time left."

Maryann's eyes filled as well. She cupped Annie's cheek. "Tom and I love you very much, Annie. We'll do whatever we can to help. All you have to do is ask."

Annie wished her mother felt the same way.

20

CORBAN HUFFED AND PUFFED AS HE MANNED ONE END OF LEOTA'S empty dresser. Sam Carter was on the other end. Annie had removed the drawers and put them in the living room on the sofa. He and Sam had managed to squeeze the piece of antique furniture out the doorway and down the short hall into the second bedroom. Annie and Susan were already taking Leota's bed apart so they could move that next.

It took the better part of the morning before they finally cleared the room of furniture and drapes, lined the floor with plastic, washed the walls, and filled in the nail holes where pictures had been hung. Annie and Susan began rolling the first coat of pink, satin-finish, waterbased enamel while Corban and Sam sat resting and refueling in the kitchen.

"How's your paper coming along?" Sam said, pouring a second mug of black coffee.

"It isn't."

Sam looked at him. "What's the problem?"

Corban shrugged. "Lost my momentum, I guess." He was keeping up in his other classes, but the project for Professor Webster was floundering. Every time he sat down to transfer his handwritten notes to his computer, Corban found himself staring at the blank screen. "Other things on my mind."

The murder of his first—and maybe only—child, for one thing. It consumed his thoughts.

The apartment was silent with Ruth gone, not that he minded that she had left. It was the guilt that kept him in turmoil. It didn't seem to matter that he had been against Ruth's having an abortion; he still felt he shared the blame for his child's death. There must've been something he could've done to stop her from going through with it. There must have been something he could've said to change her mind.

Had the baby been a son or a daughter?

Despair filled him.

Sam sat down at the table with him. "You look like something's eating you."

Corban tipped his mouth in a bitter smile. "A lot of things are eating at me."

"So long as Annie isn't one of them."

Corban raised his brows. "Are you two a couple?" Sam looked too worldly-wise for her.

"No, but I'm working on it. Just thought I'd lay my cards on the table."

"Then I'll lay mine out as well. I like Annie. I like her a lot. You might even say I'm attracted to her in more ways than just physical. Do you have a problem with that?"

Sam's expression was enigmatic. "One woman ought to be enough for any man."

"I agree."

"I heard you had a serious relationship going already."

"Not anymore."

Sam's eyes flickered, and he considered Corban for a long moment. Then he smiled slightly and raised his mug. "May the best man win."

Corban had no doubt the winner would be Sam Carter.

Annie knew all day something was bothering Corban, but there was no opportunity to sit and talk with him. There was too much to do and too little time to get it all done. When he said he was leaving late that afternoon, she followed him to the door, thanking him for all his help. He seemed so preoccupied, so depressed. She was deeply concerned about him. "Are you all right, Corban?"

"I'll survive." He gave her a self-deprecating smile. "Can I talk with you for a minute?" He glanced at Sam standing in the kitchen doorway, watching them. "Outside."

She followed him out, closing the front door behind her, and stood on the front porch waiting for him to say whatever it was he needed to get out.

He ran his hand around the back of his neck. "I don't know how to ask this without sounding like a complete jerk."

"Just ask, Corban." She was fairly sure she knew already.

"I'd like to follow this through, Annie. I'd like to know how everything turns out."

"For your report?"

His mouth flattened out. "Partly."

She saw the moisture in his eyes. "It's all right, Corban. You can admit you care about Grandma Leota. I won't think less of you because you let yourself become personally involved with your test study." She smiled.

He nodded, saying nothing for a moment. "I hope she makes it back, Annie." His voice was rough. "I really do. I hope she has a lot of years left . . ."

"She will. She's not a quitter."

"The big guns are going to be against you, and you're only eighteen."

Her heart warmed toward him because he was tender. He hadn't wanted to care, but he couldn't help it. That said something about the soul of this young man. "Grandma slipped a few cards up my sleeve. And I think I'm doing what the Lord wants me to do. With God on my side, who can be against me?"

"I've never met anyone as naïve as you, Annie." He shook his head.

She put her hand on his arm. "I talked with the doctor on Friday, and he said he'll meet with me and my mother and uncle on Tuesday morning. The social worker and physical therapist will be there, too. Would you like to sit in my corner?"

"I'd be honored."

"Eleven o'clock. Third-floor conference room. I'll meet you in the lobby at ten forty-five."

"I'll be there."

She waited to wave as his car pulled away from the curve. Corban Solsek had changed a lot over the past two weeks. Definitely for the better.

Opening the door, she went back inside. Sam was standing in the middle of the living room, his thumbs hooked into his belt loops, looking at her. "He was asking you out, wasn't he?"

Corban? Ask her out? "No. We were just talking about Grandma. He wants to be at the hospital when we have the family conference with the doctor on Tuesday. Since he's agreed to keep coming on Wednesday as my respite care, I thought it would be a good idea to have him there in my corner."

"Would you have gone out with him if he'd asked you?"

"He has a girlfriend, Sam."

"They split up."

"Oh." Sam was watching her face, assessing her reaction. Jealousy didn't look good on him. "No wonder he seemed preoccupied today. Did he say whether they might get back together?"

"No, but I doubt it," he said grimly.

"Corban's a friend, Sam. And so are you. A very dear friend."

"I want to be more."

Oh, dear. Lord, how do I make him understand?

Suzie came out of the kitchen, rescuing her from having to try. "Did I hear Corban's available? Cool!" She grinned at Annie. "Put in a good word for me, would you?" She nudged her brother. "I don't have to ask if I have your blessing, do I? Anything to get rid of the competition. Come on, Brother. We'd better go." She kissed Annie's cheek. "I put the rest of the sandwiches away. You made enough for an army. We're staying at Mom and Daddy's over the weekend, so we can come back tomorrow and help move everything back into the bedroom. Daddy said he'd come over when you're ready and put up the pole by the bed and the side bars in the bathroom."

"I'll call. I think I'll be ready for the final detailing by Monday."

Sam took her hand and drew her with him to the door. Suzie was already outside and down the steps. Sam tipped her chin. "Call if you need anything, Annie." When he lowered his head to kiss her, she turned her face slightly so his lips connected with her cheek. Even so, her heart did a little somersault. Sam stirred her, there was no denying that. But even physical attraction couldn't detract her from her calling. And the last thing she wanted to do was give Sam false hope.

Sam drew back and smiled ruefully. He ran a finger down her cheek. "I don't give up that easily."

"I don't want to hurt you, Sam."

"I'm hurting already, Annie. Maybe it'll be good for me. A growing experience."

She closed the door quietly behind him. "Lord, how can we both be so sure of our feelings and yet they're so divergent?"

Turning her thoughts back to the work at hand, Annie went back into the bedroom. She spent the next few hours painting the windowsills glossy white. When she finished, she pulled up the tape and folded up the plastic from the floor. She worked well into the evening, cleaning and polishing the wood floor. It was beautiful and it was a shame to have to cover it, but it was too slick to be safe for Grandma. Annie had purchased a lovely rose area rug at a garage sale. Dragging it into the room, she unrolled it carefully. It was four by six feet and left a nice space of wood floor showing along all four walls.

Sam had taken down the drapery rods from the front and side windows. Annie put up double curtain rods in their place and hung the sheer lace curtains. The room was high enough that no one could look in without standing on a ladder, and the streetlight was far enough down the street that it didn't flood the room with harsh light.

Standing in the middle of the room, she looked around, imagining how it would be with the furniture back in place, the few pictures rehung, and the bed made. Annie wished she had the time and money to put up wallpaper. Her grandmother would spend many hours in this room. It should be special; it should bring her pleasure and comfort.

A sudden inspiration came to her and she smiled.

She went out for a ladder and carried it back into the room. Getting her art supplies, she set to work. She wouldn't be able to finish tonight but could make a good start and add to it as time permitted.

Nora came to the conference-room doorway and saw Annie sitting at the table, Corban Solsek beside her. George had just taken his seat and was loosening his tie. The social worker and the physical therapist were talking quietly together and looking over a file. Nora felt Fred's hand touch the small of her back, not pushing her forward but reminding her of his presence. Filling her lungs, she squared her shoulders and entered the room.

She noticed Annie didn't look at her. Corban did, though, coldly. Battle lines were being drawn. Nora wondered if they were intimately involved. There was a protective air about the young man as he gave her a look of challenge, then leaned toward Annie.

"We're glad you're here, Mrs. Gaines," the social worker said. "Mr. Gaines." She extended her hand to Fred. Nora couldn't remember the woman's name. "Please sit down and make yourselves comfortable. Dr. Patterson will be here momentarily."

Nora wanted to ask why Corban was present. He wasn't family. What right had he to be here? She clenched her hands together under the edge of the table where no one could see them and kept silent. Fred reached over and put his hand over hers. His touch was warm, gentle, reassuring.

"I looked in on Mother," George said. "Her color is better."

The physical therapist nodded. "She has had several good days. We've seen marked improvement."

Nora didn't know whether that was good news or not. Either way, her mother was certainly in no shape to go home.

Dr. Patterson came into the room, all business, clearly with no time to spare. "Is everyone here?"

Nora glanced at her brother. "Is Jeanne coming?"

"She said it was up to you and me to make the decision about Mother."

"And me," Annie said quietly.

Nora cast a look at her daughter, hoping Annie would take the hint and not make trouble with irrational and emotional appeals at this stage. She and George had discussed everything in detail over the telephone. She was surprised Jeanne wasn't present. Her absence felt like a loud message that she didn't support their decision.

Dr. Patterson quickly went over Leota's condition. Stroke. Partial paralysis. Speech affected. Incontinent. Some improvement over the past few days, but a long convalescence ahead with the possibility of another stroke. The physical therapist talked about Leota's physical condition, the atrophy of certain muscles, signs of malnutrition, presence of arthritis. A nurse had joined the meeting by this time and took her turn talking about Leota's mental and emotional condition. "She seems to understand what's going on around her most of the time."

Nora noticed how Annie's eyes welled with tears, but Annie didn't ask any questions. She just sat and listened, soaking it all in.

"We recommend a convalescent hospital," Dr. Patterson said.

Annie looked at him. "What about home care?"

"Don't be ridiculous, Annie," Nora said, appalled at the thought. "Haven't you heard a word the doctor's said? She's not going to get much better. There's a good chance she'll have another stroke."

"Much of the expense of a convalescent hospital will be covered by Medicare," George said.

"I think Grandma would rather be at home."

"Well, I can't take care of her." Nora couldn't believe Annie was trying to make her feel guilty about putting Leota into a nursing home. "I have my own life to live and so does George. He has a business to run, and I have responsibilities as well."

"She's your mother!" Annie's eyes were wide and cold. "How can you even think of putting her away somewhere and letting strangers take care of her?"

Nora's lip trembled at the look of accusation on her daughter's face. "What do you know about anything? I'm doing the best I can. Why should I have to give up my life to take care of her? I have a right to some happiness."

Corban Solsek's face went white and tense. She'd never seen such a ook on a man's face. She fixed him with a glare. "Don't look at me like that. What has this to do with you? What right have you even to be here?"

Annie's response was swift and confident. "I asked him to come. I have something to say."

"You have *nothing* to say in this matter!" Nora felt as though she were choking on her anger. "George and I are her children, and it's for *us* to decide."

Dr. Patterson raised his hands. "These meetings are always highly emotional. Let's try to calm down for a minute and discuss this rationally."

Annie raised her hand. Nora glared at her. "Annie, put your hand down. We're not in a classroom."

"May I speak without interruption?" Annie said.

"You needn't be sarcastic."

Corban leaned forward. "She wasn't being sarcastic. She was asking politely for you to shut up and listen."

"Corban . . ." Annie put her hand on his arm and he sat back, muttering an apology.

"I want him out of here!" Nora said, face hot. "Now!"

"It might be better, Annie," Fred said gently.

Corban looked at Annie. She nodded and whispered something to him. He rose from his chair and left the room. "Now, may I speak?" she said quietly.

"This is just wasting time." George looked at his watch. "I have to be back at work by one. I have an important appointment."

"I'll make it brief." Annie's eyes were dark now. "I'm taking Grandma home."

Nora felt all the warmth in her body drain away. "You can't do any such thing. Of all the idiotic notions, Annie."

"I can, Mother, and I will."

Nora saw the determination in her daughter's expression. "You're just doing this in some kind of twisted effort to make me feel guilty."

"No, I'm not."

Everyone started talking at once, all protesting, all focused on Annie, who seemed unmoved by any argument.

"Enough." Dr. Patterson held up his hand for silence again. "Miss Gaines," he said with forced patience. "You are what . . . sixteen . . . seventeen?"

"Eighteen and an adult, Dr. Patterson."

"Eighteen and have no idea what you're suggesting."

"I'm not suggesting, sir. I'm informing you of my decision."

Nora protested, and George joined in. Even the social worker and physical therapist joined forces.

Annie stared at them all, her gaze unwavering. "I have power of attorney."

"What?" George nearly came out of his chair. "*What* did you say?" Nora had never seen him look so upset.

"I have power of attorney," Annie said again. "I've already moved into the house."

Nora stared at her. "What about art school?"

"I quit. The day after Grandma was taken into the hospital. I've been living in her house and getting it ready. Cleaning, painting, moving furniture, buying supplies. I've had plenty of help. Susan, Sam, Corban. Susan's mother came over and told me what needed to be done to make the house ready for long-term care. She's given me some training as well. CPR, that sort of thing. She's also given me a long list of practical nurses, home-care agencies, and government programs."

"Practical nurses, home-care agencies?" George sounded completely exasperated.

Annie went on doggedly. "Tom Carter came over and put the support bars in the bathroom and another bar in the bedroom. He also built a ramp for a wheelchair that I can put over the back steps. Corban has agreed to come in on Wednesdays as respite care so I can do shopping and other things. Everything is ready."

"Who's paying for all this?" George's eyes were hard.

"Grandma and me. She had my name added to her checking account, and I had some savings."

"That money isn't yours to spend!" George was clearly angry now. "Nora, for crying out loud, *do* something about this!"

"Anne-Lynn, you have no right."

Annie stood. "I have *every* right! I seem to be the only person in this room who *loves* her." Her eyes filled and spilled over. "Whether you like it or not, *this* is the way it's going to be. Grandma put the decision in my hands. Thank God for that!"

"Mother doesn't get enough from social security to pay for additional nursing!" George said, rising as well. "Where are you going to get the money to give her all this fancy private care?"

"It may not come to all that, Uncle George. I was only saying *if* it became necessary."

"If you plan on doing this by yourself, it will become necessary fairly quickly," the social worker put in.

"Then I'll look into selling the house to a bank that will pay out monthly installments large enough to cover—"

George exploded. "Your mother and I are not going to sit idly by and let you spend every dime of our inheritance!"

Annie stared at George. Then her gaze turned until she faced her mother. Nora could feel the heat come up from the soles of her feet to the top of her head. How could George say it like that? It sounded so appalling. What could she say now to explain it so that it sounded better? "Your uncle George doesn't mean it the way it's coming out, Anne-Lynn. He only means that Mother worked all those years and put money into social security and taxes. It's only fair the government should pay the expenses now. And they would pay the lion's share if she—"

"No." Annie's face was white. *"No!"*

"This is getting us nowhere." Dr. Patterson was clearly annoyed. "We need to be reasonable and cooperative." Nora could tell he was on George's and her side. Why didn't she feel good about that?

"The decision is made, Dr. Patterson." Annie sounded very businesslike. "I have a copy of the power of attorney. If you want to speak with my lawyer, that can be arranged. Since you recommended moving Grandma Leota to a care facility as soon as possible, I'd like to take her home with me. Today. As soon as you can arrange it, as a matter of fact."

The minute she mentioned an attorney, Dr. Patterson stiffened.

"As you wish," he said and left the room with an air of disdain. The others sat silent, embarrassed.

"Anne-Lynn, don't do this." Nora couldn't keep her voice from trembling.

"It's done, Mother." Annie looked so pale . . . and sad. She looked back at Nora, obviously deeply troubled, then at George. "May God forgive you both." She pushed her chair in against the table and walked out of the room.

Nora closed her eyes.

"Are you going to let her get away with this?" George yanked his tie off.

"I don't think there's much either of you can do about it." Fred spoke quietly and evenly. "If Annie can prove she has power of attorney, she has the legal right to make the decision for Leota."

George swore. "You'd better talk to her, Nora. Talk her out of it." He stalked out of the room. The others followed quietly.

Nora sat there, unable to move. Unable to think.

What had just happened?

Fred leaned close. "Are you all right?"

Her mouth trembled. "No." It was all she could manage without breaking down completely.

Leota was touched by Corban's presence. She hadn't expected him to be the one helping Annie take her from the hospital. He lifted her from the wheelchair and placed her carefully into the front seat of Annie's car. She wanted to thank him, but all she could do was pat his cheek. And cry.

"I'm sorry, Leota," he said, and she wondered what he meant. He lingered as Annie wheeled the chair to the back of the car and opened the trunk. He met Leota's gaze. "I was wrong about everything." He kissed her forehead, clicked her seat belt shut, and closed the door. She could feel the car bounce as he dumped the wheelchair into the trunk; then Annie was sliding into the car seat next to her. Annie was smiling brightly, eyes glowing.

"Well, we're on our way home, Grandma. I hope you like the changes I've made. Of course, we'll need to make a few more as we go along." She put the car in gear, pausing just long enough to lean over and give her a kiss on the cheek. "I love you, Grandma."

"I love you, too," Leota said, though it didn't sound just right. "I love you very, very much." Then she sat weeping all the way home.

Corban had arrived ahead of them in his own car. "Forget the wheelchair, Annie," he said, opening Leota's door and leaning in to unhook her seat belt. He scooped Leota up and lifted her out carefully. "I'll come back for it."

"Trying to impress my granddaughter," Leota said, chuckling. He didn't understand a word she said, but he smiled slightly, as though he guessed what she might be saying. He carried her right up the front steps, waited for Annie to open the door, and placed her gently in her old recliner.

Oh, Lord, it's good to be in my own home. She smiled, feeling the left side of her mouth lift. Annie was beaming. Never had anyone looked more beautiful to Leota. She could see Jesus shining right out of the girl.

Corban went out to Annie's car to bring in the wheelchair.

Annie looked at her. "We're going to do just fine together, Grandma. I've already moved into the other bedroom. Susan's mother has been working with me on the care aspects."

Leota could smell fresh paint. The living room hadn't looked so clean and polished in years. The wood on her side table was shiny. The rug had been shampooed and vacuumed. The windows were clean. Not just the one Corban had cleaned the first day he came, but all of them. Knowing Annie, Leota could imagine all the windows were so clean they looked wide open to the world outside.

"I love you, Grandma," Barnaby bellowed and bobbed his head up and down, walking back and forth on his perch.

Leota chortled.

Not only could she smell fresh paint, she could smell something wonderful cooking. For the first time since she had been taken into the hospital, she felt hungry.

Corban came to touch Annie's arm. "Anything I can do before I leave?"

"You can stay and have dinner with us."

"Not tonight, Annie. Can I have a rain check? I'll be back on Wednesday. How about I collect then?"

Annie saw him out the door. She whistled happily as she went into the kitchen. When everything was set for dinner, she came back and helped her grandmother into the wheelchair. In the kitchen Leota could see right out the newly washed windows to her garden beyond, where the leaves had been raked and additional trimming and pruning done. It was plain to see from all directions that Annie had been busy, even getting special silverware for her to use. The spoon handle was curved to make it easier for her to eat without assistance. Annie watched as she worked on the meal, but didn't interfere.

The evening was full of firsts, and every hurdle was taken successfully. Leota was touched by Annie's tenderness. Annie didn't seem the least bit embarrassed when helping her with the most personal aspects of her care. Leota was so tired, she had no strength left by the time Annie helped her into her nightgown and into her own, wonderfully familiar bed. It wasn't until Leota was lying down that she saw the pink walls and white molding, the lace curtains, the tall potted fern. As she relaxed against her own pillow, she saw Annie had painted words on the wall in exquisite calligraphy that sparked rose-sweet memories: *Sand castles. Bubble baths. Jehovah-Roi. Kisses. Holding hands. El Shaddai. Dancing. Music. Savior. Flying kites. Old movies. Nature walks. Friends. Good dreams. Rainbows. Christ the Lord. Pillow fights. Feather beds. Seashells. Jesus. Animals. Birdsong.*

Leota read until Annie leaned down, kissed her good night, and turned out the light.

And then she saw on the ceiling the fluorescent stars Annie had glued there. Leota drifted off to sleep, imagining herself staring up at the night sky from a chaise lounge in her garden.

21

LEOTA SAT IN HER WHEELCHAIR, OUTSIDE ON THE SMALL PATIO. Annie had made sure she was bundled in a warm blanket and a soft, wool hat pulled down to cover her ears. Her hands were in wool-lined leather gloves. Annie had even gone so far as to heat a flat pillow she'd filled with rice and seeds in the microwave. It lay warm over Leota's shoulders and against her back, smelling of lavender.

Her breath puffed in the cool afternoon air. She liked the feel of biting air against her skin and could see the result of it in the flush on Annie's cheeks and the red tip of her nose. Leota had longed to be outside, and only this morning, Annie had understood what she was saying.

The garden was dying down for its winter sleep. Two things were coming into their glory with the approach of the Christmas season: the holly bush and the pyracantha. As soon as their berries were fully ripe, the birds would come and have a festival. It had always amazed Leota how they knew the exact day, as though invitations had been sent out for a party. They'd swarm over the bushes, eat their fill, and flutter away like drunken sailors returning to their ship.

In January the lavender heather and white candytufts would bloom. February perked up the plum tree, and March would bring forth the daffodils, narcissus, and moonlight bloom. April lilacs and sugartuft would blossom along with the pink and bloodred rhodo-dendrons, bluebells, and the apple tree in the Victory garden. As the weather warmed, miniature purple irises would rise amidst the volunteers of white alyssum, verbena, and marigold. The roses, dahl-ias, white Shasta daisies, black-eyed Susans, and marigolds would bloom from late spring to early fall.

Leota could see it. She knew exactly where she had planted every-thing, and with Annie's tender care the garden would bloom again. She saw Annie's unique touches here and there. The funny bowling balls, looking like dinosaur eggs; the metal sculpture that was now a starburst of color; the wash bucket and wheelbarrow that served as planters. She could imagine them spilling color come spring.

In this world of New Age philosophies and El Niño weather patterns, of gambling in almost every state, of drugs, abortion, crime, gay rights, and Dr. Death, there was still an oasis.

Leota knew the Lord was with her everywhere she went—even in that depressing hospital—but she had always *felt* His presence here the most. *Is it because everything of great importance happened in a garden, Lord? Man fell in the Garden. You taught in a garden. You prayed Your passion in a garden. You were betrayed in a garden. You arose in a garden. I love this place, for when I sit out here, I see the wonder of Your creation. I smell the earth and flower-scented air, and it soothes me. It reminds me that Your hand is in it all. For I heard the voice of the Lord in the garden, calling to me.*

Instruct Annie, Lord. Teach her as You taught me.

It wasn't enough to love the flowers. Annie would have to hate the weeds that tried to choke the life from them. She would need to soften the soil and plant the seed so that she could watch the Father bring forth the growth. She would have to cut away the branches that died. It took harsh pruning sometimes to bring forth the fruit, all so that others might partake. *Oh, Father, will she see that a garden is color and propor-tion and rhythm and line and balance and focus? Will she come to under-stand that some of us are poppies, blooming bold and brief? Others are ornamental vines, passion flowers, or trumpets. Still others are shy violets and wallflowers. But we are all in the garden by Your design, each one here to proclaim the glory of Your name. Oh, Father God, teach Annie that a garden is for sharing, for meditating on Your Word, for exercising faith and experiencing the surpassing joy of Your grace.*

She closed her eyes, imagining the scent of stalk, hyacinth, sage, mock orange, gardenias, star jasmine, honeysuckle . . .

Oh, Lord, that my life could have been a fragrant aroma, a soothing sacrifice to You. Oh, that this desert of an old woman could have bloomed and brought You a bouquet of blossoms.

"I've decided to put in a vegetable garden this year, Grandma," Annie said from where she worked. "Our first crop will be this summer. Sweet corn, beans, carrots, peas, onions . . ."

Leota savored every moment, watching her granddaughter tend the garden she had loved for so many years. She knew now it wouldn't die.

Corban was standing in the corridor, next to Professor Webster's office door, when he saw the portly instructor approaching. The dark eyes looked straight at him, no hint of emotion.

"I need to talk with you, Professor. Would it be convenient now, or should I make an appointment?"

"Now would be fine," Professor Webster said, unlocking the door and pushing it open. He stepped inside, leaving the door wide open for Corban. As Corban stepped inside, he saw what seemed to be chaos. The shelves were packed with books, and more were stacked on the floor. Files and papers cluttered the professor's desk, leaving only a small work space. An old electric typewriter was on a stand in the corner. But Corban knew appearances could be deceiving: Professor Webster knew his subject.

"How's your paper coming, Mr. Solsek?"

"That's what I'd like to talk about with you, sir."

"Sit." The professor set his briefcase on the floor and took his seat behind the desk. Taking off his glasses, he cleaned them. "Go ahead. I'm listening."

"The paper is in the trash, sir. Since there's not enough time to start another, I'd like to drop the course."

"It's too late for that."

Corban had figured as much. Still, his stomach dropped. He had worked hard to hold his standing. This would cost him dearly, but he knew it was right and fair. Anyone with half a brain didn't ask for pity at a university this size. The competition didn't allow for it. "Fair enough, sir. I'll take the F. If you'll permit me, I'd like to sit through the classes until the term ends." He still had a lot to learn.

Professor Webster put his glasses back on. "What's the trouble with the paper you started?"

Corban could feel the heat climb up his neck into his face. He let his breath out slowly. "I was on the wrong track."

"The wrong track?"

"You start housing facilities for people no one cares about, and it'll become too easy to do away with them. No matter how good it looks on paper, the bottom line is there's too much government control and too much temptation to take easy solutions to long-term difficulties. With everyone griping about taxes and demanding relief, the first to be sacrificed are the ones who can least defend themselves. Right now, it's the unborn. I don't want to be part of making it easy to do away with the elderly, too."

"One old woman taught you this?"

"Leota Reinhardt *tried* to teach me, sir, but I was deaf to what she was saying. It took two other women to get in my face and show me." Ruth Coldwell and Nora Gaines. They'd never meet, but they had a lot in common.

Professor Webster leaned back in his chair. "We have a student body of brilliant young men and women here. I've had students come as puffed-up little peacocks, thinking top grades and high SAT scores make them something special. They're so full of themselves, they think they know more than anyone else, including the PhDs with twenty years' experience behind them."

Corban's face burned hot. Of all people, he knew he deserved a dressing down. "You have my apologies, sir. I've been an idiot." He started to rise.

"Sit down, Mr. Solsek. I'm not done yet."

Heart sinking, Corban sat and waited for whatever else he had coming.

"In all my years of teaching, Mr. Solsek, I can count on one hand the number of students who've had the courage to come to me and admit they were wrong and take an F without complaining."

An odd warmth filled Corban at the professor's words. "Thank you, sir."

"You're welcome to attend class. I'll give you an incomplete on the condition you enroll in my class again next term. Agreed?" The professor rose and extended his hand.

Corban stared at him for a moment, not quite sure what had just happened. Then he jumped up from his seat and shook the professor's still-extended hand. "Agreed, sir! And thank you."

The professor released his hand and smiled. "I'll be interested in seeing what you come up with next time."

Nora hadn't spoken to Anne-Lynn in ten days, not since their telephone conversation two days after her mother had gone home from the hospital. "Would you like to help me, Mother?" Anne-Lynn had said. "One afternoon a week would make a big difference."

"And if I agreed, I'd only be encouraging you to go on with this madness."

"This is what I want to do."

"Oh, so you wanted to quit art school and move away from your friends and give up dating? You *want* your life to narrow down to taking care of an old woman day in and day out for as long as she lives. You *want* that?"

"Mom, what better way can I spend my time than loving Grandma Leota?"

Nora had almost said, "You could love me," but something held her back. Maybe it was her memory of the look on Anne-Lynn's face when George had accused Leota of wasting their inheritance.

Now it had been a week since her telephone conversation with her daughter. Surely, Anne-Lynn had had more time to think things over and realize what she'd taken on. Nora dialed her mother's number and waited. Within two rings, she heard Annie's voice greeting her with a cheerful, "Hello!"

"It's your mother, Anne-Lynn, I—"

"We're sorry, but we're unable to take your call right now. Please leave a message and we'll get back to you as soon as we can. Thank you!"

An answering machine. That was a new addition. Nora listened, debating whether to leave a message or not. "It's your mother, Anne-Lynn. I was just calling to check on you." She gripped the telephone receiver a little tighter. "How are you two doing together?" She couldn't truthfully add, "Well, I hope." Unable to think of anything more to say, she held the phone away and pressed the disconnect button. With a heavy sigh, she put the receiver against her aching heart for a moment and then placed it carefully back in its cradle. She had errands to run before she attended the University Women's Literary Society luncheon. And there was Christmas shopping.

Christmas. How she hated Christmas.

Would Michael even call this year?

Did you call Leota last year?

She couldn't get away from the past all the rest of the day. Every memory that came to mind brought misery with it. When Nora finally returned home late that afternoon, her answering machine was blinking a red 5. Her dentist's receptionist had called to remind her of her appointment the next morning; Fred called to say he would be late getting home; someone from her old church had called to invite her to a women's ministry night—a cookie exchange. The next was silence and then a click. Probably another sales call.

The last message was from Annie.

"Hello, Mother. Thanks for calling." Her voice softened and became husky. "We both listened to your message. Grandma cried. We're both doing fine. We'd love for you to come by for a visit. I hope you know you're welcome anytime, Mom. If I don't answer the doorbell, just look for us in the garden."

Nora's throat closed as she listened to her daughter's voice. *"You're welcome anytime, Mom . . . just look for us in the garden."*

In the garden this time of year? The leaves were falling.

Nora remembered seeing her mother outside during the cold season, sometimes even in the rain. Raking leaves. Pruning. Putting plastic over the plants that couldn't take the cold.

The ache within Nora grew.

Walk with me. Talk with me. You are my own.

She pressed the button and listened to the message again. And again. And again.

What should I do?

She kept hearing what George had said about their inheritance. The money mattered to him because he wanted to get out from under debt. Who could blame him? Nora didn't care about her mother's possessions, and her mother certainly had no money. How had she managed to live on social security all these years? Fred was wealthy, so Nora had all she'd ever need. What did she care about the house? Maybe she could help a little . . .

George had called several times, asking if she had managed to talk some sense into Annie. Nora had found herself defending her daughter, not for her actions but for her heart. "She's not the kind of girl who's out to steal your inheritance, George. I resent you even thinking such a thing!"

She felt so torn.

"Don't you think I know that?" George had almost shouted into the telephone. "But Annie's naïve. Your daughter takes her religion a little too far! This is my inheritance she's talking about, Nora—and yours. She's going to do something stupid, like a reverse mortgage. Whatever she gets might provide a little money for the short term, but it's going to strip us of everything in the long run!"

Nora had prevailed upon Fred to talk with Annie.

"Annie assured me she's not going to do anything until the situation arises that makes it necessary," he told her after he had stopped by for a visit. "By the way, your mother looks much better. She said to give you her love." He hadn't said it to be sarcastic, she knew that, but she had felt the pinch of guilt for not having asked about her mother's condition before asking what Annie had said about money matters. She just wanted to get George off her back.

What a mess this situation had made of her life. It would've been easier on everyone if her mother had died of the stroke instead of ending up an invalid. *Invalid.* What a terrible word. What kind of life was Annie going to have confined to a little house in a ghetto neighborhood with an old woman as her only company?

Maybe a few more weeks of handling twenty-four-hour-a-day care all by herself with no help from anyone would bring Annie to her senses quicker than words could do. Nora could only hope so. She pressed another button and listened to her daughter's voice one last time before deleting the message.

"We've had a steady stream of visitors." Annie grinned at Corban. "Arba is here every day after work to collect the children." She held up another hook for him to screw into the eaves.

"You're taking care of them?" He looked at her in surprise. Once the hook was secure, he draped the string of lights. They'd look like shining icicles hanging from the eaves. Annie had already woven strings of tiny white lights through the front rhododendron bushes and the trimmed flowering plum. Devoid of foliage, it looked dramatic with the tiny lights wrapped around and around the trunk up through the center of the tree. Then she'd wrapped the two thickest lower branches outward making a cross.

"Actually, the children are helping," Annie said as she took another string of icicle lights from a box. "Grandma is usually resting in the afternoon. Did you see the new hospital bed? It makes it much easier for her to get up, and for me, too. Anyway, Nile does the reading now. He sits in the chair by the window, and the girls sit on Grandma's bed. They're almost finished with *The Secret Garden.*"

"The place looks better every time I come over, Annie." He secured another hook and draped more lights.

"I want everything to look wonderful for Christmas. Only a couple feet to go," Annie said, feeding the string of lights to him.

Corban draped the last of the lights on the last hook and came down the ladder. Annie stood back to admire his work. "Thanks, Corban. It'll make it so much easier next year with those hooks up. All I'll have to do is drape the lights." She gathered up the empty boxes. "Why don't you go on inside and visit with Grandma while I stash these in the garage. You are staying for soup, aren't you? It should be ready. Grandma likes to eat early and then have her dessert later."

"Sure. I'll see you inside."

When he came in the front door, Leota greeted him with her lopsided smile while Barnaby squawked, "911! Call 911!"

Corban laughed. "He's better than a watchdog." He closed the door and turned the dead bolt. Annie would be coming in the back. Leota motioned with her left hand for him to sit. "You're looking pretty good, Leota." He sat down on the sofa, resting in the warmth. Annie had a fire going and a new screen covering the mouth of the fireplace to keep sparks from flying out onto the rug.

"School?" Leota gave him one of her looks.

"I'm taking an incomplete and starting over on a new project next semester. I don't know what yet." He heard Annie come in the back door. "You two seem to be doing well together." He surveyed the living room. "Annie's been painting again." The drab walls glowed a warm peach in the lamplight. The mantel had been oiled and polished, and everything on it washed and rearranged.

"Corban!" Annie called from the kitchen. "Why don't you help Grandma into her wheelchair while I set the table? Supper's ready. All I have to do is warm up the biscuits."

"Where's your Christmas tree?" Corban said, wheeling Leota into her spot at the head of the kitchen-nook table. From that place, she could look straight out at the garden.

"It's on the television." Annie smiled at him as she ladled thick beef soup into bowls.

Corban glanced back. "That puny thing?" It was barely two feet tall with a few ornaments on it.

"It'll be bigger next year." She set the bowl down in front of Leota. As Annie straightened, she looked at him. He knew she didn't want him to say anything more about it.

Maybe it was a matter of money, Corban thought. Leota was living on social security, and Annie couldn't get a job and take care of her grandmother at the same time. He held his silence as Annie placed a bowl of soup in front of him. When she had her own, she sat and took Leota's hand. She held her other hand out to him. When he took it, she said the blessing. He felt comfortable in the warm kitchen. He noticed Annie had put up lights in the backyard as well.

"Are you going home for Christmas?" she said, buttering Leota's biscuit.

"No point. My mother's in Switzerland for the holidays."

"What are you going to do?"

"Hang around my apartment until registration." The soup was delicious.

"And eat what on Christmas Day?" Annie stared at him. "A TV dinner?"

"They're not that bad, but I'll probably go out to a restaurant. Live it up a little." His mother had sent him a sizable check to buy a present.

"You sound like you're really looking forward to it," Annie said ruefully.

He shrugged. What could he say? There was nothing more depressing than eating alone on Christmas.

Leota made a *harrumph*. She tapped the table with her pointer finger.

"I agree, Grandma." She looked at him. "Come and celebrate Christmas with us." She offered him a small jar of jelly.

Corban almost said he didn't want to inconvenience them, but who was he kidding? "My pleasure. What can I bring?"

Annie smiled mischievously and winked at her grandmother. "Can we ask for *anything?*"

"As long as I don't have to cook the turkey."

"No problem. We're having honey-baked ham."

"Then name it."

"A cruise," Leota said.

They all laughed, Leota most of all.

"A tree would be cheaper," Annie said. "About four feet tall, prefer-ably Douglas fir. It's the best kind because there's room between the branches for hanging ornaments, and I found some beauties in the garage the other day."

"A tree it is." Corban smiled. He was actually looking forward to it.

"There just happens to be a nice lot in front of the supermarket. All the proceeds go to charity."

Corban grinned. "I'll go get one right after supper."

Annie was putting the last strands of tinsel on the tree when Arba and the children came by to drop off presents for her and Grandma Leota. Annie served warm apple cider with cinnamon sticks and Toll House cookies. Since Arba and the children were spending Christmas with relatives across the Bay, they all decided to open presents right away.

The children helped Grandma Leota unwrap hers, then announced proudly they had all pitched in to buy the box of soft-center chocolates for Leota and the pretty bottle of bubble bath for Annie. Annie handed out their gifts, hoping they would like the dough ornaments of biblical people she had baked and painted: For Nile, she'd made Simeon called Niger; for Kenya, the Queen of Sheba; and for Tunisha, Candace, Queen of Ethiopia. She had talked about them once when Nile had told her a Muslim friend had said Jesus was a white man's god forced on enslaved blacks.

For Arba, she'd made praying hands in chocolate-colored dough. Annie was delighted to see how the ornaments pleased all four of them. She had wanted to give them something special, something that would last.

"Time to go." Arba leaned down and took Grandma Leota's hand. "You have a wonderful Christmas, Leota. You'll have a few days' rest before we get back."

"God bless." Grandma Leota spoke clearly enough to be understood.

Annie walked out onto the porch as Arba and the children left. Arba paused at the bottom of the steps. "Is your family coming for Christmas?"

"Not this year. Uncle George's family is spending Christmas in Phoenix with Aunt Jeanne's parents. They were already committed to it when Grandma had her stroke. But they do plan to come over as soon as they get back. And Mother and Fred . . ." She shrugged. "I don't know."

"I'm sorry, Annie."

"Me, too, but we had Thanksgiving. I'm glad of that. Corban's coming, though, and Susan called. She and Sam want to come over in the afternoon. We have a lot to be thankful for." Her smile wobbled. How she had wished the family would come together for Christmas! *Lord, I have prayed so hard for reconciliation.*

"Well, you and your granny have a merry Christmas, Annie."

"You, too, Arba. Drop by when you can."

"You know I will. The children've become very attached to Grandma Leota. How could they not?"

Annie waved as Arba headed for home, then went quietly back into the house. Grandma Leota was asleep in her recliner. Jimmy Stewart was wooing Donna Reed in *It's a Wonderful Life*. Annie quietly gathered the mugs and the cookie plates and carried them into the kitchen. She washed them and put them away. It was barely eight-thirty, and she was so tired. She sat down on the sofa to rest for a few minutes. Leota looked so peaceful. She didn't want to wake her yet. Closing her eyes, she leaned her head against the sofa.

Oh, Lord, there was no room in the inn for Your precious Son, and there doesn't seem to be any room in my mother's heart or Uncle George's life for Grandma Leota. I don't understand, Lord. I just don't. It's so sad. They're missing all the blessings I'm receiving. She's such a sweet old soul, and I hurt even thinking about losing her. Oh, God, please help me make this a special Christmas for Grandma. Don't let another season go by without her knowing how much she's loved.

Nora couldn't sleep. Tomorrow was Christmas Eve, and she had never felt so alone and depressed. *I hate Christmas. I've always hated Christmas. Every year I'm disappointed. When I was a child, it was because I knew I wouldn't get what I wanted. Now it's the shopping, fighting the crowds while trying to buy presents that will please everyone, decorating the house, paying good money to have lights strung all over the outside, cooking a big, fancy dinner everyone scarfs down in a matter of minutes. I'm always sick with exhaustion by the time it's over. And what's the point of it all?*

She stared up into the darkness, listening to Fred snore beside her. She resented how he could fall asleep so easily after an argument, while she lay awake for hours, going over every word a hundred times. Usually, when she was in "one of her moods," as he called it, Fred could talk her out of it. Not this evening. He'd kept silent until she'd asked him if he cared at all what she was feeling. And his response?

"Why don't you call Annie? You know you want us all to be together for Christmas."

"Here! I want her here!"

"Well, that's not going to happen. It can't happen."

"If we go over there, it'll only encourage her to keep on with this plan of hers, Fred."

He'd snapped shut the book he had been reading all evening and dropped it on the table as he rose. "How you can know so little about your own daughter is beyond me, Nora. She's committed to taking care of your mother. Nothing you do or say is going to change anything. And that's what really gets to you, isn't it? You're no longer in control."

"She's throwing her life away."

"How many years do you think your mother has left? She's not going to live forever."

"She'll probably live to be a hundred."

"You'd better hope she does." And with that cryptic comment, Fred had gone up to bed.

Now she was tossing and turning and sleepless. Nora felt the tears running down into her hair. How many had she cried over the years, starting when her mother left her to go to work?

God, I can't go on this way. Sometimes I wish I were dead. Nothing ever works out the way I want it. I called Michael this morning, and he couldn't wait to get off the telephone. She was his mother, and he didn't even care about her.

How have you treated your mother?

Nora clenched her teeth. *She abandoned me first. Michael is just like his father, Bryan.*

The silence pressed in upon her. The darkness was oppressive. Shivering, she curled on her side, tucking herself against Fred, hoping his warmth would warm her.

I loved Dean Gardner. I loved him so much I thought I'd die when he left me for that other woman—what was her name? Dominique. I kept hoping he would tire of her and come back to me. Well, he did tire of her, but then he met Phyllis and then Penny. I've lost count of the women he's had over the years. What's the name of his new paramour? Monica. She fought the tears pricking at her eyes. *God, I gave Dean all the love I had, and it wasn't enough to hold him. He was faithless.* And now Anne-Lynn was proving to be just like her father. She'd forsaken Nora just the way Dean Gardner had.

You have *forsaken her!*

I haven't. Her mouth trembled. *She'll probably marry that hoodlum, Sam Carter, and be miserable for the rest of her life.*

And if that's My plan for her, what is that to you?

Tears burned hotter as she thought about Susan and Susan's mother and father. Now that their children were grown, they never had to call and ask them to come home. Their house was always full. All through the teen years, Anne-Lynn had wanted to be at the Carters' house every chance she got. Nora used to think it was because of Sam and his "Rebel without a Cause" magnetism, but even after Sam was put into juvenile hall, Anne-Lynn kept going. She had loved being with the Carters.

Every time Anne-Lynn asked to spend the night at Susan's, it hurt me. I felt as though she were defecting. I wanted her to love being at home with me, but she was like a bird trapped in my hands. The harder I held on, the harder she fought to be free.

And now she was free. She was free. and she was never coming back.

Oh, God, what is it about me that drives people away? All I've ever done is give my children everything I never had. All I want is for my children to have a better life than I had growing up. All she wanted was for them to love her.

All you want is to be their god.

No, I didn't say that.

She could hear the grandfather clock downstairs chime four. There was no use in trying to sleep. It was almost time to get up. She eased herself from beneath the covers and slipped into her robe and slippers.

The tree lights were still on downstairs, and the soft glow lit the stairs. She had wrapped the banister with boughs of pine, putting in touches of holly berries. It looked so lovely and filled the house with a woodsy aroma. The mantel looked perfect with the silk poinsettias tucked into more pine boughs, and the tall red, green, and white candles were the perfect touch. No professional decorator could have done a better job.

It looked as perfectly arranged as any store window.

It's all for show. It doesn't mean a thing.

Christmas means something to Annie.

She remembered her daughter's telephone message. The words came back as clearly as if they'd never been erased: *"We're doing fine. We'd love for you to come by for a visit. I hope you know you're welcome anytime, Mom."*

Mom. Not Mother. *She called me* Mom.

And she'd said it so tenderly.

Nora went into the kitchen and ground fresh, gourmet-blend coffee beans. She boiled an egg, then warmed a croissant in the microwave. It was too cold to sit in the sunroom, so she turned up the heater and sat in the den, looking out the glass doors at the manicured lawn, topiary pines, and cleanly mulched and weeded ground ready for bulb planting. It would look like a park in the spring.

A park for people to walk through and leave, not a garden where visitors relaxed and lingered. A park where people had to enter through the house and get permission from the owner . . . not a garden with a back gate for neighbors to use.

Nora closed her eyes. She could see her mother outside the kitchen window, on her knees, her hands in the soil.

It had been such a shock seeing her mother in that hospital bed. She'd looked so white, so confused, so pale, so frail.

The sunrise glowed pink orange. The clock in the hall chimed seven. Where had the time gone? All the years of struggling and surviving one disappointment after another, of searching and searching for some kind of peace, some sense of accomplishment and purpose . . .

"I hope you know you're welcome anytime, Mom."

Mom. She clung to that word like a lifeline. *Mom.*

At 8 A.M. she picked up the telephone, called her daughter, and asked if the invitation was still open.

And, of course, it was.

22

CHRISTMAS EVE MORNING, A UPS TRUCK DELIVERED TWO BOXES, both addressed to Leota Reinhardt with Uncle George and Aunt Jeanne's return address. The larger box contained a VCR. "What is it?" Grandma Leota stared, completely baffled. Annie tried to explain.

The second box had a note in Jeanne's handwriting. "We're sorry we couldn't be with you for Christmas. Hope you both enjoy the movies. Love, Jeanne, George, Marshall, and Mitzi." The box was packed full of movies: *The Bells of Saint Mary, South Pacific, The King and I, Casablanca, Pocketful of Miracles, Ben-Hur, Miracle on 34th Street,* and *A Christmas Carol.*

"A treasure trove, Grandma. Which one would you like to watch first?"

"You choose."

When Annie tried to install the VCR, she realized Grandma Leota's television set was so outdated that there were no connections. How much did a new television cost? Only a couple hundred dollars, but dollars her grandmother clearly did not have. "Oh, Grandma. I'm sorry." Was this going to be a day of disappointments? "I didn't realize."

"Won't miss what I never had," Grandma said, giving her lopsided smile. "Nice thought."

Annie nodded, too choked up to speak. She'd never thought much about modern conveniences until living with her grandmother. No dishwasher, not that there was much need for one with only two people eating off the dishes, and the washer and dryer were older than she was. Annie had spent one day cleaning out the dryer vent. She had thanked God for His protection because the vent had been so packed with lint, it was a miracle it hadn't caught fire and burned the house down. In fact, there were lots of things that needed to be done. The pipe under the kitchen sink had a leak. The roof gutters overflowed with water because the downspouts were clogged with leaves. One of the back steps felt soft from dry rot, which meant there were probably termites eating away at other parts of Grandma Leota's house. The roof should be redone; Annie had noticed a ceiling stain in her bedroom.

Annie didn't want to mention these things because she didn't want to worry her grandmother. Or worse, have her grandmother mistake concern for discontent. If something had to be fixed, she'd find a way to take care of it without worrying Grandma Leota.

Lord, don't let me get distracted by all these little unimportant things. So what if Grandma's brand-new VCR doesn't work. Forgive me for being disappointed. Poor Uncle George and Aunt Jeanne. They spent so much money on something Grandma can't even use when she would have rejoiced far more over a five-minute telephone call from them. Shaking her head, Annie brought the tray with hot chocolate and cookies into the living room. After serving her grandmother, she sat cross-legged in the easy chair and sipped her chocolate.

Annie's father called at three. "I sent your present late. You won't get it for a couple of days. You want me to tell you what it is?"

"Whatever it is, Dad, I'll like it."

"You're too easy. How's Leota doing?"

"Very well."

"And you? Wearing yourself out?"

"I have plenty of help. I've told you about Corban."

"And your mother? Does she help out, too?" When Annie remained silent, trying desperately to think of something to say that wouldn't put her mother in a bad light, her father gave a derisive laugh. "Never mind, Annie. I know her better than that. What she can't control, she chalks off as a complete loss."

"Daddy . . ."

"I'm sorry, sweetheart. I'm always saying that to you, aren't I?"

"How's Monica?"

"I don't know. I haven't seen her since she moved out."

Oh, dear. "How long ago was this?"

"Last month. I thought I mentioned it."

"No, you didn't."

"She was pushing to get married. I've been down that road before and didn't want to be on it again. A few years of living with your mother—"

"I don't want to go down that road again either, Daddy." He didn't say anything to that, and she didn't want to end the call on a sour note. "I miss you."

"I miss you, too, honey. Maybe I'll fly up in a couple of weeks."

How many times had he promised to do that?

"You know you're always welcome, Daddy."

Nora and Fred pulled up in front of Leota's house midafternoon on Christmas Day. Nora groaned audibly when she recognized Corban Solsek's black sports car. "He's here again."

"Give the guy a chance," Fred said, getting out of the car. He helped her out and took her hand as they went up the walkway and steps. Annie was outside on the porch waiting for them. She was smiling, her eyes shining.

"I'm so glad you came!"

Nora's tension eased at the sight of her daughter. She looked so lovely in her long, green velour dress with a strand of pearls, her hair loose and curling over her shoulders. Nora looked for signs of strain, but saw only cheeks flushed with color and blue eyes shining with delight. And hope. It wasn't until Nora returned the hug that she felt the change. "You've lost weight."

"A couple pounds, I guess. Come in. It's cold out here, and Grandma's eager to see you both."

Nora took note of the Christmas tree first. It was right by the front door so it could be seen through the window. It was trimmed beautifully with old-fashioned glass bulbs, elves, and tinsel. Unable to look at her mother yet, she glanced around the room, amazed at the freshly painted walls, the polished furniture, the old carpet that now looked new, the table with pine branches and scented candles. A fire was crackling. The house no longer had that old smell of decay. It was filled with the pine scent of Christmas. Had the memories of this house not been so painful, she would've been utterly charmed by it.

"Corban bought the tree for us," Anne said. "And he helped string lights along the eaves across the front and along the side of the house by the drive. I put lights all through the garden. It looks like a winter wonderland at night. I'll plug them in as soon as it's dark enough so you can see it."

"Wait until you get the electric bill." Fred laughed as he bent down to talk quietly with Leota.

Nora hung back. She had avoided looking at her mother for as long as possible, and now that she did, her heart sank. She looked so *old*. One side of her face sagged slightly.

"Who gave you the VCR?" Fred said.

"Uncle George sent it to Grandma," Annie said.

Mortified, Nora wished she could hide the box of chocolate-covered cherries she had brought as a gift. What on earth was George thinking? Last year he'd sent a box of groceries. Actually, Jeanne had sent it. George didn't even bother to sign his name to the Christmas cards. Their cards always came with "George and Jeanne" signed at the bottom, in Jeanne's handwriting. And now this? A VCR? Were they trying to make her look bad?

"Do you need help hooking it up?" Fred looked eager at the idea.

Annie laughed and gave a slight shrug. "Actually, we can't. Grandma's TV was purchased before VCRs were invented."

"Oh, well, that's no problem. We'll get her a new set. Nora and I were wondering what to get you, Leota. Now we know."

Touched by his quick rescue, Nora slipped her hand into his. "You're looking much better than last I saw you," she said to her mother, and then felt the heat climbing into her cheeks. She hadn't been to visit since her mother had left the hospital.

Leota let the evening flow around her. When Eleanor followed Annie into the kitchen, Leota could only pray her daughter wouldn't say something hurtful to Annie. They were like opposite sides of a coin. Eleanor took offense at the least provocation; Annie let everything slide. Eleanor was the warrior set on battling life into submission; Annie was a peacemaker, living with the hurt, swallowing the insulting remarks, and trying to rise above it and move forward.

I tried to do that, Lord. Maybe that's why watching the dynamics of their relationship makes me want to take a page from Eleanor's book. Oh, what I would say to her now if I had the tongue to do it!

Maybe if she'd spoken up, maybe if she'd defended herself instead of keeping silent . . . Silence didn't always bring peace. Allowing someone to behave disrespectfully more often made them rude and demanding of others.

I thought I was letting Eleanor vent her frustration and that would be the end of it. Instead, her life has been focused on discontent and disappointment. I would love to be able to go back and sit down with her when she was a little girl and teach her all over again. I'd say, "This is what's happening. This is the truth. This is what needs to be done. Join forces with me and your grandmother and grandfather and let's work together to keep this family together!"

Instead, she had tried to do it alone.

For what? For the glory? To be a martyr? To show herself how much better she was than poor Helene Reinhardt, who had to piece the whole sorry mess together by herself without any help from Leota or Papa?

Lord, forgive me.

Leota heard Eleanor and Annie talking.

"Why is Mother crying?" Eleanor was asking quietly, looking uncomfortable.

"The stroke makes it difficult to contain her emotions," Annie said just as quietly.

They were acting as though her hearing had failed along with her ability to walk without clinging to someone or something! *Oh, Lord, You have frustrated me! I can't talk clearly enough to make myself understood. Except by Annie. She's just like a young mother who understands the gibberish of her toddling child. And that's what I've become. Blabbering what I can while I hang onto my walker. Lord, I'd yell at You for allowing this to happen to me if I didn't think Eleanor and George would think I was crazy and make sure I was put away for good!*

A VCR. For heaven's sake, what was George thinking? And now Fred was offering a television. Along with the box of chocolates Eleanor was trying to hide on the side table. *I wonder if she thinks I have adult-onset diabetes . . . and she's going to kill me with kindness.* Sadly, Leota could guess why they were being so generous all of a sudden. Would they be so munificent if they knew everything was already settled and filed with an attorney?

I'm not being fair. I'm wallowing in self-pity and making myself sick! I know Jeanne. And I know Fred. And they are both good and generous people. It's my children who can't see past themselves!

Lord, I can't think this way. For Annie's sake, I have to lift my chin up and take whatever comes. But I'll tell You this. I'm tired of turning the other cheek. In fact, I'm sick to death of it.

Things didn't get easier for Leota as the day wore on. In fact, things became more complicated. Corban didn't like Eleanor, and he made no effort to hide his feelings. Annie tried to make conversation, but only Fred helped keep it going. Then Sam and Susan arrived, and Eleanor's hackles went up. She was like a German shepherd with a salesman trapped on the front porch; it was a sight to see. Sam couldn't blink an eye without Eleanor observing the nuance. He certainly wasn't making his feelings a secret, either. Every time he looked at Annie, the expression on his face declared, "I'm in love with this girl." All of which only served to madden Eleanor all the more.

Lin Sansan Ng, Do Weon, and Kim stopped by, and not long after came Juanita, Jorge, Marisa, Elena, and Raoul.

Eleanor kept moving down the sofa until she was squeezed into a corner, and while Fred joined in the general conversation, Eleanor moved herself all the way to the outside edge of the family circle.

"Chris said to thank you for the information you gave him the other day," Juanita told Annie. "He said the group sounded the most hopeful. Miles is declining rapidly."

Eleanor looked at Annie. "Who are Chris and Miles?"

"They live in the house four doors down on the other side of the street," Annie explained. "Miles is very sick."

"AIDS," Juanita said sadly.

Leota saw Eleanor blanch. She could just imagine what was going on in Eleanor's mind. *Her* daughter, Annie, was living in a mixed-race ghetto with an old lady on her last legs, who would linger for who knew how long, and now, her innocent little girl was mixing with homosexuals as well!

"AIDS?" Eleanor stared.

"Annie met them a few weeks ago."

Eleanor's gaze swung to Annie, fierce with silent demand.

"They're estranged from their families. Miles is dying, Mother. I don't agree with their lifestyle, but they are neighbors and they need our help."

"Your hands are full already, Anne-Lynn. All day, every day, for who knows how long."

Annie blushed. Her eyes became fierce with warning. "I fix extra portions and take them dinner a couple of times a week. It's no big deal."

Leota couldn't allow this to go on. "I gave Annie permission to do it." Miraculously, her words were clear enough for Eleanor to understand.

Eleanor lunged forward so that she sat on the edge of the sofa, her hands like open claws on her knees. "It's all very well for *you* to be magnanimous at Annie's expense, Mother. You're over eighty. You've lived a full life. Don't you care what risks *my daughter* takes? It's not enough that she's living here with you in this crime-infested neighborhood, but you put her in contact with AIDS!"

"Mother!"

Leota used every ounce of willpower she possessed not to cry. Crying would only make things a hundred times worse. Besides, she understood Eleanor's fierceness. Hadn't she felt the same way about her children when Mama Reinhardt was dividing their loyalties?

Is that what I've done, Lord?

Annie stood stricken, looking back and forth as the battle raged around her. The poor girl was standing between the two firing lines, not sure where to find safety. It was always the innocent who were killed.

"What's not right?" Corban's face flushed with temper as he stared at Eleanor. "That, unlike you, Annie has a heart? That, unlike you, she's capable of loving someone else more than herself?"

"Now, just a minute!" Fred rose suddenly, like a knight in shining armor to shield his wife.

Eleanor aimed her animosity at Corban. "This is none of your business! Who *are* you anyway? What do you think you're going to get by coming over here and kissing up to my mother?"

Corban's face turned dark red. "It seems to me it's none of your business either, Mrs. Gaines. You bowed out of Leota's life a long time ago, and Annie's an adult. She can make her own decisions."

"*Stop it!*" Annie covered her face and started to cry. "Just stop it! All of you." She fled to the kitchen.

Eleanor's face convulsed briefly. To anyone else, it was just a flicker, but Leota saw straight into her hurting child. It was like a crack in a concrete wall around a garden. Just a second's glimpse—but she saw that a storm had ripped away at the landscape. *Oh, my child, my poor child.* Then the mortar of old resentments was poured in to repair the wall. Leota could feel Eleanor's gaze fix upon her in accusation. "Maybe this gathering wasn't such a good idea after all."

Corban's eyes flashed. "Maybe the list should've been cut by two!" He followed Annie into the kitchen. Embarrassed, Juanita quickly gathered her children, as did Lin. They went out through the kitchen, making their exit quietly. Leota knew they would make apologies to Annie before leaving.

Oh, God, my family, my precious family. Help us. We are torn asunder. The enemy has laid waste to us.

Sam sat in stony silence, his eyes on fire. Susan's chin jutted, tears running down her face, her eyes fixed on Eleanor. "Why do you always do this to Annie? For as long as I've known her, she's worked so hard to win your approval. *Nothing* pleases you."

"That's not true." Eleanor was trembling—Leota saw it in her hands, heard it in her voice. All eyes were on Eleanor now. It was ever thus. *"As you sow, so shall you then reap."* The one condemning the loudest eventually received the condemnation. Water doesn't run uphill, and Eleanor was drowning.

Helpless to do anything and unable to watch, Leota turned her face to the wall and wept.

The pains Leota had felt off and on over the past two years came again that night. She didn't ring the little bell Annie had put on her side table. She couldn't bear the thought of summoning Annie after such a devastating Christmas Day. The poor girl had wanted everything to be perfect. She had worked so hard, prayed so long. Now she needed rest. The pain eased by morning.

When Annie came in, Leota said she wanted to sleep longer. Annie looked troubled and asked questions, but Leota lied and said everything was fine. She said she had been having such a wonderful dream.

She couldn't bring herself to add to her granddaughter's misery by telling her that something was very, very wrong.

23

Annie noticed the change in her grandmother in the days following Christmas. She was always restless, shifting her body every minute or two as though no position was comfortable. Though Grandma had often been cranky since the stroke, she was more cranky than usual. Either her speech had improved greatly, or Annie was getting used to it and could more easily understand her. At first, it was funny the way Grandma Leota would talk at the television, telling the news commentator what was wrong with his shortsighted, canned presentation or that his views were "idiotic." It was when Grandma started talking cremation that Annie became alarmed. Annie tried to turn her conversation away from death, but Grandma Leota was fixed upon it. "Put me in the bulbs. They need bonemeal."

Annie called the doctor despite Grandma Leota's protests.

"I won't go!" Grandma Leota said, chin jutting. She was irascible, but Annie couldn't pretend everything was all right this time.

"Oh, yes, you will. Something's wrong, Grandma. I want the doctor to check you over."

"Nothing's wrong!"

"You're in pain! I know you are. You try to hide it from me, but I can tell."

Grandma tried charm, smiling and patting Annie's hand. "It's just my arthritis, sweetheart. I'm not a green sprout anymore. I'm ripe and ready for plucking."

Annie refused to give in. "The doctor might be able to give you something to make you more comfortable."

"I won't go! I won't! You'll have to carry me out of this house!"

Annie called Corban. He came the next morning, ignored Grandma Leota's vehement protests and downright abuse, lifted her from her wheelchair, and carried her out to Annie's car.

"It's a good thing her right arm is useless," Corban said, straightening. "I think she'd've given me a black eye."

Nora knew something was wrong when she heard the back door from the garage open. Fred never came home this early in the day. "What is it? What's happened?"

"Annie called me at the office. Your mother is in the hospital again."

Nora's heart sank. Was this the way it was going to be from here on? Her daughter unable to speak to her? Her daughter calling Fred so he could relay messages? "Another stroke?"

"The doctor thinks it could be cancer. She's undergoing tests."

Nora wilted against the back of her chair. Cancer! How was she going to face this when her life was already turning upside down? Her head ached. Her stomach was in turmoil. She felt sick in body and in spirit. She hadn't felt right since that awful Christmas Day. She should have stayed home rather than subject herself to such an emotional beating. Everyone had been against her. All because Annie had run to the kitchen in tears over something she'd said. And then her mother had cried.

What did I say? I can't even remember what I said to bring all that on. You'd have thought I was a dog making a mess on the living-room rug the way they all looked at me.

The tongue is like a fire . . .

Oh, Lord, what did I say? Sometimes, when I'm so upset I can't think straight, I say things and then I can't even remember what I said.

Is that an excuse?

"I think we should go, Nora."

"The last thing I want to do is look at my mother in another hospital bed."

"Would you rather look at her in a coffin?"

Nora recoiled. "How can you say something like that?"

"Because you may not have much time left."

She searched his eyes. "Just what did Annie say?" Was he keeping something from her?

"Exactly what I've told you, but I have the feeling time is almost up."

"My time?" Why did he have to look at her like that? As though he could see inside her and understand things about her that she didn't even understand. She looked away, uncomfortable beneath his perusal. "I don't know what you mean."

"You know exactly what I mean. You just don't want to face it." He brushed his knuckles gently along the line of her cheek. His tenderness had always touched some deep core within her. She loved him passionately, even when they didn't come together physically for a week or more at a time. She admired and respected him. And she often found herself wondering how she had been so lucky to find a man like him after two disastrous marriages. Fred was strong, but his strength didn't come from demanding his own way or believing he was always right. It came from something deep within him.

Oh, God, I know I'm not perfect. I know it! It's been driven home to me every day of my life. And it's been a hundred times worse over the past eight months since Annie couldn't bear to live with me anymore. Did I need that pounding on Christmas Day? I've always wanted to be a better mother than mine was. I've always wanted to do what's right, to rear my children to be better than anyone else. And all I've done is alienate everyone I love most. Two husbands. Michael. Annie. I'm amazed Fred hasn't left me.

She closed her eyes. If Fred hadn't been with her Christmas Day to pick up the pieces, she knew she'd have come home and slashed her wrists or swallowed a bottle of pills. She'd been knocked off her high horse and come home in tears. Again. She always seemed to come home from her mother's house in tears. That house should be called the House of Wailing. Had anyone ever been happy there?

Annie's happy there.

"I don't know what to do anymore." She looked up at Fred. "I feel as though no one in the world loves me except you." And how long would that last? How long would it take before she alienated him as well?

"Annie loves you." He smiled down at her, that sweet, gentle smile. "She loved you enough to take your abuse for eighteen years."

For the first time, Nora didn't protest at the harsh assessment. She could take the truth from Fred because words weren't a weapon for him. His touch, his voice, his faithfulness made her safe with him, open. Had anyone else said she hadn't been a good mother, she would have done battle.

Yet it wasn't easy to hear. Stricken, she closed her eyes tightly and saw in her mind's eye the look on her daughter's face before she fled into the kitchen. Even as angry as she was, Nora had realized she had crushed her daughter's heart. Just as she had on Thanksgiving Day when she threw away the turkey Annie had made. She hadn't wanted to face it. It had been Susan who slapped her with the truth, and in a small way made her willing to listen to Fred now and feel the truth of his assessment.

It is true. Susan is right. No matter what Annie did, I always wanted her to do more. Fred is right. It was abuse. Oh, God, it's because of my mother that I'm like this.

And then she remembered her mother's tears.

No, it's not my mother's fault. It's my fault. Oh, God, it is. Why do I behave like this?

Because you don't measure up. You never have, the dark voice said. And you still don't.

"What do I have to do?" Fear and anguish were choking her. "I'm so afraid and I don't know what to do."

Fred took her hands and drew her up out of her chair. He held her close for a long moment. "Just be there for both of them." She was trembling, her head aching. "I love you," Fred said. "Do you know that?"

But for how long?

Fred drew back and cupped her face. "Look at me, Nora." When she did, scarcely able to see him through her tears, he said, "I know you a lot better than I did when we courted. And I love you better now than I did on the day I married you."

"I don't know how."

His smile was tender. "*God* knows." He kissed her as though sealing a promise. "I'll get your coat."

Corban was glad he'd stayed, especially when Annie told him she'd called her mother and uncle and both were coming. She was going to need all the support she could get, especially after the doctor just told her he didn't think Leota should be going home again. Better if she was transferred into a convalescent hospital for twenty-four-hour care during her last months of life. It seemed everything was wrong with the old lady's body. Corban thought about Leota joking with him a few months back.

"I'm like an old car, chassie's dented and rusty. I'm leaking fluids and can't even get out of my chair without a jump start."

Tears burned his eyes. He held them back, swallowed them down, put on a stoic face for Annie's sake.

When had Leota stopped being *that cantankerous old hag* to him and become Leota, an old lady he loved? Hands clasped between his knees, he bowed his head and closed his eyes.

Oh, Jesus, oh, God, if You're really up there and You care, please don't let Leota die. Get her well enough so Annie and I can get her out of here and take her home. That's where she wants to be when her time comes. Let me do that much for her.

"Have you heard anything more?"

At Nora Gaines's voice, he raised his head sharply.

Annie fumbled for his hand. "No. Nothing. They said it would be awhile."

Corban held her hand firmly and met Nora's gaze in challenge. She looked back at him, but he didn't see a hint of the hostility that had been there on Christmas Day. She just looked sad. And old. It was as though she had aged in the few days since he'd seen her last. Strange. Suddenly, though he could scarcely believe it, he could see some of Leota in her. Maybe it was the eyes. He'd never noticed before.

"We came right away," Fred said. He extended his hand. "Thanks for helping, Corban."

Corban stood and shook hands with him. He couldn't see any way out of it without being rude and hurting Annie in the process. However, if the guy was dismissing him, he'd better think again. He didn't let go of Annie's hand and sat beside her again. "I'll stick around until we know more."

Fred nodded. "Of course."

Nora sat in a chair across from Annie. Annie glanced at her and then away.

I could almost pity the witch, Corban thought. *Then again, why should I? She brought it on herself. If Annie never speaks to her mother again, who could blame her?* One word from Annie would be more than Nora Gaines deserved. Susan Carter had filled in details of how Annie had lived most of her life: a puppet on strings, yanked hither and yon by her controlling mother.

Suddenly another thought lashed razor-sharp across his mind: *Weren't you the guy who had wanted to put all the poverty-level old folks in a government facility where no one would have to deal with them? Weren't you the guy who wanted to get the old folks off the street and out of sight? After all, this is a youth-oriented society. Right? Old folks could be a real nuisance.*

He swallowed hard, fighting the rush of shame that washed over him.

Admit it, Corban. You could barely stand the sight of Leota Reinhardt the first time you met her. You were repulsed by her wrinkles, her soiled polyester dress, her unkempt house in a ghetto neighborhood. You came with all the answers and wanted her to confirm them. Just so you could get an A in a college course.

It was true. All of it.

What is it about Nora Gaines you really dislike? Why not take a good, hard look at that?

He did. And he knew in an instant what it was that had roused his animosity. The reason wasn't nearly as altruistic as feeling compassion for Annie. It was far more personal. Nora Gaines had hit his sore spot. She'd recognized him for who he really was.

"Why did you come here?" The sarcasm of her question had cut his conscience wide open. Why had he come? To *use* Leota Reinhardt, to get what information he needed and then walk away and forget her.

And there was something else.

Nora Gaines reminded him of Ruth Coldwell. Ruth had said things to him on her way out that had made him see himself more clearly. And he hadn't liked what he had seen. She was wrong in what she'd done, but was he any more right in the way he'd chosen to live with her? Had he ever thought about the consequences? And with Leota, his good deeds came from purely selfish motives. Her desperate need had given him entrance into her life. No wonder she hadn't liked him at first.

Corban grimaced. *I'm more like Nora Gaines than I am like Annie. I'm self-centered and self-absorbed.*

"I shouldn't've brought her here," Annie said in a husky voice.

Nora's response was quick and gentle. "You did the right thing."

"No, I didn't!" Annie jerked her hand from Corban's and stood. She paced the waiting room. "I should've listened to Grandma. She wanted to stay home. I should never have brought her here."

"You did the right thing," Nora said again.

Fred nodded. "She needed a doctor, Annie."

"I think she knows she's dying and that's why she wouldn't tell me she was in pain."

"She's in pain?" Nora asked softly.

Annie turned, her face ravaged by conflicting emotions. "She's been in pain for years, Mother. Pain you wouldn't even understand." She turned away again.

Tensing, ready for attack, Corban waited for Nora Gaines to say something harsh and cruel. But she said nothing. She looked pale and sick. Or maybe it was the sight of her brother, George, striding into the waiting room that kept her from lacerating her daughter again. Jeanne came in behind her husband, looking weary and cautious.

"We heard the message on the answering machine." George looked from Fred to Nora to Annie. Corban smiled grimly. George's gaze barely acknowledged his existence. "We'd have been here sooner, but we had to find a baby-sitter. What'd the doctor say?"

"She's undergoing tests right now." Annie turned, squaring her shoulders as she faced him. "The doctor said it would take a few hours." She glanced at her watch. "We should hear any time now."

Jeanne went to Annie. "I'm so sorry, honey. How can we help?"

"There's nothing we can do but wait and pray, Aunt Jeanne," Annie said tearfully, receiving the hug and returning it.

"There's plenty we can do," George said, his jaw set. "We can see that Mother gets proper care this time."

Corban stood. "Now, just a minute—"

"You're not a member of this family." George ground out the words. "So butt out of our business."

"He's my friend!" Annie stepped around Jeanne.

"And it's *my mother* we're talking about."

"George," Jeanne said, her voice pleading. "This isn't the time—"

"This is as good a time as any." His face was flushed, his eyes dark. "I thought you were going to deal with your daughter, Nora. Tell her what we discussed."

Nora leaned forward in her chair and covered her face.

"We're all upset, George," Fred said calmly.

"Upset! You're right I'm upset. I get back from a Christmas with in-laws and find a message on my answering machine that my mother is in the hospital again. I just finished talking with the doctor, and he said Mother has probably been in pain for *weeks!* If she'd been where we'd wanted her to be in the first place, she would've had professional help before this!"

Annie's face convulsed.

Corban stepped forward. "Hey, man! Where do you get off talking to Annie that way?" He wanted to knock George on his self-righteous backside. "She's been taking care of Leota night and day. Where have *you* been?"

"I've got a business to run. I have a family to take care of. I'm not some snot-nosed rich kid going through college on a trust fund!"

Corban felt the heat rush into his face.

"Yeah!" George sounded positively smug. "I know all about you. Sociology major. Big paper to write. Did you think I wouldn't want to find out the whole story on some guy who just shows up one day to *help* a little old lady out of the kindness of his heart? I hired someone to find out about you."

Wrath melted into shame. "You could've asked me. What did you think? I was after Leota's massive estate? She lives from one social security check to another while her daughter lives in Black Hawk and her son—"

"Get out of here!" George bellowed. "Or I'll throw you out!"

The staff at the nurses' station looked at each other. "Do you think we should do something?" a candy striper said to one of the nurses. The medical technician stood in the supply room listening to the heated conversation. He shook his head.

"You stay out of it. I've already paged the doctor and a chaplain."

"Someone in there is going to need a doctor. They sound like they're going to start a fistfight."

"It won't be the first time," another nurse said. "Everyone trying to do what they think is right, no one wanting to take responsibility, and the poor old lady caught in the middle."

"I don't think that's what's going on," another staff member said. "The granddaughter *wants* to take care of her."

"Get real. Did you see the girl? She can't be more than eighteen. Hardly wet behind the ears and she's supposed to have that kind of responsibility?"

"Maybe if she had some help," a nurse said, writing notes on a chart.

"From what I hear, the patient and her daughter have been estranged for years, and the son isn't close to her either," said another, going into the medicine cabinet.

"It sounds like they care."

"Oh, they care all right. Put her away and let the state pay the bills. That'll leave something for them when—"

"What an awful thing to say."

"How do you know so much?" The other nurse slipped the chart back into its file.

"All you have to do is listen!"

"It's not our business what they think. Our job is to take care of the patient."

A chaplain walked by, heading for the waiting room.

"That poor little old lady."

"The granddaughter wants to take care of her," the candy striper said again.

"Doesn't sound like she'll get help from anyone in that room."

The head nurse picked up another chart. "Well, the patient won't be here long."

"Is she going to die?"

"We all die sometime, but I didn't mean that. She could last a long time. You never know in these cases. They can surprise you. And miracles still happen. What I meant was we're short on beds, and she's going to need long-term care. Dr. Patterson will have her moved into a convalescent hospital unless the family comes to some kind of agreement."

"Doesn't sound like they can agree on anything."

"How sad." The young candy striper shrugged.

"It's better than the alternative." The head nurse slipped the chart back into its place and went down the hall to check on a patient.

One of the nurses was checking over the med chart and the meds in their small paper cups. She glanced at the medical technician who was checking orders. "What do you think, Hiram?"

"I feel sorry for Mrs. Reinhardt."

Hiram knew death could sometimes be an ally. He could hear the arguing going on in the waiting room. He'd listened to the nurses without adding his opinion. He'd drawn blood from Leota Reinhardt not more than an hour ago. It wouldn't be hard to get his hands on the doctor's report and see the prognosis.

He'd helped terminally ill patients before. Maybe he could help Leota Reinhardt, too.

Leota knew something was wrong the moment Annie came into her room. Though her granddaughter smiled cheerfully, Leota could see the puffiness around her eyes, the redness of them. She was pretending everything was going to be fine.

Annie took her hand. "I'll get you out of here as soon as I can,

Grandma." Her mouth worked and she swallowed convulsively. "I'll do whatever I have to . . ."

"They giving you trouble?"

"We're just working out some details."

Leota saw the pain in Annie's eyes, the strain. She saw other things as well, things she hadn't noticed over the past weeks of being in her granddaughter's care. A pity she had to have a stroke to learn what it was like to have a loving daughter. Annie was everything Leota had hoped Eleanor would be. Kind, gentle, unselfish, honest, joyful. Eleanor had been such a sweet little girl, so eager to please. Circumstances had damaged her. Poor Eleanor had learned to lock away hurt by hiding inside herself. Maybe someone would be able to break through the walls and shake her out of herself. Maybe then Eleanor would be the woman God intended her to be.

Whatever happens, God, don't let them ruin Annie. Don't let bitterness take root and choke out her faith. Lord, would You do that for me? Put a high hedge around my granddaughter. Make a wall. Put angels in the watchtowers. I've failed You. I wasn't able to rear a child after Your own heart. How ironic that it was Eleanor who did it. No, that's not right either. I mustn't think that way. It was You. It was You all the time, Lord. It was You who made this miracle.

"Grandma?" Annie was searching her face.

Leota tried to concentrate. She mustn't let her mind wander so much. "Don't worry about me. Whatever happens, honey, you know who holds the cards."

Annie's eyes lightened, warmed, glowed. "I love you, Grandma. I love you so much." A litany from her heart.

"I love you, too." Leota couldn't begin to tell Annie how much the past months had meant to her. So many barren, lonely years. And then the idyll. "Precious . . . precious . . ." She didn't want to think about the storm coming.

Lord, I am too old and sick to dress myself for battle. You'll have to put my armor on for me.

"The doctor said he's given you something to help you rest, Grandma. I'll come back in the morning." Annie leaned down and kissed her. Someone was speaking to her from the doorway. Annie glanced up, nodded, and then looked down at her again. "I have to go now, Grandma. Hang on, please. Don't go home to the Lord yet."

George came in next. He didn't say much, but Leota could feel the tension radiating from him. Anger held in check. Had she inconvenienced him again? What time was it? Maybe he was supposed to be at work instead of visiting her in the hospital. Jeanne approached. Why was there such a look of shame on her face? What was going on? George and Jeanne wished her a good night and left.

Then Eleanor and Fred came in. *My, it's a regular family reunion. Everyone but the grandchildren.* Leota had never seen her daughter look so heartsick. Fred had his arm around her shoulders as she came closer. When Eleanor put her hand over hers, emotions flooded Leota.

Oh, Lord, she is softening. Oh, Lord, Lord, it's finally happening. It is.

Leota wept.

How long had it been since her daughter had touched her? The last thing Leota wanted to do was frighten her daughter away so soon, but she couldn't seem to hold the flood back. Annie said it was the stroke. Emotions could no longer be restrained.

Eleanor's face convulsed. She turned away slightly, but Fred was turning her back again, whispering encouragement. Before Eleanor could say anything, a nurse came into the room.

"I'm sorry, the doctor said it's best if Mrs. Reinhardt rests now. You can come back tomorrow morning and visit."

Eleanor was in control again. Or so it seemed, until she looked down, her gaze barely brushing Leota's. "Good night, Mama."

Mama. She hadn't said that since she was a little girl. *Mama. Mama!*

Leota remembered her little darling screaming after her as she was held tightly in Helene Reinhardt's arms. "Mama! *Mama! Don't go!*"

Leota wanted to travel back in time. She reached out to her daughter, but Eleanor was already turning away. *Oh, God, give me a few more minutes with her.* Why couldn't that nurse allow them another five minutes? Miracles happened in less time than that! Leota had seen Eleanor's broken spirit. Was she contrite as well? She raised her hand weakly from the bed. "Ellie . . ."

It was Fred who noticed her. He leaned down and took her hand in his. "I'll bring her back tomorrow morning, Leota. Keep the faith." He kissed her hand like a gentleman, and then they were gone.

Annie unlocked her car. Corban was with her, and she could feel the anger radiating from him. He was still fuming over the scene in the waiting room. Listening to Uncle George rant and rave, she had wondered if she was wrong and he was right. Maybe she was being thoughtless and immature. Then she had seen Grandma Leota in that hospital bed. She couldn't bear to let her live out the rest of her life in a convalescent home when it was within her power to take her home and care for her.

Lord, I know it won't be easy. Father, I know I'm near exhaustion and I need more help. Jesus, help me do the things I need to do with wisdom. I can't stand alone. Maybe some of what Uncle George said about me having a martyr complex is true. If so, get me out of that mode and make me discerning.

She'd call Maryann Carter and get a list of professionals who could help. She'd talk to the bank about a reverse mortgage or whatever was needed.

Corban took her arm. "Are you sure you're all right to drive, Annie?"

"I'm fine, Corban. Thanks for supporting me through this."

"It isn't over, Annie."

"I know. That's why I'm going home. I'm going to pray and make some phone calls, and then I'm going to rest. Tomorrow morning I'm coming back and getting Grandma out of there."

"What time?"

"Grandma usually sleeps until eight."

"I'll be here at seven-forty-five. If we have to zip her up in a body bag to sneak her out, we'll do it."

Annie gave a broken laugh. "She'd be game for that, I'm sure. It would suit her sense of humor." She took his hand in both of hers. "Thank you, Corban." She saw something flicker in his eyes. With a sense of regret, she released him. She hadn't meant to give him a wrong impression. "I'll see you tomorrow morning." She slid into her car. He closed her door for her and stepped back as she buckled up and started the engine. Giving him a wave, she backed out of the parking space and headed toward the exit. When she pulled out of the lot, she glanced in her rearview mirror. Corban was still standing there, watching her.

"Nora!" Fred called when she left him talking with Dr. Patterson and headed down the hall. All she could think of was finding Annie before she left. Nora walked as fast as she could down the corridor to the elevator. Fred caught up with her as the doors opened. "Honey, wait a minute . . ."

"I can't wait. I have to talk to Anne-Lynn." She stepped into the elevator and punched the button.

As soon as the doors opened again, she rushed out, racing for the hospital entrance. People stared after her. She didn't care what anyone thought. She didn't want her daughter to drive away without speaking to her. She'd never seen Annie look so torn or so filled with loathing. How could George lambaste Annie that way? If it hadn't been for the interference of that chaplain, Nora would have told her brother what she thought of his tirade.

The cold air hit her as soon as she went through the automatic doors. Hugging her coat closer, she scanned the parking lot and spotted Corban Solsek walking along a line of cars. He was alone. Her heart sank.

Fred came up behind her and put his hand beneath her elbow.

"She's gone, Fred."

"You'll see Annie again tomorrow morning."

"I can't leave things the way they are. Did you see the look on her face?"

"I saw," he said bleakly. "What do you want to do?"

Nora drew the fur-lined coat more firmly around herself. Still the cold seeped in. She felt chilled from the inside out. "Anne-Lynn has had all these months to hear my mother's side of everything. I want her to understand my side."

"Maybe you should wait, honey. She's upset."

She turned on him. "I'm upset, too. That's my mother in there." She understood the quiet look he gave her. *About time you realized that.* She uttered a broken sob and closed her eyes. "I never thought I'd feel this way about losing her, but it's tearing me up inside. I've never wished her to die." *Haven't you?* "Mother never cared about me. And I can see Annie doesn't think I care about her. And I do. *I do!*"

He put his arms around her. "I know you do."

She pushed away from him. "I want *her* to know it! I want Anne-Lynn to understand what it was like to live in that house. If Mother dies now, do you think my daughter will ever listen to my side? I have to talk with her *now.*" She dug in her pocket for a Kleenex and couldn't find one. Fred handed her his freshly laundered handkerchief.

People walked around them. Fred took her arm and gently drew her to one side. The wind was coming up from the Bay.

Nora felt desperate. "Please, Fred." He looked every day of his fifty-seven years.

"All right." He put his arm around her, and they walked across the parking lot to his Lincoln. As he opened the door for her, he said, "When you start talking, Nora, keep in mind this may be the last bridge. Try not to burn it."

Annie hadn't stopped crying all the way back to Leota's house. She pulled her car into the driveway, locked it up for the night, and went into the house. She flicked on the kitchen light before locking the back door and closing off the small laundry room.

She had pleaded with God all the way home to bring healing to Grandma's body so that she could have more time with her. And if that wasn't His will, she'd pleaded that she could bring Leota home to die.

It would be better if she did some chores or something so she could calm herself down before calling Susan's mother and asking for help. She had to get rid of this feeling of panic in the pit of her stomach.

Father, please. Jesus, help me. Holy Spirit, give me wisdom. Give me the words to convince—

The doorbell rang.

Annie groaned. *Oh, God, I don't want to see anyone. I don't want to talk to anyone. I need to clean up the kitchen.* The frying pan with the congealed scrambled eggs was dumped into the sink, the unused dishes and silverware still on the nook table. She scraped the eggs into the garbage can under the sink. Setting the pan under the faucet, she turned on the hot water and squirted some liquid soap into the stream.

The doorbell rang again.

It was probably Arba. She usually came by in the evening to say hello and spend a few minutes with Leota. *Oh, Lord, I forgot about the children! They would've come by today.* Shutting off the water, Annie headed quickly into the living room. She flicked on the porch light, glanced out the curtain, and then drew back in shock. In its wake came cold rage. "Go away, Mother! Leave me alone!"

"Anne-Lynn, I need to talk with you."

"I don't want to talk to you! I don't care if I ever see you again!" She turned her back and headed for the kitchen. How could her mother come here now? She had sat silently in that waiting room, letting Uncle George rant on. *"Your mother agrees . . ."* Uncle George had said. *"You were going to do something about your daughter. Did you call the lawyer?"* Her mother, the betrayer.

The doorbell rang again.

Annie stood at the kitchen sink, shaking. She turned the water on again. She let it run until the sink was almost full before shutting it off. Closing her eyes, she prayed fervently. *God, make her go away. I'm not up to seeing her now. Lord, help me hold my temper. Jesus, I*

*can't bear anymore. I think I hate her after tonight. I hate her as much
as she's hated Grandma Leota all these years.*

Shock ran cold and deep through Annie at the thought. *Oh, Lord.
Is this the way it will be? May it never be so. Only make her go away.
Make her go away until I'm calmer. Make her go away until I can
think.*

She drew a lungful of air in through her nose and blew it slowly
from her mouth. It was a technique her piano teacher had taught her
to calm the jitters before a recital. Her heart was pounding and she
felt so hot. Bloodlust instead of the cleansing blood?

Jesus, help me!

The doorbell rang again.

Something burst inside her. "Okay, Mother. If that's the way you
want it!" She strode back through the living room, unlocked the
door, and yanked it open. "Did it ever occur to you I might not want
to see you tonight?" She clamped her teeth before she screamed, "or
ever again!"

"Anne-Lynn, please, I need to speak with you."

"You never know when to leave people alone, do you?"

"This is the only time—"

"You always have to do things on *your* time schedule and in *your*
way, no matter how anyone else feels."

"Annie." Fred's voice came from behind her mother. "Please. Hear
your mother out."

The expression on his face smote Annie's conscience. Fred had
always treated her with the same tenderness he would his own
daughter if he'd had one. It wasn't fair to put him in the middle of
this. Relenting, she unlocked the screen door and moved back so
they could come in. "Five minutes, Mother. And that's it."

"Five minutes is all you can spare your own mother?"

How many times had Annie heard that faintly sarcastic whine of
self-pity in her mother's voice? Annie looked at her. "You've used up
thirty seconds."

Her mother blinked and then sat slowly on the sofa. "My mother's
turned you against me."

"That's rich, Mother, especially considering all the years you've
done your level best to poison me against Grandma Leota." Her
mother looked shocked and then devastated, but Annie had seen
that look before. How many times had her mother used that look
against her?

How could you get a B+, Anne-Lynn? I'm so disappointed in you.

*If you needed help, why didn't you tell me? I would have hired a tutor
. . . What do you mean you want to stop taking gymnastics? The
physical therapist said you could compete again next year . . . If you'd
only apply yourself a little more, Anne-Lynn, you could play that
piece without the music . . . Veronica's daughter is head cheerleader.
How can you be satisfied just being a pom-pom girl?*

Annie struggled against the resentment rising up in her, the hurt
that had sometimes almost overwhelmed her. She had toyed with the
idea of suicide the year Susan invited her to church camp. Had she
not met the Lord that summer, she wouldn't even be alive today. Did
her mother know how far she'd pushed her?

"I never meant to poison you, Anne-Lynn."

"Of course not." The bitter anger poured out of Annie, despite her
efforts to stop it. "You just took every opportunity to tell me what an
awful childhood you had and how your mother was so terrible. You
made sure I never had any time with her. God forbid that I might get
to know my own grandmother!"

"Annie," Fred said, again in that tender voice. "Who are you serving in this?"

It was enough to draw her up short. *Who am I serving? Oh, Lord,
Lord . . .*

"I came here to explain how I felt . . ." Her mother's voice cracked.

"Oh, mother," Annie said, weary and sick at heart. "You've told me
a hundred times how you felt. Dumped. Unloved. Neglected. And
you've paid Grandma Leota back in kind."

"You make it sound like I was avenging myself."

"Weren't you? As soon as you were able, you left."

"I got married."

"Miserably married. You've told me that, too. Michael's wretched
father. And it was all Grandma's fault you left home so young. You've
made no secret you hate her."

"I don't hate her!"

"Words are cheap. I've never seen you do *anything* for her in the
eighteen years of my life. I can count on two hands the number of
times we came here, and you always sent me and Michael outside as
though Grandma were some kind of disease you didn't want us to
get! And within half an hour, you'd have one of your convenient
headaches and we'd all have to go home. You'd talk against her the
whole way—"

"I can't be in this house without remembering what it was like!"

"I *love* being in this house. I *love* being with Grandma Leota."

Her mother's face jerked as though Annie had struck her. "You don't understand."

Annie had seen what bitterness and resentment had done to her mother. *Oh, God, don't let me become like her. My anger is so great, I could destroy her with it and be glad. And then what? I'd live with regret for the rest of my life because I love her. She's my mother, God help me. Oh, Lord, please, light my way. Be with us here, Lord. We need You!*

She let out her breath. "Grandma Leota has memories, too, Mother. She was hurt. You don't know anything about what was going on."

"Eleanor and George didn't understand, and it wasn't my secret to tell."

Her mother stiffened. "And you do?"

Fred put his hand over her mother's. "Maybe if you told us, Annie."

"She wouldn't listen, Fred."

"I'll listen," her mother said angrily. "I'll listen, if *you* listen."

"I have listened, Mother. I've listened to your side all my life. You want me to repeat what I know? You were three years old when Leota handed you over to Grandma Helene. And then she waltzed off to work like a single woman and enjoyed a life of her own without so much as a glance over her shoulder at the children she'd dumped. And when she was home, all she cared about was her garden. She never cared about *you*. All she ever cared about was herself." Annie dashed the tears angrily from her face. "Isn't that what you were going to say?"

Her mother's face jerked again, tears flooding her eyes. "It's the way it was."

"No, it wasn't. It was the way you perceived it through your child eyes."

"Grandma Helene said she—"

"Don't you dare blame it all on her. She's dead! She can't defend herself. And at least she had the decency to finally put it all together for herself!" Annie could scarcely believe the words had come from her mouth.

Her mother looked at Fred, her face crumpling. "I told you . . ."

"Annie." Fred looked at her, pleading. "For God's sake, she's your mother."

Shame filled her.

"Honor thy father and mother . . ."

I'm becoming just like my mother. Annie wilted into her grandmother's recliner. *Oh, Jesus, forgive me. I'm hammering the nails into Your hands all over again. What sort of witness am I of Your love? What can I do to make it right?*

Forgive her.

Her hands clenched on the armrests. *I do,* Father. Oh, Lord, I do, but I can't say it because she won't understand why I'm forgiving her. How can she? She doesn't know what she's done. She doesn't know the half of it. I feel as though I've fallen away.

Rise up.

I'm sitting in the darkness here.

Let Me be your light.

And the light is truth.

Truth!

Suddenly calm inside, Annie knew what to say. "Mom, you never understood what was going on."

Her mother raised her eyes. She looked desolate. "What didn't I understand? My mother didn't love me."

"You're so wrong. She sacrificed everything for you and Uncle George. The reason Grandma moved in here in the first place was to see to your needs. She didn't have enough money to support you on her own, and Grandpa Reinhardt couldn't get work."

"That's a lie, Anne-Lynn! My grandfather went to work every day."

"He left the house every day. And he sat on a bench in Dimond Park. He was *German,* Mother. Think this through. He was an immigrant with a heavy German accent during World War II. No one would hire him. He was using up what savings he had. He knew he was going to lose the house. And then what would happen? So he wrote to your father, who was serving overseas, and asked him for help. Your father wrote to Grandma Leota and told her the situation. She was having financial troubles of her own trying to make ends meet on your father's military allotment and rearing two children by herself. So she moved in here and went to work. She thought it was the only way they could all make it. *She's* the one who paid for the house and the food and utilities and the clothes on everyone's back."

Her mother looked frightened. "But Grandma Helene said my grandfather was an engineer."

Annie wondered if her mother had listened to a word she had said. "I don't doubt he was an engineer, Mother, but not an employed engineer. Your grandmother didn't know he couldn't find work. He was too embarrassed to tell her. He went out looking for a job every day until he realized no one would hire him."

"If all that's true, why didn't my mother tell Grandma Helene?" she said almost defiantly. "Grandma said the most awful things to Mother, and she never said anything about this."

"Because Great-Grandpa Reinhardt was her only friend in this house. If she told your grandmother the truth, what would that have accomplished? She might have avenged herself on your grandmother, but she would've shamed your grandfather in the process. So she kept silent. She thought everything would turn out all right when your father came home. Do you remember what happened? When the war ended and your father came home, your grandfather signed the house over to him. Why would he do that, Mom, if what Grandma Leota said wasn't true?"

Her mother closed her eyes. "I can remember the night that happened. Grandma Helene was screaming and crying and calling my mother a whore and a thief. She said my mother was unnatural because she didn't want her children. George and I hid under our covers and cried."

Annie's heart broke for the frightened child her mother must've been.

Her mother let out a shuddering breath. "And my father. I was terrified of him. I was so little when he went away, I didn't know him when he came home. He was so tall and broad and blond, and he had the coldest blue eyes. Just like one of those German Aryans you read about." Her face was white, her expression distant, remembering. "Once he got so mad, he put his fist through a wall. That one, right over there by the kitchen door." Her mouth curled. "He was always losing a job because of his temper. And then his drinking. He turned into a lazy drunk."

Annie uttered a broken sob at the description. She had never met her grandfather, but her heart ached for him. "Your father was a master carpenter whose life was shattered by the war. His parents asked him to look for family members when he got to Germany. He did. And he found some." *Oh, Lord, help her hear this and walk in her father's shoes long enough to understand.* "They were working for one of the concentration camps. They were supplying the soldiers who were exterminating Jews. Your father was a translator in his unit. When his relatives begged for mercy, he and another in his unit shot them down. Grandma Leota said he talked about it only once to her and never discussed the war again."

Her mother's face was white. "I remember Grandma Helene asking him questions in German, and he said he found nothing."

"Did he ever speak German again, Mom?"

Her mother closed her eyes tightly. "No. Grandma asked him once why he wouldn't, and he said he wanted to forget he was German."

"He was ashamed. He didn't understand that Germans were not the only race capable of atrocities. It's mankind. Beneath the veneer of civilization, the flesh is weak and given to all manner of sin. There, but for the grace of God, go we all."

"I never knew any of this!" her mother cried out.

"Grandma Leota said they weren't her secrets to tell. Great-Grandma Helene must've found out because Grandma Leota said she changed shortly after your grandfather died. He must've finally told her before he died. If not all, at least the part about Grandma Leota paying for the house. I don't think anyone but Grandma Leota knew about what happened in Germany. Whatever your grandfather told Grandma Helene, after he was buried, she never spoke another unkind word to Grandma Leota. They made their peace. Grandma said they loved one another in the end."

Her mother cried bitterly. "I feel as though Grandma Helene poisoned me."

"Maybe she did. Just as you've tried to poison me, Mother."

"Don't say that. Please don't say that."

"It's time you faced it. Show some compassion! All the things Grandma Helene told you out of ignorance about Grandma Leota, you've repeated to me. Not once, Mom, but over and over, year after year. This is your opportunity to change things between you and Grandma Leota. You won't have her around forever."

Grief flooded her mother's eyes, shame as well. "Why didn't my mother tell me all this years ago?"

Annie was filled with sorrow. "Oh, Mom, all you had to do was ask."

The medical technician delivered the vials of blood he had taken from several patients to the downstairs laboratory. Another technician was looking through a microscope. She straightened, rubbing the back of her neck, and glanced up at him with a smile. "How's it going, Hiram?"

"Busy day." He would go off duty in another two hours. "I'm taking my dinner break. I think I need a good jolt of caffeine."

She went back to looking through the microscope. "Bring me a cup, if you think about it. And a brownie if they have any."

The cafeteria was almost empty, which suited Hiram just fine. He needed to be alone to think. Walking along the glass-fronted counter, he picked meat loaf, mashed potatoes, corn, a piece of apple pie, and coffee. Finding a table in a back corner, he made himself comfortable. From where he sat he could see a full view of the room. He liked to be able to see who was coming in and going out.

He'd found the time and opportunity to read over Leota Reinhardt's chart. Having a premed major in college, he'd always dreamed of being a doctor. Unfortunately, his grades hadn't been high enough to get him into medical school. Furthermore, he'd had to drop out of college the last year and help his mother take care of his father, who had developed Alzheimer's. They'd finally put him in a convalescent hospital.

Every time he took his mother to visit, she came home in tears because his father's mind was so far gone that he didn't even remember who she was. It broke his mother's heart. Maybe if he'd gotten along better with his father, he would have felt the same.

Twice his father had gotten pneumonia. Both times, he tried to convince his mother to tell the hospital not to go to heroic measures to save the old man. "I can't do that. He's my husband. He's your father." Not anymore, he'd wanted to say. Whatever part of the man that had been his father was long gone. Hiram had begun to hate going to that convalescent hospital. He'd begun to hate the sight of that sick old man who was just the shell of a human being.

He felt sorry for Leota Reinhardt's family. She was half paralyzed from a stroke. Add cancer to that, along with congestive heart failure, arthritis, and a few other minor problems like borderline anemia, and her life wasn't worth living. If she did live, her granddaughter, a real beauty, would spend the next year or two or more working night and day to take care of an old woman who wouldn't even be able to carry on an intelligible conversation with her. Considering how the rest of the family was reacting, it seemed the old woman hadn't been all that nice anyway. No one but the granddaughter would miss her.

Every year there were more elderly. People were living longer and longer. All well and good if they were healthy, but, unfortunately, most weren't. Every year he saw more old people coming into the hospital, filling up the beds, and using up tax dollars he and his generation paid. He'd read that almost 30 percent of the Medicare dollars were going to the care of people during their last year of life.

Thirty percent! He'd read by the year 2040, 45 percent of the expenditures would be paid out to let these people cling to life a few more months.

It didn't make sense.

In fact, it seemed cruel to him. Cruel to make the old live longer. Cruel to make the young pay for it. You only had to look at the relatives' faces after a visit to see that it was agony watching a loved one slowly break down and die. Didn't he know it from personal experience? Some of his patients reminded him of moldering corpses that, by some accident of nature, still drew breath. They smelled of decay.

They put animals to sleep. Why not human beings?

He hated to see people suffer.

People ought to be able to die with dignity.

If the government could fund abortions for drudges and welfare recipients, why not extend death with dignity to the old? It made perfect sense to him. The arguments were the same. He carried the thought further, rolling it around some more. If people didn't want to shell out money to support crack babies and babies born into poverty or babies born with handicaps, why would they want to finance long-term care for people who couldn't pull their share of the workload anymore?

It ticked him off how much money he had to pay in taxes every year. The more he made, the more the government took. And where was it all going? To drones. How long had it been since Leota Reinhardt had held a job and paid taxes into the system? Two decades? Besides that, how many thousands of dollars of taxpayers' money were going to be spent keeping her alive for a few months longer?

Benefits and burdens should be measured.

It wasn't right to prolong life. He'd seen people suffer agonies untold with cancer and emphysema and diabetes, where bit by bit the body died off. And family members suffered right along with them. Like he had. Like his mother had. All the talk about dying being a part of living . . . If that was the truth, then what was the big deal in helping the process along?

He'd overheard enough of the shouting in that waiting room to know Leota Reinhardt didn't want to end up in a convalescent hospital. The family didn't want to be responsible for in-home nursing care, except the girl who didn't know what she was getting into. And the guy shouting didn't want to see the entire estate siphoned away by private in-home nursing care that might last as long as the old lady did.

That beautiful girl ought to be out dancing and having a good time instead of saddling herself with a sick old woman who wasn't ever going to get any better.

One injection. That's all it'd take. And all Leota Reinhardt's suffering would be over.

No one even had to know.

He looked up and around the room, vaguely uncomfortable, defensive. Sometimes he felt as though someone was watching him . . . as though someone could read his thoughts. A pity he couldn't say what he thought without risking his job. He was more compassionate than most; he cared about patients, and he hated watching people suffer. Why should he feel apologetic for wanting to help a patient die with dignity?

It had been hard the first time. He'd felt sick for days afterward. Sick with guilt, sick with fear, sick with feelings he couldn't even identify. But he'd gotten over it. He thought about it all the time and the reasons why he'd done it. It was right; he knew he was right to do it. He had made the decision after overhearing the patient's twenty-year-old daughter, hysterical and screaming at the doctor, "Can't you *do* something? Why does she have to suffer like this?"

The doctor hadn't had the guts to do what should've been done weeks earlier. But he had. During the quiet hours of the night shift, when all the visitors were gone and the nurses were working on charts and counting meds, he'd gone into the room and given the patient an injection. She hadn't even opened her eyes. She had died with dignity.

The second time had been a little easier, and with each one after that he'd spent less and less time feeling anything but relief. He'd helped ten patients in a hospital in southern California, most of them with cancer or emphysema. Then he worked in San Francisco and, over a period of three years, helped twenty more with AIDS. Seeing all those dying patients had gotten to him. All that suffering, not to mention the cost. Five, sometimes six, thousand dollars a month, just to keep one patient in medicine. How insane was that?

He had several vials of morphine and succinylcholine chloride in his locker, given to him by one of the nurses he'd gone out with in San Francisco. He wasn't alone in the way he felt. There were others, and the numbers were growing. Kevorkian was paving the way. It wouldn't be long before euthanasia was legal.

There were so many who needed help. After all, where was the dignity in being incontinent, slobbering, and half paralyzed?

If he were in Leota Reinhardt's place, he'd want someone to show a little mercy.

Nora stopped trying to defend herself and listened. Annie stopped lashing out and accusing and began to relate everything Leota had told her about those early years. For the first time in her life, Nora began to see things through her mother's eyes, and it hurt.

Oh, how it hurt.

She kept seeing that dream image of her mother on her knees in the garden looking toward the house with such longing in her eyes. Had it been a dream? Or had she seen her mother like that time and again while she was in the kitchen doing her grandmother's bidding, soaking up the bitter words and letting them take root in her soul?

"She loves you, Mom."

"She never said so."

"She showed you by working."

"I would've liked to have heard the words."

"Maybe you did, but you weren't listening."

Nora started to cry. How many tears had she shed in her lifetime? Gallons for herself. And now she was weeping for her mother, feeling the pain as though it were her own. And wasn't it? "I don't know what to do!"

Annie was crying, too. "Help me, Mom. I want to bring her home."

"The doctor said she needs to be in the hospital. She's so sick."

"The doctor said she needs extensive care," Annie said, determined.

"But you're giving up your whole life!"

Annie leaned forward, her hands open, pleading. "Mom, she doesn't have a lot of time, and I want to spend every day I can with her. Don't you want that now? Don't you want the chance to get to know her? You never did before. You never saw her or who she really was."

Nora was afraid, so afraid, of making the wrong decision. How many times in her life had she been wrong? So many times she couldn't count. And this time it mattered. It mattered so much. "I could spend time with her in a hospital. There are excellent ones, you know. There's one not far from us, isn't that so, Fred? You could come home, Anne-Lynn. We could go together and visit her."

"It wouldn't be the same and you know it, Mom. If Grandma had a choice, when the Lord calls her home, she'd want to be on a chaise lounge in her garden."

Nora felt torn. Fred put his hand over hers and squeezed gently. He was looking at her, the tenderness of his expression encouraging her. *You know what's right, Nora. You know in your heart what your mother would want. Wouldn't you want the same thing? To have your family around you . . . to be in your own home?*

"All right, Annie," she said in a broken voice. "I don't fully agree that this is best, but I'll help you."

"We'll bring her home tomorrow." Relief filled Annie's eyes—eyes so warm and thankful. Nora had never seen that look in her daughter's eyes before, at least, not for her.

"Tomorrow might be too soon, Annie," Fred said. "The doctor said she's very weak. Maybe it'd be better to wait a few days."

"Mom, please."

Nora let her breath out slowly. All the wasted years of bitterness. Maybe this one act might pave the way to a new relationship with her mother, however brief it might turn out to be. "I'll help you bring her home tomorrow morning."

Leota dozed. It was difficult to sleep with all the noise and activities of the hospital—nurses coming and going, a patient in the next bed moaning until she was given another shot that eased her pain and made her sleep so soundly she snored like a man. Then there was that medical technician who seemed to hang around. He'd just a minute ago stood in the doorway, then moved on when a nurse had said something to him.

Her mind drifted back to the years just before the war, when Bernard had been whole. She could see him in that dance hall, watching her. She could remember the wind in her face as they sat in the rumble seat riding home.

The tune of "Don't Sit under the Apple Tree with Anyone Else but Me" ran in her head. She could see Mama Reinhardt knitting socks for Bernard. She remembered the air-raid sirens going off and the block warden in his hard hat knocking on the door and telling them they had to black out the windows better because light still showed through. They'd saved everything for the war effort. Bacon grease for making ammunition, toothpaste tubes, tin cans, glass jars, newspapers and magazines when she'd finished reading and rereading them a dozen times. Nothing was wasted.

How her Victory garden had flourished! She'd grown enough rhubarb, lettuce, cabbage, tomatoes, peas, corn, beets, carrots, and potatoes to keep the neighborhood fed. Mama Reinhardt had canned hundreds of jars of cherries, plums, apricots, and applesauce.

She could still see that Jewel Tea truck come around the corner selling everything from hairpins to crackers. And the Borden's milk truck and the Swedish bakery truck. She used to sell some of her vegetables to old Toby, who came around with his pickup. He always ran out of produce long before he ran out of customers.

She thought of Cosma, her dear friend. She'd never forget the permanent Cosma gave her. *She said I looked like Rita Hayworth with all my red blonde hair in wild curls. We went shopping in San Francisco, and the sailors whistled, and all I could do was cry because I kept wishing Bernard were home to see how nice I looked. Cosma took a picture of me in that one-piece sunsuit I wore all summer long in the garden. I struck a Betty Grable pose. Bernard wrote back and said the guys in his unit told him he'd married "a dish." I wonder what I did with that sequined beret? I used to have a straw hat with giant roses and a chapeau with a barnyard of feathers. How funny I must have looked!*

She let her mind fill with memories of Eleanor and George when they were little. She loved the tiny curls on the back of George's neck, the smell of soft skin in the curve of Eleanor's baby neck. And those chubby legs.

"*Mama.*"

Let me dream about those far-off days as though they were near again. Lord, let me remember what it was like to have a whole man looking forward to a bright future and two babies, healthy and happy. Don't let my mind drift to the dark years.

And yet, they too were sweet in their own way.

Yea, though I walked through the valley of the shadow of death and I dwelt in darkness, You were light to me. My Lord and my Redeemer. All those years, when Bernard sank into his depression and used to call out for help, I looked up to You. How many times did I go out into the sunlight and walk with You in the garden and talk with You in my heart? How many times did I go out there at night and look up at the moon and stars? And You were there with me. You, the lover of my soul.

The medical technician was back at the door again. What did he want? Why was he back again? He was behaving oddly, looking down the hall one way and then the other. Was he back to take more blood? Surely the two test tubes he took this afternoon had been enough! He'd had a carrier with tubes in it when he came into her room before. His hands were empty now.

He came into the room, pausing to watch Leota's roommate sleeping. His presence distressed Leota. Something about his manner filled her with dread.

Lord, what's going on here? Why is he behaving so oddly? I'm afraid. What am I afraid of? I'm in a hospital! They help people get well here, don't they? Why this feeling of danger?

Eleanor is coming back tomorrow. Fred said he was bringing her. I could feel her heart softening. Oh, God, the years I've prayed for this to happen. Maybe tomorrow morning will be a new beginning. Maybe tomorrow morning, I can touch her hand without her pulling away. Maybe tomorrow morning, I can tell her I love her and have her finally believe me.

The man moved away from the other bed and approached hers. He didn't look her in the eyes but glanced toward the door one more time. How odd. "Just a little something to help you sleep, Leota." Why would he carry a syringe in the pocket of his coat? Any half-wit would know it could become contaminated.

For just a second, he looked into her eyes.

That was all the time Leota needed to know what the man had come to do.

Troubled, Nora stared out the front window of the car. It was raining, and the windshield wipers swished back and forth. She had no cause to worry. Fred was an excellent driver and the traffic was light this time of night. So why this strange sensation of restlessness?

"What's wrong, honey?" Fred said, flicking the headlights to bright again after a car passed by them.

"I don't know. Just a funny feeling." She felt the strong urge to go to her mother. Now. Not tomorrow morning. *Now—turn around. Go back to the hospital.* It was foolishness.

"About what?"

"I was just thinking about seeing my mother tomorrow morning and wishing I didn't have to wait that long."

"Do you want to go back to the hospital?"

Nora looked at him. "It's after midnight, Fred. She'll have gone to sleep long ago."

"And if she were awake? What would you want to say to her?"

Her throat felt so hot and tight. She looked out the windshield again.

I'd say I'm sorry. I'd say I do love you, Mother, even though it's never seemed as though I did. It was because I loved you so much that I've been so angry. I'd say please forgive me for all the cruel things I've said and done. I'd say so many things I've kept bottled up for forty-five years. She sobbed. "Mama, I've missed you. That's what I'd say."

Fred reached over and brushed his knuckles lightly against her cheek. "We can go back if you want. Say the word and I'll take the next off ramp."

She almost said yes, then mentally shook herself. What was she thinking? It was well past midnight. She was letting her emotions run away with her again. She had spent a lifetime letting her emotions control her. Besides, she could imagine what the nurses would have to say if she showed up at this time of night and insisted on seeing her mother. What was she supposed to say? *I want to make amends? I want to wake up my mother so I can say I'm sorry?*

"It's all right, Fred," she said, putting her hand on his thigh, "I can wait a few more hours."

What did one more night matter?

Oh, God, don't let him do this. Oh, please, Lord. Annie said to hang on. Fred said keep the faith. Eleanor is so close to becoming herself again. Lord, help me!

She could hardly move because of the medication already given her. She raised her hand, but the technician only smiled. "I understand," he said. "It'll all be over soon. You won't suffer anymore."

Oh, God, he doesn't understand me. He doesn't know what he's doing! I'm not alive for my benefit. I'm alive for the sake of my children. Oh, Jesus, open his eyes! Show him! Make him understand. Oh, Jesus, stop him from doing this terrible thing! I want to live. I want to see my daughter in the morning. I need time, just a little more time.

Her mind was in torment, her heart in terror.

What will happen to Eleanor when she comes? What about George? Will he withdraw more and more until he's just like Bernard? Oh, Lord, my sweet Annie. Will she think I gave up? Oh, Father in heaven . . .

She could feel the coldness of death approaching, darkness closing in around her.

"It won't be long now, Leota," the man said. "Shhh . . . don't struggle." He put his hand over her mouth. "Relax and let it happen."

Hang on! Hang on!

She tried to claw at his hand but hadn't the strength to break free. *Hang on . . .*

But she couldn't. Her mind and will were not sufficient to over-come what he had done. He lifted his hand, took hers briefly and squeezed it. "It'll be over soon," he said as though he was doing her a favor. He frowned as she looked up at him. "It's better this way, better for everyone."

Oh, this poor deluded boy. He doesn't look much older than Corban. She watched him turn away and quietly leave the room. *He must think he's done something good. Oh, Lord, forgive him. He doesn't know what he's done.*

She thought of what Bernard had found in Germany all those years ago. This boy thought she had no quality of life. He thought her life wasn't worth living anymore. She had no purpose, no value. *Is this mercy, Lord? Is it?*

Her heart broke.

Oh, Lord, Lord, I waited so long to be reconciled. I prayed a million prayers. And tomorrow might have been the day of salvation for Elea-nor. Oh, my sweet, beloved baby girl might have returned to me. Oh, Jesus, how I've longed for such a day . . .

It's time, beloved.

Light, warmth. The Presence of love was with her, raising her from the husk of her body and wiping her tears away. *I have count-ed every one and kept them in a bottle.* The Voice was within and without and all around. *Come, beloved. See what I have prepared for you.* She vibrated to the sound of love, like a harp played by the master.

Still, a part of her resisted. *What of my children, Lord? I love them so. What will become of my children?*

If they seek Me, they will find Me. He held His arms wide. *Trust Me, beloved.*

And with a sigh of surrender, Leota Reinhardt went home.

The telephone rang as Nora was finishing the last touches of her makeup before she and Fred headed back to the hospital. Everything froze inside her at the sound. Fred answered on the second ring. She had a sick feeling in the pit of her stomach. Her heart was drum-ming. Dropping the mascara, she hurried out of the bedroom and down the stairs. Who would call at six-thirty in the morning? Only Annie. Or George.

She came into the family room and saw Fred standing with his back to her. He was talking softly. He put the telephone receiver down slowly and turned toward her.

"Annie?" It was all she could manage. Her heart was pounding so hard she thought she'd pass out.

He nodded. He didn't have to say anything. The reason for Annie's call was written all over his face. "I'm sorry, Nora. I'm so sorry."

"We should've gone back last night. I should've told you to turn around!"

"You had no way of knowing."

Hadn't she? *Oh, God, why didn't I listen to You?*

Her mother was gone.

24

Annie received a call from Charles Rooks the morning her grand-mother's short obituary ran in the *Oakland Tribune*. "I have Leota Reinhardt's will as well as some documents she was having me hold for her children. I'd like to hand-deliver these. Could you contact Eleanor Gaines and George Reinhardt so we could all meet at my office? I'm located near Lake Merritt." He gave her the address and telephone number and asked if it would be convenient for them to meet the following afternoon.

"I'm sure they'll be able to meet with you, Mr. Rooks," Annie said. "I'll call and let them know."

"I need to speak with you as well, Miss Gardner."

"Me?"

"Yes. I can't meet with the others without having you present." Surprised and confused, she agreed to attend.

"There was no mention of a funeral service in the paper," Mr. Rooks said over the telephone. "If it hasn't already been held, I'd like to attend. Would that be all right with you and the family?"

Annie closed her eyes, willing herself not to cry again. "There wasn't a service, Mr. Rooks." Uncle George had said there was no point in going to such expense when Grandma Leota hadn't attended church for years. When Annie had argued that she had taken her grandmother numerous times over the past months, he said, "Has anyone called to ask about her?"

"Arba comes by frequently."

"She's a neighbor. She can pay her respects at the house."

He was adamant. Why would anyone care to attend a service for an old lady they didn't know and who hadn't been part of their congregation for more than a few months? Had she given lots of money? No. Then no one would bother. Nothing could dissuade him.

It was Jeanne who told Annie later that she didn't think her husband could get through a funeral service. Jeanne said he'd only been to one and swore after seeing his friend in the casket that he would never attend another funeral as long as he lived.

"No service at all?" Charles Rooks said.

"Not a formal service. Some of us gathered here at her home and had our own memorial for Grandma yesterday." Arba Wilson and her three children, Mother and Fred, George and Jeanne and their children had been there. No one had said very much. Annie hadn't had time enough to prepare anything in the way of pictures or mementos. Not that her mother or George would have wanted to view them.

Her mother had seemed beyond tears in her grief. Annie wondered what would happen to her mother now. She wasn't angry anymore—the resentment had been exorcised. Instead, her mother was consumed by guilt and shame for all the wasted years. And for not listening to whatever it was that had told her to turn around and go back and see Grandma Leota the night she died.

"I lost my chance," she'd said. "I'll never be able to tell her . . ."

If only Grandma Leota had been able to hang on to life a little longer! One day would've made so much difference. The doctor said he was certain she had passed away peacefully. Annie was grateful for that. She imagined her grandmother closing her eyes, going to sleep, and then waking up with the Lord. Oh, if only Grandma had been at home.

"I'd like to send flowers, Miss Gardner." Charles Rooks's voice pulled her from her thoughts. "Where is her resting place?"

"That decision hasn't been made yet, Mr. Rooks. Grandma Leota told me she wanted to be cremated." Annie would pick up the ashes when the funeral-home director called her.

"Oh."

She knew decisions would have to be made, but she didn't feel comfortable discussing them with Charles Rooks. She didn't know anything about him, other than the fact that he was an attorney who had handled her grandmother's will. She wished she could discuss things openly with her mother and uncle. Her mother had cried when Annie received the call that she needed to sign the papers for her grandmother's cremation. Her uncle said he had no idea where to have her buried. After all, what did it matter?

Annie met her mother, Fred, and Uncle George in the lobby of the office building where Charles Rooks practiced law. Her mother looked pale and wan; George looked calm. "I've contacted a real-estate firm about Mother's house," he said on the elevator ride up. That seemed to bring life back to Annie's mother.

"What about Anne-Lynn?"

"I assumed she'd want to move back in with her friend and go back to art school," he said defensively, glancing at Annie. "Or move back home. Isn't that what you were hoping would happen, Nora?"

Annie looked away. The surge of anger that rose inside her was far from godly. She knew she had no right to judge anyone, but her heart cried out against them.

"We don't have to discuss this now, George."

"There's no reason to get so upset, Eleanor." George looked at her disdainfully. "I doubt the house will sell that fast. Annie can stay for however many weeks or months it takes to unload the place. In fact, that would be convenient. Someone will have to maintain the place until we find a buyer. Annie could go on living there rent free. Of course, if you want to keep the house, Nora, we can have it assessed and you can pay me for my half."

Annie pressed her lips together and fought tears. She didn't want any of them to see the effect Uncle George's words had on her. How could he talk this way? *Unload the place.* What a terrible way to speak about Grandma Leota's home. All the years of memories bound in that wonderful little house. And the garden! Grandma's refuge. She had said once she met there daily with the Lord. Annie could imagine how much it would hurt Grandma Leota to know her son had no sentiments about her or her property. He couldn't wait to sell it and collect whatever money it would bring. Money! Bloody lucre! That's all he seemed to care about.

That can't be true. Oh, Lord, that can't be true.

"I don't want to discuss this right now." Her mother was angry, her voice cracking.

"It'd be easier on everyone if we made these decisions as soon as possible."

Uncle George couldn't wait to get on with his life. Was that it? He wanted to avoid the grief, the guilt, the emptiness he must now feel with no chance of ever working things out with his mother?

"The least we could do is wait until we find a decent resting place for her!" Annie's mother said.

"She should be next to Papa, don't you think?"

"Fine, George. Do *you* remember where Papa is buried?"

"I was in Vietnam—"

"And I was in the midst of a divorce!"

The elevator doors opened and Annie stepped out. Seeing a drinking fountain, she headed for it. She leaned down, wishing she could cool her face in the cold water. How could they go on like this so soon after Grandma had passed away? Uncle George reminded her of a carrion crow, picking at Grandma's remains. And Mother. What would happen to her mother's life now that she had no chance to ask for forgiveness?

Oh, Grandma. If only you'd lived another day, another week, another month, another year. I love you so much. I miss you. There were so many things you still had to teach me. So many wonderful stories to tell. I wanted more time. Oh, God, why didn't You let me have more time with her?

Fred touched her shoulder. "Are you all right, Annie?"

She straightened. He must think she was going to drink the fountain dry. "I'm trying hard not to say anything I'll regret." *Lord, give me strength.* And a case of laryngitis.

Fred put his hand on her shoulder. "The last few days have been very hard on your mother."

Annie could see just how hard. Annie wished she'd explained weeks before what had been going on all those years ago. "I should've had it out with her long ago." Perhaps then there would have been time for her mother to be restored to Grandma Leota. But she had been silent and patient, just as Grandma Leota had been silent and patient all those years. Now Annie wondered if her mother would ever get over the guilt and sorrow for all the years she had stayed away, nursing her grudges and refusing to seek the truth.

Will she go back to blaming Grandma, Lord? Will my mother start

*thinking Grandma Leota cheated her from a chance of reconciliation?
Like death was the last dirty trick . . .*

How she wished Grandma Leota had felt free to speak up years
ago! *I know your reasons for keeping silent, Grandma, but what good
did it do? Oh, Father, even if she had told Mother and Uncle George
the truth, would they have listened?*

Fred looked troubled. "Your mother had the feeling we should go
back to the hospital the night your grandmother died, but we didn't
act on it. I wish we had, Annie. Now it's going to be like a raw
wound. One more burden for your mother to carry, along with all
those years of bitterness."

"I'm afraid for her, Fred. Grandma loved her. I know she did."

"I've no doubt of your word, Annie, but I wish Leota had had
the chance to say it for herself. As it stands, I don't know if your
mother will ever be able to believe it. Especially considering the
guilt she carries now." He looked tired and sad. "We'd better join
the others."

Charles Rooks greeted Annie when she entered his office with
Fred. Her mother was already seated in a brown leather wing chair.
Uncle George had taken the other in front of the attorney's desk.
Annie and Fred took the sofa against the wall. The attorney intro-
duced his secretary, who offered everyone coffee. They all declined.
Uncle George was in a hurry, as usual. He had a business appoint-
ment in San Francisco in two hours. People who move fast don't
have time to think about their losses.

The secretary closed the door quietly on the way out.

Charles Rooks passed out copies of Grandma Leota's will.
Annie wondered why he gave her a copy, until he started to
explain that there was no property to dispose of in the will. It had
merely been drawn up to make sure Leota Reinhardt's wishes were
not thwarted.

"What are you talking about? What wishes?" Uncle George was
clearly confused—and getting angry. "There's an estate. Granted, it's
not much, but she had a house, free and clear. That's worth something in today's market."

"Anne-Lynn Gardner owns the house."

"What?" Uncle George turned toward her, his face reddening. A
bubble of laughter came from her mother, quickly choked back by a
soft sob.

"No, I don't!" Annie stared at the lawyer, disbelieving. "You're
mistaken, Mr. Rooks."

"There's no mistake, Miss Gardner. We discussed it at length when I met with Mrs. Reinhardt at her home. I have a copy of the deed right here, which your grandmother mailed to me."

"But that's impossible!" Annie felt all the warmth draining from her.

"Yeah, right," Uncle George said, his face mottled. "I should've known."

"She must've had you sign the papers," Charles Rooks said calmly. "I imagine she said they were for something else. She made her wishes clear to me when we talked last. She wanted you to have the house and the garden. The garden seemed to be the most important thing to her. She said you tended it the way she once did."

Uncle George glared at Nora. "I should've known this would happen. I thought it was Corban Solsek who was after something. I should've looked closer to home!" He glared at her again. "Were you a part of this scheme?"

"Think whatever you want, George. What does it matter now?"

"Mom wasn't part of any scheme." Annie didn't even try to keep the outrage out of her voice. "There wasn't any scheme. I'm telling you both, it's a mistake! Grandma asked me to sign some papers, but that was only so that I could handle paying her bills."

Uncle George stood up and faced her. "Tell me straight out you don't want her house!"

Tears welled. "I would never have asked Grandma for the house, Uncle George. Not in a million years. You should know me better than that." Clearly, he didn't know her at all.

"It's fair, George," her mother said in a broken voice. "It's exactly what we deserve. It shouldn't surprise us that Mama disinherited us. We abandoned her years ago."

"Speak for yourself, Eleanor. I've never held on to grudges the way you do."

"No, you just didn't care one way or the other. You're just like our father."

He went white and then red. "That house belongs to *us!*" He looked back at Charles Rooks. "I'm going to fight you on this."

"I'm afraid you don't understand, Mr. Reinhardt. None of this was *my* decision." His voice was cool now. "However, I'm not finished. Please, sit down and we'll get to the rest."

"The rest of what?" Uncle George took his seat. "Mother didn't have anything except the house." He looked weary and sick. "What about savings? Or a checking account."

Annie blushed, sick at heart.

Charles Rooks explained quietly. "Anne-Lynn Gardner's name is on both accounts."

"Why should I be surprised?" Uncle George's voice was riddled with enough sarcasm to tear Annie's heart to shreds. "How much was in those accounts? Are we allowed to know what's been stolen from us?"

"Grandma was living on social security." Annie couldn't keep her voice from wobbling. "There was never more than a couple hundred dollars in her checking account. She told me she'd arrange for a transfer of funds from her savings whenever insurance or taxes came due." *Oh, Grandma Leota, how could you do this to me? Is this retaliation for all the years of neglect? I can't believe it! I won't!* "I'll sign everything over to you and Mother. I didn't stay with Grandma Leota because I wanted something from her. I stayed with her because I *loved* her."

She hadn't meant to cry, but she was. She wanted to get up and run out of the room, but Fred moved closer and put his hand on her knee as though to hold her there. She'd have to crawl over his lap or the coffee table to escape.

"I'm going to fight this!" Uncle George said again.

Charles Rooks lifted his hand. "Your mother thought you might. So she made stipulations to make sure you wouldn't be able to do so. She only had to give you one dollar to prevent you from contesting the will. She made it one hundred dollars each." Uncle George started to speak. "I will say again, Mr. Reinhardt, I have *not* finished. Allow me the courtesy to proceed. All of you. Once you do, you'll find you have nothing to contest, nor would you want to do so." He looked squarely at Uncle George. "The more you say now, the more you'll have cause to regret later."

"Get on with it then."

Annie was shaking violently.

"Very well." Charles Rooks nodded. "Your mother made provisions for both of you." He looked from Annie's mother to her uncle. He lifted two manila envelopes and held them out, one for each of them. "I think you'll be pleasantly surprised at the provisions your mother made for you." He leaned back in his chair, saying no more, just watching them.

Uncle George opened his envelope quickly and slid the contents out. He leafed through the documents, his face paling, then filling with color, then paling again to a pasty white. He went back and looked at them again more slowly, studying them one by one.

Annie's mother held her envelope as though it had a snake inside it. Annie had never seen her look so uncertain, so frightened. Uncle George said the Lord's name under his breath. Trembling, her mother opened her envelope and began to go through the contents, one document at a time. A frown. Confusion, then comprehension. She looked utterly devastated as tears slipped silently down her white cheeks.

"Your mother was a remarkable woman," Charles Rooks said quietly. He leaned forward again and clasped his hands on his desk mat. "She told me she purchased those stocks years ago on the advice of a good friend. A very wise and astute friend, I would say. She had those documents in her house up until a few weeks ago. She had no idea what they were worth. When I told her, she asked me to keep them with her will."

Uncle George started reading aloud. "Standard Oil, Proctor and Gamble, Coca-Cola, DuPont, Bethlehem Steel, AT&T." He shook his head. "Goodyear, Ford, General Motors . . ." He looked as though he'd been poleaxed. He stopped reading, but he didn't raise his head. He shut his eyes for a long moment and then said, "We should get Mother a headstone. Something really nice."

Nora gave a hoarse sob, dropped the papers, and covered her face.

Uncle George winced. "I didn't mean that to sound so . . ." He looked up at the attorney. "How did she do it? I didn't think she ever made that much money."

"I imagine she invested a few dollars at a time during the years she worked for a living."

Grandma Leota had worked a long time.

Annie watched her mother tuck the documents back into the envelope as though she couldn't bear to look at them. Her hands were shaking. She scrubbed the tears from her face like a child. Annie ached for her. Grandma Leota had tried to show how much she loved her daughter. But Annie could see this inheritance had only added to her mother's burden of guilt.

Oh, Lord, will she ever understand?

Uncle George rose first. He extended his hand to Charles Rooks, thanking him as though he were the one who had poured the bounty upon him. Then he turned and looked at Annie. She saw the flicker of shame cross his face. "I'm sorry, Annie. I was out of line. I should've known better." He checked his wristwatch. "I have to run." He took a step toward the door, then paused. "Do you need me to go to the funeral home and help you make arrangements for a stone? I could meet you tomorrow."

"Grandma told me what she wanted, Uncle George. I'll take care of it."

"Tell them to send me the bill."

Her mother rose. She didn't shake hands with Charles Rooks. She held the closed manila envelope in her left hand as she turned toward Fred. Still trying to take it all in, Annie started to follow them out of the office.

"Miss Gardner," Charles Rooks said. She paused in the doorway and looked back at him in question. He came around his desk. "These belong to you." He handed her the file containing the deed to Grandma Leota's house and a short note in her grandmother's writing with the savings account number, location of her safety deposit box key, and a Scripture reference: Isaiah 40:27-31. She thanked him and went out, catching up with her mother and Fred at the elevator.

They rode down in silence. Fred kept his arm around her mother. Annie didn't know what to say. Her car and Fred's were parked side by side in the basement lot.

"I'm sorry about the house, Mom," Annie said. "I never intended for Grandma to give it to me."

"Don't apologize, Annie. You loved her. That's far more than I ever did." Her mother raised her head, and Annie saw the anguished look on her face. "Don't ever apologize." Her mother's heart had been softened, then completely broken.

"Oh, Mom," Annie said. Weeping, she embraced her, feeling her mother's anguish as though it were her own.

Annie was shocked when she saw the small, wooden box that contained Leota Reinhardt's remains. It wasn't much bigger than a shoe box and weighed only a few pounds. The funeral-home proprietor informed her that George Reinhardt had called and said he would take care of any expenses for a stone or urn or whatever Annie told the proprietor she thought her grandmother wanted. Annie had already paid for the "Direct/Budget Cremation (Noncommemorative)" before Uncle George had decided to be magnanimous.

We should get her a nice stone.

Grandma, how would you feel about having a gigantic stone cross on top of you? Or some marble angels with great big wings? They could be playing harps! A bubble of laughter came from her unexpectedly.

"I'm sorry," she said, mortified. What was wrong with her? She wanted to scream and cry and laugh at the same time. She stared at the papers. *Direct/Budget.* She felt so guilty looking at those words now. Since the doctor had been aware she had the power of attorney, all the arrangements had been left to her. She hadn't known what to do. It had cost eight hundred and fifty dollars, almost everything Grandma had left in her checking account. That had taken care of everything: filling out official documents, sanitary care of Grandma's remains, removing Grandma's body from the hospital to the mortuary, refrigeration, use of facility and equipment, transportation to the crematory, and inurnment of cremated remains. All the things Annie wished she had never known about but had to under the circumstances.

Had Uncle George learned of his windfall sooner, he might've insisted Grandma Leota be embalmed and laid to rest in the "bronze, nonrusting" casket with the "champagne whitehall velvet" interior.

I'm going to lose it, Lord. I'm going to lose it completely and become hysterical. I want to pound on this table until it cracks in two.

Poor Uncle George. What was going to happen when the truth hit him between the eyes? No amount of money would ever ease his guilt. And her mother . . . Fred had called that morning and said she wouldn't be coming to the funeral home to help Annie with the decisions at hand. Her mother was so sick she couldn't get out of bed.

Annie's eyes welled with tears. Her throat ached. Reading through the option descriptions, she realized her grandmother had been taken away in a cardboard box. *Oh, God, how could I have let that happen? Grandma, I'm so sorry.* She reached out and drew the box of Grandma Leota's ashes closer. It was hard to breathe.

"Would you like to be alone for a few minutes, Miss Gardner?"

She nodded.

The man left the book listing services, products, and prices open on the table. He had been so kind to her when she called from the hospital. What must it be like to run a mortuary and see the dead and the grieving every day?

She had to get down to business and decide on an urn. Taking a deep breath, she reined her emotions in tightly and pressed them down deep inside. Still, feelings bubbled to the surface.

Oh, Lord, did they take Grandma away in her hospital gown? I never thought of that. I should've taken something nice for Grandma to wear when she was cremated. A nice suit. A pretty dress. A wedding gown. And her Bible. Grandma would have liked to have had that in her hands.

Annie opened the book and paged through it until she found the pages with the urns. She wiped her eyes, blew her nose, and studied the pictures. The urns were in various shapes and quite lovely. Painted chests, royal blue cloisonné, ebony marble . . . urns of mahogany, cherry, maple, walnut, and poplar. The most expensive one was cast bronze on white marble and looked like a Roman vase. It was called "The Aristocrat." Annie's lips twitched. *Oh, Grandma Leota. How you would love that!* She laughed. She couldn't help herself. It just bubbled out and then died. The cost was over a thousand dollars, but that would satisfy Uncle George.

The man seemed to know the precise moment to return to the small conference room. "Have you decided?"

"Yes, I have." She turned the black binder around so that he could see the picture she tapped. "I'd like this one, please."

"A good choice."

Annie filled the first few days of Grandma Leota's absence washing sheets and blankets and remaking the beds. She vacuumed, scrubbed the kitchen floor, scrubbed the bathroom floor, washed the windows, polished the furniture, and cleaned the stove and oven. She cleaned Barnaby's cage every morning and made sure he had fresh food. He hadn't said anything for a while, and she hoped he wasn't going to get sick and die, too.

Arba came by the first night with a casserole. She didn't linger. "You let us know when you're ready for company," she said and left. The casserole was still in the refrigerator.

On the third day, Annie went out into Grandma Leota's garden.

The air was cold, the trees winter-barren, the ground hard. When Annie looked up at the lead gray sky, her chest ached so badly she thought she'd die. She almost wished she could. At least then she would be with the Lord and Grandma Leota.

She heard the gate open and saw Arba and the children entering the garden. She tried to smile, but her mouth trembled. She couldn't speak a word of greeting. The pain was still bottled up inside.

"Oh, honey . . ." Arba's dark eyes filled with tears. "You need to let it out."

She shrugged because she didn't dare try to speak.

Kenya came and wrapped her arms around Annie's waist. "Mama says Grandma Leota's in heaven."

"What do you feel like doing?" Arba said, gently pressing.

"Screaming."

"Then you do it, girl. Why should the old Israelites be the only ones to rend their clothes and wail?"

Annie started to cry.

"Ah, honey. Is that the best you can do for your granny?"

The pain burst forth then, and Annie did wail. Arba and the children surrounded her, laying hands on her, crying with her.

"That's it," Arba said over and over, weeping with her. "That's it. Let it go, honey. Let it go."

And Annie was the better for it.

During the weeks that followed, Annie went through Grandma Leota's things. Grandma had precious few clothes. In her bottom drawer, Annie found the jewelry box mentioned in her note. Annie found the safety deposit box key and put it on her key chain. There was a blue velvet box with a string of pearls and a note: "All my love forever, Bernard." Another white box held an acorn, two blue feathers, three agates, and a package of sweet pea seeds, still marked ten cents.

Annie wondered what the collection meant. None of the items were worth anything, but they must have stirred memories for Grandma. She wished she knew what sentiment they held for her grandmother. She couldn't help feeling she had lost an entire library of knowledge and wisdom when Grandma Leota had died. There was so much Annie hadn't had the opportunity to learn.

Sam Carter called several times and came over every few days. One day he smiled at her tenderly. "You're not going to let me get too close, are you, Annie? Still think I'm a rogue."

"It's not that, Sam."

"I think I understand. Except for one thing, Annie."

"What's that?"

"You're not Catholic. You can't be a nun."

She smiled at that. "You don't think an evangelical Protestant can dedicate her life to God?"

"I suppose so, but what a waste."

She laughed. "I should hope not." Perhaps one day she would marry, but for now it didn't seem to be God's plan for her. She was content.

With the boundaries clearly drawn, Sam stayed the rest of the afternoon. They talked about Grandma Leota, life, the garden, what Annie planned to do about the house.

When she saw him to the door, he gave her a rueful smile. "I should've snapped you up when you were fifteen and madly in love with me. I lost my chance." Leaning down, he kissed her cheek.

Corban came by and helped her take the boxes down from the attic again. She asked him if there was any chance he would get back together with Ruth, and he'd said not a chance in hades. Then e broke down and cried. Alarmed, she sat with him on the sofa and listened as he poured out his misery about his child being aborted. She'd cried with him then. She talked to him about the Lord and forgiveness, but he withdrew from that. He wanted to consign Ruth Coldwell to the pit and leave her there to burn for all eternity. The hotter the fire, the better, as far as he was concerned.

"We all sin, Corban."

"Yeah, right, but not the way she did. What sort of woman kills her own child?"

"There's no difference in God's eyes between Ruth having that abortion and you wishing her dead and in hell for it." She saw his eyes flicker. She didn't want him to misunderstand her. "And I'm no better than either of you with the bitterness I allowed to take root in me. Sin is sin, Corban. There's no big or small about it. It's all the same in God's eyes, and unless you confess it and lay it at the cross, it separates you from God. That's why we need Jesus, so we can be reconciled."

She got no further than that. He said he'd taken philosophy cours-es. She could see his anger. He said he knew all about Christianity. He said he was sorry to offend her, but he thought all that stuff about Jesus dying for the sins of the world was hogwash. It was too easy. And it was a crutch for people who'd messed up so badly nothing could be fixed. When they did things that bad, they ought to suffer for it. And then he was on his feet, apologizing for crying like a fool. He was out the door before she could say anything else. Annie had felt sick at heart, watching him drive away. She'd known the instant she mentioned the word *sin,* he wasn't ready to hear the Good News. She'd seen the change in his eyes. The walls went up. He couldn't get away fast enough.

Annie didn't expect to hear from Corban again after that. Then he showed up on a Wednesday morning three weeks later. She was up on the extension ladder holding an electric sander to the paint-chipped eaves. He had to shout to get her attention.

She shut off the machine, lifted her goggles, and pulled the mask down from her mouth. "Well, hi, stranger!" She grinned down at him. "Come to help?"

"Sure. I've got some spare time."

She took him at his word and put him to work.

25

NORA DREADED THE APPROACH OF EASTER.

Ever since Anne-Lynn had telephoned and said she was "opening
Leota's Garden for a party to celebrate the Resurrection," Nora had
felt sick with apprehension. She didn't know if she could stand to go
back into that house and be surrounded by memories of her mother.
Yet, there was no way to decline Anne-Lynn's invitation without
hurting her daughter deeply and risking estrangement. She couldn't
risk losing Anne-Lynn again. They were just beginning to talk, really
talk, as mother and daughter.

Since her mother had passed away, Nora had felt her life crumbling from the inside. Besides the heavy burden of guilt over how she
had treated her mother for so many years was the added shame of
finding out she was related to those who had taken part in exterminating Jews and Christians during World War II. The more she
thought about it, the more she shrank inwardly . . . and the more
empathy she felt with her father and mother.

What would people think of me if they knew? She couldn't even talk
about it with Fred. When he suggested grief counseling, Nora said
absolutely not. She would never be able to call Pastor Burnie and ask
his help. She had said terrible things to him that day she had sought

his counsel. Perhaps if she apologized . . . but why would he listen? It seemed every way she turned, she saw people she had hurt. She needed to make amends, but she was so afraid no one would give her the chance. Or, even if they did, they wouldn't believe she was sincere.

How many loved ones have I lost over the years because I thought I had all the answers? Bryan Taggart, Dean Gardner, Michael. It's a miracle I haven't lost Fred. I don't want to risk losing Anne-Lynn. Oh, Lord, seal my lips. Keep me still. I'm so afraid of ending up alone the way my mother was. I did abandon her. I wanted to hurt her the way I was hurt. And I did hurt her. I hurt her over and over again, year after year, right up to the very last day of her life.

How many Mother's Days had passed without Nora so much as calling her mother and asking her how she was? She remembered the times her mother had called and Nora hadn't even tried to hide that she couldn't wait to get off the line. So many times Nora could have included her mother in family dinners and at the children's birthday parties.

I remember things Mother said to me that filled me with anger and resentment. And now I realize she was trying to tell me something important, and I wouldn't listen. I had no idea of the burdens she carried, nor was I willing to find out. I was too busy living life my way.

Would she one day have a grandchild like Annie, who would love her no matter what she'd done? *I thought I knew more than everyone else. . . . I thought I knew everything about my mother. Why was it so easy to think the worst of her? Why couldn't I have just once swallowed my pride and listened to her side? Oh, why didn't I go back to the hospital that night? . . .*

She'd already lost Michael. *Jesus, please, don't let me drive Anne-Lynn away again.*

Nora felt as though she were locked in an elevator going down into a dark hole. There was no escaping. Fred insisted she see the doctor, but when she was given a prescription slip for Prozac, she refused to fill it. She knew the cause of her despair, and it had nothing to do with a chemical imbalance in her body. It had everything to do with guilt and shame. Why should she be spared pain when she had caused so much?

Oh, Mama, maybe if I'd had a month with you to talk everything over . . . A week would've meant so much. Even one more day. Oh, God, I would've been glad for five minutes to tell her I'm sorry and ask for her forgiveness. But that'll never happen now. You're punishing me for all

*the years I neglected my mother, for all the years I despised her and made
no secret of it. I allowed bitterness to blind me. I allowed it to choke out
every chance of a relationship with her. No wonder she could never say
she loved me. How could she when I treated her so abominably?*

Fred had finally become impatient with her last night. He said it
seemed all the energy she had expended trying to shape Anne-Lynn's
life to her specifications was now focused on torturing herself.
"You've become prosecutor, judge, jury, and prison warden all rolled
into one," he'd said in exasperation.

Maybe so, but wasn't it only fair?

"Annie's been working hard to make this a special Easter for
everyone. If you go over there and mope around the entire day, looking like death warmed over, you're going to ruin her party. One of
these days, you're going to have to *stop playing God!*"

Shaken, she made up her mind. She would pretend for Anne-
Lynn's sake that she was joyous about the religious significance of
Easter. But to do that, she needed to look her best. She needed to
smile as though she meant it, whether she felt like it or not. So she
had a massage and a facial. She went to her hairdresser and her
manicurist. Fred had suggested she shop for a new spring dress, but
she didn't feel up to that. Besides, she had a closet full of clothes
from which to choose. She could give away half of what she owned
and not miss anything. Clothing used to matter so much to her. She
had been so ashamed of her family's poverty, so determined to show
she was as good as everyone else—

No, that wasn't right. The truth was she wanted to show she was
better.

*I covered up my shame with pride. That's what I did. Isn't it, Lord?
Like naked Eve putting on those fig leaves. I've been hiding.*

Easter morning, Nora stood in her dressing room, looking
through her clothes. She felt like wearing black, but knew Anne-
Lynn would hope for something that announced spring and the
Resurrection. She finally chose white slacks and a candy pink blouse
with pearl buttons. She topped the outfit off with a mint green blazer
and long scarf in pastel yellow, pink, and green. She wore a circle of
gold leaves with pearl buds on the lapel. Looking at herself in the
full-length mirror, she was satisfied with the overall effect. She
looked fine—more than fine even.

On the outside.

Fred approved. His eyes glowed as she came down the stairs. He
kissed her when she reached the bottom. "Perfect. You look beautiful."

The word cut her heart deeply. *Perfect.* Was that at the root of her troubles? Hadn't that always been her goal? Perfection in everything. She had to look perfect, be perfect, have perfect children. What a mess she had made of everything in her constant striving for perfection!

I am a sham. All through church, Nora kept thinking about her childhood and all the ways she had tried to be better than everyone. Grandma Helene had expected perfection, but Nora knew it was unfair to cast blame on her grandmother. Grandma Helene had been miserable, and she had made everyone around her miserable.

Just as I have done. Grandpa Reinhardt sat on a bench, but my husbands ran away. I swore I wouldn't become like my grandmother, and that's exactly what I became. Hard, determined to have my way, punitive when I didn't, bitter with life, grasping for control, manipulating. I don't want to be like that anymore. Oh, God, I don't, but how do I change? Oh, Lord, I don't know what to do anymore. Help me, oh, please, help me!

After the service, Fred talked with the pastor while she went to the ladies room. Pastor Burnie smiled at her when she returned. He even extended his hand and said he was pleased to see her in church again. She said she was glad to be back. Then she gathered her courage and said, "I'm sorry, Pastor Burnie. I behaved badly."

He didn't let go of her hand, but put his other over hers. "All is forgiven."

"I'll listen next time."

She and Fred didn't say anything on the way through the hills to Oakland. Fred turned on a CD, filling the car with soothing, orchestral sounds. Her stomach was a hard knot. Fred seemed preoccupied. Was he worried she would say or do something that would cause trouble?

"It's a perfect day for a party," he said when they took the Fruitvale Avenue off-ramp.

Blue skies and sunshine. Yes, it was a perfect day for a garden party. *Oh, God, help me get through it. Help me! Help me!*

Fred drove up the road next to the freeway and took a right. At the top of the hill, at the head of Annie's street, was a new "Neighborhood Watch" sign. Nora wondered if it was her imagination, but the houses along the avenue looked neater. Lawns were mowed, and there was no litter blowing around. The bars on the windows had been removed from the house across the street from her mother's house.

No, Anne-Lynn's house, she corrected herself. Perhaps, if she thought of it that way, it would be more bearable.

Corban Solsek's car was parked in front. There were cars lined up in Annie's driveway: her Saturn, Susan Carter's old VW, and an old Firebird. Annie was going to have a full house.

The house!

Nora stared. Gone were the black water stains, the dangling rain gutters, the paint-chipped eaves. The house was a freshly painted candy pink with white trim. It had a new roof, and the small lawn was lush green, mowed short and edged. The flowering plum was in full, pale pink splendor. The trimmed and shaped camellia and azalea bushes in front were covered with pink and white blossoms. Hanging pots on the front porch overflowed hot pink and purple fuchsias. Even the white picket fence that lined the right side of the driveway was repaired and freshly painted, along with the carport and garage.

"Annie's been busy." Fred smiled at Nora as he opened her car door and helped her out.

"It looks wonderful." Nora could scarcely take in the transformation. Flowerpots filled with pink and white geraniums were on each step. Two white wicker chairs sat on the front porch, a small wicker table between them, on which sat half a dozen clay pots with tree saplings. Each pot had a white ribbon tied around it.

The front door was open, the screen unlocked. A little card that read Come in! had been taped over the doorbell.

The living room was empty except for Barnaby sitting on his perch. "Whatcha gonna do?" he said, bobbing his head. "Whatcha gonna do?"

Contemporary Christian music played quietly on the radio beside Leota's old recliner. The carpets had been cleaned, the furniture polished. There was a new painting above the mantel—a portrait of Leota as a young woman. Nora drew in her breath softly and held it, her throat aching. She remembered her mother looking like that. She had been beautiful.

On the right side of the mantel was an elegant marble-and-brass vase filled with lilacs and narcissus. The room was filled with sweet fragrance.

"Everyone must be out back."

Nora glanced at Fred and nodded, then caught her breath when she looked through the kitchen window to the garden beyond. It was like a wonderland of colors. Memories flooded back, and for a moment she thought the wave of sorrow would overtake her. Then other concerns rushed to replace them. *I have to smile for Anne-Lynn.*

She saw other guests in the garden. Corban Solsek, Sam Carter, Susan Carter and her parents, Arba Wilson, Juanita Alcala and Lin Sansan and their children. They all had reason to think ill of her. Hadn't she always thought the worst of them? She had to gather all her courage to follow Fred out the back door and face them.

"Mom! Fred!" Anne-Lynn said and came to greet them. Nora had never seen her daughter look more beautiful, though she was wearing old, faded blue jeans and a pale yellow sweater that had seen better days. Her hair was a wild mass of red blonde curls, her cheeks glowed with color. She had been out in the sun and had a golden tan. Her blue eyes shone with joy. "Oh, Mom, you look so beautiful," she said, and for just a moment, seeing her daughter's expression of pure love, Nora felt beautiful and cherished.

She and Fred greeted others and made small talk. Everyone was friendly, smiling and welcoming her and Fred. Anne-Lynn served her a tall glass of fruit punch and went inside the house to bring out more trays of food.

Nora couldn't get over the garden. She had never seen it look so beautiful, so fully in bloom. And the funny things Annie had thought to tuck in here and there made her smile. Who would've thought of using bowling balls in a garden? An old, red Flyer wagon was filled with beribboned saplings in pots.

"They're from the apricot tree," Annie informed her, following her mother's gaze as she came up with the food tray. "There's one for everyone to take home and plant."

"It's a lovely idea." And she meant it. Annie's smile was pure delight.

Nora saw Fred deep in conversation with Tom Carter. The telephone rang and Annie hurried into the house, leaving Nora on her own to wander.

The garage and apartment built at the back were painted to match the house. Shutters had been added and tole-painted with exquisite flower designs. The door was open. Nora peered in and saw several of the children playing a board game on the braided rag rug. Anne-Lynn had been hard at work here, too. The apartment had been repainted a sunny yellow, with brightly colored border designs. Gone were the old bed and couch—they'd been replaced by shelves laden with books and games and art supplies. The only furnishings were two card tables, one with a half-finished puzzle, the other with coloring books, a can of crayons, and a plastic bag of clay. The walls were decorated with childish works of art. There were two easels. One was two-sided with paint-tray holders so that a child could paint on each side. The other was Annie's.

The brick walkway had been swept and repaired with mortar. Nora's mother's old gardening clogs were by the gate, violets planted in them. Red-blaze roses covered the old fence and arbor. The scent was heady. The gate was open to the Victory garden. How many hours had her mother spent working the soil, planting, tending, harvesting? Nora remembered now how neighbors had exchanged vegetables with her mother. The lady next door had traded green beans for pearl onions, and zucchini for tomatoes. Now beneath the blossom-covered fruit trees were yellow daffodils, red tulips, grape hyacinths, and white narcissus rising from a sea of tiny indigo blue starflowers and foam white alyssum. Nora had never seen anything so beautiful.

Maryann Carter came and stood next to her beneath the rose arbor. "Amazing, isn't it? The minute I saw it, I thought this must be what it was like in the Garden of Eden."

"Yes." Nora's throat was tight.

"It smells like heaven, doesn't it?"

"Yes," Nora said, inhaling the mingled scents of roses, lilacs, white narcissus, honeysuckle, and gardenias. "I was a fool when I said Annie could never be an artist."

Maryann smiled. "People can be like Monet paintings. You have to get some distance before you can see what they are and appreciate their full beauty."

Touched by her kindness, Nora smiled at her. "Thank you."

Maryann put her hand on her arm. "Why don't we refill our glasses with punch and sit down over there so we can get to know one another better?"

Nora smiled. "I'd like that very much."

"Annie said you were graduating this June," Corban said to Sam as they leaned against Annie's car and watched the guests in the garden.

"Yep. With honors."

"Not too proud of it, are you?"

Sam grinned. "Sure, I'm proud. Not bad for a guy who barely squeaked through high school and spent a few months with the Youth Authority." He lifted his can of soda in a mock salute. "Took me awhile to grow up."

"Do you have a job lined up?"

"I've had some interviews. I'm thinking about taking a job with the LAPD. Maybe I'll get lucky and end up working with the Youth Authority again. In a different capacity, of course. But I'm planning to hold off making a decision over the summer. I'd like to do a little traveling before tying myself down to a nine-to-five or whatever. What about you? Annie said you're graduating in June, too. Magna cum laude, I hear. Impressive. Still planning to do your postgraduate work at Stanford?"

"No, Cal has a better graduate program, so I've decided to go there."

"Yeah, right. I wonder why you want to stay so close to Oakland."

Ignoring him, Corban watched Annie move among her guests. She was so beautiful she made his heart ache.

"Man, you've got it as bad as I ever did."

Corban glanced at him. "What?"

"Annie. Your tongue's practically hanging out." He watched her for a moment and then gave Corban a rueful smile. "Take some advice from someone who's been there. Give up."

"Just because you didn't get anywhere with her doesn't mean I won't."

Sam laughed. "Pretty sure of yourself, aren't you? Even if you were a Christian, you wouldn't have a prayer."

Corban's eyes narrowed. Sam Carter was full of ill tidings, not that he'd expected a rejected suitor to give him any encouragement. Still, he'd take the bait. "Why not?"

"Because she's already married."

"Married?" He glanced at Annie and then back at Sam. "What're you talking about? She's not married."

"She's as married as anyone can be, Corban, old boy. You just don't get it." He smiled ruefully. "Took me awhile, even after she told me up front I was wasting my time. I thought I could wear her down with my charm and good looks." His expression turned tender as he watched her. "Has she talked to you about the Lord?"

"Sure." Jesus Christ always came into their conversations some-where. Even when he tried to steer things down other paths, she always came back to God. "I've been taking a comparative religions class."

Sam laughed again. "Oh, that'll impress her."

Sam Carter could be more irritating than a rash. "I don't know much about religion. I thought it might be interesting to find out more."

"Religion is one thing. Faith is another entirely."

"So Annie said."

"All you have to do is watch Annie to see the difference. She say anything else?"

Corban looked away from Sam's amused expression. She'd summed up the entire course in a few sentences: *"Every religion in the world is about man trying to reach up to God, like working your way up the ladder. They're all about striving to achieve something for yourself. Christianity is the only religion about God reaching down to man and offering salvation as a free gift, with the added bonus of a personal relationship with the Creator God through Jesus Christ, who was there in the beginning."*

Corban sighed. "She talked about grace being a free gift."

Sam lifted his can of soda in salute. "It's free all right, but it didn't come cheap. And there's the rub, Corban, old man. Our sweet Annie's passionately in love with the one who paid the price for salvation." He cocked his head and smiled sardonically. "Think you're up to competing with Jesus Christ?"

"Faith can bring people together."

"True. But what's the basis of your faith?"

"I'm not sure yet." Before he met Annie, he'd never thought about having faith in anything but himself.

Sam grinned at him. "She'll make a believer out of you yet, old buddy. And then she'll cut you loose."

Corban glanced at him in annoyance. "Sounds like sour grapes."

"No. I'm just hoping the next time I meet a girl like her, she'll be the marrying kind." Sam's expression was tender as he watched Annie. "The thing with Annie is she just wants everyone to feel the same joy and sense of freedom she does." He shook his head. "She is something to watch, isn't she?"

Corban couldn't agree more. She was radiant, and some of that joy seemed to overflow to everyone she came near . . . except for Nora Gaines, who looked thinner and paler than the last time he'd seen her. Annie's mother had looked like a scared little girl when she came out the back door. Now she was sitting with Susan's mother, talking and looking less stressed out. Still pensive, but reachable. Annie joined them for a moment, took her mother's hand and squeezed it, leaned down and kissed her cheek, and then went to talk with her aunt Jeanne.

George Reinhardt was talking with Tom Carter and Fred Gaines. Corban wondered how old George was fairing now that his mother had gone on to meet Saint Peter at the pearly gates, leaving him a nice, fat bankroll. At first glance, he didn't look any happier than he had the first time Corban met him.

Annie looked his way and smiled. Much to his chagrin, she smiled at Sam Carter, too. She wasn't partial.

"It's a pity Annie doesn't need us," Sam said, straightening away from the car.

"Maybe one of these days."

"Don't hold your breath. She's got everything she wants right here in Leota's Garden."

Corban had only an inkling of what that meant.

Annie set out platters of food on the dining-room table and left the Fiesta dishes stacked to one side so that guests could serve themselves when they felt like it. Uncle George, as usual, was sitting alone in the living room, watching a football game. He had a beer beside him, one he had taken from the six-pack he had brought. Sadness filled Annie as she watched him. He had been sociable for an hour and then retreated.

At least Jeanne was having a good time, talking and laughing with Arba. And last she saw Marshall and Mitzi, who were in the game room having fun with the other children. Life was going on all around Uncle George, but he seemed blind and deaf to it.

She thought of Grandpa Bernard and the things Grandma Leota had said about him. Was Uncle George going to become like that? Locked inside himself with whatever demons plagued him?

Lord, what is he afraid of?

And what about her mother? She was trying so hard to be courteous and pleasant to everyone. Obeying the rules.

Oh, Grandma Leota, I wish you were here. She pressed her lips together and finished putting out the silverware and napkins.

Her mother had talked with Uncle George for a little while and then gone into the bathroom. Was she still in there? No, the bathroom door was open. Annie found her in the second bedroom, looking at the wall where several pictures were hung.

"I've never seen this picture." Her mother was looking at the one of Helene and Gottlieb Reinhardt on their wedding day.

"I found it in the attic. The one of Grandma Leota and Grandpa Bernard was in Grandma's bedroom. And Fred gave me a copy of your wedding picture. I had to wheel and deal to get Dad to send me a picture, and I've left a space for Michael. Maybe I could have a copy made of his graduation picture from college."

"I'll do that for you." She looked at the shadow box, and Annie wondered what she was thinking. Annie had put the Silver Star, Bronze Star, and Purple Heart in it along with some tools from a box in the garage: a measuring tape, a hammer, plans for the apartment, and some nails. Her mother's gaze moved to the plaque in the center of the wall. Annie waited, saying nothing, giving her mother time. She had spent painstaking hours doing the calligraphy, making sure every word was spelled correctly. After all, it was in German and she didn't speak it.

> *Denn also hat Gott die Welt geliebt dass er seinen, elingeborenen Sohn gab, damit alle, die an ihn glauben, nicht verloren werden, sondern das ewige Leben haben. Johannes 3:16*

"It shouldn't be so easy," her mother said quietly, guilt her mantle.

"The only thing the Lord won't forgive is the refusal to believe and accept the gift of His Holy Spirit."

"I believe, but . . ."

Studying her mother, Annie ached over the grief she saw in her face. Eleanor Gaines would bear the consequences of her behavior over the years and live the rest of her life with regrets. But she didn't have to live the rest of her life believing she had never been loved. God loved her. So had Grandma Leota. Her mother needed to know that. She needed to accept love so that she could move forward and do something constructive with her life. Grandma Leota had understood that and, with God's guidance, she had provided for it. It was time her mother knew it.

Annie walked over to the old sewing machine sitting beneath the window that overlooked the driveway and rose-covered picket fence. "Grandma said you were a talented seamstress, Mom. She told me you used to go down to the fancy dress stores and look over the new styles, then come home and make improvements on them. She said you had the talent to become a wonderful designer."

"Did she?"

"Yes, she did. She was very proud of you. Grandma said all the women in our family have been artists of one kind or another. Grandma Helene was a master with the embroidery needle and in the kitchen as a cook. Great-Aunt Joyce was a wonderful painter and graphic artist. Grandma Leota had a green thumb. You're our clothing designer." She saw the telltale moisture in her mother's eyes.

Father, is she listening . . . really listening?

Annie knew her mother was trying hard to turn over a new leaf, to be better than she had been, to be brave. But that would never be enough. She needed to relinquish herself and let God show her what He had made her to be. Would she be willing to surrender her pride for that great purpose?

Today could be the beginning. Please, Lord, please. You've softened her. Will she take the seed?

"It's yours, Mom." Annie ran her hand over the polished wood of the antique Singer sewing machine. "You can take it anytime you want it."

"It belongs to you, Anne-Lynn. Everything in the house belongs to you."

She heard the hurt in her mother's voice and knew she felt rejected despite the fortune in stocks she had been given. "Grandma Leota left things to me because she knew I'd pass them on when you and Uncle George were ready. This belongs to you, Mom. Grandma wanted you to have it."

Her mother drew in a shaky breath. "How can you be so sure?" She looked so vulnerable, so hopeful. Like a little girl desperately longing for something just beyond her reach.

"Open it. See for yourself." Annie walked over, kissed her mom, and left the room.

Nora trembled as she stood alone. She remembered the hours she had spent at that old sewing machine. She had found such pleasure and satisfaction in the work. She had lost herself in it. When had she stopped? Why? Was it the year she ran off and married Bryan? She had bought another sewing machine then, a newer one. But as the years rolled by, she had enough money to buy things off the rack. And there had never seemed enough time to sew. She was too busy driving Annie to school or music lessons or whatever else she'd planned for her to do.

Nora ran her hand over the old machine, seeing it now with new eyes. Just as her mother had retreated to her garden, she had retreated to this room, losing herself in her work, dreaming her dreams, hoping there was more to life than loneliness and rejection. *Oh, Mama, we weren't so very different, were we? Why couldn't I see that before?* Lifting the cover, Nora reached in and pulled the old machine up, locking it into position.

A white envelope was taped to the front of the machine. *Eleanor* was written in her mother's handwriting. Hands trembling, Nora opened it.

My dearest Eleanor,

I knew one day you would return to yourself and open this machine again. I'm so proud of you. I remember standing in the doorway and watching you as you sewed. You had such amazing concentration. You took such care. You were never satisfied unless you'd done the job right. And you made beautiful things, darling, the kind of things only an artist can create. Artistic talent runs in our family, you know. Your father was a master carpenter. Just look at the fireplace mantel, the apartment behind the garage, the arbor to the Victory garden. Grandma Helene could make the best strudel this side of the Atlantic. And your grandfather taught me how to grow things. You have a wonderful heritage.

I like to imagine you sitting at this sewing machine again one day and making costumes for church pageants, maternity clothing for the poor young mothers, playsuits for children, and nice dresses for little old widow ladies like me. And the Lord will bless you for it. I know He will.

You said to me the other night that I never loved you. Oh, you are so wrong, my dear. You are the daughter I prayed for, Eleanor. I loved you from the moment I knew I was expecting you. I loved you even more when I held you in my arms. I named you after a great lady, a woman of great character, the woman I know God intends you to be. Trust Him and He will mold you into His vessel. And remember . . . I never stopped loving you, Eleanor, even during all the years you believed otherwise. You are the daughter of my heart. Even when we are apart, I hold you close. And wherever I am at this moment as you're reading this letter, be reassured, my beloved,

I love you still.
Mama

Nora wept. She read the letter again through her tears and then held it against her chest, finally reading it again.

"Annie told me I'd find you in here," Fred said from behind her. He put his hands on her shoulders and kneaded her muscles gently. "She said your mother wanted you to have the sewing machine. Do you want it?"

"I do." More than anything. More than all the stocks, for they only represented cold cash. She had felt disinherited when the will was read. And now, she felt like the prodigal who was welcomed home by a rejoicing parent. She folded her mother's letter carefully and tucked it back into the envelope, then put it in her jacket pocket and kept her hand over it. She had what mattered. She had what really counted. Love.

"George brought the van," Fred said. "Maybe I can talk him into moving the sewing machine for us this evening. They could spend the night."

"They never have before."

"There's always a first time."

"We've plenty of room."

"The children could ride over in the car with us."

"That would be nice."

Fred turned her around and lifted her chin. He studied her. "Are you all right?"

"Not yet, but . . . I know now my mother loved me." *Thank You, Lord, oh, thank You.*

He leaned down and kissed her. "I love you, too, Nora. I have from the moment I met you. And I always will."

Oh, dear Jesus, I'm so undeserving, and so very, very thankful. She went into her husband's arms and rested in his embrace a long moment. "Will you do me a favor, Fred?"

"Now what?" he said in a teasing tone.

She drew back slightly and looked up at him. "Don't call me Nora anymore." She smiled. "Call me Eleanor."

Annie finished drying the last of Grandma's Fiesta dishes and put them away in the kitchen cabinets. The washing machine was going with the tablecloths and napkins and several dish towels. The left-overs were put away. She had sent German potato salad home with Arba, wedges of apple strudel with Juanita, and German potato sausage with Lin Sansan.

Smiling, Annie closed the cabinets. *Well, Lord, we had an international day, didn't we? Like a meeting of the United Nations in our backyard!*

It had been a wonderful day. Everyone she had invited had come to the party in Grandma Leota's garden. Juanita had even managed to get her husband, Jorge, to participate. He was a quiet man and rather wary among the throng of people mulling around the garden, but he had gradually warmed up when his wife had introduced him to Lin Sansan and her husband, Quyen Tan Ng. It was the first time the men had met and spoken. Amazing, since they had lived next door to each other for three years!

Halfway through the afternoon, Annie had decided to organize a block party. Summer wasn't that far away, and it would be a perfect time. When she mentioned the idea to Arba, her friendly neighbor said she was all for it and willing to help. So was Juanita. They spread the news to the other neighbors.

Lord, I want to know everyone's name by the end of summer. Men, women, and children! But it's going to take dynamite to get some of them out of their houses. People are so afraid. Father, I want this neighborhood to be like neighborhoods used to be, when everyone knew one another and people talked over their back fences.

Grandma Leota had told her what the neighborhood had been like fifty years ago. She knew it could be that way again. It was already starting. Opening the garden to the children had brought the mothers over to visit. Arba, Juanita, and Lin Sansan often sat on her patio now, talking, even when Annie was working, which was often since Arba had introduced her to Miranda Wentworth, an interior decorator. Ever since Miranda had come to see her painted trims and borders, Annie had more offers than she could fulfill. And the gallery wanted another painting. The proprietor had come over and made an offer for Grandma Leota's portrait, but Annie declined. She was thinking about painting Arba, Juanita, and Lin Sansan as they sipped tea together in the garden. They were wonderful to watch and would be even more wonderful to paint. They were all so different. Arba in her bright colors; Juanita in her old-fashioned fifties-style dress; Lin Sansan in her black pants and white shirts with mandarin collar . . . different, but perfectly matched.

Everyone loved the garden. And everyone brought something to it. Annie was always receiving potted plants, seeds, or doodads to tuck into leafy corners. Sam had brought a ceramic angel today—a silly, chubby, bewinged child that didn't bear the slightest resemblance to real angels written about in the Bible.

Grandma Leota had planned and laid out the garden. All those years she had toiled and planted, always hoping and praying this little piece of earth would become a sanctuary for those she loved. Grandma Leota had dreamed her dreams and prayed her prayers while kneeling on the earth and planting bulbs. She had believed it would all happen someday. She never gave up hope.

How Grandma would have relished this Easter Day. Annie wished she had been sitting among her flowers, seeing how everyone responded to the beauty of her garden. Sam, Susan, Corban, Arba, and the neighbor children had all shared the workload of bringing it back. Annie wanted people to feel at home in here. A garden wasn't meant to belong to one person. A garden was for sharing, for exercise, for joy, for prayer. A garden was an open-air cathedral to the glory of God, a living monument to the birth, life, death, and resurrection of the Lord. Every season was a trumpet sounding; every sunrise and sunset a daily reminder of God's glory. Here, in this small corner of a small neighborhood, Annie hoped people would come to understand a little better the way things were meant to be.

Her mother was going to be all right after all. Uncle George and Fred had carried the old sewing machine out to the van. Though Uncle George had agreed to move it, he had resisted spending the night in Black Hawk. He said he had to be at work in the morning. Poor Uncle George, debt-free, forever debt-ridden. Would he ever lay his burdens down? Annie knew Grandma Leota had written a letter to him as well.

With everything put away in the kitchen, Annie went into the living room and picked up *Kidnapped* by Robert Louis Stevenson. She ran her hand over the worn cover. Grandma Leota had told her how much Uncle George had loved to read as a boy. This had been his favorite book. Annie had put it on the side table, hoping Uncle George would pick it up and leaf through it—and find the letter tucked inside. He hadn't touched it. He had spent most of the afternoon sitting alone and watching television. She had not seen him even glance through the albums she had compiled and left open on the dining-room table. Her mother had taken one of the old scrapbooks with her.

The time just hadn't been right for Uncle George. Perhaps the next time he came, he would be ready to look around, to think back, to wonder. Perhaps he would be ready then to ask the painful questions and receive the redemptive answers. *Lord, please soften him.* Annie opened the drawer in the side table beside Grandma Leota's recliner, placed the book in it, and closed it again. God would tell her the right time to take it out. In the meantime, she would keep praying. Grandma Leota had taught her that. Never give up. Never despair. No matter what we feel or think, keep praying. Choose hope!

The scent of lilacs and narcissus filled the living room. Annie looked at Grandma Leota's portrait. Her heart had been in her throat as her mother paused to look at it before leaving. "You do have a gift,

Annie. Don't let anyone, including me, tell you otherwise." Then her mother had looked at the marble-and-brass urn that had contained Grandma Leota's ashes and was now filled with flowers. "Your grandmother loved lilacs." Her mother had touched some of the blossoms.

"Yes, she did. She loved daffodils too."

Eleanor had turned and looked at Annie. She'd smiled, her eyes filling with tears. "And roses."

Annie had smiled back. Her mother knew. "Those, too."

Oh, it was a wonderful day, Grandma Leota. And you were with us every moment of it, close to our hearts. You are alive and well and with our Lord.

Everything had been picked up in the living room. The door was locked. Annie went back into the kitchen and through to the back porch. She went outside into the cool evening air. Crickets were chirping and several frogs croaked. They were attracted to one corner of the garden, where she'd made a fountain. She had used half of a wine barrel and a small pump she'd bought from a hardware store on East Fourteenth. She'd tucked in submersible, marginal, and surface water plants. She loved the sound of running water. It was like living water, and the frogs would keep the garden free of bugs.

She walked the path to the Victory garden. The moon was out, reflecting light off the white alyssum, the gardenias, the pale blossoms on the fruit trees, the star jasmine and narcissus. The flowers themselves gave light. The darkness was broken by starlight, moonlight, and white flowers, and the air was filled with their sweet fragrance.

Annie remembered the first day she had looked out Grandma Leota's kitchen window to the garden. It had been unkempt, weed choked, barren in patches . . . the trees and bushes had been in dire need of pruning. Grandma had told her what it used to be like, and Annie had imagined it and longed to see it that way again. Under Grandma's guidance, the work had begun. The soil had been turned, softened, mulched, planted. The trees and bushes had been pruned and cut back. It had been hard work but well worth the aching muscles, broken fingernails, scratches, bruises, and blisters.

Along the way, surprises had cropped up. Bulbs Grandma had planted and forgotten years ago had appeared. Perennials long gone had left their seeds and bloomed again. New life had sprung up everywhere as though God had blessed this little patch of earth.

All day Annie had watched family members, friends, and neighbors wander around the garden, and she kept thinking how they were all like flowers. Some were poppies, blooming bold and brief. Others were like ornamental vines, passion flowers, or trumpets. Still others were shy violets and wallflowers. And all together, what a beautiful world they made. Everyone different, everyone amazing to behold.

Annie was so thankful for having had even a little time with Grandma Leota. She had never really thought about a garden's significance until she came to know her grandmother. Grandma Leota had told her once that everything important had happened in a garden . . .

"God created the garden for man and placed him in it. Adam and Eve fell into sin in a garden. Jesus taught in a garden. Our Lord prayed in a garden. He was betrayed in a garden. And He arose in a garden. And someday—" her grandmother's eyes had shone—*"we will all be reunited in the garden."*

Not all, perhaps.

Annie frowned. Corban had waited all day and all evening so he could be alone with her. She knew he was in love with her, and she had tried to dissuade him from saying anything that might later embarrass him. Yet he was persistent, determined. Far more than Sam had been. But then Sam was a Christian. He had been able to understand and accept. If only Corban would come to that saving faith and have the direction, purpose, and joy he yearned to have. Maybe then, life wouldn't be so difficult for him, so pointless and frustrating.

"I'm in love with you, Annie," he had said.

"I can't love you the way you want, Corban." What else could she say but the truth, even when it hurt him? She could see his frustration and feel his longing, but she was content. She would keep trying to turn his attention to the Lord. That's all she could do. Even when he tried to talk her out of living alone, or living in the inner city, or living for others rather than herself, she would pray for his salvation. "I'm where I'm supposed to be, Corban. I'm where I want to be. What more could I possibly want than to live in the garden?" Maybe in time he would understand what she meant.

Annie stood on the lawn, inhaling the fragrant evening air and gazing up at the night sky. It was long past midnight, the darkest time—and yet the stars shone brighter now.

This was Your day, Lord. Oh, I know every day is Your day, but this one was extraspecial, and I thank You for it. You are amazing. Oh, Father, I thought there was no chance of restoration and reconciliation when Grandma Leota passed on. I had so hoped we would have her awhile longer and Mother would have time to make amends. For whatever reason, it wasn't to be. Oh, Lord, I confess I almost lost hope when Grandma died. I thought whatever plan You'd made for my poor, broken family had somehow been destroyed by Satan. And then You reminded me of the Garden and the serpent and Your promise of a deliverer. And Jesus came. I remembered Noah and his wayward sons and how You told them to spread over the earth and multiply, and, instead, his descendants gathered together and built the Tower of Babel in rebellion against You. You went right ahead and fulfilled Your plan when You confounded their language and scattered them over the face of the earth. Man strives to do things his own way, and yet, it is always Your will that prevails.

Annie raised her hands in exaltation to the God of heaven and earth.

Oh, Lord, my God, I delight in You! She laughed aloud, so happy she felt her heart would burst with joy. *Oh, Lord, Lord, how majestic You are. Only Your plan will come to completion. Evil may seem to reign. Wars may come, and violence may spread over the earth, and man may take life itself into his own hands, but You prevail. You always have. You always will. I can rest in that knowledge. I can cling to Your promises and listen to Your voice, and walk in Your ways. I can trust You whatever the world may say or do. Someday my time will come, and however it does, I know You will not lose me. You will bring me safely home.*

A soft breeze caressed her face, and she inhaled the incense of the garden. Sighing, she lowered her arms and smiled. She went back into the house. Morning would be here soon.

And there was work to do.

ABOUT THE AUTHOR

FRANCINE RIVERS has been writing for almost thirty years. From 1976 to 1985 she had a successful writing career in the general market and won numerous awards. After becoming a born-again Christian in 1986, Francine wrote *Redeeming Love* as her statement of faith.

Since then, Francine has published numerous books in the CBA market and has continued to win both industry acclaim and reader loyalty. Her novel *The Last Sin Eater* won the ECPA Gold Medallion, and three of her books have won the prestigious Romance Writers of America RITA Award.

Francine says she uses her writing to draw closer to the Lord, that through her work she might worship and praise Jesus for all He has done and is doing in her life.

For more information visit
www.tyndale.com